# DELAYED PENALTY

By
Bianca Sommerland

Copyright 2013, Bianca Sommerland

Edited by Lisa A. Hollett

Cover art by Reese Dante

To: Robyn
Vegas 2013
#11

## Warning

This e-book contains material not suitable for readers under 18. There are situations involving sex and violence and extreme emotions as a result. It also contains scenes that some may find objectionable, including BDSM and other rather enjoyable practices. As the characters are prone to exploring their sexuality, it is advised that readers be prepared to see some lines blurred. Or erased....

Author takes no responsibility for nonexistent lines. ;)

*Author's Note: The Cobras series has a continuing arc about the franchise, players, and previous relationships. Some plots continue through the series and may involve more than the main ménage. The series is best read in order.*

# Dedication

*103 Seasons is just the beginning.*

# Acknowledgements

Spending the summer travelling everywhere from New York to Las Vegas, I've met so many people that had an impact on my work and my life that I can't possibly thank you all. For those who had a drink with me, laughed and talked, made me feel welcome in every way, I appreciate every single one of you. From authors, to readers, bellhops, and hotel staff, at conferences and for the long stretch where I was the little Canadian gypsy hopping from state to state, you all had a hand in make this summer one of the most memorable I've ever had.

To Cherise, meeting you was incredible. I am very proud of myself for not gushing—though I'm pretty sure I didn't make much sense considering I went straight to talking about our last email without introducing myself properly! Lol! I can now hear you voice saying "You can do better." And because of you, I always do.

My betas, many who I've met in person, all who are my dearest friends. Jennifer, you and your family made New York an incredible experience, please tell 'Sweetie' I miss her coffee and smiles every morning! Rosie, for my first 4th of July celebration! Heather, the things you showed me out in Kentucky had me falling in love! Can't wait to be out there again! My other betas, Lina, Missy, Bianca, and Susan, you each gave something to this story to make it even more powerful. Thank you so much!

Stacey, my dear friend, my assistant, and my savior. I can't find the words to tell you how much you mean to me. You and Doug were there to help me cope with the cloudless, hellishly hot desert, and then continued to be there when my hell went beyond the weather. From brainstorming, to research, to taking care of all the details of the job that I hate, I'm not sure I could get through a day without you!

Back to Kentucky—can you tell I'm eager to head back down? ;)—I need to give a great big shout out to the KSP, namely Easy, Carter, and Hopson, for all your insight and patience with my never ending questions. Markus, you were a wealth of information! I couldn't have managed without you guys and I can't wait to pick your brains again!

Anthony Skeans, Heather's going to give me heck for stroking your ego, but you so earned your place in this book! I don't know how often I read over the legal stuff you sent me, but it was imperative to the story and I'm so grateful for all your help. I owe you a great big hug—maybe more. ;)

To my readers, you've been awesome—and patient—as always. I went through some dark moments in this book that dragged me down, and you offered your support, lifted me back up, and helped me keep going. My every success is because of you.

Last, and most importantly, to my daughters. The way you proudly tell everyone "My mommy's an author" never fails to bring a smile to my lips. But, even more so, just you being the wonderful little people you are. I'm so proud of you too!

# Also by Bianca Sommerland

## The Dartmouth Cobras

Game Misconduct (The Dartmouth Cobras #1)
Defensive Zone (The Dartmouth Cobras #2)
Breakaway (The Dartmouth Cobras #3)
Offside (The Dartmouth Cobras #4)
Delayed Penalty (The Dartmouth Cobras #5)
Iron Cross (The Dartmouth Cobras #6) – Expected
Mid-2014

## Also

Deadly Captive
Collateral Damage
The End – Coming Early 2014

Rosemary Entwined
Rosemary & Mistletoe

The Trip

# Dartmouth Cobra Roster

## Centers

| No | Name | Age | Ht | Wt | Shot | Birth Place |
|----|------|-----|-----|-----|------|-------------|
| 27 | Scott Demyan | 29 | 6'3" | 198 | L | Anaheim, California, USA |
| 45 | Keaton Manning | 32 | 5'11" | 187 | R | Ulster, Ireland |
| 18 | Ctirad Jelinek | 28 | 6'0" | 204 | L | Rakovnik, Czech Republic |
| 3 | Erik Hjalmar | 25 | 6'3" | 219 | R | Stockolm, Sweden |
| 57 | Raif Zovko | 31 | 6'1" | 215 | R | Dubrovnik, Croatia |

## Left Wings

| No | Name | Age | Ht | Wt | Shot | Birth Place |
|----|------|-----|-----|-----|------|-------------|
| 16 | Luke Carter | 24 | 5'11" | 190 | L | Warroad, Minnesota, USA |
| 53 | Shawn Pischlar | 30 | 6'0" | 200 | L | Villach, Austria |
| 71 | Dexter Tousignant | 25 | 6'2" | 208 | L | Matane, Quebec, Canada |
| 5 | Ian White | 26 | 6'1" | 212 | L | Winnipeg, Manitoba, Canada |
| 42 | Braxton Richards | 19 | 5'11 | 196 | L | Edmonton, Alberta, Canada |

## Right Wings

| No | Name | Age | Ht | Wt | Shot | Birth Place |
|----|------|-----|-----|-----|------|-------------|
| 22 | Tyler Vanek | 23 | 5'8" | 174 | R | Greenville, North Carolina, USA |
| 72 | Dante Palladino | 36 | 6'2" | 215 | L | Fassano, Italy |
| 21 | Bobby Williams | 35 | 5'10" | 190 | R | Sheffield, England |
| 46 | Vadim Zetsev | 28 | 6'0" | 203 | R | Yaroslavl, Russia |
| 66 | Zachary Pearce | 33 | 6'0" | 210 | L | Ottawa, Ontario, Canada |

## Defense

| No | Name | Age | Ht | Wt | Shot | Birth Place |
|----|------|-----|-----|-----|------|-------------|
| 6 | Dominik Mason | 33 | 6'4" | 235 | R | Chicago, Illinois, USA |
| 17 | Einar Olsson | 29 | 6'0" | 200 | L | Örnsköldsvik, Sweden |
| 74 | Beau Mischlue | 27 | 6'2" | 223 | L | Gaspe, Quebec, Canada |
| 26 | Peter Kral | 29 | 6'1" | 200 | L | Hannover, Germany |
| 2 | Mirek Brends | 35 | 6'1" | 214 | L | Malmö, Sweden |
| 47 | Tony Brookmann | 26 | 6'3" | 212 | L | Winnipeg, Manitoba, Canada |
| 67 | Owen Stills | 24 | 6'0" | 217 | R | Detroit, Michigan, USA |
| 39 | Rylan Cooper | 25 | 5'11" | 198 | R | Norfolk, Virginia, USA |
| 11 | Sebastian Ramos | 30 | 6'5" | 227 | R | Arlanza, Burgos, Spain |

## Goalies

| No | Name | Age | Ht | Wt | Shot | Birth Place |
|----|------|-----|-----|-----|------|-------------|
| 20 | Landon Bowers ** | 27 | 6'3" | 215 | | Gaspe, Quebec, Canada |
| 29 | Dave Hunt | 21 | 6'2" | 210 | | Hamilton, Ontario, Canada |

# Chapter One

*Late December*

The icy wind drew tears to her eyes on the long trek through the snow to her car, parked at the far end of the almost empty superstore parking lot. Akira Hayashi gritted her teeth as she tightened her grip on the bags, the plastic handles having cut off all circulation from her fingers. Her toes were numb in her boots already and her arms were going to fall off. She shouldn't have gotten so much at once—no, she shouldn't have come alone.

*I shouldn't have had to. But what choice did I have?*

Maybe Sir was right. Maybe she was a little *too* nice.

*But Jami hates grocery shopping. And Sahara's working on a new routine. We needed food.*

Her roommates were perfectly happy ordering out every night, but it irked Akira to waste money like that. So she did the shopping, and the cooking, and recycled the takeout pamphlets before the other girls could get ahold of them. Her schedule made the times she could restock a little sporadic, but she managed just fine on her own. And she'd been lucky enough to make it to the store before it closed for the evening.

*"You're spoiling them, Akira."* Akira shivered as she recalled Dominik Mason, her mentor, the Dartmouth Cobras' captain—or as she most often called him, "Sir"—giving her one of his hard looks, his tone deep with disapproval. *"You teach people how to treat you. And I don't like what you're teaching those girls."*

Damn it, she hated when Sir was unhappy with her. But at the same time, she had to stop looking to him for direction. They'd both known what they were getting into when he'd agreed to train

1

her. He'd taken on two new subs recently after a *long* discussion. She'd insisted she'd be fine.

*And I will be.* She'd prove it by making decisions like this all on her own. If she wanted to do a little bit extra for her two closest friends, he had nothing to say about it.

She blew a long strand of sleek, brown-black hair away from her face as the wind slashed at her, adjusted the three heavy bags, and winced as a handle chafed her wrist above her thin gloves. Almost there. She huffed out white air, dropping the bags behind her car to fish her car keys out of her purse.

Something tugged at her purse strap. She gaped as a man loomed over her, trapping her against the trunk. A ski mask covered most of his face. A savage smile bared rotted teeth.

"Don't be stupid," he said with a growl.

Twisting away from him, she let out a shrill cry. His hand slapped over her mouth. Her knees locked and she automatically swung a fist at his face.

A sharp pain went up her arm as her fist connected with his mouth. He reared back, spitting as he swore at her. "Fucking bitch!" He yanked at her purse. "Let it go, or I'll—"

*Just let it go!* Akira released her purse and jabbed her elbow into his stomach. She dropped to her knees as he lunged for her. Scrambled out of reach, slipping in the snow, not getting far. He took a step toward her. Stopped as though just realizing he had her purse.

Then he turned and ran.

"No!" Akira sat hard on the pavement. She hardly noticed the snow melting into her jeans. Losing her wallet, her phone, her day planner, and her Kindle—her throat tightened. She hated all that, but not as much as she hated the old feelings resurfacing. He'd been so much stronger than her. He could have done anything . . .

*He didn't. Pull it together, Akira.*

She managed to haul in some cold air. But she couldn't make herself stand. Her whole body was shaking. She could taste the dried sweat and dirt on her lips from his hand. Her stomach heaved. She lowered her head between her knees.

*The man dragged her into the office down the hall from her father's. Covered her mouth with his hand, his palm slick with sweat. "You were waiting for us, weren't you, slut?" He hissed in her ear as his partner closed and locked the door. "If you scream, I'll go get your daddy. I'll bring him in here and make him watch."*

Tears burned like acid in her eyes, blinding her as a hand settled on her shoulder. They were back. They'd found her. She cowered, one arm shielding her face. She should fight, should run, but there was no point in trying to get away.

She'd never get away.

"Hey. Shh . . ."

*Look at him. You have to be able to describe him if . . . if he lets you live.* Lowering her arm, she stared up at him, staying perfectly still, needing to show him she wouldn't struggle. That she was small and defenseless.

God, he was *huge.* All the training she'd gotten, all too recently, was useless. One swing with those big hands would be no different than a grizzly bear lashing out with a giant paw.

If she didn't move, didn't breathe, maybe he wouldn't attack.

Only he didn't look ready to attack. He asked her something, but she couldn't make out the words. She couldn't hear anything beyond the pounding of her heart. Couldn't tear her gaze away from his eyes, eyes the color of her favorite stuffed frog, dull green with age. His eyes shouldn't remind her of the cuddly toy that had soaked up her tears for weeks after the rape.

But even his frown was somehow comforting. He moved his hand when she didn't answer. "Did you fall? Are you hurt?"

Muscles strained against the beaten leather of his dark brown jacket. His face was rough, like a much lighter version of his jacket. His thighs, in faded black jeans, were about the size of her waist.

He could hurt her without even trying. Literally snap her in two.

But he'd stopped touching her without her asking. He wasn't trying to drag her away somewhere—or take her right here since no one was around to stop him.

She managed to breathe. To shake her head. Then, finally, speak. "No. I'm not hurt." She ignored the hand he held out, sliding up the car for support as she stood. "Someone stole my purse. I just—"

"Someone *what?*" He straightened, hands fisted at his sides, the expression on his face so fierce she mentally advised the asshole who'd robbed her to get far, far away. She gulped when the big man returned his hard gaze to her. It softened so quickly the air rushed back into her lungs as she inhaled. His brow furrowed. "Did he do anything else? You don't gotta tell me, but I can bring you to the hospital or—"

"N-no. Nothing else. He just scared me." She let out a nervous laugh. "Not hard to do. I'm fine."

Her laugh only seemed to concern him more. His gaze went over her quickly. He shook his head. "You must be freezing. And in shock. Were your keys in the purse?"

"No, they're . . ." She glanced toward her trunk. The keys weren't there. She hadn't gotten them out. They were gone too. Her bottom lip trembled. Scott Demyan, another Cobra and her closest male friend, had gotten her the car as a late birthday present—secondhand because he'd come to know her well enough to guess that she wouldn't accept something expensive and new. And now the keys were gone. And she didn't have a spare set. And she had no idea how much getting new ones would cost.

Sniffling, she turned away from him, brushing away the single tear that trailed down her cheek. The man didn't need to see how pathetic she could be. Her stupid panic attack was done. He'd been kind enough to stop to make sure she was all right. She had to let him know she was so he could go on with his evening.

"Thank you so much for stopping, but I really am fine. I'll just call one of my friends to come pick me up and—"

"And I'll stay with you until they show up." He pulled his phone out of his pocket, his lips quirking slightly as he handed it to her. "I hope you remember some phone numbers. I couldn't even tell you my own, to be honest. Only had it for a week."

Akira grinned at the way he ducked his head, like he was embarrassed. "I've always been good with numbers, but it takes a while for most people." She dialed Jami's number. Voice mail. Tried Sahara's . . . voice mail again. Her smile slipped. She *really* didn't want to call Sir. He'd be so worried, and she hated worrying him. She nibbled at her bottom lip as she dialed Scott's number. "Why the new number? If you don't mind my asking?"

The man shrugged. "Moved back here recently."

"Ah . . ." She exhaled as Scott picked up. Tried to keep her tone light. "Hey, you busy?"

"Not really, but . . ." Scott paused. Chuckled. "Casey, your mom's gonna freak if she sees you playing with that. Grandma's crystal animals aren't really toys. One sec, Akira." The line went quiet. Scott sounded a bit more serious as he came back on. "Bit of glue and she won't even notice. Just . . . no more touching, okay? Sorry, Akira." His attention returned to her. "What's up?"

"I was wondering if you were nearby."

"Gaspe is a few hours away, sweetie. Why?"

*Ugh.* She'd thought he'd be back from Christmas vacation with the Bower family. The Cobras were lucky to have almost a week off around Christmas, but they had a game New Year's Eve. In two days. Her Ice Girls had practice tomorrow, but the Cobras' might be optional.

The point was, he wasn't close enough to help her. And she didn't want him all anxious over nothing. So she let out a dismissive laugh. "No reason. Just had some car trouble."

"Are you stuck? Call Mason—or Carter. Do you have his number?"

"I do, but I don't want to bother anyone else." Or anyone at all. The concern in Scott's tone was more than enough. Her close friends always worried when she went out alone. And she hated to do that to them. "I'll take a cab home. The car's in a parking lot, so it will be okay here for a bit."

The man, who'd stood silently beside her during the

conversation, cleared his throat. "Or I could give you a lift."

"Who is that?" Scott's tone sharpened. "Akira, don't lie to me. If you're in trouble, you have to tell me."

*So I can ruin your holiday? No thanks.* Akira frowned at the man, hoping he'd be quiet so she could calm Scott down. "I'm not in trouble. Give Casey and Amia a hug for me."

"Akira, at least give me the man's name so I can hunt him down if anything happens to you!"

"Tell him my name is Cort. Full name, Cortland Nash." The man leaned his elbow on the top of her car, his tone dry. "And let him know you're safer with me than alone out here. Kinda stupid for your boyfriend to let you come out here by yourself this late."

"Did he say Cortland Nash?" Scott laughed. "I've heard good things about him. He knows cars. Tell him to fix whatever's wrong with it, and I'll pay him when I get back."

Akira scowled. If the men were standing side by side, she'd smack them both. Did they really think she couldn't take care of herself? "I can pay for my own repairs, Scott." She turned her scowl to the big man. "And he's not my boyfriend. I don't need a bodyguard to go shopping."

Cort's brow lifted as though he thought otherwise, but he didn't comment.

*Smart man.*

Scott sighed. "Got it. You're a big girl. Let Cort take you home though, okay? It *is* getting late. If it makes you feel better, you can *borrow* the money for repairs or whatever. I know you won't touch your prize money."

"No. I won't." She didn't make much as an Ice Girl, but she could live off her salary and let the one hundred thousand dollars she'd won by becoming captain gain interest in the bank until she needed it to start her figure skating school. One good thing had come from the phone call, though. If Cort had Scott's stamp of approval, she could accept his offer and not waste money on a cab. Or embarrass herself by telling the cabbie she could only pay him once she got home.

*Yes, because that's the priority. Not being embarrassed.*

The cold from her wet clothes seeped into her bones. She trembled but kept her tone steady as she ended the call with Scott, promising she'd call him later to let him know that she'd gotten home okay. She hung up and went to put the phone in her purse. Then dropped back against her car when she remembered that her purse was gone. And this wasn't her phone.

"He knew my name?" Cort asked, making no move to take his phone back. Such a little thing, but it made her a bit more comfortable with him.

Aside from the anger when he'd learned that she'd been robbed, he'd been pretty cool about everything. Not pushy, just there. She nodded slowly. "Yes. He said you can fix my car." She rolled her eyes. "Not that he knows the only thing that needs to be fixed is new keys."

"The locks have to be changed." Cort rolled his shoulders. He gave her an unreadable look, then took a step back. "I can do that. Pay for the parts and we can both feel good about ourselves." His cheek creased slightly as he smiled. "Did your . . . friend say it was okay for me to give you a lift?"

"He did. I don't live far." She shifted her feet, eyeing her bags. Technically, she could walk, but it was cold. Getting colder by the second. And there was no way she could manage the bags all the way. "I'd appreciate it."

Cort nodded, then grabbed her bags before she could touch them. He stashed them in the trunk of his car—a classic something-or-another. Long, sleek, and black. She liked it. She bit her lip when he opened the passenger's side door for her, anxiety squeezing deep in her guts. Whatever Scott said, Cort was a stranger. Getting in the car with him could lead to . . .

"Hey, Tiny, you don't got nothin' to worry about. My intentions are . . ." His lips slanted. "Decent. I won't jump you, but I may ask you to come out for a drink with me if you don't look like you're gonna bolt." He winked. "I'll work up the courage on the drive."

Oh, she liked him. Which was weird, because she didn't "like" many men. And *never* those who would ask her out for a drink. She wrinkled her nose, slipping into the seat with her brow arched at him. "I hope you word it better when you do ask."

"I got a block or two to work on it."

"More like ten." She felt a flush rise on her cheeks. This was good. She was talking to a man without freaking out. After being mugged, she was surprised she didn't feel like going straight to the club to let Sir hold her. Remind her that she wasn't weak. That bad things happened, but she'd be okay. She *was* okay.

"Plenty of time then." Cort's lips thinned as she shivered. He reached into the backseat and brought out a threadbare, plaid thermal blanket. His knuckles brushed the side of her neck as he tried to spread the blanket over her. He let it go the second she flinched. Straightened and backed away. "It's clean. And it'll keep you warm."

"Thank you." Akira spoke so quietly, she wasn't sure he'd heard her. His brief touch had made her feel . . . she couldn't explain it, but she wasn't so cold anymore. She kept her eyes down and did up her seat belt, covering herself with the blanket as Cort closed the door. He went around the car to get in behind the wheel. She bit her lip and glanced over at him. "I'm glad you showed up when you did."

"So am I." The steering wheel creaked as Cort tightened his grip on it. "As much as I wish I could've gotten my hands on that guy, I'm glad he was already gone. That all he wanted was your purse."

Akira shivered, not from the cold this time. "Yeah. It could have been worse."

*Much, much worse.*

\* \* \* \*

The small woman hurried ahead of Cort, trembling as she opened the door to the apartment lobby. She hesitated by the buzzer, then tested the second glass door. It opened readily.

*Real safe.*

He carried the bags she'd tried to take from him up the stairs, hardly noticing their weight but wondering how she'd carried them as far as she had. One bag had either barbells or about five dozen apples in it. Another had twenty pounds of potatoes. A swing and she could have taken out the fucker who mugged her, but her arms had probably been sore. Either way, it didn't matter. She hadn't gotten hurt.

But how close she'd come pissed him off more than it should.

As they climbed up to the top floor, he took the opportunity to really look her over, if only from behind. Hell, he wasn't blind. She was a looker. Five foot nothing, if that. Long hair he ached to bury his hands in, pure black fucking silk with a sheen of dark chocolate in the light. Her army green eyes had captured him from her first glance, but he couldn't help but stare at her tiny butt, swaying a few steps above him, soaked blue jeans plastered to the nice, round cheeks. His baser urges and plain logic were at war. He'd never dated—or *fucked*—a woman as small as . . . damn, he didn't even know her name.

And, hell, he didn't want to fuck her anyway. He rarely hung around one place long enough to offer a woman more, so he knew how to get down to the basics, but this little sweetheart didn't need that from him. She needed to know he was here just to help her out. End game. He hadn't missed the fear in her eyes when he'd first approached her. That didn't come from being mugged. That fear was bone-fucking-deep.

Smart chick though, getting the okay from a friend before accepting a ride. He wasn't sure who she'd talked to—he knew a lot of people—but if the guy had given her the green light, he wasn't one of the lowlifes Cort usually dealt with. Someone who would have told her to run just in case Cort decided she'd make good collateral.

Not that he'd ever used a woman to get a man to pay up. Yeah, he'd threatened to, but his reputation was usually enough to get a man to find the money he owed before Cort had to live up to it. He wasn't proud of the things he'd done in his old job, but he'd never had to bury anyone.

Only one man that had ever crossed him had ended up in the ground.

Above him, the small woman, who he'd dubbed "Tiny," twisted a doorknob, hesitating before pushing as though she wasn't sure it was locked. The door swung open and she groaned, clearly not happy.

She shook her head, glancing back at him. "You'd think, growing up in New York, she'd know better."

He grunted, following her inside. Apparently, she didn't live alone. Two points for her, and minus about twenty for her roommate. What kind of New Yorker didn't lock up?

"Sahara?" The woman strode ahead of him, letting out a sharp sound of distress at a *Crash!* She disappeared into a room down the hall. He dropped the bags and followed her.

"I'm fine, hon, just drank a bit too much." In the room, sprawled out on the bed, a slender blonde shook her head, her cheeks wet with tears. A broken lamp lay on the floor by the bed. "I shouldn't have gone to the club."

"No, you shouldn't have." His Tiny stroked the blond woman's hair. "He was playing with someone else?"

"Of course! And he wouldn't even look at me!" Blondie sobbed, curling into a ball and holding her stomach like it hurt. "I was . . . bad. Dominik spanked me, then held me, then told me to go home. I thought he'd tell me not to come back."

*The man spanked you? And you* wanted *to go back?* Cort backed away from the door, sure the women didn't want him hearing this. Still, he couldn't help but bristle at the way Blondie talked like she'd deserved it. *What the fuck did I walk in on?*

Even from the kitchen, he could hear them clearly. Blondie wasn't exactly soft-spoken. She exploded when Tiny asked if Dominik had agreed to train her.

"No! I'm stuck with Shawn and Chicklet. And I don't want to

submit to them—there's only one man I want—"

"How much did you drink, Sahara?"

"I don't know. How much was left in the bottle of whiskey?"

"Aw, sweetie. You can't keep doing this to yourself." Tiny paused. "We have practice tomorrow."

"I took some vitamins. Drank some Gatorade." Blondie laughed. "With a sleeping pill."

"You're not supposed to drink with those."

*No kidding.* Cort scowled as he lifted up a grocery bag. He spotted a tub of ice cream at the top—decided to put it away. Then went to work placing everything else from the bags.

"My *ex* said the same thing. He didn't care that I slept just fine before him." Blondie sobbed. "I'm so tired, babe. Why can't anyone good want me?"

"They will."

"I don't know. Maybe. One day. You're so lucky. I would do anything to have a man like Dominik."

"He's not mine, sweetie. That's one of the reasons I *didn't* go to the club. I'm not used to seeing him with the other girls yet."

*What an asshole.* Cort pulverized a banana in his fist. What kind of jerk would make such a sweet chick deal with his other women? The situation was getting scary familiar. A life he'd gotten out of a long time ago, but one he'd grown up in. His mom had dealt with his asshole of a father's floozies without a word of complaint. Cort had promised her as a little boy that he'd always love only her. When he'd grown up enough to know that wasn't realistic, he'd amended his promise to her always holding a special place in his life. And if he ever got married, his woman would never doubt he was committed to her.

The girls' chatter softened so he couldn't hear them anymore. He cleaned his hands, finished putting everything away, then eyed the door, wondering if he should just go. Maybe leave Tiny a note with his number. Just in case . . . whatever.

He found a pen in a little magnetic holder on the fridge, along with a to-do list pad of paper. He'd just started jotting down his message when he heard a soft throat clearing behind him.

"Going somewhere?" Tiny stepped into the kitchen, fingering one of the empty bags he'd left on the countertop. Without meeting his eyes, she handed him his cell. "What about that drink?"

"Figured you'd want to take care of your girl." Cort stuffed his phone in his pocket and waited for the sound of Blondie puking. He had a feeling Tiny would forget all about him if she did.

Which made it hard not to smile. Nothing he respected more than a loyal friend.

Tiny sighed, nodding slowly. "I won't feel comfortable leaving her like this, but she's sleeping. This will be an issue in the morning. Sorry you had to hear that."

Shrugging, he replaced the pen. "Didn't hear nothin'."

"Liar."

"'Kay, I'll pretend like I didn't." He grinned when she laughed. Damn, that sound was the sweetest thing he'd ever heard. He pressed back against the counter, resisting the sudden urge to go to her. To touch her. That wouldn't go over well. But the drink invite . . . "So, if you're not going out...?"

Her lips curved slightly. "Then you're staying in? We have a fully-stocked liquor cabinet. And beer. What's your poison?"

*Tempting little woman?* Fuck, he'd never wanted to smile at a chick this much unless she was stripping for him. Tiny needed to strip, but mostly because her jeans were soaked. He didn't like that she'd gone to take care of her friend but hadn't taken care of herself.

"A beer would be nice if you'll have one with me." One brow arched, he looked her over pointedly. "Once you're out of those wet clothes."

"Umm . . . yeah, I should get changed." She chewed at her bottom lip in a way that made it very hard for him to stay put. Kissing was something he usually did so a woman didn't feel used, but with Tiny, he just wanted one little taste of those soft lips.

Not that he'd be satisfied with one. He bit back a grin as she scurried down the hall and ducked into another room. Guess he'd get their beers.

Moments later, she joined him on the weird, patchwork sofa, wearing black jogging pants and a big, faded Hello Kitty sweatshirt, thanking him as he uncapped her beer for her. She turned the TV on, flipping the channel from a replay of a Dartmouth Cobras game. She went through a dozen channels, not showing any interest in the late night chick flicks or sitcoms. He liked her more already.

She stopped on figure skating. Better than *"Serendipity"*. Kinda. His lips quirked as he sat back, taking a swig of beer. Tiny looked like the type who'd be into this stuff. He might be able to get somewhere offering to take her to see a show, but pretending to like something to get in a chick's pants wasn't his style. Since what was on TV was damn boring, he turned all his attention to the much more appealing sight before him. Long lashes, big, almond-shaped eyes, pink shading her soft cheeks. She was biting her bottom lip again, glancing from him to the screen as though she couldn't quite meet his eyes.

"So, you said you moved back here?" she asked as though she needed to break the silence. "Were you born in the area?"

"No. I was born in Detroit. Moved here when I was a teen." He made a face and scratched the side of his neck. "Had this crazy idea that I wanted to be a fisherman."

She blinked, shifting to sit sideways, facing him. "A fisherman? Really?"

"Yeah. Watched too much extreme fishing as a kid. The real thing wasn't all that exciting."

"But being out on the ocean, working with your hands . . ." She cocked her head, looking him over. "Yep, I can see you liking that. Maybe you should have joined the Marines instead?"

"Not really an option." He wouldn't lie to her about why, but it was a little soon to start bringing up the unsavory parts of his past. If they ever went on a real date, he'd make sure she knew the basics. Besides, he wanted to know more about her. Starting with her age—be weird to just come out and ask, though. So he tried to find a tactful way to find out if she was at least over eighteen. Likely, since she was living on her own, but he never assumed shit like that. "What about you? Got any plans for when you graduate?"

"Graduate? What, college?" She wrinkled her nose. "I never went. My mom homeschooled me since training took too much time for a regular schedule. I graduated at sixteen, then spent the next few years doing that." She nodded toward the TV. "I was good—just not good enough. I think I could teach it, though. I plan to open my own school."

"That's cool," he said, meaning it. She wasn't all down on herself for not reaching her first dream. Instead, she'd found another one. Part of him wondered, even if she wasn't too young for him, maybe she was too *good* for him. Not like he was shit under anyone's shoe, but there was a purity to her he'd ruin if he got too close. But being around her felt *too* good for him to think of leaving just yet. "I don't get the appeal of dancing around half-naked on a pair of blades, but I can tell it takes some skill. Tough competition out there. Sucks that you stopped fighting for gold, but helping someone else get there would be pretty awesome."

"Exactly." She pursed her lips, studied him for a moment, then patted his arm and pointed at the TV. "Have you ever really *watched* figure skating? I know it's not all *manly*, but appreciating beauty doesn't make you any less of a man."

Damn. He wished he'd taken off his jacket. All his muscles had tensed the second she'd touched him, as though they could absorb the brief contact. He took a deep breath, set his beer on the table, then shrugged off his jacket. "You make me want to give it a chance."

"Good." She smiled with clear approval, leaning against the sofa, just a few inches away from him. "Look at the way he lifts her up, the way she extends her body as he spins, trusting him not to drop her because she knows his strength."

He looked. Really looked for the first time. The passion in Tiny's tone was infectious. As the couple on-screen danced, pulling off impressive leaps, spinning around in time to the classical music, he had to admit it wasn't as lame as he'd thought. When the next couple came on and the music changed, he found himself actually enjoying the show.

"You see?" This time, Tiny touched his bare forearm. And left her hand there, her eyes on his face. Heat pulsed through his veins as his gaze met hers. Her cheeks were even pinker. She'd stopped breathing.

"I see." He brought his hand up to her cheek. Moved in until his lips brushed hers. So fucking soft. He smiled at the quiet, nervous giggle she let out as he kissed her. Added a bit of pressure as her breath caught. He tasted her lips, eased past them with his tongue when they parted. Her hands flattened against his chest as she rose up on her knees. She kissed him hard, desperation in the way her fingers bunched up in his shirt.

Then made a frustrated sound in her throat when he gently wrapped his hands around her arms and eased her back. "What's wrong?"

"Nothing, Tiny. Just slow down a little." He kept her in place as she tried to flounce off him, tightening his grip just a bit. Then he curved his hand under her jaw. "Hope you don't think I need a show of gratitude or anything. You're cute, but I would've done the same for any lady who looked like she was in trouble."

"This isn't gratitude, it's . . ." She groaned, pressing her eyes shut as she shook her head. "Please let me go."

He released her, not sure what to make of the way she scooted back to the corner of the couch, arms wrapped around her knees. He'd seen chicks get emotional before—usually his cue to leave— but he didn't like seeing *her* upset. What did he have to do to get her smiling again?

"Tiny, did I—?"

She frowned at him. "Why do you keep calling me that?"

"Because you're . . . tiny." He grinned at her huff. "And you never told me your name."

"It's A—Ace." She was blushing again. *Cute little liar.* But "Ace" suited her well enough.

And would probably annoy her less than "Tiny." He inclined his head. "All right, Ace. Just had to clear things up. I said 'slow down,' not stop. Get back over here."

\* \* \* \*

Akira's eyes widened. She giggled and crawled back across the sofa, gasping as Cort pulled her into his lap. Something purely magnetic about him made it impossible not to give in to the pull. He wasn't handsome in a conventional way, but his smile made him absolutely gorgeous. Her lips hovered over his as she slipped her arms around his neck. Being near him felt so natural. So right.

*Why though? What makes him so different from the other guys that hit on you?*

Good question. One she couldn't answer. All she knew was she was drawn to him in a way she didn't want to fight. She'd told the truth; she wasn't doing this out of gratitude, but, in a way, he'd been her hero. Not just because he'd saved her, but because he'd been exactly what she'd needed out there, alone in the cold. And he was exactly what she needed right here, right now. A man who was interested in her, physically, mentally, and not through mutual pain. She loved Sir for all he'd done for her, but he'd never be hers.

Maybe . . . maybe Cort could be.

*You can't know that. Not yet.*

No. But she had him in this moment. And for the first time ever, she didn't want to be slow and careful.

She wanted to dive in and see what happened.

Cort placed one hand on her hip and ran his thumb across the waistband of her jogging pants as he teased her lips with his. His other hand moved up her side, his palm skimming the curve of her breast. Her nipples drew into sensitive little points, begging to be touched.

"Mmm." She pressed against him as he cupped her breast in his hand, stroking her tight, throbbing nipple through her sweatshirt. He shifted his lips to her throat and his hand to her waist. Slowly slipped his hand under her sweatshirt. Grazed her with his fingertips.

He slid his hand over her breast. "Fuck, you're gorgeous."

"Cort . . ." Akira tipped her head back as he lifted her sweatshirt to expose her breasts, closing his mouth around her nipple. The jolts of pleasure had her writhing against him. Her fingers delved into his hair, tugging slightly even as she held him in place.

He sucked hard, barring one arm behind her back to steady her as he undid the tie string of her jogging pants. He worked his hand down until his fingers touched her moist heat.

"Baby, you're so wet." He rubbed gently over her clit, then slipped the tip of his finger inside her. Her whole body quivered as his thick, callused finger sank into her all the way. She whimpered as he brought his mouth to her other breast. Cried out as he began to thrust his finger and flick his tongue over her nipple while holding it between his teeth. She became pure, sizzling liquid as he held her gaze, gradually easing two fingers inside her. He smiled as her lips parted. Moved his free hand to the back of her neck to pull her close and whisper in her ear, "Ride my fingers, sweetie. I want a visual of how you'll look when you're riding me."

*"When." Oh God, yes!* Shifting without displacing his fingers, Akira straddled his thighs. She gasped as he added yet another finger, then lifted up slightly, until only the tips of his fingers were inside her. She lowered, then rose, finding a nice rhythm, lost in the naughty pleasure. She shouldn't be doing this. Not with a stranger, no matter how easy it was to take everything he gave her. No matter how good it felt to—

"Ah!" Her pace faltered and she gripped his shoulders as her pussy clung to his fingers, clenching as she teetered right on the edge. "May I . . . oh God! I need to come, please!"

He wrapped her hair around his fist and bit her throat as he fucked his fingers up into her. Then he pressed his fingers in as deep as they could go. "Do it, baby. I want to feel you coming hard all over my fingers."

She convulsed around his fingers, letting out a ragged sound as white heat erupted in her core. The flames spread, reaching beyond the depths, swallowing her whole. Her throat felt raw from the noises she'd made. She shuddered as he slid his fingers from her, burrowing her face against the side of his neck.

"That was . . . that's not something I usually do. I'm not a slut."

He hugged her tight. "I know you're not. You had a rough night. You used me to make it better. I'm good with that."

Letting out an incredulous snort, she sat up, catching his face between her hands to kiss him. Damn, this felt good. Everything he said, everything he did, made taking this chance with him seem less reckless. And more like an opportunity to have something wonderful. Her lips curled slightly. "I don't believe in using people."

"Oh, yeah?" He gave her a hooded look as she reached between them to unzip his jeans.

"Yes." She slipped off his lap and knelt between his thighs. His hot flesh filled her hand, and she couldn't get a good grip on him. All the past girl-talk about how size *does* matter came back to her. *Size isn't supposed to be scary!* Her tongue flicked over her bottom lip. "You're . . . very big."

He chuckled, petting her hair as she wrapped her hands around him. "So I've been told. Not trying to be cocky, but I've had to learn how to deal with being such a big man. I promise I'll be careful with you, little one."

*Little one.* She smiled, loving how casually the endearment slipped out. For some reason, she didn't think he was a Dom. And yet . . . he could easily fit into that role.

*But does he want to?*

She would find out. Eventually. But for now . . . "I believe you." She pressed a soft kiss to the tip of his dick, then swallowed as she gently stroked him. "Just . . . don't move. I'm not sure how much of you I can take."

"Keep your hands just like that. Fuck, you touching me feels amazing." He slid his hand over hers, encouraging her to tighten her grip. "Your pretty lips don't need to go any farther than your hands."

"It's enough?" She peered up at him as her tongue swirled around the head of his cock.

He traced her bottom lip with his thumb. "More than enough."

\* \* \* \*

Preening as though Cort's words pleased her, she took him in her mouth, sliding down slowly until her lips met her top hand. There was something about her expression, the way her lashes lowered, the way her wet lips tightened as they glided up, then down, that made it seem like she enjoyed doing this as much as he enjoyed having it done. Innocent and wanton all at once, not going too fast or too slow. Not trying to get him off as quickly as possible.

He let out a low groan of approval as her tongue fluttered over the sensitive underside of his cock. A flush spread across her cheeks, and she pressed her tongue on that spot as she bobbed her head. He fisted his hands by his hips, resisting the urge to grab the back of her head and thrust in as his pulse thrummed harder, right between her lips. He wanted to last longer, but his girl was determined.

Her gaze on his face as she moved did him in. Pleasure rocked up from his balls, shuddering through his muscles like the goddamn earth was coming apart under him. He tipped his head back, cursing at the fucking mind-blowing sensation of her swallowing around him. She licked the last glistening white trail from the slit of his dick, then sat back on her heels with a satisfied smile on her lips.

The woman had killed him. But as good as she looked down there, he wanted her closer. Which was weird, because he wasn't the snuggling type.

*Fuck it.* He crooked his finger at her. "Up here, you little brat."

He did up his jeans, then threw his arm over her shoulders as she curled up beside him. "Not sure I want to know how you got so good at that."

"With one man, Cort. Only one." She took a deep breath. "I'm still. . . involved with him, in a way. We should probably discuss—"

"There's a few things we should probably discuss. But not tonight. Let's watch the rest of the show." He kissed the top of her head. "Save the ex-talk—or not-quite-ex-talk—for our first dinner and a movie stint. I can't stay much longer. I came to help out a friend, and I want to check in since I'm crashing at his place for a bit."

"I can live with that." She let out a happy sigh. "This was . . . nice."

"Nice?" He wasn't sure if he should be insulted. "Nice" wasn't high on his list of compliments. "Remind me to work that 'nice' up to an *unbelievable* next time. Because that's what you did for me."

"Aww." She rubbed her cheek against his arm like an affectionate kitten. "I wouldn't have taken you for a sweet guy."

He snorted, not quite sure what had come over him. He *wasn't* a sweet guy. "Believe me, anyone who knows me would be shocked."

"Maybe they don't know you all that well."

"Baby, you don't know me at all." He gave her a one-armed hug when he noticed the show was over. He wanted to stay, wanted to take what he could from tonight because who knew if she'd *want* to get to know him once she learned a little more. He stood, scratched his chin, then went to the kitchen. Jotted his name and—after checking his phone—his number on the fridge pad. He went still when he heard her come in behind him. For some reason, it bothered him that his next move might end things between them before they'd even begun, but she needed to have her eyes wide open if she was going to get involved with him. "You've got my name. A quick Google search will tell you plenty. Call me if it doesn't scare you off."

She folded her arms over her chest and shook her head. "Or

you can just tell me. You said dinner and a movie, right?" She tore off the slip of paper with his number, then wrote her number on another. "I'm free Wednesday and Thursday. I actually *like* action movies—just so you don't feel stuck watching a chick flick. Let me know what you want to see. And what restaurant you want to bring me to. I'm not a big fan of Chinese food or anything too spicy, so choose carefully."

He grinned, folding the paper she handed him and stuffing it in his pocket. "Steak and potatoes?"

"Mmm. Yes to both. I also love buffalo wings and beer during hockey games."

*The girl's a hockey fan.* He'd dated a few gushy ones who didn't watch the game. They just creamed over the players. And had meltdowns when "their men" got a few bumps. He didn't see his girl doing that, but he could be wrong. "You don't cry when players get hit, do you?"

Cocking her head, she frowned at him. "Why would I? Unless they don't get up after a hit, it's all part of the game."

"What about football?"

"Love it."

Could she be any more perfect? He gathered her in his arms, kissing her until she was gasping and pressing against him in a way that got his dead dick twitching with new life. *Down, boy.* "If I don't scare you away, there's a few things I want to do with you."

Her teeth dented her bottom lip. Her brow furrowed. "Say that again after our talk. I might be the one who scares *you* away."

It was cute that she thought that. He tapped her tiny nose. "Not happening, Ace."

"We'll see."

He inclined his head. "Yeah, we will. Wednesday. I can't wait longer than that to see you again."

Out in the hall, after making sure she locked the door behind him, Cort leaned against the wall, shaking his head, not quite sure what had come over him. He was acting like a fucking chump. Going soft. Over a woman he hardly knew.

21

Didn't matter. He could be that for her. Find a way to keep her away from the rougher parts of his life. Hopefully.

He'd know once Ford told him what kind of trouble he was in. Much as he wanted to get to know his little Ace better, his best friend came first.

# Chapter Two

C ort called Ford's phone again, wondering if Ford had changed his number. He made his way up the metal steps in the alley leading to the man's apartment, right above the bar, which looked like it had been closed for a while. The darkened windows were streaked with dirt, and Cort knew Ford kept his bar fucking spotless. If he didn't have the money to hire someone to do the cleaning, he'd do it himself. He was too proud to leave the place looking this bad.

Ford calling him was enough of a clue to let Cort know something was wrong, but this had him really worried. He stopped in front of Ford's door and pounded on it, ready to give the kid shit if he was inside acting like a goddamn pussy 'cause he had a cold or . . .

The curtain that usually covered the small window in the heavy oak door was gone. Cort shielded his eyes and squinted to see inside. The place was trashed.

"Fuck." Cort pulled his small tension wrench and pick from his wallet. Within seconds he had the door open. Picking locks was a trick he'd learned as a kid after his stepdad, Sutter, started locking him out when he missed curfew. Rather than yell at Cort, Sutter had offered him a job. Trained him to do tougher work over the years. And that training would come in handy if anything had happened to Ford.

Droplets of dried blood on the floor made Cort's gut clench. He searched for a number on his phone even as he strode through the apartment, silently praying Ford wasn't still here.

Living room wrecked. TV smashed. Leather sofa cut up.
More blood.

Bathroom in order. Kitchen covered in broken glass. Bedroom . . .

Empty. More blood on the sheets and the black-and-white-striped area rug.

"Cort?" The voice on the phone sounded nervous. Ford's bartender, Reggie, knew something was up.

"Where. Is. He. Reggie?" Cort ground his teeth at the pothead's long silence. If he was too strung out to answer, Cort would hunt him down and make sure he'd never be able to light another spliff. "Talk to me, punk. I have zero patience for you spacing out right now."

"He's at . . . uh . . . ." Reggie mumbled something. Probably to himself. The loser's brain couldn't retain his own name half the time. He finally spoke, all excited, like he'd come up with the answer in a Final Jeopardy round. "The General. One of the waitresses called him an ambulance when she found him."

*Jesus, Ford! What the fuck happened to you?* He pressed his fist against Ford's padded, leather-covered headboard. "How is he?"

"How is he? Don't know, man. Didn't see him. Angel gone brung him flowers and a card though, so I'm thinking he's not dead."

Cort hung up, heading straight out. He managed not to break anything else before shutting the door behind him, even though he was tempted. Losing it wouldn't help Ford. Getting to him, finding out the names—or at least the descriptions of whoever had messed him up would.

*Me being back won't hurt either.* He'd taken off because he didn't want to spend any more time "inside." A few years for shit he hadn't even done had taught him to take the . . . well, not high road. More like *any* road.

But Ford was on this one, and he'd crashed and burned. If he made it out of whatever this was alive, Cort planned to be riding by his side. From this fucking point on.

\* \* \* \*

24

A soft, cold hand on Ford's chest jolted him awake. His eyes shot open. He chuckled as his pretty little redheaded nurse leaned over him. He cringed at the sharp pain in his side, taking deep breaths as he shifted his position without giving in to the urge to wrap his arms around his guts and never fucking move again.

"Sorry, sweetie." The nurse made a soft, crooning sound. "I didn't mean to wake you."

"It's all right." Damn, she probably thought he was pathetic. The painkillers kept him out of the fetal position, but she'd seen him curled up and trying not to shout when the doctor had checked him out. Time to redeem himself. He toughed out a weak grin for Nurse Aggie. "I like waking up to such a beautiful face."

She blushed and ducked her head. "Oh, you are a smooth talker. You have a visitor. I told him to wait until you woke up. He's been here for hours."

*A visitor?* Ford swallowed hard. The men who'd come after him hadn't wanted him dead—that he was still breathing proved it—but they might want to make sure he'd gotten the message. They weren't his "dad's" regulars, so they'd been a little . . . *overenthusiastic* about the job.

Kingsley hadn't bothered to warn him personally. Since his mother's death, the man he'd believed to be his father his whole life, the one who'd raised him, hadn't spoken to him at all. Ford's eyes burned as he recalled his mother's last words. "Take care of each other." Her stroke had come so suddenly he'd made it just in time to take her hand and watch her slip away.

The look Kingsley had given him then should have been warning enough. His *father* had held back for *her.* He had no reason to anymore.

"His name's Cort. Is he a friend?" Aggie straightened, frowning. "I can call Security if he's—"

"He's my *best* friend." Ford rested back on his pillow with a sigh of relief. "If he's around, I won't need security."

Aggie inclined her head, her features tense with doubt. Then she spun on her heels and walked out.

The beeping on Ford's heart monitor sped up a bit as Cort appeared in the doorway. Seeing the brutal, tough bastard made Ford want to sit up and do something stupid like ask for a hug. Damn it, he'd missed the man. He'd *needed* him. Cort had been like a big brother to him since he was sixteen. Gotten him out of all kinds of trouble in the almost ten years since. Watched his back even after Ford was big enough to watch his own.

Cort didn't look like he was in the mood for a hug, though. He looked like he wanted to kill someone.

Ford chanced a smile, hoping it would get the man to relax a bit. "Hey, pal. Nice to see you."

"You stupid bastard." Cort shook his head and stormed across the room so quickly Ford shut his eyes and braced himself for the shaking he knew he deserved, but wasn't sure he'd survive. Instead, Cort shocked him by squeezing his shoulder. Carefully. "You fucking scared me, kid. You knew something was gonna go down, but you were all cool on the phone last week. I get nothing but a 'Might need your help, buddy'?"

"Mom died over a month ago. He didn't say nothin'." Ford couldn't meet Cort's eyes. But he could feel his friend's level gaze on the side of his face. "I thought I could handle it."

"Like I said. Stupid." Cort shook his head, moving away to pull a chair up to the side of the bed. "You knew he was fucking ripping about you selling your shares of the team. And the goddamn Forum. Who'd he send after you? And what did they ask for?" Cort's brow furrowed. "You've got nothing left."

"But my sister does. Her and her man own forty-nine percent of the team between them. Kingsley could use that."

"What *exactly* did they ask you to do?"

"See what I can get out of my sister. My dad thinks she'll give me her shares—and she might if I pushed. Tell her she can't handle it. I'd have considered it just to get him to back off, but . . . Silver's fragile. She's getting stronger, but who knows what the wrong trigger would do to her." Ford scraped his bottom lip with his teeth, staring at the ceiling. He hadn't seen his little sister much lately. His half sister, who'd once hated him and now invited him over for family dinners. To her daughter's baptism. For the first time, he'd felt like he had a real family. But he'd had to push her away after the first call from Kingsley's men. "I gotta say, he gave me more chances than most, even if he didn't give me a heads up. I got three . . . *messages*. Two over the phone. The third at the club ..."

Bile filled his throat. His waitress, Angel, had been raped in the alley. She'd begged him not to call the police, but he'd called Laura, the cop he'd met at the BDSM club he'd started going to months ago. Laura had convinced Angel to go to the hospital. Managed to convince his waitress that she'd be safe.

"You better tell me everything, kid." Cort sat back, perfectly still as Ford gave him all the details of what had happened over the last few weeks. His eyes narrowed as Ford trailed off at explaining how the thugs had shown up at his door and forced their way inside. "Go on."

"What else is there to tell? They put me here." Ford held out his arms to indicate the hospital—instantly regretting it. Sharp pain rose over the cushion of drugs, causing his stomach to clench, which made him hunch over, gasping for air. "I don't want to talk about it."

"Too fucking bad. If they . . ." Cort's chair toppled over as he stood. He raked his fingers through his short, brown hair. "Damn it, Ford, I know how this works. I wanna kill them for what I can see. I'll kill 'em slow if they—"

"They didn't. They threatened to. Copped a feel while they did." Ford shuddered as his balls shrank at the recollection. A big body on him. Hands all over. He wanted to skin the men who'd done so much worse to Angel. "Kingsley would have been real specific about that shit. I might not be his *real* son, but that's how everyone sees me. It would look bad on him if someone made me their bitch."

"But they hurt your girl. She was under *your* protection, Ford."

"I know that."

"Do you? You've got no one to back you. This *can't* happen under your watch." Cort paced, shaking his head. "Your girls deserve better. And it makes you look weak."

"I'm out, Cort. I don't want to deal with Kingsley and his 'connections' anymore." Ford frowned, wincing at the tug on broken flesh held together with string. He had enough stitches in his face for the scars to rival almost any of the hockey players on the team Kingsley wanted to control. He took a deep breath and met Cort's eyes. "I thought you wanted out too?"

Cort nodded slowly. "Yeah, I do. Did when I got free, but you still needed me."

*Fuck.* Ford thought about when Cort had gone to jail for two years. Not because of his job as an enforcer, but covering for Ford's brief stint as a car thief. Ford had wanted to turn himself in after Cort got caught cleaning up his mess, but Cort pulled the "you owe me" card. Of all the bullshit he'd had on Ford, he'd brought up the time they'd liked the same woman. Shared her. She'd chosen Ford, and he hadn't even been that into her. He was a stupid seventeen-year-old, and she'd been closer to Cort's twenty-six. Cort had stepped aside after warning Ford that she'd move on to the next "made man" who could get her out of her stripping gig. Said he'd let Ford make his own mistakes this time, but next time Ford would "fucking do what he was told."

At nineteen, Ford had still been dumb enough to think he could repay Cort by going straight—well, as straight as someone like him could be. He'd talked to Cort once a week when he'd gone to visit him in jail, taking all Cort's advice. He'd gotten his college degree in business. Shown Kingsley he'd be ready to take the reins when the old man stepped down, handle the legit shit *and* the family business. Drug smuggling and gambling just scratched the surface. What Kingsley was into made Ford's dealing pot and jacking cars nothing but child's play. But his father didn't trust him while he was playing at being a petty criminal.

While Cort was in jail, Ford had become the perfect son. He'd gotten along real well with Kingsley. Things were calm for a while.

Cort got an early parole and had a stable job as Ford's bodyguard and bouncer at Ford's bar. Everything had been fine until Ford found out he wasn't Kingsley's son.

Ford dropped his gaze to the rumpled sheets covering his legs. His chest tightened. He mumbled his next words so low he wasn't sure Cort would be able to hear what he said. "I still owe you."

Cort barked out a laugh. "Fuck that! Kid, I *am* out. But that's because of you. You think I didn't know how much you looked up to me? A little punk still hanging on to his mom's apron strings while trying to be all badass. If you'd done time, you'd be dead. Or worse. Ruined. My older brother tried to go legit to show me better, but he couldn't. I came a lot closer. To show you."

"Yeah, I really fucked that up." Damn, he was tired. And fed up. Kingsley managed to destroy anything good he tried to do. Everything Cort had tried to accomplish. With Kingsley out of the picture, Ford could have his bar, his real family, and the girl he . . .

*No point in thinking about her. She fucking hates you, man.*

True, but Cort could have his garage. They could both have good lives.

But Kingsley wouldn't let that happen.

"Kid, you did something I never would have done. You brought the cops in for that girl. You're on your way to the straight and narrow. Legit." Cort turned his chair, straddling it, a big grin on his face. "Just what I wanted for you."

*Great. So I get to walk away free and clear? Again?* Ford stifled a cough with his hand, shaking his head. "What about you?"

"I'm here, aren't I?" Cort shrugged, his gaze slipping from Ford's for the first time. "Might have a reason to stay clean anyway. And she's a lot less trouble than you are."

*A woman? That Cort's serious about?* Ford smiled, biting back the pain that tore at his stitched-up cheeks. "What are you doing here then? Go get her!"

"You really are a fucking idiot. You think any woman can keep me from checking on you?" Cort stood again, shoving his hands into his jean pockets. "I broke into your place. Saw the blood and .

. ." Cort tipped his head back, eyes shut. "Don't ever do that to me again. I thought you were done for. Reggie wasn't much help. He was 'thinking you weren't dead.' And I'm thinking of beating him sober."

*Reggie.* Ford laughed and it hurt. Bad. Reggie was a good bartender. A pothead, yeah, but they'd been friends when Ford was dealing, and Reggie was the only person who had stuck around when Ford wanted clear of that shit. He wasn't sure Cort would get that. Or that he could explain how much the few friends he had left mattered. His eyelids were dragging. "Don't. People love him. He always comes in fine. Never fucks with the cash like some of the girls. I think he went off the deep end when he found out I was messed up. I cleared some of his debts because he's solid."

"Not solid enough to keep things going while you're laid out."

"That's why you're here. I called you because I was gonna lay low for a bit." Ford pressed his eyes shut tight, trying to push past the weight of the drugs urging him to let go. "I'm still a manager with the Cobras. Handle the paperwork Silver doesn't have time for anymore, go to meetings, stuff like that. And I've got my bar. I need you to take over for me. I'll make it worth your while."

"Shut up." Cort patted his arm. "Ford, I've got you. Get some rest, and I'll handle anything you need me to. But get better quick. If I have to wear a suit for more than a month, I'll lose it."

"You won't. Give me a week and I'll be—"

"A week?" Aggie slipped into the room quietly, giving Cort an assessing look. "I apologize, but I couldn't help overhearing that. There's no way you're getting out of here for at least two. There were complications in your surgery. That drip I keep refilling isn't for show. Honey, your kidneys need time to heal. The infection alone almost did you in. From what I heard, you were lying on that floor for hours before—"

"Please give us a moment." Cort growled, all the color leaving his face as he stared down at Ford. He waited for the nurse to step out before continuing. "You stay. You stay until you're better. *I* deal with everything else. Got me?"

"Cort—"

"Say 'Yes, Cort.'" Cort bent over him, a hard glint in his eyes, his voice a harsh whisper. "Say it, and I won't kill anyone until you're on your feet. I have a feeling you'll want to lay those fuckers low yourself. I'll sharpen the knife for you. They dared touch you? They *will* pay."

"What about your girl, Cort?" Ford didn't want to kill anyone. Not even the guys who had wanted to rip open his asshole. They were pathetic douchebags on a payroll. On the payroll of the man he'd called "Daddy" for most of his life. But he knew Cort wouldn't let this go for him. For him, he'd dig them a grave near the ocean. Hopefully this chick meant enough for Cort to use his brain. "She the 'conjugal visit' type?"

"No. But I'll steer clear of her if I have to."

"You don't have to."

"We'll see." Cort sat back in the chair, like he was settling in for a while. "Get some sleep. I'm pretty sure you haven't been doing so good knowing 'Daddy' might send some flowers. Or another fist to the gut."

He hadn't been, but he didn't want Cort to feel like he had to stay. "That's not how he works, Cort. He sent his message. I got it. And I've got time before he'll expect an answer."

"Yeah, I've got his answer." Cort shocked Ford by grabbing his hand, squeezing hard before releasing it. That same hand had steadied Ford when he was young and got drunk, keeping him from walking into traffic. Or any kind of danger Ford couldn't see coming. "He can go fuck himself. I know how you feel about your sister. When you wake up, we'll talk some more about keeping someone at your door. And finding someone to keep an eye on Silver. Until then . . ." Cort dropped his boot on the table by the bed. "I'm staying."

# Chapter Three

Something pounced on Akira's bed, and her heart leapt out of her chest. She sat up, bringing her pillow with her as she spotted Jami, kneeling over her, howling with laughter. Akira thunked her with the pillow.

"You scared me!" She shook her head as Jami caught her breath, trying to say something. Akira could guess what. "Revenge?"

"You're damn right! At least I didn't knock you off the bed like you and Sahara did to me last time!" Cheeks red, Jami shifted to sit cross-legged, facing Akira. "And neither of you was nice enough to bring *me* coffee."

"Coffee?" Akira scooted up, bracing her back against her headboard as she retrieved the mug from her night table. Black, rich-scented coffee, so fresh just the aroma woke her up a little. She took a tentative sip. "Mmm, I love you, Jami."

"Oh good, because I felt real bad when I saw all the stuff you got." Jami's brow furrowed. "I should have come back last night to help you with groceries—but you said you'd be okay! I thought you were just getting salad or something."

"I was okay." Akira took another sip, then sighed and set the cup back on the table. When Jami had gotten hurt, she'd gone quite a while without telling Akira, or anyone else, about everything her stalker had done. Akira had told her off for not sharing that very important info with either her boyfriends or . . . well, Akira. It would be a little hypocritical to pretend like nothing had happened last night. "Actually . . . I wasn't. But it's not your fault."

"What do you mean? Did you get hurt?" Jami sprang off the bed and ripped the blankets off Akira's legs. "Did you twist your

33

ankle? Hon, you can't perform hurt. I won't let you. Sahara can take care of practice while I—"

"I'm not hurt. I was . . ." *No other way to say it.* "I was mugged."

Jami covered her mouth with her hand, paling. "You . . . what? Oh my God, Akira! Baby, I'm so sorry." She slipped onto the bed, pulling Akira into her arms. "Are you okay? He didn't touch you, did he? I'll kill him! I'll find him, then I'll kill him." She paused long enough to breathe. "Did you call the police?"

"Umm . . . not yet." Akira rested her forehead on Jami's shoulder, relieved to find there was no lingering fear from the night before. Only . . . her cheeks heated. She quickly answered Jami's question. "Laura will find out. And she'll tell Chicklet. And Chicklet—"

"Will tell Dominik." Jami rubbed Akira's arms soothingly, easing back. "Maybe you should tell him before she has to. You have to report this."

"I know." Ugh, that brief moment where she'd been able to think of the good that had come of last night was gone. Now she had to focus on talking to Dominik. And the police. Replacing her bank cards, her ID. She'd make a few calls to notify her banks and stuff, but the rest could wait. "Are you coming with me and Sahara?"

"Naw, I want to stay here and clean a bit." Jami lifted one shoulder, a sheepish smile on her lips. "Least I can do after what you went through. But before you go *anywhere,* you're gonna tell me why you're blushing."

"Am I?" Akira's cheeks were burning now. She wouldn't be able to keep this from Jami either. But for some reason, she didn't want to give details just yet. She knew Jami wouldn't judge her, but she might question Akira moving so fast with a virtual stranger. Akira fiddled with a loose thread on her blanket. "I met someone."

"Really? Who? When?" Jami bounced up on her knees. "Oh, I was hoping you would ever since Dominik started training those twits." She rolled her eyes. "You can hear them across the club when he plays with them. 'Master! Oh, oh, oh, Master!'"

Akira giggled, shoving Jami lightly. "I can hear you just as loud when you're with your guys."

"Touché." Jami stuck her tongue out. Then nudged Akira's shoulder with her fist. "Stop changing the subject! Tell me about your new man! Is he hot?"

*Very.* Akira chewed her bottom lip. Actually, he might not be hot by Jami's standards, but everything about him appealed to Akira. She let her gaze drift past Jami, a small smile creeping across her lips. "He's . . . amazing. Actually, he found me after I got mugged. I kinda freaked out. I was sitting in the snow—"

"Oh, sweetie." Jami's face crumpled and she took Akira's hand. "I should have been there."

"You couldn't have known that would happen, Jami. Besides, it turned out all right. He came to check on me. Stayed while I called Scott to see if he could give me a lift—" She held up her free hand when Jami's lips parted. "I figured Scott would be the least likely to freak out. Scott's still in Gaspe, but he knows the guy and told me he was safe. So I let him drive me home."

Jami nodded slowly. "He didn't just drop you off, did he?"

"Ah . . . no." The heat on Akira's cheeks spread to her ears and down her chest. "We hung out here for a bit."

"Uh-huh." Jami pursed her lips. "Scott knows him? Not so sure that's a good thing. What's his name?"

"Cortland Nash." Akira took her cooling coffee off the night table and took a big gulp. Tried to ignore her own reaction to just saying his name.

It was impossible to ignore Jami's reaction, though. Her eyes had gone wide. Her lips gaped open. "Cort?"

"*Yes* . . . do you know him?"

"Yeah. He saved me from . . . he's the reason I wasn't raped." Jami hugged her knees to her chest. "I thought I'd told you about—"

"You told me about the man who killed your stalker with a baseball bat! You never told me his name!" Akira groaned, draining the coffee as she threw her legs over the side of the bed. Her brain couldn't process the information. Her skin flushed hot, then ran cold. "He works for Ford. Oh God, I . . ." She laughed, rubbing one hand over her face. "I lied about my name. I thought it would be better to not give away too much—well, too much information anyway. And being someone different for a change . . . I didn't think about anything else."

"What are you talking about, Akira?" Jami slid up beside her. "Did you sleep with him?"

"Not quite."

"Not . . . oh, honey, he's bad news. You have to stay away from him." Jami took her hand again. "I'll talk to Ford, make sure Cort knows he can't—"

Okay, now *that* pissed Akira off. Did Jami think Ford was somehow better than Cort? Jami could be friends with Ford, but Akira had to stay away from a man who worked for him? Her eyes narrowed. "I don't need you to talk to Ford. Cort saved you. He was there for me. How is he bad news? You told me the guy who *saved* you was a bouncer at Ford's bar—does he even work for Ford anymore?"

"I don't think so, but—"

"Then he's a smart man." Akira stood, her cup clinking hard on the night table as she set it down. She paced away from the bed. Scowling, she went to grab her Ice Girl practice uniform from the closet. "I don't know how I'm going to handle this yet, but whatever I choose to do will *not* involve Ford."

"All right, but please be careful." Jami came up behind her, speaking quietly. "I don't want to see you get hurt."

Damn it, she couldn't be mad at Jami about this. Jami was blind where Ford was concerned, and she was just being a good friend. Akira turned and pulled Jami in for a hug. "I'll be careful. And . . . I think Cort expected me to find out a bit about his past. Enough for me to want to stay away from him."

"You're not going to though, are you?" The short blue strands of Jami's hair tickled Akira's neck as she shook her head. "He got to you. You'd already decided to see him again."

"Yes. I don't know what it is, but I can't stop thinking about him." Akira took a deep breath. "What he did for you makes him seem better, not worse."

"He killed a man, Akira. He didn't even hesitate."

Akira's lips slanted slightly in a tight smile. She patted Jami's cheek. "I wouldn't have either."

\* \* \* \*

The scent of leather as he crossed the threshold to the Blades & Ice BDSM club made Cort smile. Country music played low in the background—a little off in this setting, but whatever. The place was pretty empty. He paused by the coat check, looking over the tiny woman wearing nothing but a strip of what looked like duct tape over her breasts and pubic area. She didn't meet his eyes as she took his leather jacket. *Interesting.*

"I need to talk to some guy named Dominik. He here?" Cort asked. He'd left Ford under the watchful eye of his new bouncer, Cam—Dominik's brother, actually. The man had been damn pissed that Ford hadn't called him because he "didn't want to cut Cam's time with his family short." Cort liked the guy already. He was the one who'd suggested coming here to talk to Dominik about how much Ford's sisters needed to know.

And whether or not Cort *really* needed to take over Ford's management position with the team. Cort secretly hoped Dominik would say no.

"He's right back there. With Cheryl."

Cort looked to where she pointed and cursed under his breath. He rarely forgot a face. *Never* after he pulled a gun on someone.

In the far corner of the bar, the big, black man had a large, leather flogger in his hand and was using it to redden the shapely ass of a woman strapped to a high, padded bench. Cort's first instinct was to go over there and protect the woman, but he hadn't been living under a fucking rock. This shit got some people off, and the woman was making some happy noises every time the leather licked her flesh. Dominik Mason, who'd come to Ford's bar once with Silver, was shirtless, his skin glistening with sweat. Big guy, built a lot like Cort, which was why Cort hadn't hesitated to draw his piece when the man had gotten too close to Ford.

A fistfight would have been a lot more fun, but Cort didn't fuck around when it came to Ford. He'd been paid to protect the kid once. He still considered it his job to protect the man.

*More than a fucking job. No one fucks with my boy.*

Setting the past aside—he hoped Dominik would as well— Cort took a minute to take in the twisted decor. Lots of chains and crosses and whips lining the walls. Some stuff he didn't even wanna think about being used on another human being. The cages made him grind his teeth. No fucking way he could see being locked up as erotic.

He inhaled slowly through his nose, drawing in the familiar smell of leather again. Reminded him of his dad's bars. Got him nice and calm, because that's how he had to be around the bikers. His dad wouldn't put up with Cort losing his shit over a trigger like a cage. He could almost feel Sutter's grip on his arm, painfully tight, a subtle warning that he expected better from his son.

*I'm good. Let's get this bullshit over with.*

He would've thought a place like this would be closed on a Tuesday, but Cam had told Cort his brother was training a nurse as a submissive and had the club opened different nights to accommodate her schedule. Decent of him. Cort had a feeling he'd like the guy from the little his brother had said about him.

Too bad they'd gotten off to a *really* rocky start. Maybe the guy would understand if Cort was straight with him. He looked back at the coat check girl. "Should I be bugging him while he's doing that?"

"Ah . . ." She blushed, glancing up at him quickly as she shook her head. "Not unless it's important. I'm sorry, I'm new at this. Master Dominik will play with me later, but he asked me to watch the door in case any of the other guys came in. As you can see, none did. They lost against the Sabres. Never a good thing."

*Yeah. Whatever.* He didn't really give a shit who the Cobras lost to. The Red Wings were doing just fine, and his home team was the only one he ever rooted for. But the man might be in a mood, which could be an issue.

He didn't want to interrupt, but . . . fuck, Ford was in the hospital. He needed his sisters. Or, at least one of them.

Dominik could get his goddamn freak on later.

There was no reason to be a jerk about it though, so Cort crossed the room, moving to a spot where Dominik could see him, but Cheryl wouldn't. He leaned again a large, polished wood X with his arms folded over his chest. And waited.

Not for long. Dominik stiffened as he noticed Cort. His grip tightened on the flogger. His eyes narrowed and he glanced toward the front of the club. "Katie, please come help me with Cheryl." He stroked the curvy woman's back, then bent down to kiss her cheek, giving her his full attention, which Cort thought was pretty damn decent. "How are you feeling, pet? Can you sit with Katie for a bit while I take care of something?"

"Yes, Sir." The woman let out a soft, blissful sigh. "I feel wonderful. Thank you, Sir. I will wait for you if you want to give me more."

Dominik chuckled. "I'm sure you will." He undid her restraints. "There's my good girl. Up with you."

Ignoring Cort, Dominik helped the naked woman settle on a big, circular chair with the coat check girl, Katie. Only once both women were comfortable did he acknowledge Cort. He nodded toward a short hall with several doors and small windows.

Cort followed him into one, not taking his eyes off the heavy flogger still held tight in the black man's fist. He closed the door behind him. No need for the women to be disturbed if things got violent.

"So . . . care to tell me why you're here?" Dominik eyed Cort as he laid the flogger on what looked like a teacher's desk. The room had a blackboard on the wall and three old-fashioned desks, with chairs attached, in front of the big one.

For some reason, the setup made him think of his tiny in a cute little schoolgirl outfit, sitting at one of those desks while he paced in front of her, playing the tough teacher. Fuck, he'd never done any role-playing shit, but he suddenly wanted to.

*Focus, Cort.* Cort tore his gaze away from the desks and met Dominik's eyes. "I talked to your brother. Cam told me you'd be here. And that I should talk to you about contacting the Delgado sisters."

Lips in a hard, thin line, Dominik took a step forward. "About what exactly?"

"Their brother. Ford's in the hospital. Kingsley had him beaten."

"Jesus." Dominik took a deep breath. "Why? How bad is it?"

Cracking his knuckles, the image of how Ford looked in that hospital bed flashing behind his eyelids, Cort did his best to keep his tone level. "Can't give you details yet. But pretty bad. They kept him in because he was pissing blood. He looks like shit. With Silver's condition, it probably wouldn't be good for her to see him like that. Part of the reason I came to you first."

Dominik nodded slowly. "He needs Oriana."

*Man doesn't need a paint-by-number. Good.* "Yeah."

"I've gotta say, I'm a little surprised you cared about protecting Silver, but maybe I shouldn't be." Dominik rested his hip against the side of the big desk. "You're Ford's man. She wasn't a threat to him, but I was. Did you bring a gun here?"

Cort had a feeling the man already knew the answer. But he gave it anyway. "No. Don't need it. You want a go at me, that's fine. I'll try not to hurt you."

Laughing, Dominik looked him over. "Not saying you could, but why try not to?"

"My boy loves his family. The team's all wrapped up with the Delgados, so messing up one of their players would probably be bad." Cort studied Dominik, realizing he was vaguely familiar. And not just from the time he'd held a gun on him. "You play defense?"

"Yeah. You watch hockey?"

"Sometimes."

"Which team?"

"Detroit."

"All right, no accounting for taste." Dominik grinned, standing and hooking his thumbs to the pockets of his leather pants. "I'll talk to Richter about Silver. And give Oriana a call—she's still in Calgary, but I know she'll come. Thanks for letting me know about this first. Ford didn't want to tell anyone, did he?"

"No." Cort scowled. If Ford wasn't already laid low, he'd be tempted to kick the kid's ass himself. "Your brother's pissed that Ford didn't call him. And I'm not too fucking happy that I was only called in for the bar and the goddamn team."

"The team?" Dominik's brow shot up. The desk creaked as he pushed away from it, but it didn't move. Apparently it was bolted to the floor. Dominik's tone became dangerously low. "Why would you have anything to do with the team?"

Cort shrugged. "Well, Ford's a manager. Not sure how important a part he plays, but I'll step in if I *really* need to. And I'm good to have around if Kingsley decides to start putting pressure on the new owner or the Delgados."

"Yeah, I can see that . . ." Dominik's jaw ticked. "Like I said, I'll talk to Richter. The GM."

"Got it." Cort inclined his head at the other man, then turned to leave.

"Hey . . . I didn't get your name," Dominik said as Cort's hand touched the doorknob.

"It's Cort. Cortland Nash." Cort glanced back at Dominik, giving him a half-smile. "Should probably apologize for pulling a gun on you."

"That's in the past." Dominik made a vague gesture at the room. "Like what you see here?"

Cort shrugged, not wanting to seem too interested. He was still processing the whole flogger thing. "Still deciding."

Dominik nodded. "Well, let me know. Since you're gonna be around, I wouldn't mind showing you the ropes."

Yeah, the man was pretty cool. Cort was glad he hadn't shot him. He grinned, looking back at the desk. Never been interested in this stuff before, but something about the kinky shit he'd seen so far . . . he inclined his head.

"I might take you up on that."

# Chapter Four

"Thanks for calling, Dominik. Yeah, I'll talk to her. No . . . calling me was better. This is gonna be rough either way, but I might could smooth things over a little."

Max Perron finished up his conversation with Dominik, then put his almost dead phone back on the charger. Both Oriana and Sloan were watching him across the dinner table, but he couldn't look at them. Not yet.

And he couldn't sit still much longer either. He rose, tucking his chair back under the table after he stepped away, then went to the fridge for a beer. He held two up, finally meeting the steady gaze of his wife and his best friend. He brought the beers to the table when they both nodded.

Then he cleared his throat. "We're going home."

"You're fucking kidding me." Sloan gnashed his teeth audibly, shoving away from the table to stand. "Just like that? Fuck, Max! You know I can't just take off. Some of us have a job."

Oriana covered her mouth with her hand, paling. "Sloan, please don't—"

"It's okay, sugar. I know how Sloan feels about me not signing with the Flames." Max rolled his shoulders, leaning the one he'd messed up in a rodeo over the summer casually against the fridge. He knew it would piss Sloan off to see him all calm, but the man could suck it up. This went beyond what Sloan wanted. "I'm healed. And we're needed in Dartmouth."

"Because you still want to play for them?" Sloan pressed his eyes shut and tipped his head toward the ceiling. "You couldn't have said so months ago?"

Max shook his head. "No. This is what you wanted. And what

Oriana needed at the time. But now her—"

"Bullshit! Are you trying to tell me you were good with how things were? You put her through all this just to change your mind?"

*Well, fuck. You really aim to go there, pal?* Max crossed the room in three long strides. "*I* didn't put her through anything. None of y'all asked me what I wanted. I came here for *her*. I gave her the choice I don't reckon you could've." Damn it, his accent was getting thick. This kept up and neither Sloan nor Oriana would be able to make out much of what he was saying. And they needed to understand every goddamn word. "While you and Dominik were playing tug-of-war with my wife, I was trying to be the man she needed me to be." His jaw hardened. "I didn't want to leave my fucking team!"

"Max, sweetie, we could have stayed. I would have . . ." Oriana came to his side, tears in her eyes as he took her in his arms. "All you had to do was tell me."

"You had to get away from there, love." He kissed her forehead. "It wasn't Dominik. It wasn't even just how badly things were going between the four of us. I couldn't stand to see how much power your father still had to hurt you. But that doesn't matter anymore. It's Ford who needs you now."

"Ford?" Oriana swallowed hard. "Is he okay?"

"I don't know. He's no better than Silver in telling everyone he doesn't need anyone. But Silver has Dean and Landon. And the team. Ford has no one but the people who work for him." Max hated that his words put pain and regret in Oriana's eyes, but he couldn't sugarcoat this. "I can't tell you what to do, Oriana. I couldn't before either, but I will tell you what I've seen with you here. You've lost your love of the game. You're in school, and that's awesome, but . . . you could go to school anywhere. I saw how hard it was for you to leave your sister the last time you visited. I know you want to make peace with your father, and—"

"And Ford needs me." Oriana pressed her forehead against his chest. "Max, I want to go home."

"So do I." Max met Sloan's hard eyes. "What about you? You

gonna stick with this team? They just sold to a new owner. He won't keep you on. And they ain't making the Cup, no matter how hard you work them."

"You think I don't know that?" Sloan rubbed his temples, then shook his head and went back to the table to grab his beer. But he didn't sit as he finished it. "The thing is, I can't play, Max. And I can't just quit. Being a coach is the only shot I've got at being part of the game."

Oriana groaned. "Damn it, I can't do this again. I'm not choosing between you." She lifted her head. "Yes, you're my husband, Max. But I love Sloan, too. And I won't—"

"I'm not asking you to." Max pressed a finger to Oriana's lips, then kissed her nose. "Our man will be unemployed soon. Then he'll come home and we can take care of him while he's bitchin' about 'the ol' days.'"

"Yeah, fuck you, Max." Sloan walked over to the window, pressing his fist to the windowsill, rocking his knuckles over the chipped, white paint as he nodded. "You're probably right, though. About me ending up unemployed. If that happens, I'll go work with my dad."

"Then I'll never see you!" Oriana pulled away from Max and approached the table. "You could be an assistant coach for the Cobras. I'll talk to Richter."

"No thanks." Sloan inclined his head as Max brought him another beer. His brows drew together. "They won't welcome me back now. I doubt they'll be happy to see you either, Max. The Cobras have had a pretty crappy season."

Max frowned. "And this is somehow my fault?"

"Yes!" both Sloan and Oriana exclaimed before laughing.

*Real funny.* "Reckon I'm missing somethin'."

"They didn't call you 'The Catalyst' for nothing, man. Lots of strong personalities on that team. You knew how to handle us." Sloan rubbed the back of his neck, his expression showing he knew he was one of the men Max knew how to "handle." "Tim is phenomenal. I love the man, but he's not on the ice when egos start getting in the way."

"But you don't think they'll welcome me back with open arms?" Max couldn't see them doing anything else. They all understood why he'd left . . .

*Didn't they?*

"Max, Sloan is right." Oriana rubbed his arms. "They won't be all warm and fuzzy. And the press will have a field day with how you shafted the Flames." She took a deep breath. "You still want to go? I will either way, but I can leave and come back and—"

*Well, ya ever find yourself in a hole, best thing to do is stop diggin'.* Max was still pretty damn sure the men would be happy to have him back on the ice, but Sloan and Oriana would have to see it to believe it. So he shook his head and grinned. "No need, darlin'. We're both going. Sloan will come along shortly."

"And what if I can't?" Sloan tipped his beer to his lips. Went still, then inhaled noisily. "Damn. If this is even half of what Dominik felt, I owe the man an apology."

"You *do* owe him an apology. You were an asshole to him and y'all were friends." Max didn't hold back. He loved Sloan like they were blood, but the man hadn't even had the gumption to say goodbye. To Dominik or the team. "We'll be fixin' that when you join us."

"You can't fix everything, Sir." Oriana's tone became soft as she gazed up at him, giving him that look that said she needed him to be more than a husband or a lover. A role he too often left to Sloan—and at one point, Dominik. Because she often needed a harder Dom, a stricter Dom, than he knew how to be. Her voice caught as she spoke. "I want you to be happy. Whether that's here, or back home—"

"I know, sugar, but enough talk now. I know you. You'll be fretting about this until we get ourselves on that plane. And likely for a while after. Close your eyes for me." He smiled as she closed her eyes, then turned her slowly to face away from him. "Get me my ropes, Sloan."

Sloan's eyes narrowed for a split second. Then his lips slanted and he stood. "Right away, *Sir*."

"Oh my God, what did you do to him?" Oriana laughed, a hint of nervousness in her tone.

Max spoke close to her ear. "Not a thing, pet. We're both here to give you what you need. I'm thinkin' he's just as eager as I am to do just that."

\* \* \* \*

Joining his brother in the coach's office, Dean Richter inclined his head as Tim offered him the chair behind the desk. Some might question Tim giving up his chair to his older brother, but Dean knew Tim. His submissive urges sometimes came out when he was uncertain. He needed Dean to take the lead.

Dean didn't waste any time before stating what he saw as the obvious. "You don't think I should have taken Perron back."

Not a question. Dean didn't see anything else bothering Tim this much. Especially since the man in question was waiting outside the door to speak to them after taking a red-eye flight.

But Tim shook his head. "It's not that. I'm glad to have him. We *need* him. But . . . damn it, I'm not sure how to present this to the men."

Dean looked his brother over, still seeing the boy who'd worn his first suit at nine years old on the way to a hockey game. He remembered fixing Tim's tie and assuring him that, yes, he did look stupid in a suit. Their mother had cuffed Dean upside the head and pinched Tim's cheek, telling him not to listen to his nasty big brother.

They'd had a great childhood, but Tim was still a little OCD. About his appearance. About the team's schedule. About what the men would think about things they should just deal with.

At least Dean could help him with this little issue. "They want to make the playoffs. Perron can help them do so. Very simple."

Tim stared at him as though Dean had just informed him he really could train a donkey to skate. Then he burst out laughing.

"Dean, you should go back up to your office. Deal with the paperwork. Not sure you get anything that has a pulse—besides Silver and Bower, which is surprising. How's your man anyway?"

"You know how he is. He skated with the team yesterday."

"That's not what I mean."

"That *better* be what you mean." Dean's tone sharpened. "You are overly invested in your players' love lives. I suggest you don't do the same with mine."

"Understood. Your love life with one of my players is none of my business." Tim grinned, calling out before Dean could reply. "Come in, Perron!"

Perron stepped into the office, still in his sharp, dark blue suit since he'd been asked not to go to the locker room yet. His long, dirty-blond hair was pulled away from his face in a slicked-back ponytail. Dean had seen him earlier that morning to sign his contract with the agent the man had chosen at the last minute to represent him. Everything had happened much faster than Dean liked, but with little time to close the gap to a playoff spot, there were no other options. Every game counted.

"Please take a seat." Easing back into the chair, Dean studied Perron, taking note of his easy smile and relaxed posture. The man didn't seem at all uncertain about returning. If anything, between his words earlier and the barely restrained excitement that lit his eyes, he was eager to leave the office and get out on the ice. Very good. "You haven't played for a while due to your injury, so it may take a few days before we put you in the lineup."

"Or not." Tim arched a brow at Dean's frown. "He'll skate with the team as soon as the doctor takes a look at him. I'll meet with the doctor and the trainers after practice to decide whether he's ready for the game on Thursday. I see no reason for him not to play on Saturday, latest."

"Perhaps. Let's see what the doctor has to say first." Dean wasn't sure what to make of his brother's sudden shift from concern over the team's reaction to wanting to shove Perron down their throats so quickly. "Mrs. Pearce has scheduled a press conference for later today. I'll brief you both before we get in front of the cameras. If there's nothing else, I will—"

"Just one thing before you go." Tim smiled, but there was something in his eyes Dean didn't much like. His question pissed Dean off even more. "Perron has a three-year contract with a no-trade clause?"

"Yes. That is what I told you."

"Just making sure you weren't getting anything for him from Calgary if he signed with them." Tim shrugged, moving to take his chair back as Dean stood. "The trade deadline isn't that far off."

Dean stepped up to his brother, speaking low even though there was no way to prevent Perron from hearing every word. And no point in asking him to step out now. "Do you honestly believe I'd sign him just to see what kind of deal I could get shipping him off to another team?"

Tim's smile never wavered. He met Dean's eyes, his tone cold. "I believe you're a businessman, Dean. You always go for the best deal. This contract means you don't think you'll get a better deal on another player. I needed to know where we stand. Now I do." He paused. "Maybe my team should simply accept that Perron can help us reach the playoffs, but there's more involved and we both know it." He glanced over at Perron, who hadn't moved, but now looked tense instead of eager. "I'm going to be straight with you, Perron. I want to see you on the ice sooner rather than later because there are some issues to work out, and I don't want them ruining whatever chances we have left. We could get away with losing a couple of games and still skid into 8th spot. Hopefully we can get through the 'honeymoon' period by then."

Perron nodded slowly. "I got you, Coach, but I think you're wrong. The game comes first for all of us. I ain't seeing there being a whole lotta issues."

"The game does come first; I agree." Tim ignored the chair Dean had vacated and rested his hip on the edge of the desk. "But what you're missing is that there is no 'us.' Not anymore." The softening of Tim's tone and the understanding in his eyes as Perron frowned lessened the harshness of what he was saying. He straightened and nodded as though pleased to see Perron understood. "We'll work on getting back there though, all right? If anyone can help us get there, it's you."

"Right." Perron stood, rubbing his hands on his pants before holding one out to shake Dean's hand, then Tim's over the desk. "I appreciate being given another shot, Coach. I'll go see Doc, then suit up." He cleared his throat before Dean could excuse himself. "Sir, did you happen to speak to Dominik?"

Dean's brow furrowed. "No. Why would I?"

"He called last night. I didn't want to mention nothin' in front of my agent—that's why I didn't tell you before," Perron said. "Ford's in the hospital—got a bad beating. Has something to do with his father. Not too sure on the details."

"I see. Thank you for letting me know." Dean ran his tongue over his teeth, thinking fast as he strode out of his brother's office and headed up to his own. He and Landon had kept a lot from Silver because of her heart condition—it had become something of a habit. At this point, all she knew was that the team had a big investor who had helped bring the franchise out of the black. She still didn't know Lorenzo Keane was running the team. He and Landon had planned to break it to her—very carefully—sometime this week. Before the meeting he'd scheduled among the investors. Ford had stood in by proxy for Silver during every other meeting, but Silver wanted to get more involved.

*"She wouldn't if not for your brilliant plan. I told you we didn't need a nanny." Landon had just left the nursery, where Silver was rocking Amia to sleep. He spoke in a hushed voice even after they'd gone to their bedroom and closed the door. "Silver loves staying home with our daughter. Things are going well. Why mess with a good thing?"*

*Shaking his head, Dean had squeezed Landon's shoulder. "I know you love how devoted she's become to our baby. So do I. But it's also a good thing that she wants to get back into the flow of her life. She's getting just as bad as you are with hovering over Amia. We all need to find some kind of balance."*

*"I don't want someone else raising my daughter." Landon tried to jerk*

*away from him, but Dean tightened his grip. The flash of challenge in Landon's eyes stirred his blood.*

*Dean moved closer, his tone rough. "Neither do I. The nanny is here to help Silver. You'll be back on the ice soon. Feeling stuck won't improve the situation for our woman."*

*Landon glared at Dean's hand. Spoke through partially gritted teeth. "Careful, Dean."*

*"Careful of what?"*

*"You're not the only dominant one in this relationship. If you want balance . . ." Landon firmly pulled Dean's hand off his shoulder. "I suggest you don't try to exert your control over me. You and Silver overruled me on the nanny thing. Fine. But from this point on, I expect to be treated as an equal. Whether it comes to our woman, our daughter, or—"*

*"Or?" Dean waited, having a feeling he knew what Landon meant. Landon wanted to be an equal in* their *relationship, but he wouldn't say that because he didn't know what kind of relationship they had. Hell, Dean wasn't sure what to make of how things had changed between them. Not that either of them would ever act on it, but there was a tension that hadn't been there before.*

*"Or nothing." Landon scowled and took a big step back. He held up his hand, making a cutting motion before Dean could speak. "Leave it alone. This is about Silver. I don't care if I'm on the road or whatever. We make decisions together."*

*"Agreed," Dean said, perfectly fine leaving "it" alone. Things were complicated enough.*

And were about to get even more complicated. Silver had to be told about Keane, about her brother, and, Dean had to admit, Landon might have some good ideas on how to bring up both without Silver getting too agitated.

Either way, they had a lot to discuss. Landon was skating with the team, but Tim wouldn't mind letting him come up to talk to Dean about something this important.

Shortly after, Landon was sitting behind Dean's desk, raking his nails through the sweat-soaked spikes of his short brown hair. His face was red from the exertion of training, and water marks stained the front of his gold practice jersey. Landon hadn't moved since Dean had finished explaining the situation.

But he finally spoke. "What do you suggest?"

"Does she know Oriana's back?" Dean wasn't too concerned about Oriana saying anything just yet. She was a smart woman, and she'd consult Dean and Landon—and perhaps Silver's doctor—before she'd risk upsetting her little sister.

Landon let his hand fall to the arm of the chair and nodded. "Yeah. She called Oriana this morning to show her pictures of Amia sitting up on her own." All the strain left Landon's features. He sat up straight and grinned at Dean. "I wish you'd been there. Amia was so proud of herself."

Dean smiled, finding his hand in his pocket before he realized he'd left his phone on his desk. Silver had likely sent him photos as well. He hated missing moments like this, but at least he knew either Landon or Silver would record everything for him to see later. He found his phone under a pile of files his assistant had left for him.

"God, she's beautiful." Dean glanced over as Landon stood beside him. "She has your eyes."

"Yeah, but check out the look on her face. So focused." Landon nudged Dean's side with his elbow. "She gets that from you."

"You're quite focused yourself, Landon."

"Not like that. Here—" Landon pulled out his own phone and played a short video of Silver sitting in the center of their king-sized bed, holding Amia's hands as their daughter pulled herself up. Amia's big gray eyes were wide, her tiny nose wrinkling as she released Silver's hands. She swayed a little, then righted herself.

"Look at Mommy, Amia! Smile for Daddy D!" Silver was calling out as she shifted away a few inches, holding up her phone to take some pictures. "Landon, try to get her to look at you."

"Where's my girl? Amia . . ." Landon was laughing as Amia held out her arms, refusing to look at either of them, concentrating so hard on staying upright. "She doesn't want to get distracted. Oh, watch out, she's gonna tip over."

"I've got her." Silver smiled toward the camera as she swooped Amia up in her arms. "Such a big girl. Wave to Daddy D." She moved Amia's hand in a wave. "Say 'Miss you, Daddy!'"

His grin even bigger, Dean gave Landon a one-armed hug as he turned off the video. "Thank you for that. I wish I hadn't left so early, but this helps."

Landon reached around Dean, curving his hand over Dean's shoulder. "Not a problem. You'll do the same for me when I'm on the road."

"I will." Dean rubbed Landon's arm, thinking back on the original problem. "We should tell Silver tonight. If not sooner."

"I agree. There's no point in putting it off any longer." Landon idly tapped his fingers on Dean's shoulder. "We can make sure she's very relaxed before we bring it up."

"I've no doubt we can." Dean pretended not to notice the way Landon stiffened at a knock at the door. He moved away from Landon and took his seat behind the desk. "Come in."

Oriana slipped into the office, then cast a curious look over at them. A glance at Landon made it clear why. He had the expression of someone caught doing something either immoral or illegal. He'd worn that same expression when his father had come into the room to find them sleeping "a little too close."

*Another subject not to be discussed.* Dean's lips slanted wryly. He gestured for Oriana to take a seat. "I take it you've come to discuss Silver?"

Oriana toyed with the end of her long, smooth, bronze ponytail as she perched at the very edge of the seat. Then she shook her head. "No. I trust you both to tell her the *right* way." She took a deep breath. "I'm here to discuss Max."

"Are you really?" Landon placed his hands flat on the table, his tone taking on a dangerous edge. Dean managed not to laugh at the nervous glance Oriana shot his way as Landon continued. "Does your Master know you've come behind his back to speak on his behalf?"

"No, but—" Oriana started to rise.

Dean arched a brow at her. "You haven't been excused. You were saying?"

Her eyes narrowed. She sat forward, her knuckles white as she clung to her tiny black purse. "Don't *do* that! I need to know Max is going to be okay." She turned pleading eyes to Landon. "The men respect you. You're their goalie and you made your way into the inner circle faster than anyone. You can—"

"I think your husband would prefer to deal with the men his own way." Landon straightened and folded his arms over his chest. "I know I would in his position. And I wouldn't appreciate my fiancée trying to make things easier for me."

"And Silver knows better," Dean added, amused because he knew very well Silver wouldn't have quietly come to speak to one player on Landon's behalf. She'd likely confront the entire locker room if she thought a single man would mistreat one of the men she loved.

But Landon went along with it. He inclined his head. "That she does. However, since I consider you family, I won't say a word about your misjudgement. Though I expect you'll tell your Master yourself."

"Max?" Oriana had paled slightly, but a pretty pink blush stained her cheeks. An interesting contrast. Silver had the same way of being scared and . . . well, something else all at once.

Dean didn't want to think about his love's sister being aroused by the slight taste of dominance he and Landon couldn't help exerting. So he smirked. "No. Actually, I believe Callahan would come up with a much more suitable punishment."

Oriana's lips parted. She sidled up and out of her chair. Stopped. Moved as though to sit back down. Groaning, she crossed her arms over her chest. "May I go, Sirs?"

"You may." Dean waited until she'd reached the door. Then cleared his throat. She froze. "Will you be joining us for dinner tonight?"

"Ah . . ." Oriana glanced back at him. Swallowed at his hard look. "I'll ask Max."

"See that you do."

After she disappeared into the hall, Landon punched his shoulder playfully. "That was mean."

"It was." Dean inclined his head, chuckling. "I expect a thank you from Mr. Perron sometime this evening."

"Yeah, well, you know I'll back him anyway, right?" Landon sighed, meeting Dean's eyes. "You brought him back into the fold. Despite everything else, I will respect that."

"Which I appreciate."

"Really?" Humor lightened Landon's tone. "How much?"

*Damn the man.* Dean opened his mouth. Closed it. He'd keep his comments to himself. The younger man didn't mean anything by his teasing. Months ago, Dean wouldn't even have considered anything implied beyond perhaps chores being taken over in appreciation. Which was likely exactly what Landon *was* implying.

"I'll take over the shoveling for the week." Dean opened one of his folders, needing the distraction of work. And not the other man. "Now, if you'll excuse me, I have some calls to make and—"

"Like I'll let you shovel, old man," Landon said, the affection in his tone the only thing that kept Dean from taking his "old man" cane and cracking the cocky goalie with it. Landon put his hand over the papers in front of Dean, his lips tightening slightly around the edges. "That's not what I meant."

Dean gave Landon a hard look. *Leave it alone, my ass.* "What *exactly* did you mean then?"

Landon shook his head. Shrugged. Then laughed as he backed toward the door. "I'll let you know when I figure it out myself."

\* \* \* \*

Gasping and laughing, Akira ran down the last steps between the bottom rows of the Forum seats around the ice, collapsing into a chair, smiling back at her girls as they took the opportunity to do the same. Sahara dropped into the chair beside her, groaning.

"I need to stop drinking. My head is pounding and you're

insane!" Sahara fixed her bun, then fell back into the chair dramatically. "I'm getting too old for this."

"You're what, twenty-six?" Akira propped her foot on the back of the chair in front of her, grasping her hands around the bottom of her running shoe and bringing her head to her knee for a deep stretch. "Stop whining. And yeah, you really should cut back on the drinking. Jami won't like the drool stains you left on her sofa. She loves the funky old thing."

"I didn't drool! And I'm only gonna be twenty-five in April, thank you very much!" Sahara rolled her eyes. "But damn, that sofa is ugly! I got a nice one in storage, but Jami wants to keep hers."

"It was her grandmother's. On her mom's side. She was the only person on that side of Jami's family that she was close to. The rest are just like her mother." Akira eased out of the stretch, shaking her head. The only reason she knew about that was because Jami got really maudlin the rare times she drank. Which she had—a lot—after the last time she'd spoken to her mother. Her mother had invited Jami to her baby brother's first birthday, then called again a week later to uninvite her because, "They were going to Florida to celebrate with Jami's stepfather's family, and Jami wouldn't feel comfortable around them." Jami's mother hadn't *asked* how Jami would feel; she'd simply played it off like no big deal.

Jami did just fine without her mother, but those odd calls, the little *effort* her mother made to be "close," tore her apart.

Akira thought the sofa was ugly too, but she knew what it meant to her friend.

And now Sahara did too. There was no point in leaving it to Jami to tell her. Jami didn't bring up her mother or her mother's family unless she was in a really bad place. And Akira wanted to make sure Sahara could help Jami get through those times if she wasn't there.

Sahara bit her bottom lip. "Damn. Okay, I've heard a bit about her mother, so thanks for telling me. I won't say another thing about the sofa."

"That would be good. She didn't even tell her dad about the conversation with her mother. She doesn't want to bother him since he's got the baby to take care of—I told her he'd want to know, but she wouldn't listen." Akira considered the way she'd pulled back from her parents when they'd taken in a few foster kids. Not because it bothered her, but she didn't want to be a burden. Her father had seen right through her after a bit, and both her parents had sat her down to clear that right up.

She was sure Mr. Richter would do the same with Jami. Once he knew what was going on.

"So Jami doesn't talk to anyone in her family anymore?" Sahara sat forward, concern in her eyes. "What about Silver?"

"She talks to Silver, but everyone's careful about what they say to Silver, so . . ." Akira shrugged. "I think she talked to Tim."

"Oh, that's good. Tim will tell her dad."

"Not if she asks him not to." Actually, Akira was pretty sure Jami *had* talked to her uncle. She'd had lunch with him anyway, and had come home looking much more relaxed. "Maybe we should— hey, is that . . . ?"

"Max Perron!" Sahara stood, as did all the other Ice Girls. They jumped around, flailing their arms and cheering.

The chill from the ice was nothing compared to the looks some of the men cast their way as they stopped practicing. Akira paused, halfway out of her chair herself. She'd always been a big fan of Perron. And Callahan. She'd been heartbroken when they'd left, and the possibility that Perron was back on the team thrilled her.

But that was the reaction of a fan. The team obviously didn't feel the same.

"Bring it in, boys." Tim skated to the center of the ice, gesturing for the team to join him. Perron stood by his side, his expression hard to read behind his visor.

A panting breath and a thump brought her attention to the girl who'd joined them, kicking up a folding chair so she could stand close to the glass. Jami's back was to her, but Akira could imagine the tense look on her face.

"Luke better not give him a hard time." Jami shoved her hands in the pockets of her thick, black parka. "If he's back, that means Oriana is too. And Mom—I mean . . . I mean, Silver will be so happy." Her voice caught. "Max being here is good. Really good."

"I'm sure Luke will be fine," Akira said, reaching forward to put her hand on Jami's shoulder.

Of course, Luke had to prove her wrong.

His voice could be heard clear across the ice. "Are you fucking kidding me? So who loses their spot? Richards? White? *Me?*"

"Perron plays well on defense. I haven't said *anyone* is losing their spot." Tim didn't shout, but his voice carried well as he faced Luke. "He was an important part of this team for years. He will be again."

"Sorry, Coach, but I agree with Carter." Tyler Vanek, a young right wing who'd been out of the game for over a year due to a concussion, slid up to Luke's side, glancing around as some of the men nodded. "I know you were disappointed in how we played last game, but we can do better."

"Where do you boys get the idea that this is up for discussion?" Dominik moved to stand beside his coach, and though Akira couldn't see him clearly, she knew his eyes were hard. Cold. She wasn't sure how he'd feel about Max—and likely, Oriana—being back. Right now, he was focused on the team. And his expression showed he wasn't pleased with those who followed Luke and Tyler's lead. Disappointed didn't cut it. She shivered, glad that she'd rarely given him any reason to turn that look on her. It *had* happened, but usually when she was being a brat just for fun.

Which didn't happen often. She wasn't sure *why* she did it— sometimes she was just looking for a reaction. For . . . more.

More what exactly? She couldn't say.

Luke's venomous comment interrupted her thoughts. "Right. So we don't get a say. How 'bout we get back to practice while you guys work on fucking up this team even more."

"*Niño*," Sebastian Ramos, Jami's other lover, both her and

Luke's Master, said sharply. Akira had watched enough practices to know Sebastian didn't use that tone with Luke on the ice. *Ever.*

She found herself going still in response. But Luke just laughed.

"You know what? Fuck you. *Sir.*" Luke's skates cut into the ice as he drove toward the other end of the rink. He took a few wild shots at the net, then just tossed his stick and headed off the ice.

Jami hooked her fingers to the rim along the glass separating them from the rink and whispered under her breath, "Damn it, he can be such an asshole sometimes."

Before Akira could think of a thing to say to comfort her friend, Tyler made things even worse with his own comment. Sliding away from the other men, he gave Perron a mock bow. "Welcome back, man. Apparently the big guys think you can 'fix' the team. Good luck with that."

As Tyler turned, Perron nodded, then spoke up sharply enough to stop Tyler in his tracks. "This is still my team, boy. A few months didn't change that. Life happens. You should know that better than anyone."

Tyler fisted his hands by his sides. Turned slowly. "I didn't have a choice when I couldn't play with the team, Max. You did. Don't compare the situations."

"I'm not. But I won't apologize for doing what I had to for the woman I love."

"No one's saying you should." Tyler glared at Perron. "But you have no right to call this your team."

Tim put his hand on Perron's shoulder before he could follow Tyler off the ice. He shook his head and said something Akira couldn't make out. Max tightened his grip on his stick as he replied.

"Prove it right here, Perron. That's all that counts." Tim blew his whistle and shouted to the other men. "Anyone else want to be a healthy scratch for the next game? We've got forty-five minutes left to get our shit together. Let's go!"

Akira glanced back to see her girls trailing up the stairs, talking quietly amongst themselves. Sahara hadn't moved. And neither had

Jami.

"This isn't fair," Jami whispered, hugging herself. "At least he came back. He cared enough to come back."

Exchanging a look with Sahara, Akira climbed over the seats to stand beside Jami. Sahara squeezed in on Jami's other side. They both wrapped their arms around her and watched the rest of the practice. Something was off about it at first, but then Scott Demyan hissed something to his boyfriend Zach Pearce and took the Zamboni exit. Pearce watched him go, then joined the short scrimmage as the team split into two groups.

There was something . . . different about the way the men played. More obvious on the team donning white and gold practice jerseys with Max. The black and gold jerseys took up the challenge and met them with a passion the team hadn't shown in months. By the time they were done, half the men were slapping Perron's back and talking excitedly about the next game. Dominik hugged him tight, skating by his side as they made their way to the bench where the coach was waiting.

Tim looked over to where Akira, Jami, and Sahara stood, crooking his finger in a "get over here" gesture.

The three of them rushed up the stairs, then took the elevator down to join the men at the benches. Tim took Jami aside, leaving Akira and Sahara with Dominik, Pearce, and Sebastian—the latter didn't pay any attention to them. His entire focus was on Jami.

Dominik tugged at a loose strand of Akira's hair, cocking his head as she glanced up at him shyly. He nodded slowly. "Is this how it will be now, little one? You've stopped calling me."

"You've been busy." Akira shook her head when Dominik frowned. "No. Before you ask, the other subs don't bother me. I just . . ." She looked over to Sahara, who was flirting with Pearce, and rolled her eyes. "I've been busy too."

"Have you considered what I said?" His focus narrowed on Sahara. His jaw hardened. "She's a sweet girl, but she's . . ."

"Trouble? Oh, Sir, I know." Akira flattened her hand on Dominik's chest, curious about the fact that the "Sir" still came so easily when she spoke to him, but he was now just "Dominik" in her head. The sudden shift . . . she wasn't sure it was a good thing. But she managed an impish smile as she peered up at him. "I'm still a good girl."

Snorting, Dominik wrapped an arm around her and kissed the top of her head. "I sincerely doubt that. I like that you've relaxed enough to be a little naughty—even though I don't enjoy playing with a brat. And I do understand wanting to be there for your friends. But take care of yourself as well."

"I will, Sir." Akira considered telling him about Cort, but thought better of it. What had happened on the ice meant more than discord amongst the team. She curled her fingers over Dominik's collar, resting her head against his chest. "What about you? Are you taking care of yourself?"

"Yes." Dominik nudged her chin up with his fist. "Why do you ask?"

No better way to put it. So she took a deep breath and didn't hold back. "You seem fine with Max, but . . . Oriana's back, right? How do you—?"

"I haven't seen her. But I'll be fine."

"That's good." Akira rose up on her tiptoes to kiss his cheek. "You will tell me the truth before we see each other on Friday."

Dominik gave her a lazy smile. "You're coming to the club?"

She nodded, her pulse racing a bit as she considered how that would go over when she saw Cort tonight. When she told him what she knew about him. And what he needed to know about her.

"Good." Dominik slid his thumb into her mouth in the strangely possessive way he did that made her melt inside. He whispered in her ear, "I will expect some truths from you as well. Something's changed."

He was right, but she could do nothing but nod again as he let her go. Something *had* changed. With his help, she'd stepped out of her shell, but he'd given her a new safe place to hide. With Cort . . .

She wasn't hiding any more. Well, not really. Her fake name was her last childish fort built of couch cushions and sheets. All those fragile walls were toppling over around her, but she wasn't afraid. Because she could face the world again. All on her own.

So long as Dominik held her hand for that final step. She blinked, catching his hand, needing to really *feel* that he was still there. Maybe she wasn't ready. Maybe she was going too fast. Maybe she would fall on her face, and who else would be there to pick her up and dust her off? She still needed Dominik. Damn it, she should have gotten over relying on him when she gave the okay for the other subs.

"Akira, look at me." Dominik framed her jaw, not giving her a choice but to meet his eyes. "I'm still here. For as long as you need me."

"Thank you, Sir." She felt herself trembling and was grateful for the strong arms he wrapped around her. And she gave him all the truth she could. "I still do."

# Chapter Five

Ford tried to sit up in his hospital bed, the effort making his side feel like a knife was being twisted in deep. A low growl from Cam, a laugh from one of the two big guys that he'd blocked outside the door, had Ford wondering how far it was from the window to the ground. Fuck, he wasn't the type to run, but he was in no shape to defend himself. Cam could only do so much against those thugs. Ford had never seen Cam really tested—he handled fights in the club well enough—but the guys who wanted to "see" Ford would be armed.

*Cam's got a gun.*

Yeah, but would he use it? Kingsley's men wouldn't hesitate.

*Shoulda considered that before you hired him. Idiot.*

Another voice came loud and clear from the hall and Ford grinned, sliding back a bit to rest against the headboard.

"Problems, Cam?" Cort asked, sounding amused.

Cam snorted. "Nothing I can't handle."

"Good to know."

"If you guys were smart, you'd clear out. Kingsley wants us to give his son a message," one of the thugs said, not sounding so cocky anymore.

Ford smirked. They'd probably thought their odds were good against one guy no one had ever heard of. They wouldn't fuck with Cort.

"Ford got his message. Care to give Kingsley my answer?" Cort's tone took on a sharp edge. One of the thugs yelped. "Tell him 'I'm back.' You know who I am, right?"

"You're breaking my fucking arm!"

"Noticed that, did you?"

"Oh! Oh, please stop!" The familiar voice of Ford's nurse, Aggie, made him wince. Her next words had him trying to get out of the bed again. "If you don't leave, I'm calling Security!"

Shit. Security meant the cops. As far as Ford knew, the case of how Jami's would-be rapist had died was still open. Cort was a person of interest because of the fact that he'd disappeared right after Lee's death. Because of his connection to Ford—who'd been cleared. If he got arrested for fighting here, the police might take the opportunity to look into what had happened a little deeper.

"Shut that bitch up!" the thug who wasn't yelping snarled.

A *thunk* and quiet. Ford swore, managing to slip halfway off the bed before Cort spoke.

"Go take a walk, Cam. I'll clean this up."

"You don't talk to women that way." Cam sounded like he was about to lose it. If he hadn't already. "These are probably the assholes who roughed up Ford."

"Probably. We'll deal with them somewhere private. I know you're new at this shit, but put the fucking gun away. You ain't shooting him in the goddamn hospital."

"Right." Cam's voice faded away. Ford sucked on his teeth, shaking his head.

*Guess Cam* would *use his gun.* Thank God Cort was here, though. Last thing Ford needed was his new bouncer in trouble with the law too.

This was getting to be too much. Maybe he should call his da—Kingsley. Make some kind of deal. The man wasn't showing his usual patience. The team winning games wasn't worth someone getting killed.

He looked up as Cort came into the room with the nurse. Past the open door he could see security guards, some orderlies, and a doctor. The nurse pushed the door shut behind her and leaned against it.

"I told them your friend helped stop a fight, but . . ." She shook her head, bringing one hand to her throat. "I don't understand! What did those men want?"

Cort replied before Ford could, dragging over a chair, his guitar case under one arm. "Best you don't ask, sweetheart." He sat, giving the nurse a reassuring smile. "The one Cam knocked out will leave as soon as he's awake. Neither will be back now that they've seen me."

"That's good." She pressed her lips together. "But you can't stay here all the time."

"Cam's coming back, right?" Ford looked over at Cort, relaxing at his nod. Which made him feel even more pathetic. But he knew without either Cort or Cam to watch over him, he was as good as dead.

The nurse shook her head. "I know it's none of my business, but Cam couldn't keep them away before—"

"They don't know him. He's a live wire. They'll think twice before fu—before trying him again. I wouldn't leave if I didn't trust Cam to keep Ford safe."

All right, that was quite enough. Ford rolled his eyes. "Now that we're done making sure I've got babysitters lined up, you wanna tell me why you brought your guitar? I need a lullaby too?"

*He says yes and I'm gonna deck him.*

Cort gave Ford a lopsided grin. "Naw. Me and your doc talked. He said you're doing good, but your sulking isn't 'conductive to healing.' You used to like singing while I played."

"I was a kid. Doing anything with you was cool." Ford's face heated as the nurse gave him an indulgent look. "I'm not sixteen anymore."

"Yeah, you're a big boy. We get it." Cort smiled at the nurse. "You wanna stay?"

"If you don't mind?" She kept her eyes on Ford as she asked, which made him like her a little more. A blush spread across her cheeks. "I find a man who sings very attractive."

*Well now.* Ford winked at her. It was gonna be a long time before he got out of here—'least a week. Making his pretty nurse happy could work in his favor. "In that case, I guess we could do a song or two. What you got in mind, Cort?"

Taking out his guitar, laying it across his lap, Cort shrugged. "How about 'Only God Knows Why'—Kid Rock?"

"Fitting." Ford cleared his throat. Closed his eyes as Cort strummed out the first few notes. He'd always loved the sound of the guitar, even though he couldn't play. And it sounded . . . different when Cort played. Music was one of the reasons they'd become close friends. With all the other shit in their lives, it was their one escape. Neither had the ambition to make it big—no way would either of them get away from their pasts, find the time to dream.

But they could have the song. The melody. The lyrics. No one could ruin that for them. Make it into something violent and cold. He felt the rhythm seep into his bones and sang, letting each word free from his fucking soul.

The nurse hadn't moved. She just stared at him with an awed expression on her face. Which made him feel pretty damn good. He finished the song. Then laughed as Cort started another, "The Joker" by Steve Miller Band.

Cort grinned and let a note trail off. "Reminds me of that girl. Might play it for her some time. Too bad I can't sing like you."

That was some compliment. Cort didn't give those out lightly. Ford inhaled slowly, thinking of the girl the song reminded him of. His heart beat a little faster, but his blood ran cold as he considered her reaction to him even trying to get close enough to serenade her. Didn't matter how good he sounded. She'd probably throw something at him.

*I'm not the man for her.* Which made the song even more appropriate. To Akira, he'd never be anything but a joker. Not a man to take seriously. Not a man worth her time of day.

He'd still never stop wanting her for his own. Might be pointless, but he hadn't given up just yet. Which made the lust-filled gaze the nurse was giving him much less appealing. Hell, he was becoming a decent candidate for sainthood. Kinda. The last time he'd fooled around had been on the cruise that summer.

With an Ice Girl who'd made Akira's team.

Another drunken mistake to add to the many. Didn't earn him any brownie points with the girl he couldn't forget—no matter how hard he tried—but he was trying to be a better person. That had to count for *something*.

*Does it, really?* Ford's level tone trailed off. He was completely drained. Wasn't thinking straight. No more fucking singing. He couldn't think of a single song that could get the "I'm sorry I almost got your friend raped" message across. Or a single thing he could say to make it right.

He'd tried. And he couldn't even say why he'd tried so hard. Nothing but a moment of . . . something had passed between them. And still, every woman he met, every time he thought he might be able to move on, all he could see was her face. The only thing that kept him from dwelling too much was knowing Cort had found someone.

And by how often Cort brought her up—either on the phone or while visiting here—she was special.

Ford couldn't think of much that mattered more to him than earning Akira's forgiveness. Cort's happiness was way up there.

"You're seeing her tonight, aren't you?" Ford made a face at how weak he sounded. He could see his nurse going into . . . well, nurse-mode. She walked over to check his monitors. But surprised him by leaving without another word. He focused on Cort. "Where you bringing her?"

"Dinner and the new G.I. Joe movie." Cort pulled out his phone, a crooked smile on his lips. "She's pretty awesome. Told me straight-up I didn't have to sit through a chick flick."

Quite a catch, but still . . . G.I. Joe? Ford shook his head. "Seriously? Cort, you've got to stop fucking sweet butts. Unless she's—"

"No. She's not biker pussy. Fuck, Ford, you get brain damaged during that beating?"

*Touchy much?* Ford shrugged. "All right, but those are some lame-ass plans. What's she into? Can't you bring her to . . . I don't know, a musical or something? Chicks like those."

"She's into figure skating. I might bring her some time, but it's a bit last minute." Cort tapped the strings of his guitar. His lips slanted. "Doesn't matter. We'll have fun."

"So she's easy."

"Boy, you're asking for it." Cort shook his head as he put his guitar away. "We need to find you a nice girl of your own. Maybe then you won't be so fucking miserable."

"We're talking about your girl and what you're gonna do with her before you fuck her."

Cort lifted his head, eyes narrowed. "Watch it, Ford."

"Oh, relax. I'm just messing with you." Ford cocked his head. "Why don't you bring her skating?"

"I can't skate."

"So what? She can teach you." Ford snorted. Cort didn't look uncertain often, but right now Ford might as well have asked him to put a Hemi engine in a Smart Car. Like it technically *could* be done, but . . . why would you want to? And Ford wasn't about to ease up on him. "She'll think it's cute and sweet that you're making the effort."

"Cute, I can't see. Sweet?" Cort nodded slowly. "Yeah, I'll be sweet for her."

"Fucking gag me."

"I'm sure Dominik could lend me a nice big, red ball to stuff in your mouth." Cort stood, bringing his guitar case up with him. "We'll wait until you're all healed up before I gag you, tie you up, and hand you over to that Domme you like so much."

"Hey, don't get all kinky on me now." Ford's brow furrowed. "Things went well with Dominik? You were really vague on the phone."

"Yeah, I was. Don't worry about it." Cort put his hand on Ford's shoulder. "I'm taking care of things. You just get yourself better and get out of here."

"Will do." Ford could tell Cort was worried about him. Which was the last thing he wanted. So he latched on to the one subject that he knew would get Cort to get out of there. "You're meeting your girl in an hour, eh? Better go change and shave. Make yourself look decent."

"I shaved this morning asshole. And I look fine." Cort hooked one thumb to his leather belt, glancing down at his dark blue jeans. He was wearing a white T-shirt that was actually *white*. No grease stains from working on cars.

As well put together as Cort usually got.

But Ford wanted Cort to impress his girl. She'd clearly gotten under his skin. From what Cort had told him, this was their first date. Wouldn't hurt to make an actual effort with his clothes. And his five o'clock shadow was comparable to some guys not shaving for days.

Not like Cort would take his advice if he was direct about it. So Ford shrugged. "You're right. She probably likes you enough to ignore the scruff and all. Forget I said anything."

Cort frowned. Then shook his head and laughed. "Got it. I'll go change and whatever." He went to the door, gesturing someone inside. Cam came in, nothing in his expression to betray his temporarily almost losing his freakin' mind. He nodded to Cort, then went to stand by the window in full bodyguard mode.

Nice guy, but way too serious. Time for a nap. Ford plumped up his pillow and dropped onto it, suddenly beat. He gave Cort a sleepy smile. "Have fun, man."

"I will." Cort looked at Cam. "Take care of him."

Their voices faded away as Ford drifted off. A brief thought of talking to Kingsley seeped into his half-conscious brain, but he let it slide.

*Cort's back.* He let out a sigh of relief. *Things are gonna be good.*

\* \* \* \*

The doorbell rang and Akira jumped. Sahara groaned, jerking the eyeliner away from Akira and shaking her head. Akira bit her bottom lip as she glanced at Jami's vanity mirror and saw the ragged line going up to her eyebrow.

*I shouldn't have let her talk me into wearing so much makeup.* Akira gave Jami a helpless look as she pushed off the bed behind them.

"I'll stall him." Jami winked. "Stop stressing, girl! Men are used to waiting for their girlfriends to pretty up."

"Cort's not like most men." Akira held still as Sahara carefully cleaned the line using a Q-tip moistened with makeup remover.

"You forget, I *know* Cort." Jami patted her shoulder before heading toward the hall. "He doesn't do picking up girls at their front door for a normal date. He usually just goes home with the ones he meets at a club."

"Jami, that's not helping." Sahara pursed her lips, the Q-tip pinched between her fingers. "Just get the door."

"What I meant is he's doing it for *her*. Which makes her special." Jami paused, her hand on the doorframe. She caught Akira's eye. "Don't forget that. You don't need to . . . *do* anything to keep him. You deserve a man who will treat you right. And I'm still not sure he's—"

Akira rolled her eyes, waving Sahara back as she met her best friend's steady gaze. "Jami, I like him. And I want to see where this will go. He'll treat me right; I can feel it."

"Sure . . ." Jami's brow furrowed as she shrugged her shoulders back. "But you're still 'Ace'?"

"Yes." Akira's gaze shifted. She knew lying about her name didn't really prove how comfortable she felt with Cort, but she'd have to tell him the truth soon enough. And she wanted to be Ace just a little longer. The girl who hadn't panicked when he'd touched her. The girl who'd wanted him to.

Sahara arched a brow. "Ace?"

"I'll explain later." Akira glanced back over at Jami. "Please, just trust me."

Jami nodded. "All right. But I think you're making a big mistake."

"It's my mistake to make."

"Ugh, now I know how my dad felt when I told him about Sebastian." Jami giggled and toyed with a short strand of hair by her ear. "I'm the last person who should be giving advice. I hope it works out. And you know I'll cover for you."

"Thank you." Akira exhaled as Jami disappeared into the hall. She let Sahara finish with her eyeliner, listening to the conversation as Jami let Cort in and offered him a beer.

"No, thanks." Cort's smile was clear in his tone. "I didn't know you were Ace's roommate. How've you been doing, kid?"

"Good," Jami said, her tone light. "You?"

"Can't complain. But . . . have you heard about Ford? I've been dealing with a lot, but I should have called you."

*Ford?* Akira frowned, holding up a hand for Sahara to stop, leaning forward to hear Jami and Cort better.

"I haven't heard from Ford in a while." Jami's tone tightened with concern. "What's going on?"

"He's in the hospital. I can't give you details, but he'll be okay. I just came from there."

"Is that him talking, or you? I know how Ford is about admitting he's hurt. Remember when he broke his hand—with his phone in it—after talking to his dad?"

The whole past thing annoyed Akira for some strange reason. Not that she should care about Ford's past. Or present. It was probably just bugging her that Jami and Cort were being so friendly.

*She said she'd stall him. I didn't know that meant flirting.*

Flirting? Ugh, what was wrong with her? Jami wasn't flirting. She was asking about Ford. Who she still cared about despite everything.

*Well, I don't.*

Still, she held her breath as Cort laughed. "Yeah, I gave him shit for that. This is worse than a broken hand, but he's in one piece. Why don't you go see him tomorrow?"

Sahara tapped Akira's cheek. "Relax your lips, sweetie. I'm just gonna put on a light lip stain."

Akira made her lips soften, but she tensed as she waited for Jami's reply.

"I'm going to see him now. The idiot should have called me." Jami huffed. "Ak—Ace is almost ready. Just wait for her here. Is he at the General?"

"Yeah, but—"

"Wait here. I'm going to—"

"Jami. No." Cort's tone took on a hard edge that had both Sahara and Akira lifting their heads, eyes wide. They'd both heard that tone before. At the club. From Doms.

*Oh my.* Akira felt heat seep down from her belly, spreading fast. One of the things she had to tell Cort didn't seem like such a big issue anymore. Maybe he could give her *exactly* what she needed. She exchanged a look with Sahara, whose cheeks were red. Sahara swallowed hard, pressing her hand to her lips.

Jami let out a nervous laugh. "You can't tell me what to do, Cort. Ford is my friend."

"I know that. But I'm more than his friend. It's my job to look out for him, and he needs his rest." Cort's voice returned to the laidback one he usually used. "You'll go tomorrow and he'll be happy to see you." He cleared his throat. "You ready, Tiny?"

"It's Ace!" Akira giggled, then hugged Sahara and bounded out into the hall. Her breath caught as she watched Cort rise from the sofa. He was in all black, from his jeans to his crisp cotton shirt. His hair was still damp, unruly, but utterly charming. His jaw was smooth, and, as she moved closer to him, she caught the scent of his spicy cologne. He held out his hand and drew her into his arms.

Then he tipped her chin up with his big fist, bending down a bit so he wasn't looming over her. "You're a horrible liar. We have a few things to tell one another tonight. I like calling you 'Tiny,' and you don't mind it as much as you pretend to. It's either that or your real name. Ready to share?"

"Not yet," Akira whispered, knowing she'd just confirmed everything he said, but she couldn't find it in her to keep up her deceit while trapped in his level gaze. Besides, he was right. The way he called her "Tiny" did something to her pulse. She could be his Tiny without losing the freedom she'd found from her damaged past. But there was something she needed to know now. And she didn't care who was around as she asked. "Are you a Dom?"

"Honestly, I have no idea. I'm not surprised that you're interested in . . . the lifestyle?" He gave her a half-smile when she nodded. "Does it make a difference? Are you like our girl Jami? Is it something you need?"

Akira bit her inner lip, wrinkling her nose at Jami's expectant look. "Can we talk about this later? Alone?"

"Absolutely." He put his hand on the small of her back, leading her toward the door. He ran his hand down her side as she slipped her feet into her boots. His lips brushed her ear. "You look really pretty. I'm glad you dressed comfortably. I have a surprise for you."

Her dark blue skinny jeans and simple, white V-neck top with a thick brown belt low on her hips had seemed rather plain for a date, but she'd thought Cort would like it. Knowing he approved made her feel all glowy from the inside out. She didn't have to put on a show for him. She could be herself.

She *should* be herself. She met his eyes as he took her jacket from her and held it open for her to slip her arms in. "I should tell you—"

"You will." He grinned, then leaned close to kiss her nose. "But I think you had your reasons for what you've told me so far. Have they changed?"

"Umm . . . maybe?" She placed her hand on his chest, loving how strong, how solid he was. From more than all that muscle. It was just him.

"Take your time, sweetie." He zipped up her jacket, then placed her hand in the crook of his elbow. "There's no rush. Tonight, we're gonna get to know one another better. Let your friends know I may keep you out all night. But they don't have to worry. I'll take real good care of you."

Akira blushed, then forced herself to look at Sahara, who smiled at her and made a "go ahead" motion with her hand.

Jami folded her arms over her chest. "I'll wait up."

"Don't, Jami." Akira hugged Cort's arm. "I'll be just fine."

\* \* \* \*

Cort laughed out loud as his Tiny finished her story, then he reached across the table to take the cherry off her piece of Black Forest cake and hold it to her lips. She gave him a naughty smile as she slid her lips over his fingers.

"I guess your girls know better than to drink the night before practice after that?"

"I hope so. Sahara was pissed, but she admitted after that she would have done the same." She licked some chocolate icing off her lips. "I felt bad that she got sick after all those sprints across the ice, but she knows we all have to stay in good shape. The team needs us. It's hard to believe that Mr. Keane credits us for a twenty percent increase in seat sales, but it's true. People who weren't fans of the game come to see us. And now they follow the team."

"You should be proud of yourself." Cort put his hand over hers on the table. He'd gotten her to open up a lot over the last hour while they ate at a local pub. She wasn't just a hockey fan. She was a big part of the Cobra franchise, and he couldn't help getting caught up in her passion. He'd never be a big Cobra fan, but he wanted the team to succeed. For Ford. And now for her.

He tried to keep Ford out of his head, needing to focus on the time he had with his Tiny in blissful ignorance, but Cort wasn't a stupid man. It didn't take much to put two and two together and figure out exactly who this girl was. There was a sense of loss that he felt deep in his bones, an immediate feeling of knowing what he should do. Should . . . but wasn't sure he could.

No need to face it, though. Not just yet. That would come soon enough.

"I am proud of myself. And of my girls." She turned her hand to hold his. "Enough about me. I really need to be honest with you."

"All right." So much for not facing it yet. Might as well get the truth out of the way. He forced a smile. "Shoot."

"I know who you are." She dropped her gaze to the table. "Your father's a biker. He's in jail. And you have a reputation."

His muscles tensed as he fought not to pull away from her. Maybe who *she* was wouldn't be the issue after all. "I've been in jail."

"I know." Her brow furrowed. She gave him a hard look. "But I don't think you did it."

He shook his head, the laugh he let out tight and rough. "Babe, don't do that. Don't try to make me out to be some kind of innocent man wrongly accused. I'm not. I've gotten away with stuff that would get me behind bars for a lot longer."

"Maybe. But I still think you're a good person. We've all done things in the past that we regret."

"And some things we don't."

"Are you trying to scare me away?" She squeezed his hand. "You were more honest with me than I was with you. You gave me a chance to learn everything I could before going on a date with you. I wouldn't have come if I was afraid."

*So sweet. And innocent.* He shook his head again. "I don't want to scare you away. And that's selfish of me. But I think you're looking at me too much as the man who was there when you needed someone. *Anyone.* You've gotta look past that and decide if you really want to get mixed up with a guy like me."

"I probably shouldn't want to. I mean, you work on *cars* for a living. If I want a sugar daddy, you're a very bad choice." She smirked. "Good thing that's not what I want."

"You know very well that's not what I mean." He frowned at her, letting his disapproval of her making light of everything harden his tone. "I'm all kinds of trouble, Tiny."

She gave a mock shudder. "Oh, *now* I'm scared!"

He snorted. "And you were asking about me being a Dom? Not sure I'd put up with you being such a mouthy brat if I was."

"Really?" She leaned forward, eyelashes fluttering. "What would you do?"

The possibilities thrilled him. Damn, he couldn't help picturing her as *his* sub. Bending over one of those benches in the club, her little butt wiggling as she pushed for him to lay out some kind discipline. He shifted as his dick hardened, reaching across the table to frame her jaw with his hand, a slow smile crossing his lips as she went still. "I'd spank you. Which is why you're playing this way, isn't it? You need to know if I can do that for you. You're really into that stuff, aren't you?"

"I am." She drew in a deep breath. "Can I be really honest with you?"

"Yes." No question about it. He didn't want this to end, but there was no point in going any further without honesty. Once she laid it all out there, he'd know the next step to take. And he knew that might be straight to his car to bring her home. And never look back. "I like spending time with you, Tiny, but sometimes things just can't be—"

"I was raped."

His stomach dropped. The waiter who'd served them all night came over, but Cort made a sharp motion with his hand to get rid of him. He pressed his eyes shut and took a deep breath. "When?"

"I was sixteen. I'm over it." She dropped her gaze to the table. "I'm okay, but sometimes . . . it's hard to explain. If I didn't feel the way I do about you, I wouldn't tell you any of this. But since I do, I needed to say it. Needed you to know."

"I'm glad you told me, but—fuck, I wouldn't have—"

"Yeah, but I wanted you to." Even as he was condemning himself for going so far with her, she was tugging at his hand and glaring at him. "I didn't want you to see me as some delicate victim. I was so relieved that I could just go with it and you didn't know enough to be all careful. But I can't promise it will be like that all the time. I have flashbacks. I trip up. I . . . I don't want to scare *you* away."

"Not scared, Tiny. Nothing you say will scare me away." He stood, still holding her hand, nodding at the waiter so the man could bring the bill. After paying for them both, he helped Tiny with her coat, sliding it over her slender arms, feeling her soft skin. He walked with her out to his car, keeping her close to his side the entire time. He couldn't get those words out of his head. "I was raped." He wanted to take that away. Wanted to make it so that had never happened to her.

He'd been able to stop it from happening to Jami. He hadn't meant to kill the man, but he didn't regret it. Not for a fucking second. And he'd love to know who'd dared hurt his Tiny so he could take out the bat again. He'd do more time to get some justice for her.

"You look pissed." She drew away from him, facing him as he opened the passenger's side door of his car. "Cort, it's over."

"It's not over. It never will be. I saw how you looked after that guy mugged you. You were relieved that your money was all he wanted."

"Yes."

"Never again." He raked his fingers through her silky hair, staring into her beautiful green eyes to make sure she got what he was saying. "Whether or not you want this to go any further, I need you to know I'm here. You're safe."

"I feel safe with you."

"Good."

"But don't treat me differently. That would be horrible." She ducked her head. Her cheeks were blazing red. "I like the way you were with me last time. Like it was okay to just go with it. Do what felt right."

"That won't change, Tiny." He had to practically choke out the words without making it obvious. He wanted her; his body didn't give a shit where his brain was at, but she really didn't get it. He folded his shirt cuff over his wrist, bearing the number thirteen in Roman numerals, with a ½ beside it. "But you need to understand what you're getting into."

She paled a little as she stared at the tattoo. Twelve jurors. One judge. Half a chance at going free. She couldn't understand. But she shook her head like it didn't matter. "That's not you."

"Yes, it is. This is me. I've killed a man. And I would do so again if I had to."

"If you *had* to," she repeated very clearly. Maybe she did get it. Her chin jutted up. "Most people are capable of killing to protect themselves or the people they care about. I'd like to think I am."

"Let's hope you never have to find out." He rested his hand on top of the passenger side door, in no hurry to move away from her. "Is there anything else you wanna tell me now? That you wanna know?"

"Now? No. Let's just have some fun. This conversation is getting depressing." She wrapped one arm around his waist, hooking her thumb to his belt. Damn, having her this close felt incredible. Such an affectionate little thing, so delicate, but she had some spirit.

Which made the fact that she didn't pull away, didn't act all tough like some of his exes, damn satisfying. She didn't have to put on the hard front to stay on the level with him—a mistake too many women made. She proved she was strong enough to be a little vulnerable. She was slowly bearing it all, and he was amazed at himself for not wanting the date to end so he could get some play.

That changed the first time he fell on his ass. But her tinkling laugher made the bruises to his pride—and the rest of his body—so fucking worth it.

* * * *

Akira had been all ready for snuggling while watching a movie, but Cort's surprise was so much better. He'd parked near an outdoor skating rink she'd been to a few times, assuring her they could go to the movie instead if she wanted.

She'd caught the uncertainty in his tone, but didn't know what to make of it until they were both on the ice in their rented skates. He strode onto the ice with feigned confidence, and she'd found herself glancing back for him when she'd ended up halfway across the rink alone.

Cursing under his breath, then apologizing at a dirty look from a big woman with a pair of toddlers, Cort latched on to the boards surrounding the rink, trying to haul himself up. She'd rushed to his side, laughing as his skates slid out from under him.

"Why didn't you tell me you couldn't skate?" She held out her hand, helping him up and staying close to him as he clung to the boards. "Are you okay?"

"I'm fine." His jaw hardened as he straightened. His skate blades cut into the ice. "Thought you'd like this. And . . . hell, little kids can do it. I'll figure it out."

He pushed away from the boards fast, and she glided up to his side before he could fall on his face. Apparently he thought this was something he could conquer with brute force. His skates dug grooves into the ice. She shook her head, trying not to laugh again.

"Use the boards to start off. Get used to the ice." She gave him a hard look when he opened his mouth like he'd argue with her. "If you were teaching me to shoot, would you just hand me a gun and say go for it?"

"Tiny, I'm never handing you a gun." He frowned as she eased him back to the boards. "Why would you need a gun? Keep some Mace in your purse if you want, but I'll—"

"Protect me?" She sighed. "Don't start that, Cort. You can't be with me all the time. And that's not the point. This isn't about guns. I have experience. You don't."

He inclined his head. One hand on the board, the other clasped with hers, he slowly made his way around the edge of the rink. Then he groaned, watching a little kid speed past them. "I look pathetic."

"You do not. You're learning, and I'm sure everyone thinks you're a big sweetheart for coming out here with me." Akira grinned as an elderly couple skated by, arm in arm, the old woman smiling at her and the old man giving Cort an approving nod. Some teens were snickering a ways off, but hopefully Cort didn't notice them. "I think it's hot."

"Hot?" Cort tripped forward, letting out a rough laugh. "I

make a hell of an ugly Bambi." He smirked as she rolled her eyes. "But I think I'll be pretty sore by the time we're done."

The implication in his tone had warmth rushing over her, and she was sure her cheeks were red. She gazed up at him, tonguing her bottom lip. Flirting didn't come naturally to her, but it was so easy with him. She couldn't wait to be alone with him. To run her hands all over his hard—and soon-to-be aching—body.

"I have a few ways to make you feel better." Her breath caught as heat flared in his eyes. "But . . ."

"But what?" He chuckled. "There's not much I won't do for you, Tiny. *Obviously.*"

"I can see that. But I'm not sure you can pull this off." She let out a dramatic sigh, then ducked away from him. "If you can catch me, I'll do anything you want."

His broad laugh had her grinning as she skirted across the ice, doing a few easy spins just to warm up. Being on the ice without needing to work out or practice was wonderful. She felt so alive and free, and having Cort with her made it that much more special. She alternated between zipping around the ice and coming to Cort's side to help him try a few steps away from the boards. After about an hour he could slide a few feet without tipping over, but there was no way he could keep up with her. And the temperature had taken a nosedive.

She tried not to shiver, but he had a tendency to watch her very closely, and he caught her hand as soon as she glided close to him. The rink was almost empty. He managed to push off the boards and reach the part between them fairly steadily. He held her hand as he walked on his blades to the small wooden shelter where they'd left their boots under a row of benches.

After putting on his own boots, he settled his big hand on her shoulder, leaning close. "In case you missed it, I caught you."

Her lips parted. She wrinkled her nose. "That's cheating. You wouldn't have caught me if I wasn't coming over to see if you'd had enough."

"I was doing just fine." He grinned. "We're leaving because

you're cold."

"You're so full of it."

"And you're adorable when you pout. Don't be a sore loser. I won't ask you for slave labor." His brows lifted slightly. "Unless you're into that?"

She snorted. "Umm, no. Doing dishes isn't one of my kinks. And if you ever smack my butt and tell me to 'Go make me a sandwich, Tiny,' I'll . . . do something nasty."

"First of all, I *never* talk to women like that. Even when it's what they're used to. Second, if I'm smacking your butt, I won't be sending you off to do anything." He ran his knuckles down her cheek. "However, I would like to know what the 'something nasty' would be."

*Ugh, idle threat much?* She tongued her bottom lip, a sharp shiver almost making her bite it. The best she could think of was giving him a dirty look and *maybe* a smart-assed remark. She finally shook her head. "I have no idea."

He pulled her back to what she was beginning to consider her nice, comfy place against his side. And kissed the top of her head as he took her skates. "I'm sure you'd come up with something. I am duly warned. Let's get you into my car, all nice and warm, so I can consider what my reward for catching you will be."

"But you didn't!" She laughed, skirting away from him, spinning as he called out and tossed her his car keys. She got in the car and blasted the heat while he returned their skates. The cold seemed to have set in deep, and the heat couldn't quite reach her. Even as the numbness left her fingers, tiny shards of ice seemed to stab inside her toes.

She didn't want the night to end, not yet, but she was looking forward to changing into nice comfy pj's and slipping into her bed under a dozen blankets. As Cort climbed in behind the wheel, she glanced over at him, then ducked her head. There was only one way to get everything she wanted, but maybe asking would be too forward. Too . . .

Damn it, she didn't want him to think she was a slut. But no matter how great of a guy he was, there was no way he'd take her asking him to come home with her as anything other than an invitation for more.

*So don't ask.*

Cort turned to study her face, creases forming in his cheeks. "You look exactly like I do when I'm considering splurging on a new part for my car that I know I can't afford. Want it so bad, but it would be irresponsible. Reckless. 'I really shouldn't . . .'"

"What do you do? Do you buy the part?" She leaned forward, bunching her hands in the bottom of her jacket. "Some things have to wait, right?"

"Some things do, yes. But sometimes you've got to go with your gut." He cocked his head as though thinking over his words carefully. "If I can get a better deal holding off, I will. If taking on a few extra jobs will get me out of the hole quick, can make it so I won't regret the buy, I lay the cash down and walk out with a heavy chunk of happy."

Now *that* wasn't helpful. She smiled, nodding as though she understood. "You seem like a hard worker. I'm sure you don't regret things often."

His lips thinned. "I am a hard worker. I also know how to make a good deal. People respect me, so they don't try to screw me over. That respect is the reason I don't often regret things." He put his hand on her knee in a way that wasn't even remotely sexual, not with the way he held her gaze. "I respect you, Tiny. Be straight with me about what you want. I'll do the same and you can decide from there."

All right, that *did* make sense. It was like she wanted something without knowing the price. And he was willing to negotiate. Her chin rose. "I'm cold. I want to go home and . . . and I want you to come with me. For the night. I know how that sounds, but—"

He pressed a finger to her lips and shook his head. "Do you want to know what it sounds like to me?"

She nodded.

"It sounds like you want to be close to me, want to be wrapped up in my arms without being groped. Want to feel safe and warm, and you think you can feel that way with me." His tender smile softened the hard angles of his face. "I'd like that. I won't lie and say I don't want more—eventually. But after what you told me, it's pretty fucking awesome that you'd trust me enough to even *consider* asking me to spend the night."

She giggled, all the tension from before gone so fast she felt a little light-headed. "You swear a lot."

His lips slanted ruefully. "Yeah, sorry about that."

"Don't be. I don't mind." She put her hand over his on her knee. "I'm sold. I know exactly what I'm buying—not sure you know what you're getting into, though. I was thinking a nice, long massage to settle our debt." She ran her fingers over the back of his hand, her head tilted in thought. "So although I expect you to keep your hands to yourself, I won't be doing the same."

He groaned, then laughed. "Damn, girl. You're gonna test me, aren't you?"

"I won't mean to," she said playfully. "Why? Are you afraid you're gonna fail?"

Taking the car out of park, he shook his head, bringing both hands to the steering wheel as he pulled out of the parking lot. "Nope. Not an option."

\* \* \* \*

Cort muffled a groan in the pillow beneath him as Tiny dug her fingers into the tight muscles of his thigh. His dick pressed into the bed, hard as molded cement, but he did his best to ignore it. The massage was damn satisfying, even if parts of him didn't agree.

When they'd gotten here, his Tiny had quietly led him to her room without even letting him take off his boots. She'd knelt to remove them, but he'd stopped her, insisting she change into something nice and comfortable before she did anything for him.

*Big* mistake. Thankfully, she'd taken her clothes to the bathroom to change, but the flashes of her cute little creamy pink nightie under her long, white night robe made keeping his hands off her challenging. Worse, she'd had him strip down to his boxers, so he could feel the bare skin of her legs against his thighs.

It reminded him of all the pop quizzes he'd failed in high school. He *knew* the right answer, but his mind raced and his brain stalled. Best if he didn't move. Didn't speak.

"Tattoos used to scare me," she whispered.

He sucked in a breath as she ran a finger from the beginning of the tattoo on his back, starting at the base of his spine, all the way up to his shoulder. Full patch members of his stepfather's MC got the club logo—which reminded him a lot of Ghost Rider and was pretty lame—tattooed on to show dedication to the gang, but his mother had begged him not to. And even though he'd been young and idolized his dad, he'd made her that promise. Actually, she'd given her permission when he turned seventeen to get the tattoo Tiny was tracing with her fingertip. His mom's brother was a tattoo artist and had done the job free for Cort's birthday.

Since his Tiny was Asian, he wasn't sure how she'd feel about his having used a lotus flower and koi for the tattoo covering the expanse of his back, but he'd been obsessed with the symbolism ever since the only teacher who'd ever gotten through to him—a Korean teacher in grade nine—showed Cort his tattoo and explained the meaning. Overcoming obstacles, strength, rebirth, there was so much to the legends that he used for direction when his life went to hell.

His other tattoos meant just as much. His whole arm looked like car parts coming out of his flesh because working on cars was the only thing he was good at that didn't darken his goddamn soul. He hadn't seen much in his future beyond the lifestyle he'd grown up in, but his skin, both his arms, his back, was artwork that showed where he wanted to go. So many times he'd peeled off a bloodstained shirt after a rough night, feeling a little dead inside from how far he'd go to get someone to settle a debt. A flash of the tattoo in the mirror and he'd crash for a bit, then get his ass to the garage to put in insane hours for shit pay, loving every fucking second. He'd spent his whole life like that, sometimes swimming upstream, rising from the depths.

And sometimes he turned around and dove back in.

Maybe it was too late for him to leave all that shit behind him, but as he turned his head to meet Tiny's eyes, he couldn't help seeing a little of what she saw in him. Not a man damned.

Just a man.

"I can guess why they scared you, but . . . mine don't?" He rolled on to his side as she climbed off him to lie on the bed.

"No. Actually, the one on your back was the first I noticed besides the one you showed me." She ran her thumb over the tattoo on his inner wrist. "I don't think you'd put that on you for nothing. And I think this one was a reminder."

"Perceptive." He lowered his head to his arm on the pillow, reaching down to pull the blankets over them both. She tucked her feet between his thighs, curled so she faced him. He smoothed a loose strand of hair back from her face. "There's a reason behind everything I do. Not always the right reason, but it's there."

"And this?" Her eyes drifted shut as he stroked her cheek. "Is there a reason for you being here with me, right now?"

"Yeah, 'cause I want to be." He shifted to his back, drawing her close so her head rested on his shoulder. "Pretty simple."

She let out a sleepy laugh. "And yet, not simple at all."

He stared at the ceiling, barely holding in a sigh. Simple was a bit of a stretch.

*What the fuck am I gonna say to Ford?* He'd backed off one woman for the man he considered a brother. Hadn't thought twice. *What if that's what he wants? Can you do it again?*

Not a fucking chance.

*Delayed Penalty*

# Chapter Six

"**Y**ou're starting tomorrow night."

As soon as Dean spoke, Landon paled and stared at the tiny socks he was trying to fold together. So small in his big hands. Landon clearly knew it wasn't a question, but still, Dean almost wanted to take the words back. To make them untrue. *Unnecessary.*

If he thought it would do Landon any good, he'd leave it alone. Let Landon stay home with their daughter. Never mention the game again. If he didn't know better, he'd be convinced Landon would be fine staying home, devoting his life to doing nothing but making sure Amia was never alone for too long. That her cries never went unanswered.

But she needed to cry sometimes. She couldn't be in Landon's arms all the time. Dean and Silver had worked hard to get Landon to sleep through the night without getting up a dozen times to check on their baby. Which would be funny if it wasn't so sad, because Amia was such a good little girl. She settled in just fine the few nights Landon wasn't hovering, sleeping right through to morning, waking with giggles and smiles. She was doing fine.

Landon, however, wasn't. If he wasn't hovering over Amia, he was cleaning, or in the kitchen making sure Dean prepared the baby food according to all the parenting books they'd all read. It was Silver, not Dean, who had lost her patience and told Landon using store-bought baby food wouldn't hurt Amia. He'd grudgingly agreed and backed off a little.

Then the other issue came to the fore. Landon was fit to play. And wanted to, by the way he stared at the screen when the Cobras played. But he was torn.

Dean wasn't sure what bothered Landon more. The thought of

being away from Amia for any length of time, or the fact that she might not need him around.

What Dean had seen less than an hour earlier made the former more likely. And there was no mistaking Landon's reasons. Dean had walked into the bathroom to see Landon with a towel draped around his waist, staring at the tattoo on his ribs, a phoenix and the same poem that was engraved on his son's tombstone. Landon had walked by Dean, going to their room to pull on a T-shirt and boxers, but his hand subconsciously drifted back to his ribs even as he turned to Dean with a fake smile on his lips.

Dean had no doubt that Landon understood that Silver's postpartum depression wasn't her fault. But Landon still suffered some PTSD from finding the mother of his first child dead in his bathtub. And some serious issues about the loss of his son. The way Landon looked at the tattoo proved the fear thrived. He was still afraid for Silver, even though she was doing well.

Leaving their daughter to play the game he loved wouldn't be easy.

"Tell me you know Silver will be okay. She's a damn good mother." Dean clenched his teeth, fighting not to let his aggravation at the flash of uncertainty in Landon's eyes show. Fuck the internet and all the "knowledge" Landon had gained from it. Those horror stories weren't the norm.

But the fact remained that Landon had driven the doctor insane with questions for the first month after Silver had started her treatment. Landon needed to know Silver would be safe from herself. That Amia would be safe with her mother.

After the doctor, *and* the psychologist, had assured Landon that Silver was stable, Landon had stopped being quite so paranoid, but Dean still ended up waking in the middle of the night to a sense of something missing. He'd leave the room and find Landon either standing in Amia's door, watching her sleep, or sitting at the kitchen table with a bottle of beer he usually let go warm while he stared at the wall.

From talking to him, Dean knew exactly what Landon saw,

what he felt, while seeming to look at nothing. He felt the weight of his son's body in his arms. Saw the blood of the baby's mother darkening the water around her. And believed he'd failed them both.

"Landon, look at me." Dean kept his voice low, well aware of Silver upstairs, trying to get Amia back to sleep. "You're playing."

"Tell Tim to put Hunt in. I can't do it." Landon dropped the socks on the coffee table and lowered his face to his hands. "I'm going to retire. Silver's doing a lot better, but she needs me. Amia needs me. I—"

Dean shackled one of Landon's wrists in his hand and lowered his head as Landon looked up. "You are twenty-five years old. You're too young to retire. You have a contract."

"Fuck the contract. I'm a father."

"So am I."

Landon's eyes narrowed. "I know that. But why should both of us work? You be the breadwinner. Me and Silver will be the stay-at-home parents. Or I will be since you think Silver wants to work."

"The men are looking forward to having you back." Dean gritted his teeth, trying not to get frustrated. For a while it had looked like Landon was ready to start living again. He talked about playing with longing, as though he missed it, but then he'd backtrack—almost as though he felt guilty about wanting anything for himself. Dean was done with handling the younger man gently. It was getting them nowhere. "Is this the example you want to give our daughter? When things get hard, give up?"

Jaw ticking, Landon picked up the socks again after wrenching free from Dean's hold on his wrist. "You're a grabby, pushy, fucking asshole. Don't you have a meeting with Keane and everyone tomorrow? Go to bed."

"I do have a meeting. And Silver *will* be there." Dean stood. "I'm going to talk to her now. Are you bowing out of that as well?"

"Damn it, you've got to back off, man." Landon rubbed his hands over his face after giving up on the socks. "Why is it so horrible that I want to be a stay-at-home dad?"

Dean took a step back, thinking of the one time Jami's mother had tried being a stay-at-home mom. Granted, some people could do it. And be happy. Others would be miserable, and Dean wasn't about to stand by and let Landon become one of them. Amia deserved a father who felt whole.

"Tell me something." Dean grabbed the basket of clothes Landon had already folded, ready to bring them upstairs to Amia's room. He glanced back at Landon, trying to gentle his tone even though he was running out of patience. "You're amazing with Amia when you're with her, but do you think she gets anything from you when you're staring at the team stats in the morning, wishing you'd been the one between the pipes, knowing you could have saved the game?" He shook his head when Landon dropped his gaze to the floor. "Other players have kids, and you can tell they're proud of their daddies. Cheering them on out there, wearing their numbers and bragging to all their friends. Your niece does it. I want that for Amia. I don't want her to see you pissing away the few years that remain in your career, sitting at home with nothing but regrets. And the way you're going, that's all you'll have left."

*But maybe that doesn't matter. And if it doesn't, I still have a job to do.*

Heading up the stairs, Dean mentally went over Hunt's stats. And Ingerslov's. Ingerslov wasn't old, but he'd proven to be injury-prone over the last year. He'd also gotten sick again—his immune system was not good. The doctors were looking into it, but it was likely that the man wouldn't play for much longer. Hunt had talent but lacked maturity. If Landon didn't return to the team, Dean would have to look for another experienced goaltender. Which the team couldn't afford. Keane's money gave them a bit more leeway, but they were still barely above the league's salary floor of forty-four million. Which Keane would be bringing up tomorrow at the meeting.

The man was a billionaire, so maybe he could invest more than the Delgados had, but that would all depend on what the team needed. And what Keane was willing to invest. From their dealings so far, Dean knew Keane was a savvy businessman. He wouldn't throw money around needlessly.

*We need a goalie we can rely on.*

They had Landon. He could bring the team to the playoffs.

*Landon needs the team. The team needs him. I have to make him see it.*

As a general manager, dealing with all the issues players brought to the table was easy. He could handle egos and agents. But this thing with Landon was a little more personal. Pushing too hard made Dean uncomfortable. He had to separate what the team needed from what he expected from the most important man in his and his youngest daughter's life.

"Dean."

Dean stopped halfway up the stairs, glancing back at Landon over his shoulder.

"You're right. I miss the game." Landon hunched his shoulders and sighed. "And it makes me feel like a shitty father for wanting to get back out there."

Nodding slowly, grip on the basket tightening as Landon's words offered a sliver of hope, Dean watched Landon step up to his side. "But you don't think I'm a bad father for going to work every day? I did the same with Jami as I'm doing with Amia. And I raised Jami alone, for the most part."

"You're an amazing father, Dean. You know that."

After seeing how distant and tired Jami had been lately, Dean wasn't so sure, but he'd leave that for now. He put his hand on Landon's shoulder as they neared Amia's room, holding the basket of clothes against his hip. "Think of it. Amia has you, and Silver, and me. And we're all doing everything we can for her. You have to trust that Silver and I will take care of her when you're not around. And that every moment you're here will be no less precious."

"You make it a little easier to see that." Landon held his breath as he approached Amia's crib, the tender expression on his face making it hard not to understand where he was coming from. Blankets kicked off, Amia slept completely sprawled out, smiling in her sleep. Standing here, just watching her sleep . . . nothing else seemed all that important right now.

There were times when Dean hesitated by the door after he kissed Amia's cheek, straightening his tie and meeting Silver's knowing eyes before grinning and heading to his car. As Landon fussed with Amia's blankets, then went to check the long heater under the bedroom window, Dean stood by the crib, struggling with the urge to pick Amia up and hold her close. He forced himself to go to her dresser to put her clothes away. He'd been through this before, but it never got old. He knew how fast babies grew up, how quickly the time came when you had to let them go.

Landon shook his head as he came to Dean's side. His tone was soft. "I wish I could tell you why I worry so much. I just—"

"I know better than almost anyone, Landon. I'm here." Dean shook his head and drew Landon out into the hall when the man simply nodded. "No, don't just pretend you know that." He curved his hand around the back of Landon's neck, his pulse racing at the feverish heat against his palm. But he managed to get the words out that he needed to say. "I. Am. Here. Not just for Amia and Silver. For you. I know you are trying to understand what Silver went through with her PPD, but you're fucking stubborn about dealing with your own problems. I've stood by you at your son's grave. I've sat up with you when you've had nightmares of bloody bath water. Of Silver in the place of your ex. I've been here through it all." He had the urge to hold Landon against the wall outside their bedroom until the man did more than nod. Until he said *something* that would assure Dean his words were getting through that thick, puck-dented skull.

"I know you're here, Dean. I couldn't have done any of this without you."

"Damn it, I don't believe that." Dean lowered his voice, hearing Silver shifting around beyond the closed door. "Do you know what scares me?"

Landon swallowed hard, refusing to meet Dean's eyes. "Nothing?"

*I'm going to strangle him.* Dean inhaled slowly, keeping his tone level. "I'm afraid of what will happen when you wake up after a nightmare without me or Silver around. They've gotten worse since Amia's birth. You're better after you see her."

"Then don't make me go." Landon's voice broke. His muscles relaxed under Dean's hand, then he shuddered. He turned his head to stare toward the darkened hall, blinking fast. "If I'm here, I can always see her."

"You can't live like that. Maybe you should . . ." Dean dug his fingers into the sides of Landon's neck, pressing closer when Landon tried to jerk away. "We both told Silver to see someone. And she has. It helped her. You're a hypocrite for refusing to do the same."

"Then I'm a hypocrite. Silver has issues because of her past and having a baby. I'm okay."

"No. You're not. But I can't force you to see anyone, anymore than I could force Silver." Dean released Landon's neck, knowing full well he shouldn't be touching him like that. Nor should he be smoothing his hand over the front of Landon's shirt, feeling tense muscles jump against his light touch. "At least Carter will be with you. He tells Ramos everything, and Ramos will tell me." An edge crept into his tone, almost taunting as he smiled at Landon. "Having subs has been rather beneficial to this team, don't you think?"

"Try it, Dean." Landon latched on to Dean's wrist, turning to back Dean into the bedroom door. "Try to Dom me. I need a good laugh."

"Why so defensive, Landon?" Dean gave Landon a hard look, still smiling. "I'm a sexual dominant. There's nothing sexual between us. And if there were . . ." Dean let a slow smile slip across his lips, and he reached behind him for the doorknob. "I don't believe there'd be any power play involved."

Landon jerked Dean away from the door before he could open it. "Then what would there be?"

Sweet revenge. Dean liked being straightforward, but Landon

made it difficult. So he shrugged. And pushed Landon's hand away to open the door. "I'll let you know when I figure it out."

As the door swung open, Dean met Silver's eyes. Then frowned as he saw the team ledgers spread out over the bed. So far both he and Landon had managed to keep her on a "need to know" basis concerning the team. Even Oriana had done her best to distract her younger sister. Silver had seemed happy to stay on the outskirts of team management, hearing that the Ice Girls were doing well, that the team had made it through half a season with decent stats. She stayed off the internet after reading a nasty article from the vindictive gossip columnist, Hayley, about how her figure had suffered from childbirth.

Thankfully, that was all Silver had seen. Until now.

"We don't own the team anymore." Tears spilled down Silver's cheeks, wetting lips that had held nothing but smiles for so long. Dean stared at the books as she bowed her head, wishing he could have burned them before they'd hurt her. But she shoved them off the bed, the bitterness in her tone making it clear what was written on those pages wasn't what caused her pain. "We haven't owned the team for months. You *both* lied to me!"

"Fuck," Landon muttered as he stepped into the room. He drew his shoulders back, spine stiff. "Silver, we were afraid what the shock—"

"My condition. *Right.*" Silver's eyes were glowing with a dangerous light. Dean almost wished she'd thrown the books at them. That he could have handled. Her light laugh was nerve-racking. "Is that going to be an excuse for you two keeping things from me forever?"

"No." Dean stepped up to Landon's side. He squeezed the other man's shoulder, just to reassure him, then went to the bed, taking a knee close to Silver by the side of the bed. "Listen to me, dragonfly. I know what this team means to you. How hard you've tried to keep it going. Ford's decision to sell his shares to Keane surprised me. I didn't know the power the Kingsleys held. Or that Ford could change that by using his shares and getting to the investors."

"That bastard." Silver glared at him, but her rage was all for her half brother. "I was actually starting to like him. I should have known something was up when he pulled away from me and Oriana. He took *everything* my father worked his whole life for."

Dean hated defending Ford, but in this case, he had no choice. "Ford gave his power away. Oriana kept him in as management, but—"

"Oriana knows?" Silver slapped the hand he held out to her away, shaking and hissing at him as she shoved herself against the headboard. "So everyone thought I was too weak for the truth. Damn it, I can't blame you. Who wants an ex-druggie making decisions? I might as well just have kept getting high and—"

"Silver, please—" Landon took a step back, away from Silver. From Dean. His expression showed all the fear Dean had tried to get him past. "—please don't say that. You're better."

"Am I?" Silver gave Landon an incredulous look. "You don't believe that. You don't trust me with our daughter. You won't leave unless someone else is here to keep an eye on me."

"That's not true!"

It was, but Dean wasn't going to get into that now. Both Landon and Silver were hurting. And lashing out at one another because they couldn't deal with the pain. He wouldn't let that happen.

"Enough." He sat on the edge of the bed, latched on to Silver's wrist, giving her a moment to respond to his sharp tone. To his solid grip. She resisted at first, but when he brought his hand to her jaw and made her face him, her body went soft. He pulled her close and met Landon's eyes. "Come sit down, Landon. We will discuss this like adults. No shouting. Silver paced the floors for an hour to get Amia to sleep. Wake her up, and you'll sleep downstairs on the sofa while I bring her to sleep between me and Silver." Dean's jaw hardened as Landon took a deep breath to start on one of his parenting rants. "Yes, I know neither you or Becky even slept in your parents' beds, but Tim, all my brothers and sisters, and I took turns doing so. And none of us were smothered. Jami spent many a night on the sofa with me, and she's clearly fine."

"Damn it, I get it. You know what you're doing." Landon paced across the room, then threw his arms up in the air. "There's no reason to wake her up. But I'll sleep on the floor in here before I sleep on the sofa."

"Because you don't trust me." Silver lifted her head to scowl at Landon. "Very clear. And I hate you for that."

*Ouch.* Dean stroked Silver's arm, trying to calm her, but knowing she and Landon needed to hash things out. Apparently in the most brutal way possible.

"You hate me?" Landon looked like someone had driven a spike into his heart and was slowly twisting it. He took another step back, knocking so hard into the dresser that several of Silver's perfume bottles fell over, several cracking and letting out a pungent wave of spice and sweetness. "Silver, I love you. And I'm trying to—"

"You're trying?" Silver pressed against Dean's side. "This is you trying?"

Landon approached the bed cautiously. His leg touched Dean's but he kept clear of Silver. "I *am* trying. But Dean's right. Maybe I need help too."

Dean blinked even as Silver stared at Landon, all the righteous anger seeping out of her body. Landon's admission shocked the hell out of him. And suddenly he was afraid Silver might say the wrong thing and ruin whatever progress they'd made. Damn it, the two of them were difficult enough for *him* to need therapy.

"Landon, please come here." Silver held out her hand, her head on Dean's shoulder as Landon took it. She sighed as though the rage had taken the last of her strength. Or maybe she was ready to cast it aside. "I'm . . . I'm sorry I wasn't there the last time you visited your son's grave. I've been selfish."

"No. Silver, none of this is your fault." Landon knelt and brought Silver's hand up to his lips. He kissed her knuckles. "At least Dean was here to help you when I couldn't. I know me and you planned to walk down the aisle and make this all legal, but he would make a better husband."

Silver's lips quirked. "To us both."

Landon frowned. "Don't start that again."

*God help me.* Dean did *not* want the conversation to go *there.*

"Start what?" Silver arched a brow, pulling free of them to rest her elbows behind her on the mountain of pillows on the end of their bed. "I know when I have competition. I went through this with Asher and Cedric. Just wanna catch it before I'm left out again."

Dean chuckled, moving up onto the bed and latching on to Silver's wrists with one hand. He drew them over her head, holding her down so he could kiss her. "Those men didn't know what they had. I bet they're regretting letting you go now."

"I doubt it." Silver sighed as Dean held her wrists and drew her nightgown up over her breasts. "But it's nice to be with two men who actually *like* women."

"*Only* like women." Landon rose up on her other side, brushed his lips over Silver's, then lowered to take a tight nipple in his mouth. He took hold of Silver's wrists, moving in perfect sync with Dean as though he'd sensed Dean wanted to shift his attention to thoroughly distract their woman.

Silver arched her back, trembling as Dean kissed down her belly. "We agreed to be honest with each other, Landon."

"That we did." Landon cupped his hands under Silver's breasts, moving over her so his hard thigh pressed against Dean's side. "I've missed you."

"But you and Dean—ah!" Silver cried out as Dean thrust his tongue into her moist depths. He already knew what Landon's answer would be. And he didn't need to hear it while enjoying the body of the woman he loved. She tasted so sweet, was so hot under his lips. The way she tightened and released as he pushed his tongue in deep made it easy to forget everything else. He grabbed her ankles when she moaned, shifting her legs even as her hips rose to him. She was trying to get closer. Get away. Mindlessly.

*Utter perfection.*

Silver panted as he licked along the slit of her pussy. "You're trying to distract me."

"And doing well." Dean smiled as he pushed two fingers into her. She tossed her head from side to side. "Don't come, dragonfly. I want you begging."

Silver whimpered as Landon restrained her wrists, leaving her no choice but to accept whatever Dean gave her. Ever since making love had been safe after Amia's birth, either he or Landon had taken her gently. And alone. This was the first time the three of them had come together in far too long.

She licked her bottom lip, then bit the tip of her tongue. "I won't beg. Not until you both come clean."

His lips curving, Dean eyed Landon as the other man sucked hard on Silver's throat. Landon still wore his boxers and a snug white shirt with a Cobra logo centered on the chest. He struggled to remove both as he licked and sucked every bit of Silver's skin he could reach. He seemed oblivious to Silver's words, but Dean knew better.

Silver wanted them to come clean. But why? Dean rose up to align his body with hers. He unzipped his dress pants and pressed hard and firm against her moist slit, rolling her to her side to face him, drawing one thigh up to his hip as he thrust in deep. Landon had moved over to the side of the bed to find something in the night table drawer.

Dean took the opportunity to whisper in Silver's ear as he held her tight against him, telling her what she needed to hear, but Landon didn't. "How long have you been fantasizing about me and him together, pet? Do you pleasure yourself while you imagine how he would look under me?"

"God, Dean!" Silver cried out as Dean drew out almost all the way. Her core convulsed as though she was nearing the edge of release. "Please . . . Sir. More!"

"More what, pet?" He drove into her hard, then held her still as Landon positioned himself behind her, preparing her with lube-slicked fingers. "Details? Nothing's happened. But if it did, I would still want this. I would still need you, and so would he."

"You don't know that! I don't want to hear it!" Silver panted as Landon slowly pressed deep into her from behind. She fit snugly around Dean, her body reacting even as her mind retreated. He made a soft shushing sound, conscious of how close Landon was. Feeling the pressure of him filling her. And he didn't need to hear this either. Teasing became irrelevant as Silver raked at Dean's back with her nails. "Make me come! I'm still mad at you, and this isn't helping!"

"You mean *let* you come, don't you, pet?" Landon kissed Silver's throat over the mark he'd left, then grinned at Dean. "Didn't we make a rule about never going to bed mad? Maybe we should all get up and go discuss this in the kitchen?"

"Not an official rule, but a very good idea," Dean said, giving Silver a slow smile. "Don't you think, dragonfly?"

"Don't you fucking dare." Silver let out a mountain cat-worthy growl. "You leave me like this, and I'll kill you both in your sleep."

"Now that isn't a very nice thing for a sub to say to her Doms." Dean clucked his tongue, easing his dick out of her hot cunt. He placed his hand over Silver's mouth before she could say anything else to get herself in trouble. His dick didn't appreciate the cool draft brushing over slick flesh, but it had been too long since he'd exercised any real control over Silver. There was no better time than the present to do so. "Landon, please hold her on top of you, legs wide open. We've been too indulgent, too gentle. That needs to change."

Silver's eyes widened. As Landon shifted so she lay with her back to his chest, spreading her legs with his hands hooked under her knees, she shook her head. Her hand flattened on Dean's chest as he knelt between her parted thighs. She blinked fast—a nonverbal sign that she was overwhelmed—and he moved his hand. "Dean—*Sir*, you have been gentle. I don't know if I'm ready for . . . it might hurt."

Dean studied Silver's face, taking note of the flush of her

cheeks and the way her pupils dilated even as she voiced her fear. She might be a little afraid, but the fear aroused her. If he backed off completely, she'd be disappointed.

*We can't have that.*

He inclined his head. "If you behave, I won't gag you." He angled his dick to her moist slit. "Latch your hands behind Landon's neck. We both know you can't stop me, pet. And that you don't really want to."

"Don't speak, little one." Landon met Dean's eyes and nodded, his way of telling Dean they were on the same page. They often communicated this way during a scene, a brief look, a touch, some gesture either to say all was well, or not. Few words were needed with how easily they read one another. Landon returned his attention to Silver, speaking low as he ground his dick into her ass. "Safeword if you need to, but otherwise, relax and take whatever he gives you." He kissed her cheek as she gave a short nod. "I'll feel him through you as he pounds into you. And I want it rough."

*Fuck.* Dean groaned, tasting the beads of sweat on his lips, the aroma of his own musk, Silver's sweetness, and Landon's heady aroma almost undoing him. Landon smirked at him, but a long, hard thrust wiped the smirk right off the cocky young man's face. Landon's legs were stretched out on either side of Dean's knees, and Dean could feel his thigh muscles tense. Silver's hips rose to take Dean in deeper, then jerked back as Landon moved in and out. She shuddered, and it wasn't long before she was making pleading, incoherent sounds.

But she didn't come. She wouldn't until given permission.

*Good girl.* Dean kept his pace going hard and fast, framing Silver's jaw with his hand to take her mouth in a rough kiss. His balls tightened and his pulse thrummed erratically up the length of his dick. He pressed his eyes shut, determined to retain control. He never expected more from Silver than he could manage himself. Once he couldn't hold back anymore, he'd let her find her release.

A firm, callused hand gripped his upper thigh, and his steady pace faltered. Landon's unspoken rule was that they didn't touch one another. It was his fucking rule, and his timing in breaking it was horrible. That grip tested Dean's control because it was unexpected. He cursed under his breath as his eyes shot open. Landon did not touch Dean when they were in bed together—at least no more than necessary to be with their woman. Contact was usually casual. Or unintentional.

From the glazed, steady look Landon gave him, this was intentional. And more than Dean could take. He spoke against Silver's lips. "Come for me, love. Let it all go."

Silver bucked and let out a scream that Dean silenced with a long, gentle kiss, even as violent pleasure tore through him. His breath caught and heat erupted from the base of his spine, straight through his dick as Landon's grip on his thigh tightened. He could *feel* the way Landon's cock jerked inside her, and it was almost too much. Physically, emotionally, he was raw and without any resistance. His brain tried to speak past the erotic haze, but he let the pleasure drown out any logic it wanted to throw in. Every last ounce of strength he had left went to not collapsing on Silver, to holding still as her inner muscles undulated around his sensitive, slackening cock.

"Mmm." Silver wrapped her arms around his neck, sighing happily as Dean carefully pulled her off Landon and lay on the bed with her in his arms, not quite ready to leave her. "May I speak now, Sirs?"

"Not until I get my brain functioning again." Landon laughed, pressing a light kiss on Silver's hip before pushing off the bed. "Damn, that was amazing. Let me clean up and call Tim. I'm not sure I'll be in any shape to play tomorrow. The two of you did me in."

Dean rolled his eyes as he lazily stroked Silver's back. His mind couldn't come to grips with how far away Landon was. He did his best not to react to it and go with the conversation as though Landon not being in the bed didn't matter. "Don't tell my brother that. He'll assume you're sore and blame me."

"Don't be ridiculous, why would he—" Landon cut himself

off. His eyes narrowed. He gave Dean a curt nod. "Right." He cleared his throat. "I was joking anyway. I said I'd play."

From bed to business. Which shouldn't bother Dean at all. He'd wanted Landon invested in the game again. "That you did."

Landon nodded, then shook his head and disappeared into the bathroom attached to the master bedroom.

Silver's fingers curled around the collar of Dean's shirt. She peeked up at him, her tongue touching her upper lip in thought. "You know I appreciate how much you've been there for him while I couldn't be?"

"I care about him too, Silver." Dean kissed her forehead, almost wishing he could remind her of Landon's request that she not speak until he returned. But he wouldn't impose speech restrictions just because he didn't want to hear what she had to say. He saw the hesitation in her eyes and could pretty much read what she hadn't said. Best she say whatever she was thinking out loud. "What is it?"

"I was only half joking before. When I brought up Asher and Cedric." She lowered her gaze, then swallowed hard. "I'm not sure how I feel about you and Landon . . . I mean, if you—"

"A very big 'if,' pet." Dean absorbed the "if," then shelved it. No point in even considering what would never be. His lips formed a stiff smile she couldn't see as Landon returned to the room in a towel, changing into a fresh pair of dark blue flannel pajama pants while covered, as though he didn't strut around bare-assed in the locker room every day. As though Dean had never seen him naked before. Refusing to let it bother him, Dean eased Silver onto a pillow, sitting up so he could strip off his shirt and pants. He pulled his boxers up for Landon's sake. They'd all slept in the nude before, but he had a feeling his doing so now would make Landon uncomfortable. He let out a dry laugh as he settled into bed beside Silver, Landon on her other side. Whatever closeness had been between him and Landon before was gone. "I don't think you have *anything* to worry about."

# Chapter Seven

There was something different about waking up next to a man. Akira smiled as she leaned up on her elbow and watched Cort's big chest rise and fall. She'd spent the night with Dominik on the cruise—maybe a couple of times after—but it wasn't the same as being with Cort. The bed wasn't just warmer, more comfortable. The whole room seemed brighter. And unlike all the times with Dominik, they were in her space.

Which meant she had all the control. She got a say in what happened next.

Or what didn't.

And she wasn't so sure how she felt about that.

She almost laughed at herself as she glanced over at her phone on the nightstand. Calling Dominik to ask what she should do wouldn't go over well. Dominik probably wouldn't be too happy about her having Cort spend the night. Even though nothing had happened.

*You don't need Dominik to tell you what to do. Get the man some coffee or something!*

Coffee. Right. But did he even like coffee? She couldn't remember their talking about it. There was still so much she didn't know. Having him here would give them a chance to get to know one another better, but she didn't want to wake him up just yet. He seemed so peaceful.

The clock on the nightstand read 9:00 a.m. Which was late for her even on the weekend. Unheard of on a Thursday. She couldn't go back to sleep, but she refused to disturb him. She didn't know what his schedule was like. And she didn't have anything to do until the game tonight.

Pulling on her housecoat, Akira slipped out of the room, quietly closing the door behind her as she caught the sound of raised voices in the kitchen.

"I said I was sorry!" Luke made a sharp, aggravated sound, and Akira paused in the hall by the doorway as he paced across the kitchen, his attention on Jami and Sebastian who were sitting at the kitchen table. "What the fuck do you want from me?"

"Why did you have to act like such an asshole to Max? Him leaving had nothing to do with you!" Jami slammed her fist on the table, moving to stand, then dropping back down as Sebastian put his hand over hers and shook his head. "Sebastian, you were fine with Max. Tell me you don't agree that Luke is being an idiot."

Surprisingly, Sebastian said nothing. He simply held her hand and gave Luke an expectant look.

"Yeah, Max leaving had nothing to do with me. Or the team! An idiot? You have no idea what you're talking about, girl. Leave the game to the men."

Sebastian's jaw ticked. Oh, he so wasn't happy. But for some reason, he remained quiet at Jami's side.

"Umm, how about you go fuck yourself, Luke." Jami grabbed the bouquet of flowers off the table and threw them at Luke. They hit his chest with barely a sound, then separated in to a colorful mess on the floor, petals everywhere, only wet splatters left on Luke's white T-shirt to show they'd hit him. Jami jerked away from Sebastian and strode across the room, shoving Luke toward the front door. "Get out!"

"Fine! Let me know when you're off your goddamn rag!"

Akira put her hand over her mouth, not sure whether she should try to restrain Jami before she killed her boyfriend, or be a good friend and find a good spot to bury the body. She felt warmth behind her and a firm hand on her hip. Sebastian had already gotten to Jami and was speaking softly to her as Luke stormed out, but all Akira could see was Cort.

"Good morning, Tiny." He kissed her nose, amusement in his tone. "Did they wake you up?"

Shaking her head, Akira glanced back at Jami and Sebastian, not sure whether to chance going into the kitchen or just head back into her room until things had calmed down. "I was going to get some coffee. Do you want some?"

"I do." Cort placed his hand at the base of her spine, guiding her into the kitchen as though he sensed she couldn't make that step without some encouragement. "Don't worry. Her fights with Ford were much worse. And I was there for most of them. If she doesn't want to see anyone, she'll hide in her room."

"I know that." Akira frowned at him. She wasn't sure what bothered her more. His bringing up Ford, or the past he had with Jami. She found herself stepping away from him, not even glancing toward the couple at the table, and opening the cupboard door a little too hard to get the mugs. She winced as the back of the door hit the side of the fridge. "Sorry."

Jami lifted her head from where it had been pressed to Sebastian's chest. "Oh, Akira. I didn't mean to be so noisy." She pursed her lips as she noticed Cort. "Ugh, really, Cort? You spent the night?" She let out a heavy sigh and gave Akira a pointed look as she moved to slip off Sebastian's lap. "Can we talk for a—"

"Sure." Akira folded her arms over her chest but didn't bother heading for the door. Jami's comment to Cort didn't have Akira feeling very accommodating. "What was that all about? I've never seen you get that angry with Luke."

"He's being a dick."

"I agree. Bringing up a chick's rag is never smart." Cort moved around Akira to take the coffee mugs and fill both. He smiled at her. "Sugar?"

Akira nodded, then turned back to Jami. "He shouldn't have said that, but you're not being fair. He's allowed to be upset that Max abandoned the team."

"But he didn't! And I'm not on my rag!" Jami dragged out a chair and dropped into it. Her nails gouged her palms. "I should have punched him. Or kicked him in the balls. Fucking jerk."

"*Gatita*, stop." Sebastian pried her hand open, then held it within his own. "Have some coffee. I'll bring you to work so we may speak alone."

Cort cleared his throat, the challenge in his green eyes as he eyed Sebastian over his coffee cup contrasting with his deceptively calm tone. "And you'll be having a chat with your boy. He doesn't talk to her like that. You tell him or I will."

Sebastian moved away from Jami, his lips thinning. He was only a couple of inches taller than Cort, but the rage that darkened his eyes made him look dangerous. Akira almost wanted to pull Cort back. Face Sebastian because she knew he wouldn't hurt *her*, but she wasn't all that happy with Cort taking Jami's side and threatening Luke. Sebastian had every right to stand up for the man he loved.

*Cort asked for it.* She stepped sideways, not too keen on catching a fist if things got nasty.

"My gratitude only goes so far, *hombre*." Sebastian's tone was the smooth slice of a freshly honed blade. "You do not get involved. You do not touch Luke."

Jami slipped between Cort and Sebastian, her hand on Sebastian's face, drawing his attention to her. "He won't. Cort's just being overprotective." She snapped a glare over her shoulder at Cort. "You really need to go now."

Akira slammed her mug on the counter. The handle broke and a jagged piece stabbed into her palm. "Shit!" She waved Cort away, grabbing a piece of paper towel to staunch the blood as she scowled at Jami. "This is my house! I asked him over, so don't tell him to leave."

Cort looked impressed, but Jami and Sebastian just stared at her like she'd suddenly grown fangs and started sparkling. Jami's bottom lip trembled.

She gave Akira a curt nod. "Fine. Then I'm leaving."

"Jami, that's not what I'm saying." Akira put her hand to her throat as Jami strode down the hall, grabbing her jacket and shoving her feet into her boots. She slipped past the men and touched Jami's arm. "I would never do that to you. I let Luke and

Sebastian come over whenever they want and—"

"*Let* them?" Jami snorted. "And here I was thinking paying a third of the rent made this my place too. My mistake."

"That's not what I'm saying either!"

"You know what? Right now, I don't think I care." Jami walked out. Sebastian followed, giving Akira's shoulder a little squeeze before following.

What the hell had just happened? Akira's whole body shook hard as she stared at the closed door. She and Jami *never* fought. Not like that. Maybe she should have stayed in her room. Kept her mouth shut.

"Tiny, come sit down." Cort waited a beat, then, when she didn't move, came to her side and guided her back into the kitchen. He lifted her up to sit on the edge of the table. "You're her best friend. You know she has a temper."

"So do you." Akira stared at her bare, dangling feet. "You need to leave Luke alone."

Cort sighed. Kissed her cheek. And whispered, "You're right. I shouldn't have said that shit. I just get a little worked up when guys talk to women like that." He shook his head as she peered up at him. "Not as bad as Ford's new bodyguard. That man would have laid Luke out. I've grown out of that."

"I thought you were just sticking up for Jami." *Ugh, you've got to stop that. Things with Jami are bad enough without your being jealous.* She just couldn't seem to help it.

Frowning, Cort took her wounded hand and gently moved the paper towel. "I would have done the same for Sahara. Or any other woman. Except you."

*Real nice.* Akira tried to pull away. "Got it. Look, I really need to—"

Cort continued as though she hadn't spoken. "For you, I would have just clocked him."

"Really?" Damn, that should sound horrible. She didn't want Cort punching anyone for her. And yet . . .

"Really. What kind of man lets a guy swear at his woman? Do

you have a medical kit?"

"Here." Sahara stepped into the kitchen, holding out the big, white metal box. She wouldn't look at Cort as he took it. Just edged close to Akira, giving her a one-armed hug and resting her hip against the table. "I heard everything and started coming in, but it looked like it was gonna get violent, so I chickened out and went back to my room."

"Are you okay?" Akira let Cort clean her small cut, grateful for how carefully he kept away from Sahara. The amount of attention he gave her hand was sweet, but that he'd caught on to Sahara being uncomfortable around him was very much appreciated.

"Yeah, I was just . . . Grant used to yell at me when we fought. He told me I was a bitch when I was on my period." Sahara bowed her head. A teardrop landed on Akira's knee. Her throat tightened as Sahara shook her head and wiped the rest of her tears away. "I *am* supersensitive when I'm on it. Jami's probably starting soon. And so are you. You'll both make up over some brownie chunk ice cream tonight, right?"

Akira's cheeks heated as she glanced at Cort, who had a big grin on his face. She nudged Sahara's arm. "Not a discussion to have in front of my new . . . boyfriend."

Oh, she really liked the sound of that. And from Cort's broad smile, he liked hearing her say it.

Sahara laughed. "Well, it's only fair that he knows when to avoid this place." She finally looked at Cort. "I call it Shark Week."

"Shark Week?" Cort's brow raised as he smoothed a Band-Aid over Akira's palm.

"The uterus looks just like a shark's brain. One of my friends shared the image with me on Facebook." Sahara rolled an elastic off her wrist and put her long blonde hair up in a ponytail. "So it's fitting."

"I agree." Cort sighed as his phone rang. He checked the number. "Sorry, girls. I gotta take this."

He went to the living room to take the call.

Fetching them both some coffee, Sahara slid into a chair,

smiling at Akira as she lowered onto another. "I don't know what Jami's problem with him is. He seems nice enough. I give my temporary stamp of approval."

"Temporary?" Akira warmed her hands on her mug. She needed to turn up the heat—or put on some gloves. She tried to keep the electricity bill down by not blasting the heat, but maybe she was going too far. "Ugh, it's chilly in here, eh?"

"Just a bit." Sahara popped out of her chair, sliding across the floor in her socked feet to turn up the dial on the wall. "And yes, temporary." She slid back into her seat and leaned forward, tone low. "Soon as he pisses you off, he's on my shit list."

"Sounds fair." Akira giggled, glancing innocently at Cort as he returned. She bit her bottom lip at his strained expression. "What's wrong?"

He shrugged. "Gotta get myself a suit. Silver's gonna be at the meeting today, and seems best if I'm there to represent Ford. He'll wanna know how she's doing and what else is going down."

Akira nodded sympathetically. "You didn't want to go to the meeting."

Leaning down, he kissed along the side of her throat, murmuring. "I wasn't in a hurry to leave."

"Mmm." Akira almost wanted to ask him to play hooky. But she wouldn't like it if he did that to her. So she simply turned her head to steal a quick kiss before speaking. "Maybe, if you're not busy tonight . . . do you want to come watch me and the girls perform?"

"Think I will." He pulled her to her feet. "See me to the door?"

"Sure." She went with him, letting out a surprised laugh as he held her against the wall, groaning as he kissed her until her whole body hummed with need. She bunched her hands in his hair and sighed. "That just made it harder to let you go."

"Good. Makes it just that much better when we get to see each other again." He winked, stroking her lip with his thumb. "I'll call you later."

"Okay." She backed up so he could open the door. Then yelped as he grabbed her and kissed her again.

He chuckled against her lips. "I laughed at men who acted like I am after just a few days." His cheek slid along hers and he whispered, "You did this to me, Akira."

Her heart stopped. She gaped at the door, long after it had closed. It took Sahara joining her to get her brain working again. He hadn't called her "Tiny" like he usually did. His buying that her name was Ace had been a joke. It took Sahara saying Akira's name with concern for her to get the words out.

"He knows."

\* \* \* \*


Cort hated the way the stupid, shiny black shoes sounded on the pavement as he strode up to the Delgado Forum. Might as well be wearing fucking tap shoes. His suit was plain, black jacket too snug on his shoulders because he hadn't had time to get one custom-made—not that he would have forked out the insane amount if he had. White shirt, black tie. He looked like a damn stiff.

*Just put me in a casket and call it a day.*

Suits weren't his thing, but after the call from Cam, he knew he couldn't ditch the meeting. There was a whole lot of drama going on with the Delgados, and the only way to keep Ford out of it was for Cort to deal with it himself. He wasn't quite sure what he could do to keep Silver from stressing, or protect Ford's negligible position with the team, but that didn't matter. He wasn't a planner. Spur of the moment was more his style.

A long town car he immediately recognized pulled up in front of the Forum and he paused midstep, eyes narrowing as a short black man with large, thick, brown-framed glasses stepped out of the front passenger's side seat. He gave Cort an expectant look but didn't speak as he opened the back door of the car.

"Want something from me, Patty?" Cort shoved his hands into the pockets of his jacket. His fancy shoes felt like thin ice encasing his feet, but he wouldn't let his discomfort show in front of Roy Kingley's little assistant-slash-weasel. "Kinda busy."

Patty's dark skin took on a hint of red—hard to catch, but the sun glaring off the snow into his face brought out the color. He pressed his thumb to the bridge of his glasses and cleared his throat. "Mr. Kingsley would like to speak to you."

Cort snorted. "Good for him."

Cort put his hand on the long metal door handle, ready to step into the Forum and clue Roy in to exactly how much the summons meant to him, but then Patty spoke up, his nasally tone sharp. "I received an update from Ford's doctor this morning. He's resting well. I would hate to have him disturbed."

*For fuck's sake.* The bastard would do it too. Cort shrugged as he made his way to the car, keeping his strides slow and relaxed— despite the urge to put Patty's head through the window and send the car rolling off the closest cliff.

He gave Patty a lazy smile. "I'll talk to him. Seeing your ugly mug wouldn't be good for my boy's health. Not sure it's good for mine."

Nostrils flaring, Patty drew himself up as much as he could, his forehead almost level with Cort's chin. "I suggest you treat Mr. Kingsley with more respect than you've shown me. His patience is wearing thin."

"Yeah? Well, mine's shot. Get the fuck out of my way, Urkel." Cort slid into the backseat, slouching as he glanced over at the old man. Roy looked well put together as always in a sharp, dark gray suit, his almost pure white hair slicked back. His face was so sharply angled his wrinkles didn't soften his features at all. The shadows under his eyes made them seem even darker. Like the narrowed eyes of a snake spotted in a deep, dark hole.

"You've ignored my calls, Cortland." Roy pulled a gold cigarette case from his thick, wool jacket and plucked a thick cigarette out with shaky, age-spotted fingers. His hands betrayed his age much more than his face. But his tone was as cold and steady as ever. "Some would say that was rather unwise."

"I don't work for you anymore, Roy. And some would say what you pulled with Ford was damn stupid." Cort was tempted to take the week-old pack of smokes out of his pocket and light one up, but that would make him look nervous. And he wasn't. He could manage this old fucker without a drag.

"How I deal with my son is none of your concern."

"You've made it pretty damn clear you don't consider him your son anymore."

"I raised him. He owes me some loyalty for that at the very least." An icy smile slit Roy's lips. "Besides, you know me better than that, Cortland. He is mine until I have no use for him. As are you."

"Is that so?" Cort laughed, the muscles in his forearms twitching as he realized he'd taken out his pack. Putting it away now would look worse than lighting up, so he shook his head, casually placing the filter between his lips. He flicked his lighter, then laughed, letting out a wisp of smoke. "I think you're forgetting, you can't intimidate me, old man. I put up with you because I liked your kid. And you hired me because you wanted my connections. Starting shit with me is not something you want to do."

Roy arched a brow. "I believe you're overconfident in your 'connections.' Your stepfather is one of the many who benefited when the games were fixed. Perhaps you should speak with him to see where he stands on the issue."

"Yeah, maybe I will." Cort knew his dad liked gambling once in a while, but if they wanted to talk loyalty, he knew exactly where Sutter Nash's lay. With his family. "We done here?"

"No. You're a smart man, but sadly uninformed. Ford took what didn't belong to him. I will not let that slide. Consider carefully before you dismiss my offer. I am a proud man, and you know very well how I handle those who've wronged me." Roy snuffed his cigarette in the ashtray on the door. "Ford becoming close to his sisters has given me a way to make him pay for defying me, but he knows that. Which is likely why he contacted you." His head tilted slightly. "Seeing Delgado's relaxed treatment of his daughters has misled my son. Perhaps he needs a reminder of how I do business."

"I think he got that." Cort's jaw hardened. "I'm warning you, Roy—"

"Perhaps you need a reminder as well. Do call your stepfather. I hope he can reason with you before I must take action." Roy made a dismissive gesture with his hand. "You may go. We will be speaking again shortly. At which time you will tell me how this team will benefit me. It will be unfortunate if I have to find a way to make it profitable on my own."

"You better be clear, Roy. You threatening me?"

Roy laughed. "Now, that *would* be stupid of me. As you pointed out, you are very well connected." He stroked his chin thoughtfully. "But I can make you pay in a way that won't be worth Sutter—or any of his associates—getting involved. In a way that will be *very* clear. This isn't Detroit, Cortland. You are quite isolated here. So much can happen to you and yours. Think on that before you turn down my offer."

Cort had to clench his fists to keep from shaking with rage. The son of a bitch was right. Cort might be able to intimidate Roy's thugs to a point, but there was only so much he could do to protect Ford. Or anyone else.

That Roy hadn't tried to use Akira in the negotiations was good. He would have if he knew about her. Cort had to make sure he never did.

"You haven't given me an offer." Cort managed to keep his tone light. A dark part of his mind wondered if just reaching over and snapping the old man's neck would put an end to all this, but the sane part of his brain kept him in check. Even if he got away with another murder, Roy's death being tracked back to him would have repercussions. The Kingsley family was big, and Roy's brothers were even more dangerous than he was. Roy's recent actions made it obvious that Ford snatching the team out from under him had a bigger impact than the profit made by fixing games.

The big investors had probably been using their "investments" to launder money. Now that they'd gotten out, Kingsley was stuck with a lot of traceable cash. Gambling it would clear that up, but he wouldn't risk the proceeds without some guaranteed payoff.

Roy's next words confirmed his suspicions. "The team must start winning. I know you've stepped in for Ford, and you have a better business sense than he does. All the information I have on Lorenzo Keane is that he is very cautious with his investments. He'll hesitate to make big moves before the trade deadline because he doesn't believe the team will make the playoffs. Convince him otherwise. If the team makes the playoffs, the stakes will be high."

"And what do I get out of this?" Cort mentally cursed at Roy's smirk. The man knew he had Cort by the balls. He'd play Roy's game until he could figure out a way to stop. Without anyone getting hurt.

"I would hate to see you behind bars again, Cortland. You're a good man. It's a shame to see you looking over your shoulder all the time, second-guessing your every move." Roy was using that fatherly tone that had always irritated Cort. Only because he knew what kind of father the man was. "I can make it all go away. Lee deserved to die. There's no reason for you to suffer for seeing it done."

"Right." Cort opened the door, desperately needing the bite of cold air. He felt like he was being roasted alive in that car, like he'd just stepped into the devil's office and signed away his soul in blood. "I'll be in touch."

"I'll let Patrick know to put you straight through to me. No need for you to work with underlings." Roy let out an airy laugh. "It's always such a pleasure working with you personally."

Cort nodded, then got the fuck out of the car. There was no mistaking what Roy meant by "personally." It wasn't often that Roy got one over on Cort. Now he knew he could use Ford, and the threat of jail time, against him.

*But not Akira.* Cort didn't bother acknowledging Patty as he cut

114

across the sidewalk and straight into the Forum. There was no need to even put Akira at risk. Or put Ford through any more. Roy was right. The team needed to start winning. Then some "unexpected" losses would get them out of this mess.

He'd find a way to control the outcome of the game—as much as possible anyway—and keep everyone he cared about safe. That was all that mattered. And anyway, if the team was gonna survive, they needed all the help they could get. Dirty or not.

Then again, if the league got wind of it, the team would be toast. But there wasn't much he could do about that. He had his priorities.

*Fuck the goddamn team.*

\* \* \* \*

Dean nodded to Keane as the other man pulled out a chair for Silver to the right of his seat at the head of the long conference table. Silver gave Keane a regal look, smoothing her black skirt down as she folded gracefully into the high-backed, armless leather chair.

The sun shone so brightly through the floor-to-ceiling windows in the conference room that it hardly seemed necessary to have the lights on, but for some reason, the room seemed gray. Cold. The meeting wouldn't start for another half an hour, but Silver had wanted a few minutes to speak to Keane beforehand. And she wasn't the only one who expected a briefing before they got started. Dean held up a hand as his brother approached, clearly wanting to have a word. He drew Tim out into the hall.

"I get it. You're worried that Silver will go for a big move to show she still has some control. Or that Keane will start selling to get us good draft picks for next season." Dean grinned at Tim's curt nod. He knew his brother too well. How protective Tim was of his players was one of the reasons that Dean had second-guessed putting him in as head coach. And the very reason Dean had decided to keep him in that position. "We have a good, solid team. I like the idea of first-round draft picks, but I'm not ready to give up on this season."

Tim nodded, as though happy that Dean agreed. "Good, then let me talk to them. They don't know the men like I do—don't know what they're capable of."

"Tim, *I* know the men. Trust me, okay?" Dean shook his head when Tim let out a heavy sigh. His brother trusted him, but it was in his nature to grumble when he couldn't get his own hands dirty. Once, Dean and two of their dads had been in the backyard using axes to chop dead roots out of the area where their mother wanted to plant a garden. Tim was too small to pick up an axe—and their mother was afraid he'd get hurt—so she kept him back. Tim had been told he could plant and weed and do everything else, but it wasn't enough. He didn't want to do only the "easy stuff." Their mother had managed to distract him by having Tim make sure their little sisters were all safely out of harm's way. Dean would use the same method to distract Tim now. "Listen, I need your help. I've convinced Landon to play tonight, but he's . . . this isn't easy for him. Keep an eye on him for me?"

Tim nodded again, slowly this time. He gave Dean a shrewd look. "You know I will. But tell me something."

"All right. What?"

"You love him, don't you?"

Dean took a deep breath. The way Tim asked wasn't casual. Wasn't about Dean caring for the man he shared a woman, and a child, with. This hadn't come suddenly, and Tim listened to all the things Dean didn't say, had been listening for quite a while. There was no simple way to explain how or why it had happened. With Landon it was . . . it was all the things he'd never thought possible. And Tim was probably the only person he could openly admit his true feelings to. The only person who would make Dean face them himself.

"I love him." Dean lowered his voice as he spotted Cort coming off the elevator. "And I'm worried about him. Not all the men share rooms on the road anymore. I need you to make sure

Landon isn't alone. You don't know how he is in the middle of the night. It's bad, Tim."

"All right . . . I'd put him with Carter, but the boy needs Ramos to keep him in hand. What about Vanek?"

*The blind leading the blind. Not a good idea.* "If it wouldn't be so disruptive, I'd have Chicklet on the road to take care of Vanek. He's been temperamental ever since he came back."

"I agree. But he's a team player. And he's got issues with Perron coming back. Getting him past that would distract Landon."

"I think Vanek would be better with Mason. He needs a firm hand, and he'll respond well to how steady Mason is." Dean's brow furrowed. He could go on the road with the team and watch out for Landon himself, but he wasn't sure Silver was ready to be alone for that long. "Maybe you should just play Hunt."

Tim patted Dean's shoulder and shook his head. "Landon is our only real shot at the playoffs. If we're making a run, we need him." He cocked his head. "What about Perron? He's on the outs with a good half of the team, but Landon seems to understand why he left. To be happy that he's back. I used to have Callahan and Perron room together because Perron is a calming influence. Callahan never talked much, but Perron was good when he needed to. He could do the same for Landon."

"Yes. I think that will work." Dean squeezed his brother's shoulder as Tim sighed like he'd grudgingly accepted that he'd done all he could for his men. "Thank you."

"Hey, you might love him, but he's still one of my men." Tim gave him a half-smile and leaned in for a hug. "Good thing you know how to share."

"I suppose." Dean gave his brother a little shove. "Tell Madeline I enjoyed our last scene."

"Ha! Just so you know, just touching the bruises you left on her butt gets her ready to go. I should be thanking you!"

"Remember that if we end up trading one of the men." Dean hated to shift things from their easy banter, but it had to be done.

He refused to let his brother be caught off guard. "You can't keep them all."

"I'd debate that. Quite well." Tim frowned. "You sure you don't want me to stay? I can speak for any man on my team."

"Again, you need to trust me. I can speak for them as well." Dean stepped aside so Cort could go into the conference room. "I know who we can give up. And who you can't."

Tim inclined his head. "Got it. And I'll smile for the press even though this whole thing pisses me off. We haven't rolled over just yet."

"Good. Don't. The men need that attitude to keep them going." He pulled the door open behind him, wincing as he heard Silver swearing at Keane. That didn't sound promising. "I'll deal with this. Come to my place before the game. I'll make some lasagna. Amia's missed you and Madeline."

"My night to make dinner, how can I refuse?" Tim winked. Then sobered abruptly. "Besides, it will do Maddy some good to snuggle with that sweet baby after the last false positive. Me and my fucking lame swimmers are making this tough on her."

"I thought you were looking into—"

"No. Maddy wants to do it naturally. You know how she is about 'if it's meant to be.'" Tim's face reddened. He swallowed hard. "Ah, if it wouldn't make you uncomfortable, we could try—"

"Damn it, Tim. You know Madeline and I don't play like that. And I'm not sure Silver would—"

"Forget it." Tim retreated a few steps. "Just . . . the doctor told her it's unlikely I could get her pregnant without help. And if I can't do it—anyway, doesn't matter. She's right. If it's meant to be, it *will* happen. I just . . . I know how badly she wants this. And she'd be an amazing mother."

"She would be." Dean studied his brother's face. "Weren't you looking into adoption?"

"We have, but nothing yet. There's a teen we might take in for a bit, though. Just waiting for the paperwork to go through."

"Good. There are a lot of kids out there you can help."

"Very true. But now the only 'kids' I have to worry about are on my team."

"Trust. Me." Dean left his brother in the hall and went back to the conference room. Silver had quieted down, but her cheeks were crimson, which put Dean on alert. The only people invited to this meeting were Dean, as the general manager, Silver—mostly as an indulgence—Cort on behalf of Ford, and Oriana, who came in a few minutes before the meeting started. Dean had to respect Keane for including Oriana. Out of the Delgados, she was probably the easiest to deal with, but unless she fought her father in court, she didn't have a legal say in what happened with the team.

Then again, neither did Ford.

Keane acknowledged them all individually before beginning on the very topic Dean had expected him to. "This team is floundering. There are holes in the roster which I believe can be filled with some sacrifices."

Dean inclined his head. "Granted, but as I've told you, I've considered this carefully. I gave you an outline of the moves I plan to make before the trade deadline."

"Yes, but there are a few names missing from that list that seem logical choices." Keane opened a folder and tapped it with his forefinger. "Now that Tyler Vanek is healthy, I don't believe we really need Luke Carter. And I've seen the offers that have crossed your desk. Is there a reason we're hanging on to him?"

"He's performed quite well this season." Dean kept his cool, even though he could just picture Jami's reaction to even the possibility of Carter being traded. "He's one of the many young players I believe we can build the future of the team around."

"Perhaps. And Ramos? He was a good choice when the team was making a playoff run, but that's not the case now."

Dean's eyes narrowed. It was no coincidence that Keane had chosen to spotlight those two players first. This was a goddamn test. So he reacted as any other general manager would. "We haven't clinched a playoff spot, but we're only a few games out. Handing up one of our best defensemen would be as good as waving the white flag. I wasn't aware that we were doing that just yet."

"We aren't." Keane sat up straight, glancing at Silver as though surprised that she hadn't spoken up. His lips quirked. "If we're going to make a run, there is the issue of a goaltender. Hunt isn't ready."

Cort cut in before Silver could. "Ingerslov isn't on injury reserve. Haven't the Leafs and the Blue Jackets shown interest? If the doctor can clear him in the next week or so, we can get something for him."

"I've been considering that." Keane sat back in his chair. "The question is, is Hunt ready to take a backup role to Bower permanently? And is Bower ready to be our starter once again?"

"He's ready." *Damn it, I hope he's ready.* Dean didn't like the idea of losing Ingerslov after six years, but it was a smart move. The few years Ingerslov had left to offer another team could buy them a good slot in the draft pick. Maybe even a solid defenseman which they needed for depth. And better Ingerslov than one of the others. He was unattached. A strong man who could do well with another team.

Dean couldn't say the same for Carter. And—damn love the man for it—Ramos would likely retire before leaving Jami.

"Very well. So we will trade Ingerslov. Our hopes rest on Bower. With that settled, if we are making a playoff run, we should make a bid for a strong offensive defenseman. I trust you to find us a suitable candidate—I don't want to give you the impression I intend to be a meddlesome owner—" Keane paused as Silver made an angry sound in the back of her throat, but then smiled as Dean silenced her with a hard look "—but I need you to know you will have a bit more leeway financially. I'm prepared to meet the cap."

Silver sucked her teeth. "You do know you can't throw money at the Cup to win it, right? A little thing called faith might help, though."

Oriana put her hand over her sister's. "Silver—"

"Is quite right," Keane said. "And if I didn't have faith in this team, I wouldn't have bought the shares from your brother." He gave Silver an indulgent look. "Did you have anything to contribute, Miss Delgado? You clearly aren't pleased with my plans for the Ice Girls."

"No, I'm not." Silver moved to stand, then glared at Dean when he cleared his throat to get her attention. "This is my project! And it's worked so far! Cutting the advertising and limiting tryouts to right before next season ruins my plans for another show."

"The show cost more than it brought in. Giving the Ice Girls segments in the Cobras' show will strengthen their connection to the team and lower the astronomical expense of location shoots."

That made a lot of sense. Dean hadn't wanted to stress Silver with the details, but renting a mansion for a week for a show that had been a complete flop had serious financial repercussions. Several networks had backed out of airing it. The cruise had been a success, but the players had been involved.

Despite the logic, Dean expected Silver to argue. He wasn't sure she'd be able to help herself. But she surprised him by folding her hands on the table, meeting Keane's eyes as she spoke calmly.

"I'll give you that, but I need to have some control over the Ice Girls and how they're run. You brought in Sahara without discussing it with me or any of my management team. I like her and I think she's great for the team, but an unintrusive owner wouldn't acquire a player without running it by the general manager." A blush stained her cheeks, but thankfully no one brought up *her* acquiring Scott Demyan, so she continued steadily. "I'd appreciate the same respect."

"You will have it." Keane's lips curved into a genuine smile, as though Silver had impressed him. "I'm willing to contribute to the Ice Girls' success. Please don't hesitate to come see me if I can help in any way, but rest assured that from this point on, I will leave the girls to you."

Silver blinked, then returned Keane's smile with a genuine one of her own. "Thank you."

"Now that that's settled, I would like to broach a more . . .

personal matter." He turned to Cort. "I appreciate your attending this meeting on Ford's behalf. I hope he's doing well?"

Cort winced, glancing over at Silver as the color left her face. Dean held his breath as Oriana—who'd been quietly observant so far—left her chair and went to kneel by Silver's side, speaking softly to her.

Keane frowned and gave Dean a disapproving look. "I wasn't aware that Silver didn't know about her brother's injuries."

"This is a private matter." Dean took Silver's hand, ignoring Keane and Cort as they discussed Ford's condition. "Dragonfly, with how upset you were about your family losing majority ownership of the team, I didn't want to bring up anything else to upset you. Ford is fine."

Lips thin, Silver jutted her chin up and stared at him. "No more. You don't get to decide how much I can handle anymore. Either of you." She snapped her gaze to Oriana, who nodded quickly. Clearing her throat, Silver stood. "Please excuse me. I hope you understand, but I really need to see how my brother's doing for myself."

"Absolutely." Keane stood, walking with Silver to the door. "I will write up an outline of anything else we discuss and email it to you by the end of the day."

"I'd appreciate that." She let out a tight laugh. "I was surprised by everything, but I have a feeling you're gonna do good things for this team." Her eyes narrowed as Dean stepped toward her. "Don't, Dean. Stay here and do your job. We'll talk tonight."

Oriana moved to stand by Dean's side as Silver walked out. Strangely enough, she was grinning. She snickered at his questioning look. "I wouldn't want to be you, but if you put how pissed she is aside, you'll see what I do." She took a deep breath and let it out in a sigh of relief. "Silver's back."

The meeting continued, but Dean had a hard time focusing on the discussion, even though Keane riled Oriana up a bit by bringing up Perron and asking about the terms of his no-trade clause. He had the impression that Keane was feeling them all out, and he couldn't hold it against him. Besides, only one thing really mattered to him at the moment.

Oriana was right. Silver, his spunky, mouthy, fearless woman, was back.

# Chapter Eight

Ford sat back in his bed, lips slanted with amusement as Silver drilled his nurse. In her cream colored silk blouse under a matte black suit jacket that matched her skirt, hair up in a no-nonsense bun, she looked very professional and demure, but the edge to her tone ruined the image. After his little sister sent the nurse away, she folded her arms over her chest, tapping her foot and glaring at the door, waiting impatiently for his doctor to come speak to her. His relationship with his younger sister was touch and go, but she had this motherly thing going for her now. A mother who bared her fangs if you fucked with her cub. She'd fussed with his blankets and told the nurse the room was too cold. After pouring him a glass of water, she finally took a seat by the bed.

Then burst into tears. "I was so mad at you for selling the team. I'm sorry!"

*Umm* . . . Ford patted her shoulder, not sure what he should say. His mother used to have emotional outbursts, which was why he and Kingsley had coddled her. His throat thickened as he remembered his mother's abrupt death. Silver's health wasn't good. He should be careful.

"It's okay, Silver. You had every right to be upset." He smiled as she looked up at him. "But you're not anymore? You still love me?"

She let out a watery laugh. "Never thought I'd say this, but yes, I love you." She scrubbed away her tears with her fists. "Sorry for falling apart. It's just . . . you look horrible, Ford."

"Thanks," he said dryly, even though he knew it was true. "And don't worry about it. Oriana started crying the second she saw me. I haven't talked to her yet—she came while I was sleeping. My nurse was going to wake me up, but Oriana wouldn't let her."

"Good." Silver straightened, shooting a dirty look toward the door. "That nurse seems like a twit. She was giving you doe-eyes while answering my questions. She wants to fuck you."

Snorting, Ford grinned at his little sister. "Blunt much?"

"But, it's true! And you're a dog, so I'm sure you're not smart enough to turn her down. You need your strength to get better."

"Yes, Mommy."

Silver stuck out her tongue at him, then frowned abruptly. "I did some research while waiting to come in. Why didn't you tell me about your mother?"

"I didn't want to upset you." Ford's lips twisted as her frown deepened. "You've been hearing that a lot, eh?"

"Yeah. From everyone." She hugged herself, staring at the floor. "I'm better, Ford. Really. I need you to trust me."

"I do." He surprised himself by saying so without a second's hesitation. And meaning it. Oriana and Silver were the only family he really had anymore. He wasn't too proud to admit that he needed them.

"Good." Silver fidgeted with the edge of his sheet. "So tell me what happened to you. Who hurt you?"

Biting his inner cheek, Ford inhaled slowly. As much as he trusted his sisters, he wouldn't let them get involved in his problems with Kingsley. He wasn't sure how much Oriana knew through Dominik, but hopefully not much. "The bar was robbed. Cam was away with his family for Christmas. I got a little cocky and paid for it."

Silver nodded, not seeming too surprised. "You have to be more careful."

"I will be. Believe me, I learned my lesson." That was the truth. He wouldn't give Kingsley another chance to come at him. Or anyone he cared about. He wasn't sure how to deal with the man yet, but he'd figure it out. "So how's my niece?"

The topic of her daughter distracted Silver for the rest of the visit. She got to talk to his doctor, then gave Ford a kiss on the cheek and promised to visit every day. And call. And get updates. That kind of fussing would have irritated Ford once, but he found himself grinning and pulling her in for a hug.

"Give Amia a kiss for me. And . . . yeah, I'd love it if you'd visit." He kissed her forehead. "It was pretty cool—spending time with you."

"It was." Silver glanced over her shoulder as the door opened. "Hey, Jami."

Ford swallowed as he took in Jami's pale face. Shadows under her eyes. Hair a tangled mess. Wearing faded jeans and Ramos's old practice jersey. He held his arms open as Jami crossed the room, holding her, not surprised to feel her tears soak through the shoulder of his hospital gown.

"I'm okay, sweetie." He made a hushing sound as she shook, choking back her sobs. "Hey, where's my tough girl? Look at me, babe."

Jami turned her head, wrinkling her nose at him. "You shouldn't call me that. Only Luke calls me that."

"You better not tell him then." Ford smirked. "That little punk comes after me, Cort might not be too happy. Hate to leave you with just *one* boyfriend."

"So not funny, Ford." Jami eased back after a nod to Silver and a promise to swing by the house before the game tonight. She turned back to Ford as she settled in the chair by the bed. "How you doing though? *Seriously*? I talked to Cort, but you're not missing any limbs, so I'm not sure if a 'he's fine' from him means much."

"I'm *fine*. Just a little roughed up." He cocked his head, brushing her cheek with a fingertip. "How about you, kid? You look like you haven't been getting much sleep."

"It's nothing, just my mom and . . ." She rolled her eyes. "Akira. She's got a new boyfriend and she's different. She actually got mad at me for getting mad at Luke, and I had every right to! You should have heard her. She actually *defended* him."

Ford forced his face to remain neutral. He refused to react to the "new boyfriend" thing. This guy couldn't be much worse than Dominik. And if he was coming between Jami and Akira already, he wouldn't last long. So Ford focused on what Jami obviously needed to get off her chest. "Why you pissed at Luke? Do I need to bash his head in?"

"No! He's just being an asshole about Max coming back, acting all betrayed. Akira says he has every right to feel that way, but—"

"She's right." Damn it, he should have kept his mouth shut. Just nodded and been all sympathetic. Jami's glare had him ready to take his words back, but then he considered how miserable Akira must be without Jami. And how much Jami would need her best friend if she was having issues with her mother. He grabbed Jami's hand before she could rise and storm out. "Listen to me before you get all bitchy. You love Luke, right?"

"Of course I do! But I don't have to like how he's acting!" Jami *humphed,* then folded her arms over her chest. "I'm happy Max is back."

"And that's fine, but look at it from Luke's point of view. The team's struggling. They had to manage with both Sloan and Max leaving pretty abruptly. Whatever their reasons, it had a big impact." He took note of Jami's pursed lips relaxing slightly and plowed on. "Luke's very devoted to the team. He won't understand someone not taking the game as seriously as he does. He's frustrated because the Cobras are in a slump, and he's not going to be all grateful that Max is just stepping back in like nothing happened."

"He isn't though! It's so obvious that Max feels horrible about leaving."

"And that makes it all better?"

Jami opened her mouth. Shut it. And sighed. "No, I guess not."

Ford smiled. Jami might be a stubborn little thing, but she was a smart kid. He ruffled her hair affectionately. "I can't see Akira saying anything unless you completely lost it in front of her. Go make things better. With her and Luke. You'll be much happier, and I don't like seeing you all upset."

Lips curving slightly, Jami nodded. "And you probably won't object to me letting Akira know *you* were the one who got me to see reason?"

"Not at all." Ford winked, speaking in a conspiratorial tone. "So, you don't like this new guy? You think it's gonna last?"

Chewing at her bottom lip, Jami looked away from him and shrugged. "Hard to say. He's no good for her, though." She snickered as she got up and gave Ford a quick, gentle hug. "But you wouldn't be either."

"Better than him?"

Jami cocked her head. "Maybe. Just a little."

"Well, thanks for that." He shook his head. "Just put in a good word for me."

"Stud, I don't think anything short of a miracle will get her to think any better of you." She grinned, cuffing his shoulder lightly. "I'm a little surprised you asked. Getting pretty desperate?"

The bed creaked as Ford shifted to make himself more comfortable. He winced at a painful twinge in his side. "Almost dying does that to a man."

"Milk it, why don't you?" Jami squared her shoulders, nibbling on her bottom lip now as she looked him over. "I won't ask what happened to you—pretty sure I can figure it out. But this is a good time to maybe get Akira to understand why you did what you did. Maybe then she'll forgive you."

He couldn't meet Jami's eyes after that reminder. "I'm not sure *you* should have forgiven me."

"It wasn't your fault, Ford." Jami squeezed his forearm. "You can't control your father. Or his men." A shadow stole through her eyes, and her jaw ticked as she stifled a shudder. "You got out. That's all that matters."

Long after Jami was gone, all Ford could think about was those words "You got out."

He had gotten out. Which meant he'd given up whatever power he'd had to prevent what had almost happened to Jami. And what *had* happened to his waitress. His muscles clenched, the sickness he'd felt every time that came up before shifting into a tension that made all his muscles tighten, his hands shake. As if his body thought this was something he could physically fight. But it wasn't. And becoming an outstanding citizen wasn't doing anyone any good. But he wouldn't give in to Kingsley, to use the team and his sisters to make the man money.

*Then what are you gonna do? Not like you've got many options.*

No. But he did have one.

*"I need a man who's in control of himself, his life. You're not. I'm not sure you ever will be."*

When Akira had said that, Ford had truly believed he'd surprise her. He hadn't known when. Or how. But he finally had an idea.

There was only one way to stop Kingsley from doing any more damage. He fisted his hands to stop them from shaking. Only one way for Ford to take complete control of his life.

He had to find a way to bring Kingsley down.

\* \* \* \*

Akira bit the tip of her tongue as the end of the iron grazed the edge of her palm. Her eyes teared at the sharp, searing sensation spreading across her hand, but she waved Sahara back as the other girl made a sound of distress and rushed to her side. "It's nothing."

"Damn it, Akira! I can iron my own skirt." Sahara unplugged the iron, then set it aside, gently latching on to Akira's wrist and drawing her across the kitchen to run cold water over the small burn. "What's going on? You're been cleaning all day. You don't have to do Jami's and my laundry. Why don't you rest for a bit? You're going to be exhausted tonight."

"I enjoy doing things for you. It's no big deal." Akira forced a smile, looking over Sahara's baggy, gray sweatpants and worn, pale blue Cobra T-shirt. Sahara looked good even without her makeup or hair done, but it was rare that she spent over half the day not all dolled up. A bit of teasing was in order. "You *are* going to shower and change before the game, right?"

"Oh my God, yes!" Sahara laughed, making a face at her own clothes. "If I leave the house like this, all the tabloids will go on and on about how I'm 'wasting away' without Grant."

"At least they dropped the whole scandal with you and Mr. Keane." Akira hissed in a breath as Sahara dropped her gaze and nodded. She dried her hand on her own jogging pants as she pulled Sahara in for a hug. "See, I don't think. I should just keep my mouth shut. I'm so sorry, sweetie."

"Don't be. It's just a stupid crush." Sahara hugged her back. "He's just so . . . untouchable. But he noticed me, and I guess I thought—doesn't matter. The subs he plays with at the club are all *perfect*. I'll never be like them."

"You shouldn't try to be. You'll find a man who loves you for you."

"Yeah. A Dom who likes a brat." Sahara blew irritably at a strand of hair that fell over her eyes. "The last time I went to the club, Dominik asked me if I was *sure* I was even interested in the lifestyle. How is it Silver and Jami can be over-the-top troublemakers and get away with it, but with me it means I'm not serious about learning?"

Akira nibbled on her bottom lip, considering carefully. "I've been a brat with Dominik, so I don't think that's the issue. Maybe he just sees you trying so hard to get Mr. Keane's attention, and he's worried that you're into this for the wrong reasons."

"But I'm not! Everything I've seen gets me really hot." Sahara blushed and pressed her hands to her cheeks. "Totally T.M.I."

"Like we haven't shared dirtier details than that!" Akira bumped hips with Sahara. "Remember when Jami told us about how she can get off with nothing but Luke using his ropes on her? How a tight knot placed just right can get her to come when she wiggles?"

"Mmm, was I the only one wondering if it would be crossing friendship barriers if I asked him to tie *me* up?"

"No! God, I almost asked, but then . . . yeah, hard to tell

what's okay with them. Sebastian lets them both play with others so long as he trusts the Dom. And Luke *does* do demonstrations. But . . ." Akira shrugged. "Might be a little weird to face Jami after having a mind-blowing orgasm because of her boyfriend."

A snicker brought both their guilty gazes to the kitchen doorway. Akira's face blazed as Jami dropped her schoolbag by the fridge, shaking her head as she opened the fridge and took out a beer. "Wouldn't be weird at all. You've both seen me all wrapped up and . . . stuff. Akira, you saw Dominik spank me bare-assed once when I mouthed off at him, and Sebastian wouldn't play with me until I begged the man for a punishment. Playing in front of my dad or my uncle would be weird, but I'm cool with everything else."

"That's good . . ." Sahara gave Akira a pointed look as Jami guzzled half her beer without pausing to breathe. "I need to take a shower. You two need to talk." She flashed Jami a grin. "You've given me a lot to think about. I wouldn't mind finding out if Luke is as good as you say."

"Better." Jami's lips curved mischievously. "But if you play with him, I get to watch."

Sahara stuttered something incoherent, face bright red, then rushed off to the bathroom.

Akira cleared her throat. "Jami, I'm—"

Jami held up her hand. "Don't apologize. I've been a raging bitch lately, and it's not fair to you or Sahara. Or Luke." She rolled her eyes. "And it's not just because I'm about to start my period. It's . . ." She rolled her eyes again, but this time a few tears spilled down her cheeks. "All the guys were there for me when my mom took off. Max, most of all. I knew my dad was going through a lot, so I didn't want to add to his problems—even though I kinda did by drinking and doing drugs. I'm not sure how to explain . . ."

"Take your time, sweetie." Akira faced Jami, reaching up to dry Jami's tears with her thumbs. "You never really said anything when Max left."

Shrugging, Jami took another swig from her beer. "Why would

I? People leave."

"But they don't always come back." Maybe that was why Jami had been so mad at Luke. Akira had a feeling if Jami's mother came back to her, Jami would welcome her with open arms. But she never did, so Jami knew she didn't care. Max's return proved he cared.

Akira seriously hoped Jami's mother *never* came back. From what she'd heard, the woman was flighty and she'd break Jami's heart when she lost interest in playing mommy.

Not that Akira would ever voice those thoughts to Jami. That would be cruel. All Jami had of her mother right now was a shallow trace of hope. Akira wouldn't take that away from her.

"Sometimes they don't come back at all." Jami hunched her shoulders. "I should be grateful for who I have, though. Ford kinda made me see that."

"Ford told you to be *grateful?*" *What an asshole.*

"No!" Jami looked horrified. She put her hand on Akira's shoulder, her tone firm. "I was whining about how you'd defended Luke. Once I explained everything, Ford told me you were right."

"Am I supposed to be impressed?" Akira bit her lip at Jami's wide-eyed stare. "Sorry, now *I'm* being bitchy. I'm glad you can talk to him, but him agreeing with me doesn't change what he did."

"*He* didn't *do* anything."

"Exactly! He should have!"

"Ugh, you are the most stubborn person I've ever met! If you saw what happened to him because he defied his father, you wouldn't be so hard on him. If he'd known what would happen, he would have stepped in." Jami rubbed Akira's arms as Akira dropped her gaze to the kitchen counter. "He didn't know."

"He knows what his father's capable of." Yeah, maybe she was being stubborn, but she just couldn't let it go. She was still a little shell-shocked by how quickly she'd let him in the first time he'd touched her cheek. The first time they'd spoken. Back then, most men had scared her. But not him. He'd put her at ease with a smile and a few words.

And *that* had scared her more than anything.

Jami's grip on her arms tightened. She pressed her forehead to Akira's. "I've seen some of what Mr. Kingsley could do, Akira. But seeing Ford in that hospital bed . . . that man is capable of anything. No one wants to believe that of their own parent. He might not be the man's real son, but Ford didn't know that before."

Akira swallowed. Her hand drifted up to her throat. She tried so hard to pretend like she didn't care what happened to Ford. *Told* herself she didn't care. But she did. "He looks that bad?"

"Don't feel sorry for him. He'd hate that. He's a tough bad boy, remember?" Concern creased Jami's forehead. "But yeah, someone roughed him up really bad. Maybe even more than Mr. Kingsley wanted, but I don't think he gives a shit that they almost killed the man he raised."

"Damn it." Akira's lips thinned. She still had a clear image of Ford's smile and the intensity of his golden eyes when he was close to her. She shook her head hard to get rid of the image as she strode into the hallway, grabbed her coat and tugged on her boots. "Don't think this means anything, Jami. I just need to see for myself because otherwise, I'll think the worst."

"Uh-huh."

"Stop it." Akira frowned at Jami's knowing smirk. "You know I'm with Cort. And you telling me he's no good for me makes *absolutely* no sense with you trying to play matchmaker between me and Ford. His past is no better."

"But that's the thing! It's his past! I can't see Cort ever really getting out of his father's business. You've never seen how those biker chicks throw themselves at him and—"

"Are they any worse than the puck bunnies that throw themselves at Luke and Sebastian?" That ended that conversation. Akira gave Jami a quick hug while Jami's mouth still hung open. She tapped under Jami's chin before opening the front door. "I'm seriously considering being on speaking terms with Ford again. I know you two are still friends, and this will make things easier on you. But I'd really appreciate it if you'd stop pushing for more."

"All right, I'll stop." Jami had the grace to look embarrassed. "I have been a little pushy about it. Guess I just want to see you both happy."

"I think . . ." Akira nibbled at her bottom lip, not sure she should share her suspicions. But maybe it would end the meddling once and for all. "You and Ford ended bad because of the drugs and everything. Without that, you might still be together. Maybe you're trying to fix things for him because you feel like it's your fault that things went bad. You couldn't be the kind of girl he needed and you think I can."

"You think I'm trying to use you as a replacement for me?" Jami's eyes narrowed. Her face reddened a little as she pursed her lips. But then she went still, her tone uncertain. "I wouldn't do that."

"Not intentionally." Akira's phone beeped, letting her know she had two hours left to get ready for the game tonight. She'd have to keep the visit with Ford short. "It's okay as long as you stop. Ford will find someone, but it won't be me."

\* \* \* \*

The temperature inside the hospital made the cold outside seem tepid in comparison. Akira stuffed her hands in her pockets as she made her way past the waiting room, dodging stretchers and a mother pacing with a child whose face was blotchy, either from fever or his pain-filled screams.

She'd been pretty lucky so far, never having spent much time in the hospital herself, and visits for friends and family had always been short because the wounds or illnesses hadn't been life threatening. She'd seen worse injuries in the Cobra locker room than she'd been exposed to in her whole life.

But after following a nurse's directions to Ford's room and stepping inside, she realized the worst of that was nothing compared to the damage that had been done to Ford. Her heart stuttered as she took in the dark brown and purple surrounding one of his eyes. The stitching on his cheek, his forehead, along his jaw, all surrounded by more bruises. He sat up quickly when he saw her, and the strain in his features proved his face held the least of his injuries.

Jami hadn't been exaggerating to gain Ford sympathy. Akira felt sick to her stomach considering that his own father—damn it, Roy Kingsley *was* his father despite the truth of DNA—had done this to him.

"Hey, shorty." Ford pushed himself up to prop his back against the headboard. The tube trailing from the back of his hand made soft wispy sound against the blankets as he adjusted them. "It's not as bad as it looks."

"It's so much worse than I expected." She approached the bed, stopping about a foot away from him. She spotted movement from the corner of her eye and saw Cam—Dominik's brother—standing by the window. He inclined his head to her, then walked out. Her throat tightened. "Cam's here to make sure they don't come back, isn't he?"

"The less you know about that, the better." Ford ran his fingers through his hair, glancing toward the chair by the bed. "You stayin' for a bit? You can come sit and tell me how things are going with the Ice Girls. And with you."

His eyes met hers and she felt exactly as she had when they'd first met. When he'd touched her cheek and they'd shared a moment in their mutual concern for Jami. And something more. Something that made it so hard to keep the distance between them now.

She lowered to the chair, trapped in his gaze. His eyes were the color of amber in the sun, warm with an entrancing glow. His skin was pale under the bruises, but despite that he didn't look weak. She could sense his inner strength, and it made it impossible to pity him. He would heal, and once he did, he'd get out of the hospital even tougher than he'd been before.

Ready to face his father, which suddenly made her very afraid for him. She didn't want to talk about the Ice Girls, didn't want to have an idle chat about her life.

She needed to know he wouldn't do anything stupid. Before she had a chance to think about what she was doing, she'd stood and taken his hand in hers. "You need to get better, then you need to leave. Get far away from your father and everything he's involved with. Don't give him a chance to—"

"I can't do that, shorty." Ford dropped his gaze to her hand as he lightly stroked her knuckles with his thumb. "But I'll be okay. He caught me off guard this time. That won't happen again."

"He's dangerous. If you're going to stay, you need to get the cops involved. Tell them everything you know." Actually, she liked that idea. His father couldn't hurt him from behind bars. "I know you don't want to tell me anything, but you should think about it."

"I have." Ford gave her a slanted smile. "But it's not that simple. And you're right. I don't want to get you involved in this at all. I'm just happy you don't hate me anymore."

"I never *hated* you." She laughed as his brows shot up. "Okay, maybe I did." Recalling why, she withdrew her hand and looked away from him. "You should have spoken up about what he was doing then. It would have changed so much."

"I know."

"And you're doing the same thing now. There'd be cops outside your door instead of just Cam if you'd reported this." Of course, having Cam for protection was no small thing. Except, it meant Ford was no further removed from his father's business. Voluntarily or not. "When will you learn—"

"I have learned, Akira." Ford's tone turned sharp. He shoved away from the pillow, his relaxed posture gone. "You might think what happened to Jami didn't affect me, but it did. I loved her once. I still care about her, very much."

Back to him and Jami. Damn, those two had a lot of unfinished stuff to work through. Not that what they did or didn't have mattered to her in the least. She crossed her arms over her chest, glad that she hadn't taken off her jacket. There was no reason to stay any longer.

"Why are you looking at me like that?" Ford let out a bitter laugh. "Did I do something else to piss you off?"

"I'm not pissed."

"You're a liar."

*Arg!* The man was infuriating. "I am not a liar, you fucking—" She covered her mouth with her hand. And all the angry heat that had spread through her body seeped out, giving way to cold. She knew better than to swear at people. Her mother would be shocked. Her father would give her one of those disappointed looks, letting her know he expected better. She inched closer to the bed. "I-I'm sorry. I need to go."

"Don't be sorry. I love that spunk." He took her hand in his, her fingers against his palm, and pulled her toward him. "You're so much stronger than you were just months ago. Not afraid to speak your mind. Don't stop now. Tell me why you're upset." He leaned forward, drawing her so close that his lips brushed her cheek as he spoke. "There's nothing but friendship between Jami and me. There's only one woman I want."

"That has nothing to do with me." She should push him away, but she didn't want to hurt him. And didn't really want to move. Something stirred inside her as she stared at him.

"It does. You're that woman, shorty. You always will be."

"No." She swallowed, turning her head so his lips grazed her chin, rather than her lips. "Ford, I'm with someone. You need to let me go."

"Ask me to and I will." He gave her a tender smile when she didn't move. "You can't, can you?"

"I shouldn't have to."

He took a deep breath, then nodded and released her hand. She swallowed as he reached up and tucked a strand of hair that had come loose from her ponytail behind her ear. "Now I need to be saying sorry. You took a big step just coming here. Why don't you stay a little longer?"

"Because I can't." She made a face, aware by the knowing look in his eyes that they were both thinking the same thing. She couldn't have asked him to let her go. She hadn't wanted him to. Squaring her shoulders, she did her best to hold his gaze without letting him see how hard it was to maintain her distance. Her words were as much a reminder to him as to herself. "I'm with someone."

"You keep saying that." Ford shrugged as though it really didn't matter. "I'll wait."

She scowled at him. "Don't. If things go the way I hope they will, you'll be waiting forever."

"If that was true, you'd be gone already."

"Oh, I'm going. I should just tell you, he's—" Her lips snapped shut. She couldn't tell him, not without speaking to Cort first. They were friends, and she didn't want to ruin their friendship because she'd said the wrong thing while she was irritated with Ford. But she had to say *something*. "He means a lot to me. Just . . . just remember that. I don't want you getting all upset when—"

"I won't. And . . . fuck, I'm being a jerk. Let's call a truce." He gave her his most charming smile and her heart melted a little. "Maybe give the friend thing a try?"

*It would have been so much easier if you'd kept being a jerk.* But she let out a sigh of relief and nodded. "I'd like that."

"Can I call you?"

"Yeah. Or . . ." Her lips slanted as she recalled the first time he'd asked for her number. "You could try smoke signals."

His laughter made their rough start a little easier to forget. And not being mad at him released a tightness in her chest that came whenever he was around. Maybe being friends with him would help when he found out about her and Cort. Maybe he'd just be happy for her. For his best friend.

She said goodbye, then left, her steps just a little lighter. Once she reached the parking lot, she took out her phone and saw two missed calls. One from Jami.

The other from Cort.

She called Cort back first. "Hey! How'd the meeting go?"

"Not bad. Keane's got everything in hand. Got nothing but

good stuff to tell Ford when I talk to him."

Akira held her breath. Then spoke in a rush. "I just saw him, but I didn't tell him anything. We agreed to be friends though, so I think it will be fine. I'll talk to him if you want, but it might be better coming from you."

Cort was silent for a long time. His sigh couldn't mean anything good. His next words weren't promising. "I'll talk to him, but I don't think anything's gonna make this go over well."

"Why not? We're *just* friends. He'll have to accept it."

"He won't. But let me deal with it."

"Cort, this doesn't have to be complicated." Who was she trying to convince? Cort or herself? "It's my fault for lying to you about who I was."

"I'm not sure it would have mattered, Tiny." He let out a low chuckle, easing some of the tension. "I was hooked from the moment I found you sitting out in the snow." His tone turned rough. "But . . ."

"But what?" She fumbled with her borrowed car keys. "You know him better than I do. He won't lose it, will he?"

"No, he knows better. He'll just calmly ask me to do what I always have."

"And what's that?" She knew. She already knew. But she needed to hear it from him.

Cort let out another sigh. "He'll ask me to step aside."

The resolve in his tone made her stomach clench. She couldn't speak past the lump in her throat. However she reacted with Ford, he wasn't the one she wanted. But her wants didn't change the way things worked. She'd watched enough biker shows to figure out what Cort would do.

"You still there, Tiny?"

She swallowed hard. "Yes."

"Good, then listen to me very carefully." He paused and she held her breath. "My answer will be no. Now, I dropped your car off—locks changed and all—in front of your place. Slipped the new keys under the door. I gotta go, but I'll see you tonight."

She must have whispered something to make him think the conversation was over, because she heard the click as the call ended. Her mouth was dry and her emotions were all over the place. She was still a little worried about how Ford would react, but only one thing stuck out in her mind.

*No.* She bit her lip hard and hugged herself, loving the sound of that word. *His answer will be no.*

*Delayed Penalty*

# Chapter Nine

Cort checked his watch and quickened his pace along the hospital hallway. He'd promised Akira he'd be there to watch her perform before the game, but he was cutting it close. Unfortunately, this couldn't be put off any longer. Ford finding out that Cort was dating Akira from someone else would only make things worse.

The nurse stopped Cort in the hall to Ford's room. "His doctor told him it would be good for him to get out of his room for a bit." She gestured toward the elevator past the nurse's station. "He went to the cafeteria with Cam. Second floor."

"Thanks," Cort said before heading to the elevator.

He didn't find Ford and Cam in the crowded cafeteria, but he knew Ford well enough to check the outside smoking sections, set short distances away from the hospital in intervals. The boy shouldn't be fucking smoking in his condition, but Cort wasn't gonna tear into him about it. Yet.

Maybe after he dropped the bomb about him and Akira, though. He pulled out a cigarette of his own as he joined the other men.

"Hey, Cort." Ford puffed away, smiling as he let out a stream of smoke. He was off his IV and wearing his own clothes under his thick black bomber jacket. Hopefully a sign that he'd be released soon. "Didn't think you'd make it today. You going to the game?"

"Yeah, just have to talk to you first." Cort met Ford's eyes, which narrowed as though he knew whatever Cort was about to say, he wasn't going to like it. Might as well cut to the chase. "I'm dating Akira."

Ford blinked. Cam frowned.

Cort waited.

"*You?*" Harsh red stained Ford's cheeks as he stepped up to Cort, hands fisted at his sides, half his cigarette snapped in the snow. "You're the one she's seeing?"

"Yes." More waiting as Ford fumed, pacing away from him, then back. The way Ford clenched and unclenched his fist made Cort wonder if the younger man would take a swing. He'd let him get in one, but that was it. He didn't want the kid hurting himself.

Bringing one hand to his mouth to rub his lips, Ford let out a sharp laugh. "That's what she meant by 'I don't want you getting upset.' And . . ." He tipped his head back and dropped his hands to his sides. "Jami gave me a few hints. Jesus fucking Christ. Anyone else know you were fooling around with my—"

"Your what, Ford? From what she's told me, you guys *just* became friends. I know how you feel about her, but shit happens. By the time I figured out who she was, I was in too deep to end things." Cort shrugged, well aware that the way he was laying things out was harsh, but he didn't sugarcoat. "It is what it is."

"Fuck that! Cort, I know you! You got bored of the chicks that hang out at the clubs. You found someone fresh and innocent, and you'll fucking play with her until you get tired of her too."

"No. She got to me, Ford. I can't say how long it's gonna last, but if I gotta end things for any reason, I'll be gentle." And he couldn't see that happening. Unless Roy became an issue, but he wasn't bringing that up with Ford. Not yet. He watched Ford pace a bit longer, then dropped his cigarette and approached the younger man. "Give me some fucking credit, man. If I wasn't serious about her, I wouldn't be having this conversation with you."

"Yeah, but you just proved my goddamn point. 'If you gotta end things.' You'll find a reason. Might take a couple weeks, a month, but it'll happen." Ford stopped in front of Cort, his eyes hard. "Spare her the fucking pain and end it now. Me and her are friends, but that's just a start. With you out of the way—"

"Let's get one thing straight, kid." Cort hooked his thumbs to his pockets, his tone level, his expression as calm as he could make it. "I'm not going anywhere. If there's something between you two—*if* she chooses you—then . . ." He shook his head. He wouldn't let her go that easily. "I'm willing to fight for her, Ford. I don't want to have to fight you."

"Then you should back the fuck off." Ford raked his fingers through his hair. "Why bother? You're thinking with your fucking dick."

"Careful, Ford."

"What? Not like I can stop you. Just make sure you can still do the fucking job I'm paying you for."

"Since when are you paying me for any of this? I was doing you a goddamn favor." Damn it, the anger he could handle. He'd figured Ford would get mad. Shout a bit. If he was gonna start sulking and toss their friendship over a woman, they'd be having a very different conversation shortly. "Don't be an idiot about this, boy—"

"Boy? You know what, when we were friends, that didn't bug me so much. But now?" Ford sucked his teeth, a sound he knew pissed Cort off. He was obviously looking to push Cort, but Cort refused to take the bait. Even though the bullshit Ford was spouting brought him to the fucking limit. "We're not. Have some fucking respect. You were my dad's lackey. Shoulda taught you how to speak to your boss."

"You arrogant little shit." Cort shook his head slowly. "You've got so many friends you can stand to lose me?"

"You asking if I need you, Cort? If so, yes. You're the perfect employee—when you know your place." Ford's arrogant tone matched the one Roy used with anyone he considered beneath him. It had been a long time since Cort had seen Ford trying to live up—or rather *down*—to his "father's" image.

Fucking sad that he was back to that. Maybe Cort should have expected it, but he'd thought the kid had grown up enough to be his own man.

*Guess I was wrong.* A gruff laugh escaped him even as his guts clenched with regret. "I'd be very careful if I were you, Ford. Your dad knows exactly how far he can push me. And he's got the backing to pull it off. You've got no one but me. Keep it up and you'll lose that."

"Some loss." Ford snorted. "We're done here. I'll have Cam bring you a check once I'm released and your services are no longer required."

"Don't bother. You know what I'm worth, *boy*." Cort reached out before Ford could turn away and patted his shoulder. The gesture lacked the usual affection he showed the younger man. And by Ford's wince, it wasn't as light a pat as Cort had intended. Cort took a step back before he gave into the urge to shake some sense into the kid. "You can't afford me. Stop while you still can, go back to your room, and calm the fuck down." Cort inhaled the cold winter air to help settle his own nerves. Everything would work out once Ford had time to think things over. *I fucking hope so anyway.*

Ford pulled out his pack of cigarettes and tapped one into his palm. "Don't make me repeat myself, Mr. Nash."

Cort stuffed his hands into the pockets of his leather jacket, torn between needing to get the fuck out of there and the impulse to get right into Ford's face and crack the Kingsley-grade ice his once best friend, his *brother* in every way that mattered, had put between them. But he was fucking pissed and this was going nowhere good. He gave Cam a brief nod and turned his back on Ford, heading to the parking lot, not willing to test his own control any longer. One more word and he would have laid Ford out. Kid had some fucking balls, Cort would give him that.

Their friendship might be done with. Not what Cort wanted, not over a chick.

*Not just any chick. Any other chick and it wouldn't have gone this far.*

Maybe it was good, though. Ford had shown his true colors and let Cort know exactly what their friendship was worth to him. Fair enough.

Akira was worth the loss. And so much more.

\* \* \* \*

Ford dropped onto his hospital bed and lowered his head to his hands. His rage had faded, but all that left him was a numbness he couldn't shake. He wasn't sure why it bothered him so much more to learn that Akira was with Cort than it had when she'd been with Dominik. It could be because the way Akira talked about Dominik, the way the two scened at the club, made their relationship seem like a temporary haven.

Dominik had helped Akira heal. He was the reason she'd found her inner strength. Ford couldn't be anything but grateful.

Cort was an entirely different story. Akira spoke as though she was falling hard and fast, and Cort . . . Cort *might* not be playing her at all. If he wasn't, he'd make Akira happy.

*That's what I want for her.*

But the chance that Cort was using her—even unintentionally . . .

*I won't let that happen.*

Not that there was much he could do about it. He pressed his eyes shut as he pictured Cort taking Akira's small body in his arms, making love to her, kissing her, and telling her everything she needed to hear. Then crushing her when she didn't fit with his plans anymore. Cort had no ties to Dartmouth other than Ford. He might stick around for a while to make sure Ford had everything under control, but they both knew the longer he stayed here, the bigger the chance that he'd have a run in with the law. If a cop recognized him, they'd bring him in for questioning—at the very least.

He *knew* Cort. Cort would head back to Detroit as soon as possible to avoid the risk of ending up back in the joint. If he was still interested in Akira when it happened, he might ask her to come with him.

But Akira had so many people she loved here. Jami and her family, the Cobras, Sahara, some of the other Ice Girls. He wished he could include himself on that list, but that wasn't important. All that mattered was Akira wouldn't go and Cort couldn't stay.

Telling Akira all this wouldn't get him anywhere. Jami had tried to warn her best friend away from Cort. The only thing either he or Jami could do was stand behind Akira, ready to catch her when Cort pulled a cut and run.

*She won't want you there. She barely tolerates you now.*

That was something he could change. He would be the best goddamn friend she'd ever had. He wouldn't say one fucking thing about what he thought of her and Cort together. He'd pretend he was happy for her.

Pretend there was a reason to be.

He lifted his head, not surprised to see Cam by the window again, looking out rather than watching Ford. Once Cam got the hang of dealing with the kind of thugs Kingsley sent around, he'd be the perfect right-hand man. Maybe better than Cort because he didn't have a reputation, so the cops wouldn't constantly be tailing him.

The thought brought on the sensation of swallowing a lump of cold oatmeal that stuck in his throat. Cort had been the one constant in his life, the one person he could always count on.

Until now.

Which meant he had to stop relying on Cort to handle the bar. Had to get out of this fucking bed and take his life back.

"You wanna find my doctor, Cam?" Ford rolled his shoulders to release some of the tension that had settled between them. "I'm checking out."

Cam frowned and his lips parted as though he wanted to object. But then he gave Ford a sharp nod. "No problem, sir."

Ford's brow shot up. "Sir?"

With a humorless laugh, Cam shrugged. "You *are* paying me, boss. I happen to like my job."

"Yeah . . ." *Shit, I don't want this.* Ford pressed his eyes shut, thinking about how he'd asked Cort to act like an employee. He shouldn't have done that. He'd probably sounded like Kingsley, and that was the last thing he wanted. He was still too mad to care about the impact his words had on Cort, but he had to clear things up with Cam since the man had witnessed the whole fucking thing. "Well, then don't fucking call me 'sir.' You got an opinion, speak up. Otherwise, nothing's changed."

"You want my opinion?" Cam's level gaze was so like his older brother's Ford could practically picture him tapping the leather strands of a flogger against his thigh as he spoke. "Checking out of the hospital early isn't gonna improve the situation. It's easier to keep an eye on you here." His lips quirked. "And, much as you don't want people to pity you, I saw the way Akira looked at you when she saw you in that bed. A little sympathy from her wouldn't hurt."

*Sneaky.* Ford snorted. "So you're not gonna tell me I'm wrong for trying to get Cort to leave her?"

"Hard to say. I wouldn't want my sister with a guy like him." Cam gave Ford a pointed look. "Or you."

"Then why are you taking my side?" Ford's lips curved into a dry smile. "Besides the fact that I'm paying you."

"I'm not taking sides. My brother wouldn't have gotten involved with the girl if she was stupid. I'm kinda hoping she'll ditch you both and stick with him."

"Not gonna happen. She's not in love with Dominik."

"You sure about that?" Cam chuckled as Ford frowned at him, approaching the bed to squeeze Ford's shoulder before heading for the door. "You've got a bit of competition, man. Still want me to get the doc, or should I just grab us some coffee?"

"Coffee." Ford settled into his bed and crossed his arms under his head. He wanted to get the fuck out of there, but Cam was right. He wasn't in any condition to leave yet, and staying did have some advantages.

And he needed every single one he could get.

\* \* \* \*

In the Ice Girls' brand new dressing room, Akira strolled along the mirrored wall, with a dozen swivelling stools set before the short, white-tiled counter, where her girls were doing their makeup. Her youngest girl, Justina, shook hard as she brought a wide blush brush to her cheek.

Akira took it from her and gently spun her on the stool to help her. She tipped the girl's chin up and swept the brush over her round cheeks. "Nervous?"

Justina blushed, her soft, black bangs falling over one eye. "Maybe a little." She took a deep breath, then blew it out and grinned. "But I'm ready."

Such an adorable baby face, with big, bright blue eyes that retained their brilliant light even when she couldn't get a new routine just right. Justina had been put on callback after the competition since she'd barely skimmed by the age requirements and hadn't really impressed the judges. After their last spare was injured during a routine, twenty girls were called in and given one last chance to "stand out."

Akira, as team captain, had been on the judging panel. As had Sahara. Justina performed last and neither Akira nor Sahara would let the other judges consider anyone else. Justina was spunky, sporty, and so full of energy there was no looking away from her when she let it all out.

The problem was *getting* her relaxed enough to shine. Akira grinned, then tapped Justina's nose with the brush. "I brought you something."

Fetching her purse from her locker, Akira returned to Justina's side and handed her a small box of candy Nerds. Justina giggled, opening the top of the box and pouring some of the colored candy into her palm. "You remembered!"

"I remember everything about my girls." Akira glanced back as one of their trainers stepped into the room, then moved to shield Justina's treat. She spoke softly. "I know they've been on you about eating healthy, so make it quick."

Justina covertly popped the candy into her mouth, stuffing the rest into her makeup bag. She leaned closer to Akira and whispered, "You're not gonna get on me about eating sweets?"

"No. I think you're perfect. I do agree you should eat your veggies, but you've gotten better with that." Akira toyed with a bouncy curl on Justina's shoulder, making it spring in a way that had the younger girl giggling again. "The lectures make them feel like they're doing something. Don't take it so hard."

"I can't see them telling you to go on diet pills." Justina fidgeted with the base of her halter top, which bared her stomach. "I want to be part of the team, and if I'm not careful—"

*Oh,* hell *no.* "Sweetie, listen to me. There's absolutely nothing wrong with your weight. Anyone tells you otherwise, you send them my way." Not that Akira would wait for that to happen. She'd find out who was making Justina feel insecure and give them *one* chance to change their attitude. Then she'd . . .

Depending on who the person was, she might have to go right to the top. Maybe even speak to Mr. Keane himself. And the man was intimidating.

But she'd do it. *No one* mistreated her girls.

"Thank you, Akira." Justina drew in another deep inhale, then stood. "I'm gonna go stretch. That routine you've got for the opening is . . . wow!" She laughed. "Something special we're celebrating?"

Akira grinned. "Bower's in nets. Perron's back. The Cobras have a real shot at the playoffs now. I want the fans just as excited as we are!"

"I second that!" Sahara shouted from the other side of the room, leaping up with her knees bent like a cheerleader—which was basically what they were. She *whooped!* then waved the girls to their feet. "Ten minutes, girls! Go get warmed up!" Leaving the girls to warm up and chatter excitedly, Sahara moved to Akira's side as Justina joined the rest of the team. She folded her arms over her chest. "They're on her back again, aren't they?"

Tugging her sleek, gold skirt straight, Akira met Sahara's eyes, not hiding her displeasure. "You knew about this?"

"Hey, I only found out yesterday. I passed by the performance director's office and heard Ms. Plant and a couple of the trainers *reminding* Justina that most of the girls are in an extra small and having a uniform made in medium just for her was troubling. They were 'worried' that having to get her one in large if she didn't watch her weight would embarrass her."

"That . . . *bitch*!" Akira didn't hesitate long before spitting out the insult. Her father might not like her swearing, but she knew in this case, he'd approve. "Okay, this is going to be an issue. Ms. Plant has always been hard on us, but she's gone too far. One girl quit because of her. I didn't think too much of it, because she had a hard time keeping up with the schedule. Maybe I should have done something then."

"Doesn't matter. We'll do something now." Sahara bent closer, her tone low. "Silver's back. One word to her, and Ms. Plant is gone."

"Good." Akira liked the idea of talking to Silver much more than approaching Mr. Keane. She was also glad that she hadn't had to bring up his name to Sahara. She nodded for Sahara to follow her to her locker, one eye on the girls as she stuffed her things inside and clicked her lock shut. "Do you know if Silver's here?"

"Bower's first game back? Probably." Sahara shrugged. "I haven't seen Jami, so she's probably babysitting."

"All right. Let's put on an awesome show and go find her."

"Works for me."

Akira heard her phone ringing inside her locker and groaned. She glanced over her shoulder at Sahara, their unofficial timekeeper.

"Grab it, you've got a couple of minutes."

Quickly unlocking her locker, Akira fished her phone out, not even checking the number before answering breathlessly. "Hello?"

"Hey, shorty." Ford's deep laugh sent little tingles all over her flesh. "I know you don't have much time, but I'm sitting here, waiting to watch you go out there. Just wanted to tell you to rock it."

"We will." She held the phone close, turning away from the other girls so she had a bit of privacy. "Jami gave me the idea, actually. So hope the girls don't kill each other swinging around hockey sticks!"

"With you leading them?" Ford went quiet. She had to hold her breath to hear his next words. "They'll do great."

"Thanks." Akira leaned against her locker, not sure why she couldn't stop smiling. She jumped when Sahara tapped her shoulder. "I gotta go, but, Ford?"

"Yeah?"

"I like knowing you're watching." She bit her bottom lip, hoping he didn't make too much of the admission. "But don't stay up too late. You need your rest."

"I won't. Just have to see this." He cleared his throat. "I, uh, never miss your performances. You're something else, shorty."

Hearing that meant more than it should have. Akira quickly ended the call after making Ford promise to call in the morning. She stashed her phone with barely any time to spare before dashing out with her girls, each of them grabbing a stick from the equipment manager before they hit the ice in their special non-slip sneakers. A wide carpet-like dance floor was set up in the center of the rink. She took her place at the tip of the triangle formation, holding the stick as though taking a face-off. She threw her body into motion, twisting around the stick and tossing her hair in time to AC/DC's "Shoot to Thrill."

The complicated dance moves were cut in sections to give the girls a chance to lay down their sticks and simply jump up and down, waving their arms to get the crowd involved. Justina did some impressive flips, showing more strength and finesse than the others, making Akira feel like maybe she'd boosted the girl's confidence just enough to let her shine. Everyone in the stands left their seats. The chorus faded to let the fans sing in an excited roar. Five girls—including Akira, Sahara, and Justina—flipped across the carpet for the finale.

Deafening applause followed the performance. Above, the Jumbotron showed flashes of the more enthusiastic fans. Then the screen showed the owner's box. Dean Richter and Silver standing side by side, grinning and applauding. Several of their staff clapping behind them. And farther back . . . Cort, his eyes filled with pride as he cupped his hands around his mouth as though cheering loud. She couldn't hear him, but she could feel his approval deep in her veins like a sugar rush. In her bones like the deep thrum of a bass drum.

Her heart raced as she took a bow with her girls. For that moment, everything was perfect. And the reason why seemed so very wrong. She'd never admit it out loud, but she could admit it to herself.

Knowing both Cort and Ford had seen it all, had watched her put on one of the best performances of her life . . .

The sensation was a brownie chunk ice cream, top grade, lottery winning rush. The only thing that could have made it better would have been to see her parents in the crowd. To see them just as proud as Cort was of her.

She shook away the depressing thought of knowing they'd never make it here. Never see her up close, living out her dreams. Even if they found the time to get away from work and their foster children, the expense of the trip was just too much.

But she'd send them the clips like she always did. And they called when they could, but the conversations were always short and awkward. She preferred the letters they sent, which told her that they loved her. That she'd done well.

On her way to the dressing room, she flashed Sahara a broad grin, happy that the other girl returned it without question. She'd have to be careful not to act too excited whenever the mailman stopped at their apartment. Neither Jami or Sahara knew how desperate she was to have some kind of contact with her parents. How often she wondered if she'd been forgotten as they carried on their lives across the country with all the children they cared for.

She wasn't jealous. But she needed to know she still mattered.

That all the wrongs she'd done in the past, all the shame she'd brought to her family, didn't overshadow what she'd finally done right.

# Chapter Ten

Max stretched his neck, back to front, side to side. He looked up from where he sat hunched in his stall as Carter passed, not all that surprised that the younger man never even glanced his way. Some would say Carter, Demyan, Vanek—and hell, some of the less vocal players—were being unprofessional by giving him the cold shoulder, but Max was starting to get it. During the video coaching session a few hours earlier, he'd felt the tension in the room as sloppy plays were dissected. Shortly after, there had been a lot of grumbling as the lines were drawn up on the whiteboard in the locker room. He was being played on the left wing and Dexter Tousignant had been sent back down to the minors. There was something unspoken going on here.

Almost as though the coaches were saying the team couldn't manage without him. Not just him—there was plenty of underlying excitement about Bower being back—but in his case, it was almost as though the players agreed.

Which explained why their young backup goalie, Hunt, looked so damn miserable.

An enthusiastic shout from one of the assistant coaches got all the men to their feet. White stood by the door, giving each player a mock check as they walked by. Max nodded to White when the gritty forward didn't check him, wanting to make sure the man knew that Max got he had to earn his way back into the team's tight inner circle.

He barked out a laugh when White grabbed him from behind, giving him a hug that lifted Max clear off his skates.

"Fuck those whiny bitches, Perron." White cracked his helmet against Max's. "You were the first one to have my back after I got suspended. I missed you, man."

"Right back atcha, bruiser." Max grinned at White, slapping the other man's shoulder as they both made their way down the hall to the rink. "Still thinkin' it was a clean hit."

"Hey, I'll admit it was questionable. Hit the guy in the numbers. Glad he just lost a couple of teeth to the boards."

To most, losing teeth would be no small thing, but White's broad smile showed the upper incisor he'd lost. He never tried to hide it—somehow it gave his smile more boyish charm. The two molars that had shattered from a vicious cross-check had given him more trouble, but he'd finally gotten those fixed after the pain started interfering with his love of medium-rare steaks.

"You planning to keep your gloves on tonight?" Max chuckled at White's snort. They were playing the Broad Street Bullies. Might as well ask White if he'd try vegan for a day.

"If it helps, I'll wait for Tim's go-ahead." White cocked his head as they reached the end of the bench. Tim looked up from his clipboard, inclining his head at them both before fixing White with a warning stare. White took it in stride. "Uh . . . maybe."

Max nudged White toward the ice for the warm-up skate. "Go with your gut, pal. Usually works for you."

White skated backward, giving him a sharp salute with his gloved hand. "Best advice ever."

On the ice, Max did a few quick laps to get his blood pumping, then fired several shots toward Bower, wincing at the ring of the pipes. He hadn't let himself go physically, but it would take more than one practice to get him as sharp as he had been. Unfortunately, he didn't have the liberty of slowly readjusting to the game. The team, the fans, would be watching his every move. The fans might hate him one day, then love him the next, but the players . . . they needed a good reason for his being back in the lineup after leaving them and taking the place of someone who'd been there through the worst.

"Hey, Perron!" Bower called before Max could skate away.

Bower pushed his mask off his face as Max skated up to his side. "Just a heads up since you're on the second line. Demyan and Vanek can't read each other all that well. Not sure why Tim put them together—you three had one good play during practice. Might want to keep an eye out for wild passes."

"Got it." Max leaned against the side of the net, watching Demyan and Vanek as they stood side by side near the benches. Demyan was saying something as he brought his water bottle to his mouth. His laughter could be heard clear across the ice.

Probably teasing Vanek. Trying to loosen him up before puck drop.

From Vanek's scowl, he didn't find whatever Demyan had said all that funny.

"They hang out off the ice?" Few would think it mattered, but Max knew how to read plays by knowing his teammates. He didn't know Demyan very well, but he did know Vanek. The kid could take teasing from a teammate that was little more than an acquaintance much better than he could from someone who had actual dirt on him.

Bower arched a brow. "They used to. They were roommates for a while."

"What happened?" Max flashed Bower an apologetic smile. "Feel free to tell me it ain't my business."

Shrugging, Bower nodded to the stands behind the team's benches. Chicklet sat close to the glass with her girlfriend, Laura. "Don't know details, but I heard Chicklet showed Demyan the curb."

"Got it."

"I think they're still friends, though." Bower's brow furrowed. "Seems day-to-day."

*This could be interesting.* Vanek was still young enough to let personal garbage affect his play. But as the game started, he paid attention to Demyan's comments and observed how Vanek's face grew red with agitation.

Demyan smacked the boards, surprising all the players sitting

157

close to him. "Now I remember! The slogan was 'Do it like Zovko.' Gotta admit, he looked pretty hot in that white silk shirt and those tight boxers."

A few feet away, Zach Pearce looked over at Demyan and shook his head. "Funny. Didn't think you liked silk, Scott."

Wiggling his eyebrows, Demyan gave Pearce a hooded look. "I like it on you."

"Head in the game, boys," Tim said, his tone sharp.

"Zovko is an amazing player. Does everything have to be about sex with you, Demyan?" Vanek ignored Tim's warning glare and sat up, facing Demyan. "Fuck, I can't tell you anything."

"Sure, you can. I think it's cute, that's all. You got all excited when you found out he was available." Demyan turned his attention back to the play when Tim put a hand on his shoulder. "Head up, Richards! Fuck!"

"Available for a trade, you sick freak!" Vanek shouted before hopping over the boards for a shift change. He missed a pass from Mason, still too wound up from the argument to focus on the game.

Max retrieved the puck, then dodged a Philly forward, cruising across the neutral zone, mentally mapping out potential plays as Demyan and Vanek reached the blue line a step behind him. He met Vanek's eyes a split second before snapping the puck to him.

Vanek cupped the pass and took three long strides toward the net. Cut the puck across the goal crease to Demyan.

Who tucked the puck straight between the goalie's pads.

"Nice set up." Demyan's tone held some grudging respect as Max and Vanek slammed into him to congratulate him for the goal. "Good to see you haven't lost your touch."

"Don't give him all the credit." Vanek kept pace with Demyan, not looking at Max. "Sweet goal, Demyan."

The game progressed with another goal from their line and two from Carter and the first line. Bower made some awesome saves, but his expression didn't change as he kept glancing at the clock like he couldn't wait for the game to be over. Tim called a time-out after one save had Bower down for a few seconds longer than usual. He spoke at length with Bower, glancing down at Bower's legs as the goalie shifted his weight.

"I'd tell you if I wasn't okay, Coach." Bower gave Tim a tight smile. "Little twinge in the muscle. I'm good."

"All right." Tim looked over the team, nodding slowly, clearly not having much to say since they were leading 4-0. He glanced at the Jumbotron which showed they were in the last five minutes of the final period. "We got two days before we're on the road. Let's finish up and enjoy our time off."

"Best idea I've heard all night." Bower skated away from the rest of the team, taking a solid stance between the pipes before striking each with his stick.

Max took a deep breath, shaking his head as he lowered to the bench. If this was how Bower acted during an at home game, how would he handle being on the road?

Last year, Max would have talked to Sloan about it. Or Dominik. But Dominik seemed distant and distracted despite his welcoming behavior at practice, and he'd likely tell Max that Bower was fine anyway.

*So long as he stops the puck, who cares how anxious he is to leave?*

That's exactly what Dominik would say, but Max could see Tim watching their goalie with the same concern he felt. If Bower couldn't maintain his passion, his focus, how long would it be before he couldn't stop the puck?

"I get this in, top shelf, and you're buying me a beer, Demyan!" Vanek called out as he leaped over the boards to join the play.

Demyan gave Vanek a thumbs-up with his gloved hand, then looked over at Carter. "You still coming?"

"Yeah, Jami and Seb are driving up to Montreal to see some musical tomorrow." Carter grinned. "I got out of it by reminding them that I got Seb all to myself for a few weeks this summer. I'm gonna take Jami to play laser tag next time we get some time off. Not Seb's thing."

Max smiled, thinking how he and Sloan split time with Oriana

159

in the exact same way. Oriana had recently developed an interest in opera, which Sloan couldn't stand, so Max would bring her. The music wasn't much to Max's taste either, but he loved watching her while she let the long, pure notes, the emotion, pull her in. Her whiskey eyes shone with tears as the drama played out onstage and she would hold his hand so tight, as though needing to feel him close during the tragic death scenes. As though she relived her own losses and needed to know he was still with her.

Back in Calgary, Oriana had school and him and Sloan, but he'd sensed that she was lonely. She didn't make friends easily, and those she did make had very different lives. Sometimes he wondered if she'd never been invited to their houses because her married friends couldn't come to grips with the fact that she was living with two men.

Here, she had her sister. And all her friends in Montreal that had known her long enough to accept her no matter how she chose to live her life. She'd mentioned staying over at Silver's tonight so she could spend some time with her niece.

Leaving him without much to do. Unless . . .

"So Ford asked you to check on the bar?" Carter leaned close to Demyan, his brow furrowing slightly. "That's weird. With Cort back, you'd figure Ford wouldn't be worried about it."

"Yeah, guess you haven't heard." Demyan lowered his voice, the two men looking like schoolgirls exchanging gossip. All that was missing was the giggling. "Akira's dating Cort."

"Oh, fuck." Carter's eyes widened. He glanced across the bench at Dominik. "But I thought—"

"Mason's playing with other subs now. Him and Akira were never really a thing."

"This could get interesting."

Inhaling slowly, Max forced his attention back to the ice. A brief thought of how things would go with Dominik single and Oriana being back weighed on his mind, but he pushed it aside. One problem at a time. He needed a way to get back into the team—and not just with his name on the roster.

"I haven't gotten a chance to see Ford's new bar." Max chuckled as both Carter and Demyan lifted their heads, staring at him as though they'd forgotten he was sitting so close. "I could go for a beer. First round's on me."

Demyan ran his tongue over his teeth, nodding slowly. Then he shrugged. "I never say no to free beer."

"You never say no." Carter snorted, bumping Demyan with his shoulder as he stood for a line change. He cocked his head, looking back at Max as he climbed over the boards. "Make it first round and fifth and I'm in."

*Fifth?* The young man was going to get plastered. And if he knew Carter as well as he thought he did, that meant a very loose tongue. By the third beer he'd tell Max exactly why he was so pissed about Max coming back. So Max inclined his head. "You got it."

The Cobras finished the game, 5-1, Bower losing his shutout in the last seconds of the game on a softie. He was the first one out of the locker room—no surprise there. Demyan and Carter told Vanek Max was coming with them to the bar, which got them nothing but a blank look. Vanek told them to wait for him while he went to let Chicklet know he'd be out late.

A bit of ribbing about being pussy whipped and they let him go. Meanwhile, Ramos came to Max's stall, speaking to him while several of the players jostled at the other side of the room, celebrating the win.

"Luke says you are joining them at the bar?"

"Yeah." Max gave Ramos a slanted smile as he shoved his helmet onto his shelf. "Those three ain't my biggest fans. I'm thinkin' we all should have a chat."

"Good. I dislike seeing him bitter and angry. But . . ." Ramos shook his head and laughed. "No, I would ask you to keep him out of trouble, but I'm not certain that's possible."

Barking out a laugh, Max reached over and squeezed Ramos's shoulder. "Can't make you no promises, but I'll do my best."

Right then, a *Whoop!* came from the player's lounge and Max went to the door, letting out a deep sigh as Carter roughly hugged Vanek with one arm while holding up a flask.

"To Chicklet for letting you off your leash!"

"Keep it out of the locker room, Carter!" Tim slid past Max, his arms crossed, expression firm, but his tone making it clear he was trying not to laugh. "No practice tomorrow, boys, so have fun!"

"To Coach!" Demyan grabbed Carter's flask before the younger man could take a swig. "For letting us *all* off our leashes!"

All the men laughed and Tim gave Demyan a mock punch in the gut. The energy in the room buzzed through Max's veins, giving him a rush like how he felt on the back of a bucking bronco, like how he felt when he made love to Oriana. Like he'd always felt in this very room after a win.

It was fucking good to be home.

\* \* \* \*

In between periods, Silver had taken Akira and Sahara to her office to hear what they had to say about Ms. Plant. The way Silver's eyes had flashed with rage made Akira confident that the situation would be handled.

But she hadn't expected Silver to ask her and Sahara to be present when she called Ms. Plant in to meet with her after the game. Cort remained by her side as they headed up to the offices, taking the stairs so Akira could rid herself of some of her nervous energy.

Before leaving her in the hall to continue to Ford's office, Cort put his arm over her shoulder and whispered in her ear, "Soon as you're done, come to the office."

A little chill ran up her spine even as heat descended between her thighs. There was no mistaking the hunger in Cort's tone, but the idea of doing anything in an office . . . she swallowed, forcing a smile as she peered up at him. "Okay."

"Wait." Cort's eyes studied hers. He frowned. "Are you afraid to be alone with me?"

"No! Not at all!" Akira flushed as Sahara glanced back at her, one hand on the doorknob. Akira waved Sahara on, lowering her voice as the other girl opened the door to Silver's office. "It's just . . . what happened to me . . . they brought me to an office and—" She cut herself off as his gaze hardened with understanding, grateful that she didn't have to say any more about the rape. She took a deep breath. "I'm just afraid I'll have flashbacks or something. I'm sorry."

"Don't be." He leaned in, pressing a gentle kiss to her lips. "We can go to your place to watch a movie if you want."

She wrinkled her nose. "Sahara's having a few girls over." Her cheeks flushed as she pressed against him, and for a split second she was wondering if the words in her mind were too bold. But feeling Cort's hard body against hers made it impossible to hold anything back. "There's always your car. The backseat looks comfy."

His body shook with laughter. He kissed her again, longer, slower, then spoke against her lips. "It's *very* comfortable. I'll meet you here and then we can go for a ride."

"A long ride?" She took a few steps back, biting her lip before giving him a mischievous smile. "Are you all right driving with distractions? I can't promise to keep my hands to myself."

He grinned, smacking her butt as she spun around. "Get going before Silver starts thinking I kidnapped you."

"I think I'd enjoy being kidnapped by you."

His hooded look had the flush of her cheeks spreading all over her body. The hallway was cool, but she felt like she was standing in a sauna whenever he was near. As though water poured over her skin would evaporate like it did on the heated stones.

He winked, moving away like it took an effort to do so. "I'll keep that in mind."

Sure her face was beet red, she took a minute to compose herself before going into Silver's office. Ms. Plant was already seated in the chair in front of Silver's desk. Sahara had taken one of the two chairs set off to the side near the window and Silver stood beside her, looking every inch the businesswoman in her pale gray slacks and jacket, her hair pulled back in a sleek updo.

Silver nodded for Akira to sit beside Sahara. Then she turned to Ms. Plant.

Who spoke before Silver could get a word out. "Miss Hayashi, it shows a great lack of respect for you to take your time joining us. I'm sure Miss Delgado asked us here to discuss how unprofessional you've behaved, and I must say, I agree."

Lips in a tight, thin line, Silver stepped forward. "That's not—"

"Sahara may be Akira's friend, but the favoritism she's shown is unseemly." Ms. Plant turned her nose up as though Akira and Sahara had done something disgusting. She nailed Akira with a hard stare. "Any other girl showing up with a hangover even once would be given a warning. The trainers have told me you wanted to handle it yourself, but you clearly haven't. Your relationship is—"

"Will you shut up!" Silver slapped her hand on her desk and glared at Ms. Plant. "We're here because of you."

"Me?" Ms. Plant brought her pale hand to the light blue scarf on her neck. "I don't understand."

Silver shrugged. "That's not my problem. It may have been acceptable wherever you worked before to bully young women and make them feel insecure about themselves, but I have zero tolerance for it here. One of the many charities the Ice Girls are involved in is to support women with eating disorders. You clearly don't fit with what we're trying to accomplish."

"Is this because of that chubby girl?" Ms. Plant frowned at Akira. "Did she complain to you about my showing interest in her health? Why didn't you speak to me? This is ridiculous!"

"'That chubby girl?'" Silver's jaw ticked. "Lady, first of all, you're fired. Second of all, I'm giving you two seconds to get out of my office before I slap you."

"Before you—?"

"One." Silver took a step toward Ms. Plant.

Ms. Plant let out a shocked cry, then scurried out of the room, slamming the door behind her.

Mouth open, Akira stared at Silver. Sahara was doing the same.

"Damn, that felt good." Silver went around her desk, pulling her chair out and lowering into it, pulling the clip from her hair before leaning back and propping her feet up on the desk. "Anyone else you want me to get rid of?"

*Silver freakin' rocks!* Akira decided Silver was her new idol. She felt hysterical laughter bubbling inside her, but was too stunned to let it loose as both she and Sahara shook their heads.

"All righty then. Enjoy your night, girls." Silver grinned as she picked up a folder off her desk and placed it on her thighs. "I've got to think about who I'm gonna have fill Ms. Plant's position as Performance Director."

Akira stood, not sure what to say other than "Thank you."

"No problem. I'm glad you told me." Silver shook her head. "What a bitch."

"I agree." Sahara paused by Akira's side. "Do you have anyone in mind? For the position I mean?"

"I might." Silver gave Akira a look Akira couldn't read, then sat up and picked up her phone. "Don't worry, you'll like this one." A broad smile crossed her lips as whomever she'd called answered. "Hey, bro. Did I wake you up?"

Sahara pulled Akira out into the hall, speaking in a hushed voice as she eased the door shut. "Tell me her calling Ford right after me asking if she had anyone in mind is a coincidence?"

"Umm . . ." Akira nibbled at her bottom lip, not sure what to say. This was Silver. She'd done crazier things than hiring her brother to take over as Performance Director. Hopefully Silver would have to run it by Mr. Keane first, but Akira wasn't going to bring *him* up to Sahara. So she simply shrugged. "Maybe Ford won't want the job."

Brow raised, Sahara walked backward to the elevator. "Sweetie, this gives him a chance to see you almost every day. You really think he'll turn it down?"

"We're just friends. He's not going to take a job just to spend more time with me."

"Uh-huh." Sahara pressed the button to call the elevator. "You waiting for Cort?"

"Yeah." Akira ducked her head as she felt her cheeks heat, sure her plans for the night were written all over her face in explicit detail.

The way Sahara wiggled her eyebrows made Akira wish she had a mirror to check how obvious it really was. Sahara backed into the elevator, calling out before the doors closed, "I won't wait up!"

# Chapter Eleven

Cort rested his forearms on the desk, glancing down at the old team roster, nodding slowly as Tim finished a brief recap of the whole scandal from a couple years back when the former team coach and a couple of players had helped rig games for the Kingsleys. He'd used the excuse that Ford wanted to know exactly how involved his "father" had been, but what he really wanted to know was if there was anyone he might be able to approach.

It made him feel sick to his stomach to even consider bribing or threatening anyone—that wasn't *him*. Not anymore. But as bad as things were between him and Ford, he wouldn't risk the young man he'd looked out for since he was a boy getting hurt again. At least this way, Cort could tell Roy he was looking into it. Give him a fucking name.

Unfortunately, the Cobras all seemed too fucking tight to single one out. Cort had considered Max Perron, but Tim had just brought up how the man had gone to jail rather than betray his team. Every other player had been questioned and had stated clearly that they would have reported any attempt at bribery.

His only hope was one of the rookies, the new player being brought in, or . . . he studied the coach's face as Tim finished giving him the last details of the investigation. "I take it you were questioned as well?"

"About Paul? Yes." Tim scowled. "Made me feel like an idiot. I never suspected a thing."

"You never wondered why the goalie was so inconsistent?"

"Why would I? Some are, and you have to work with them. Hunt might end up being like that. He's an emotional player and tends to lose momentum after a soft goal." Tim scratched his jaw. "It was smart of Paul to use the goalie, though. No one really questions when a goalie has a bad game, and it's hard for the team to come back if too many go in. As a coach, you've got to be ready to pull him if he can't get his act together."

"But sometimes you leave the goalie in to finish the game, right? Like, they win or lose as a team?"

"Exactly." Tim stood, reaching across the desk to shake Cort's hand. "Hope that's it? Not to cut things short, but my wife's waiting for me and I want to take advantage of all the time we have left before the road trip."

"Not a problem." Cort smiled at the other man. He was hard not to like, even though he was making this even more difficult. "Thanks for talking with me."

"Sure thing. Glad you could be here for Ford. He's not a bad kid. It's good that he's clear of Kingsley."

"I agree." Cort stared at the closed door after Tim left, pressing his eyes shut. He wouldn't put up with anyone else talking to him like Ford had—fuck, he'd either cut them out of his life or beat the shit out of them. But he'd worked too damn hard to get the kid on the right path to give up on him now. And damn it, he still considered Ford a brother.

*Gonna make sure he stays clear of Roy. Then . . . we'll see.*

He took out his phone and called Roy's house, wasting no time with pleasantries after the man picked up. "It's gonna take some work, but I might have something."

"Excellent." Roy's usually composed tone held a hint of anxiousness. "A player?"

"Not yet, but just getting a player would be useless."

"I'm not sure what you mean. All we had last time was the goaltender."

Cort rolled his shoulders. "That's not what I heard."

"Then . . . ah, yes. Paul." Roy let out a soft laugh. "You've approached the coach?"

"Yes." Cort inhaled quietly, keeping his tone level so Roy

wouldn't hear the lie. After speaking with Tim, Cort didn't get the impression that the man could be bought. Which left only one option, and . . . *fuck*. He needed to buy himself some time. "I'm working on it. Let them win some games, then I'll put some pressure on him."

"Very well. You have until they clinch a playoff spot," Roy said with faux pleasantness. "I appreciate your cooperation, Cort, but if it proves to be too difficult, I may have to send in my own man."

"Your own—" The dial tone sounded. "Son of a bitch!" Cort slammed his phone down on the desk. He'd gotten the time he needed, but he didn't like not knowing what the fuck Roy's plan B was. "Send in my own man" could mean a lot of things.

None of them good.

"You okay?"

Akira stood by the open door. He hadn't heard her come in.

And he really hoped she hadn't heard anything. Damn it, she'd hate him if she found out what he was doing.

But the concern in her face made it clear she didn't know. She approached him, wrapping her arms around his neck. "Tell me whoever that 'son of a bitch' is—" Her cheeks grew pink as the words left her mouth, as though she felt naughty saying them. She kissed his cheek. "—didn't stress you out too much. I may have to hurt him."

What should have been funny made his gut clench. Cort was happy she hadn't questioned his intense focus on the game while they were in the press box. She'd likely thought he was just doing his job, but he'd been a little concerned that she might come over to him—hug him or something right there where the cameras might catch them. The fewer people who knew he and Akira were together, the better.

*How long can you keep that up, Nash?* He inhaled slowly and pulled her into his lap, holding her close. Fighting Ford for her seemed so simple, but keeping her might put her in danger.

Ford thought Cort would end things because Akira didn't fit into his life.

And maybe he was right. Because she didn't. Shouldn't.

He was the son of a bitch. The best thing he could do for Akira was break things off with her now. Before she got too attached. But part of him hoped that he'd find a way around Roy. If he could give Roy a few fucking games, make him some money . . . he ground his teeth, stroking Akira's back, already finding it hard to imagine not having her around, and hating himself for it. There was no guarantee he'd ever get away from Roy. Not without leaving Ford out to dry.

*Not fucking happening.*

So he'd do what he always did. Live day-to-day and handle whatever shit came at him. He and Akira had right now.

He let out a rough laugh. "No more work talk. Tonight is ours. Already forgot about the ass—about who I was on the phone with."

"Good. Deal with the asshole tomorrow." She wiggled off his lap, tugging at his hands until he stood. "Fuck him."

"I think I'm a bad influence on you." Cort grinned as she stuck out her tongue at him, then framed her chin in his hand and bent down to trace his tongue over her damp bottom lip. "Don't swear and I'll try not to."

"It doesn't bother me." She pressed her hands to his chest, going up on her tiptoes to reach his chin, nipping him lightly. "I'll just try not to do it in front of my father."

"Or how about you keep those nasty words out of that pretty mouth." He tightened his grip on her jaw, kissing her hard until she gasped and fisted her hands in his shirt. Then he kissed the tip of her nose. "Only use them when you can't help yourself."

She cocked her head as he grabbed his jacket from the back of his chair. "Why wouldn't I be able to help myself?"

"Because I'll work very hard to make you lose control." He joined her by the door, wrapping his arm around her shoulders, his dick so damn hard it practically led the way to his car. He waited until they got out of the elevator in the parking garage to speak again. "'Oh fuck! More!' is perfectly acceptable."

She giggled, sounding nervous and excited all at once. "You're bad."

"And you love it." He opened the passenger's side door for her, sliding his lips up the length of her throat before she got in. There was something about being around her that didn't make him feel "bad." Like if things were different, he could be real good for her.

Maybe he would be. He had to believe if there wasn't a chance for them, if there was no hope for him to find a way out of the mess he was in, that he'd have ended things already.

He would if there was no other option, but he hadn't gotten there yet.

They drove out aimlessly for a while, the ocean to the right, the view of the snow-blanketed city fading away on the left. Akira's small hand covered his for most of the drive, then shifted to his knee. He could practically feel her hesitant gaze on the side of his face as her hand drifted up a little higher. His throat worked as she reached his belt.

"I've always wanted to do this." She spoke softly as she undid his belt. Then unbuttoned his pants and pulled down his zipper. "I'm not distracting you, am I?"

"No, I'm good." He tightened his grip on the steering wheel as she freed his dick and brought her lips down to his throbbing flesh. This wasn't the first time a girl had gone down on him while he was driving, but with Akira it was different. Fucking sinful, like corrupting an angel.

And as her soft lips slid down his hard length, all he could think was he didn't want to stop.

* * * *

Akira's breath caught as Cort placed his hand on the back of her head and the car stopped moving. Giving him pleasure was easy. She loved the feeling of his thigh muscles hardening under her hand. His pulse racing against her tongue. Dominik had helped make going down on a man feel like something erotic, like a gift of pleasure. She never had flashbacks while doing this with either man. It was when they wanted to return the favor that the darkness fell over her, that the memories loomed like an evil specter, tainting the perfect moments with dread.

"Akira."

She bit her lip as she sat up and met his level gaze. Was he mad at her? She'd stopped while her thoughts had wandered. What man wanted that?

"Aw, Tiny, don't give me that look." Cort raked his fingers through her hair. "I think we need to clear something up."

"I'm sorry." She wasn't even sure *why* she was sorry. Mostly because he must be disappointed.

He shook his head. "See, that's what I'm talking about. I'm not upset. We're getting to know each other, and I can see when you're thinking hard. When you're worried. I just can't always figure out why."

She stared at the dashboard. "It's nothing."

"That's not helpful." He tipped her chin up with a finger until she had no choice but to face him. "Have you ever been tied up?"

Her brow furrowed. "Yes. Loosely."

"Would you trust me to tie you up?"

Without thinking, she nodded.

He shook his head. "No. Not yet." He stroked her bottom lip with his thumb. "You'd panic. You're not ready." His eyes softened and her heart melted like a candle too close to a blazing flame. "I won't make love to you tonight."

The way he said it . . . from some men, it might have sounded odd, but from Cort the statement was gentle. As though he wanted to take very special care of her.

Which was nice, but she was still hot. Fairly burning up in all the places her stupid brain couldn't ruin things for them. She wanted him so badly it hurt.

He grinned as though he'd somehow caught the thought. "A gentleman returns the favor. No sane person would call me that, but I'll be one for you."

"You're incredible." Her fingers curled around his stiff shirt collar, and the warmth of the brief contact with his skin beneath it shot straight to her core. She rose up on her knees. "You don't have to—"

"I know. I've been doing some reading. Dom's pleasure can be more than enough for a sub." He chuckled as her eyes widened and he fisted his hand in her hair. "I'm not a Dom. *Yet*. But even if I earn the title, there's some things I won't do. Like the whole orgasm denial thing. I'll find better ways to punish you if you're a bad girl. Now get in the backseat."

She scrambled between the seats, watching him as he got out of the car to join her. "Better ways? Like what?"

"Good question." He drew her up to her knees and pulled her panties down from under her skirt. He left the door open and the cold from outside clashed with the heat of the car. "It'll be something good. Something that will make you think twice before disappointing me."

"I think knowing I've disappointed you would be enough." She let out a little squeak as he wrapped his hands around her hips to pull her closer. "What are you—?"

"Lie back and enjoy, Tiny." He lowered his face between her thighs, kissing the side of one. "I don't want to have to think of a punishment just yet."

She lay back and closed her eyes, swallowing a gasp as his mouth covered her. His thick tongue pressed in deep, then slid over her clit with just enough pressure to make her squirm. The pleasure escalated as his grip tightened on her hips, forcing her to take the way he slowly tasted every bit of her blazing flesh without letting her rise up to take more. She trembled as all the sensations coiled into a sizzling core of erotic energy, growing with each spark of her nerve endings, tightening until she blazed within and without.

Cort slid his lips up to the top of her mound, laying a soft kiss there as the cold air from outside rushed in to caress her damp folds. Her insides convulsed as though trying to latch on to the release that had been so close. When he slicked his fingers through the moisture between her pussy lips, her hips jerked. As he slowly pressed two fingers inside her, she threw her head back, lips parted as she tried to gasp in air, her body trapped on the precipice of ecstasy, close enough to take the plunge or stumble back onto level ground.

A lazy glide of Cort's tongue over her clit had her crying out, tipped closer to the ledge. He dragged his fingers out and closed his lips around her clit. Pulled lightly with his mouth and thrust his fingers in deep.

Her next cry scored her throat as her body thrashed and she lost control. Boiling waves kissed by electric currents crashed over and over inside her, the sensation so intense the muscles in her thighs tightened and her eyes teared. Cort shifted, pulling her to him with his fingers still inside her. The movement set her off again, and she buried her face against the side of his neck as she rode out the last wave, everything solid within washed away with the tide.

The sensation of being boneless, limp and helpless, stole the air from her lungs. She stiffened, shoving at the heavy weight on her shoulders, blindly grasping around for a way to escape. Darkness seized her mind and all that she could see was that she was trapped.

"You're okay, Tiny. You're with me." The weight left her shoulders and a gentle, warm hand cupped her cheek. A soothing, familiar tone reached beyond the smothering shadows, leading her back to where she could open her eyes and see Cort. Cort, whose tender smile let her know she was safe. "There we go. Back with me?"

"Yes." She curled up on his lap, resting her head against his chest, just listening to the sound of his heart beating at a steady rhythm. Breathing in the cold air while he held her, keeping away the chill. Once her pulse almost matched his, she looked up at him. "Sorry about that."

"Why? It's not your fault." He smoothed his hand over her hair and kissed the top of her head. "Is it usually that bad?"

"It's been worse." She shuddered, recalling the times where she'd actually seen their faces in the place of any man who came too close. "Dominik's the only one who's ever been able to bring me back that fast."

"Is he the first one you slept with?"

"Yes. I wasn't sure I'd ever be able to let a man touch me after . . ." She swallowed, slipping her fingers between the buttons of his shirt, needing the contact with his skin, the feeling of him real and warm and near. "All the therapy couldn't make it okay to let a man close. But he did." She bit her lip, finally considering what she was saying. "Ugh, I shouldn't be bringing up another man while I'm with you. Not after—"

"He's an important part of why you can be with me, Akira. These are things I need to know, whenever you feel comfortable telling me." He held her for a while longer, then gently eased her off his lap. "Let's get you home. I don't want you getting cold."

"Would it be too much to ask . . ." *Or too pathetic?* She scowled, hating how worried she was about what people would think. About the mocking voice in her head with the sneering lips calling her too needy.

"Ask." Cort's lips thinned when she shook her head. His eyes were hard as they locked on hers. "Communication is important with this 'lifestyle.' Fuck, it's important in any relationship. Don't shut me out now."

"I'm not, I just don't want you thinking I'm a silly, desperate, little girl." She folded her arms over her chest, the disappointment in his eyes sinking straight in and leaving a painful ache. She caught her bottom lip with her teeth as it trembled.

"I'd never think that. My answer won't always be yes, Tiny, but I'm making this my first official rule as your potential . . ." His eyebrows drew together slightly as though he was searching for the word. "Top. I want to try out the scene thing sometime, but I need to know you're not afraid to talk to me about anything."

175

"I'm not afraid."

"Good. Then what were you going to ask?"

"If I can keep you." She blushed at his grin. She'd spoken too fast to think her words over. "I mean, I liked having you in my bed. You're nice to snuggle with."

"I like being there." He ran his fingers down the length of her throat, then nodded. "No harm in spending another night. Jami might start wondering if I plan to move in, but that's her issue." He drew a crooked line down to the deep V of her shirt, causing her to shiver and lean toward him, a different ache settling in her core. His lips slanted. "But I have one request."

"Yes?" A question, and her answer. She couldn't see herself saying no to him. *Ever.*

"This time, you have to keep your hands to yourself." He patted her cheek, then got out of the backseat. Glancing at her through the rearview mirror once he'd taken his place behind the wheel, Cort spoke in very serious tone. "I need my sleep."

Chewing at the inside of her cheek, Akira made her way to the passenger seat beside him. She considered Cort for a moment, wondering what he'd do if she disobeyed. She had a feeling he wouldn't be disappointed.

This was his way of telling her he expected nothing. That he'd come home with her for the simple reason that she'd asked him to. And that made her feel all fuzzy and tingly. He was incredible.

*Your move, Akira.* She sat back and put on her seat belt, inclining her head. "I'll try my best, but I should probably tell you something."

"Go ahead."

"I usually sleep naked." She tilted her head as he arched a brow at her. "That won't be a problem, will it?"

"I like this game. A problem?" He let out a rough laugh and shook his head. "Not at all, Tiny. I'm ready to play whenever you are."

The hairs on the back of her neck rose. She felt like she was stepping off a bridge with nothing but an elastic rope keeping her from crashing to the earth. And Cort was that rope. He wouldn't stop her from taking that leap, but she had to trust him to catch her before she fell too far.

She shouldn't. Not yet.

But she did. She gave him a sly smile. "My game, my rules?"

He chuckled and the little rush became a dizzying high as he put his hand on her wrist, shackling it with his fingers. He was more than the rope. He was the harness restraining her, snug and secure, and his next words let her know he'd hold her even as she soared.

"Your game for now." He brought her hand to his lips, never taking his eyes off the road, and kissed her palm. "Always my rules."

# Chapter Twelve

A dull, serrated blade, working its way through the tight, throbbing mess of his knee, pain so sharp, Dean's stomach almost rejected the cold water he'd just downed. He eyed the painkillers on the dresser across the room, which he'd brought to the bedroom after saying goodnight to Silver and Oriana. The ladies were downstairs, watching a movie, eating ice cream, and catching up. Thankfully, Silver had been too distracted to observe his strides with her usually sharp eye. Or maybe he'd hid it well.

No chance that he could have managed that after reaching the top step. The rapid drop in temperature had made his knee sore enough for him to use his cane, but the pain had been bearable until tonight.

Silver would have told him to take his meds. Both she and Landon knew he disliked taking anything unless absolutely necessary, but their opinion of when it was necessary and his were quite different.

He'd finally given in, but his knee buckling had forced him to set down the painkillers and the bottle of water to take the weight off his knee by sitting on the bed. Any attempt to stand was pure agony.

*I'll be fine in a minute.* He bent his knee to test it and cold sweat covered his flesh. Gritting his teeth, he latched on to the wooden post of the footboard and rose, using his left leg. His head spun and he cursed under his breath as the door opened.

"Forget these?" Landon picked up the pills, gently closing the door behind him, then coming over to the bed. Fine creases formed in his otherwise smooth forehead as he opened the pill bottle and tapped three into his palm. "Wish you'd said something before it got this bad."

Dean shook his head as he lowered back down to sit on the bed. "It wasn't until I got up here."

"And you just needed a minute for it to pass." Landon pressed the pills into Dean's hand. It was unsettling how well the man knew him. Landon's next statement proved it even more. "Silver didn't suspect a thing, did she? You made sure of it."

Tossing back the pills and taking a gulp of water from the bottle Landon uncapped and handed to him, Dean shrugged. He pressed one fist into the mattress as pain tore through his knee. "You know I like dealing with this alone."

"Right. But you don't have to." Landon's gaze hardened. He sighed, taking a knee and beginning to unbutton Dean's suit jacket. He made an irritated sound when Dean tried to stop him. "Let's get you comfortable. I have an idea."

Once his jacket was off, quickly followed by his shirt, Dean leaned back on the pillows, inhaling slowly as his pulse beat hard enough to outdo the steady throb in his knee, the slice of arousal holding the perfect edge of pain. He choked out a laugh as Landon's hands moved to his belt. "Not sure that will help, but I'm in no condition to stop you."

"Funny." Landon carefully pulled his pants down, leaving Dean in nothing but his boxer briefs. He tossed the pants aside, his bearing almost detached as he helped Dean straighten his right leg. His jaw ticked when Dean stiffened. "Does that hurt?"

"The edge will come off as soon as the medication kicks in." Dean rested his head on the pillow, breathing in and out slowly, evenly, as blazing heat stabbed deep into the center of his knee. He tensed as Landon's hands surrounded his knee and the heat changed, surging up into his swelling cock. Not wanting to make the younger man uncomfortable, he gestured for Landon to leave him. "Massaging it won't help."

"I didn't think it would." Landon lifted his head, but didn't move his hands. "The muscles are tight. If I could get them to loosen up—"

"I have pills to help with that."

"Yeah, sure it helps a lot when you won't take them."

"Says the man who stopped taking morphine the day after surgery." Dean closed his eyes as Landon idly rubbed his rock-hard thigh muscles. When the pain was this severe, every muscle in his leg tended to tense up. The muscle relaxers did help, but . . . "I don't like how drowsy I am after taking the Valium. I know Amia mostly sleeps through the night, but still, I like knowing I won't sleep through her crying if she needs something."

"I get that. I hated being stuck in bed after surgery." Landon slipped off the bed and went to the closet. He came out with a large, metal box. "I've been looking into something . . . wasn't sure if you'd go for it." He gave Dean a crooked smile as he placed the box holding his TENS unit beside the bed. "I know I usually use this to have fun with Silver, but that's not what it's really meant for."

"My doctor suggested this type of therapy, to be honest." Dean let out a self-deprecating laugh. "I may have refused strictly *because* I've seen how the stimulation can be used."

"You're weird, man." Landon chuckled as he opened the box and took out two large electrodes and two small ones. "I've never seen someone come up with so many excuses not to get help. You spend less time in your doctor's office than most people do at a fast-food joint."

"He understands that I'm a busy man." Rather than sounding direct, Dean had a feeling he sounded like a grumpy old man. And being around Landon certainly didn't make him feel any younger. It had been a little easier to deal with when Landon had been the one who needed to be taken care of, but with his looking so young, strong, and virile, Dean couldn't help but look down at his own damaged body and wonder how things would be if he was closer to Landon's age. And if Landon hadn't made the limits of their relationship so very clear.

Landon pulled the paper backing off one of the electrodes. "Not too busy to get on me and Silver's case about taking care of ourselves."

"It's not the same at all." Dean narrowed his eyes at Landon, tempted to grab him and shake him hard enough to get that smirk off his face. He automatically used the same tone he used with Silver when she became obstinate. "You both have your full lives ahead of you. You're much too young to—"

"Does that make you ancient?" Landon placed one hand on Dean's knee. "You're fourteen years older than me, Dean, but I don't see it. All I see is a strong man I respect more than anyone besides my own father."

"I appreciate that." And he did. Dean knew Landon didn't say things like this lightly. He watched Landon silently setting up the TENS unit, only looking away when Landon stood to take off his black t-shirt. But even staring at the wall, he could picture those thick arms. The tanned flesh smoothly sliding over the solid swell of muscle. Picture the movement of those sculpted abs, the large body maintained by the meals Dean prepared to help keep Landon in the shape he was now.

*Easy there, Richter.* He bit back a wry grin as the image of Landon licking rib sauce off his fingers with gusto flashed through his mind. Any thought of Landon eating was not conductive to keeping their relationship unchanged. Perhaps, somehow, he could see Landon as he was sure Perron saw Callahan. For years he'd seen the two men grow closer, become like brothers.

But Dean had brothers. And his feelings for Landon were very different. His only option was to deal with them as best he could without letting them disturb the balance he and Landon had found with Silver and their daughter.

"How does it feel when I touch you here?" Landon sat by his side, one hand high on Dean's thigh, the other beneath his knee. His lips quirked as Dean glanced at the hand on his thigh. He pressed a little under Dean's knee. "The meds kick in too much?"

"No, I feel it." *Fuck.* There was no way Landon would miss how Dean's dick had pressed long and hard against his boxer briefs. They were too snug and Landon was too close. But he cringed as Landon's fingers pushed into another spot. "Damn it, don't do that again."

"I won't." Landon placed a small electrode right over the spot, then another above Dean's knee. The other two went on in a way that would have the charge crossing through his knee. "Twenty minutes, and if we're lucky, the pain should be gone for at least a few days. Maybe longer."

"Twenty minutes." Dean licked his bottom lip as Landon attached the cables and plugged them in to the unit. As soon as the unit was turned on, he felt the electric stimulation triggering his muscles and nerves. The strange sensation wasn't enough to draw his attention away from the other, very *obviously* stimulated part of him. "Thank you for this. Maybe you should check on Amia while it does its work."

"Weren't you the one who told me to stop hovering over her?" Landon pulled something out of the drawer by the bed. He poured the lightly sweet-smelling almond oil into his hand, then knelt on the bed, looking Dean over with a curious slant to his lips. "She's fine. You, however, are quite tense."

"Quite." Dean agreed, his eyes drifting halfway shut as Landon's slick hands slid over his chest. Between the painkillers and the massaging sensation of the TENS, he was feeling much too relaxed. Mentally, if not physically. He wasn't sure what he would do, or say, if Landon kept touching him. "You should stop."

"Ask me to." Landon pressed his fingers hard into the knotted muscles of Dean's pectorals. "Ask and I will."

The urge to pull Landon down was overwhelming. Dean ground his teeth, locking his elbows to keep his arms by his sides. He opened his eyes in narrow slits. "Stop."

Landon went still. Then leaned closer, his tone low and husky. He spread his hands over Dean's chest, rubbing even as he spoke. "Guess I lied. Wanna try a safeword?"

"Fuck." Dean groaned as his muscles gave under Landon's careful manipulation. His dick was fully erect, but he wanted more than just a quick fuck. Something he'd never have even if they crossed all the erratic lines Landon had drawn. Only, he was losing the will to stop this. His body sank into the bed, and all he wanted was for Landon to continue. "Just like that, you bastard. Damn it, that feels good."

"Yeah?" Landon let out a soft laugh as he shifted again, straddling Dean without putting any weight on him. "Does your knee still hurt?"

Not feeling a thing other than his painfully hard dick and Landon's hands on his chest, Dean mouthed "no," not sure he could find the air to voice the word. Lying there and letting Landon stroke his hand down his chest, then over his twitching stomach, felt oddly decadent. Right and so wrong all at once, because Landon couldn't know what this was doing to him. How much it confused the unspoken boundaries.

But if crossing those boundaries remained just as unspoken, perhaps it wouldn't mean a thing.

"Shit." Landon's breath on Dean's face brought his eyes open. The younger man's eyes were wide, his face flushed, and the confusion Dean had felt reflected in Landon's gaze. His hands were flat on Dean's chest and his inhales and exhales raced with the pulse that pounded between them. "I should have stopped when you asked me to."

"Yes." Dean studied Landon's face, wondering why Landon hadn't pushed off the bed and put space between them the second he'd become aware of what he was doing. He reminded Dean of a young Dom using a flogger for the first time, both aroused and afraid of how good it felt when a sub struggled against their restraints. As though it *shouldn't* feel good.

And no one could tell them how to deal with that internal battle. No one could determine the outcome.

Landon had enough experience to know that. So it wasn't as surprising as it should have been when he brought one oil-smoothed hand to Dean's face. Testing his own responses. And Dean's.

"Should have, but didn't. I think we both know why."

Landon's lips curved as he stroked Dean's jaw with his thumb. "You need to shave."

"So do you." Dean couldn't lie there passively anymore. He pushed up on his elbow until they were breathing in each other's exhales. And he spoke plainly because he knew no other way. "What do you want, Landon?"

"I—" Landon swiftly shoved up, swinging his legs off the bed as the door cracked open. He bent over Dean's knee, checking the connections as though he'd been doing so all along. "I think this has been on long enough."

Silver stood in the doorway, shaking her head as Landon put the unit away. She said something over her shoulder—likely to her sister—then pushed the door shut. "Don't do that. I'm not stupid."

"Do what?" Landon straightened, his shoulders stiff, his throat working as he swallowed hard. "Dean's knee—"

"You fucking coward." Silver strode up to Landon, stabbing her finger into the center of his chest. "Why don't you just say it? You want him."

"Silver, that's enough." Dean tested his leg as he stood, pleased that the pain was all but gone. But much less pleased with Silver's attitude. Both he and Landon had shown patience when she wanted to try something new, like needle play or a fucking machine. Understanding when she decided not to try it at all. Landon had earned the same consideration, no matter where things went from this point on. "You will not speak to him that way."

"He needs you to talk for him, too?" Silver sniffed derisively. "I'm sure you'll enjoy this. Now you've got two subs."

"No." Landon stepped toward her in a way that had Silver taking a big step back, her lips parted, eyes wide. "Is that what you're afraid of Silver? That I'll somehow take your place?"

"You won't take my place. I just won't have one with you." Silver's lashes clung together with her unshed tears. She hesitated, moving as though to go to Landon, but instead came to Dean's side, latching on to his hand as though he was the shore and facing Landon was like facing a storm trying to drag her out to sea.

Dean drew her closer, but didn't say a word. They might all be together, but this issue was between Landon and Silver. The best he could do was be here for them both.

Silver hauled in a breath that sounded close to a sob. "I'm losing you. I know it sounds selfish, but I could handle being the one between you. The one you both loved. If that changes . . . if it's Dean between us and nothing else . . ." She shook her head, letting out a bitter laugh. "No. Wait. We have a kid."

"'A kid'?" Landon glared at Silver, and Dean suddenly understood Silver's fears. The child that should have brought them closer together had instead driven them further apart. "Amia. *Our* daughter. Yours, mine, and Dean's."

"I know that." Silver practically spat out each syllable. "Haven't you heard? Two daddies can raise a child just fine."

"That is very true." Landon closed his eyes. "Is that what you want? Are you tired of being a mother already?"

"I was never *tired* of it, you asshole! I was sick!"

"I know that! I'm trying to understand what you're getting at! I don't understand why you hate me so much!" Landon brought his hands to his short hair, raking his nails over his scalp. "One minute, everything's fine, then *this*! There's nothing . . . nothing between me and Dean that you need to worry about! I just . . ."

"Just what?" Silver tightened her grip on Dean's hand, her whole body shaking against him. "Say it."

"I love him." Landon stopped breathing and went perfectly still. He stared at Dean as though he'd shocked himself and desperately needed Dean to make it okay. But Dean wasn't given a chance. "I love you, and I love him, but it's different. Does your sister worry about Max and Sloan?"

"No. They might as well be brothers."

*Don't, Landon.* Now it was Dean who stopped breathing. Silver had just given Landon a way to make all the emotions that confused him so much go away. An excuse to put up a wall that might never come down.

And Landon took it with a firm nod. "Dean and I are no

different."

"Really?" Silver looked doubtful, but hopeful. She glanced over at Dean. "You don't kiss your brothers."

Dean shook his head, not sure what he'd expected. Landon and Silver had too much to work through to add further complications. And that was all he could call what he'd imagined between *himself* and Landon. "Landon and I have never kissed." He gave Landon a level look, letting the other man know he accepted the choice he made. But not letting Landon see how much he hated it. "And we never will."

\* \* \* \*

Max leaned his elbow on the bar, glancing around at the pressing crowd as Demyan planted a loud, smacking kiss on Vanek's cheek while Carter ruffled Vanek's golden curls.

"You're so cute." Demyan told Vanek while refilling the four shot glasses on the bar, having temporarily taken over bartending duties since the waitress had let them into the bar. The bartender who should be here, Reggie, was late. And Demyan was taking full advantage of his absence, and the liquor.

Apparently, Ford wouldn't mind.

"He really is." Carter propped his elbow on the bar, sliding a little as he tossed back his shot. He sat up, raising his voice to be heard above the noisy throng, half the patrons surrounding them, demanding to know why they hadn't gotten their drinks yet. They all looked annoyed at Carter distracting Demyan from filling their orders. "Zovko's on! Halo boy's gonna wanna hear this."

Vanek, who hated all the angelic nicknames the team gave him, made a face as he choked down his own shot. "You guys should wanna hear this, too. The Cobras are on the list of teams he's willing to be traded to."

Demyan turned up the volume. Then looked over the crowd. "No more drinks unless everyone shuts up!"

*Well, that worked.* Max nursed his beer and lifted his head to watch the interview on the huge screens above the bar.

"Zovko, is it true you put the Dartmouth Cobras at the top of the list of teams that interest you? *Above* the Pens?"

"Yes." Raif Zovko gave the young reporter a rakish smile, which made the woman blush. His unruly brown hair fell over his forehead as his dark brown eyes locked on the camera in a way that made it seem like he was speaking to his audience and not to the reporters. "The team is very appealing. I've told my agent to accept *any* offer."

The reporters started shouting questions at him, but Zovko didn't speak again until they calmed down. He nodded to an older man.

"Do you believe you'll fit in with the team's . . . proclivities?"

"I do." Zovko laughed as the reporters began firing questions again. "Am I kinky? Shall I show you?"

*Damn.* Max shook his head, glancing over at Demyan who was snickering and Carter who was showing some random girl pictures of his puppy. Vanek had his empty shot glass against his lips and was swallowing convulsively.

"You okay, kid?" Max reached over and smacked Vanek's shoulder to get his attention. "Had a few too many?"

Vanek shook his head. He motioned toward the screen with his glass. "He's flirting with them. The men and the women."

"That he is." Eyeing Demyan and Carter, Max moved a little closer to Vanek, not sure how the other two men would react if Vanek said the wrong thing with his inhibitions shot. Demyan's jaw had hardened and he'd turned the TV off. Carter had turned his back on the girl he'd been chatting with. Max shot an easy smile at both, then focused on Vanek. "I might've heard a few rumors about him being bisexual. Makes sense he'd want to join the team."

"But he was engaged." Tyler's face fell, as though the revelation bothered him. "He was dating this cute little country singer. They looked great together. I didn't think he was—"

"What? Gay?" Carter noisily gritted his teeth. "Shit, Vanek. I didn't think you were a fucking bigot. Is it only cool when it's two hot chicks?"

"Fuck you. I'm not a fucking bigot like your dad, Carter." Vanek slammed his shot glass in front of Demyan, staring at him until he filled it. Then he slurped it back, shuddering as he wiped his mouth with his hand. "I just . . ." He hiccupped, then laughed. "I thought Chicklet would like Zovko's girlfriend, and we could all hang out or something."

Demyan grinned, taking a swig right from the bottle. "That's hot. Chicklet, Laura, and Maggie whatever-her-name-is." He looked Vanek over and his grin broadened. "No getting in bed with a man though, right, Vanek? Guess you and Zovko would just watch?"

There was no mistaking the implication in Demyan's tone, so Max laughed and patted Vanek's back. "Nothin' wrong with watching."

"Says you." Vanek made a face as he stole Max's beer. "It's hot the first few times, but Laura isn't big on sharing."

"So you and Laura don't—" Carter frowned abruptly. "Hey, what were you saying about my dad? Don't bring up that asshole. I'm not his son anymore since he found out I'm with Seb." He smiled, placing his phone on the bar. "I love Seb. And Jami." His smile faltered. "Jami's mad at me." He turned to Max. "All your fault."

Max's brow shot up. Looked like Carter was drunk enough to start sharing. Taking his beer back from Tyler, Max spoke as he brought the rim to his lips. "My fault?"

"Yeah, she don't like that I'm pissed at you—hey, where's my beer?" Carter gave Demyan a dirty look. "You drank it, didn't you?"

"You weren't drinking beer, dumbass." Demyan went to the fridge at the other end of the bar and returned with four beers. He uncapped the bottles, then handed them out. "I got a hard time from Zach, too. Becky says she's staying out of it." He shrugged, glancing at Max. "I'm over it, I think. Just . . . hell, we needed you. Things kinda fell apart after you and Callahan took off. Hard to just make things okay because you decided we're worth your time."

"We're not." Vanek mumbled into his beer, shoulders hunched. "He didn't come back for us. He came for her. If Oriana wanted to stay in Calgary, Perron wouldn't be here."

"Exactly." Carter grumbled, rubbing his eyes with one hand as he gulped down half his beer. "We could've managed without you. I'm fucking sick of people saying how important you are to the team. We've got lots of good people. You can't just come back and expect everything to be cool."

"Like your dad." Max wouldn't have taken that approach if Carter was sober, but the buzz of the alcohol had the young man reacting slower. And more honestly than he would otherwise. Max knew enough about Carter's past to put two and two together. "He came back to claim all the glory after you and your mom struggled for years."

"Fuck him." Carter took a deep breath. "I hate him. But I almost . . ." He pressed his eyes shut. "I almost forgave him for what he did to my mom. For cheating and everything. Took a while, but I thought I should. Then I told him the truth and he decides I'm no good anymore. So fuck him. And fuck you."

"Luke." Max wrapped his hand around Carter's wrist, using his first name to get his attention as he stopped Carter from taking another swig of beer. Carter stared at him, his eyes glistening. "I didn't want to leave, but I'm back. I love this team and I'm fucking proud of y'all for keeping the team going after me and Sloan took off. I know it wasn't easy for you to tell your dad that you're in love with a man. You're right, though. Fuck him. You're good and tough and I'm happy that you found people who love you like you deserve. Ramos and Jami." His lips twitched. "Gotta tell you though, Jami's like a little sister to me. So you better treat her right."

Carter nodded solemnly. Then lunged into Max's arms. "I take it back. I love you, man."

"I love you, too." Max laughed, rubbing Carter's back as the kid hugged him. He should have known Carter's "daddy issues" had something to do with his resentment. Luckily, the young man had enough invested in the game to "love" what Max could bring to the team once he let the rest go. "We good now?"

"Yeah, we're good." Carter ducked his head. "Sorry I was a dick."

"I'm not sorry." Tyler tried to stand, but ended up tipping sideways off his stool. He sputtered as half his beer spilled over his face. "You were supposed to make Oriana happy. She won't be happy here."

"Yes, she will." Now *this* was unexpected. Max had figured Vanek was over Oriana. Was too happy with Chicklet and Laura to focus on her. But maybe some of his old feelings lingered. He set his beer down and helped Vanek back onto his stool. "Where is this coming from, kid? I thought you and Oriana were fine as friends."

"We are, but Sloan hurts her." Vanek stared at the bar, fidgeting with his beer. "Dominik could have kept her safe, but he's not with you anymore. And all you do is watch. You can't keep her safe."

*There we go.* Max shook his head, pressing his hand to Vanek's cheek to force the boy to look at him. "I don't need to. Oriana knows what she wants. And I trust Sloan."

"I don't." Vanek cleared his throat. "But it's none of my business. That's what Chicklet said."

"She's right." Max softened his tone, recalling the last time he'd seen Vanek like this. His mother had a habit of dating abusive men. Vanek had grown up knowing just when to get the ice pack to tend to his mother's latest swollen lip. Not long after Vanek had been drafted, he'd asked his coach in the minors for some time off so he could check on his mother in the hospital. When he'd returned, he'd been brought up to the Cobras to replace an injured player. He'd been only eighteen and overwhelmed.

He'd gotten drunk that night and Max had taken him aside when he started crying. He'd held Vanek as the boy whispered that he was no better than the men who beat his mother. Because most of them got drunk all the time.

Max had told him, drunk or sober, he'd never be like them. Because he knew how they treated his mother was wrong.

It had taken some time, but Vanek had finally started seeing that there were good men out there. And that he was one of them. But that wouldn't change how he'd react to seeing a sadist with a masochist. Consent wouldn't matter. All Vanek would see was abuse.

Oriana's return brought it all back. But Vanek wouldn't focus his anger on the woman. He might have reacted to seeing Dominik not part of the relationship, but when they were gone, it was easier for him to accept that there was nothing he could do.

Vanek probably thought there was something Max could do. And resented the assumption that Max would do nothing.

There was no way Max would justify the dynamics of his, Oriana's, and Sloan's relationship. But maybe he could say something to make Vanek feel a little better.

"Has Chicklet ever punished you?"

Vanek sat up. He inhaled sharply. "Yeah. I hate the cane. It hurts."

"But that's not abuse?"

"No! Chicklet loves me." Vanek's cheeks reddened. "I feel better when she shows me what I did wrong. Makes me pay. Then it's over."

"Not everyone would agree." Max paused, letting his words sink in before he continued. "*You* need to know you've taken the penalty and made things right. You've *consented*. So it's not wrong."

Inclining his head, Vanek blindly reached for his beer. "It's not wrong."

"And when she uses the flogger? And you enjoy it?" Max assumed Chicklet had done so. She wasn't a tender Mistress. But Vanek might not see pain a woman gave as equal to the pain she received. "Is that wrong?"

"Nothing Chicklet does is bad. It's not the same." Vanek propped his head on his hand, sliding until his elbow met Carter's.

He frowned at Carter, who seemed completely distracted by the texts he was sending. Then he sighed. "When I spank Laura . . . it's bad, but not. Because it's what Chicklet wants. Which can't be wrong?"

*Oh boy.* Max gently took Vanek's beer away. He liked that the boy was relaxed enough to speak openly, but any more and he'd pass out. "It's not wrong. Are you ready to go home?"

"Reggie!" Demyan shouted before Vanek could answer. Demyan swayed as he crossed the space behind the bar to meet the very late bartender. "What's all this?"

The skinny man with bright blue hair dropped his bags on the floor. "Sorry I'm late. Had two full sleeves that ran long. Didn't even stop at home to drop my stuff off."

"You any good?" Demyan braced himself on the bar, staring at the bags. "I want a tattoo."

"Hey, I'll give you a good price since you covered for me." Reggie took out his phone and showed Demyan a few pictures. "This was the last one."

"Nice." Demyan dropped into a chair and rolled up the sleeve of his T-shirt. "I want a doe—like, the outline. And Casey's birthday in Roman numerals."

*Very sweet.* Max had never pictured Demyan as a daddy, but he was obviously fully invested in the role. The doe idea was questionable, but getting his stepdaughter's birthday on his arm wasn't something Max thought Demyan would regret.

"I can do that." Reggie started pulling out his equipment. He grabbed a pen from the bar and drew on Demyan's arm, holding his tongue between his teeth. "Something like that? What's the date you want?"

"Oh, you're good." Demyan took a deep breath and gave Reggie the date. He nodded once the drawing was done. "Perfect. Do it."

Shaking his head as he studied the picture, beautiful as it was, Max put his hand on Reggie's arm to stop him. The tattoo was pretty *big*. And Demyan was in no condition to decide on something this permanent. "Can you trace it and do it tomorrow? Just so he's sure this is what he wants?"

Demyan frowned. "Fuck, Perron, really? It's a tattoo for the woman I love and my baby. You think I'll change my mind?"

What to say? Max felt the weight of his phone in his pocket. He should call Pearce. Or Becky. But Demyan was a little old to need permission.

"I want one too. *Cats*." Carter cocked his head. "I think that's Jami's favorite musical. Something from that."

"I've got the perfect idea for you." Reggie picked up the pen. "But . . . how old are you?"

Carter stared at the man. "Seriously? I'm old enough to drink in the States. Just do it."

"What about you?" The skinny man seemed to see the three drunken players as a payday He turned to Vanek and all Max could think was that he liked his balls. And Chicklet would kill him if he let the boy get a tattoo.

Vanek cocked his head. "No ink. Thanks."

*Good boy.*

Reggie smiled. "Piercing?"

"Nipples!" Carter folded in half, laughing so hard he couldn't seem to breathe. "Jami will love it if I get mine pierced!"

"Oh, that's hot. You do that?" Demyan asked.

"Yeah, got all my stuff and some nice silver rings—a few new barbells too." Reggie jerked his chin at Vanek. "You in?"

"Sure." Vanek straightened, slightly, though his stance was somewhat slanted. "Does it hurt?"

Reggie shrugged. "Didn't bother me."

"Come on, you wimp." Demyan pulled off his gray T-shirt. "Max is paying."

"I am?" Max considered Chicklet's reaction. And Ramos's. Standing by while their subs desecrated their bodies was bad enough, but paying for it?

Then again, a playoff run would be worth the ire of both. Forgiveness was priceless. And letting the trio go for it would get him just that. So he eased back onto his stool and nodded to Reggie. "Two tattoos and three sets of piercings. If none of them cry, I'll give you a nice tip."

"Cry?" Demyan snorted and braced his arm on the bar. "You wish."

"Piercings are faster. You don't wimp out when I pierce your nipples, and I'll do the tattoos." Reggie took out a blue sheet and went over to the far end of the bar where he'd be less likely to be disturbed. He laid out the alcohol pads, antibiotic gel, a metal clamp and a container holding rather large needles, all individually wrapped. Another container with different rings and barbells.

Clean equipment at least, though Max wasn't so sure about the piercings being done in a crowded bar. He watched Demyan stand in front of Reggie as Reggie pulled on some latex gloves and figured he should probably speak up. "You sure you don't want to wait 'til closing? Ain't he supposed to lie down?"

"I can do it with him sitting up," Reggie said, shrugging. He held up an alcohol pad. "Would you rather wait?"

"No, I'm ready." Demyan's jaw hardened as Reggie ripped open the package. "Let's do this."

Max chuckled at Demyan's wince as the alcohol swab touched his nipple. "Shall I man the bar?"

"Would ya?" Reggie held his tongue between his teeth as he dotted each side of Demyan's nipples. He pulled over a chair and had Demyan sit. "Take out a Red Bull for him—just in case he gets dizzy."

Demyan scoffed at that, but once Reggie had the clamp in place, his face had lost most of its color. Max held up a finger as a group of men called out for some beer and went over to set the can of Red Bull on the bar, out of Reggie's way.

The hiss Demyan let out as the needle pushed through his flesh made it impossible to look away. Suddenly, Max couldn't see the men anymore. He pictured Oriana in Demyan's place, Sloan in Reggie's, his big hand around Oriana's breast and the gleam in his eye as the sharp needle broke through her skin.

Stepping up to his side, Carter nudged him, bringing him back to the present. "I'll take care of the bar. You go ahead and watch."

Max nodded his thanks, swallowing as the sharp needle tip came through the other side. The act in itself wasn't erotic, but knowing how Sloan would feel doing this to Oriana, being there to see her eyes glaze with pleasure as the pain shifted inside her . . .

Fuck, he was hard. He grinned at Demyan's questioning glance. "It ain't you."

"Well, damn. Way to crush a man's ego." Demyan inhaled roughly, inclining his head when Reggie asked if he was ready for the second one. Once both barbells were in, Demyan stood, staring down at them with a crooked smile on his lips. "Looks good, don't it?"

The silver against Demyan's smooth, tanned skin did look good, but Max imagined it would look even better against the swell of Oriana's beautiful breasts. He licked his lips and decided he'd bring the idea up to Sloan when he got back to the hotel.

"You know it looks fucking sexy. Your ego don't need no more stroking." Carter laughed, handing Max a paper with an order to fill out for one of the waitresses. "My turn."

Vanek leaned over the bar, chewing at his bottom lip as he stared at Demyan's piercings. "Was it painful?"

"Nothing I couldn't handle." Demyan rolled his shoulders, barely hiding a wince. Then he reached out and squeezed Vanek's shoulder. "Don't do it if you're nervous, though."

"I'm not."

"Not worried about what Chicklet will say?"

Max missed Vanek's answer as he was filling all the orders. Once the crowd around the bar had thinned, he returned to observe Carter's reaction as his second piercing was put in. The young man's expression was almost dreamy. He twitched when Reggie dabbed on the antibiotic gel, shifting his hips as though sitting still was becoming uncomfortable.

"That was . . ." Carter shook his head hard, likely to clear it. "Damn. Wish Jami was here. Or Seb."

"Why?" Vanek came around the bar, hesitating as Carter moved so Vanek could take his place. "You not feeling good?"

"Too good." Carter gave Vanek a lazy smile, looking him over. "Hell, even you're looking good right now."

"What—?" Vanek frowned when Max lifted his hand and shook his head. Vanek peeled off his shirt and dropped it onto the other two on the counter behind the bar.

Without making it too obvious, Max gently pulled Carter aside and got him to sit on a stool. He studied Carter's face, very familiar with this behavior from Oriana when Sloan got her in the right headspace. Carter was floating on endorphins. The second Max pulled out some beers at a call from a waitress, Carter grabbed one and tried to open it.

"Water." Max used the firm tone that usually got through to Oriana when she was spacey. He smiled at Carter's contrite look, pleased when the young man quietly took a water bottle from him. It was getting near last call, so most of the people in the bar were clamoring for a few more drinks. Max served them all, surprised when Reggie joined him.

"Might want to go check on your boy," Reggie said grimly.

That didn't sound good. Max turned to see Demyan crouched down in front of Vanek, while Vanek slumped against the bar, one hand over his very pale face. He was shaking hard, skin slick with sweat. When Max got to him and moved his hand, he could tell the boy was close to either throwing up or passing out.

"Call Chicklet, Demyan." Max rubbed Vanek's back, his voice low and soothing. "Tell me how you're doing, kid?"

Vanek hiccupped, staring at the bar top. "Don't call Chicklet. She gonna be so mad."

Would have probably been good if the boy had considered that before going through with the piercings, but there was no point in bringing that up now. He needed to keep Vanek calm. "All right, reckon you can break this to her tomorrow. Can you sit up for me? Might could see if this Red Bull helps any."

After a few gulps, Vanek made a face. "This stuff's nasty."

"Drink up." Max glanced over his shoulder, opening his mouth to ask Demyan for a damp cloth. Reggie caught his eye, then nodded toward the dance floor. Where Carter and Demyan were dancing with two young women.

*Well, shit.* Max rubbed his face with one hand. He needed to get them all home. He took out his phone and called the one person who might be able to get them all rounded up and out of here before they got themselves in trouble.

"Damn it, Perron. Do you know what time it is?"

"Sorry, Coach." Max groaned as the waitresses started getting the customers to clear out. All except for the crowd Carter and Demyan had herded to the bar. Reggie served them all, then set up everything he needed to do Demyan's tattoo. "I might could have a problem here."

Tim sighed and the sound of his mattress creaking came clearly through the phone. "Are you drunk?"

"Had a few, but that's not the problem." Max cleared his throat, feeling more than a little guilty having to drag the coach out of bed to deal with a situation *he'd* let get out of control. "Kinda brought the boys out and—"

"Which boys?"

"Demyan, Carter, and Vanek."

"Are you insane?" Tim groaned, then spoke away from the phone. "He brought out the trouble triplets—stop laughing, Madeline, it's not funny." Despite his words, a hint of amusement lightened Tim's tone. "Where are you? I'll get there as soon as I can. Keep them from doing anything stupid for the next hour or so. I'm a ways out of the city."

Max told Tim where they were, then returned his focus to Vanek, who appeared to be sleeping. He tried to call out to Reggie to stop giving the boys alcohol, but the music seemed to have been turned up even louder than when the bar was open.

By the time Tim arrived, the tattoos were finished and Demyan and Carter were both stripped down to their boxers. Dancing on tables. The coach took one look at them, then brought his fingers to his lips and let out a sharp whistle that cut right through the music.

Carter and Demyan froze. Vanek sat up.

Reggie shut off the sound system.

Arms folded over his chest, Tim glared at Carter and Demyan as they climbed down from the tables. "This ends up in the papers and you're both getting fined." He made a sharp motion with his hand when Demyan tried to speak. "*You* should know better. Now get your goddamn clothes back on."

"Don't be mad, Coach." Carter slid sideways and put his arm over Tim's shoulders. "We were celebrating Perron coming back."

"Which is the only reason I don't punish the lot of you with a 6:00 a.m. skate." Tim looked over at Carter, his brow slightly raised as he studied the tattoo on the side of Carter's neck, sharply defined despite the redness and the shiny ointment. "Music notes?"

"Cats." Carter gave him a dopey grin. "Jami's gonna love it."

Tim snorted. "And Ramos is gonna kick your ass."

Carter's grin vanished. Worry clouded his overly bright eyes. "You really think so? You don't really have to tell him, do you?"

"Don't worry, I won't." Tim rolled his eyes at Max, who did his best not to laugh.

They got the three drunk players into the backseat of Tim's Range Rover, not speaking much until they'd gotten all three to Tim's house and settled them into the spare bedrooms. A few phone calls to their significant others so they wouldn't worry, and Max joined Tim in the living room.

He was sure Tim would tear into him, but Tim simply slouched back into the sofa and burst out laughing.

"You ain't pissed?" Max asked, more than a little surprised.

"No. I think this was good for the team." Tim folded his hands behind his head. "Those three needed to let loose. Doing so with you will get them past whatever issues they had." His lips slanted. "This team has always been pretty tight. Having you back . . . I like our chances for the playoffs. They might get some flack over the ink and the table dancing—Chicklet and Ramos might want a word with you over it too."

This was why Tim was the best coach in the league. He saw not only the big picture, but all the little details that would get the team where it needed to be. He might not have liked being called away from his wife on a rare day off, but so long as he saw results, he'd let it go.

Max would see to it that he got those results. He couldn't stop smiling as he thought of how a few—okay, more than a few—drinks had diluted the bitterness the trio had toward him. In the end, it felt like old times with the team. "I'll deal with the fallout, don't worry." He stood as Tim did, reaching out to shake Tim's hand and give him a firm hug. "Thanks for helping me out."

"Glad I could." Tim grinned, hugging Max a little harder. "I'm a little surprised you're sober. I'd half expected you to be hanging on me like Carter was, telling me how much you love me."

Laughing, Max patted Tim's back before letting him go. "Don't need to be drunk to tell you that. I love you, Coach. We all do."

"You'd better." Tim brought a hand to his mouth to stifle a yawn. "Dragging me out of bed in the middle of the night." He shook his head as he made his way out of the living room. "See if you still love me at our next practice."

# Chapter Thirteen

Exhaustion had taken Akira the second she'd climbed into bed with Cort, but it was 5:00 a.m. and she was wide awake. She rolled on to her belly, braced her elbows on the bed, and smiled at the big man in the bed beside her. He let out a soft, sleepy groan and dropped an arm over her back.

She giggled as he picked her up by the waist and laid her over him. "I thought you were sleeping!"

"No, I was waiting for you to follow through with your threats." He placed his hands on her hips, his thumbs lightly stroking the curve of her pelvis, waking her in a different way. All that was between them were his boxers and her panties. The swell of his erection pressing against her had her melting with pure, hot desire. He gave her a knowing grin. "I spent the first hour considering all the things in your room I could use to tie you up if you got out of control."

"Mmm, I think it's too late." She grabbed his wrists and pulled his hands over his head, leaning down to kiss the length of his neck. "You can't stop me."

"Not sure I want to." He easily freed one hand, slipping it around the back of her neck and guiding her up so he could give her a long, slow kiss. The way he ground up against her made her breath catch as heat throbbed down low. Then he slipped his lips along her cheek to whisper in her ear. "The first time would be easiest with you on top. Then I'll know how much of me you can take."

"I'd say you're bragging." She inhaled his clean, arousing scent, sure she could get drunk and high on him alone. He was rain in the spring mixed with pure, deep notes of musk. Like standing on a mountain during a downpour, the air around her earthy and rich. She lifted her head as his fingers trailed up her spine under her nightshirt. "But I've had my mouth on you. I can't take you all the way in."

"Such a dilemma." He made her sit up and pulled her night shirt up over her head. "I guess we'll have to go very, very slow."

Her eyes drifted shut as he covered her small breasts with his huge hands. Brought her back down so he could suck a nipple into his mouth. The tug of his lips, the flick of his tongue, had her trying to get a good grip on his hair so he wouldn't stop. His hot breath moistened her flesh. He slipped one hand between her thighs, rubbing gently at the moist swatch of cloth covering her.

"Not too slow." She whimpered as he slid a finger under the material and pressed it inside her at a torturously languorous pace. Part of her was a little nervous about taking him into her body, afraid it would hurt. Some women might think bigger was better, but Cort was big enough that he'd have to be careful whenever they were together.

If she didn't trust him, she wouldn't even risk it. But she did, and right now his finger just wasn't enough.

"Hmm, I guess not." He withdrew his finger, glistening wet, and brought it to his mouth, making a hungry sound as he sucked it. "Fuck, I could just eat you. You taste so good."

She held her breath, torn between wanting his very talented mouth on her once again, and taking as much of him into her body as she could. Shifting restlessly, all kinds of naughty words on the tip of her tongue, she spoke quietly. "I want this, Cort. I want you."

He sat up, wrapping his arms around her. "Your last request of the night." He glanced at the clock and laughed. "Or should I say, morning. But we do this my way."

"Yes, Sir." She batted her eyelashes, wiggling her hips a little to tease him. "I am yours to command."

One brow arched, he set her aside, then stood. He reached down to take his wallet out of his jeans on the floor, pulling out a condom. "Right now, I have only one command, Tiny."

Her lips held tight between her teeth, she looked up at him expectantly as he placed the condom in her hand.

His fingertip brushed down her cheek. He bent down and grazed her lips with his. "Don't let me hurt you."

"You won't." She said the words with complete confidence, but sensed his doubt as she knelt in front of him to pull down his boxers. He climbed onto the bed as she took off her panties, then hauled her onto him, tangling his hands in her hair as he kissed her. Something about the tenderness in his kiss made her want to assure him it would be all right. She cupped his cheek in her hand. "I'm tougher than I look, Cort. Don't worry."

"If I didn't believe that, I wouldn't be here now." Cort loosened his grip on her hair as she glided down his body, taking him in her mouth to distract him. He groaned, moving his hips to match her rhythm as she took him in a little deeper than any time before. "Fuck, baby. I'll never get enough of you."

She smiled as she slid her lips off him. "I like hearing that."

Being with him was so easy. So natural. She put the condom on him, trembling as she rose above him and positioned him against her. She wasn't sure she could have gone this far, this quickly, with anyone else. But as the blunt end of him penetrated her, only the very tip, she froze. Swallowed over and over, trying to get air past the rapid pulse in her throat, pounding in her chest.

"Don't move." His tone was hard, but not angry. He sat up and wrapped one arm around her waist. "Does it hurt, or is your head somewhere else?"

His voice slowed her stuttering heart, made it easier to breathe. She had to think about her answer, because she didn't know what it was. The stretching was almost too much, but . . . yes, for a split second her body had made the penetration a bad thing. She needed to get out of her head a little bit, but she wasn't sure how. She wanted to feel, not think.

"Talk to me, Akira." He wound her hair around his fist and tugged until her eyes widened and she stared at him. "We can stop.

Don't force yourself to—"

"Dominik." She shook her head quickly when Cort's eyes darkened. "No, I wasn't thinking of him. It's just . . . when I'm with him, he's completely in control. There's no room for anything but giving myself to him." She held her breath, not sure Cort would understand. "I want to give myself to you. Completely."

"Red." Cort let out a husky laugh when she frowned at him, confused. He drew her hands up, placing them behind her neck. "That's the word, isn't it? You'll say red if it gets to be too much. Otherwise, you've given me this sweet little body to play with." He latched on to her hips and eased deeper into her. "And I plan to do just that."

He hadn't given up on her. His saying, "say red if . . ." might have got her wondering if she'd need to, but instead it brought her to the scene mentality. She trusted him. She could let go.

"That's it." Cort stroked her side as she let the muscles in her thighs relax. "Such a good girl."

The thickness of him spread her open. She was wet enough to let him glide in half his length easily, but she had to force herself to relax to take more. The full sensation was exquisite, but a shallow thrust made her lips part. He hit something inside her that hurt.

"There we go. You don't need to say it." Cort kept one hand on her hip and fisted the other at the base of his dick. "Deeper than this is too much, but you feel so good, it doesn't matter. Move with me, baby." He gave her a positively evil smile as she moved to drop her hands to his chest. "Keep them there. Let those strong little legs do all the work."

*Oh God!* All the muscles in her thighs worked as she rode him, but it was *that* tone that almost set her off. The tone of a Dom taking over, using her exactly as he pleased. Leaving her only the power to hand herself over to him, to sink into that place where she knew only her surrender would satisfy him.

Or her.

Fingers twined behind her neck, she rose and fell, faster, harder, moaning as he dug his fingers into her skin and lifted up to meet her. The feeling of his fist keeping her from going too far somehow added to the rough ride, almost bruising as she slammed down on him. But the pain was so damn good. Raw and brutal as they both gave in to what they'd been wanting for days. Pleasure laced through her like a fiery, silk ribbon, whipping in and around her core until it burst out and she dropped down on him, grateful for the arm that held her as she came apart.

The arm was like a steel bar across her back as Cort joined her, letting out a soft curse into her hair as he came hard. He didn't move the hand that kept him from going deeper until his dick grew slack inside her, and when he moved it, he didn't pull out. Which allowed her to take the rest of him. To slowly glide over him until a second climax shuddered through her. Her heart stuttered again, but this time, it wasn't from her body and mind working against her. Her whole being seemed to have come to the same decision as she lay in his arms.

This was where she belonged.

"Fuck, Akira." He spoke quietly, kissing her cheeks and holding her close as he rolled to his side. "How can I ever let you go?"

"Don't." She nuzzled his neck, hissing as he slipped out of her, only now realizing how tender she was. "I give you permission to never ever let me go."

"It's too soon to say that, Tiny." He released her, sliding over to the edge of the bed to remove the condom and wrap it in a tissue from the box on her night table. Then he dropped it into the small trash can by her bed, keeping his back to her for a few long moments. "I'll hang on for as long as I can, but maybe he's right." He shook his head, laughing. "Fucking awesome time to bring *him* up."

She knew exactly who he meant, but had to ask anyway. "Him?"

"Ford." Cort took a deep breath, letting it out in a sigh. "We should have discussed this before. He's the reason you didn't tell me your name."

"Not the whole reason." She pursed her lips, not too happy that she was having this chat with Cort's back. "Look at me. Did you talk to him?"

He turned and met her eyes. "Yes."

"And he said something to piss you off." Typical Ford. And, naturally, he'd pretended everything was fine when he'd called her. She brought the sheet up to cover her breasts, scowling at her bended knees. "Let me guess. How dare you take what's his?"

"No." Cort took her hand between his and stroked his thumbs over her pulse. "He's worried that I'm using you. Because I'm bored of the biker chicks I usually go for."

"But you're not. And he's your best friend, so he should know better." She was a little surprised that Ford's concern was more about her than about some kind of territorial BS. But she didn't want to give him too much credit. "I want to be friends with him—for Jami, if nothing else, because they're still close. That can't happen if he can't accept me and you."

"I'm not all that concerned about what he accepts." Cort dropped back down onto the bed, bringing her with him. "He's my boss, that's it. He's made that clear."

"He. Did. What?" She shoved away from Cort, sitting up and placing her hands on her hips. "Oh, no. You two are not losing your friendship because of me." She moved to get out of bed. "I'm going to talk to him."

Cort grabbed her and dragged her to him, shaking with laughter. "Not so fast, Tiny. Pretty sure his nurse will have a fit if you wake him up this early."

She glanced at the clock, then sighed. "Fine, but I *am* going to speak to him."

"I'd rather you didn't."

"You don't get a say." She pressed her hands to his massive chest, happy that he let her hold him down, needing to make something very clear. "See this bed? You're only in charge when we're in it."

"Really?" He chuckled, flipping her over onto her back,

pressing himself between her thighs, hard again. "What about when I take you in *my* bed. Or my car. Or up against any hard surface I can find?"

"Then too." She gasped as he thrust his fingers into her, blazing again as though his touch was a match dropped into a pool with oil floating on the surface. "But not with him, Cort. I need you two to be okay."

Cort grabbed his wallet, found another condom, and quickly rolled it on. He wrapped his hand around the base of his dick, then filled her with one hard thrust. "For me, or for him?"

The way he took her, as though she belonged to him, made it impossible for anything but the truth to cross her lips. She cried out as he restrained her wrists in one of his hands over her head, never letting up on his solid thrusts. "Both. I need it for you both!"

His pace faltered at her words, and she almost wished she could take them back. But then he dragged one fierce orgasm out of her. Continued until she had another.

"A Dom gives a sub what she needs." He growled into her ear as he came. "So I'll give you this. But I meant what I said."

"I know." She wasn't sure which part, but she believed him. Right now, she was pretty sure he could say anything and she'd believe him. "I know, Cort."

"I'm not letting you go. Not for anyone." His tone was rough. A little broken as he held her close. "Not unless I have no other choice."

\* \* \* \*

Cort waited two days to go see Ford, distracting himself with crap work at the auto body shop, taking out dents and changing windshields until his muscles told him to back the fuck off. A call from Ford's nurse letting Cort know Ford had been released prompted the visit. The man being strong enough to go home was perfect. Sure, Ford wasn't in any condition to go a few rounds with him physically, but he could stand on his own two feet. Wouldn't lash out as much because he wouldn't feel so vulnerable.

Maybe, this time, he'd be speaking to his best friend, and not the boss's son. Either way, he had to talk to Ford before Akira felt like she had to step in.

And he couldn't put her off much longer.

"Cort," Ford said, his tone cordial as he let Cort into his apartment. "I wasn't expecting you."

"It was either me or Akira." Cort tried to keep his tone level, but by Ford's frown, he wasn't pulling it off. He shrugged. "Don't think it's right for her to have to get involved."

Ford shook his head, scratching his jaw. "Too easy. I could say she *shouldn't* be involved with you at all, but why bother? You want a beer?"

It was just after noon, but what the hell. This was normal-like, and he could work with that. Cort nodded. "Sure."

Bringing their beers to the kitchen table, Ford sat, almost managing to hide the tension of pain as he lowered into his chair. Cort felt rage flare up as Ford paled, wishing he could go after the assholes who'd hurt the man he'd protected for so long.

As angry as he'd been at Ford's attitude, that protective instinct hadn't gone away. But all Cort could do was make sure Roy never hurt Ford again. And see if he and Ford could be civil-like. He opened his beer. "Where's Cam?"

Lips quirking, Ford sat back. "Checking the block to make sure no one's watching my place. He somehow found out one of the orderlies was listening in to his calls to his brother. Made him paranoid."

"That's good." And that explained how Roy had known Cort was filling in for Ford. He hadn't thought too much about it at the time—Roy had his ways to get whatever information he needed—but if Cam had inadvertently been the leak, it was good to have that patched up.

"Hey . . ." Staring at his beer bottle, ripping off little pieces of the label, Ford cleared his throat. "You know, some of the shit I said—I was an asshole."

*An apology?* Cort opened his mouth, ready to make a joke about the whole deal, not wanting to rehash all the bullshit. But then he pressed his lips shut, mentally going over how he'd considered their friendship over. Maybe they both needed this to fucking clear the air. "You were, but I kinda expected it."

"You're not a goddamn employee."

"No kidding?"

"Fuck off." Ford grinned as he finished stripping his beer bottle. "You need me to tell you I love you and all that, or are we good?"

*Cheesy motherfucker.* Cort rolled his eyes. "We're good. Need it in fucking writing, man? You know the people I hold grudges against aren't still walking."

"Very true." Ford cleared his throat again. "So . . . how did I come into the conversation?" His tone was relaxed, but Cort sensed some hope there.

The man wanted to know Akira hadn't forgotten him. That he still had a way in.

And everything inside Cort wanted to cut that off. Crush it. Except for the part that still cared about Ford. That part wanted to break it gently.

But break it nonetheless. "She doesn't want to be the reason we're not friends anymore. She won't listen to me when I tell her she's not."

"That's because she's smart." Ford gave him a tight smile as the doorbell sounded. "Speaking of which—she called just before you showed up. Guess she doesn't trust you to 'deal with me' on your own."

"Don't go there, Ford." Cort stood as Ford slowly eased out of his chair. "I've earned her trust."

"She's a sweet girl, but obviously she gives her trust too easy." Ford moved past him to answer the door. "Hey, shorty."

Akira looked over at Cort, seemed to read his expression, then hiked up her chin. "We need to talk."

"Come to the kitchen," Ford said, his tone guarded. Maybe he was finally getting it. "We're all friends, right?"

"Yes." Akira took a seat at the small kitchen table, then folded her hands in front of her. "Let's make one thing clear. This is my fault."

*No.* Cort refused to let Akira take this on herself. He pulled his chair close to her before sitting. "Tiny—"

"Tiny? Really?" Ford let out a bitter laugh. "'Tiny' and 'shorty.' Glad you were all original, man."

"Ford, you need to shut up." Akira took one of Cort's hands in hers and faced Ford. "Neither of us did this to hurt you. I'm sorry you don't see that. It happened, and you need to deal with it."

"Akira, listen to me. As a friend." Ford waited for Akira's nod, then continued. "He'll hurt you. That's what bothers me, not that—"

"That I'm not with you?" Akira's bottom lip trembled, which had Cort sitting up a little straighter. Seeing Akira and Ford in the same room was very different than hearing about it. There was an undeniable pull between them. Almost painful to see, like flesh stitched together being torn apart. He pressed his eyes shut even as Akira spoke. "You'd hurt me, Ford. You hurt me when you do this. When you try to fight everyone in the world because I didn't choose you."

Ford's chair scraped across the floor as he stood. "Then don't choose me! But choose someone worth you! That will be good for you!"

"He is! He's everything I need!" Akira shoved her chair back and it fell with a solid *Thunk!* on the floor. "Be my friend and be happy for me! Be his friend despite everything, because otherwise, what kind of friend are you? One who leaves when he doesn't get what he wants?"

"He's like my brother! He always has been and I don't want that to change!" Ford glanced at Cort, then swallowed hard as he brought his gaze back to Akira. "But I love you, and I can't stand by and let him destroy you!"

Akira took a step back and put her hand over her mouth. Cort shot out of his chair, catching her elbow as she stumbled. "Please don't say that. How are we supposed to be friends if you say that?"

Ford held still. "Your other friends don't love you?"

"It's not the same."

"Let it be the same." Ford returned to his chair, looking defeated. "I'm not sure I can forgive him if he hurts you, but until then, I'll stay out of the way, all right?"

"That's what friends do. But you have to promise me one thing." Akira swallowed audibly as Ford nodded. "Things won't change between you and Cort. I couldn't live with that. I can't be the reason you lose what you have."

"You won't be." Ford finished his beer and pressed his hand to his side. "Hate to cut this short, but I gotta take my meds and they knock me out."

"Oh, Ford." Akira moved away from Cort and approached Ford, reaching out to him, then dropping her hands to her sides. "Get some rest, but . . . call me if you need anything. I need to know we're *real* friends."

"We are." Ford gave Cort a hard look as he spoke. "Don't get me wrong, shorty. I'm not just around when I get what I want. I'm in for the long run."

"*That* is what I need from *you*." Akira's soft face was tight with the need for more, and Cort had a feeling she wanted to hug Ford.

That she would have if Cort wasn't there. And fuck, he wouldn't have her holding back for him. He wouldn't have Ford coming between *them,* and the easiest way to do that was to make their friendship perfectly acceptable.

He smiled, placing his hand on her back and easing her closer to Ford. "Go ahead, hug him. I'm glad we finally hashed this out." His smile broadened slightly when Ford's brow shot up. "Look, I get it, ki—man. It's not like I've always been a nice guy. She makes me wanna be one."

"Good." Ford swallowed hard, putting his arms around Akira as she carefully hugged him. "I . . . ah, I'd appreciate it if you'd keep things going at the bar for a bit. I'll swing by when I'm feeling up to it, and you can catch me up on the goings on with the team."

"Sure," Cort said.

Akira took Ford's hand, squeezing it and gazing up at him so sweetly as she whispered, "Thank you."

Ford inclined his head, then trailed them to the door. He put his hand on Cort's shoulder before Cort could follow Akira out. "Well fucking played, Cort."

Cort didn't bother commenting on that. He'd won this round.

No goddamn need to rub it in. He wasn't even tempted after taking one last look at Ford's bruised face.

Not knowing what Ford had lost.

# Chapter Fourteen

They had about an hour before the team was meeting up for the road trip, first up Vancouver, then LA. A couple days rest before the game in Nashville, then the last stop in Detroit before heading home. The men were never called in even a minute early when they were going away for that long.

Which was Max's first clue that something was up.

His two days with Oriana had been well spent giving Sloan a chance to play the voyeur on Skype. A pair of nipple clamps while he'd told his wife and best friend about the idea of Sloan piercing her nipples had Oriana going off like a firecracker, shuddering deliciously as she finally came down and asked, "How soon?"

Nothing but good consequences for him from the boys' night out. He smiled as he recalled how Sloan's face had lit up. The way the man had completely opened up as he'd asked Max to give him some time to learn from a piercing expert in the area. He'd even brought up the house prospects Max and Oriana were looking in to, a wicked gleam in his eye as he mentioned space for a dungeon in the basement. A soundproof dungeon.

Ever since Max and Oriana had gotten married, things had changed between him and Sloan. He'd wanted to make sure Sloan felt included in every way, but that often led to him stepping aside so his wife could get her needs met by the other man. Without Max. It excited him to consider taking a step in a different direction, to become part of fulfilling those needs.

Losing Dominik should have given him the incentive to take that much-needed step, but there was no point in looking back now. All he could do was focus on the present. On how incomplete things felt without Sloan. And how good it felt to know he'd be coming home to them soon.

The Flames had fallen to last place. It shouldn't be long.

Max stepped into Tim's office, frowning as he looked around the room and saw Vanek and Carter sitting in front of the desk like two boys called to the principal's office. Demyan stood at the other side of the room, leaning against the wall by the whiteboard with his arms folded over his ribs. Tim was reclined in his seat behind the desk, a casual smile on his face as he gestured to the chair closest to his.

"Sorry to call you in early, Perron, but I want this cleared up before we head out."

"No problem." Max sat, casting a questioning glance at Tim. "I haven't heard anything from Chicklet. Or Ramos. Is this why—?"

"Seb was cool with it." Carter ran his tongue over his teeth, leaning forward to rub his hands on his thighs. "He loves the piercings and the tattoo."

"Is that what he said?" Tim's tone was relaxed. Casually curious. "I only spoke to him briefly."

"You want details?" Carter let out a nervous laugh. "He played with the piercings every time he kissed me. Every time he—"

"We got it, Carter." Vanek ducked his head. "Chicklet . . . didn't seem to mind. She didn't get mad or anything."

Demyan snorted. "My money's on them both biding their time. Glad I'm not a sub. Becky and Zach let me do what I want."

"Let you?" Carter smirked. "Yeah, you're a free man."

"Fuck off, you know what I mean." Demyan's gaze shot to the door as it opened. A soft smile spread across his lips as Becky came in, closely followed by Pearce. As they stepped aside, Ramos and Chicklet entered, Chicklet shutting the door firmly behind her, her eyes on Vanek.

Who seemed to be trying to become one with his chair.

"Gentlemen, this will seem a little unorthodox, but none of us in this room really knows the meaning of the word, so it's irrelevant." Tim sat forward, folding his hands on his desk. "You're fortunate that Ford won't allow the press in his bar—I'm assuming there's no need to discuss why he's strict with that policy?" He glanced over at Demyan, who nodded. "The fact remains, your actions were irresponsible." He held up his hand when Max frowned. "Perron, I understand your intentions, and I have no issues with you doing whatever was necessary to fix things with you and the boys." He gave Max a level look. "But can we agree that it went a bit too far?"

*Good question.* Max thought about the table dancing and Vanek half passed out on the bar. But the ends justified everything, far as he was concerned. So he shrugged. "No harm done."

"Are you joking?" Chicklet stepped up to Vanek's side, curving her hand around the back of his neck in a way that seemed both possessive and comforting. "Would you feel that way if I took Oriana out and let her get that out of control?"

Max took a deep breath, reminding himself that Chicklet was Sloan's friend. And a very strict Domme. So he chose his words with care. "Oriana and I don't have the same kind of relationship you and Vanek do. I made sure he was safe, which is no more than I would expect if you—"

"*Safe?*" Chicklet made a rough sound in her throat. "You let someone put fucking holes in his body while he was drunk. In a goddamn bar!"

"The needles were clean." Carter cringed when Ramos gave him a dark look. He sank a little lower in his chair. "Well, they were."

"My body, Luke." Ramos approached Carter at a slow, ominous pace, sliding his hand around the side of Carter's neck, tipping his chin up with his fingers as he loomed over him. "You do not allow others to mark it. Least of all in such a reckless way."

"You two gonna give me shit, too?" Demyan scowled at Becky's sigh. Then jutted his chin at Pearce. "If Becky wanted to get a tattoo, and you came down on her, I'd clock you."

"Scott, do you have any idea how upset Casey was when you weren't there for breakfast?" Becky's face crumpled as she turned her head, as though she couldn't face Demyan anymore, either because of his attitude or what she had to say next. "You don't have to be there at all, but—"

"I want to!" Demyan shot out of his chair and pulled Becky into his arms, speaking softly. "Why didn't you say something before? You've been so quiet—"

"I asked them not to say anything." Tim stood and came around the desk, then braced his hands behind him against it. "This wasn't a private thing. The three of you had issues that were affecting the team. And your own lives. One thing that I love about you guys is how devoted you are to the team. You all have people in your lives who understand that, but there needs to be some kind of balance." He held out his hands as to include everyone in the room. "What happens on the ice means nothing if you're not okay. These people trust me to make sure you are. I couldn't bring you along on the road trip without letting them know you will be."

"I appreciate that, Tim." Chicklet chewed at her bottom lip, shaking her head. "But I have my own ways to deal with things like this. Carter and Demyan have their men on the road with them, but I have to know Tyler feels me with him, even when I'm not."

Tim nodded slowly. "The thing is, Chicklet, I can't have Tyler hampered by your kind of discipline. Not while we're still fighting our way out of the bottom rankings. I need you to trust me to give him the control he needs. He'll be rooming with Mason."

Chicklet's expression lightened considerably. "Oh, that'll work."

"No, it won't!" Vanek shot a pleading look at Chicklet. "Last time me and Laura were 'bickering'—" he made quotations with his fingers in the air "—at the club, you let him put me in the stocks and use a tawse on me!"

"I used the tawse on her. In the stocks beside you." Chicklet arched a brow. "I don't see a problem there."

"He has your permission to punish me!"

"He does." She slid her hands down Vanek's chest, pressing hard enough over his nipples to make him cringe. "And he's creative enough not to let it ruin your game."

The situation seemed to have been handled, quite efficiently, but Max suspected his presence was part of Tim's plan to assure all present that a lesson had been learned. At the very least, he owed them all the courtesy of an apology. He looked from Pearce and Becky, to Ramos, then finally, to Chicklet.

"I might could've done a little better with the boys." Max bit back a grin at Demyan's eye roll. He was only a year or so older than the man, but sometimes it felt like a decade. "It won't happen again."

"I do not expect you to keep Luke in line." Ramos tightened his grip on Luke's throat in a way that had the young man's eyes glazing over, his breath catching as a dark flush spread across his cheeks. "As Chicklet mentioned, I will be there to do so myself. But I appreciate that you will not stand by and allow this again."

"A call next time, Perron." Pearce had one hand on Becky's shoulder, the other on Demyan's, as he met Max's eyes. "That's all I ask."

"*I* should have called you," Demyan said quietly, turning his face to nuzzle Pearce's throat. "I'm sorry."

Pearce slapped Demyan's arm and chuckled as he cursed. "You will be."

Chicklet did nothing but incline her head in acceptance of Max's words as she crouched down in front of Vanek, holding his face in her hands. The touching scenes made Max's heart ache for Oriana. He'd said goodbye to her early that morning before she went to resume her internship with a sports doctor connected to the farm team.

If they'd stayed in Calgary, he would have seen her even on the road while she was training with the team's doctors. The decision to return meant more time apart, but she was happy. The tension in her from being away from her sister was gone. She'd even managed to see her father, which had done wonders for her even though she'd admitted he didn't know who she was. Through the whole visit, he'd called her Adona—the name of an aunt Oriana had loved and lost during her teens.

All that seemed to matter was that he hadn't sent her away.

"So, are we all good?" Tim went around the room, lightly tapping the men's shoulders and hugging the women. "I can personally guarantee there will be no further body modifications on my watch."

Carter drew in a sharp inhale as Ramos whispered something to him. He cleared his throat. "And no more drinking."

"For a while." Demyan kissed Becky. Then laughed and kissed Pearce. "Damn it, I fucked up. I get it. I'm a daddy now and I need to do better."

Becky's eyes glistened. "You are. And she's going to miss you so much."

"I'll call every day. And write. I know she likes the letters me and Zach send." Demyan lowered his voice, but not enough that every person in the room couldn't hear him clearly. "Gotta admit, I get a little teared up whenever I get one from her. Tell her every goal I get is for her." He kissed Becky again, speaking against her lips. "And you."

"I will." Becky blinked fast and took a big step back. "I better get to work. Get ready for the winning streak." She took a deep breath. "This is always hard, but it makes me feel a bit better to know Zach is with you in case—" She cut herself off and shook her head. "Just in case."

"I'm better, Becky." Demyan caressed Becky's cheek, something in his eyes so open and honest Max had to look away. From the rumors he'd heard, Demyan being better meant a lot. He'd changed, despite his actions of the other night.

Vanek seemed enfolded in his Domme, looking like he never wanted her to let him go. But sturdier now that she was there. Now that they'd gotten past his slipup in one piece. She was disappointed, but made her love so very clear.

A soft knock at the door had them all looking up. Jami slipped into the room, then went straight over to her uncle, leaning into him as though all her strength had been taken from her.

"My mom called. She's pregnant again." A tight, bitter laugh escaped her. "I said all the right things. And I'm okay. Just sorry I'm late."

The scent of hard liquor came off her in waves as she rested against her uncle's side and looked over at Carter. Her gaze had seemed unfocused and her stance unstable, as though Tim was the only reason she was still standing.

"Damn it, Jami." Carter rose from his chair, reaching for her. "I'm a selfish jerk. I didn't know—"

"I said I'm okay." Jami's bottom lip trembled as she went to him, but her whole body shook until Ramos put his hand on her shoulder, lending her his strength, his expression troubled. "You . . . you need to be careful. I know what your dad said got to you. Don't do anything stupid, and I promise I won't either."

Carter straightened and gave a hard nod. "I swear I won't. But . . . why don't you come with us?" He looked over at Tim. "Can't she? Wives come sometimes. It won't be no different."

Tim stroked Jami's arm, then kissed her cheek. "You're more than welcome."

"I need to work." Jami rested her head on Tim's chest. "But I'll come if you want me to."

"I do." Tim kissed the top of her head. "Find someone to cover your shift." He laughed at Jami's hesitant stare. "Get going!"

Jami glanced up at Ramos, who hadn't shifted from his solid stance behind her. "Sir?"

"There's nothing I want more than to have you with me." Ramos patted her cheek, whispering something for her alone before kissing the tip of her nose. "You can help me keep our boy out of trouble."

"Yeah, like that'll happen." Jami stuck her tongue out at Carter, then dashed out of the room.

Carter slipped an arm around Ramos's waist, resting his head on the man's shoulder, clearly comfortable enough with those present not to hold back. "I'll do better. For her. She needs us both."

Max didn't hear Ramos's reply. His thoughts went back to

Oriana. And Sloan. Both of whom he'd be leaving behind. All that the meeting had proved was how much he was missing without them by his side. At least he'd see Oriana soon. With the whole issue of his handling other's subs poorly, he needed Sloan here. Telling him he hadn't fucked up too badly.

Sloan would have told Chicklet her boy was still becoming a man. Told Ramos his boy needed to live his own life. He probably wouldn't have had much to say to Becky and Pearce, though he may have shown some longing when Becky mentioned her daughter.

Oriana had gone off birth control. The three of them wanted a child. The only person who knew they were trying was Tim. Oriana spoke to him almost every day. She'd told him about her one miscarriage.

Which explained why Tim held Max back once the others left.

"We're in the same place, Perron. Max." Tim laughed when Max blinked at him. It was rare that the coach used a player's first name. "That's why I got us all together. I know where you're coming from. You love the team. But you love them too—Oriana. And Sloan. You're torn in two and that's where I'm at." Tim cocked his head and shrugged. "This would have been an issue if I hadn't made them all put it out there. Now you've just got to worry about the game." He took a deep breath. "And the people you love. Which is no small thing."

"They both put the game first, Tim." Max leveled his gaze with Tim's. "You know that."

"I do." Tim shrugged and placed his hands on Max's shoulders with a bit of pressure. "But that's not how it should be. And I've known you long enough to say you know that."

Max pressed his tongue to his teeth. He'd never admitted this to anyone. Never even brought it up to Sloan after months of trying. But Tim was the one person who might understand. "After Oriana lost the first child, I wanted to believe it was somehow my fault—that just stepping aside would make it all work out. The doctor knows everything and he said . . . he said it's not me. Or

Sloan. Nothing with the chromosomes. Oriana may never be able to carry to term. I'd rather it be my fault. I hate seeing her blame herself. The game isn't first anymore."

"It's no one's fault, Perron." Tim's eyes were haunted, and Max wished he'd kept this to himself. The coach had enough of his own problems to deal with. But, as always, Tim made him feel foolish for even thinking that. "Madeline and I want a child more than anything. And physically, it *is* my fault. But the team is our baby. When I come home, she asks me about you all as though you're all our children. The team has a bond that will last beyond the next season. We give our all, or we don't bother. And when it comes to the personal stuff, we give no less. Always."

"I agree." Max forgot how Jami would be with her men. How Oriana wouldn't be with him. How Sloan was so far away. But the three of them still had everything. Because they had one another and that would never change. "Thanks for making me see that. Oriana doesn't need to feel my doubts. And Sloan . . . after Dominik, I think he's worried that he's expendable. And he's not."

"If anyone can prove it, you can." Tim moved behind his desk. "I did try to work out a way that Oriana could be one of the medical staff on the trip, but the sports doc said she has some tests to pass before she's licensed to work. Bringing her along would delay the process."

"I refuse to do that. I'll be just as good out there knowing she's watching."

"I know you will. But I wanted to have her there for you." Tim gave a rueful shake of his head. "There's been all kinds of reactions about you being back. Mine is this. I'm grateful. We need you."

"I aim to be all you need." Max stepped up to his coach, hugging him as tight as he had when he'd been drunk. Because the tie between them was just as real as it had been in a liquor haze. "But thank you. For believing in me. Makes it all just that much easier."

"That's how it is for us." Tim cocked his head, grinning. "Life can be easy compared to the game, depending how you look at it.

In life, you can make mistakes and earn forgiveness, come back from behind. That doesn't always happen on the ice."

\* \* \* \*

Dean held his arms out as Landon finished covering Amia's face with kisses, laughing as Amia's eyes widened and her attention immediately went to his steel-gray tie. She settled in Dean's arms and brought the end of the tie to her mouth.

Silver went to Landon and wrapped her arms around his neck. Not much had been discussed about how she'd found Landon and Dean in the bedroom, but she seemed much less insecure since they'd reassured her she had nothing to worry about. She'd spent most of the day with Landon, going out for brunch, then a matinee movie. Things were much more relaxed between the two, and Dean was happy to see the warmth in Landon's eyes as he looked down at her.

But he blinked at Landon's next words, not sure he'd heard right.

"What?" Silver stared at Landon. Apparently she wasn't sure either.

Landon went down on one knee. "Marry me. I know we're already engaged, but the wedding's been put off so often . . . I love you. Between you and Dean and Amia, I have everything I could ever want, but I need to see you walking down the aisle while Dean stands at my side as my best man. To know the vows we exchange include all three of us."

"They will, but . . ." Silver made a frustrated sound and pulled at Landon's hand until he stood, his expression a little hurt. "Landon, I love you too. But I don't think getting married will fix anything. Let's make a date for this summer and see what happens."

"What do you think's going to happen? Do you think I'll change my mind about spending the rest of my life with you both?"

"No. I just . . . ugh, why did you have to bring this up right before leaving?" Silver folded her arms over her stomach. "Now I feel bad."

"I didn't ask to make you feel bad." Landon's tone was hard. He took a step back and grabbed his suitcase. "I thought this was something you wanted. A big, elaborate wedding. We can't plan that overnight."

"Damn it, then forget the big wedding. Why don't we do like your sister and have a quick wedding?" Silver's lips thinned. "Maybe things would be better if I did everything nice and efficient like she does."

"Do you have to bring my sister up every time things don't go your way?"

*So much for things going better.* Dean shook his head and rubbed Silver's arm, Amia braced carefully against his hip. "The two of you need to stop this. Silver, why don't you just tell him how much you'll miss him and kiss him and say goodbye. Landon, we'll make a date for this summer. You're right, nothing will happen between now and then to change anything, so take her roundabout answer as a yes."

It took a few moments for both to stop glaring, but then Silver nodded and laughed and Landon grinned. Silver put her head on Dean's shoulder and caressed Landon's cheek with her fingertips.

"It was a yes. I guess I'm a little afraid to make plans." She pulled Landon closer and rose up on her tiptoes to kiss him. "Something always comes up."

"Not this time." Landon dropped his suitcase and drew her up against him, making a low, hungry sound in his throat as he sucked at her bottom lip. "Unless Dean or I manage to make Amia a little brother or sister. But you can waddle down the aisle if you have to. You'll still be the most beautiful woman in the world."

"Should Dean and I start trying while you're gone?" Silver wiggled a little closer to Landon, teasing him with the press of her hips.

"Mmm, I think you should." Landon glanced over at Dean, the

heat in his eyes making Dean's pulse speed up, something in them telling Dean the arousal in them was from more than Landon picturing their sexy woman in the throes of passion. But, as always, Landon seemed to catch himself. He looked away as he released Silver. "I better go before I'm late. But this is better. I hate fighting with you, *mon amour*, and without Dean, I think that's all we'd ever do."

"Then I better thank him for us both." Silver took Amia from Dean, cooing to their daughter as she gently pried Dean's tie out of her hands. "Naptime, baby girl. Say bye to Daddy."

Amia giggled and latched on to one of Silver's hoop earrings. Silver winced, carefully extracted her earring from Amia's hand, then blew Landon one last kiss before heading up the stairs.

Getting the door for Landon, Dean stood aside as Landon carried his suitcase out to the porch. There were many things he wanted to say, but instead, he smiled as Landon turned to him. "Make us proud, goalie."

"Dean . . ." Landon's brow furrowed. He set his suitcase down and slid one hand behind Dean's neck, pressing their foreheads together. "I wanted to tell you I'm sorry. I made this harder and that's not what I was trying to do."

"No harm done, Landon."

"Right." Landon swallowed audibly, then backed away, stepping out into the cold. "No harm done."

Hours later, Dean sat at his desk, unable to focus on the player stats laid out in front of him, his thoughts slipping to his and Landon's last exchange. The wall Landon had put up wasn't as solid as he'd first believed. With some effort, he could break it down, but did he want to? With what the man was going through, he needed Dean to be strong enough to set the boundaries. To give him and Silver a strong foundation to rebuild their fragile relationship. His own feelings were irrelevant. He had to be the person they could lean on.

Without coming between them.

# Chapter Fifteen

Tyler found himself shaking with nervous energy as Doc shone a bright light in his eye. So stupid, needing to come get an exam for a damn headache, but that was the deal he'd made with Chicklet when he'd gotten cleared for play.

*"I have to trust you, Tyler."* Chicklet had pressed his head against her *thigh as he knelt before her, gently stroking his rumpled curls. "And I do. But there will be no toughing it out."*

The guys might call him pussy whipped, and sometimes it pissed him off, but when he submitted to Chicklet, it wasn't just an act to get some. He'd never felt anything so powerful as the peace that settled inside him when his Mistress took control and let him just be. He didn't have to wonder if he was making her happy. She had so many ways to show him.

"All good, son." Doc smiled, taking a few notes down on his clipboard. "You haven't felt dizzy or sick, so I see no cause for concern." He handed Tyler a small sample pack of Advil. "Take these before the game. If the headache gets worse or you experience other symptoms, come back and see me. Otherwise, you're good to go."

Grinning at the doctor, Tyler hopped off the table, throwing back both pills right there where the doc could see because he knew the rules. After Richards had gotten caught leaving his fish oil pills under his lettuce, Doc had been pretty mad. He couldn't control what they did at home, but on the road, either he, a trainer, or one of the coaches had to be present when the players took any medication or supplements. Everything was written down.

A little crazy, but whatever. Tyler started for the door.

Then stopped short as it opened, his jaw practically hitting the floor.

*No fucking way!*

Hell, he wouldn't lie. He wouldn't be this starstuck if he met Dwayne "The Rock" Johnson. Okay, maybe that was a stretch— he'd been a wrestling fan since birth—but still, this was *Raif Zovko*. The man fans called Midas because of his mad skills. With his hands, unless you shut him down the second he got the puck, he struck gold. The man *never* missed the net or hit a post.

"Hey, kid." Zovko flashed Tyler a smile as he passed, nodding to the doctor as Doc gestured for him to take a seat. "You look familiar."

Tyler's lips parted, but not a sound came out. All he could do was stare at the man like a brainless dolt. White silk shirt with the first few buttons undone, rich olive skin, broad shoulders. Dark hair, gleaming like polished mahogany, kinda messy, like the man had just climbed out of bed, but it still looked perfect. The man couldn't look anything *but* perfect.

*Stop staring, Vanek! Be cool!*

He cleared his throat and managed to make a sound kinda like, "Hey."

"You all right?" Zovko's dark brows drew together. He had a slight, smooth accent with a gravelly edge Tyler couldn't quite place. It never came across this well during interviews. Zovko sat up as the doctor placed the blood pressure thing on his arm. Then he snapped his fingers. "Ah, I remember. You took a bad fall two seasons ago. Glad you're back, but there are setbacks sometimes, yes?"

"No, no setbacks." Tyler shook his head hard. He needed to get the hell out of there before the man started thinking he was brain-dead. "Sorry. Nice to meet you. Coach—Coach is waiting."

"Sure thing. I'll see you in the locker room." Another smile and Zovko turned to the doc to answer some routine questions.

Face burning, Tyler darted out of the training room, making a stop in the bathroom to splash some cold water on his face. If Carter and Demyan saw him like this right before Zovko joined them, they'd never let him live it down. But . . . damn, he couldn't help it. Zovko was his freakin' hero. Tyler had watched him play for the first time when he was nine or ten, and had gone from being pretty into hockey to deciding he wouldn't stop until he went pro. His mom had bought him Zovko's jersey for Christmas a couple of years later, and Tyler still had it in a frame in his game room.

And now Zovko was a Cobra.

By the time Tyler got to the locker room, Zovko was there, being greeted by all the players. Tyler went to his stall, head down, hoping to avoid the two men who wouldn't be his friends for long if they said anything stupid. Richards sat beside him, his eyes wide as he watched their teammates taking turns introducing themselves. The eighteen-year-old rookie was trying to tape his stick, but he couldn't seem to keep his eyes off Zovko.

Which made Tyler feel a bit better about his own reaction. He laughed and took the stick from the rookie. "You're making a mess."

"That's Raif Zovko." Richards reached back into his stall and pulled out a stack of cards wrapped in a thick elastic band. "Do you think he'd—"

Tyler shook his head, leaning close to Richards and speaking low. "Ask him in private or the guys will bug you about it."

Blushing, Richards ducked his head and stuffed the cards back in his sports bag. "Good idea. But . . . is this for real? Man, if he's with us, we're so getting the Cup."

"My thoughts exactly."

"Hey, Vanek, did you see who's here?" Carter called out. "Funny how we were just talking about—"

"Luke." Ramos stepped up to Carter, his tone sharp. "Stop."

Carter pressed his lips together and nodded.

Demyan, standing a few steps away from them, snorted and winked at Tyler. Tyler grinned at him, deciding Demyan was pretty decent after all. He didn't have a Dom to make him behave. So long as he didn't bring anything up *in front* of Zovko, Tyler could take it.

"Pearce." Zovko moved away from the other men, a broad smile on his lips as he crossed the room. He hugged Pearce, slapping his back in that manly way guys did, perfectly appropriate for the locker room. "It's been a long time."

"It has. Good to have you with us, Raif." Pearce laughed, leaving his hand on Zovko's shoulder. "I'd heard rumors, but wasn't sure I'd get to play with you again."

*Again?* Tyler frowned, noticing how Demyan's eyes narrowed as he watched the friendly exchange. He couldn't recall Pearce and Zovko ever being on the same team. And he was pretty sure he knew everything there was to know about the man.

Apparently the two knew each other pretty well. Pearce had called him *Raif.*

"We had some good times in Hamilton, Zach," Zovko said, his tone casual, but something more beneath it.

Tyler wasn't the only one who caught the shift. Demyan stiffened, and from the corner of his eye, Tyler noticed Tim straightening from where he'd been crouched in front of White, going over some plays on his laptop.

*Things could get nasty.*

But Demyan simply stepped up to Pearce's side, holding out his hand to Zovko. "Scott Demyan. Zach's boyfriend."

"A pleasure." Zovko shook Demyan's hand, his expression unreadable. "I'd heard Zach had come out. There was no mention of you, but I have seen your face in several papers. You have an . . . interesting reputation, Demyan."

"Yeah, but this man got me to clean up my act. Not much I wouldn't do for him." Demyan gave Zovko a tight smile. "Awesome to have you on the team, though. *If* you're as good as everyone says, you're a decent purchase."

"I'm worth every cent."

"Great that you think so."

"Scott." Pearce put his hand on Demyan's arm and pulled him aside. Tyler couldn't hear what he was saying, but there was no mistaking the tension between Zovko and Demyan. They might as well be fucking growling at each other.

All this drama wasn't what Tyler had expected to happen if Zovko joined the team. He'd pictured everyone being excited. The team coming together and being a goddamn force to be reckoned with on the ice. Maybe . . . maybe getting up the nerve to ask Zovko to show him a few moves.

Kinda hard to do when the man was all up on Pearce.

He was glaring at his own stick, finished taping it, when a shadow fell over him. He jumped as a cool hand brushed his and gaped up as Zovko took his stick from him.

"Not bad, but a little thick, no?" Zovko unwrapped a length of tape. Then he knelt and put Tyler's stick between his knees. He held out his hand to Richards, who passed him the wax he'd been using to cover his stick blade. "Hope you don't mind I use your stick to show the rookie?"

Tyler shook his head.

"Wax is good, but make sure it's even, like this." Zovko quickly waxed over the tape on both sides, then watched Richards tear the tape off his stick and redo it, finishing off with a much smoother coat. He stood and handed Tyler his stick. "Let me know if I can help, all right?" He gave Tyler a shrewd look. "I want to be a good part of this team. First impressions aren't always the best."

Thinking of the first impression *he* must have given Zovko, Tyler nodded. "Yeah, I don't usually stare at people. I was just . . . I watched you as a kid."

"No worries." Zovko put his hand on Tyler's shoulder, glancing back at the noisy locker room before leaning close and lowering his voice. "You should have seen me the first time I met 'Le Gros Bill.'" He chuckled. "I forgot my own name. I think you and I will be good friends. Maybe have a beer sometime?"

Despite swearing to himself just last week that he'd never drink again, Tyler quickly agreed. Out on the ice for warm-up, he noticed that Zovko steered clear of Pearce. Actually, he spent a lot of time with Tyler and Richards, demonstrating shots while they helped

Bower warm up. The goalie had gone from distractedly blocking to really putting it all out there after Zovko sailed a few easy shots past him.

Bower snatched the last snapped puck out of the air, then tipped his mask off his face, really smiling for the first time since he'd returned from his injury. "All right, *uncle*! Keep that up and you're gonna show the other team all my weak spots!"

"You don't have many." Zovko saluted Bower with his stick blade, then skated off to the bench.

The energy Zovko brought to the team did exactly what Tyler had hoped it would. Within the first period, Vancouver's goalie was pulled in response to the five goals in eight shots. The backup goalie didn't fare too much better. In the end, the Cobras completely *destroyed* the Canucks. And then headed off to LA without any more drama.

First thing the next morning, Tyler found the headline online from the *Dartmouth Herald* reading "The Cobras got the 'Midas' Touch" and got the pretty receptionist at the hotel to print it out. He'd do like he'd told Richards and ask privately, but he needed to get Zovko to sign this.

The man was still his freakin' hero.

\* \* \* \*

"Where is he? No, I don't need to talk to him *instead* of you. I just want to know what's going on!"

Max stood in the open doorway of the hotel room he was sharing with Bower and considered turning around and heading back down to the hotel lounge, but they had a game in just over an hour. He needed to get his things.

*And get that man calmed down some.* He quietly shut the door behind him.

"You probably should have talked to him before—no, I'm not saying he's right. Goddamn it, Silver, don't you—"

A quick side step was the only thing that kept Max from

getting hit by Bower's phone. Bower kicked his bed, then pressed his hands to either side of his head and groaned.

"Deep breath, Bower." Max approached the other man as he dropped heavily onto the second bed. He shoved his hands in the pockets of his gray slacks, not sure what kind of comforting Bower needed. If any. He might just need to be left alone. "You want me to call Tim and—"

"No. Fuck no." Bower let out a gritty, agitated laugh as he pushed off the bed. "I play. That's what I do. That's what they want me to do."

"All right, then we better go." Max inhaled slowly as Bower moved around the room at a dragging pace, looking like a man with his soul half in the grave. Tim had given Max the heads up that Bower had some nasty nightmares, but since the man hadn't slept, that wasn't an issue.

The win had given Bower a brief spark of life, but that had faded after they'd gotten on the plane to LA. He put on a decent show in front of the team, but his brief talks with Richter and Silver seemed to drain the last of his spirit. He didn't eat with the team. Had missed the morning practice.

If Tim didn't know what was up, it was about time he did.

Bower grabbed Max's arm with brutal force and gave him a sharp look as they started for the door. "Not a fucking word to anyone. Hear me?"

"I hear you." Max jerked his arm free, his jaw clenching as he faced the other man. "But you better cool it. No point 'n gettin' all bowed up wit' me." He gnashed his teeth when Bower frowned at him, likely confused. Max's accent was getting thick as his tolerance frayed. He had all the patience in the world with his friends and teammates, but none when things got physical for nothing. He was usually the coolest head on the team, but he'd been raised to know when the civil line was crossed. "I ain't the one you're mad at."

"I'm not mad, I'm . . ." Bower shook his head and pressed his eyes shut. "I'm sorry. Fuck, I would have knocked you out if you'd grabbed me like that."

"I might've been tempted." Max slapped Bower's shoulder, more than ready to forget the slip. And get on the ice where he could burn off the adrenaline sizzling in his veins. "If I didn't suspect you were hoping I would."

Stupid, but he did end up keeping his mouth shut. And it took about half of the first period for him to regret it. Bower's head wasn't in the game.

Gasping in a lungful of ice-sweetened air, Max threw himself into a rapid glide across the ice, pinching in the offensive zone to retrieve a missed pass from the Kings' defensemen. Playing defense, he knew to make sure one of the Cobra forwards read his play before going in so deep. He quickly snapped the puck to Zovko who buried it in the back of the net.

3-2 for the Kings.

Tim left the line on for the center ice face-off. Carter won, but his backward pass was too hard for their German defenseman, Kral, to stop. The Kings' speedy forward dashed across the ice between Max and Kral, shooting right over Max as he dove to block the puck.

4-3.

Not a goalie's game. It happened. But during the break, Bower disappeared with his phone into the bathroom and barely made it back in time to start the second period. As Max sat on the bench, cursing as two more goals went in, Tim came up behind him, one hand on his shoulder.

"He's done, isn't he?"

"He was done before he got out there." Max sighed and glanced over his shoulder at the coach. "I should've told you."

"Yeah, well, I would've given him a chance if he'd asked for it, too." Tim inclined his head to Max, letting him know he understood, then shifted over to speak to the assistant coach. He signaled to the ref. Then to Bower.

Hunt stood, ready to take Bower's place. Kudos to the kid for not looking too excited about it, but before he could step on to the ice, Bower skated up, his face slick with sweat and red with rage.

"Don't fucking pull me, Coach." Bower shoved his mask off his face. "Twenty shots on net in the first period. How about giving me some goddamn defense?"

"We're not discussing this now." Tim waved Hunt on. "Take a seat, Bower. Save whatever you have to say until after the game."

For a second, Max was sure Bower would storm off, head to the locker room rather than take a seat at the end of the bench. But then Bower nodded slowly and got off the ice. He spent the rest of the game staring at the play, but not like he really saw any of it. They lost, 5-4, and not a man felt like talking as they gathered in the locker room.

Bower was already gone.

Max found him in their room, halfway through a bottle of whiskey. Thankfully, they didn't have a game the next day, but he gently eased the bottle out of Bower's hand, sitting in front of him on the floor.

He took a swig himself, not saying a word, determined to just be there in whatever way the man needed him to be. Even if it was only to make sure Bower didn't make himself sick.

"I can't lose her. And not just because of Amia." Bower dropped his head back onto the edge of the mattress. "I love her, but she scares me. All I seem to do is make her mad."

"It happens." Max spoke carefully, more to ease the man into letting the shit out than to give him advice. "Oriana gets right fit to be tied with me and Sloan sometimes. That woman's got a temper."

"But she's never . . . never talked like she wants to give up." Bower's face crumpled. He turned his head to the side, away from Max. "Silver says things sometimes. I just don't ever want to find her—damn it, if she thinks she has no place with me and Dean . . . she doesn't really believe Amia needs her. But my baby needs her mommy. And I need Silver."

*Christ.* That didn't sound good. No wonder Bower was a wreck. Oriana had told him and Sloan a little about Silver's postpartum depression, but he'd never gotten the impression Silver would try to end her own life. "I thought Silver was seeing someone."

"She did." Bower shrugged. "No one can stop you when you get to that place."

"Maybe you should go home, Bower. Be with your family."

"She has Dean. She'll be fine as long as she knows she has him. I just wish I didn't—didn't feel like I do about him." Bower reached for the bottle, then struggled to stand when Max placed it out of reach. "I did this to her. I could have prevented it."

"Bower—Landon." Max shot to his feet as Bower tripped over the side of the bed, almost cracking his head on the night table as he went for his phone. "You need to get some sleep."

"I need to call her." Bower squinted at his phone. "I need to make sure—"

"She's not your ex, Landon." Tim was suddenly beside them. Max hadn't heard him come in. But he nodded as Tim took the phone, set it aside, then latched on to one of Bower's arms. "Silver's strong and she has a lot to live for." Tim grunted as he and Max dragged Bower onto the bed. "I've seen her. Spoken to her. The therapy helped and so did the medication. She's not the one who needs it now."

"She knows I love him and it's killing her, Tim." Bower hauled in a rough breath, shaking violently as he sat up. "Shit, I'm gonna be sick."

Max snatched up the small black garbage pail just in time for Bower to toss up most of the alcohol he'd guzzled down. It wasn't long before Bower was leaning against him, covered in sweat, out cold.

"Stay with him. I'll get the doc." Tim combed his fingers roughly through his hair, his face pale and drawn with concern. "Just . . . just stay. Damn it, I should have known he wasn't ready."

"I ain't going nowhere, Coach, but I need to know something real quick." Max lifted his head, hardly able to get the words out. "Do you think Silver would—"

"No. Absolutely not." Tim rubbed his hand over his face. "I'm not sure she ever really got to that point, but after finding the mother of your dead child in a bath full of blood. . . Silver got the help she needed." The look Tim gave Bower was much like a father would give his very own child, one whose pain he couldn't take away. "Landon hasn't. But I'm going to make sure he does."

"I think the man needs to go home. If I felt like he does, I'd need to hold Oriana. Fuck, I'd need Sloan." Hell, he needed to talk to both now. Bower was a strong man. Seeing him in this condition was hard. "We'll take care of him."

"Yes, we will." Tim rested his hand on Max's shoulder. "I know that look. He's out. Go ahead and call your woman. Silver's gonna need her sister if things go down like I think they will." The fine lines around Tim's lips drew taut. "I'm going to call my brother."

Richter. Yes, that was an excellent idea. The man was a rock. He could get Bower through this the same way Sloan would do for Max if he ever dropped this low. Alone in the room with Bower, Max dialed Sloan's cell phone, inhaling and exhaling evenly as it rang again and again. Sloan would help get him level enough to speak to Oriana. Hell, he didn't want to scare her.

"What's wrong?" Sloan didn't bother with "hello." They'd known each other long enough to know Max wouldn't call this late without a reason.

Sloan remained silent as Max explained the situation. Then breathed out loudly into the phone. "All right, listen to me. Tim's got this. Bower's gonna be okay. But, yeah, Oriana needs to know what's going on. Just talk to me for a minute. This got to you."

"They're family, Sloan." Max dug his fingers into the tense muscles of his brow. "I wasn't here. For any of them."

"*We* weren't there. But you are now and I will be . . ." Sloan made an aggravated sound. "As soon as I can. Don't you dare start blaming yourself. And don't let Oriana either."

"I won't."

"You'd . . . you'd talk to me, right? If things were that bad?"

Max had never heard this kind of uncertainty in Sloan's tone.

Not in all the years he'd known him. He smiled a little, the answer coming easily. "I would. We don't got no secrets, man. I trust you to use a whip on my wife. I know you love her, even when you make her cry. Make her bleed."

"Sounds fucked up when you say it like that."

"It ain't fucked up. It's ours." And knowing that, deep in his fucking bones, made it so he was sure he could talk to Oriana calmly. Aware that nothing could shake what they'd built together. Even without Sloan close, their bond held strong. "I love you, Sloan."

"I love you too, Max. You're my brother in every way that counts." Sloan's laugh was hesitant. "Ah . . . if there's more, we can talk about it. Can't promise it wouldn't be weird, but you can—"

"There's more than enough in what we've got. Don't worry, I ain't looking to ride you, pal. Watching you with our woman does me just fine."

"Good, because you'd make a lousy fucking bottom. I've seen those ass muscles at work. You'd rip my dick off."

"You trying to make me laugh?"

"No. I'm trying to make sure you're all right," Sloan said quietly. "Are you?"

"I am now."

"Good. Call me after you talk to Oriana. And . . . give Bower a hug for me when he's conscious. I like that man."

"So do I." After Max hung up, Tim returned with the doctor, who assured them both Bower was fine. Physically.

And Max was able to call Oriana with Sloan's words in mind. *Tim's got this.*

* * * *

Cort frowned at his phone, then glanced over at Akira, who'd stayed in his hotel room rather than going back to her own place. His phone was on vibrate, but he knew it didn't take much to wake her.

And when he saw the number, he was grateful the call hadn't. He left the bed and went to the bathroom, closing the door and turning on the shower even as he answered. "Fuck, Roy. Really?"

"They lost." Roy's tone was on the jagged edge of outright panic. Considering that he'd given Cort a month, his behavior was odd.

Not to mention that Roy Kingsley *never* fucking panicked. Cort scratched his jaw. "I saw the game. The goalie was having a bad day or something. It happens."

"They were supposed to win."

"Tell me you didn't bet on the game." Silence was answer enough. "Shit, will you give me some time to get this sorted out?"

"You said you were talking to the coach. I need results. See what you can do with the younger goalie—he played well after the starter was pulled." Roy's voice sounded a bit calmer, as though he was confident his idea would work. "One of my manufacturing companies is receiving a large shipment of parts. It's imperative that you get the books organized."

*Jesus fucking Christ.* Cort wasn't sure whether he should laugh or get in his car and head to Roy's place to bust the man's face in. The greedy motherfucker wouldn't have his own family's support if this went south. His "parts" were fucking guns. Not the first time he'd dealt in them, but the rest of the Kingsleys were more interested in the drug trade. Less fucking risk. If Roy was getting nervous, the shipment must have gone smoothly. It was the money he had to deal with now, and he couldn't filter it through the team anymore. Gambling would do the job, but every bad bet meant losses Roy would have to make up to his partners.

He was getting desperate. And stupid. If the team didn't make the playoffs, Roy was a dead man.

Cort "getting the books organized" meant he had to give Roy some guaranteed wins and losses so the man could even things out. Since he didn't actually have the coach—or anyone else—the best he could do for now was get some insider info to increase the odds.

"Give me until the end of the day, and I'll let you know which way we've got to go to make the bottom line." *Which is gonna take a fucking miracle.* But he'd figure something out.

Roy made an affirmative sound, but his next words proved he wasn't about to put all his faith in Cort. "From what I hear, Ford is doing much better. Perhaps his experience has him rethinking approaching his sister."

"You listen to me very carefully, Roy." Cort's pulse quickened, his tone dead calm despite the rage that ripped through him. "Involve Ford again and the deal's off."

"Very well. There are things you will do that Ford is too weak to even attempt. But I expect to hear from you tonight."

"Not a problem." Cort hung up, then placed his cell on the bathroom counter and his hands on the ledge. He dropped his head, eyes closed, and seriously considered just killing Roy. Ending this before shit got out of control.

*Not worth jail time.*

But Ford's life was. Roy had stooped to hiring cheap thugs to handle his son. He would do so again if given *any* reason. Cort's options were to keep the man happy, or put him in the ground.

A soft rap at the door had him standing up straight and glancing back at the shower. Hell, he might not be able to tell Akira everything, but he wasn't gonna start playing stupid games. He turned the shower off, then opened the door.

She stopped unbuttoning the white dress shirt she'd borrowed from him to wear to bed. Her teeth dented her bottom lip. "I was going to join you, but . . . you weren't taking a shower, were you?"

"No. I was on the phone."

"And you didn't want me to hear what you were saying." She backed into the bedroom, holding up her hand before he could speak. "With who your father is, I'm sure there's some things I don't *want* to know. But you have to tell me one thing."

"Akira, I can't—"

"Are you dealing drugs? Or anything like that? I enjoy being with you, but I can't be with . . . with a criminal." She hugged herself as though she was afraid of his answer. Then continued. "I'm fine leaving whatever you've done in the past. But I don't want to have to worry about the cops showing up to arrest you someday."

"They might, Tiny. Not because of anything I'm doing now. My stepfather knows I'm out of . . ." He chose his words carefully. "The 'family' business. He respects my choices." Reaching out, he brought her closer to him, needing to hold her for as long as she'd let him. He wasn't quite lying to her, but he couldn't give her the full truth. "I killed a man. The cops know it wasn't an accident. They could bring me in and—"

Akira's eyes flashed. "He deserved to die. You saved Jami— they can't punish you for that."

"That's not how the world works, baby. I understand you not wanting to be with a criminal, but that's what I am." He sighed as she shook her head with a stubborn look on her cute little face. In her world, there was good and bad. She didn't understand all the gray space between. And she shouldn't have to. "If I were a better man, I'd tell you to get lost."

"Yeah, that sounds like something a 'better' man would say." She frowned up at him. "I shouldn't even have asked. I know you wouldn't do any of the terrible things I see on TV. I just . . . sometimes I watch those biker shows or movies and I'm like, I'd never be like those women. All okay with their man coming home covered in blood and stinking of the whores they fucked."

Cort covered her mouth with his hand, all the dire thoughts from before tossed as he backed her into the wall. He wasn't angry, but he hated how easily she was swearing lately. It wasn't her. He moved his hand to curve it under her jaw. "What did I say about those words?"

"I was just trying to make a point." She swallowed hard, peering up at him with big eyes full of excitement—and a trace of fear. "You f-fucking swear all the time."

"'Fuck' was one of my first words. 'Bitch' a close second." He gave her a lazy smile as her lips parted, her expression no different than if he'd told her his mother had bottle-fed him beer. "I had to be taught not to speak like that at school after doing it at home for years. My first girlfriend slapped me when I affectionately told her, 'You're one beautiful bitch.'" He brought his other hand up and began to undo the buttons of the shirt she wore. "So yes, I still swear, but I'm trying to stop."

"Fine. I'm sorry." The fear faded from her eyes and she suddenly looked disappointed. And a little surly. "I'll try to be a good girl, Daddy."

"'Daddy'?" He barked out a laugh, which had her scowling at him. He finished removing the shirt and let it fall to the floor. "I'm sure your daddy would have washed your mouth out with soap. Turn around and put your hands on the dresser."

"*What?*" She gaped at him and brought her hands up to cover her breasts as he stepped back. "Why?"

"Because this discussion is over." He spun her around when she didn't move, using one hand on the nape of her neck to bend her forward. His "good girl" was being naughty to get a reaction. One she may not like. He kissed her shoulder to ease the harshness of his words. "I've been handling you all wrong, Tiny." He slid his lips up her throat, then whispered in her ear, "But I won't make that mistake again."

\* \* \* \*

Akira braced her hands on the dresser and held her breath. This . . . this loss of control was exactly what she'd wanted. But she wanted her nice, easygoing Cort to take it from her. Maybe kiss her to shut her up, then toss her on the bed and take her. His bending her over, naked, felt a lot like when Dominik disciplined her. A little too much like it . . .

Or maybe just enough.

He covered her butt with both hands, molding her cheeks, the tips of his fingers grazing her moist slit. His low growl made it clear he was thinking of doing something other than spanking her.

Something a lot more fun.

She liked that idea. Spreading her legs a little more, she flipped her hair over one shoulder and wet her lips with her tongue. "Cort?"

"Sir." He gave her a crooked grin. "Call me 'Sir.' At least when we're doing stuff like this. I wouldn't want to get distracted."

"It's okay to get distracted, Cort." Akira wiggled her butt under Cort's hand, needing him too much to start a play punishment scene. She wouldn't *dare* pull this with Dominik, but she didn't see any problem with Cort easing his way into the lifestyle. Very, *very* slowly. She hissed in a breath as his fingers pressed against her. "Please, please just—"

Two fingers filled her even as Cort set his teeth into the flesh of her neck. The pain and pleasure swirled through her body, and her nails scratched at the dresser. She could spend all her time with this man naked, with his hands on her, and be perfectly happy.

"Does your other Dom get distracted so easily?" Cort withdrew his fingers, then kissed the curve between her shoulder and her neck. "No wonder you're so naughty."

His hand connected hard with her ass; the sting made her yelp as she absorbed the impact. She stared at him. "That fucking hurt."

"This blog I read suggested starting slow. Like five smacks." Cort cocked his head as though considering. "I think you can take more, don't you?"

Another resounding smack and she kicked him in the shin. "You fucking bastard! That's too hard!"

He went still. "I thought there was a word for that."

"There is, but I'm not using it."

"Why?"

*Because I don't really want you to stop. Because I love the fact that you're ready to take this step with me.* But there was no way she could say all that. So she simply shrugged and did her best to stare him down.

"Your thoughts are all over your face, Tiny." His eyes hardened and her breath caught as he latched on to the nape of her neck and laid another stinging slap on her ass. "You don't want me to stop. But you're not getting the point either. If we're gonna do this, if I'm going to give you what you need—" The next slap came across both cheeks and her eyes teared at the pain. His tone was rough, but controlled. He hadn't lost his temper, which was good. But he didn't sound happy. "—you need to be real with me. Would it help if I talked to your Dom?"

She shook her head quickly. Having both Dominik and Cort disappointed in her would be unbearable. "He's not my Dom anymore. You—"

"I'm not. But I want to be." He inhaled roughly. "I'm doing this all wrong."

"No, you're not! You're trying and I love it!" Her whole body shuddered as she gulped back a sob. Tears dripped from her chin to the dresser, glistening in the light glaring through the part in the curtains. "I'm the one who's not trying. I need . . . I need to feel the limits you place on me. To know they're there."

"They are. But . . ." He barred one arm across her stomach, kissing between her shoulders. "I'll stop if you ask me to. I don't want to go too far. Just looking at how red your ass is makes me feel like shit."

She giggled as he groaned with his mouth against her back. It was kinda funny, him swearing while punishing her for doing the same. But then she thought about what he'd said. He was raised with cursing as the norm. She hadn't been. He'd liked who she'd been from the beginning. From shy to tentatively bold. With all her issues and her occasional clinginess. He wanted that person, not the one she was trying to be.

"Co—*Sir*—my butt being a little red is okay." She let the tension out of her arms, still facing him over her shoulder, but lowering her eyes to offer her submission. "Dominik's left bruises for less."

"That son of a bitch, I'll—"

"No! No, it's not a bad thing!" She turned now, framing his hard jaw with her hands. "He knows my limits. You will too. He made sure I knew when to use my safeword, so trust me to if I can't take any more."

"This shi—stuff is complicated." He picked her up and carried her to the bed. "Let's consider this first punishment a complete fail. Are you sorry for your dirty mouth? Your attitude?"

"Yes, Sir." She gasped as he dropped her on the bed, his hands on her inner thighs, pressing them apart. Her head fell back onto the pillows as he covered her with his mouth. "Ah! I shouldn't—"

"Shouldn't what?" He gave her a positively wicked grin as he lifted his head. "Let me guess. You were a very bad girl, and I shouldn't reward that kind of behavior."

"You shouldn't." But she fisted her hands in his hair as he trailed his tongue along her heated flesh, desperately hoping he didn't agree and wouldn't stop.

He ate her like a starving man, thrusting and sucking until she squirmed mindlessly. Then he let out a low, humming sound and brought his head up again. "This isn't your reward. It's mine. Spanking you, rather than tasting you, was torture."

"I'm yours, Cort. You can take me, then spank me, or just . . ." Her body arched as he licked her like her body was dripping with sweet syrup. "Just keep doing that."

"I like that idea." He pressed his lips against her hard, dipping his tongue in deep. Then replaced his tongue with his fingers. "Love how wet you are, baby. I could do this all night."

"Please, please just let me—" The heat of his mouth left her. She sat up as he stood and held out his hand. "What are you—?"

"I never got to take my shower." He smiled pleasantly as he drew her to her feet, pressing her mouth closed with a finger under her chin and raising his brow when her eyes narrowed. "You can join me, but don't worry. I'll let you come." He gestured her ahead of him to the bathroom, laughing softly into her ear. "Eventually."

\* \* \* \*

All the distraction had been more than welcome, but Cort had work to do. He dropped Akira off at her place just after noon, hating to see her go, yet knowing he couldn't do what he had to with her making him feel like he could do no wrong.

Because he could. He had to. He might not be doing all those things she thought were too much to deal with. Drugs, whores, blood . . .

But she might consider what he *was* doing just as bad.

# Chapter Sixteen

Every inch of the bar shone, the place was packed, and Ford was damn happy to be back. He'd started slow his first few days out of the hospital, but that didn't keep him busy enough. Paperwork at the Forum took up most of his mornings, and now he could burn his empty nights surrounded by liquor and noise. See familiar faces.

And try not to think of the faces he wished he could see.

He avoided his sister's steady gaze, one that said she knew something was up, and surveyed the crowd. Despite the celebratory mood of the night, people were starting to grumble. He had two waitresses working the floor, but only one was actually doing her job.

The Cobras winning three games in a row was awesome, but Ford was starting to wonder if he'd need to hire a new girl. Angel had gone to see some family in Nashville and had somehow met Dave Hunt, the Cobras' young backup goalie. After what she'd gone through, Ford hadn't expected her to jump into another relationship, but over the last week that they'd been dating, Hunt had been treating her real good.

And he'd better continue doing just that, or the Cobras would have to bring up yet another goalie from the minors. Ford finally glanced over at Silver as he placed the last of the glasses in the dishwasher under the bar, taking note of her hesitant smile as Dean held his hand out to her. Ford watched his sister follow Dean to the dance floor, the way she relaxed into the man's arms as a slow song began. Nice to see her not so damn stressed.

Silver had told him a little about the situation with Landon. The Cobras' starting goalie was seeing the team's shrink, and wouldn't play again until he worked through his issues. Local fans were grumbling that the Cobras would never make the playoffs with Hunt in the nets, but Ford didn't really give a shit if the team didn't make it to the postseason. He knew Silver wouldn't be happy without Landon, and she wouldn't have him until he was well. Which he wasn't.

The front door opened and a cold draft rushed in before Cort pushed it shut behind him. He inclined his head to Ford. Ford returned the gesture, trying not to show that he was fucking happy to see the man. Things were still a little off between them, so Ford was relieved when Cort went to one of the pool tables in the back, probably to challenge someone to a game. He grinned when he saw Cort lay down a twenty.

*Bad idea, pal.* Ford remembered Cort teaching him to play in his teens. How quickly Ford got the hang of the game. And how easily he'd started beating Cort. Unless the competition was pathetic, Cort would lose. But he knew that. He just liked to play, and setting down money was easier than being all friendly.

Cort didn't call many people friends. He kept few people close, which made Ford feel more than a little guilty about letting their friendship get all strained and shit. He should do something about that.

He didn't get a chance. Screams drew his—and everyone else's—attention to the drama playing out across the bar.

"I saw you looking at her! You want her! You'd be fucking her right now if I wasn't here!"

Ford frowned as Angel stormed away from Hunt. He'd never heard the waitress raise her voice, never mind scream like that. The petite brunette was usually friendly, soft-spoken with a tinkling laugh that drew customers in almost as much as her smile. That had changed a bit over the last week because she spent most of her time draped over her new boyfriend, but they were still in the honeymoon period. And Ford was pretty sure Hunt wasn't even aware of a single woman besides her.

Which was probably why Hunt looked lost as he followed her

to the door. "I wasn't looking at anyone, babe. I swear!"

"You're a liar! I can't even stand to be near you right now!" Angel disappeared into the staff room where she'd left her coat, then came back out, still seething. "You've got a game tomorrow, so you're probably going to have those sleazy puck bunnies all over you. I don't know if I can do this anymore. I thought you were different."

"I am! Angel, please just tell me—"

"Not right now, Dave." She jerked away from Hunt when he reached for her. "Maybe I'll call you tomorrow. Maybe I won't. Just . . . don't call me. I need some time to think."

Several of the Cobras approached Hunt as he slumped at the bar on a stool, but he ignored them all. "Can I have some vodka, Ford?"

*Vodka? The night before the game?* Ford opened his mouth to suggest something else. Like Pepsi—except the kid didn't usually drink anything besides orange juice or water.

Suddenly, Cort was beside him, pouring the drink. "Just one. And don't worry, your dad won't find out."

"Shit, my dad . . ." Hunt scowled at the drink. He rolled his eyes, shook his head and let out a bitter laugh as he drained the tumbler in a single gulp. "Screw it. He's already pissed that I'm dating her. Give me another."

"She told you what happened to her, right? Just give her some time." Cort hesitated, then refilled Hunt's glass. "Last one. We need you focused on the game tomorrow."

"She told me and—hell, how am I supposed to focus on anything? I think . . . I think I'm in love with her."

*Well, that didn't take long.* Hunt was young, so it wasn't all that surprising, but the timing was horrible. Would be so much easier to let it slide if Ford still didn't give a shit about the team, but since he did, he was more than ready to show the kid the door.

"Buddy, how about you wash that down with some water and listen for a sec." Ford uncapped a bottle of water and placed it in front of Hunt. "You don't have to understand why she's pissed.

Just that she's hurting, you know? Find a way to make her feel good again. She loves big, romantic gestures and foreign films. Get her two dozen roses, write her a poem—hell, copy one off the internet if you've gotta—and tickets to one of them boring flicks."

"You really think that's gonna work?"

"Sure. She wouldn't be flying off the handle if she didn't like you, right?"

"Guess not," Hunt said, sounding hopeful.

The little talk was kinda awkward since Ford and Hunt weren't friends. Thankfully, Cort convinced Hunt to leave after he'd finished the water—and the vodka. Cort returned after making sure the kid got in a cab, helping Ford close up like he always had.

"He's a good kid, fucking talented, but emotional, you know?" Cort shook his head as he polished the bar. There was a tension in his every movement, and Ford wondered if Cort was starting to get invested in the team. He might be a Red Wings fan, but being with Akira might have split his alliances a little. Cort's lips tightened as he dropped the rag into the sink. "This thing between him and Angel isn't straightened up by tomorrow night and a loss is pretty much guaranteed."

"Yeah. Maybe I should talk to Silver—or Tim." Ford thought on the last performance of the farm team goalie who'd been brought up as backup. He was decent. With the way the new guy, Zovko, was scoring, the team might manage a win. "Hunt keeps to himself a lot. They might not know—"

"It's no one's business, Ford. Just leave it." Cort flashed an apologetic smile when Ford's brow shot up. "Sorry, Angel just told me how much pressure the kid gets from his dad. He doesn't need anyone else meddling."

"Got it." Ford took a deep breath, nodding to Silver as she headed out with Dean. He grinned as she stopped and came behind the bar to hug him. Pressing a kiss on her cheek, he searched her face for some sign that she was okay. Since he couldn't tell, he just asked, "How you doing, little sis?"

"I'm fine, but . . . I feel a little guilty." She rested her head on his shoulder, seeming more comfortable with him now than she'd ever been. Things had changed for the better between them since his little trip to the hospital and he liked it. Having sisters was pretty cool. Having two who didn't hate him even better. Silver sighed. "If I'd seen how bad things were for Landon sooner . . ."

"Hey, don't do that. You were both dealing with your own shit. If he's any kind of man, he'll understand once his head's on straight." He hugged her tight. "If not, just give me the word, and I'll kick his ass for you."

Ford spotted Dean giving him a dirty look from the corner of his eye and smirked until Silver playfully slapped his chest. The stab of pain wiped the smirk right off his face.

"Oh God, Ford! I'm sorry!" Silver pulled away, covering her mouth with her hand. "I should be asking how you're doing. You really should come stay with us so I can take care of you."

He pretended to consider just so he could watch Dean's jaw tick. The man really needed to chill out. Smiling, Ford patted his little sister's cheek. "I appreciate the offer, but I'm all right. Got my nurse coming in almost daily to check on me."

"A nurse?" Silver grinned. "How respectable of you. Is it serious?"

*No comment.* Ford just shrugged. He wouldn't tell Silver, but he couldn't think about any woman besides Akira. Which made Cort hanging around after Silver said goodbye even more awkward.

And the bastard got straight to the point, as usual. "Good to see you're moving on."

"I'm not." Ford laughed bitterly as Cort's eye narrowed. "Don't worry, I'm not going to be stupid about it. Akira's with you. I don't like it, but I'm dealing. I promised her I'd be her friend and that hasn't changed."

"She wants me to go with her to the club tomorrow. You okay with that?"

*Fuck no!* His guts twisted as he imagined Akira kneeling to the man who'd once been his best friend after how long Ford had been working to be the man who earned her submission. But he gave

Cort a stiff nod. "I've had to watch her with Dominik. Seeing her with you won't be no different."

"You don't have to be there." Something like regret darkened Cort's eyes. He looked away. "If it's too hard—"

"I used to go to the club every weekend. Started it for her, but found out it's something I need too." It had taken a few months. Playing gopher to the club's Masters and Mistresses had almost gotten him to say "fuck it," but then Chicklet had taught him how to use a whip and Carter had given him some lessons with the ropes. The more people saw he was serious, the more willing they were to help him out. He'd slowly gained confidence and the subs responded well. He'd kept his play light—no sex—but maybe that would change. There were a few cuties he could have fun with. Just the thought felt wrong, but the crooked smile he gave Cort was almost genuine. "Makes you feel any better, I won't be there watching the two of you. Pischlar was talking about doing a chemical play scene. Might get in on that with him."

"Chemical play?" Cort's brow furrowed. "Sounds dangerous."

Ford laughed. Damn, the man was clueless. "Most of it's natural stuff. Some's even edible." He wiggled his eyebrows and Cort grinned. "A pretty little sub tied up while me and Pischlar suck cinnamon-flavored nipples. Mint where she's all hot and wet and juicy—" Fuck, he missed talking to Cort like this. About anything. "Could be fun."

"Never thought you'd share a woman after what happened with Jami." Cort's grin faded. "How's she doing, anyway? Haven't seen her lately."

"She's doing better. Spent a few days with her uncle, then went to Ramos's place and 'made up' with Carter. Didn't want details!" Ford pulled on his jacket and walked out with Cort, locking the bar behind them. "As for sharing . . . well, I lost control of things with Jami. I couldn't be with a girl who could be with just anyone. At the club, it's different. When I play with a chick, we negotiate and have some kind of connection, even if it's just temporary. She's trusting me. Pischlar's a good Dom, so I won't be all paranoid about how he'll treat the woman. That was a big issue with me and Jami. I knew I wasn't protecting her from those losers, and she didn't want me to."

"Yeah, well, you and Jami were a hot mess."

"Sure were. But she's happy and I'm happy for her."

Cort nodded slowly. "Maybe you and Akira will be able to have that t—"

"Yeah, maybe." All the good feelings were snuffed out like a healthy flame covered in dirt. What he'd had with Jami had been a wild ride on a highway in a fast car with no headlights. They were both lucky to have gotten out in one piece. He and Akira had almost had . . . damn it, he couldn't even put a label on it. He'd really thought she was *the one*. Part of him still did.

But *that* wasn't something he could discuss with Cort. So he cut the conversation short, suddenly goddamn exhausted. Cort wanted to sit in on the team management meeting tomorrow and he was welcome to it. Once Ford had told him as much, he headed up to his apartment.

His place had never felt so empty. There'd been times where he'd enjoyed having his own place to crash without anyone bothering him, but not anymore. He was actually relieved to hear Cam come in a few minutes after he'd dropped into bed. Cam hadn't been at the bar since Cort was there, but Cort had probably called him before leaving.

Much as he hated needing a bodyguard, he wasn't in the frame of mind to complain tonight.

He was so fucking tired of being alone.

\* \* \* \*

Akira tried on her third outfit and groaned as she turned from side to side, looking herself over in the mirror. It was Saturday night and the first time she'd be going to the club with Cort. She knew the kinds of things Dominik liked to see her in, but she wanted something different for Cort. Wanted to wear something to please him.

But what? He'd seen her in everything from sweats to skirts, jeans, pajamas, her Ice Girl uniforms. He never seemed to notice her clothes, whether she wore a bit of makeup or none at all. He only saw her.

Which was wonderful. She got all warm and fuzzy when she thought about how he looked at her when she'd come out wearing one of his shirts. He'd be happy no matter what she settled on, but she wanted to render him speechless.

"You look really sexy, Akira." Jami held her breath as Sahara tightened the white corset with pretty, pale blue ribbons she'd chosen to go along with the short, fluffy white pettiskirt she was wearing. She rarely went to the club, but since neither her father or uncle would be there tonight, she'd finally given in and agreed to go with Akira and Sahara. Her cheeks were flushed and there'd been a bounce to her step all day.

*I missed this Jami.* Akira smiled at Jami, then smoothed her hands over the sides of the white latex dress. "Thanks. Do you think he'll like it?"

"I don't think you'll be wearing it long enough for it to matter." Jami winked, thanked Sahara, then moved to stand in front of the mirror with Akira. She toyed with a curly strand of the black wig which covered her short, light brown hair. She'd gone back to her natural color, but her own hair still didn't quite reach her shoulders. Jami looked adorable no matter how long her hair was, but she'd recently admitted she missed having it long. Not that she regretted her choice to give Luke's mother her hair. She was just eager for it to grow back. Which explained why she'd insisted both Akira and Sahara wear theirs loose.

Akira worried her bottom lip with her teeth. Jami had straightened her dark brown hair for her, and it looked nice and sleek. She wasn't really feeling the dress, though. "Is it weird that I *want* it to matter?"

"Not at all." Sahara sat on the edge of her dresser, using her thumb to push up the red horn-rimmed glasses that completed her slutty secretary outfit. She cocked her head and held her tongue between her teeth thoughtfully. Then she hopped down and laughed. "I got it! OMG, why didn't I think of this before?"

"I hate it when you talk like a text." Jami followed Sahara to the closet. Her tone changed from grumpy to excited again as Sahara showed her whatever she'd pulled out. "That's perfect! Damn, I so have to be there when he sees her in this!"

"What?" Akira spun around, her eyes widening as Sahara held up a studded leather bra and skirt. And a leather biker hat with a thick silver chain running across the base of the rim. She arched a brow at Jami. "I thought you were worried that he'd treat me like one of those biker chicks."

"He hasn't so far, and I don't think this will make him start." Jami giggled, dashing across the room as Sahara handed Akira the outfit. "But if you want a reaction, this will definitely get one. Now hurry up!"

Alone in Sahara's room, Akira fidgeted with the studs on the leather bra, wondering if she had the guts to pull this off. It wasn't that much more revealing than some of her uniforms, but . . . was this how she wanted Cort to see her?

She recalled how she'd been a little bold with him. A bit naughty at times. He might not like her swearing, but he seemed to like that side of her. The side that wasn't afraid to live in the moment.

He might not be a biker anymore, but she could still see him pulling up on a Harley, waiting for her to climb on behind him so they could go for a ride. She'd never been on a motorcycle, but she could picture hanging on to him as the wind whipped through her hair, practically smell the leather of his jacket, warm from his body, soft against her cheek.

Taking a deep breath, she stripped off the white dress and changed quickly. She could hear Sebastian's deep voice and Luke's laughter in the other room. She found a pair of six-inch heel thigh-high leather boots to complete the outfit, a tad big since Sahara wore a size bigger than her, but not too bad. They'd keep her legs from freezing anyway.

*That's it. I'm ready.*

A rough, familiar chuckle had her freezing with her hand on the doorknob.

Cort was here.

*Oh God! I'm not ready! What if he hates it?*

Too late to change again now. With one last glance at herself in the mirror to adjust the hat, she stepped out into the hall. The men all turned to look at her. Luke's lips parted. Sebastian smiled.

And Cort choked on the sip of water he'd just taken. His eyes widened and he opened and closed his mouth several times. Tried to speak and coughed.

Sebastian slapped Cort's back, his lips slanted in amusement. "A Dom typically shows more composure, *hombre*. You'll have your sub thinking she can wrap you around her little finger with a reaction like that."

"Done deal, man." Cort came toward her, his eyes drinking in every inch of her in a way that made her feel like she was bathing naked under the blazing sun. His hands on her waist, pulling her to him, had her forgetting that there was anyone else in the hall. He was already hard beneath his black jeans, and his tone was thick with lust. "Damn, Tiny. I'm glad we ain't going to a biker club. I'd be fighting all night to keep those fu—those dirty bastards away from you."

"No one will touch me without your permission tonight, Sir." Akira flattened her hands against his chest in the part of his leather jacket, loving the way his heart raced under her palm. Knowing she had the same effect on him as he had on her was a heady feeling. "You won't have to fight at all."

"Good. I don't want you to see what a caveman I can be." He accepted her jacket from Sahara with a "thanks" and held it for her while she slipped it on. When she did up the last button of the long, black wool coat, one of those sexy, wicked grins stole across his lips. "You know what, I lied."

"About what—Cort!" She squealed, then laughed as he threw

her over his shoulder. "Put me down!"

"No can do, Tiny." Cort carried her to his car, smacking her butt when she tried to wiggle free. The others followed, Sahara getting into Sebastian's car with Luke and Jami, all acting like they were completely oblivious to her struggles. Cort placed her into the passenger seat, curving his hand around her throat and giving her a bruising kiss as he whispered, "Rough or gentle. That's the only choice you get tonight."

Scary options if she thought about it, but it took less than a second to realize she didn't have to. She met his eyes and said softly, "However you want to take me, Sir. I'm yours."

\* \* \* \*

The club was louder than the last time Cort had been here, the bass of the music booming through his bones, the heat of all the bodies around him almost stifling. As he took Akira's jacket at the coat check, he saw the other men checking her out, both Doms in their leathers and subs in . . . well, some of them wore leathers too. The only way he could really tell them apart was the Doms met his gaze head-on and the subs dropped theirs the second he glanced their way. One familiar Domme—Chicklet—came over and smiled at Akira before turning to him.

"May I? It's been a while."

"May you?" Shit, was the woman asking to play with his girl? They'd just fucking walked in! "Listen, lady, I—"

Stepping up behind him, Sebastian put a hand on his shoulder. "She wants to greet your sub, Cort. Asking is a show of respect."

"Ah, yeah." Cort rubbed his jaw, feeling pretty fucking stupid. From what he'd heard about Chicklet, she was kinda a big deal here. Being an asshole to her straight off wasn't the smartest move. "Sorry. Go ahead."

Chicklet's lips thinned as she hesitated in front of him. She moved toward Akira, then stopped. "You were expecting swapping or something? If that's what you thought happened here, why did you come?"

"I know it *does* happen. And that not everyone does it. I'm not *quite* as clueless as I came off." He chanced an apologetic smile. "I'm here because I want to learn more about what Akira likes."

"Fair enough. You're forgiven." Chicklet leaned close to him, her breath cold and minty, her red lips slanted playfully. "If your girl was into women, I'd have played with her already. Might have kept her because she's such a cute little thing. But she's not." She glanced pointedly across the club, to where Dominik was widening the rope barrier around a large wooden frame. "A little tip since I'm a nice gal. He's the only one she's ever played with here. Things will go a lot smoother for you if you give him the courtesy of speaking to him before you drag her into a full scene."

"I planned to."

"Good. I like you more already." She lowered her voice, eyeing Akira who was chatting excitedly with Jami and Sahara. "There's only one other person you have to worry about with her, but I expect you know that already."

"There's nothing to worry about." Cort looked over at the bar where Ford was handing out drinks and marking the bracelets of those he served. Ford inclined his head when he spotted Cort, but nothing in his expression showed resentfulness or anything else. "We've all worked things out."

"Right. Well, good luck with that." Chicklet joined the girls, hugging all three. A pretty brunette trailed after her, looking familiar somehow.

Not a biker. Not one of the Ice Girls. But he'd met her somewhere . . .

"Cort, come to the bar for a sec, man!" Ford called out, urgency in his tone. "Just wanted to run something by you!"

Cort glanced back at Akira, decided she was safe enough with her friends, and strode up to the bar. "Yeah?"

Ford dried his hands on a rag and came around to the open end of the bar. "Laura—Chicklet's sub—is a cop. You might wanna steer clear. There's enough people here that she might not notice you if you mingle."

The warning came as a surprise. Shouldn't Ford be sitting back and hoping the cop would recognize him and haul him in?

*Fuck no. Ford's better than that.* And damn, he hated that this whole thing with Akira gave him any doubt. He squeezed Ford's forearm. "Thanks for the heads up."

"No prob. Oh, and the goalie, Hunt—he's really not bad, but he and Akira had a nasty run-in. She's not really comfortable with him."

*Fucking dead man.* Screw stupid head games to throw the kid off his game. The next loss would be just as certain with the goalie in intensive care. "What the fuck did he do to her?"

"Relax, killer." Ford's laugh cut short as though he'd suddenly caught that the old nickname wasn't so funny anymore. "Listen, I beat the shit out of him once, and it just made Akira hate me more. He knows better than to touch her here, but I just thought you'd want to know about any triggers she has. She gets into a zone when she's with Dominik . . . he's really good at not letting anything yank her out. You'll have to learn to do that for her. Keep it to light scenes in the main area. Anything more in the private rooms. Don't bring her in the office and—"

"Why are you telling me all this?" All right, he knew Ford wanted to be her friend, but he didn't think the man was going for sainthood. "If I screw up, you might get a shot to—"

"If you screw up, she might not feel safe here anymore. If you screw up, you'll take away the one thing that helps her feel okay with being close to men." Ford dropped his hand, his eyes a hard, cold shade of gold as he fixed them on Cort. "So don't."

*Well, damn.* Cort nodded and watched Ford return to his duties behind the bar. He sensed Akira slipping up to his side and put his arm over her shoulders. Whatever his motivations, Ford was right. This place, these people, had given Akira so much. Because of them she was strong and sassy and passionate. She might not be with him if it wasn't for all that.

Which brought to mind Chicklet's suggestion. Cort kissed the top of Akira's head and guided her across the room. "There's something I have to do, Tiny."

"What's that?" Akira's cheeks got nice and pink, her mind obviously in a very different place than his was. "Did you see something—"

"Someone." He took a deep breath as they drew closer to where Dominik was laying out an array of whips on a short folding table. "Someone I need to thank."

\* \* \* \*

*Oh, Dominik doesn't look too pleased.* Akira chewed on her bottom lip as Cort held out his hand and Dominik just stared at it. The man she'd called "Sir" for months shot her a look that she wasn't sure held disapproval or concern. Maybe a bit of both.

"You were supposed to come to the club two weeks ago, little one." Dominik squared his shoulders and took Cort's hand. "We've met."

"We have, but I didn't know I had you to thank for this." Cort's lips curved slightly as he glanced over at her, his eyes holding something so intense her heart began to beat like a frightened little bunny's. "I'm falling in love with this girl. Figured it would be decent of me to let you know she's in good hands."

Her little bunny heart skipped and stuttered as she stared at Cort. And then burst open because it didn't have to be a cautious, tough little organ any more. It could do what it was meant to and feel without restraints. This man wouldn't just catch her if she fell. Wouldn't just hold her tight and keep her safe.

He'd take the plunge right along with her.

Dominik shook his head and put out his hand, palm up. He smiled when she placed hers in it. "If I didn't believe him, I'd find a way to take you away from him. You know how much I care about you, how hard I worked to help you accept how strong you really are." He stroked her knuckles with his thumb. His lips curved at one edge. "He's not the kind of man I'd have chosen for you, but I wanted you to be strong enough to make that choice on your own. And I can't think badly of anyone who can make you look this happy."

"Thank you!" Akira threw herself into Dominik's arms. She couldn't deny that if he hadn't accepted Cort, moving on would have been that much harder. *Oh God, what does Cort think about me hanging all over another man?*

She tried to duck away from Dominik, but he held her in place, speaking to Cort almost as though she wasn't there. "You didn't come to me just for my approval."

"No." Cort put his hand on the small of her back, and her pulse quickened again as the sensation of being trapped between them seized her. "I can't give her what she had from you. Not yet. But I'm willing to learn."

"Commendable. But how involved do you want me to be?" Dominik pressed his hand to her cheek, tilting her head up and giving her one of his dark smiles. "This sub has never been shared. Is that your intention?"

*Shared?* Akira swallowed hard as Cort's hand slid down over her butt. She figured he'd be possessive. She knew he wanted to learn, but that meant workshops or watching scenes, didn't it? The possibility of his accepting other methods was a little frightening. And thrilling. And . . . and, oh God, he wanted to learn from *Dominik?*

"You know how to handle her. She can be a bit of a brat." Cort chuckled as he nuzzled her neck, his body against her pressing her even closer to Dominik's hard chest. "My first attempt at punishment didn't work out all that well."

Dominik clucked his tongue, grazing his scruffy cheek against hers as he spoke in her ear. "Earning punishments already? Naughty girl."

"You work with other subs; I take it you can keep this as strictly a lesson?" Cort squeezed her ass, which caused her bare stomach to rub against Dominik's leathers. And the thick swell beneath them.

"Absolutely." Dominik teased her lips with his and smiled. There was tenderness in his eyes. "One last time, little one. I'll show him what you need."

One last time. She blinked fast, wondering if it hurt him to let her go. This wasn't the first time he'd been forced to do that. And the last thing she wanted to do was hurt him. She owed him so much.

"None of that." Dominik wiped away the single tear that spilled free. "We both knew what we were getting into from the start. I was afraid you'd gotten too attached, but you told me you were fine with the other subs I was training. I'd hoped you would find someone to give you what I can't give anyone, and you have."

"You can, Sir! You have so much to offer—" Akira's throat locked as Dominik looked past her, his jaw ticking slightly. She had to rise up on her tiptoes to see past Cort's shoulder. *Oriana and Max.*

Neither had come to the club since they'd returned to Dartmouth. For all her fears of hurting Dominik, Akira knew she couldn't bring him the pain Oriana had. And she couldn't help but hate the woman a little for that.

To top it off, Oriana was standing by the bar, hugging Ford and looking at Akira like she was . . . trespassing? She had no goddamn right to any opinion on what Dominik did. And with whom.

If Cort hadn't been holding her so close to Dominik, she might have hesitated, but he'd made his intentions pretty clear. Which gave her the opening for a great big "fuck you" that she didn't dare voice.

Hooking her fingers to Dominik's belt, she nipped his jaw and gave him an impish smile. "Do you really think you can teach my Dom how to 'handle me,' Sir?"

The pain left Dominik's eyes. He blinked, then barked out a laugh. "Someone has to. Bring your pet, Cort. And please, let me know how the punishment failed. And what she did to deserve it. I usually recommend immediate discipline, but we can make an exception."

"Wait! *What?*" Akira's breath whooshed out as Cort flung her over his shoulder for the second time that night. "I'll be good, I swear!"

"Swearing is what got you in trouble, Tiny." Cort's whole body vibrated with laughter as he carried her to one of the theme rooms. "Might want to avoid it now."

*The classroom!* Akira swallowed spastically as Cort put her down in one of the student's desks. She sat up straight as Dominik snapped a long, flexible ruler against the large desk at the head of the class.

"Lock the door please, Cort." Dominik pulled a set of keys out of his pocket and tossed them to Cort.

Cort went to close the door. Locked it and handed the key back to Dominik.

No one was allowed to lock the doors unless one of the club's Masters was present. If a DM walked by and looked in the small window that was nothing but a mirror from this side, they would see Dominik and keep going.

She was trapped. And a little nervous. Her most intense scenes with Dominik had all been during role-play. Doing this with Cort and Dominik was . . . almost overwhelming.

But she wasn't afraid. She trusted them both.

"Swearing and dressing provocatively. This behavior is unacceptable, Miss Hayashi." Dominik sauntered up to her desk and slapped his hands down on it, making her jump. "Do you have anything to say for yourself?"

*Maybe I* should *be afraid.* She shook her head quickly.

"No? Perhaps a color?" Dominik studied her face, clearly waiting for her to absorb his words.

It took her a full minute to understand them. A color. Like red. Which she could use at any time.

But she didn't need to. Actually, what she needed to do was show these men she wasn't a little mouse. Not anymore.

Leaning back into her seat, she put her boots up on the desk and smirked. "I have nothing to say, Sir. Do your worst."

Cort moved to Dominik's side, arms folded over his chest. "You sure about that, Tiny?"

His tone made her both want to back off and press on. Her whole body shook as she sucked her teeth, deciding to just go for it. "I'm sorry, Sir. Is your hearing aid on low? I know old men have difficultly—"

Shoving her boots off the desk, Cort fisted his hand in her hair and pulled her to her feet. "You asked for it."

\* \* \* \*

Cort's Tiny was, well, *tiny*, but her wiggling made her quite the handful. He was pretty damn sure she didn't really *want* him to let her go, but he didn't like the idea of using brute force to hang on to her. A little hair pulling was one thing, but when he had to latch on to her arms to keep her from taking a swing, all he could feel was how fragile she was.

Too easy to break. He loosened his grip, his lips thinning as he met Dominik's steady gaze.

Dominik sidestepped when Akira tried to dart by him, then framed her jaw with one big, black hand. His tone was low and firm. "Enough."

Akira stilled, eyes wide, practically panting as she stared up at her former Dom. "Sir, I—"

"You want to play pretend, and that's fine, but is there nothing in you that wants to please him?"

"Everything in me wants it! I want him to know it's okay to—"

"It's not. I'm not comfortable restraining you that way." Cort wasn't sure he could face the other man anymore. Fuck, he had no goddamn clue what he was doing. All he knew was focusing on not leaving bruises on her arms wasn't much of a turn on. "If you want someone to wrestle with, it ain't gonna be me."

Dominik let out a deep, dark laugh, full of danger and passion. "She doesn't want to wrestle with you, Cort. She wants to be overpowered. Which can be done without hurting her." He slid his hand up the back of Akira's neck, combing his fingers into her hair, then fisting his hand close to her scalp. Ignoring her yelp, he barred one arm across her stomach and forced her facedown onto the desk. "Much."

Akira's cheeks reddened. "Stop!"

"Do you mean 'red'?" Dominik asked like he sincerely doubted it.

Cort's Tiny wrinkled her nose. "No."

"Then be silent. And don't move." Leaving her there, Dominik retrieved two packaged ropes from a desk drawer and placed them on the desk by Akira's head. While Cort observed with his arms folded over his chest, Dominik pressed Akira's legs together between his knees, handling her as though she was a prop as he spoke to Cort. "There are many different opinions about topping from the bottom. Personally, I don't like it. I can't see you enjoying it either. Many subs—not all, but I've dealt with several—will try to top from the bottom without even knowing they're doing it. They may be bratty or demanding. From my experience, it's because they need to see who's in control."

"She knows I'm not."

"Exactly. But she wants you to be, don't you, pet?" Dominik tapped Akira's cheek, grinning at her little scowl. "I've played games like this with her because it's easier for her to leave her comfort zone. Which means sometimes I have an unruly little sub on my hands." His teeth flashed as he set them into the side of Akira's neck. She jerked, then moaned, squirming under the press of his body. "In this scene, you are her teacher and she needs to please you to pass."

Cort's lips curved slightly. He had a feeling the other man recalled his original interest in this very room. Probably wasn't too hard to put two and two together. What man didn't have some kind of fantasy about the naughty schoolgirl? Not a real one—teenage girls were confusing creatures and he didn't do kids—but a woman playing the part?

*Oh, hell yeah.* He nodded, then jerked his chin at Dominik. "If I'm the teacher, what does that make you?"

"The principal. I'm ready to expel our little delinquent biker wannabe, but you've convinced me to give her another chance."

All right, this he could do. Oddly enough, it didn't bother him to see Dominik handling Akira. No matter how sexual things became, this was nothing but a way for Cort to become the man Akira needed. He felt strangely comfortable with Dominik—maybe because the man was straight-up about his intentions.

The fact that he had other subs helped too.

"Sir, he's lying to you." Akira batted her eyelashes and gave Dominik a sweet little smile. "My grades are excellent. I pass every test."

"You got an F on the last one." Cort rested his hip against the teacher's desk, his own smile sly. "You're a smart little thing, but you must think I'm stupid. I see the way you look at me. You tease me, wearing those short skirts with no panties, sucking on those lollipops to make me hard before you leave with those boys who follow you like little puppies. I've been patient, but I'm done."

"Y-you can't do—" Akira pressed her lips together, her brow furrowing as though she was considering how far she really wanted to take this. Then she rolled her eyes. "Fuck it. You're an asshole if you fail me just because I won't suck your fu—"

Dominik slapped his hand over her mouth and arched a brow at Cort. "You allow your students to speak to you this way?"

"No." Cort frowned at Akira, which took an effort because her little pout when Dominik moved his hand was adorable. "That's another issue I've had with her. The language."

"She deserves to fail. And to be expelled." Dominik straightened and shook his head. "Such a shame. With my recommendation, she could have gotten in to Harvard."

Akira shook her head quickly. "No! Please, Sir! You'll ruin me!"

Dominik smirked. "I'd like to, but the way you flaunt yourself around, I'm not sure you can give either me or Mr. Nash anything worth having."

"I can! I might tease a lot, but I don't sleep with those boys. I only want . . ." Her teeth worried her bottom lip as she lifted her eyes to meet Cort's. And damn, that look melted his heart. That look wasn't part of the game. "I only want you."

"And I want you, but you've been so very bad." He couldn't stand aside anymore. He had to touch her. Smoothing one hand over her cheek, he tilted his head to one side. "You need to be punished."

"Then punish me. I'll do anything—just don't fail me." She pleaded with him with her eyes. "Don't send me away."

Taking the rope out of its plastic wrapping, Dominik glanced up at Cort. "I'll leave this up to you, Mr. Nash. If she will accept my punishment, and you are willing to give her a pass, she may stay."

Cort trailed his fingers down Akira's throat, over her shoulder, then down the bare expanse of her back. She looked all hot and badass in the biker chick costume, but, somehow, still delicate and . . . so damn gorgeous. Not just her body, but the little things, like the quiver in her lips as she tried to stay serious about playing her part. The glow of excitement in her eyes as she waited for him to make his decision. Yes, she trusted him not to hurt her, but there was more to it. She was trusting him to follow through. To go down a dark path with her, balancing on a kinky fucking line of things most people wouldn't understand.

But he understood. As her eyes drifted shut, he could sense the peace coming over her. She felt safe with him. Not only physically, but emotionally. This place, these people, took her away from all the things that haunted her.

And so would he.

"She'll take the punishment. I think this one's got potential." He kissed her cheek, then backed away, falling into character. "If you can make her a little more manageable, I think she'd make an excellent little sex toy."

"I agree." Dominik rolled her skirt up over her ass, then

laughed. "Apparently she only forgets panties on test days. She remembered them today."

*Kill me now.* All the leather and metal and she was wearing a transparent. white lace thong. The contrast made him feel like he was taking something pure. And really, he was. No matter how many times he was with her, she retained that innocence. How could a girl be kinky and yet come off as almost virginal? He traced a finger down the soft edge of the thong along the soft curve of her ass. *You're fucking damned, man.*

His lips quirked.

*"Highway to Hell" has always been one of my favorite songs.*

"Do you have a knife?" Cort's jaw tensed when Akira stiffened. Fuck, so much for just going for it. He'd fucking scared her.

Dominik shook his head even as he pulled a folding knife out of his pocket. "I do. And I like the way your mind works. She won't be needing these."

Cort watched Dominik stroking Akira's back, not saying a word, but somehow getting her to relax. She didn't move as he slid the blade under the thin strip of lace on her hip.

Shit, he didn't want to pull her out of her zone, but he had to ask. "Bringing up the knife bothered her, but you used it anyway?"

"I know Akira's limits. It's good that you noticed, but a reaction doesn't always mean you have to stop. If it makes you more comfortable, vocalize your concerns. Make sure she hasn't forgotten her safeword." Dominik tugged at Akira's hair. "What color, little one?"

"Green." Her eyes held a daze that made Cort smile. He hadn't ruined this for her. "But I *was* bad. Will it hurt?"

"Not this time." Dominik continued his instructions even as he took a knee behind Akira, rope in hand. "Akira and I have played together for months. She can read my intentions, feel assurance from the slightest pause. I gave her enough time to remember that I would never use a knife on her flesh." He began wrapping the rope around her thighs, over her knees. "You'll know when you reach that point."

"Okay. But if I have to ask, it won't be as intense as it is now." Cort looked down at the ruined panties, crumpled on the floor near Akira's feet. "I don't want her to feel like she has to teach me."

"She won't have to. Besides myself, there are many Doms here that can help you. If you want to keep some anticipation in your play, do the negotiations with them in private. Your discussions with Akira can revolve around any current issues she has. Lingering pains. Insecurities. Anything about your last scene that didn't work for her." Dominik neatly tied the rope midway down Akira's calves, then went to the head of the desk to tie her wrists together. "You're impulsive, and that will work for her, but you have to find a way to manage your own doubts. And your limits. She can't set them for you any more than you can set hers."

"Got it." The way the man put it was so fucking logical. But he didn't make Cort feel like an idiot. Dominik was a lot like Cort's auto body teacher in high school. The teacher knew Cort wouldn't graduate—his stepfather's lifestyle was too tempting with all the money and the women—but he'd seen something in Cort that he wanted to reach. That teacher was the reason Cort had gone back to trade school so he could work on cars for a living instead of using pain and threats to collect debts.

Akira could do better than him. She could find a man whose only prospects didn't involve coming home covered in grease every day. But taking this step toward learning to be her Dom gave him an edge. Because other men may have more to offer financially. And in breeding and all that crap. But they couldn't give her this.

Dominik studied him for a moment, then grinned and smacked Akira's butt. "Lines on the chalkboard, girl. 'I will not swear. I know my manners.'"

"Okay . . ." Akira shook her hair away from her face as she stood up straight. Then she looked down at her bound wrists and legs. "But how am I supposed to—"

"I've hobbled you before, pet. You know how," Dominik said.

"Ugh! Fine!" Akira jutted her chin up, moving with stilted

steps to the blackboard. She struggled to position the chalk in her hand, the way her wrists were bound making it difficult. "How many times?"

"Until we think you've learned." Cort didn't wait for Dominik to take the lead. He had his own expectations. He wanted to see the submission he'd earned on a few wonderful, rare instances. There was no way he'd miss that coming from her if it was real. But he knew his own limitations. "Or if we can't keep our hands off you any longer."

Akira pouted as she lifted her hands, chalk at the ready. "Meaning you can now?"

"Meaning I will. It's gonna be tough." He kissed her shoulder and let out a heavy sigh. "But you deserve better than a pushover. You need a man." He forced himself to put some distance between them so she could carry out her punishment. "And I will be that man."

\* \* \* \*

Being hobbled was *horrible*. Akira hated having to take tiny steps, hated the restricted movements, hated the ropes digging into her thighs and making it almost impossible to bend her knees.

And yet . . . she loved it.

Her biggest fear in submitting to Cort *and* Dominik had been that they would be an unbending force that would smother her, take all the fun out of what she had with Cort. Instead, they'd managed to set up a nice, big playground for her to let loose in. Not in a way that she could run wild, but in a way that she could truly express herself. Feel the give and take of a D/s relationship.

Still, she was a little pissy about having to write lines with chalk she couldn't hold right and every restricted step along the length of the blackboard a struggle. She could picture both Cort and Dominik behind her, Dominik reclined in the big chair behind the teacher's desk. Cort propped up on one of the smaller desks. Here she was, sizzling inside and out with desire, and they were just watching her. Waiting.

She hated the waiting more than anything. Because sometimes it was hard to know what was expected. Would pushing for another punishment be more fun? Were they waiting for her to act up so they could step it up a notch?

But no, she knew Dominik better than that. Her wrist grew sore as she moved on to the fifth line. The ropes around her legs dug into her skin. He was behaving pretty relaxed—for him anyway—but there was no mistaking this for "funishment." He might not have made it obvious to Cort, but he wasn't happy with her.

*"I will not swear. I know my manners."*

The words hadn't meant much before, but looking at them— *really* looking at them for the first time—she suddenly understood. She wasn't being fair to Cort. She'd said as much, but the "I know my manners" was Dominik's way of saying he'd taught her better than this.

Cort's interest in the lifestyle stemmed from pleasing her. As a sub, she craved her Dom's approval, but had she ever really tried to earn his? After all he'd done to earn her submission, her respect . . . her love.

A single tear traced a warm path down her cheek. Then another. Cort had given his all, but she hadn't done the same. And she had no excuses. She'd been spoiled by a Dom who could cut her off at every wrong turn. And had taken advantage of one who couldn't.

"'I will not swear. I know my manners.'" She said the words even as she wrote them, blinking away the blinding tears. "'I will not swear. I know my manners.'"

"That's enough." Cort strode up to her and took the chalk out of her hand, tossing it aside. His brow creased as he held her face between his hands. "I'm not mad at you. Do you get that? I'm not crazy about you swearing because it's not you, but . . . whatever. Just tell me you're okay."

Her bottom lip trembled as she tipped her head back to look

into his eyes, darkened with a fierce protectiveness she'd never expected. Dominik had given it to her, but she never *expected* it. Not from anyone. Her father loved her, but even he couldn't stop what those men—

*No! Don't think of them!*

But it was too late. She was already hearing their words. Their threats. Her father was so close, but even if he knew, he couldn't stop it from happening. He hadn't even been able to testify at the trial because he knew the men's families. Anything he said could mean his death. If the men who had raped her condemned themselves without his testimony, only they would pay. But if he got involved . . .

Thankfully, the prosecutor hadn't needed anything other than Akira's statements. And the reports from the doctors about the damage that had been done. She'd needed stitches because they'd—oh, God, she could almost feel her flesh tearing again as they ripped into her body—

"Akira, now is when you say red." Dominik's wide chest filled her vision. Through the corner of her eye, she saw Cort, whose face was pale, as though he believed all this was his fault.

But it wasn't. And she didn't want to say red. She didn't want to stop. Her whole body was shaking, but she refused to give the men who'd hurt her that kind of power five years later.

But she had to say something. Dominik had taught her not to ignore her reactions. Had taught her how to face them head-on. She swallowed and pressed her eyes shut. "Yellow. I need a second. I saw . . ."

"Tell me."

That sounded like something Dominik would say, but it was Cort who made the request, his tone gentle, his eyes full of concern. She managed to bring herself back to that room. A playroom in Blades & Ice.

"I saw them taking me. R-raping me." She shook her head before either Cort or Dominik could think it was anything they'd done. "The way you both look at me—like you want to protect me

. . ." Damn it, Cort would believe this was all on him. But she'd been here before. "It's happened with you, Dominik. I'm really okay."

"I know you are." Dominik approached her, then brought her head to his chest. "In cases like this, it's better to continue slowly, but continue nonetheless. She's with us. There's no point in letting her dwell. It's good that she feels we could have protected her, but the present is what she needs."

"Fine, but she's been punished enough." Cort's tone held a finality Akira had never heard before. No one questioned Dominik.

She wasn't sure how she felt about Cort doing so now.

Dominik frowned. "If you let this shift the direction of the scenes, it may do so in the future. She needs consistency."

"She'll have it." Cort nuzzled her cheek, putting a bit of pressure on her shoulder to bring her to her knees. "She knows I won't punish myself for her mistakes. And I want her now. If she's very good, I may let her enjoy it."

On her hands and knees, Akira looked from one man to the other, unsure of who was in charge. Which made the solid floor under her hands unsteady. Her instincts led her to Cort, to trying to anticipate his desires. But he was so hard to read. Her palms slipped on the floor as she remained where he'd placed her, waiting for a clue of what she was supposed to do next.

"How much is an A worth to you, Tiny?" Cort was still in the game, but not completely. He knelt behind her, his knees outside hers, and held his body close. "Can I have you? Can I use your body and let the man who brought you to me take whatever I can spare?"

"Yes." *Oh yes.* And she loved him so much more for wanting to give Dominik that much. "I-I can say nothing but yes."

"That's all I need, babe." The sound of Cort unzipping his jeans made her breath catch. The rip of a condom wrapper, then a . . . buzzing. A firm, blunt round thing pressed against her clit, and Cort pushed the end of the vibrator between her thighs. If she relaxed, it slipped away from where it needed to be. So she tensed to keep it there even as he kissed his way down her spine. The sound of a zipper had her anticipating . . . anticipating . . .

Cort stood and his footsteps receded a few paces. Dominik stepped up to her side. The hot raindrop lick of the flogger hit the fleshy part of her ass. She jerked, struggling to hold on to the vibrator as the flogger hit her twice more.

"Move your wrist like this and control where each strike falls." Dominik's hands curved over her butt cheek, several inches apart. "See if you can hit between my hands."

Pure torture. Dominik had Cort flog the same area over and over until the stinging sensation almost overpowered the forceful pleasure of the vibrator. Then he moved to the other side, correcting Cort when the lashes didn't fall right. Dominik's fingers dug into her flesh every time she wiggled, keeping her from giving in to her need to reach the building climax. She half wanted to beg, to cry that it was too hard to keep waiting while Dominik gave his lesson, but the submissive part of her took over. Drowned out the impatience. Brought her to the sweet, calm, giving place that was so much more fulfilling than surrendering to rash urges.

She stilled under Dominik's hand, practically glowing from the inside out as he stroked her butt and whispered words of approval she couldn't quite make out. But she didn't need the words. She could sense how pleased he was. Feel the atmosphere in the room change as Cort's confidence grew.

The heat covering her skin as the flogging continued sank in deeper and deeper. As the lashes came a little harder, she became more aware of her tight, sore little clit, almost overstimulated at this point. Her senses drifted to the scent of leather and sweat. The aroma of light, fresh cologne and pure masculine musk. She could taste the saltiness of her own sweat on her lips, breathe in the scent of sex.

Her arousal bloomed like a flower of flame, and she took slow breaths to tamp it down. Her hair was wet and cool against her cheeks, and she dropped her head down to keep it out of her eyes. The hands she pressed flat against the ground were slippery.

Focusing on these little things kept her from letting go. From taking what wasn't hers.

Dominik—no, *Cort*, would tell her when he wanted her release.

"Such a good girl." Cort bent down behind her, turning off the vibrator. He kissed one blazing hot butt cheek. "If that didn't earn a pass, I don't know what will."

She bit back a groan as he gently took the vibrator away. Any movement came close to setting her off, but she wouldn't let go. "Thank you, Sir."

"How you doing, Tiny?" Cort pressed his fingertips into the fire covering her ass, causing it to flare up. "Sore?"

"Oh, no. No pain. Nothing but you." Would he understand what she meant? Her fuzzy brain wanted to know, but he'd tell her if she'd done bad. But she knew she hadn't. The knowledge made her smile. "I didn't fail."

"No, you didn't. You're definitely an asset to this school." Dominik knelt in front of her, his curved hand on her cheek bringing her head up. "Is your mouth dry? Can you tell me if you need a minute?"

Need a minute? As in stop? Panic almost took hold, but a quiet voice in her head told her it was all right for him to ask. All she had to do was answer to let him know she wasn't too far gone to continue. It took an effort to get the words out. "I don't need anything, Sir. I want to stay here."

Cort smoothed his hands over her sides. The ropes on her thighs suddenly loosened and fell away. Those around her wrists quickly followed. "She sounds different. If I didn't know better, I'd say she was drunk."

"She's doing well. Floating a little in subspace, but not so much that you have to worry about taking advantage of her."

"So she could say no if this wasn't something she wanted?"

"Yes and no. She's more in tune to your pleasure than her own, but that's not a bad thing. She's completely surrendered to her trust in us both, and she won't regret anything that happens."

The men's voices were clear, and she understood what they

were saying, but none of it shifted her from the breezy, relaxed feeling of being exactly where she needed to be. The moisture in her mouth matched the hot slickness down low and told her she was ready for them. More than ready.

All the emptiness ached. But then Cort said something to her and she felt him, thick and hard, pushing into her. A slick, stretching glide and he settled in as deep as he could, his fist positioned at the base of his cock. He reached down to pull her bra up above her breasts, squeezing one as he eased in and out.

"I can go now. You've proven yourself to be competent, despite how new you are." Dominik leaned over to press a light kiss on her lips as she gasped at the slow drag of Cort's dick. "She's all yours."

Cort stopped moving, petting along the arch of her back, his tone low and firm. "We started this scene together, and I know her well enough to say she won't feel right if you walk out without . . . a token of our gratitude."

Dominik chuckled. "A token? Most men wouldn't offer up a 'token' from their girlfriend so freely."

"What about most Doms?" Cort slid out almost all the way, then thrust in so hard her lips parted at the violent rush of pleasure. "Give him your mouth, Tiny."

*Yes!* She kept her lips parted, not sure she could love Cort any more than she did right now. This had all begun with Dominik, her ability to be touched. To feel passion without feeling dirty and afraid. It ending with nothing but a few kisses and touches would leave her feeling like things were left . . . not quite unsaid, but *unexpressed.* She couldn't take all Dominik had given her without giving something back.

Something only she could give. He could have a thousand subs who would never thank him in a way that had him looking back and smiling at the memories. She needed him to be able to do that when he thought of her.

The one thing about Dominik she'd never questioned was how quickly he could really see what she needed when she was in full giving mode. Without speaking again, he unlaced his leathers, freeing his fully erect dick. He held her jaw and guided himself between her lips. She savored the taste of him, hot and slightly salty and sweet. He always tasted fresh, like a gulp from a sun-heated spring. But it was the way he held her gaze as he glided into her mouth that was her true reward. As though he understood why she was doing this.

Which let her fall into the pleasure the two men gave her. The giving, the receiving, the amazing place where she could simply go with it all. Cort matched Dominik's pace as it grew rougher, faster. And she sped toward climax as though she'd just taken a dive off a board high above a pool that would be tranquil until she made contact. But the fall came in slow motion, her desire to offer up her release rather than take it prolonging her body's crash into the water below.

"Tell her." Dominik made a gruff sound in his throat as he thrust into her mouth. "Tell her to come."

Cort latched on to her hip with one hand, moving faster. "But a woman can't just come on demand. She needs me to—"

"This one can. She won't until you do."

*I won't! I can't!* She couldn't let her body's betrayal take over. Her pleasure had to come from the man she gave herself to. Willingly. Because if not—

"Akira, show me." Cort pistoned in and out, spreading her open, grinding out each word. "Show me what he's taught you. Show me that you can give me that part of you, that you can't hold back anymore."

A request, rather than a command, but her mind didn't get a say in this. She clamped her lips down on Dominik, swallowing as he came, her eyes tearing as her body crashed into wave after wave of viscous pleasure, more like diving into the ocean during a storm than a pool from any height. She was grateful when Dominik pulled away, because she could let out the scream that reminded her that she could breathe. That she wouldn't drown in the sensations threatening to drag her under.

But it wasn't enough until she felt Cort's dick pulsing inside her with his own release. Only then was she completely satisfied. Sated.

And drained.

Her legs were wobbly as Cort hauled her to her feet. He seemed to notice, because he picked her right up and sat her in his lap as he sat behind the teacher's desk.

Dominik pulled a bottle of water from the top drawer and handed it to Cort. Then dropped a bag of Hershey's Kisses on the desk before him. "She never really *needs* it, but she enjoys being fed some treats after a scene." He bent down as she curled up in Cort's lap. "Thank you, pet. The next time I see you, I will be no different than any Dom here who's not yours, but we will always have this."

She laid her head on Cort's shoulder, feeling a little drowsy, but so happy. Smiling, she let out a contented sigh. "Not like any other Dom, but not mine. And it's okay, because you'll belong to someone special. Like I do."

"You do." Dominik moved toward the door, pausing for an instant to return her smile. "I feel good about leaving you with him, but if you ever need me . . ."

There was no doubt in her as she nodded, her eyes drifting shut. Cort's hard chest under her, his arms around her, made this the perfect place to be. Not only now, but always. "I feel good knowing you're there. For us both."

But after Dominik was gone, even as she giggled while Cort fed her the chocolate and made sure she sipped the water, one thought haunted her. *Who* would be good enough for the man she'd called "Sir" when every other man scared her so much? She had to be as accepting of whoever he chose as he'd been for her.

Only . . . would he ever choose anyone? Or would he simply keep giving without asking for anything lasting in return? That was one thing she couldn't give him. That he'd never asked from her. Because he'd chosen once. And ended up with nothing.

At least she'd left him with something, but he deserved so much more.

*He'll get it. He has to.* She nuzzled her face into Cort's neck, happy that she'd found the one that she could give the *more* to. Because he deserved it too.

And seemed to read exactly where her thoughts were at.

"A man like him won't be alone long, Tiny. Not with all he has to offer." Cort kissed her forehead and fed her some chocolate that had begun to melt between his fingers as she was lost in thought. "As soon as he allows it, he'll have someone who can make him happy."

"As happy as we are?" Akira's mind was perfectly clear now. Which left her fixated on absolutely everyone being happy and— okay, maybe she was still floating a little. She was grateful that Cort was so comfortable to cuddle with. That he made getting up and annoying everyone with her idealistic haze a to-do-later thing. "Sorry, I'm in a spreading the joy mood."

"Good, because so am I." Cort chuckled as she tipped her head back and raised one eyebrow. "Hey, you think you're the only one wondering if it's okay to go out there smiling? With how things went with the . . ." Guilt darkened Cort's eyes, and what he said next made it seem like he thought he had much more control than he did. "With the last game. Damn. You made me forget, Tiny. People put that stuff aside here?"

"Sometimes." She grinned because it was sweet that Cort was worried about the players who were present tonight. He wasn't a fan, so he was either worried because of her or . . . or Ford. She wrinkled her nose as she considered what Ford was doing tonight. Was he practicing with the whip? Doing a scene with a pretty little newbie sub who was all impressed with all he'd learned? She didn't see him too worried about the loss. Like every other night, he'd be the chatty bartender all the girls flocked to. Or the Dom-in-training all the subs wanted to experiment with.

For a second, she wondered if he'd watched her leave with Cort and Dominik. If it had bothered him.

Because she didn't want it to. She didn't want any reaction from him at all.

She wanted him to move on. *Really*. It would be best if he did.

"Some are better with the losses." She took a deep breath as she fixed her clothes and pushed off Cort's lap, even though she wanted to stay right there all night. "Some hold on and get all bitter. It's kinda sad to see."

Cort stood and caught her wrists, studying her face. "Does that bother you? We could go back to my place. Or yours. I know you're invested in the team. I don't want anything to ruin where you're at now. Seeing them—"

She shook her head. Seeing *Ford* all pissy about the loss wouldn't bother her at all. And if he was sulking behind the bar, she'd just handle it like she always did. She'd ignore him. He didn't have the power to take her out of her happy place. "I'm good. More than good. Because of you."

"Any Dom that don't like to hear that?"

"None that I know of." She kept close to Cort as they left the theme room, positive nothing could ruin her good mood.

Until she saw that Ford was perfectly fine. Without her. And crossing boundaries he shouldn't. And wouldn't again, if she had a say.

# Chapter Seventeen

ord would never see breath strips the same way again. He almost grinned as he recalled the way the pretty, bound sub had moaned as he let it melt on her clit under his tongue, but the tears now soaking through his T-shirt made him feel like a jerk for even thinking about smiling. The scene had ended with her using her safeword after Pischlar slid a small butt-plug-shaped piece of ginger into her ass.

Apparently, some found it pleasurable, and she'd been all for trying it, but it was just too much for her. So now both he and Pischlar were sitting on a sofa near the bar, doing their best to comfort her. Pischlar wanted to take her home to soak in a bath and get rid of the lingering pain. She refused to budge. Seemed moving only made it burn more. So she'd curled up on Ford's lap while Pischlar spoke softly to her and petted her hair.

*Poor thing. Hope it goes away soon.*

Only once her tears had stopped did she lift her head, giving Ford a shaky smile. "Sorry for being such a baby about this. I liked everything else."

"Don't even worry about it, Sahara." Ford kissed her cheek. "I'm glad you wanted to play even though it didn't go so well. You looked so sad before."

She wrinkled her nose and glanced over at an intense whipping scene being led by the Cobra's new owner. Keane had paused the scene when Sahara had safeworded, giving Pischlar a hard look, then a nod of approval when the other Dom efficiently ended the scene and began aftercare, but Ford didn't think telling Sahara about that would do her any good now. It wasn't a secret that she had a thing for the older man. Or that Keane had no interest in taking her on. The man tended to choose experienced subs closer to his own age.

Sahara obviously wasn't beneath his notice, but she might as well be. She didn't need a reminder that Keane was looking out for her the same way he would any sub here. Doing scenes with other Doms rather than just watching them all was a good first step away from wanting someone she couldn't have.

Except that step had turned into more of a trip.

"Is it horrible that I want to stay? I feel a bit better." She cleared her throat. "I really like watching. Imagining what I could be—" She cleared her throat again. "Ah—"

"Is your mouth dry, sweetie?" Ford let his grin loose as Sahara ducked her head and nodded. "You wanna stay with Pischlar while I—"

"No! Don't go—" Sahara made a face and rolled her eyes. "I am so pathetic."

"Stop that." He felt a bit better knowing his holding her was helping. "You want Pischlar here too?"

Pischlar smiled and stood. "I'll just be a sec, pet, then—"

"Ugh, I'm hopeless. It's just . . . I did the scene with both of you. I . . . having you both here all calm and being so sweet makes me feel like I didn't screw up too bad."

"Can't say I don't like hearing that." Pischlar kissed her shoulder, then called out. "Akira, can you get us a bottle of water, honey?"

One look at Akira's narrowed eyes before she strode off to the bar had Ford's pulse picking up a notch. *She isn't fucking pissed off, is she?* He caught Cort's eye as his friend stopped short, watching Akira as she got the bottle of water. Cort frowned and seemed to inhale very, very slowly. He moved to cut Akira off as she returned.

"Akira—"

"Excuse me, Sir." Akira sidled past Cort.

Ford eased Sahara out of his lap into Pischlar's, standing before Akira could get too close. He wasn't sure what her problem was, but Sahara didn't need to be in the line of fire. "Hey, is there something—"

Akira slammed the bottle of water into his chest. "Here's your fucking water. And—and I hate you again. How could you say all that shit to me, then do this?"

*This?* He had no clue what she was talking about, but that really wasn't the issue right now. He took the water, his lips thinning as he met her flashing eyes. "Go home, Akira."

"Don't play the Dom with me, Ford." Akira hissed out a breath, speaking low. "Does she know you only became a Dom to get with me? That you're using her to—"

"Not another word, shorty." He moved toward her, forcing her back a few paces, surprised that Cort hadn't stepped in yet. Or even Dominik, who was within hearing of her little outburst. "I *am* a Dom here. I earned the position. And I'm in the middle of aftercare."

Behind him, he heard Sahara whisper Akira's name.

"Pass me the water, Ford." Pischlar took the water, then picked Sahara up. He had one hand pressed over her ear as he stopped by Ford's side. "I'll be in The Office if you want to check on her."

"I will." He gritted his teeth as Pischlar disappeared with Sahara down the hall past the main room. Then turned his attention back to Akira. "I earned a lot of you being pissed at me from the thing with Jami, but I don't deserve this."

"Stay away from my friends." Akira jutted her chin up, hands on her hips, looking like a little, dark avenging angel in all that leather.

But despite how hot she was, her words made him laugh. "Don't go there. Seriously."

"You fucking bastard! You're going to compare—"

"Stop." Dominik held up his hand, though it took only a look to get Akira to snap her lips shut. And to replace the anger in her eyes with shame. He glanced at Cort who seemed stunned to silence, then shook his head and turned to Akira again. "You've embarrassed your Dom. He's very new, so I can let him not taking you in hand slide, but you *know* better."

"I'm sorry, Sir. I just—"

"Silence." Dominik gave her his back, focusing on Ford and Cort. "Cort, you're her Dom. I know you're uncomfortable with punishments, but I won't let this behavior slide. Either you discipline her, or she has to leave until you can."

Cort rubbed his jaw, his shoulders tense, as though just the thought of punishing her—or maybe of her getting kicked out of the club—bothered him. But then he nodded slowly and rolled his shoulders back as he dropped his hand to his side. "I think Ford should punish her."

Ford only heard the agreement in Cort's tone at first, but then the rest registered and he could only stare at the man. "What?"

"She interrupted the aftercare you were giving. She insulted you." Cort's gaze leveled with Ford's. "She needs your forgiveness. Not mine."

*Fuck. Just . . . Fuck!* In what messed up parallel universe would Akira ever need *his* forgiveness? Yeah, he wasn't too happy about what Akira had pulled, but punish her? He glanced her way and his throat tightened at the pleading in her eyes. She'd been told not to speak, so she wouldn't, but he could tell she wanted him to do it. To find some way to take away all her guilt with a few strikes of the cane or a belt or kneeling on unsharpened pencils he'd forced her to line up perfectly . . .

He could come up with a dozen ways to punish her. Could probably make her cry with a few harsh words at this point.

*No.*

If she submitted to him, even for this, he wasn't sure he could simply walk away after and keep pretending he was happy for her and Cort. He'd punished other subs, held them after, and told them it was all better now. But he wasn't in love with them.

*I can't do this.*

"Ford—Sir?" Akira blinked fast and swallowed audibly. "Please. I'm sorry, please just—"

"No." He took a step toward the bar, stopped, spun around

because he needed to make sure Sahara was okay. He couldn't look at Akira again. All he could do was put the responsibility back where it belonged. "I'll be satisfied with whatever your Dom decides."

"I've made my decision," Cort said, his tone hard.

"Then you'll have to live with it." Ford moved out of hearing, hesitating at the end of the hall to see Cort leading Akira to coat check. Then out of the club.

* * * *

Two weeks had gone by since the scene at the club—namely the one that made it so Cort couldn't return with Akira—and he was fucking fed up. Ford was handling stuff at the Delgado Forum again, fully involved now with his position as Performance Director and assistant to the community relations director, which meant that he was always at the Forum.

And Akira wasn't dealing with that all too well.

Since Cort worked mostly at night at the bar and work was slow at the shop, he was able to meet with Akira for lunch whenever she had practice and pick her up after. She used the Forum gym daily, so her chances of running into Ford were high. And every time she did, it was bad.

This time was no different.

Standing in the hall, holding Akira's skates while she searched her gym bag for her ringing cell phone, Cort spotted Ford coming out of the coach's office. He quickly fished his own cell out of his pocket and handed it to her.

"It's probably Jami—weren't you supposed to meet her later to go shopping or something?" Cort really hoped Ford just got on the elevator and out of sight before Akira noticed him. He couldn't take much more of them sniping at each other. "I'll drop you off after we eat—"

Akira shook her head, finally pulling her phone out from under a few neatly rolled up towels. She stood, expression composed, and tugged her wool coat straight over her blue skinny jeans. "I see him, Cort. Don't worry, I won't say a thing. He's not worth it."

"Good to know." Ford joined them, nodding to Cort before giving Akira a bland smile. "I do need you to say something, though. Your name isn't on the list of girls signed up for the mentorship program with the girls' club. I thought it would be something that would interest you."

"It does." Akira's face went red. "I didn't know there was a sheet."

"I told you last week."

"Yes, well, I usually block out your voice—you rarely have anything important to say." Akira's tone didn't match her harsh words. Cort could tell she was finally getting that this grudge she had with Ford was going too far. She tugged at her bottom lip with her teeth as she glanced up at Ford—who thankfully hadn't commented on her little jibe. "I'll go sign up now."

"Thank you." Ford moved to walk past her, pressing his eyes shut when she put her hand on his arm. "What is it, Akira?"

Akira jerked her hand away as though just realizing she'd touched him. "Is that all?"

"That's all. I told you I wouldn't bother you anymore." Ford's jaw tensed slightly. "I meant it."

She didn't budge until Ford was out of sight, but Cort could read the emotions crossing her face so clearly she might as well have screamed them. She was confused, hurt, and she wanted to fix things with Ford. But she didn't know how.

Cort hated seeing her like this—hated feeling like there was nothing he could do. He'd let her make Ford a topic they couldn't discuss for too long. That was about to change.

Taking her bag, then her hand, Cort led her out to the parking garage, speaking softly. "This can't go on, Tiny. I need you to tell me how to help you. If it's because of the club, I'll speak to Dominik."

Letting out a heavy sigh, Akira hesitated by the passenger's side door he opened for her. "But you won't punish me?"

"No. I'm sorry, Akira, but I don't think that would do you any good—even if I was willing to." He tried to keep his tone neutral, with a little bit of sympathy slipping in that he couldn't quite contain. He didn't want his reactions leading what she chose to share.

It took half the drive to her place, but she eventually started spilling. "It should be Ford punishing me anyway. It's pretty obvious why he won't."

"Is it?" Cort kept his eyes on the snow-slicked road, but his grip tightened on the wheel. *Here we go.*

"He doesn't care about me anymore," Akira said, her voice small. "I got what I wanted."

Cort didn't reply at first, because he wasn't sure what the hell he could possibly say to that. Not just her words, but all that was behind them. A longing, an emptiness, the same kind he saw in Ford's eyes every time Cort caught him watching her. The two people who meant more to him than anything in the world were tearing each other apart.

He pulled up in front of Akira's apartment, reaching over before she blindly opened the door and pulling her close. He tipped her chin up with a finger and kissed her lips until some color returned to her pale cheeks. Then he smiled. "You didn't get what you wanted, Tiny." He put his finger over her lips before she could interrupt. "But you will."

\* \* \* \*

"I want a baby."

Akira's head shot up from where she lay on her stomach on the floor, flipping through a catalog of designs for uniforms Silver had asked her to look at. Sahara knocked her glass of wine over on the coffee table.

Jami didn't seem to notice their reactions. "Can you picture it? A little boy with Sebastian's eyes—or . . ." She laughed, a dreamy expression on her face. "Luke with a little girl. They'd both make amazing fathers, and . . . I think I'd be a good mom." She took another sip from her wine glass. "I'd be there anyway. That's something?"

Sahara gently took the wine away from Jami and slipped off the sofa. "All right, I think you've had enough."

"That was my first one." Jami frowned. "What? It's not a bad idea. Luke's mom hints about it every time I see her. It's adorable, really. If I ask for seconds at supper, she gives Luke this little happy smile."

Akira closed the catalog and pushed back onto her knees. "I know you love Luke's mom, sweetie, but you can't have a baby just to make her happy."

"It's not just about her. I love them. I want to make a family with them, and why not do it while I'm young?" Jami leaned her elbow on the arm of the sofa, resting her head on her hand. "I talked to my doctor and he got me to do a bunch of tests. I shouldn't have the problems Silver had. I'm healthy and everything." She blushed, wetting her lips with her tongue. "I didn't get my last birth control shot."

*Oh, this isn't good.* Akira inched closer to Jami, taking her hand. "Did you tell Sebastian? Or Luke?"

"Of course I did! I'm not trying to trap them." Jami pursed her lips. "Sebastian decided both he and Luke will wear condoms all the time now. Until we 'discuss it further.'"

*Jami's Master is a very smart man.* Some of Akira's worry eased up. But she wanted to keep Jami talking. Yes, sometimes Jami decided things out of nowhere. Nothing like this, though. Which meant she'd been thinking about it for a while. Akira eased up onto the sofa beside Jami, thanking Sahara quietly for refilling her glass of lemon water.

"Have you talked to your mother recently?" Akira took a sip of her flavored water to get the bitter taste of bringing up *that* woman out of her mouth.

Jami's brow lifted. "Who? Silver? Yep. Just last night. Landon's therapy is going well, Amia learned how to say 'puck'—she hopes—and she thinks I'm too young. I hung up on her."

"Oh, Jami." Akira sighed. "I meant . . . ugh, never mind. What about your dad?"

"Dad would freak!" Jami shook her head quickly. "I'll tell him when—*if*—it ever happens. Then he has to be happy and can't kill his grandchild's fathers."

There was clearly no talking Jami out of this crazy idea. And trying would probably get her storming into her room. Akira was only a year older than Jami, but sometimes it felt like a lot more. Jami still had some growing up to do. Sometimes she could be very mature, but other times . . .

"Hey, I meant to ask—are you and Ford still fighting?" Jami's lips curled up slightly at Akira's groan. "What? I thought we were sharing drama?"

"There's nothing between me and Ford!"

"I didn't say there was!" Jami huffed out a laugh as she pulled Akira into her arms. "Don't get all upset. We are *not* breaking up as best friends again. I almost rebounded to Braxton Richards, and the boy can't do anything but stutter when a girl talks to him!"

"He's shy." Akira grinned, all too ready to move on from the baby—and worse, *Ford*—topics. "Did you see the segment of 'Following the Cobras' when the guys were ribbing him about his mom buying his suits? His face was so red! I was glad that Luke and Tyler stuck up for him."

"Yeah, but now they're calling them 'momma's boys united'!"

"Better than the 'trouble triplets'!" Akira couldn't stop laughing at that one. Jami had told her a little about what had happened when Luke had finally gotten home the day after the drunken piercing and tattoo incident. Sebastian hadn't punished the young man, but had casually warned Luke that Chicklet may want his balls on a platter for corrupting her sub. And Sebastian hadn't decided whether or not to stop her from taking them. She cocked her head thoughtfully. "I wonder if they have a nickname for us."

"Yep. Bunnies on Ice." Jami shrugged as Sahara and Akira stared at her. "Hey, I didn't come up with it. I'm trying out again, you know."

"You are?" A broad smile brightened Sahara's face and made her eyes sparkle. "That would be awesome! We can help you practice routines and—"

"One sec." Jami checked her buzzing phone, then stood as she answered. "Hey! Yeah, she's—gotcha. Don't worry about me. You take care of *her*." She hung up and cleared her throat. "Sahara, you wanna come help me make those . . . umm, cupcakes? For the bake sale at Casey's school? Becky's swamped with work, and she asked if I'd mind."

"Ah, how about I cook and you lick the spoon." Sahara headed for the kitchen. "You coming, Akira?"

"No!" Jami hooked her arm with Sahara's, dragging her forward. "She's busy."

*I am?* Akira watched them go, then froze as the front door creaked open. All she saw at first glance was a whole lot of leather. Black ropes in one big fist. A roll of duct tape in the other. Her gaze inched up to Cort's hard stare and her stomach took a nose dive.

"Come here," Cort said in a tone that had her skittering up to him before the fearful urge to make a mad dash the other direction took over. He pointed at the floor and she dropped to her knees. "You can safeword out at any time, Tiny, but otherwise, we're going to play." He used the end of the wrapped-up rope to tip her chin up. "Do you trust me?"

"Yes." The ropes, the tape, scared her. But he didn't. There was only one problem. "If you cover my mouth, how can I—?"

Cort grinned and pulled a small bell out of his pocket. He made it jingle, then placed the ring holding the bell over her finger. "Hold this in your palm to keep it quiet. Make it jingle to replace your safeword."

"You thought of everything." Which was perfect. She wanted to experience all he had planned without feeling like she had to be his guide. The presence of another Dom might pave the way a little more smoothly, but it was so much more exciting to see where

Cort would take this on his own. Besides, she couldn't think of anyone besides Dominik that she'd feel comfortable sceneing with. And that door had been softly shut behind her.

Without any further discussion, Cort tore a piece of duct tape and placed it over her mouth. He took a knee and bound her arms to her sides with the rope, then helped her to her feet. Her palm grew moist around the little bell as he put her jacket over her shoulders, doing up the buttons so the ropes were hidden.

Panic made her breath come out fast through her nose. Would the jacket muffle the sound of the bell?

After holding her boots for her to slip into, Cort straightened and curved his hand under her chin. His brow creased slightly. "Ring the bell, Tiny."

She shook her hand hard and a faint jingle could be heard. *It's fine. He can hear it.*

Cort nodded. "All right, that's not too bad. Feel free to clear your throat if I don't catch the bell fast enough."

She inclined her head, his attention to all the little details making it a bit easier to relax.

"I'm going to walk you to my car. Keep your head down and don't draw any attention to yourself." His voice was gruff, almost cold, and she realized he'd gone into character. "If you behave, no one will get hurt. Blink once if you understand."

One blink and she followed him out into the hall, keeping her head down. It was late enough for both the halls of the apartment and the streets beyond to be pretty much empty. They made it to the car without any trouble.

He opened the door to the backseat and gestured her in. After putting her seat belt on, he leaned close and whispered in her ear, "I've planned this very carefully—kidnapping you and playing with you for a few days. No one will even know you're gone. You're completely at my mercy."

*Which is exactly where I want to be.*

# Chapter Eighteen

Cort carried Akira into the cabin after an hour-long drive and brought her to the largest bedroom—the only one with an attached bathroom. He undid the ropes and placed a pair of soft cuffs around Akira's wrists, linking them behind her back. He hadn't had much time to organize everything after renting the cabin, but he hadn't needed much. Food and necessities. A few toys, some ropes, and a door handle he'd installed on this room which could be locked from the outside.

Akira hadn't used the bell yet, but he still looked her over before leaving the room, checking her coloring, her pulse, and her wide eyes. She seemed more excited than anything—probably wondering what kind of kinky games he had planned. Sex had been pretty tame over the last two weeks, and he knew she was waiting for him to spice things up.

*Just gotta take care of something first, Tiny.* He left the bedroom door open as the doorbell sounded, recalling Dominik's firm warning never to leave a bound sub alone.

Ford stepped in, shaking snow from his hair and brushing it off his jacket. His eyes were hard as he looked up at Cort. "I take it whatever you wanted to talk about is bad if you had me come all the way down here?"

"Nothing bad. But it's important." Cort waited for Ford to take off his boots and jacket, then gestured for him to follow. "There's something you need to take care of."

"Yeah, what's—" Ford froze in the doorway of the room, staring at Akira. Akira stared back. Ford spun around, his eyes blazing with rage. "What the fuck do you think you're—?"

Cort grinned and moved forward, backing Ford into the room.

"You two are going to work this out. You're a Dom, so I trust you to respect her safeword if she uses it."

"You're missing a little thing called consent, asshole. I didn't agree to this, and by the look on her face, neither did she."

"She came here willingly. So did you. The rest . . ." Cort shrugged. "You're both too damn stubborn to deal with this thing between you on your own. You can walk out now and forget the whole thing, or . . ."

"Or?" Ford took a deep breath, then went to Akira's side and carefully removed the duct-tape gag. "I need you to be fucking clear about what you expect from us."

"Or you can stay and use this opportunity to make up. You can both curse me out for forcing the issue if you want, but unless I hear 'red,' neither of you are leaving until you can play nice." Cort met Ford's eyes and saw the instant when what he was offering registered. He gave Ford a tight smile. "I know why you wouldn't punish her. It's not a problem anymore."

"How is it not a problem? Are you leaving her?"

"No."

"Then—"

"I think it's pretty obvious what he's suggesting, Ford," Akira said softly. She studied Cort's face for a moment, then sighed and turned to Ford. "I'm surprised you never thought of it, considering both your sisters are—"

"I'd never share you if you were mine." Ford crossed his arms over his chest and took a seat on the bed beside her. "So no, it wasn't even in the cards."

"I'm not yours. And I can't see that changing." Akira shot Ford a dirty look, rising gracefully from the bed to approach Cort. "I understand your reasons for this, Sir, but I can't promise to do anything besides tolerate him while we're stuck in here."

"Fair enough." Cort pulled her close, kissing her, tasting her sweet lips and the heat of her mouth. Then forced himself to let her go. "I won't be far. Say the word any time and I'll let you out."

Akira's lips slanted. "He'll safeword before I do."

"Not likely." Ford pulled his feet onto the bed, stretching out with his arms folded behind his head. "Is there a time limit on this, Cort, or does she just get to bitch me out until she loses her voice?"

"I won't be 'bitching you out.'"

"Really? What's changed?"

"You'll be lucky if I say anything to you, you . . ." Akira sucked in a harsh breath, shook her head, then peered up at Cort, a rueful smile on her lips. "I will make an effort, Sir. But only because I love *you*."

If he doubted that, even for a second, he wouldn't risk letting her and Ford explore whatever this was between them. He kissed her cheek, then retreated from the room. "The only reason I'm doing this is because I love you. And because I know he does too."

\* \* \* \*

Ford groaned as he watched Akira pacing the room, wishing she'd just sit down and chill until Cort got tired of this stupid game. He spotted a pile of books and magazines on the dresser and went over to check them out, hoping one would help pass the time.

He dropped the first one with a snort. *You've gone mental, Cort.*

The themes of all the books and magazines were either BDSM or hockey. "This is stupid. Is this his way of telling us that we've got stuff in common?"

Akira came over, her cheeks growing red as she glanced over the titles. "No, I think those are for me."

"*Tough Guy* by Bob Probert? Give me a break."

Her nostrils flared. "Oh, but the romance novels don't surprise you?"

"Ah . . ."

Tugging hard at her wrist cuffs, Akira got one hand free, then grabbed the non-fiction hockey book. "He knew you'd bore me. It was thoughtful of him to give me ways to entertain myself."

"Yeah, sure. Guess that makes up for him bringing you here

under false pretenses."

She plopped down on the bed with the book open on the pillow, her brow raised as she glanced over her shoulder at him. "What false pretenses? He was kidnapping me for nefarious purposes. This qualifies."

Strange, but it was actually kinda fun butting heads with Akira when it was more a battle of words than bitterness. He sat on the dresser, his gaze drifting from her idly swaying feet to the gentle curve of her cute little ass in her tight jeans. His lips twitched at her words. "I know, it's horrible. Being forced to be around me for any amount of time—"

"You're smarter than you look."

"—'cause when it comes down to it, you're going to have to stop pretending to be okay with this."

"I *am* okay with this. When you say something worth hearing, I'll listen."

He lowered from the dresser and moved to the bed, leaning down with his hand braced close to her elbow. "You're going to have to beg me."

She snickered, casting him an amused glance. "Yes, I'll get right on that, *Sir*."

*Cheeky little brat.* He shoved away from the bed, lifting his shoulders in an offhand shrug. "All right, but I believe the whole point of this is for you to receive your punishment. You've been nagging me to give it to you for two weeks—"

Akira slammed the book facedown on the pillow. "I never nagged! I just don't understand why you refused! You were going to the club because of me, and then when you got a chance to—"

"It's not just for you! Not anymore!" He pressed his lips shut, inhaling slowly and picturing her strapped down, ass up, able to do nothing but take as many lashes from the cane as he chose to give her. Chicklet had taught him that trick when he'd asked her why she never raised her voice at Tyler. When the boy was in brat mode, he could try the patience of a saint. With his exhale, he found some much-needed calm. And recalled how much Akira needed to see her Dom was in control. He chose his words carefully, his tone measured. "Do you honestly think I'd just take any opportunity I was given? That I could punish you, then just hand you back to your man?"

"Why not? You do it with other subs?"

"No, I don't. I spend time with the subs I discipline. They don't hate me when I'm done." He stared at the window, black beyond the pale lilac curtains. "I've had them curled up in my arms, happy with what I can give them."

"I'm sure you give them a lot." Akira's bottom lip trembled. She glared at him as she sat up. "I really don't need to hear about all your conquests."

"That's not why I'm—ugh, this is pointless." Ford held his arms out, palms up. "Forget the begging. Just ask me to punish you and I'll do it. A few swats on the ass with your jeans on, and we can tell everyone you learned your lesson."

"All this might be fake to you, but it's not to me. I'll accept a punishment, but only if it's real."

"It can't be real!" *No yelling at the sub, Ford.* He gritted his teeth. "You want me to stay away, don't ask for real."

"I'm asking." Akira gave him a derisive once-over. "What are you afraid of?"

*You.* He almost laughed at how quickly the answer came, if only in his head. *You fucking terrify me, shorty.* Out loud, he managed a slightly better response. "I'm afraid you're biting off more than you can chew, little girl."

Her lips parted. She strode up to him, lifting her hand like she'd either shove him or slap him. But she seemed to catch herself at the last second and did neither. Her lips curled away from her teeth. "You fucking pussy."

*Too goddamn tempting.* He shook his head, laughing as he went to knock at the door. "Nice try, shorty." He cleared his throat. "All right, you had your fun, Cort. I'm ready to leave."

He could hear Cort walking down the hall and stopping at the other side of the door. "Safeword?"

*You've got to be kidding!* Ford latched on to the handle and rammed his shoulder into the solid wood door. "Enough with this shit! Open the fucking door!"

Akira chuckled softly behind him. "Did you forget the word?"

"No, I didn't forget it." Ford rested his head against the door. "Cort, this is fucking illegal."

Cort actually burst out laughing. "So?"

"So open the door! Come on, this isn't fucking funny!" Only, it sorta was. Ford knew Cort, and his best friend was about as moveable as Everest when he got an idea in his crazy head. "I'll do it, man. I'll punish her, and then I'll have her screaming my name. Is that what you want?"

For a long time, Cort didn't say a thing. Ford almost thought he'd left the hall. But then Cort spoke, so quietly Ford had to hold his breath to hear him. "If that's what she wants, we'll both learn to live with it."

Akira strode forward, her eyes hard. "It's not what I want. You know what, Ford's right. This is getting us nowhere. Open the door."

"At least you're agreeing on something. That's progress." Cort let out a heavy sigh. "Funny thing is, if you weren't both so full of it, one of you would have said 'red.' But you haven't, so get comfy." He laughed again. "And quit shouting for me. I'm in the middle of a *Big Bang Theory* marathon."

*The man's lost it.* Ford backed away from the door, looking around the room for something he could use to pick the lock. He spotted some bobby pins in Akira's hair and moved to snatch one.

She slapped his hand away. "What are you doing?"

"Picking the lock. I need one of those, then we're both out of here." He scowled as she skittered out of reach. "Stop messing around."

"My Master put me in here. I'll leave when he lets me out." She put her hands over the pins when he tried for one again. "Don't touch me! Damn it, you're obnoxious. It's like being stuck in a room with an annoying brother."

"A brother?" That was quite enough. He stepped into her personal space, speaking with his lips over hers. "Would you let your brother do this?"

One hand wrapped in her hair, he tilted her head back as his lips came down, silencing her protests with a bit of pressure. She shoved at his chest, then bunched her fists in his shirt, gasping as he teased the seam of her lips with his tongue. He wanted more of her, more of the honeydew sweetness, of the barely restrained passion. His blood carried a charge through his veins that sparked as he dipped his tongue into her mouth and touched the tip of hers.

*She's not yours. When this is over, Cort will take her back.*

He probably would. For all Ford knew, Cort wanted to get him out of her system. But that meant he was there.

Which meant he could stay.

Not like this, though. What he felt with her was blazing hot, close to a flash flame that could die once it stole all the oxygen from the air around it. For this to last, they needed more.

"Not yet, shorty." He took his lips from hers, smiling down at her. "I know what you want, but—"

"You know what I want?" Akira stiffened against him, her eyes shooting poisonous little darts. "Because I let you kiss me? You arrogant bastard. I've kissed a lot of men, and it didn't mean anything until Cort."

"Uh-huh." He smirked, knowing it would get her even more aggravated. "May I finish now, my dear?"

"Don't be all patronizing with me, Ford." Akira retreated a step, then another as he moved toward her. "You have this one opportunity. Take it or leave it."

He continued backing her up until they'd entered the bathroom. Then he cocked his head. "After I've punished you, right?"

"Like you could, you coward." She sneered at him. "All you have is kisses and pretty words."

"You couldn't handle more."

"Really? Try me."

"All right." He picked her up and put her in the bath, reaching down to turn the shower on. And blast the cold water. He held her in place, grinning as she screeched. "Count to ten, pet, and I'll consider the punishment served."

\* \* \* \*

"I could kill you! Let me out, it's cold!" Akira yelped and latched on to Ford's arm as her feet slipped. "A goat and an—an ape! That's who y-you call your mom and dad! That's why you're so stupid!"

"Very creative, shorty. I'd call my 'father' worse than an ape, but that's irrelevant." Ford smoothed her wet hair away from her face. "Count and it will be over soon."

*He's serious.* She sniffled, turning her face away from the icy spray. "O-one."

Ford rubbed her arm, then bent down, adjusting the temperature of the water so the cold wasn't quite slicing at her, but was still uncomfortable. "You get all fired up and speak without thinking. I was happy to find out you weren't lashing out at Sahara the next day. I checked on her and she—"

"Two." Akira swallowed, staring at him through the hair clinging to her face. "I hated seeing you with her."

"I know."

"Not for the reason you think. Three." Akira's chest ached as she pictured Ford, holding Sahara so tenderly. But she made herself finish talking. "You'll hurt her. You don't care about her."

"You know that's not true. I played with her because I'd already agreed to do a scene with Pischlar, but I wouldn't have done it if I didn't care a little."

"You care about—" *Doesn't matter!* Her throat tightened. "Four."

"I care about all the subs I play with in some way." Ford traced his thumb over her wet bottom lip. "But I don't love them."

"Five." Akira took a deep breath as her heart pounded and her flesh heated despite the cold raining down on her. "Six. And I asked you not to say that."

"Try to stop me. It won't ever change." Ford moved close to her, almost as much of the icy water hitting him as was covering her. But it didn't seem to affect him at all. "I love you."

"Stop."

"Seven." He kissed her, his lips chasing away the cold. "Eight."

"Ford . . ." Tears mingled with the droplets spilling down her cheeks. She wanted to tell him she couldn't love him back. She'd been hanging on to hating him for so long. Had barely accepted that maybe she shouldn't. And then things had gotten confusing. And now it was too late. "I love Cort."

"Nine." Ford inhaled slowly. "Can't say I don't wish you didn't. But . . . he could have kept you to himself. I gave him every reason to."

She was shaking all over, but she wasn't sure this punishment was good enough anymore. How could it be when Ford had spent the whole time telling her everything she hadn't even dreamed possible? It couldn't be true.

She turned away from him, hugging herself.

"Ten." Ford turned the water off. "Come here."

Letting him hold her, she took tiny steps with him into the bedroom, reeling with the thoughts of all that had led to this. The way she was talking to people lately . . . not only Ford, but Jami. And even Cort! She was swearing and being mean. That wasn't her!

Two big towels were draped over her. And Ford's arm. She wasn't sure she should accept his comfort. He'd been too easy on her.

"Hey, talk to me." He used one of the towels to soak up the moisture from her hair. "You've been punished before and you know how this works. All's forgiven. You'll be able to go back to the club."

"Took me a lot longer—" her teeth chattered, her jeans and T-shirt molding to her body like a thick coat of ice "—to forgive you."

"What I did was a lot worse." Ford faced her, hooking his fingers under the hem of her shirt. "Arms up, shorty. You'll get sick if you stay in these wet clothes."

"Right." She lifted her arms, feeling a little numb. He'd want to make love to her now. She had a feeling she'd enjoy it, but she was too emotionally drained to work up any excitement. She didn't say anything as he peeled off her shirt, then her jeans, leaving her in her damp, white bra and panties. As he moved her onto the bed and pulled the blankets over her.

But when he crossed the room and tapped on the door, she went still. Listened to him speaking softly, making out only one word before the door opened. *"Yellow."*

"I know you're not big on planning, but please tell me you brought a change of clothes?"

Cort frowned and glanced over at her, then back to Ford. "Why are you wet?"

"I punished her. I'm not leaving this room until I give her aftercare, but she needs to be comfortable." Ford pulled his own soaked shirt away from his chest. "I wouldn't mind getting out of this either."

"There's stuff in the dresser." Cort hesitated in the doorway, his steady gaze on Akira's face pulling her out of the numbness, giving her a feeling of longing that almost overshadowed the guilt that made it so hard to breathe. He shook his head and came to her side, taking her hand as he knelt by the bed. "You look so lost, Tiny. Was this a mistake?"

God, she loved him, but she couldn't wait for the day when caring for her didn't make him second-guess himself. She shook her head quickly, sitting up with the blanket held to her chest. "It wasn't a mistake. I just . . . I don't know what comes next."

"We get you all nice and warm." Ford came over with pink and purple cupcake pajamas that still had tags on them. He tugged off the tags, then held up the long sleeve, flannel top. "Then I'll hold you for a bit before you start deciding you hate me again."

"That won't happen." Akira's brow shot up when Ford gestured for her to turn away from him. She did so without question, then blushed as he undid her bra strap. Cort sat on the bed and pulled her bra off. Ford held the shirt for her to slip her arms in. Cort did up the buttons.

*All right, now I'm confused.* This all seemed backward. Shouldn't they be working on getting her clothes *off* rather than on? She got out of her wet panties, the length of the shirt making it easy not to flash anyone, and quickly pulled on the pants. Being fully clothed gave her some strength, but she wasn't sure she wanted it. *I would have done anything they wanted before. Why change that?*

"It's simple, shorty." Ford pressed his hand to her cheek, his whiskey-colored eyes reflecting the light like the golden liquid would shimmer under the sun. And those eyes seemed to see right through her. "Just being this close to you is more than I could have hoped for. When you've had time to absorb everything, you can tell me whether or not you want me. Because I won't take what you're in no position to give."

"I can give you myself, Ford." She licked her bottom lip, the idea of him taking her much more appealing without the cold, without the feeling that it would be rushed. And with Cort here, she wouldn't have to wonder if he'd regret setting all this up. It would be no different from when he'd shared her with Dominik. "We have tonight. Take it or leave it."

"I never said you had only tonight, cutie." Cort kissed the side of her throat before shifting off the bed. "Yellow to pause a scene, not end it, right?"

Ford nodded. "That's right."

"I'll take off then. Let me know if—"

"No. You should stay." Ford shoved Akira back onto the bed, pressing his hand to her shoulder when she tried to sit up again. "Just turn off the lights before you join us."

"You sure you don't need more time?"

"I'm sure. I got a few seasons of *Big Bang Theory* on Blu-ray. We can all watch it together when we get home."

"Works for me."

*But* . . . Akira bit the tip of her tongue as Ford stretched out beside her. The light went out and shortly after, Cort's weight settled on her other side. She held her breath as Ford pulled her up to rest her head on his shoulder. As Cort's arm went around her waist. Having them both with her was wonderful, but . . . but it shouldn't feel so . . . *normal.* Part of her could see nights from here on ending the same, with her between them, feeling like someone so precious these men were willing to share her, just to have her.

*That's not how life works.* It worked for Jami. For Becky. For Silver. But in her mind, all she could see was what had happened to Dominik when he'd given his heart to a woman who wasn't his alone.

"I don't know if I can do this." She reached down to lace her fingers with Cort's. He was the only one here she was certain of. He hadn't acted differently toward her after the scene with Dominik. He'd be her man tomorrow. And every day after. But Ford . . . she'd seen his jealous rages. She couldn't see being a Dom changing him enough for him to want a relationship like this. But could she walk away from him again if he did? "Cort, I love you so much, but what if I'm not strong enough to be the woman you both need?"

Ford was silent, but she could feel his pulse pick up under her cheek. Behind her, Cort rose up on one elbow, smiling as he looked down at her.

"Close your eyes, Akira."

She closed her eyes.

"You've seen how things can go wrong, and I get that, but I want you to tell me how this feels. From here." He placed his hand over her chest, just above her left breast. "I didn't make this decision with my head. I did it from the only place that counts."

From his heart. And she could see that as she followed his instruction. He loved Ford like a brother, she could hear it in his voice every time Ford was mentioned. Choosing her over Ford would have been hard for him, but doing so when he'd clearly seen there was something between them . . .

But how did it feel for her? To know she could have everything she hadn't even known she wanted?

"It feels right." She grinned as she sensed the tension leave Ford's body. Having him not being all cocky at being in bed with her was the sweet, whipped icing with a cherry on top. Lying on her back, she wrapped her hands around the back of Cort's neck and pulled him down for a kiss. "But you'll make him behave?"

"Oh yeah, that'll be easy." Cort snorted. "Wanna ask me if I'll make her stop being a brat, Ford?"

Ford chuckled in a low, sensual way that made the hairs on the nape of Akira's neck stand up. "Naw, I like it when she's a brat. I had a feeling when she stopped running from me, she'd come at me swinging."

"You better believe it!" Akira rolled over, spooned close to Cort, and swatted Ford's chest. "And for your information, I'm not a brat!"

Both Cort and Ford laughed, but Cort was quick enough to grab her arms before she could smack him too. "You're our beautiful, fiery, passionate little brat. And I wouldn't want you any other way."

"Our?" It was too fast. And not fast enough because she'd wasted so much time being angry. She had a feeling if she'd faced her own feelings sooner, she could have come to this place with Cort and Ford before this, but . . . but maybe not. Maybe everything had happened as it was meant to.

And maybe she read way too many romance novels. Because she truly believed that this was meant to be.

"You are ours." Cort gathered her in his arms as Ford's body curved against her from behind. "But quiet now. I'm tired, babe."

"Let the old man get his rest, shorty." Ford breathed softly into her ear. "I'll try to behave, but I'm not sure how much longer I can keep this up."

"Until morning, Ford, that's all I ask." She smiled as she closed her eyes and felt him settling comfortably with his hand on her stomach and his cheek close to hers. "Let me wake up and see I'm not dreaming."

Ford made a soft sound of agreement before he grew heavy against her. She heard Cort's breaths slow, how quickly he'd fallen asleep making her feel that much better about accepting what he'd offered her. Tomorrow, she'd know for sure, but right at this moment . . .

Life couldn't be more perfect.

# Chapter Nineteen

The next morning, Akira woke before the men, but she could tell one of them had gotten up at some point because her jeans and T-shirt had been left to dry over the heater in the bathroom. After getting dressed, she went to the kitchen, happy to find a decently stocked cupboard and fridge.

For someone who didn't plan, Cort had managed to think of all the essentials. Really, they could end up stuck here for days and have everything they needed. She'd found a week's worth of fresh panties in one of the drawers. Plain cotton—comfortable, nothing fancy. The other drawers she'd gone through to find them had revealed boxers in extra-large for Cort, and medium—clearly for Ford. There were more pajamas like she'd worn last night, and some T-shirts and jeans that would fit each of them.

She wasn't sure why that bothered her. She didn't think Cort planned to keep them here long, but the efficiency of it all was troubling. As though Cort could leave any place at the drop of a hat given the right reason. Find all he needed and never look back.

After making some coffee, she poured herself a cup, pulled on her coat and boots, and went out to the back deck. She brushed snow off a wooden bench so she could sit, then sipped the hot, rich liquid as she took in the scenery. They weren't close to the ocean, so all that could be seen from any angle were trees weighed down with glistening white. No visible roads, only the far reaches of winter surrounding them, nowhere close to letting go. They were completely isolated, with no one to answer to. No worries besides the ones brought with them. Which was plenty.

Thinking back on the night before, she considered how peaceful it had been. Then wondered if it would still be as they took this further. Cort could say he wanted this, but would he feel the same after she gave herself to Ford? And would she after he let Ford take her?

Behind her the door to the deck opened, and she glanced back over her shoulder as Ford came out. He lifted his coffee mug, taking a long sip and letting out a pleasure-filled sigh as he came over and propped one foot on the bench beside her. "You make damn good coffee, shorty. I should have you teach my secretary."

She rolled her eyes. "Sure, I'm right on that."

His brow rose slightly. "Not a morning person?"

"I love mornings. And here . . . well, it *was* nice and quiet until you came out."

"Damn it, Akira. What did I do now?" Ford raked his fingers through his hair and stared at her like he just couldn't figure her out. "I gave you a compliment."

"Sorry." She dropped her gaze to the steam rising from her cup and let out a heavy sigh. Ugh, why did she let him aggravate her so easily? He probably didn't think anything of bringing up another woman after spending the night with *her*. And maybe she shouldn't care about his other women, since he'd be sharing her with Cort. She planted a pleasant smile on her lips. "You know how busy I am. But there's a great little café down the street from the Forum. Have her get your coffee there."

"Yeah, I'll do that." He studied her face for several long moments. A slow grin spread across his face. "You're jealous."

*As if!* She snorted, pushing off the bench to go back inside. Ford ruined the scenery anyway.

"Don't walk away from me." Ford followed her into the kitchen, taking her mug from her and putting it with his on the counter. He placed his finger over her lips when she scowled at him. "We made a lot of progress last night, but I think we've still got some things to work out."

She brushed his hand away. "Like what?"

"Like how quick you assume I'm a fucking dog playing the field. My secretary is a lovely woman, with two sons my age, and she's been happily married for thirty years. You don't have to be jealous of her."

"I'm not jealous! Being jealous would be stupid considering what we're thinking of—"

"I don't think it's stupid." Ford picked her up by the hips and sat her on the counter, the movement so abrupt she didn't have a chance to object. He placed his hands on the cupboards at either side of her head, leaning close enough so she had no choice but to look directly into his eyes. "You're not sure of me yet, and that's okay. I'm gonna work my ass off to give you a reason to be."

"But . . ." She bit the tip of her tongue. Fighting with Ford had become a habit that was hard to break. But it was a lot harder to keep an argument going when he was being so reasonable. She shook her head slowly. "You're right, I'm not sure of you. But I'm not being fair."

"No. You're not." Ford curved a hand around the back of her neck. He grazed his lips over hers, smiling against her mouth. "But I'm ready to learn how to deal with that side of you. With all the sides of you."

That made her laugh. "You don't know me as well as you think you do."

"You're wrong. I knew you when you were still vulnerable and a little broken. I was there while you struggled to put all the things that had hurt you in the past. I quietly cheered you on because I knew you wouldn't want to hear my voice." His lips brushed her cheek. His breath stirred the hair he tucked behind her ear. "You didn't want to see me, so I kept my distance. But I always saw you."

He was incredible, but for once, that didn't sound as negative in her head as she usually meant it. Most men would have given up on a woman who treated them like Akira had treated Ford. He'd been a presence in her life, and no matter how often she'd told him she didn't want him around, part of her had been comforted by the fact that she didn't have to look far to find him.

And now he was right here. All hers.

Only . . . she had no clue what to do with him.

"What am I supposed to say to that, Ford? I wasn't ready for you then." She closed her eyes as his lips hovered a breath away from her throat, wishing he'd kiss her, or touch her. His being so close brought on the edge of heat, like sitting by a fireplace after coming in from a day out in the bitter cold, frozen to the core. She needed to burn to melt the shards of ice inside. "But I don't want you to keep your distance anymore."

"Good." The scruff along his jaw lightly scratched her cheek as he drew back. He framed her chin with one hand, teasing her lips with little flicks of his tongue, refusing to give her more even when she tried to lean forward and groaned in frustration. He sucked her bottom lip gently, his eyes on hers even as he added a bit of pressure with his teeth. His hand delved into her hair as she fisted her hands in his shirt to jerk him closer. He tugged at the tangled length of her hair and smiled at her. "So demanding."

"Kiss me, Ford." She pulled harder at his shirt, glaring at him when he refused to move. "You're starting to piss me off."

"I know." He chuckled as she hissed and changed tactics by trying to shove him away. "I can't help it. You're so cute like this."

"You won't think I'm cute when I kick your ass." She planted both hands on his chest and pushed herself off the counter, smirking as his firm stance faltered. Up on her tiptoes, she latched on to the back of his neck, and dragged him down to nip his bottom lip. *Hard.*

"Is that how you want to play?" His smile was vicious, his grip on her hair painful. He bent her backward, claiming her lips in a bruising kiss. Her eyes teared, but she didn't want him to stop. Everyone she knew was always so careful with her. As though she was still so fragile she might break.

She needed that with Cort because he didn't like these kinds of games, and she craved his pleasure at her sweet submission. But if she was going to have two men, why not have fun with the one who'd give her some slack on the leash?

Or would there be a leash? She'd loved the security of the

collar when Dominik had placed one for training around her throat. Cort wasn't deep enough into the lifestyle yet to even consider collaring her, but Ford was. Except, if he was happy to let her run wild, why bother?

The conflicting thoughts had her shaking with nervous energy as she twisted, dropping her weight the way they'd taught her in self-defense. Caught off guard, Ford released her hair, grabbing at thin air as she darted out of reach. She skidded into the living room, panting as she faced him with the coffee table between them.

Ford squared his shoulders and placed his hands on his hips, looking her over, his lips slanted in amusement. "You don't really expect me to chase you around the cabin, do you?"

"How else are you going to catch me?" She skittered sideways in the opposite direction as he took a step around the table. His dark look had her shaking even harder and her cheeks heated as her panties became uncomfortably damp. She jumped as he strode toward her, scrambling to keep away, even though her body screamed for her to throw herself at him. Her tone was sharper than she meant it to be. "You're not very good at this game."

"Because I'm still trying to figure out how far you want this to go. What happens when I catch you, shorty?"

"You win." She swallowed and braced to make a run for it. Maybe she was thinking too much. The limits would come in time. In this moment, all that should matter was one of her needs was being met. She didn't have to give in. Ford would make her.

His next step had her tripping sideways, swiftly plotting her escape, but then his sharp tone made her freeze. "Stop."

Trembling, she fisted her hands by her sides as he came to her. She yelped as he picked her up and dropped her on the sofa, the landing causing the air to whoosh out of her lungs. Before she could gather her wits and spring back up, he had her trapped.

"Cheater!" She laughed and slapped his chest, then bit her bottom lip, not sure if she'd gone too far.

He shackled her wrists with his hands and pulled them over

her head, laughing softly as she squirmed beneath him. "I can't cheat at a game neither of us wants me to lose." Holding her wrists in one hand, he brought the other down to her throat with a light pressure that had her holding completely still. "One day, during the summer, I'll bring you out into the woods and let you run as far as you can. And when I catch you, I'll take you right there in the dirt, no matter how much you struggle." He spoke against her lips. "But we're not ready for that yet. I wanted our first time to be somewhere a little softer than the floor."

And there it was, Ford doing what everyone else did. Telling her she wasn't ready. She ground her teeth and turned her head. "Softer is good. And you better be really gentle. Otherwise, I could shatter."

"Gentle?" Ford moved his hand from her throat and reached down to undo his belt. He pulled it from his jeans in one smooth motion, then brought it up to bind her wrists. Then he flipped her over so she was kneeling on the sofa, her bound wrists held firmly over her bowed head. "I never said I'd be gentle."

She couldn't help struggling against the restraints, but Ford didn't give an inch. He undid her jeans with one hand, working them down to her knees. She heard him undo his zipper. The distinct sound of a condom wrapper being torn open.

The blunt head of him breached her, dipping in and out without filling her until she was ready to scream. Her breath caught as he finally slammed in and held there, letting her adjust to having him inside her. He never let go of his grip on the belt holding her wrists, but he stroked her with his other hand, running it up and down her side soothingly, then along her thigh as he began to move in steady, even thrusts. His fingers slipped between her folds, at either side of her clit. She trembled as the sensations reached a fever pitch, so close to igniting she knew she couldn't hold back for long.

But then he whispered in her ear, "So easy. All I have to do is get inside you and you're all mine."

*"All mine."* She shook her head, shocking herself with the low

growl that came out of her as she bucked against him, not sure if she wanted to throw him off her or take him deeper. She hadn't forgotten Cort. She didn't belong to Ford.

And yet, she did. Because Cort had allowed it. She stiffened, breathing hard, mindlessly seeking out *her* man. She cried out as Ford pistoned into her, the pleasure trying to drag her under, but an emptiness kept her from letting go.

*I belong to Cort.* So how could Cort not be here? He must have heard them. He was doing this for her. For all she knew, he was in the room, pacing the floor and just waiting for it to be over so he could come out. He'd known it would come to this, but did it bother him?

"I've lost you." Ford pulled out and flipped her over again so she was facing him. "Why?"

"I'm afraid." But she wanted him back. She wanted Ford inside her, making her forget everything else. Only . . . she couldn't forget. Cort was part of her. Nothing would ever change that.

"Don't be afraid, just tell me what you need."

"You'll hate me." She drew her knees to her chest, her arousal fading as she came to realize how badly she'd messed up. "God, I'm sorry!"

"I get it." Ford knelt in front of the sofa, lowering his head to kiss her clenched hands. "I should tell you off for not saying yellow, but I understand."

"Then explain it to me, because I don't." She hugged herself, not even caring how exposed she was with her jeans around her knees. She'd had this man inside her. And that didn't bother her. Only . . . something was missing. No, *someone*. Cort. "He knows, and he's okay with this."

"Cort? Yeah. He's reading one of the books he got for you. And . . . hell, I'd feel better if he was here too." Ford rubbed his face with his hand. "Which is messed up. We're both more into the lifestyle than he is. I'm supposed to know what I'm doing. You're the only one who makes me feel like I don't."

"He gave you to me. I mean—"

"No. You were right the first time. I feel the same." Ford shook his head and glared at the floor. "There's only one way about this. It's the three of us, or it's nothing."

*Yes!* Those words felt so completely right she could only swallow and stare at Ford because voicing those words would only hurt him. And that was the last thing she wanted to do.

"Cort! Red!" Ford let out a bitter laugh. "Fuck, I am the most pathetic Dom ever. I'll be tagged 'the safeword man' at the club."

"It's my fault."

"Stop it."

"It's true!"

"You two are giving me a headache!" Cort strode down the hall, laughter underlying his every word. "What's the problem?"

"This ain't gonna work unless you're here. She can't stop thinking about you." Ford snorted at Cort's broad grin. "Asshole."

"You're lucky I'm in a good mood, Ford." Cort came over and ran his finger over her swollen bottom lip. "You hurt her."

"We played rough. She loved it." Ford pulled her to her feet, removing the belt restraint which she took as a sign that the fun was over. He flashed her a knowing smile as he drew her shirt up and off. He had her step out of her jeans, then trailed his finger down her cheek, his words for Cort. "But you're always there."

Cort placed his hand on the base of her spine and all the uncertainty dwindled away to nothing, leaving only the warmth of his touch. "I always will be. You good with that?"

Ford inclined his head, no resentment in his eyes, only the same question she was thinking as he looked at Cort. "So what's next?"

"Breakfast." Cort nudged her in the direction of the kitchen. "I'll have a bowl of cereal. Seems to me you've already chosen yours."

Not sure what he meant, Akira let herself be led to the kitchen, a little voice in her head nagging at her that she shouldn't allow them to talk around her like she wasn't even there. But the rest of her was sinking into the still pool of submission, letting the feeling of being there for their pleasure drown out the urge to question anything. Ford had more experience with the lifestyle, but Cort knew *her*. He seemed to sense that she didn't want a part of the negotiations. Her limits were set, and she was perfectly happy going along with whatever they had planned.

But when they reached the kitchen and Ford swooped her up onto the table, she couldn't help but gasp and stare at him. And then at Cort.

*What are they going to—*

"Breathe, Tiny. Just breathe and let him have you." Cort brought a box of Cap'n Crunch, some milk, a bowl, a spoon, and a glass to the table. He set them off to her side as Ford laid her down. "And try not to spill my milk."

Easy enough. She remained motionless as Ford ran his hands up her thighs, then breathed in slow, measured breaths as his fingers trailed over her hips and found a sensitive spot low on her belly. Her whole body quivered as he molded her breasts in his hands. She giggled as she heard Cort crunching his cereal.

Ford smiled at her. "Better?"

"Yes." A little hum of pleasure escaped her as he kissed along the same path as his hands. He rose up to remove his shirt, tossed it aside, then lifted her calves to his bare shoulders. His muscles, his smooth, hot skin against hers as he lowered his head between her thighs, added an intimacy that hadn't been there before. He watched her as he tasted her with a long, languid stroke of his tongue. She whispered his name as something more than pleasure stole inside her.

Another crunch, quieter this time. She swallowed and turned her head to see Cort, watching them, his hooded gaze and lazy smile drawing out the sweet sensations like melted chocolate drizzled on her tongue. As Ford dipped his tongue into her, she arched her back, sucking in air as the pleasure saturated every nerve. Her whole body was so sensitized that every time his tongue left her she felt a dull ache. She needed the pressure of him inside her, needed . . . needed more.

She reached down blindly, lacing her fingers through his hair, pulling him to her. He thrust his tongue in again and again and his hands wrapped around her thighs, his fingers massaging the straining muscles. The table grew slick with the moisture beading on her skin as a spark lit within, catching quickly and growing like she was made up of the perfect kindling. There was no chance to ask for permission to come. Ford didn't give her a choice.

She thrashed on the table, bringing her hands to her sides to claw at it, crying out. Her thighs clenched against Ford's face until the strength left her trembling as wave after fiery wave hit her. Her body shook hard as Ford brought her calves down, gently bending her knees by his hips and filling her in one smooth thrust. The aftermath of her climax still held her, making her tight and slick around him.

"Are you with me, Akira?" Ford slid in deep, resting an elbow by her head as he covered her with his body and kissed her. He stroked her hair as she nodded, rocking his hips in a shallow motion that stirred all the heat all over again. "We can keep going, just like this."

"Don't be . . ." She gasped in air, bringing her arms around him and pressing her hands to his back to keep him near. "Don't be careful with me."

"I won't." His lips came down for a rough kiss, his tongue and teeth leaving her lips tender, a promise that her body would soon feel the same. He rose up, taking her hands from his back and drawing them over her head. "Can you hold her, Cort?"

Cort brought his breakfast to the counter and returned, firmly shackling her wrists with his hands. He bent down to kiss her sore lips, his voice rough with passion as he spoke against them. "It would be my pleasure."

Stretched out on the table, Akira held her breath as Ford pulled out almost all the way, rasping out her exhale as he drove back in. His hands on her hips kept her still as he fucked her, and her rasps became wordless screams of ecstasy.

His grip was bruising, but it only added to the feeling of being taken without restraint. The exquisite friction as he hammered into her, the fullness, was almost too much. Yet when she finally managed a word, it was "More!" She'd never get enough.

No longer a fire, the pleasure boiled up like a volcano that couldn't be contained, spilling lava before it finally burst and lit up the sky. Mindlessly tugging at her wrists, unable to get free, kept the flaming liquid flowing for what seemed like eternity.

Ford slapped his hands on the table, letting out a low growl as he dropped his head to her stomach. His arms shook, and as she came down to level ground, her lips curved a little in feminine satisfaction. Making a man like Ford come completely undone ranked right up there with the decadence of Black Forest cake or a day spent basking in the sun.

"Are you all right, Sir?" she asked in a sugary sweet voice as he drew out and dropped into a chair. Cort had released her wrists, so she sat up and scooted over to the edge of the table, her smile growing even bigger as Ford tipped his head up and arched a brow. "Maybe you need a nap?"

Laughing, Ford stood, taking her face in his hands to kiss her. He nodded solemnly as he tucked her hair behind her ears. "It's been a while, so I probably need some time to recover." His lips slanted in a wicked grin. "Good thing you've got two of us."

Her eyes widened as he stepped aside and Cort came toward her. She hopped off the table, squealing as Cort caught her. He lifted her up and headed straight for the bedroom.

"Cort! I can't—not yet!" But she squeezed her thighs together as arousal pulsed over the delicious ache. Maybe she *could*.

Cort dumped her unceremoniously onto the bed, climbing over her even as she tried to scramble out of reach, his hands on her thighs keeping her right where he wanted her. The material of his jeans was rough against her inner thighs, but feeling him hard and ready had her holding on to him tight, eager for more.

He kissed her throat, chuckling as she wiggled under him impatiently. "Tell me what you need."

"You." She licked her bottom lip as he shoved up to his knees, crawling out from under him so she could undo his jeans herself. She took him in her hands, kissing the feverish head of his cock, suddenly wanting nothing more than the soft, gentle loving he could give her. But only after she gave him a little something of her own. "I'm greedy today."

"You won't hear me complaining." He petted her hair as she glided down along his length, taking her time with him, savoring his taste, the steady thrum of his pulse under her tongue, his body so familiar to her now. A body, a man, who still belonged to her.

Nothing had changed. She spent hours in his arms, in Ford's, and the connection she had with Cort remained the same, seeming to grow even stronger with Ford by their side. All that she'd feared became a thing of the past. What they had together was solid, and she could see it lasting forever if they stayed just like this.

The three of them, right here. Because going back to the real world would be a challenge.

One she wasn't ready to face just yet.

\* \* \* \*

They all ended up having a midday nap, but as usual, Cort heard Akira up and about way before he'd even considered opening his eyes. He grinned as he heard her giggling with one of her friends—probably Jami or Sahara. She suddenly told them she'd call back and pressed a button to take the other line.

His grin faded as he remembered that he'd left her phone with her purse back at her apartment. Which meant she was using his.

"Hey, Angel! Yes, he's right here, I just borrowed his phone for a . . . hey, are you okay?"

Cort schooled his face and held out his hand. "Let me talk to her."

Akira frowned at him, but nodded. "I'll pass you to him, one sec."

There were so many questions in Akira's eyes, and he couldn't answer any of them. He also knew leaving the room to talk wouldn't help, but he didn't have a choice. This wasn't a conversation he could have in front of Ford and Akira.

"Hey, Angel." He made sure to keep his tone light, even though her calling had him uneasy. She wasn't supposed to contact him unless there was a problem. "What's going on?"

"I broke up with Dave. I'm so sorry!" She let out a broken sob. "He's just . . . he's so sweet and I can't do this anymore. I feel like a whore, and it didn't bother me at first—I needed the money. But he's trying so hard, and he knows something's not right even when I'm playing the perfect girlfriend. I even considered doing this for real, only . . . I don't feel anything for him. Every time he tells me he loves me—"

"I know, sweetie. And *I'm* sorry. I shouldn't have asked you to do this."

"But I told you I could! You've trusted me with stuff like this before, but it just feels so wrong."

Cort took a deep breath. He should have expected this, but he'd been desperate. And still was. The Cobras had a game tonight. Maybe he could figure something else out if he had a bit more time. But it made him feel sick to ask. "Could you have dinner with him? Maybe tell him you're willing to give him another chance?"

"Damn it, Cort, why do you hate the kid so much? That would destroy him. I made a clean break. It's over."

"I don't hate him." This was just business. The fucking business of keeping Ford alive. Maybe using the young goalie to do it was heartless, but . . . damn it, didn't matter. He didn't have that option anymore. "Forget it. You're right. This has gone far enough."

Angel sighed. "You don't have to give me the last payment. I know I made a mess of things—"

"You did everything you were supposed to. I'll pay you—give you a bit extra so you can go on a trip." His lips thinned as she quickly agreed. He knew she understood the reason for the trip. If she wasn't around, her guilty conscience was less likely to lead to a confession. He couldn't handle that on top of everything else.

Both Akira and Ford were up when he returned to the room. Akira chewed at her bottom lip as he began packing up.

Ford tugged on his jeans and then stepped up to Cort's side. "What's going on?"

"We're going home." He shrugged off the hand Ford placed on his shoulder. "You know how it is, kid. Don't fucking ask."

"Don't give me that shit. You're out." Ford moved quickly, blocking the door with his arm before Cort could leave the room. "Angel is one of my girls. If something's wrong—"

"Angel's fine. And we both know I'll never be out. Not completely." Cort squared his shoulders, staring at Ford's arm. "Get out of my way."

Akira made a soft, pleading sound. "Don't fight. Things are . . . they're better."

"It's not a fight, shorty," Ford said, holding Akira's gaze until she nodded and settled back on the bed to watch them warily. Then he turned back to Cort. "She knows your stepdad. If it's him, I get it. I won't ask." Ford moved his arm, his tone sharp as Cort strode by him. "But you'll tell me if there's anything I can—"

"You know I will." Cort felt an icy calm settle over him as he latched on to the one thing he knew would get Ford to back off. He dropped the bags by the door. "Not trying to be an asshole, man. Just . . . there's some things you don't need to know."

# Chapter Twenty

"**M**ax?"

Max sat up, rubbing his thighs and smiling at Oriana as she crossed the locker room. Damn, he loved the way she blushed, trying not to look at the men lounging around the room in different states of undress. The game was gonna start in about half an hour, and usually Tim didn't let any women in here— too distracting—but Oriana had been spending a lot of time with the team doctor. Doc seemed to be wavering on taking her on as an intern.

*The blushing ain't gonna help.* He inhaled sharply as Pischlar called out to Oriana and walked up to her wearing nothing but his jockstrap. Doc was checking on Richards, prodding the shoulder the rookie had thrown out in practice, but he paused his exam to watch Oriana's reaction.

"Hate to bug you, hon, but the rest of the guys are hogging the medical staff." Pischlar gave Oriana a sheepish smile. He reached over his shoulder, poking at a spot on his back. "Can you check this for me? Feels a bit stiff."

Oriana nodded and had Pischlar turn around. She pursed her lips as she dug her fingers into the muscle. "I feel it. Nothing a massage won't fix. Get on the table."

Pischlar moved toward one of the tables a trainer had set up. Then he stopped and glanced back at her. "You don't have to—"

"No, but your shot's going to suck if I don't. And like you said, everyone else is busy." Oriana nudged Pischlar until he was spread out on the table. "Let me know if it hurts too much."

Within seconds, Pischlar was groaning, an expression of pure bliss on his face as Oriana worked the knots out of his back. He murmured something about being in love with her and Oriana laughed.

"You say that now, but you might feel differently after a bit of time in an ice bath. I think you need to spend more time on your core muscles at the gym. Looks like you're working on your arms more than your lats or your traps."

"I agree." The doc joined Oriana in exploring the muscles of Pischlar's back, approval clear in his tone. "I'll speak to the sports therapist about getting you on a new PT regimen. How does it feel? Sit up and stretch a bit."

Max winked at Oriana as she glanced over at him, so damn proud of her for showing the doc how good she was without a hint of the nervousness he knew she felt. Doc was as big a part of the organization as any one of the owners—more actually because he'd been here from the start and he was the one constant. Everyone knew Oriana being a Delgado didn't mean a thing when it came to becoming part of the medical staff. Keane and Richter were smart enough to leave Doc fully in change.

Doc walked with Oriana over to Max when they were done with Pischlar. "I take it you didn't come here to try to convince me to give you a permanent position?"

"No, doctor. Actually, I came to talk to Max."

"I see." The doc inclined his head at Max. "Have you both settled in well?"

"Just signed a new mortgage, Doc," Max said, knowing the doc wanted to make sure they were sticking around. "Nice school district and everything."

"Excellent." The doc's attention shifted to the other side of the room. "Vanek, enough with the Red Bull! One can a day! Can't you read the label?"

While Vanek stuttered an apology, bouncing on his soles in a way that made it obvious he had *way* too much caffeine in his system, Max pulled Oriana to sit beside him on the long bench in front of his stall. He reached back into his stall to grab the Tiger

Balm Oriana had gotten for his shoulder. He laughed when she snatched it out of his hand and began to apply it to exactly the right spot.

"Sweet of you to come down here just to take care of me." He teased, knowing full well that wasn't why she was here. "The guys are lucky I don't mind sharing."

"Ah, but Sloan won't be too happy if you're too generous." Oriana let out a dreamy sigh. "He might beat me if I tell him the thoughts that went through my head when I saw Pischlar's tight ass."

"He wouldn't beat you, he knows how much you like it." Max chuckled as he pictured Sloan's reaction to Oriana gushing about another man. "I'm thinkin' he'd have you write Pischlar a nice, long letter, telling *him* how much you like his ass. And make you present it to him. At the club. Naked."

Oriana gaped at him. "That's something *you* would do. Don't give Sloan any ideas."

"I don't need to. He's quite creative. If he thinks you want to play with Pischlar, he might let the man use some toys." Max cocked his head, recalling the last scene he'd seen Pischlar do. "Or volunteer you for a chemical play demo."

The color left Oriana's cheeks. "I don't like doing demos."

"I know."

"And I don't want to play with Pischlar."

"Are you sure?"

"Positive." She gave him a look so full of lust he instantly hardened in his own jock. "Besides, I prefer a little more meat on my men's butts."

His blood had abandoned his brain. He checked the clock on the wall. Hell, there was no time to enjoy his wife being the one exception to the locker room rule. He grabbed a nearby bottle of water and dumped it over his head.

Better. Not much, but he could make it through the first period. He swiped the water from his face and laughed at Oriana's little smirk. "Behave yourself, darlin'. What can I do you for?"

She opened her mouth, then shook her head and giggled. "Too easy. I got a call from Sloan. He wanted to tell us both something. Not sure there's enough time to—"

Apparently, Sloan had managed to play whatever it was off as something that could wait. But Max knew Sloan a bit better than Oriana. He'd call before a game for only two reasons. Either to wish Max luck, or because he needed to talk. The Flames had a game tonight too, so . . .

*Shit.* Max stood and held out his hand. "Got your phone, sugar?"

"Yeah." Oriana pulled her phone out of her purse, but hesitated before handing it over. "He said everything was okay. He wouldn't lie to me."

"Not saying he did." But Sloan's definition of "okay" was damn vague. Max gestured for Oriana to follow as the phone rang. He went straight to Tim's office.

Tim met his eyes and let them in, closing the door behind them.

"If you're trying to call Callahan, I doubt you'll get an answer." Tim gestured to the small flat-screen TV on the wall by his desk. "They just announced that he was fired. He's popular, so he'll be getting offers from across the league."

"Are the Cobras making an offer?" Oriana pressed against Max's side, her question little more than a whisper. She likely felt guilty because this was what they'd been hoping for—and yet, Sloan losing his job as assistant coach after less than a year couldn't feel good. And neither she nor Max had really considered the possibility of Sloan going anywhere besides Dartmouth.

"As soon as we can get through." Tim grinned. "Hey, I want him back almost as much as you two. And it so happens that one of my assistant coaches is looking to retire. Keane and his people will have Callahan here by the end of the week. Don't worry."

"Thanks, Coach." Max hugged Oriana, catching Tim's pointed look. "Reckon I'll go get warmed up."

"Reckon you should." Tim chuckled as he followed them out

322

of the office, a playful southern drawl added to his tone. But his whole demeanor changed as he entered the locker room.

Max looked over at their rookie goalie who was starting tonight even though Bower was back in the lineup. He caught the back end of the conversation Hunt was having with their eighteen-year-old forward.

"Twins, man. Remember how you were saying like three people have bought your jersey? Well, the one in the thigh-high boots looked like she wasn't wearing anything *but* your jersey! Told her to wait for us after the game."

"You . . . you mean it? But I thought you were with someone?" Richards's eyes were wide as he stared up at the man he seemed to idolize even though Hunt was only two years older than him. "She's okay with—"

Hunt snorted. "One thing you gotta learn, kid. These bunnies lose interest real quick. I thought she was—doesn't matter. I'm a single man. So are you. You in?"

"Yeah. Of course I am!" Richards jumped as Tim cleared his throat. "Sorry, Coach."

"No, please don't let me interrupt. Ask Demyan, this kinda stuff does great things for your reputation." Tim's gaze fell on Demyan, who seemed to find inspecting the tape on his stick blade suddenly imperative. Max snorted, covering with a cough as Tim squeezed Richards's shoulder. Tim patted Hunt's arm, studying the young goalie for a moment. "Your head in this, sport?"

"Where else would it be?" Hunt shrugged Tim's hand away and stormed across the room to grab a can of Red Bull. He ignored Doc's narrow-eyed stare.

"All right, let's do this!" Tim shouted. He stood by the door, slapping the men's backs, stalling Bower before he could go out to the ice and speaking quietly to him. Bower nodded to whatever Tim said.

Max went out last, not all that surprised when Tim stopped him a few feet from the benches.

"Richards steers clear of Hunt from now on. Got it?"

"I'll take care of it, Coach." Max watched Hunt skate back and forth along the goal line, his jaw hardening as the young man ignored Dominik's encouraging tap with his stick. "You sure he's gonna be all right?"

"Hard to say. I've never seen him like this." Tim shook his head, his jaw hard as he stared across the ice. "He's a pro. Let's see if he can act like one."

By the end of the second period, the Cobras were down 5-1. And Hunt was losing it. The crowd was booing . . . no, Max winced as he realized what they were doing was so much worse.

They were chanting. *'Bower! Bower! Bower!'*

Hunt drew a penalty by slashing one of the opponent's forwards after letting in the sixth goal, seconds after the period ended. He made it to the hall toward the locker room before he cracked his stick into the wall.

The men spoke low amongst themselves as they converged on the locker room, but Max didn't join them. He headed straight to Tim's office, ducking just in time to avoid getting clocked by the water bottle Tim threw.

"Coach, he's a pro." Max slammed the door behind him, not really giving a shit that this was none of his business. Hunt didn't want anyone's help. But he was gonna get it anyway. "He's not made of fucking stone. You heard them."

"Yeah, I heard them. Probably before you did." Tim let out a sharp laugh. "After the first goddamn goal, and it just got louder. I should have pulled him sooner, but I didn't want him to feel like I blamed him. Three of those goals were bad defense. Bower wouldn't have been able to stop them."

"You can't put Hunt back out there."

"I know that. But it's going to tear him apart to sit on the bench and listen to them howling for Bower."

"You ain't got a choice, Coach."

"I could dress you. Too bad this ain't the OHL." Tim rubbed his hands over his face, groaning. "Team therapist is gonna need a raise."

"Naw, you've got me." Max punched Tim's shoulder, tempted to tell the man he loved him again just to make him laugh for real. But taking care of Hunt would be the next best thing. "I'll talk to him. Remind him that some of the best goalies in the league have gone through this."

"You do that." Tim stepped out of his office, looking around the locker room and groaning again. "Just kill me now. Where the fuck is Bower?"

\* \* \* \*

"Defense, Silver."

"You always want defense! Look at this kid's stats!"

"I agree, he has potential, but if we get a good draft pick, I want to strengthen the blue line." Dean's lip quirked as Silver's brow furrowed, ready for her to give him hell for using terms she didn't understand. "I'm sorry, dragonfly, what I mean is—"

"Same thing you started on. Defense, blue line, got it." She wrinkled her nose at him. "Nice try, smart-ass. Now, from what I've seen looking over last year's draft picks, we might get lucky and get him in the second round. Can we grab him then?"

"Absolutely." He dragged her from her perch on the edge of his desk, laughing as she fussed about how he'd wrinkle her suit. And his. Sitting her on his lap, he carefully straightened her pale blue jacket, then wrapped his arms around her, kissing her throat until she melted into his arms. "You've come a long way from signing men because they look hot in a magazine spread."

"Perhaps, but it was still a good decision. I give you full creds for Zovko, though." She toyed with his lapel, a mischievous smile on her lips. "Can't say you didn't choose him for the same reason. He's pretty hot."

Dean snorted as he slid his hand under her jacket to palm her breast. "My tastes lean toward the softer sex, pet."

A firm knock and his office door opened. Seeing it was Landon, Dean kept his hand where it was.

Silver's lips slid across his cheek, brushing his ear as she whispered, "Liar."

The hairs on the back of Dean's neck stood on end. The word didn't sound like an accusation. If anything, her tone was pure temptation.

But that could be wishful thinking, so he let it slide as he focused on Landon. "Does Tim know you're here? He'll have a fit if he—"

Landon held out his hand and pulled Silver to her feet. He kissed her hard, holding her head in his hands as he looked into her eyes. "I love you. It didn't take therapy to know that, but I haven't shown you it for a long time. Not really. You gave me and Dean our beautiful daughter, and I've been acting like she's just mine. But she's ours."

"She is." Silver wrapped her arms around Landon's neck, staring up at him. "You've said this before. I know why you were having a hard time. We're better."

"We are." Landon nodded and finally let her go. "I just . . . I'm ready to get back out there. For real this time. I just needed to see you first." He turned to Dean, something in his eyes causing Dean's heart to beat like he'd just raced up four flights of stairs. "I needed to see both of you."

*Nothing's changed. We're all better. And he needs to get on the ice.* Dean stood and gave Landon a curt nod. "You've seen us. And now the team needs you."

"They can wait." Landon shifted away from Silver, looking from Dean to her, then back. "I said things, and I didn't mean a fucking word."

*Not now.* Dean could only guess, but if he was right, this wasn't the time. Or the place. Landon had to focus on the game, and Silver . . . Silver was happy. Truly happy for the first time in much too long. Anything Landon had to say about what he "hadn't meant" could ruin it.

"Understood." Dean shoved his hands in his pockets, jerking his chin at the door. "We'll discuss this later."

"We'll discuss it now." Landon inched closer, and Dean could see the war being waged within in his eyes. And he could tell which side won as Landon latched on to the front of his shirt. "Right fucking now."

There was no discussion, only Landon's lips on his in a brutal kiss, as though Landon felt he had to fight Dean himself to take it. Dean shoved Landon against his desk, his hands fisted in Landon's jersey. He held Landon in place, forcing him to accept a gentler response. Looked into Landon's eyes as the lips beneath his softened. He'd never really considered how things would be if they came together, but part of him had prepared for a struggle for dominance. Instead, he found Landon meeting him as an equal. Not submitting, not taking control. Simply giving everything he took.

Until Landon became *aware* of everything. Aware of Silver, watching them with an unreadable expression on her face. Landon dropped his hands to his sides. "Silver, I didn't mean—"

"Stop." Silver approached them, at first like she wasn't sure she should, then like nothing could stop her. She put her hand on Landon's cheek. "Don't spoil it to try to make me feel better. What you have with Dean is . . . beautiful. It scares me less when you're not trying to hide it."

"I wasn't, it's just . . . I'm not . . ." Landon glared at the floor. "Hell, I don't care what my father thinks. This is us. It feels right."

Dean couldn't agree more. He took Silver's hand, then framed Landon's jaw with his hand, kissing him again just to prove to himself that this was real. That he could do so without damaging the man in some way. "This is right. And your father doesn't need any more details about this than he does about how often you spank your fiancée."

"Yeah, that would freak him out too." Landon leaned into the next kiss, then turned his head to claim Silver's lips before whispering. "I don't want this to hurt you."

"It doesn't. So long as you two don't forget about me . . ." She rubbed against Dean as she shoved Landon toward the door. "I should thank you. It's hard to distract him, and you did a very good job of it. You go out and play while I take care of him." She blew Landon a kiss as he chuckled, reluctantly backing out of the office. "I'll let you do it next time."

"I'm taking you up on that." Landon gave Dean a hooded look, hesitating with his hand on the doorknob. "I'll make you a deal, old man. I win this game, I top you. If I lose . . ."

Dean held up his hand. *These two are going to kill me.* "Damn it, one kiss and you want to fuck?"

"Dean, I've wanted this for a long time." Landon's lips quirked up at the edges. "But if you want to be crude about it, yes. I'm still young. I rarely think about anything else."

"I believe it." Dean snorted, but thinking of the game and what the team had to lose made him frown. "Focus on the game, Landon."

"I always do when I'm on the ice." He glanced at the digital clock on Dean's wall that showed both the time and counted down to the next period. "Five minutes until we start. Twenty minutes for the last period—closer to forty if you count commercial breaks. Longer if there's penalties and—"

"Go before I tell my brother he doesn't have a goalie to put in! You're worse than she is!" Dean pushed Landon out into the hall and shut the door in his face. He bowed his head, hiding his smile as he heard Silver giggle again. She really was okay with this. He turned to her, his expression as stern as possible as he crossed the room. "What were you saying about taking care of me, pet?"

"Oh, did I say that?" She curved into him, nipping his throat even as he combed his fingers through her hair. Her fingers tugged at his belt. "Do you know why I'm not threatened by him anymore?"

"Because you know we both love you?"

"There's that." She dropped to her knees, forcing him to loosen his hold on her hair. "And he's got a lot to learn." Her nimble fingers curved around his dick. Her hot mouth slid over him once before she tipped her head back to give him a taunting smile. "I can't wait to teach him. To teach you both. It's going to be fucking hot to see him just like this."

Dean should have been embarrassed by how quickly he came, deep in her throat, but he wasn't. Silver had found a way to feel included in the next step he and Landon took together. And there was no better way to express how it felt than what Landon had said.

*It feels right.*

\* \* \* \*

The loss wasn't a surprise, but Max found it hard to set aside as he joined Demyan in Tim's office. He could tell Tim had already put this game behind them.

"I'll only say one thing about tonight. 6-4 isn't bad. Landon gave us a shot to come back, but it's gonna be one hell of a battle to get to the playoffs." Tim pointed to the calendar on his desk. "That aside, you've both heard about the charity events coming up. Both are for a good cause, but I understand why most of the men signed up for the charity ball. It's close to Valentine's Day. The thing is, you're both at the top of the list for the mentorship program. Most of the Ice Girls are going, and I need to show the team is committed to these girls. They come from underprivileged homes. Yeah, they're cheerleaders on ice, but they love the Cobras. Some are just Ice Girls for their high school hockey team because they only allow guys to play. I have pamphlets for a local girls' team, one we're sponsoring, but it doesn't get much attention . . ." Tim scowled at the glossy pamphlets he set before them. "I've set up funding for equipment, travel—most calls are from kids. Only one parent. Doesn't feel like I'm doing enough . . ."

"I'll be there." Max picked up half the pamphlets, exchanging a look with Demyan, happy to see the same determination in the other man's eyes. "It's something, Coach. These girls don't have much, but they're given a way to get on the ice. If they want to play the game, if it's in their blood, we'll help them."

"Is that a yes?" Tim asked, as though he hadn't been sure about asking in the first place. "Hell, I know any one of the guys would do this if I told them to, but the ball is important too. The money we'll raise will go to victims of domestic abuse. Scott . . ." Tim's use of Demyan's first name showed his reluctance. "It's your cause. I wouldn't have asked if so many of the girls hadn't put down your name."

"The rest of the guys can dress up and dance and bring in the money. I know where these girls come from. I want to be there for them. Where I can really make a difference." Demyan grabbed the rest of the pamphlets. "Give me a time and place, Coach."

"Friday. Around four. They'll all meet up after school. The ball is from five to eight. You might be able to—"

"Zach will be there for Becky. I'm not rushing this." Demyan grinned. "You know there'll be fans swamping the place. We can't ignore them, but I won't give them a second of my time until I've talked to all the girls. Like . . . to encourage them. Nothing bad." His grin shifted to a scowl. "Damn, maybe I shouldn't go. Teenage girls . . . people might think—"

"The last headline you were featured under had a 'Daddies of the Year' over it. With you, Pearce, and Casey. People don't see you as the playboy anymore. You didn't just come out as bisexual, you came out as a man who went through hell as a child. You've given kids someone to look up to." Tim went over to Scott, who was staring at the floor, and gave him a little push. "Head up, man. You should be proud."

"I am, just . . . my life wasn't something to want until lately."

Max bumped against Demyan's side. "Lately is what counts."

"True." Demyan gave them both a stiff smile. "So that it? If I know Casey, she's pretending to sleep until both me and Zach are home."

"A good half of the Ice Girls that are going don't have cars. I figure we could drive them between the three of us." Tim counted the girls out on his hands. "Three in my car. Four in yours, four in Perron's. Two are maybes, but they have their own cars."

"Works for me." Demyan saluted to them both, answering his buzzing phone as he headed out. "Figured that!" He laughed. "Put my baby on the phone . . ."

Tim spoke before Max could follow Demyan out. "Max, I hesitated asking you, but mostly because I know Oriana wants to go to the ball. And she'll be alone."

"She loves this team. And they love her." Max could already see Oriana, all dressed up, dancing with every player while talking about the game. "I'll ask her, but we both know what her answer will be."

"Sorry, give me a sec." Tim answered his buzzing phone. "Yes? No. I'm not sure what you mean." Tim paused. "Yeah, I was given that offer. A couple of years ago. And my answer hasn't changed." Hanging up, Tim dropped his phone on the desk and sighed. "I'd feel better if Sloan was here."

"So would I." Max let his curiosity about Tim's odd conversation slide. And concentrated on the matter at hand. Sloan could move on from the loss. Tell him he'd dance with Oriana and convince him the season wasn't over. But from what Tim had said, Sloan would have been getting calls all night. He'd have turned his phone off, hopefully having made his decision.

The man was a Cobra. This was where Sloan—and Max—had started. And as far as the game went, this was where it should end.

# Chapter Twenty One

A fancy hotel ballroom, with round, white linen-covered tables circling the huge, glossy pale wood dance floor, crowded with the hundreds that had come for a chance to be close to the Cobras. Women who giggled behind their silk gloves, men who spoke loud after a few too many drinks. A band that switched between classical in slow rich tones, to covers of old and new songs, both a male and female singer that did pretty impressive covers. The music made the whole thing almost bearable.

But this still had to be one of the lamest things Cort had ever done. The tuxedo Ford had rented for him was too fucking tight—the idiots hadn't measured him right. The buttons holding the jacket together were straining. If he bent over he was pretty damn sure the pants would rip.

And . . . shit, the drool from the chicks throwing themselves at him was gonna leave stains. The "ladies" were all fucking bunnies and they thought he was a player. Or someone connected to the team. He got a bit of a chuckle every time they asked if the Cobras had a chance for the Cup, and they gaped at him when he said the Red Wings would take it.

Yeah, maybe that made him an asshole, but he hadn't asked to be here. He didn't *belong* here. Fuck, he was the reason the team was gonna lose whatever slim chance they had at making the playoffs. The idiots would have to go on an impressive fucking winning streak to clinch a spot, and he didn't see it happening. He glared at the starting goalie, the man who the fans had screamed for during the last game. Yeah, he'd kept the other team from scoring again in the third period, but so what?

It should have been a win. He'd told Roy it would be a win. And now the goddamn sociopath wouldn't answer his calls. Which meant he was dealing with the unexpected loss in his own way.

*I need to get Ford out of here.* Cort watched Ford bowing low to Jami in mock formality as "Crash and Burn" by Savage Garden began. In a pearl white gown, her short brown hair swept away from her face in a cute little updo, Jami looked so young, and too fucking fragile. She gave Ford a little shove, laughing at him until he straightened. Ford offered her his hand after looking to her father, and Sebastian Ramos, for permission. Both men nodded and Ford spun her around the dance floor. Holding her as though she was an old friend and not the girl who'd almost ruined him. Or who he'd almost ruined.

Hell, Cort couldn't tell anymore. He half wished Akira was here to give him something to do other than watch Ford like one of the dancers was gonna pull a gun on him. Ford was probably safe enough here. The team's security detail was pretty efficient. They were dressed in dark suits and blended pretty well, but Cort had seen them closing in on the groups of men near the refreshment table when things got rowdy. Besides, Akira would be here soon enough. Her mentoring thing should be almost over.

But when she came, he'd have to keep his distance. With all the camera crews hovering around the crowd—damn it, all he needed was for Roy to catch one image of Akira in his arms. There was no way Cort could pretend she was just another woman. He couldn't hide how he felt about her. They'd been lucky so far, but Cort's luck had a tendency to run out pretty fucking quick. Things were about due to go to shit.

*I fucked up.* Roy would make Cort pay for the money he'd lost on the "sure bet." Cort needed to know when. *How.* But there was no way to tell. He'd been awake for three days, sleeping on Ford's sofa with a gun in his hand, sure Roy would try to use his son again.

After a flask full of whiskey, Cort had even called Ramos,

asking about Jami, probably sounding like he was fucking crazy. Roy had sent someone after her once. He wouldn't put it past him to do it again. Ramos hadn't laughed him off and hung up like Cort had expected. He'd asked a bunch of questions that Cort couldn't answer, and from the shadows under his eyes as he watched Jami in Ford's arms, the man hadn't slept much either.

Twice now, Ramos had turned to look at Cort, like he wanted to have a chat. And both times Jami's other man, Carter, distracted him. Once by taking a glass of champagne from a waiter passing with a tray—Ramos immediately retrieved the glass and returned it to the tray. The second time, Carter cut in on a dance, playfully taking Vanek away from the old lady who was groping him. Ramos shook his head, smiling at the boys as they danced in a tipsy two-step.

When Ramos caught the eye of Vanek's Domme, Chicklet, and got a nod, Cort knew the man would head right over. He had the sudden urge to grab the closest lady and get in on the dancing himself, but he couldn't avoid this. He couldn't look out for both Jami and Ford. The man needed to know enough not to let his guard down.

Ramos didn't say anything at first, simply stood beside Cort, his gaze trailing Jami and Ford's progress around the floor. His jaw hardened as he glanced over at Cort, his arms folded over his chest. "You understand, I cannot protect her if I don't know what the danger is."

"Roy Kingsley. Pretty sure I told you that on the phone." Cort rubbed his lips with his fist, trying to figure out what he could give the man. If he told him too much . . . he shook his head. "You saw what he did to Ford. That was just a warning."

"He wants Ford to work for him again. Jami mentioned that she suspected as much," Ramos said. "Ford clearly refused. It's been over a month. What has changed?"

"He thought he was getting what he wanted. Then you guys lost."

"It is the way of the game."

"I get that, but there are ways to make it lean a little more in your favor if you're a gambling man." Cort was getting close to spilling more than he should. He chose his next words carefully. "All I can say is he's done giving warnings. His next move will either be to make sure he's taken seriously, or—"

"Or what?" Ramos turned to face Cort, his tone dangerously low. "I am not a stupid man, Mr. Nash. You clearly attempted to pacify Roy Kingsley in your own way and you failed. What will he do now?"

"I don't know." Which was the truth. In the state of mind he was in, Roy could do just about anything. There was only one sure way to stop him. He gave Ramos a tight smile. Might as well let him in on the rest. He didn't see the man having any objection. "He wouldn't be able to hurt anyone else if he was dead."

Ramos inclined his head, not looking at all shocked by the statement. He stared out at the dance floor as he quietly spoke. "Jail would likely limit his power as well."

"It would. But I go to the cops, and I'll end up behind bars myself. I won't be able to protect Ford while Roy's lawyers are sweeping whatever shit I can give them under the rug." A dull ache settled between Cort's eyes. He tried to rub it away with his finger and thumb. Rats didn't have long life spans in jail. Even if Cort gave up enough to condemn Roy, he'd never make it to trial. "I should grab Ford and get the fuck out of here."

"Perhaps you should discuss that with Ford. I doubt he'll be willing to leave the others at risk behind." Ramos's expression turned grim. "The problems didn't disappear the last time you ran, Cort."

"No, but I've told you plenty. You can make sure everyone else watches their back. Ask for a fucking trade and get Jami and Carter out of here."

"And what of Akira? Will you leave her to 'watch her back'? Or will you force her to abandon everything she's worked for to hide with you?" Even though Cort didn't so much as blink, Ramos seemed to read something in his expression. Ramos's jaw ticked.

"There is a reason you're not as worried about her. Roy doesn't know she's involved with you. You aim to keep it that way."

"Yes." Cort inhaled deeply, but he couldn't get enough air. It was like someone had pulled a bag over his head, and he'd just taken his last breath. He'd had it good for a while, but it was over. "You'll keep an eye out for her? She'll probably go back to Dominik—he's a good man."

The music changed and Carter met up with Jami and Ford at the edge of the dance floor, offering Ford Vanek in exchange for Jami. Ford laughed and ruffled Carter's hair before calling out to his sister. Oriana joined them and Vanek's face went red. He looked to Chicklet, who motioned for him to go ahead.

Oriana whispered something to Vanek that made him laugh and stole the tension from his body. He took Oriana's hand and led her in a slow waltz. So much history between all these people, and Cort didn't know all of it, but he did know Akira was happy here. So was Ford, but Ford's staying wasn't an option.

Ramos surprised Cort by putting a hand on his shoulder. "He is a good man, but you are the man she loves. I owe you much for saving Jami, and I will repay that debt in part by telling you this. Give those you love the truth. Do not make this decision alone."

"Right." Cort watched Ford make his way along the table with a charming smile for all the rich old ladies who called out to him. A year ago he could have almost guaranteed Ford would agree to however Cort decided to handle things. Ramos was right; Cort had to talk to Ford. But he was more than a little reluctant because Ford would probably tell him the same thing Ramos had. *Don't run.*

As Ford approached them, Ramos squeezed Cort's shoulder, saying one last thing before he walked away. "We will speak again. Hopefully when I come to the police station to post bail."

*Shit.* Cort frowned at Ramos's back as Ford stopped, his expression making it clear he'd caught the last words. Ford jerked his head toward the door leading outside. Once they were away from all the smokers huddled on the recently shoveled path, Ford faced Cort, shoving his hands in his pockets to grab his pack of cigarettes and his lighter.

He offered Cort one and sucked his teeth before placing the cigarette filter between his lips, speaking around it as he lit the tip. "Time to fucking talk, man. Why you need bail?"

Cort lit his own cigarette, watching the cloud of smoke that left his lips slink into the darkness. "I had to warn Ramos that your da—that Roy might come after Jami. We got to talking about how I've been working for the son of a bitch. And how I fucked up."

Ford went perfectly still. Dropped his cigarette in the snow. And punched Cort in the face. "You dumb fuck! Why didn't you tell me? That shit the other day had nothing to do with your stepfather, did it?"

Jaw throbbing, Cort swiped a trickle of blood from the edge of his lip, tamping down the instinct to strike back. "No."

"How long has this been going on?" Ford took out his pack, put it away. Started pacing as he raked his fingers through his hair. "Wait, don't bother answering, I can figure it out. He came to you while I was in the hospital."

"Yes."

"That's why he hasn't approached me again. He already had you." Ford glared at Cort. "Were you paying off someone? You must have done something to keep him happy."

"I did." Cort stared at the dirty snow at the edge of the path, his guts churning, almost as disgusted with himself as he knew Ford would be. "The rookie goalie—"

"You had him throwing games? But he doesn't seem like the type who would . . ." Ford's eyes snapped. He looked ready to punch Cort again. "Angel. You had her playing fucking head games with him? That's just sick, Cort. You're messing with some kid's career just to make my old man some money?"

"I did it because he almost had you beat to death the last time you stood up to him. He knows I killed Lee, so I didn't have too many fucking options!"

"You stopped Lee from raping her! No way you'd do time for that!" Ford's hand came out fast, but instead of punching Cort, he latched on to the front of his tuxedo jacket, speaking through his teeth. "I know you don't wanna go inside again, but you gave that bastard too much power. Is all this shit worth avoiding a couple of years inside for involuntary manslaughter?"

Cort wrenched Ford's hand from his jacket and jerked him close so the stupid kid wouldn't miss one goddamn word. "This ain't about me not wanting to do time. There's nothing standing between you and him if I'm inside."

"Then let's put him away!"

"I plan to put him in the fucking ground."

Ford let out a rough laugh. "Yeah, because two bodies, rather than one, will make this whole mess go away."

Letting Ford go, Cort took a step back. "You got a better idea?"

"Actually, I do. All that education you made sure I got is good for something." Ford rolled his shoulders and straightened his jacket. "You're gonna turn yourself in. And I'm going to make a deal to get you cleared—if the law don't work in your favor anyway. Either way, I can get plenty on Kingsley."

The kid was living in some kind of fantasy world. If Cort didn't know better, he'd ask if Ford was high. "You can't get shit on him. I was working for him, and I don't got nothing solid."

"He's desperate, right? If you get taken in, he'll know he can't use you. I tell him I want back in the fold, prove to him that I can rig the games, he'll jump at the chance. He never hid anything from me before." Ford smirked. "It'll be just like old times."

"And how exactly do you plan to rig the games? I thought you cared too much about this team to fuck with it." There had to be some way to talk Ford out of this crazy plan. Cort thought of all the people Ford loved here and had his answer. "Your sisters, Jami, they'd fucking hate you if they found out—"

"My sisters are gonna know what I'm doing. Jami doesn't need to be involved." Ford scratched his jaw. "Besides, I'm not gonna need to actually rig any games. If I get someone in and can call even one game—"

"With your psychic fucking powers?"

"No, using the fucking odds. He wants the team in the playoffs. We need a winning streak. To make it seem real, I can talk to Tim—see if he can get the guys to hold back a little in the first period without letting anything in. Tell them not to burn themselves out too early or—"

"How many people you plan to get involved in this?" Cort asked irritably. He could just see Roy taking down the names of all the people who knew too damn much. All the people that would be in his way. "This can end now with no one else getting hurt. If we leave—"

"We're not leaving. You're gonna fucking trust me." Ford put his hand on Cort's forearm. "You trusted me enough to let me close to the only woman you've ever loved. Trust me with this."

*Low goddamn blow.* Cort tipped his head back and sighed. "I trust you, but I'm not sure how you think this will play out. Best scenario, I'm in jail and you start working for your dad again for real. And you never piss him off because I won't be around to watch your back."

"No. Best scenario, you get cleared, and he's out of both our lives for good." Ford grinned like he was so damn sure it was gonna work. "You come home every day stinking of grease, and I come home looking all sharp in my suit. And Akira is there, waiting for us both."

"Barefoot and pregnant?" Cort chuckled, half ready to pack up his shit and move into Ford's little dreamworld. "Or does this fantasy involve her waiting on her knees? Naked?"

Ford shrugged. "Either way. Don't think she'll want kids for a few years since she wants to open that figure skating school, but I ain't in no hurry."

"Good to know." Cort sighed and rubbed his hand over his face. He'd pretty much just agreed to all the insanity. Once he confessed to the cops, there'd be no turning back. Ford would be on his own. And Akira . . . fuck, they had to keep her safe. He couldn't do this unless he knew she'd be safe. "Think we can get

Akira to go on a trip?"

"No, but I've got an idea to make sure my dad don't know she's with us." Ford got out another cigarette, his hand shaking slightly as he brought it to his lips. Just enough to show Cort he knew how serious this all was. "I'll have her stay with Dominik."

"Dominik would be good. He'll take care of her." Cort took Ford's lighter and lit the cigarette for him. "Just . . . promise me something. You won't take no stupid chances. Roy is fucking unstable, and if he thinks you're setting him up—"

"I promise." Ford looked around quickly, then grabbed Cort and gave him a tight, backslapping hug. "Pisses me off that you didn't come to me sooner, but I get it. Guess I wasn't in any condition to deal with the old bastard while I was still pissing blood."

"Still not sure you can, kid." Cord shook his head. "Sorry, I know you hate when I call you that. You're not a kid anymore. Fuck, you grew up to be a better man than I'll ever be."

Ford laughed and slugged Cort's shoulder. "Enough of that crap. You'll have some interesting stories to tell our grandkids about being their godmother's hero."

"Some hero." Cort shook his head, his lips slanting in an amused smile. "You and Jami have been spending too much time together. Stop with the baby talk before Akira decides to have you fucking neutered."

"Thanks for the warning." Ford grinned, then sighed and took a big step back. "Guess we should stop looking so friendly. How you gonna do this?"

Cort turned back toward the door to the ballroom with an offhand shrug. "Might as well take advantage of the fact that there's a cop right here. Don't think she's got cuffs under that little red dress."

"Chicklet might have a pair to lend her."

"Real funny."

"No, not funny at all." Ford stopped him at the door, his brow furrowed. His throat worked as he stared at the door. "But you're doing the right thing. And even better, you did it before it was too late."

Cort gently moved Ford aside and opened the door. "Just tell Akira I'm sorry. And I love her."

"I will."

"But—" Cort hung his head and closed his eyes. "Make sure there's no one around. And make sure she understands—"

"I will, Cort. I've got this."

"Right."

Inside the ballroom, Cort looked around until he spotted Laura. She wore a knee-length, crimson silk dress, her light brown hair in fluffy curls, her face glowing as Chicklet fed her a cherry from the top of her fruity drink. She laughed as she caught her Mistress's wrist and sucked the juices from her fingertips.

Chicklet lifted her head as Cort stopped in front of them. She gave him a hesitant smile. "Hey, Cort. Everything okay?"

"Yeah." He turned his attention to Laura, and his lips quirked as her eyes narrowed. "Take it you know who I am?"

"Yes." Fine creases formed on her forehead. "You're aware that you're wanted for questioning? I have to call someone to bring you in."

"How about I give you one better? I'm ready to confess." It was fucking weird, but he felt kinda good. This shit wouldn't be hanging over his head anymore. He cleared his throat. "I'm the one who murder—"

"Not another word." Laura took her phone out of her small, black beaded purse and gestured for him to follow. "First of all, murder is a charge, not an action. Even *if* you killed Charles Lee, there's no need to discuss it with me. Or *anyone* until your lawyer tells you otherwise."

"Yes, ma'am."

"Don't call me ma'am." She made an irritated sound as they reached the hotel lobby. "Why now? I've seen your file. You don't have a reputation for cooperating with law enforcement."

"Guess now would be a bad time to tell you I'd be gone

already if I didn't have a reason to stay?" He gave her a rueful grin when she scowled at him. "I shouldn't be discussing this with you?"

"No. But I haven't given you the Charter of Rights—damn it, you're from the States, aren't you?" Laura paused while dialing on her phone. "It's a little different from Miranda rights, but the basics are the same. You have the right not to incriminate yourself with anything you say. So just don't say anything."

"Got it."

"This won't take long." She kept her eyes on him as she made the call. Then led him outside. The second the cop car pulled up, Cort felt all his muscles tense. He had to force himself not to make a run for it.

Cameras flashed from somewhere off to the side. Cort turned his head, but they were everywhere. He clenched his jaw as someone stepped up behind him.

"Give me your jacket, Cort," Ramos said.

Ramos's big body blocked Cort from one side. His sub, Carter, blocked Cort's other side. Cort let Ramos take his jacket, all the noise around him, the curious onlookers, the reporters trying to get closer, the cops talking to him, all jumbling together so he couldn't make out a single word. He nodded when the cop asked, "Do you understand?"

The metal of the cuffs on his wrists was ice cold. More flashes, but his jacket was suddenly hanging over the cuffs. He stared at Ramos as the man backed away.

"You get one phone call, Cort." Ramos gave him a bracing smile. "My number is in the pocket of your jacket. I will provide you with legal counsel."

"You don't gotta do that, man." Cort laughed as the cop shoved him toward the squad car. "Fuck, I turned myself in. No need to be pushy."

"Shut up, Cort!" Carter backed up a few more steps when Laura frowned at him. "If you piss them off, they'll, like, beat you with phone books or something."

"That's not a bad thing." Vanek had joined Carter on the sidewalk, cutting off the reporters even more as Cort was placed in the backseat. "Claim police brutality. You'll be out tomorrow!"

"Tyler, get back inside." Laura looked past him to Chicklet. "He's not helping."

"Sorry, sweetheart." Vanek's tone seemed to set Laura's teeth on edge. And the kid moved even closer to the door before the arresting officer could close it. "You helped Jami. The team's behind you. Don't take any shit."

Chicklet pulled Vanek back. The door was slammed shut. Cort rested his hands on his lap, thinking on Vanek's words. Sounded like exactly what his stepfather had said the last time he'd been arrested.

*"The club's behind you, Cort. Don't you fucking worry. You won't be in long."*

The club hadn't been able to do a goddamn thing. Not for him, and not for his biological father, who was doing life. But Cort had done okay in jail. He wasn't as built then as he was now, but he'd held his own. He'd gone two years without getting raped or any kind of shit like that, but he'd spent plenty of time in SCU, or solitary, for "disorderly conduct." Cracked one guy's skull in the showers for grabbing him. Got in more fights than he could count.

It was the hotbox that had almost broken him. The walls so close, like they'd crush him. As a kid, his mom had let him run wild in the fields outside his dad's club. As soon as he was old enough to ride, his only limits were where the road ended. But waking to those walls around him was a constant reminder that his freedom was gone.

And he might never get it back.

He'd done everything he could to avoid going in again. Until now. Now he'd let them put the cuffs on him. He'd gone willingly.

*Stupid.* He barked out a laugh that had the officer watching him warily through the rearview mirror. *Why didn't you fucking run, Nash? You should have fucking run.*

He pressed his eyes shut and let Ford's words play over and

over in his head as the car pulled up in front of the station. *"You trusted me enough to let me close to the only woman you've ever loved. Trust me with this."*

"I trust you, Ford." Cort mumbled to himself, trying to block out the confines of the cop car. Trying not to think about the cell he'd be sitting in shortly. Or the hospital bed Ford would be lying in again if he made the wrong move. "Just watch your back, kid."

The cop turned to him as he parked. "You say something?"

Cort shook his head, glaring out the window. "Got nothing to say without my fucking lawyer."

"You heard what I said before, right?" The cop's tone was calm. Almost comforting. And so low Cort had to listen close just to hear him. "You have the right to apply for legal assistance if you need it."

Ramos had offered to get Cort a lawyer. And, hell, maybe he should take him up on it. If there was any chance he could get out—fuck, even on bail . . .

"I think I've got a lawyer." He didn't move as the cop came around the car to open the door. Got out nice and peaceful-like, because that would look good. And since the cop wasn't being an asshole, Cort didn't laugh when the guy slipped on a patch of ice. He just stood there and waited for the man to bring him through the sally port. "Can I make a call?"

"After I book you." The cop's tone hardened a little as he brought Cort to a small room and handed him an orange jumpsuit. Cort knew the drill. He changed and gave the cop his tuxedo.

*No big deal.* Cort went numb as the cop brought him to the booking desk. *Just like coming right back fucking home.*

# Chapter Twenty Two

Not all the Ice Girls were going to the charity ball, but those who were had gathered in the bathroom of the large arena beyond the rink where they'd skated with the high school girls. Akira came out of one of the changing stalls in her dress and joined Sahara at the sink, placing one hand over her exposed chest as she looked in the mirror.

"Very daring, Akira. I like." Sahara winked at her as she swept another coat of mascara over her lashes. She faced Akira, looking over Akira's low cut, V-neck sky blue halter gown, then down at her own pale gold, strapless dress. Sahara brought one hand up to her elegant topknot, then smoothed her fingers over the tendrils framing her face. "How old do I look?"

"No more than twenty-two." Akira sighed when Sahara frowned. "Oh, sweetie. Don't try to look older."

"I'm not. Of course I'm not." Sahara's chin jutted up. "Why would I?" She grinned. "Think Pischlar will ask me to dance?"

"I think he'll ask for more than that."

Sahara laughed and bumped her shoulder against Akira's. "So naughty. You better let Ford and Cort dance with you at least once before you drag them home. I bet they both look lickable in a tux."

"As if I could drag them anywhere. I am a good little sub." Akira winked as she slicked some peach-flavored gloss on her lips. "I do as my Master commands."

Their youngest Ice Girl, Justina, stared at Akira as she approached the next sink, fussing with the fluffy skirts of her black gown, her hand covering her chest as well above the pink-beaded sweetheart neckline. "I can't get used to *you* calling anyone 'Master.' You're just so . . . strong."

Madeline, the wife of the Cobras' head coach, came up behind Justina and hugged her. "Akira is very strong. It takes a lot of strength to trust a man that much. And to find the one who deserves it."

"Like Coach." Justina glanced back at Madeline. "I hope I find someone just like him. He's amazing."

"He is, but he's not my Master—unless I ask him to be." Madeline chuckled. "Between us girls, he's just as happy kneeling to me as he is when I submit to him. There's all sorts, honey. You'll find someone right for you."

"Maybe." Justina tugged at the bodice of her dress. "Some guys like big girls, right?"

"Don't make me take out my whip, little girl." Madeline lightly slapped Justina's shoulder. "You're speaking to an old lady who is about fifty pounds heavier than you. If you're a 'big girl,' what does that make me?"

*Oh, I love her!* Akira wrapped her arms around Madeline's waist. "You're not old!"

"I second that!" Sahara pushed her breasts up and shook her head. "And please let me come over to dinner sometime! I need to gain some weight! Right here!"

"You girls make me so glad I'm not young and silly anymore." Madeline gathered them all in a hug, giving all the other girls she couldn't reach a big smile. "You're all beautiful." She looked at Justina. "And I heard what that nasty bitch said to you. Don't you dare believe a word of it."

"Oh, I don't! Sahara and Akira took care of that." Justina blushed and ducked her head. "I'm just . . . I'm happy I finally made it. I've never been part of anything this amazing." She bit her bottom lip. "Did you see my brother out there? He was mad that my parents made him come, but when Scott talked to him—"

"He was the adorable little redhead, right?" Carey, a quiet little brunette, a few years older than most of the girls, asked in a whisper. "He reminds me of my son. Pierre loves the team too."

"Yeah, but I hope he's not bugging Scott too much. He was

still with him when we came in here," Justina said.

"I don't think Scott minds at all. He's got his own kid, so he's used to it." Akira had seen Scott with Casey. From playboy to super dad. When she'd found out he was coming, she'd known all the younger ones in attendance would be fine. "I think everything worked out perfectly. I'm gonna ask Silver if we can do this again next year."

"Already done." Madeline shooed them out of the bathroom. "You're all perfect. Now let's give our boys someone to dance with besides rich old ladies!"

Outside in the parking lot, Akira waited with a few other girls who'd gotten a lift from Scott as he spoke with Justina's brother while turning his keys in his ignition, his tone light even though he must be getting annoyed at the whine and stutter noise his car was making. Justina pulled her car up in front of Scott's to give him a jump start. It wasn't working.

"I'd love to stay, kid, but I'm supposed to be somewhere," Scott said to Justina's brother before dropping back into his seat, groaning. "What the hell!"

"I can bring some of the girls back with me." The father of one of the Ice Girls approached, leaning on the door of Scott's car. "They're not all going to the ball, are they?"

"No." Scott looked up at Akira. "Split the girls going between Max's car and Mr. Slogan's. Tim will have too much equipment in his car for more than one person if he's gotta take the stuff I brought."

Max came up to the car and stood beside Mr. Slogan. "You gonna head back with Tim?"

"Yeah." Scott chuckled as the crowd around the barrier security had set up thickened. "I'll go sign some stuff and meet up with you guys in a bit. Tim's the man, but they don't really want the coach signing their jerseys."

"Maybe I should stay?" Max followed Scott's gaze to the fans. "I hate walking away from our admirers."

"They'll live. Look at these girls. They're all prettied up." Scott got out of his car and shut the door behind him. "If I don't get there in time . . . just make sure Becky never leaves the dance floor. And tell her I'll take her out dancing sometime soon to make up for it."

"Will do." Max hugged Scott, then waited for Akira to sort out the girls who were going to the ball.

Akira put her hand on Justina's arm before she could follow Scott to the crowd. "Aren't you coming?"

"In a bit. I know my dad will bring my brother home, but I have to admit, I love seeing him following Scott around. He gets in a lot of trouble at school. He kinda likes hockey, but he's not serious about anything." She smiled as her little brother gazed up at Scott while Scott spoke to an adoring fan. "Maybe he will be now."

It took an hour to drive to the hotel in Dartmouth. When they got there, all the girls spread out on to the dance floor, pairing up with the players. Akira spotted Ford. She moved toward him, but he held up his hand and nodded toward Dominik.

She swallowed, not sure why he wouldn't come see her first. It was hard not to feel a little rejected. Maybe Ford was busy. This was a charity event, after all. But still, wouldn't he want to be near her after the time they'd spent apart?

"Don't look at him, Akira." Dominik's solid arm came across her back. His cheek pressed to hers as he whispered, "Right now, as far as everyone is concerned, you're still with me."

"But . . ." *What?* That didn't make any sense. "I'm with Cort. And Ford. What's wrong with that?"

"Cort was arrested tonight."

*No!* Akira's blood ran cold, as though all her veins were filled with melting ice. She went stiff, tried to turn, but Dominik held her firmly as he moved her in a slow dance to "Desperado" by The Eagles. And the song itself made her want to push him away and scream at him. Not Cort. He hadn't done anything wrong. Why would he let this happen?

"Let me go, Dominik. I have to go talk to Ford." Tears streamed down her cheeks as she pushed at his chest. "He'll know what to do."

"He was the one who asked me to keep you away from him." Dominik made a soft shushing sound. "He's trying to help Cort. To help the team. But he can't if he's worried about you."

"He doesn't have to worry! I'm fine!"

"Be still, little one." Dominik's arms tensed around her. "Ford's father—Kingsley—doesn't know about you. If he did, he'd use you. He'd have someone hurt you so much worse than he hurt Ford."

She trembled, pressing her face against Dominik's chest as she saw Silver looking over at her, concern in her eyes as she danced with Dean.

"If . . . if people see me with you, Ford and Cort will be okay?" *Please tell me they'll be okay.* She couldn't stand the thought of Cort in jail. And what had happened to Ford . . . that couldn't happen again. "I need to do something."

"You're doing it. Smile, pet. Make it as real as you can." Dominik kissed her cheek. "Kingsley will be watching. Be my strong girl and don't give him anything. We don't know if there are pictures out there with you and Cort. Or you and Ford. If Kingsley sees you with me, not reacting to Cort's arrest, not even looking at Ford, he'll move on."

"He'll try to use Silver. Or Oriana." Where was Oriana? Akira spotted her on the dance floor with Max. Max was pressing his hand to her cheek, saying something to her. "Or . . . damn it, Ford cares about the team now. Kingsley can use anyone!"

"Shh . . . not you." Dominik held her head against his chest. "All I can do is make sure it's not you."

Akira couldn't smile. She wasn't that good of an actress. But she did lean into Dominik, letting him lead her in one dance after another. Whatever Cort and Ford were dealing with, she didn't want to be a distraction. Or a weakness. So she clung to Dominik and ignored everyone else, as though he was the only man she wanted.

And prayed that would be enough.

* * * *

Dean tightened his grip on Silver as they circled around the dance floor, not missing the tears in Akira's eyes. Or the way Oriana tried to pull away from Max, her eyes on her brother. There was something very wrong. Something he didn't know anything about.

What though? This night had been planned so well, most of it by Silver herself. She'd taken care of every little detail. He tried to think of the very worst thing that could happen and came up blank. Yes, the team had lost a few games, but that was nothing new. He could see someone bringing up the Cobra's failings bothering Oriana, but Akira would take it in stride. Because the Ice Girls would be on the ice until the last game, no matter what happened.

He'd mark it off as something personal for Akira, but that didn't explain Oriana's reactions. Or the way Ford was standing at the edge of the dance floor, careful not to look at Akira, looking like he expected . . . something.

"Dean?" Silver cupped his face in her hand, seeming to sense his concern. "What is it?"

Dean shook his head. "I don't know."

Their life had been difficult enough. Silver had healed from her wounds. Landon . . . Dean spotted him near the refreshment table, standing by his sister who was on her phone. Becky covered her mouth with her hand. Her phone hit the floor.

Zach kept her on her feet by wrapping his arms around her. He spoke in her ear.

"Dean?" Silver latched on to Dean's arms as he stopped moving. He reached for her hand and moved across the floor.

Landon tore his gaze away from his sister as Dean approached them. He looked torn, but he left his sister with Zach and met Dean a few feet away from them. "Dean, Becky just got off the phone with one of the reporters covering the mentorship program. There was an accident—"

"Is it one of the girls? One of the players?" *Oh God. Scott.* Dean took a step back, bringing Silver with him. "Max is here. But Scott—"

"Scott was with Tim and Madeline." Landon moved with them. Put his arms around Dean. "Dean . . . your brother—"

"Scott was with them. Then he's okay." Dean carefully lowered Landon's arms. Tim would have kept an eye on Scott. It was ridiculous to think Tim would let Scott drink and drive—and why would Scott be drinking at an event with children anyway? No wonder Becky was upset! What kind of father did that? "If Scott got drunk, we'll suspend him. Give him a fine. He'll learn. He loves your sister, but he still makes mistakes."

"Dean—"

"We all make mistakes. Scott's getting better."

Becky was grabbing for her phone as it rang. She sat on her floor, the skirt of her mauve gown bunched around her knees. "They didn't find him in the car? Then where . . . oh God! Are you sure?" Her bottom lip trembled. "Are they sure it's . . . ? Okay. Thank you." Becky let Zach help her to her feet. Let him hold her. "Dean . . . I—I'm so sorry."

"Why?" Dean smiled at her. Clearly, Scott was okay. That was good. Scott was a good man. His whole body shook, but that was just nerves. The players . . . he cared about each and every one. Tim would be happy to know Scott was okay. The Ice Girls had arrived, so Tim should be here any minute. "With what Scott's been through, I was a little worried that he'd done something foolish. But he is all right? The accident—"

Zach looked to Landon. Who hadn't taken his eyes from Dean.

"An accident. The roads are icy. It happens." Dean put his arms around Silver as she pressed against his side. She worried too much. With what she'd been through, it wasn't good for her. "I should make a statement in the morning. Was anyone hurt?"

"Dean." Landon placed both his hands on Dean's shoulders. Made him stop moving. Made Dean face him. "Tim . . . he was on his way back with Madeline. A car turned into them. They went off the road—"

"Tim is a very good driver. I taught him." Dean shook his head as he saw the pain in Landon's eyes. He wanted to keep Landon from hurting. There was no reason for Landon to look so upset. "We were . . . he was sixteen. Middle of winter. I took him out in my mom's car and he ended up in a snow bank. But he got better. We fixed the dents and she never knew—"

"Dean—"

"Next drive I went on with him—all black ice on the road—"

"Dean, the car was hit too hard. It flipped—"

"He righted the car. I was impressed. He listened to me, you know." Dean's throat locked. He forced out a laugh. "He knows how to handle himself out there. He was just sixteen, but he looked up to me. He knows how I am about bad drivers. He knew I wouldn't let him go out on his own until I was sure he could handle himself."

"There was nothing he could have done—"

"No. No, I taught him." *What is he saying? He isn't saying it's Tim. He can't be saying that. He wouldn't dare.* "But he's hurt? Where is he? I should go see him. I know my brother. He'll try to be all tough."

"They tried, but Tim and Madeline—they were already gone."

"So he's out of it. He looks bad. I can deal with that." Dean knew Tim would be worried about Madeline. And the other driver. "Stay with Silver. And make sure Oriana is okay. I know they'll be all worried about him, but I know my brother. It will bother him if anyone's upset. The assistant coach will take care of the team. And we'll make sure everyone else can deal with this. He'll want to know we're dealing with this."

"Dean—"

"Landon, I love you, but I need to see my brother. Need to know he's okay."

"Dean."

"Say that again and I'll punch you, you bastard!" Dean pushed Landon away. Held his hand up to stop Silver when she tried to come to him. "Where is my brother?"

"He's . . . let me take you to him." Landon's tone faltered. "I'll go with you."

*I don't need anyone to come with me. Tim is hurt. He needs me. Only me.* Dean shook his head as he turned toward the door. His knee buckled. And there was a hand there to catch him as his strength gave out. Silver at one side. Landon at the other. *Mother. Mom needs to know.*

"Mom. Give me my phone. I need to tell her Tim . . ." *He's hurt. They haven't seen him.* "I'll tell her I'll be with him."

"Let me call her, Dean. She likes me." Silver took his phone as they went into the hall. "Stay with Landon. If you need to see Tim . . . Landon will be with you."

"Of course I need to see Tim. You should see him too. He's family."

"He is." Silver hesitated. "Do you want Jami to come with you?"

*No.* Dean quickly shook his head. If it was really bad . . . Tim had been a father to Jami when Dean couldn't be. Dean wouldn't pretend otherwise. He'd focused on his work, and Jami hadn't had a mother. And there was always Tim. Tim who wouldn't judge him but would tell him his daughter needed him to *see* her. And Dean hadn't understood what that meant until now. Until he knew, Tim needed to tell him what he'd missed in his own daughter's life.

"I need to ask Tim, he wanted to tell me—" *What if he can't? What if it's too late?* Dean pressed his fingers against his closed eyes. "Silver . . . let me tell Jami."

"I will. Do you want me to come with you?" Silver stood between the door back into the ballroom and where Dean and Landon were standing. He had to tell her where to go. He wanted her with him. But he didn't want Jami to be alone. "Where is Jami?"

"Sebastian and Luke are with her." Silver's voice broke. "They know . . . they won't leave her."

"Good. Good, she needs them. But I have to be the one to tell her . . ." He shook his head again. Landon. Silver. They wouldn't be acting like this if Tim was okay. And if Tim was . . . Mom needed to know. "Damn it, what do I say? I can't believe he's— why upset them if he's going to be fine?"

"He isn't, Dean." Landon put his hand on Dean's shoulder. "But you need to see him. I understand. I'll drive you to the hospital."

The door opened behind Silver. Jami came into the hall holding Sebastian's arm and Luke's hand. She moved away from them both. "Dad? Are you okay?"

His baby. God, his poor baby. She was worried about him and he couldn't allow that. His eyes were moist, but he managed to hold back tears as he pulled his daughter into his arms. And knew what he had to do.

"Jami, I was given some very bad news. Your Uncle Tim and Aunt Madeline were in an accident." Dean inhaled slowly. Jami was looking up at him. Waiting for him to tell her they'd be all right. He wished he could, but that would hurt her more when she learned . . . when she learned the truth. "They died."

Jami's face lost all color. Dean held on to her, not sure if she'd pass out from the shock. Sebastian and Luke shifted a little closer to her. But she stayed on her feet, eyes wide. Drew in a sharp breath.

And let it out in a sob as her face crumpled. "No, Daddy . . . No! He can't be. I just saw him this morning!"

"I know, baby." He couldn't breathe again until she returned to him, burying her face against his chest, trembling so violently he wanted to cradle her in his arms. Bring her home and tuck her into her bed. Find the words to make all the bad things go away, like he had when she was little. But he couldn't make this better for her.

"Where is he? Can I see him?" Jami scrubbed her tears away with the heels of her palms, giving Dean a stubborn look that reminded him of his mother. And Tim. She wouldn't take no for an answer. And her words weren't that different than his had been. "This could be a mistake. Have you seen the body? You couldn't have—you were here . . ."

Dean turned his gaze to the wall as those words "the body" shattered something inside him. Glass shards that didn't cut, but became ice, freezing everything around them. Everything within. He managed to face Jami again. To nod. "You can come with me to see him. I'll have to call the hospital to make sure it's okay."

"Let me take care of that, Dean," Landon said softly, pulling his cell phone out of his tuxedo jacket. He glanced over at Luke. "Can you get Jami's coat?"

Luke blinked at Landon, then nodded quickly. "Yeah. Yeah, I'll go get it." He leaned over to kiss Jami's cheek. "I'll be right back, boo."

Jami stiffened, her eyes on Luke until he disappeared into the ballroom. She chewed at her bottom lip. "He can come, right, Daddy? Luke and Sebastian? Can they both come? I'm afraid if anyone goes . . ." A fresh tear trailed down her cheek. "Anyone goes, I might not see them again."

"They can come." Dean stroked Jami's hair, waiting for Luke to return and for Landon to finish on the phone. He felt strangely calm. Almost as though they were waiting for an appointment with a lawyer. Or someone in the media. Something unpleasant, but something they could deal with quickly.

Until Landon hung up, his brow furrowing as he approached. "It will be a few hours before they'll let anyone see . . . before anyone can see Tim. There's an investigation and they have to examine the—examine him."

"I didn't approve that, Landon. I didn't say you could approve that." *You'll scare your daughter, Richter. Keep your cool.* He would just call them back. "Let me speak to them. Tell them there's been a misunderstanding."

Landon swallowed hard, his gaze shifting from Dean's. "It's procedure, Dean. They don't need the next of kin to approve it."

"Procedure." *Of course. There's procedure for these things.* "Then we'll wait. We'll go to the hospital and . . . wait."

Time passed in a blur once they left the hotel. At the hospital, in the waiting room, every time he looked at the clock it seemed like a huge gap of time had been stolen. Jami paced, then sat with him, then went back to her men. An endless cycle. Silver had called his mother, and in the next instant, she was there with his father. Tim's was away on business. Dean should call him.

He recalled telling his mother he would make the call. Take care of anything she needed him to. And then they were allowed into the room. A private room.

To see Tim.

Only it wasn't really Tim. The same face he'd seen smile at him so many times—laughter lighting up hazel eyes, now closed forever. Because what Landon had said . . . what he'd said at the very beginning . . .

It was true. Tim was already gone.

# Chapter Twenty Three

Watching Akira leave with Dominik, tears black with mascara running down her white cheeks, was one of the hardest things Ford had ever done. He'd stayed until the very end, saw the news spread. The players had all reacted differently. Dominik, thankfully, had nodded grimly when Luke had stopped to talk to him, then had taken Akira aside to tell her.

Across the room, a glass had shattered. Tyler's dress shoes crunched through the glass as he'd tried to walk away from Raif Zovko. Raif hadn't let him go far. Ford was a little surprised when he brought Tyler to the refreshment table, had him sit, and gave him a shot—but then again, Ford might have done the same. He'd wondered where Laura and Chicklet had gone, but hadn't had time to dwell. Oriana had caught his eye, her own red-rimmed and still wide with shock. She'd slipped out of Max's arms, as though to go to Ford.

The next hardest thing. Ford had turned and strode off in the other direction. Informed the waiters, and those in attendance, that due to the recent tragedy, the charity ball was over. He'd thanked one and all for coming. Told them there would be a press conference in the morning. He couldn't be any closer to his sisters than he could be to Akira. They were already in danger. Being around them would only make things worse.

He'd have to handle things from here on alone. Couldn't react to Tim's death. Damn it, the man had been . . . just knowing him had changed Ford's life. He wanted to be with his family, to take a fucking minute to let the loss set in, but the "car accident" was a little too conveniently timed. And if Kingsley had anything to do with it . . .

*I have to be my father's son right now. Just as cold and heartless as he is.*

He'd been raised that way. There was no room for emotion. No loss, only . . . opportunities. The Kingsley motto got him out of there, on the road, but his guts twisted even as he pulled his car up in front of his father's house. Seeing the lights on didn't surprise him. When the man took action, he brooked no delay. Not even for sleep.

The butler answered the door at Ford's first knock. Let him into the dining room, where his father was sitting with dozens of files spread out in front of him. The old man was a mess. His hair wasn't combed. The wrinkles on his face looked even deeper, furrowing into the gray flesh around his eyes and his pursed lips. His dark blue suit wasn't so perfectly fitted to his broad frame—as though he'd lost a drastic amount of weight.

Ford knew it was twisted, but it gave him some dark pleasure to see the bastard wasn't doing well. It tightened his throat, but part of him wanted to see Kingsley just as broken as his *real* father, Anthony Delgado. Or worse. As much as the man deserved to suffer, the world would be a better place if he just fucking died.

But Kingsley's tone was as strong and sharp as ever as he fixed Ford with a hard stare. "What do you want?"

"What do you think?" Ford dragged out the chair to his father's right, slouching back, lazily taking out a cigarette and lighting it before he continued. "Cort fucking turned himself in."

"Cort is an idiot. But that doesn't explain why you're here."

"Because I'm *not* an idiot. You know why I called him back. I figured he could do the dirty work." Ford let the smoke stream from his lips and cocked his head. "Jesus, Dad. I was trying to play nice with the fucking Delgados until the old bastard keeled over. Then you go and send those thugs after me."

"You showed no interest in working with me after your mother died. You ignored my calls." Kingsley slammed his fist on the table. "You sold our shares of the team!"

"Made me look real good, didn't it?" Ford smirked. He knew he was pushing, but his father was used to him either caving or being defiant. Defiance would work in Ford's favor. If Kingsley was as desperate as Cort said, he'd be more than willing to buy the prodigal son act. With a little twist. "I'm not one of your goddamn lackeys, but . . . shit, Dad, I kinda like being alive. Can't do much for you if I'm dead."

Kingsley nodded, scrubbing his face with his hands and groaning. "My intention wasn't to kill you. I was angry. A man should be able to rely on his son."

For a second, Ford wanted to remind the man *he'd* taken every opportunity to point out that Ford wasn't his son. But no. This was good. Ford had his way in. "You can. The team's going down. We don't need to go down with it."

"It still has its uses." Kingsley lifted his head, studying Ford for a few long moments. "More now. I take it you've heard they are without a head coach?"

*I should be fucking taping this.* Then again, Kingsley was being purposely vague. He wouldn't trust Ford enough to tell him straight-out he'd had a hand in Tim's death. *Not yet, anyway.* So Ford shrugged. "Sure it won't take them long to find another one."

"This is an excellent opportunity to put in our own man."

"It is."

Kingsley stood, pushing his chair in and pacing along the head of the table, raking his fingers through his hair irritably. "Or . . . they will likely use one of the assistant coaches temporarily. One is ready to retire. He might be willing to consider an offer."

"He might, but I don't think they'll go into the playoffs with a temporary fix."

"You're assuming they'll make the playoffs?" Kingsley stopped. Stared at Ford. "Do you think there's still a chance?"

*I've fucking got him.* Ford smiled slyly, letting out a wide circle of smoke. "Dad, I can pretty much guarantee it."

\* \* \* \*

Akira's hands shook as she accepted a mug of warm milk,

sweetened with sugar and a dash of nutmeg, from Dominik. He sat across the round table from her, elbows on the surface, chin on his clasped hands. They hadn't said a word to each other since she'd stopped crying. And thinking of what had made the dam break had her shaking even harder.

*Tim . . . and Madeline.*

How could they just be gone? She didn't understand. Didn't want to try. All she wanted was for Cort to be here, telling her . . . telling her it would be okay. Even though it wouldn't.

Or Ford. He'd been right there, but she couldn't go to him. He'd left her with Dominik.

*He had to.*

But . . . she didn't *want* Dominik. Which made her feel horrible. Dominik had been all she'd needed for so long, and suddenly, he wasn't enough? It wasn't fair to him. And, yet, she wasn't in the mood to be fair. Anger had settled deep in her stomach, like a meal that wasn't sitting well. She couldn't say why she was so mad. On a basic level, she understood why things had to be this way. But the understanding couldn't keep away the irrepressible need to lash out.

"Say something, Akira." Dominik reached out one hand to take hers, his lips turning down a fraction when she kept her hands around her cup and just stared at him. "Pet—"

"I'm not your pet!" Akira slammed the mug down on the table and shoved out of her chair. Then she slapped her hand over her mouth, her eyes tearing yet again. Shaking her head, she whispered, "I'm sorry. Sir, I'm—"

"I'm not your 'Sir.' You will call me so at the club, but right now, I'm Dominik. A man who still cares about you very much." He stood and came around the table. Curved his hand under her elbow before she could back away. "Your men can't be here for you. But I am."

She groaned, leaning toward him, shifting away. "There's nothing you can do."

"What would Cort do?"

Eyes shut tight, she pictured Cort, with her instead of locked away somewhere. He'd wrap his big arms around her and everything pent up inside her would spill out, and she'd come apart, and maybe, just maybe, feel a little better. But she didn't want to be held.

Rubbing her arms, she shook her head. "He'd try to comfort me. Listen if I needed to talk, but that's not what I—"

"And Ford?" Dominik drew her a little closer. "He wouldn't handle you the same way, would he?"

"No." A little tension burrowed between her brows, and she could practically feel Ford, putting his hands on her shoulders, making her look at him. "He'd tell me not to hold everything inside. Not to hide how I feel. And I'd get mad at him—" She let out a shaky laugh. "I get so mad at him! But it would work, because I *am* mad and I just want to . . ." Her jaw ached as she ground her teeth together. She opened her eyes and glared at Dominik. "Why are you asking me these things? Neither of them can do anything!"

"You're right. Ford is dealing with his father. And he told Cort to stop hiding too. So neither of them can do anything."

"And you have to keep reminding me?" The rage was boiling over. She dropped her hands to her sides. Fisted them. And forced herself not to hit him like she so desperately wanted to. Like she'd hit Ford. Like she might even hit Cort. "Why don't you just leave me alone?"

"That's not going to happen." Grabbing her wrists, Dominik pressed them against his chest. "Go ahead, Akira. Let it out. Either tell me why you're so angry, or show me."

The last tendril of restraint holding her back snapped. She wrenched her wrists free. Hit Dominik's solid chest with both fists. "They're keeping something—*everything*—from me! Tim is dead and Cort chooses tonight to turn himself in? Ford's father is involved. I know it! But they've left me alone to think the worse!"

"You're not alone, sweetheart." Dominik gathered her hair in his hands even as she continued to strike him with weak, little punches. He dried her tears with his thumbs and kissed her forehead. "You will see them soon. And you'll have a chance to tell them all this. A chance to demand answers."

"Don't you want answers?" She peered up at him, jamming her fists against his chest and leaving them there. He was still wearing the black shirt and crimson tie from the charity ball, hadn't bothered changing even though he'd given her one of his big white Cobra T-shirts when they'd gotten here so she could get out of her dress. He looked well put together. And calm. So goddamn calm. Her eyes blurred with unshed tears. "How can you be like this? You knew Tim for so long and—"

"And it hurts like hell to know he's gone." Dominik's jaw ticked. He stared past her, at the wall. "I could be getting drunk with some of the other guys. I could easily start looking around my house for things to break—God help me, it's tempting." He took a deep breath and shook his head. "But this, just being here for you, makes me feel like I'm doing something. I wish you could be with your men. I know you need them, but I'm glad you're here."

His . . . logic, for lack of a better word, deflated her anger. She suddenly felt tired. And useless. Dominik had found comfort in taking care of her, but all she'd done was lash out at him, demanding answers he couldn't give. She leaned into him, relaxing a little as he hugged her. Maybe she wasn't completely useless. At least she could give him this.

"I get it. I'd be doing the same if I could. Be nice to focus on something besides how much it hurts." She sniffled and Dominik reached over to the table to hand her a tissue. She mumbled thanks, then drew away from him to blow her nose. "I don't suppose I can get you to talk about how you're feeling?"

Dominik gave her a weary half smile. "I don't feel much like talking, sweetie."

"Do you want to go to bed?"

"No. Do you?"

She shook her head.

"Well . . . I'm not sure how much good it will do, but I know Pischlar took Sahara home. Would you like to see if they're still up?

Have them come here?" His smile grew a little. "We can sit together and not discuss anything."

"I'd like that." Akira lowered back into her chair, finishing off her milk as Dominik made the call. They sat together in silence until the doorbell sounded, then they all went to the living room after hugs and a few quiet words.

Didn't make a huge difference, but Akira found herself dwelling less on Ford and Cort as she brought out some beer for everyone after a soft request from Dominik. As she wrapped her arms around Sahara when the other girl broke down in sobs. And finally, as she went and got some sheets for Pischlar when he gave in to Dominik's insistence that he stay for the remainder of the night.

She shared the bed in Dominik's guest bedroom with Sahara, and though she couldn't sleep at first, she felt so much lighter just being there to comfort Sahara. As though her grief had shifted a little. Not gone—it wouldn't be gone for a long time. But she'd found a place for it for now. A way to handle the flood of emotions so they wouldn't drown her.

Still lying there awake after what seemed like hours later, Akira heard the door creak open and looked up to see Dominik. He nodded toward Sahara, who'd been drifting in and out every ten minutes or so. "How is she?"

"I think she'll be okay." Akira smoothed the blanket over Sahara's shoulder when she shivered. She bit her bottom lip as she remembered the last thing Sahara had said. "She was very close to Madeline. Especially after . . ."

Dominik nodded. His lips thinned. "I know. Madeline was the one who went with Sahara to get the rest of her things. She made sure the cops were with them. I still can't believe her ex got away with what he did to her."

"Neither can I. But she's safe now."

"She is." An ominous shadow passed through Dominik's eyes. "We're playing the Islanders in two days."

*Damn it, what is he thinking?* "Dominik—"

365

"Get some rest, Akira." He hesitated on his way out. "And tell Sahara, in the morning, that I'm here if she ever needs . . . just tell her I'm here."

"I will." Akira sighed as the door was eased shut behind him. There was no point in arguing with him about his new cause. He probably wasn't the only one who'd be targeting Sahara's ex, Higgins, during the game against the Islanders. Tim had likely been the only one keeping the Cobras from going after the man before.

Being captain of the team, Dominik *should* be the one keeping the men in line, but he was obviously using Sahara's abusive relationship as a distraction. Unless . . .

As she rested her head on the pillow, she could almost see Madeline, smiling down at her from heaven. Akira wasn't very religious, but she had to believe Madeline had gone on to a beautiful, wonderful place. She'd been such an amazing woman. And Akira knew Madeline would approve of *her* new cause.

Which was making sure two people she loved ended up happy.

Together.

# Chapter Twenty Four

Everything from the third shot on was a haze. Tyler felt numb. Dizzy. Sick.

Then *cold*. Like someone had taken him out of the nice, dark room he was pretty sure he'd passed out in and dumped him in a snowbank. Only the snow was pelting his back and a firm hand was rubbing his bare skin.

*Fuck, am I naked?* Tyler pushed the hand away, scrambling, then slipping out of reach. In the bathtub. He was in a tub with light glaring down on him and his head was pounding.

"Sorry, kid, didn't mean to make it so cold. Just wanted to get you cleaned up a bit." Warm brown eyes met Tyler's and a big hand came out to help him stand. "I'd hoped you'd come to as well. Be best if you call your Mistress before she and her girlfriend hunt me down for taking you."

"Taking me?" Tyler's head spun as he straightened under the spray. Rubbed one hand over his dripping wet face. Damn, his mouth tasted like sour nastiness. His eyes raw all around, like he'd been crying. He braced his hand on the tiled wall, filling his mouth with water, swooshing it around and spitting it out before he spoke again. "I got pretty drunk, didn't I?" He swallowed hard. *What did I do?* "Never gotten so drunk that I did anything—fuck, I said I'd never drink again. She forgave me for the stupid piercings, but this—"

"*Jebem ti!* That is a grave insult, young one." Raif crossed his arms over his chest, his expression almost as scary as Chicklet's when she got mad. "You had a shock. I tended to you. I take advantage of no one. I have no need to."

*Good going, Vanek.* He tried to apologize, but the words seemed to trip over his tongue. "Wasn't saying you would! Just, maybe I was—" Was what? Not like he'd come on to a *man*. Wouldn't matter how plastered he was . . . would it? Damn, what a mess. He hung his head. "Sorry."

"You would be if I was any other. Or sore at least." Raif's lip quirked. "Virgin?"

Tyler scowled. The man might be his hero, but that was pushing it. "Fuck no! I'm with two women—"

"But you've never been with a man?"

"No. I'm straight." Tyler turned off the water, grumbling thanks as Raif passed him a towel. Having this conversation with the guy, naked while Raif was standing there in jeans, was weird. All right, sure, he would have probably felt different if Raif had fucked him, but . . . well, he hadn't. So they didn't need to be talking about stuff he'd never experience. He draped the towel around his waist and got it firmly in place. "You said I had a shock?"

Raif paused with his hand on the open bathroom door. His shoulders stiffened. "You don't remember."

"I . . ." Tyler's feet snagged on the hall carpet. A giant claw ripped into his chest. He wanted the numbness back. Wanted another drink. Or twenty. Dead . . . Tim. Coach. He couldn't be. Air thickened in Tyler's throat, almost as though he was breathing in exhaust fumes.

"Come." Raif put an arm around his waist and guided him to the sofa. "I did not know Tim well, but he made me feel welcome. He will be missed."

"I can't . . . can't believe it. I've known him since I was on the farm team. He was the one I went to when things were bad, you know? When Oriana didn't love me back. When I started with Chicklet, and Laura . . . anyway, he was always there." *But now he's not. Not anymore.* Tyler chewed at his bottom lip as it trembled, but he couldn't stop the tears. "Shit." He scrubbed the tears away with his fists. No wonder his eyes were so raw. He'd probably been doing this all night. "Sorry."

"Why be sorry? It is a great loss. There's no shame in tears for a man of such great worth." Raif patted his cheek, his accent adding a lulling quality to his tone. "No need to 'man up' for me. You are a teammate. I appreciate that you are comfortable with me."

Teammate. The word reminded Tyler that there was still a game. A game he'd be expected to play. But how could he? Every time he looked over at the bench, he'd be expecting to see Tim, cheering him on—or tearing him a new one if he did something stupid.

"Feels like it's over. I just can't see how any of us can go on without him." No, the others would. They'd put on their skates and play the game. Things happened, right? But Tyler couldn't even picture walking into the Forum, knowing Tim wouldn't be there. "I never told him . . . I should have, but I didn't."

"Told him what, young one?"

"I'm not that young." *But I am. Tim always said I'd learn. That I was just getting started . . .* Tyler covered his face with his hands as his voice cracked. "I was gonna show him I could do better."

"And you will. You will, Tyler." Raif's hand curved around the back of Tyler's neck. And for some reason, that firm grip helped him breathe. As did Raif's words. "I believe those we love leave this world in peace because they know they can still watch over us. You will show Tim all you learned from him. And you will feel how proud he is of you."

"For real?" That sounded good. Tyler wanted to believe that too. He could play if he could picture Tim still watching. Wherever he was.

"Yes. How about you promise me one thing?" Raif gave him a slanted smile. "Every game we play counts. When the game is in your blood again, when you sense his presence, you will score a goal for him. And we will celebrate together."

Tyler's smile was shaky, but he managed to nod. He could do this. "Deal."

"Now." Raif held out his cell phone. "You dropped yours in

the toilet. I called Chicklet so she wouldn't worry, but she needs to hear from you."

"Right. And I need to talk to her. Just hearing her voice will make everything . . . I don't know, better I guess. It always does."

"She is a strong woman. She will help you through this." Patting Tyler's back, Raif stood and went to the mini fridge. He took out two bottles of water. "Assure her that you are in good hands."

"Yeah." Tyler stiffened against an involuntary shudder as he took a bottle. Weird that Raif's words had him thinking dirty things. Maybe it was because he knew Raif was bi. But some of his teammates were bi, and he'd been naked around them without anything getting . . .

*What? Kinky?* He let out a shallow laugh as the phone rang in his ear. No reason things would be any different with Raif. He hadn't reacted at all to "handling" Tyler naked. And it must be the shock that had Tyler feeling a little bitter about that. Carter had hit on him once and Demyan flirted playfully sometimes, so it wasn't like men didn't find him—

*Raif thinks I'm a kid. Guess I'm just not his type.*

Pearce was, though.

*Yeah. And Pearce likes guys.*

Tyler had a feeling he was losing his mind. The endless ringing set his teeth on edge. No answer. Chicklet was probably sleeping. He pressed end, then dropped the phone on the coffee table. "I should probably go home."

*Home where I can see Chicklet. She'll help me put my head on straight.*

Raif cocked his head. "Do you know that she is there?"

"Well, no, but—" Tyler tried to stand and the bottle of water sloshed over his bare chest. The phone rang, but slipped out of his hand when he grabbed for it. He felt like he'd gone a few rounds with the biggest man in the league. Beaten and bruised and bloody. So weak he'd have to be helped off the ice.

In a swift motion, Raif took his phone, answered, and held it to his ear. "Yes. He is better. I watched over him. I wouldn't have let him drink, but considering—" Raif's lips quirked. "I agree. The boy should not drink at all. Would you like to speak to him?"

Tyler held his breath as he took the phone. Chicklet was gonna be mad. He wasn't sure where she'd gone, but she would have expected him to be there when she'd returned. He tried for a light tone. "Hey, Chicklet."

"Where are you? Laura only had a couple of glasses of champagne, but I was the designated. You know she won't drive if . . . damn it, where are you?"

"I'm . . ." Fuck, he didn't even know. He looked over at Raif. "Where are we?"

"I have leased a condo close to the Forum. I will give her directions when you are done."

"Hear that? Everything's fine."

"It's not fine. I don't know this guy. And you—Tyler, I know what Tim was to you." She let out a heavy sigh. "Laura can probably drive over and pick you up. Been long enough since she drank—"

Frowning, Tyler fidgeted with the end of the white towel on his knee. He didn't want Laura to pick him up, she was always so cold when she was alone with him, and he couldn't deal with that now. "Can't you come?"

"No. I got in touch with Sloan last night and he took a red-eye. I'm waiting for him at the airport."

"Already?"

"Tyler, it's 7:00 a.m."

"It is?" Tyler searched the room for a clock. Damn, he'd lost the whole night. He looked over at Raif. "I sleep all full of puke in your bed all night?"

Raif chuckled. "I wouldn't have allowed that. You managed most in the garbage pail last evening. It was only when I tried to wake you an hour ago that you didn't make it in time."

"He took care of you through all that, my boy?" Chicklet's tone was soft, as though she'd been worried about him, but felt a bit better knowing he'd been okay with Raif. "Tell him I appreciate it."

Tyler told Raif, who simply inclined his head. "It was my pleasure."

Chicklet sharply cleared her throat. "Was it really?"

"Nothing like that, Mistress." However messed up his head was, he couldn't bear the thought that Chicklet might believe he'd cheated on her. "I wouldn't—"

"I don't think you were in any place to avoid it if he'd wanted you."

"He doesn't."

She let out a surprised laugh. "That answer was quick. How do you know? Did you ask him?"

"Why would I? I'm not like that, Chicklet. Wouldn't make a difference if he did." Tyler ground his teeth as Chicklet chuckled. "I don't see what's so fucking—"

"Careful, boy. I'll put up with a lot because I know you're upset, but you don't use that tone with me." Chicklet's voice was hard, and he knew better than to test her when he hit her limits. And right now, he was pretty sure he'd gone way past that. Best to pick his fights. Like with what she said next. "I'll have Laura there within the—"

"Please, Mistress, if you don't mind . . ." His mouth went dry as he heard the irritated sound she made in the back of her throat. "With your permission, I'd like to stay."

"With my permission, eh?" She laughed. A few seconds went by with him holding his breath, wondering if he'd gone too far. Then she continued. "Fine. But remind him he needs mine."

"For what?" *Watch your tone, Vanek!* He swallowed and spoke calmly. "I'm sorry, but I don't understand why I need to—"

"You don't need to understand. Do as I say."

His cheeks were blazing hot as he met Raif's eyes. He licked his lips and took a deep breath. "My Mistress wants you to know you need her permission."

Raif arched a brow. A slow smile spread across his lips. "I understand. Say goodbye, Tyler. I'd like to speak to her again."

"But I—"

Chicklet clucked her tongue. "You're being very difficult, boy. Must you question every command? Goodbye. I love you. Now put Raif on the phone."

"I love you too, Chicklet. And I miss you."

"There's my good boy. Behave yourself, all right? Obviously you trust this man, so I will too."

Once he'd passed the phone to Raif, Tyler sat on the sofa with his throbbing head in his hands, wanting to sink into it and disappear as he listened to one side of the conversation. He'd said it before, but this time, he meant it.

*I'm* never *drinking again!*

Raif took a seat on the armchair across from Tyler, his eyes never leaving Tyler's face. "I have no designs on his innocence, if that's what concerns you." He grinned. "No, I didn't say that. I may touch him, but it will be strictly . . . how do you say—yes, platonic. I will handle him as though he were my own child."

*Someone freakin' shoot me.*

"I am aware that he is not a child. But he is not mine, and I have no interest in making him so." Raif laughed. "Oh, I probably could, but that is not a game I play. His lack of experience keeps him safe from me."

*Again with the virgin shit. Fuck you, man!*

"Yes. There is no need for concern. Ah, I see matters within the locker room are common gossip. But I don't care to discuss the history Zach and I have with you." Raif smirked. "No, Zach's lovers have no need to worry right now. Yes, I do mean right now." His eyes went over Tyler in a way that made Tyler's pulse jump. "And neither do you."

After hanging up, Raif stood and held his hand out to Tyler. Tyler stood without taking it, glaring at Raif as he tried to figure out what game the man *was* playing. "What did you go and say that for? She was cool with me staying here."

Raif cocked his head slightly, studying Tyler's face. "And you think she won't be after our conversation?"

"Not likely! You made it sound like eventually something might—"

"I did no such thing. She's a delightful woman and she was testing me. We have an understanding."

"I don't get it."

"You don't need to. Come." Raif held his arm out, gesturing to the bedroom. "There is a team meeting in several hours. I will see to it that you are well rested before then."

Tyler rolled his eyes and strode past Raif into the bedroom. He glanced over at the bed, then down at his towel. "Mind if I get dressed?"

"There's no need." Raif folded over the thick comforter. "Get in."

Being in nothing but a towel had Tyler feeling a little vulnerable. Not a feeling he liked without Chicklet around. But he was damn tired. And as he crawled into the bed, rolling his eyes again when Raif tucked him in, the ache in his chest returned. There would be a team meeting today. Probably to talk about how they'd go on without Tim.

He gave Raif his back as the man stretched out on the other side of the bed, on top of the blankets. Pressing his face into the pillow, he ground his teeth as the urge to break down again smothered him.

"None of that. Come here." Raif pulled Tyler close and made him turn. Brought Tyler's head to rest on his shoulder. "I can offer you comfort, young one—"

"Stop calling me that." Tyler wasn't sure he liked that he was so comfortable lying next to Raif. The man was acting like a Dom, and Tyler couldn't help but respond. He held himself stiff, mentally counting out all the reasons this was wrong. "I have a name."

"But I will choose my own for you. We are friends, no?" Raif sighed when Tyler shrugged. "You, my boy, need your Domme very badly. I am a poor substitute, but I will do my best."

Tyler didn't say anything for a while, but then it started hurting again and he had to talk just to prove he could still breathe. "Can you make the pain go away?"

"I wish I could, Ty." Raif smiled as Tyler tipped his head back, the stiffness leaving him. His friends in high school had called him "Ty." "The name suits you?"

"Yeah. I like it."

"Good." Raif squeezed Tyler's shoulder. "Sleep. And remember what I told you. He is watching, even now."

Tim was watching. Tyler's throat felt tight and narrow as he imagined Coach being so close, but so far away. But at least Tim wouldn't be worrying about him. Tim wouldn't care who Tyler was with. He'd always made one thing very clear, each and every time he sent them out on the ice.

*"We're family. We win or lose together. That's the one thing you can never forget. Do your best, but you're not out there alone."*

\* \* \* \*

Max lifted his head at a tap on the door. He'd been sitting on the edge of the bed he shared with Oriana, holding her hand and watching her sleep after she'd finally exhausted herself crying. He eased his hand from hers and went to answer the door.

Then choked on a laugh full of relief as Sloan crossed the threshold. Grabbing Sloan's wrist, Max jerked him forward for a rough, backslapping hug. "Fuckin' good to see you."

"I got here as soon as I could." Sloan stepped aside to let Chicklet in. Chicklet nodded to Max and went straight to the bedroom without even stopping for a hello. He could hear the women whispering softly. Within seconds, Oriana joined them. She wrapped her arms around Sloan's neck, hiding her face against his chest as fresh tears spilled. Sloan spoke softly to her, then met Max's eyes. "How's everyone holding up?"

"I don't know. We've been . . . here." Max felt a little guilty about shutting himself away with Oriana, but he couldn't find the strength to do anything else. "There's a team meeting today. Around one."

"Good. Fuck, I wish I'd come sooner. I wish I could've—" Sloan's eyes were haunted, full of the pain they all felt, but he didn't look like he'd been crying. Max knew if Sloan had cried—or would cry—he'd be alone. He watched Sloan square his shoulders and the resolve tighten his features. Some might think Sloan was being cold, but Max understood his best friend. He'd handle his grief with action. "I'll speak to Keane. See if he wants me at the press conference. Richter . . ." He shook his head and his brow creased. "Richter needs to be with his family."

Max nodded slowly. It would be good if they could take some pressure off Richter. He couldn't imagine how broken the man must feel, losing his brother like that. Just grasping losing Tim as their coach, their leader . . .

*As my friend.* Max couldn't think of anyone besides Oriana and Sloan that it would be harder to lose. He had to open his mouth just to draw in enough air as it really hit him that he'd go to the Forum today and Tim wouldn't be there. The world had tilted on an unstable axis and every step was a challenge.

Oriana shuddered, but straightened to look into Sloan's eyes. "The team won't welcome you. They would be bitter no matter what, but this will make it so much worse."

"I know." Sloan inclined his head in the direction of the kitchen. He didn't speak again until they were all seated around the table. "Some will lash out, because there's nowhere else for their pain to go. But I'll take it. They're right to be angry. I abandoned the team."

No. Max couldn't sit by and let Sloan take this on. Sloan was hurting too, and the backlash would leave him emotionally battered. No one had the right to do that to him. Max wouldn't allow it. "We need you. They have to see that!"

"They will, but it's going to take some time. And that's fine. I'm not a masochist, but part of me needs this. I need their rage. Need to earn their forgiveness." Sloan tucked Oriana to his side as she dragged her chair close and put his hand over the one Max had fisted on the table. He smiled at Chicklet as she placed her hand over theirs. Some might think she shouldn't have stayed, but she was the only reason Sloan had made it here. She had a way with Sloan, could keep him from losing himself to the darkness when no one else could reach him. Which meant Sloan had to feel the pain like the rest of them, but at least he was letting himself. "I don't need a fucking welcoming committee. I'm back. And I need to prove that means something. Tim wanted me here, and that's all that matters. I'm gonna make him proud."

Max felt like his ribs were being cracked open to expose his heart, beating hard, so stubborn because it was like the blood-filled organ wanted to remind him that he was still alive. That he had to keep living.

And he would. Sloan's words took a while to reach him, but when they finally did, he lifted his head, not trying to hide the tears that came even as they spilled down his cheeks. Both he and Sloan had strayed, but they were back where they belonged. And the Cobras would make it.

"The point is, you're back."

Sloan's lips hitched up at the edges in a hesitant smile. "Yeah. I'm back."

# Chapter Twenty Five

Ford settled in his office, spreading out all the accounting papers for the Ice Girls, the folders containing the names of the hopefuls and all their stats, all kinds of straightforward shit on his desk. Stuff he knew how to deal with. But every figure, every word, was a blur.

Not that he'd really expected to get much done today. He just had to look busy. His hand shook as he picked up a pen to sign approval on an advertising contract for the girls. He glanced up at the clock above his door. Shouldn't be too much longer now.

*It'll be fine.*

Only, it wouldn't be. There was no taking back what had happened. No preventing how easily Kingsley had removed any obstacles without a second thought. All Ford could do was make sure the man paid.

But there were a lot of ways this could go wrong.

*I have to try.*

He pictured Tim, smiling at him with some deep knowledge in his eyes. As though he really *saw* Ford. *Accepted* him. Few had done that. Oriana had been the first, but he hadn't wanted her to. He'd done everything in his power, without really meaning to, to make her reject him. He'd never had siblings, never had anyone who would love him unconditionally besides his mother. Facing Silver's rejection had been so much simpler than actually letting himself feel Oriana's pure acceptance. But with Tim . . . all the shit Ford had done didn't matter. Almost as though Tim believed in the man he could be and would support *that* man. No matter what.

Who else would do that? Ford lowered his head to his hands as he thought of Cort. Because Cort was that person. No matter how hard Ford pushed, no matter what he said, Cort would always be there. They weren't blood, but they might as well be. Loving the same woman had brought them even closer once they'd dropped the alpha dog bullshit.

Only . . . Cort wasn't here now. He'd taken Ford's advice and turned himself in. He hadn't wanted to because he was worried about Ford. And really, he was right to be. What had Ford ever done without Cort watching his back? Without his father's money and power?

*I finished school. I got my bar. And my job here.*

None of which mattered.

*Maybe not. But this will.*

Raised voices outside his office brought his head up. He checked his watch. They were early.

Ford took a deep breath as his secretary shouted that she was calling a lawyer. A "Step aside, ma'am" had Ford cutting across his office and swinging the door open before his secretary could say or do the wrong thing and get herself in trouble.

"It's all right, Rosie." He moved toward her, placing his hand on her shoulder and giving the two cops standing in the reception area a tight smile. "Can I help you, officers?"

"Ford Delgado, you are under arrest for the charges of obstruction of justice and aiding and abetting in the murder of Charles Lee. I wish to give you the following warning." The older cop, with sharp green eyes and a head full of bushy gray hair, faced Ford. "You are not obliged to say anything, but anything you do say may be given in evidence. It is my duty to inform you that you have the right to retain and instruct counsel in private. You may call any lawyer you want—"

Ford widened his eyes. Laughed and shook his head. "You're joking, right? Why would I need a lawyer? I've been through all this shit before. I was cleared."

The second cop, mid-thirties and buff with a shiny bald head, grabbed Ford's shoulder and pushed him over Rosie's desk. "You aren't planning to add resisting arrest to the charges, are you, Mr.

Delgado?"

"I'm not resisting—this is fucking mental! Get the fuck off me before my father's lawyers sue you, you goddamn pig!" Ford winced as baldy put the cuffs on him. *Tight.* He toned down the struggling as the officer pulled him up straight. "It's fucking February! You gonna get me my jacket or what?"

"I'll get it, Mr. Delgado." Rosie frowned at him before heading into his office, her head held high. "They have nothing on you. Try to relax. I know you're upset, but you don't want to make things worse."

"Listen to the lady. She's smart." Baldy shoved Ford toward the elevator and Ford tripped, landing hard on his knees. The older cop's tone tightened with irritation. "Hey, cool it, Hayes."

Down the hall, a few office doors opened. Silver's secretary stared at him as he got back to his feet. Rosie ran down the hall to hand his jacket to the older cop before they got on the elevator. Ford stifled a smile as she quickly returned to her desk and started making a call.

The elevator door shut. Ford scowled at baldy, Hayes. "You wanna loosen them up a bit? Be good if I make it to the station with both hands."

Hayed looked down at Ford's hands. "You'll be fine."

"I say red and that dumb expression on your face is gonna become permanent, eh?"

The older cop coughed loudly, keeping his hand over his mouth as he eyed Ford. "You're pushing it. Save the act for the cameras."

"I'm serious. My hands are going numb." Actually, at this point, Ford could hardly feel his hands at all. He clenched and unclenched his fists to get some circulation back. "Should get Laura to teach you to do it right."

Laughing, the older cop put his hand on Ford's shoulder to lead him from the elevator, through the lobby on the main floor of the Delgado Forum. "I taught her."

"And you left this idiot to fend for himself?" Ford squinted as a camera flash blinded him. There were only a few reporters present since the press conference wasn't happening for a few hours, but those who were there immediately got out their mikes and cameras. Before they reached the end of the lobby, the number of reporters had doubled.

"Ford, what are the charges?"

"No comment." Ford took a deep breath, carefully turning his wrist to take some pressure off a spot that was getting pretty raw. Outside, three cop cars blocked the street, lights flashing. This was going to end up breaking news.

*I hope.*

"Mr. Delgado, does this have anything to do with the death of the Cobras head coach, Timothy Rowe? Are you a suspect?"

Ice water filled his veins. His jaw hardened. "Tim's death was an accident."

"But there's still an investigation?"

"Will this affect the Cobras' game on Tuesday?"

"Do your sisters know about this? Were they involved?"

"No comment." Ford bowed his head as the older cop put him in the backseat of the squad car. He kept it down as the door was slammed shut. Didn't sit up until they were at the police station. Then he shot the older cop an apologetic smile before he straightened, jerking away from Officer Hayes, who'd come to collect him. "I'm a goddamn Canadian citizen. You can't treat me like this. I'll sue you if there's a fucking mark, you hear me?"

"I think everyone on the block can hear you. Are you done?" Officer Hayes asked.

"I'm done. Just let me talk to my lawyer."

"We've got a few things to take care of first." Officer Hayes strong-armed Ford from the car all the way into the booking room. While the older cop spoke to another officer, Officer Hayes led Ford past the main area to a long hall.

Then shoved him into one of the many interrogation rooms. Baldy shut the door behind them.

And Ford's lips inched up at one side as he spotted the familiar face inside. "I take it they're letting you take the case?"

"Yeah." Laura shook her head, gesturing for Ford to sit across from her. "Why insist I be here, though? The fact that we've hung out at the club won't have me treating you any differently."

"Maybe not." Ford planted his boots flat on the floor, trying to get comfortable on the metal chair. Sitting back seemed impossible, so he ended up hunched forward near the table, facing Laura as she settled on the large, red padded chair. Officer Hayes sat in the other, closer to Ford. Both staring at him like they were waiting for a confession. He ran his tongue over his teeth. "Laura, you know Jami. You know my sisters. I figured you'd be a bit more careful to keep them safe than just any cop."

"This careful enough for you?" Laura held her hands out, palms up, to indicate the room. "I'm not sure why you wanted the arrest to be so public, but you don't have to worry about anyone hearing anything you say in here besides me and Hayes."

"Good." Ford shifted his shoulders, trying to get the tight ache between them to let up. "So how do you want to do this?"

Smoothing her hands over the front of her dark blue uniform as she stood, Laura came around the table, then lifted one eyebrow at the other officer. "You didn't uncuff him?" She sighed at Hayes' shrug, bending down to unlock the cuffs herself. "Sorry about this, Ford. This isn't my usual gig, but the detective will be here any minute. Hayes will stay on as your handler and make things as publicly difficult for you as possible. It's pretty much the norm for him."

"Thought he looked like a *real* asshole." Ford rubbed his wrists, biting back a wince at the burn of broken skin.

Hayes grinned and threw his feet up on the table. "You're just lucky you aren't a 'real' criminal." He glanced over at Laura. "Or isn't one anymore? Not clear on that."

A man in a dark suit who'd been coming in as Hayes spoke gave the officer a hard look. "I hope you're not giving my new informant a hard time." He held his hand out as Ford stood. "I'm Detective Sargeant Hamilton." Once they'd shaken hands, the detective motioned for Ford to take Hayes's chair. "Hayes, go out and stall his lawyers."

"Lawyers?" Ford leaned forward as Hayes strode from the interrogation room. Just a few steps away from the door he spotted his father's lawyer—who he'd expected to show up—and . . . he blinked. Asher? He bit into the side of his tongue to keep from laughing out loud. The *last* person he'd want representing him was Silver's ex-boyfriend, no matter how good of a lawyer he was.

And Silver knew that, but she hadn't liked not being able to help him with "whatever messed up plans he had" when he'd warned her he'd be getting arrested today. She'd offered to post bail, but he told her to let Kingsley do it. That he needed whatever time he could get in here.

Which apparently *was* something she could help with. He could hear Asher putting up a fuss even as Hayes started barking at them to keep it down. "He's a *Delgado*! Do you have *any* idea what that means?"

Detective Hamilton shook his head as he went to firmly close the door. "This has turned into quite the production. I hope you know what you're doing, Mr. Delgado."

"Call me Ford. And if you know who my 'father' is, it ain't hard to figure out why I needed to get arrested to talk to you guys." Ford cracked his neck, his gaze on the detective as the man sat in his abandoned chair. Then he glanced over at Laura who was taking notes. He was glad she was here, but it seemed like she was just going to sit back and let him deal with the detective. Ford swallowed hard. "Look, I'm willing to testify in court or whatever you want, but I need some assurances first."

The detective rested his elbows on the table and steepled his fingers. "Such as?"

"Cortland Nash was arrested yesterday. I get you Roy Kingsley . . ." This had to work. He'd take all the risks if it would set Cort free. "You drop all charges."

Eyes narrowing, expression dark, Detective Hamilton straightened and shook his head. "No deal. Nash will take care of his own shit."

Ford pushed out of his chair. "That's it?"

"Sit the fuck down." Detective Hamilton looked more likely to rip Ford's throat out than make him any kind of offer. Ford had seen Cort switch from calm to growling rage just as quickly.

So he didn't say another word until he was sitting. And tried to keep his tone level. "You're telling me you'd rather take down a man who stopped that disgusting bastard from raping a young woman than a criminal who's hurt so many people?"

"Speculation is useless. Do you have any proof?"

"I told you I was willing to get it." Ford brought his head to his hands, tugging at his hair with his fist. This couldn't be happening. "Tell me what you want me to do."

Shoes making a clipped sound on the white-tiled floor, Detective Hamilton walked over to the door, opened it briefly to listen to Asher arguing—loudly—with Kingsley's lawyer, then closed it and returned to stand over Ford, thumbs hooked to his belt. His jaw worked as he studied Ford.

"Why are you doing this? We never charged you because your story checked out. Jami confirmed that Lee was dead when you arrived at the scene. From this point on, your involvement in Cort's case is over. You understand?"

*Fuck that.* If Cort needed Ford's testimony, he'd give it. "That's up to Cort's lawyer."

"This is a waste of my fucking time. And Laura's. I don't know what problems you have with your father—or the man who isn't really your father." The detective shook his head and let out a rough laugh. "Whatever. The family drama is your problem. We're not starting an investigation because you want your muscle back."

"He's my best friend." *And I can't do anything for him.*

"Good for you. If that's all—"

"No." A stone fist grabbed hold of Ford's windpipe. His eyes burned as he glared at the detective. "Tim is dead. Because of my father. I'm sure you've all written it off as an accident, but—"

Detective Hamilton met his gaze with a hard one of his own.

"We know it wasn't."

"My fath—Kingsley did this! He wants control of the team, and he couldn't get it through Tim! He won't stop until he gets what he wants!"

"Tell me why you're doing this! You can accuse your father of anything under the sun, but I need to know why!"

For Cort. For Jami. For . . . for Tim. But none of those answers really explained his reasons. It was for all of them. And more. He'd stood by and watched the man he'd called "Daddy" hurt so many people. He couldn't do it anymore.

Staring down at the floor, Ford spoke softly, closing his eyes when the threat of tears scalded them. "Jami was almost raped because I didn't stand up to my father. One of my waitresses *was* raped. Cort tried to get out of all this bullshit, but I brought him back in. And now, Tim is dead. That's on me. This keeps going, and I'll be no better than *him*. I wanted to be out of his shadow, but I'm still walking through the blood he leaves behind."

The detective stood there, silent for a few moments. His tone was direct when he finally continued. "All right, here's the deal. I'll keep you as a confidential informant. We know very little about the Kingsleys, but they have been investigated in the past. Your uncles more than your father. They'll kill you if they find out you're doing this."

"I don't care."

"Then, again, you're wasting my time. You can't stop your father from doing anything if you're dead."

Ford almost stood again, but recalling the detective's reaction last time, he stayed put, gritting his teeth. "I don't want to die. I want to stop him from hurting anyone else. And I want him to pay."

The detective nodded. "And this conversation would be over if I didn't believe you. How much do you think you can get from him? Do you know what he's involved in? Do you have access to computer files, anything solid?"

A tiny glimmer of hope sparkled through the murkiness within.

Ford inclined his head. "I can get that. Once I can get him to trust me again, I can get pretty much anything."

"Good. I'll let Laura work out the details with you. There's not much more to discuss, but the two of you can meet at your bar— or that club you both go to." Detective Hamilton's lips quirked. "She'll get you hooked up with a wire. Might be best if she shows you how to use it there. No one will question her touching you."

For the first time in a while, Laura spoke up, after rolling her eyes. "Hamilton, you don't know what you're talking about. I don't play with Ford."

"But you can, can't you? Your . . . Mistress? Isn't she the one that got Ford's message to you?" The detective's cheeks reddened a little. Fuck, the man was human after all. "She'll let you play with him if it's important?"

Laura snorted and took a few last notes on her pad. "If he's willing to submit to her? Maybe."

"I see. Well, good luck with that. The woman is pretty . . . impressive." Detective Hamilton chuckled. "Now, if there's nothing else—"

"Just one thing, if you don't mind." Ford got it. The detective didn't trust him yet. But he could work on that. So he put all the respect he could into his tone as he started to rise, waiting until Hamilton nodded before pushing completely off his chair. "I'd like my phone call."

\* \* \* \*

The bar should be closed. After the scene that had played out on the big screen showing Ford's arrest, Akira couldn't really explain why it wasn't. The team was meeting in an hour, but a good half of the Cobras were in here. Some drinking hard. Some staring at the walls. All shattered men.

And yet she wasn't feeling much of anything. It was like the pain had reached the point where her body had to shut it out. All she could do was observe all those around her, her core hollow, emotions like a distant echo.

Neither Dean nor Landon were present, but Silver had come with her sister. Sloan and Max were sitting with them. Akira was at the bar with Sahara after deciding that noon was close enough to five for a couple of shots. And by the nod Dominik gave Reggie, the bartender, he agreed. The glasses were filled.

The music changed. Silver stood and joined the band. Akira's brow creased. She'd never heard Silver sing, but the woman seemed so comfortable up there on the stage, it was hard not to believe she belonged there.

Silver cleared her throat before speaking into the mike. "For my big sister. Fuck, I'm not sure I should be here. Maybe none of us should be. But looking at all of you, there's nowhere else I'd rather be. I can't imagine how you feel, but he was there when I . . . when I wasn't, sweetie. I just know it hurts. Bad."

Tears glistened beneath Silver's long, black lashes as the band started playing. Her smile was tight, but big and real as she began to sing "Here's to Us" by Halestorm.

Dominik swallowed hard at Akira's side. He shook his head, squeezed Akira's shoulder, then went over to Oriana's table. He hugged Max, then Sloan, speaking softly to both before holding out his hand to Oriana. Akira's throat locked as she saw the sheen of moisture on Dominik's cheeks. He kissed the top of Oriana's head.

And held her as she whispered to him, nodding slowly. Akira could hear him over the emotional lull of Silver's song.

"It will get better."

Akira had to look away from them. Not because she was jealous. She knew it was over between Oriana and Dominik. Akira could hang on to Dominik for as long as she needed to. He'd allow it.

But she shouldn't need to. She hadn't fucked up. And she wasn't sure either Cort or Ford had either. But they weren't here. She caught something special pass between Sahara and Dominik as he released Oriana and gave her hand one last squeeze. He returned to the bar, standing a little closer to Sahara than to Akira, nodding at something Sahara said. Almost smiling when Sahara dried his tears with her fingertips.

She didn't want to be in Sahara's place. Didn't want to dry Dominik's tears. She wished her friend all the best, but part of her wanted . . . Her chest tightened even more as she saw Sebastian in the shadows, his arms crossed over Luke's chest. Tyler near the back of the room with Chicklet, his forehead rested on the cushion of her breasts. The Cobras with wives sat with them, accepting their comfort.

And no matter what anyone said, Akira was alone. Both her men were behind bars. The one thing she'd told Cort she couldn't deal with, having him picked up by the cops one day . . .

Now it was him *and* Ford. And she wasn't sure which was worse. She suspected part of the reason Cort had let Ford in was so she'd never feel like this. She'd always have someone.

But she didn't.

Her phone buzzed in her purse. She ignored it at first, but it started again. It could be anyone. One of her girls, calling like others had, to tell her they couldn't come today because it was too hard. She glanced at the number. Didn't recognize it.

The phone kept ringing.

She couldn't face the people around her anymore. Heading to the back of the bar, she ducked into the small hall with a single door for the bathroom. She pulled the phone out of her purse and answered, abruptly numb. "Hello?"

"Damn it, I'm sorry. Just hearing your voice . . . I really messed up. Again."

*Ford.* Her bottom lip quivered. "Ford?"

"It's me, shorty."

"Why? Why did you—I mean, what happened?" She wasn't even sure what she was asking. Only that she needed him here. Now. "You didn't do anything. Why did they arrest you?"

"Babe, I'm only telling you this because I'm on Laura's phone. So it's safe. But don't say anything people can hear. Both me and Cort are doing everything we can to keep you safe."

"I know." Cort wouldn't have hesitated in leaving her with Dominik. But Ford might have. Ford was so afraid to lose her. So afraid he didn't have her. "Ford . . . I don't care. Being safe means I'm all by myself."

"You have Dominik."

"But I don't have you."

"You will. I hate that you've had to deal with all this, but it won't take long. I only went in because . . . Akira, I'm ending this. Kingsley is involved in a lot of the things that have gone bad."

Her blood ran cold. "Tim and Madeline . . . ?"

"Yes. It wasn't an accident."

"Oh God." She pressed her fist to her lips, leaning against the wall when just standing became difficult. "But . . . Ford, King—"

"Shh, please, baby, don't say his name. Or mine. I don't know how secure the bar is anymore. Kingsley thinks I'm on his side now. I'm going to work on getting him put away for a long time." He inhaled sharply. "And before you ask, Cort had to turn himself in to stop Kingsley from using the threat of prison against him anymore."

"Anymore?" She didn't understand. Kingsley had threatened Cort, but for what? She needed to know, but she couldn't voice her questions. Not if doing so could put Ford in more danger. She held the phone closer, whispering. "When will I see you?"

"Soon. I don't know how yet, but I'll figure something out that won't put you at risk. I know it must have been scary to see me on the news, being hauled in, but it was staged. I should be out in a few hours."

"Good. That's good." She scraped her bottom lip with her teeth. "And then you'll come to me?"

"I will." He went quiet, spoke to someone else, then sighed. "I have to go, but I promise you, this will be over before too long."

"I miss you." Her voice sounded small, but she didn't care. She was scared. For Ford, for Cort, for anyone else Kingsley could hurt. And it didn't make her feel any better that her men had made sure she wasn't one of them. The pain of losing Tim and Madeline was still so raw, she knew she couldn't take losing anyone else.

Hearing Ford's voice helped, though. No matter how afraid she was, she knew he'd find a way to come back to her. And find a way to bring Cort home.

"I miss you too, shorty. And I love you."

Her lips quirked a little as she thought of all her past replies to him saying those three words. Tears clung to her lashes, blinding her. "I love you, too."

"Do me a favor. Go back to Dominik and tell him something for me."

"Okay."

"Tell him, thank you," Ford said quietly. "Thank you for taking care of someone who means more to me than my own life."

"Don't say that." She wasn't sure what scared her more. The implication of what he'd said, or the fact that he might take foolish chances to prove it. "You have to—you have to be careful."

"I will be."

"And I'll be waiting for you. So hurry and get out of there."

"But you'll tell him?"

Such a simple request, but she understood why it was important to him. He needed Dominik to know, true, but she had a feeling her acknowledging how precious she was to him mattered more. So she nodded. Smiled a little. "I'll tell him."

Back in the main area of the bar, Akira watched the men gathering near the entrance, where Dean was coming in with Landon. She hadn't expected Dean to be here today, but he was hugging the men and the women, nodding as everyone gave their condolences. Landon went over and spoke to the waitresses standing near the bar. They all nodded and began to move the tables to the center of the room in a close cluster.

After everyone was seated, Dean rose from his chair at his table with Landon and Silver. He bowed his head for a moment, hands on the table. Then he straightened and squared his shoulders. "I know you all expected to meet at the Forum, but . . . I thought it would be better here. I'm sure I'm not alone in feeling that the place won't be the same without Tim. Going there for the game tomorrow will be soon enough."

The players nodded, some with their heads down, some never taking their eyes off Dean. A few of the women stifled sobs behind their hands. Tyler's shoulders stiffened, and it looked like Chicklet's grip on his hand was the only thing that kept him from getting up and walking out. He rubbed his face with one hand, clearly trying to hide his tears.

"My brother—" Dean's tone hitched. He took a deep breath, pressing on. "My brother loved this team. Each and every one of you meant so much to him, and he was never happier than when he was watching you on the ice, putting your blood, sweat, and tears into the game. I-I wasn't sure I could come here today. Wasn't sure I could look at you—but I'm glad I did. My brother didn't have any children, but you guys, you are his legacy. He's not really gone because everything he taught you, how hard he worked to make you the very best, is still here."

Everyone went still, as though absorbing that statement. As though they'd all just realized there was still a reason to go on. They wouldn't be playing the game without Tim. They'd be playing it for him.

Akira looked over at Sahara as the other woman took her hand. Her vision was a little blurry, but she could easily read Sahara's smile. The Ice Girls would do the same for Madeline. She'd been an unofficial part of their own team, but integral. Always looking out for them, always around to offer a kind word or a shoulder when they needed it. Even when Akira or the trainers had to be hard on the girls, Madeline was there with a wink and a little smile that said "you can do it."

And Dean hadn't forgotten her. "Not all the Ice Girls are here, but Madeline would understand. Hell, she'd have made sure I understood if some of the players hadn't shown up. I hope you're here because you're finding some comfort in each other. It's going to be hard for a while. Madeline. Tim. They were the heart and soul of this team. No one can replace them, but they both gave us so much, I believe the best thing we can do to honor their memory is to keep their dreams alive."

"By playing the game?" Tyler didn't meet Dean's eyes, but his tone made it clear he didn't think that was enough. "I'm sorry, I just—"

Blinking fast, Dean observed Tyler for a bit, nodding to himself before he spoke again. "Don't be sorry. I understand the game might not seem all that important now. But as a team, we're in a position to do a lot of good things. My family is setting up a charity in their name in partnership with The Rose Campaign, the charity Scott Demyan is a spokesman for." He inclined his head in Scott's direction, his throat working as Scott looked up at him, letting his tears fall freely. "The Rowe Foundation will both provide education toward preventing domestic violence and contribute toward giving victims a fresh start. While my brother and his wife were working with several charities, they found many abused women returned to their abuser because they were afraid they couldn't make it on their own. Some children who are mistreated their whole lives stay with their parents for the same reason. We want to make sure they know they have other options."

The men seemed to like that. They talked quietly amongst themselves as Dean spoke to Landon and Silver. His shoulders sank as he nodded, then shook his head. He looked like he'd hefted up a boulder and was determined to carry it alone, but Landon and Silver wouldn't let him.

Akira leaned over as Sahara whispered to her, "Do you think he's all right?"

"No." Akira watched Dean lower to his chair as Silver stood. He clearly didn't have the strength to carry on with the professional front. There was more to be said, but he was letting Silver take over. Which was good. Maybe part of him had needed to come this far, to show the team he was still standing, still moving forward. But no one expected him to do so with even strides. And he had people who would make sure he took the time to heal. "But I think he will be."

# Chapter Twenty Six

D ean closed the front door of his house and leaned against it. He could hear his mother and Jami in the living room, playing with Amia, his mother's laughter soft, but genuine. He'd seen her fall apart, then pull herself back together, one piece at a time over the past couple of days. Sometimes she would leave family gatherings abruptly, and after giving her a few minutes because they knew her well, his father and Tim's would go to her.

Landon and Silver did the same with Dean. So many times, he found himself alone, not even sure when he'd walked out. He'd be outside without a coat, but he couldn't feel the cold. All he could do was stare at the snow, seeing Tim as a boy, picking up handfuls to throw at him. He actually *saw* his brother. Sometimes he wondered if he was losing his mind. But then Silver would be there, her arm around his waist, her head on his chest. She wouldn't say anything until he spoke. It was almost as though she didn't want to disturb those memories.

And he knew that's what they were. Memories of his brother, so real, his own way of hanging on to Tim, just a little longer. He mentioned it to Silver once.

*"When I first moved here, middle of winter, there was a snowstorm. The power went out for a couple of days. Jami was fourteen and bored and I didn't know what to do with her."* He let out a bitter laugh. *"I had brought some work home, and she wouldn't stop complaining. Tim came over to see how we were doing. He made lunch on the barbeque and then got Jami to come outside. Tried to get her to play in the snow like we did when she was little, but she acted like she was too cool. So he just started building a snow fort. I heard her laughing, and when I came out, they were having a war game."*

395

*"He was great with her." Silver hugged his arm and looked up at him. "She was lucky to have him. She's hanging on to that as much as you are."*

*"I know, but . . . damn, I remember standing right here, and it just hit me that his smile hadn't changed. Something about him was exactly the same as when we were kids. So full of li . . ." His voice broke. But he got the word out. "Life."*

*"He was. He didn't waste a single moment, Dean. I don't think he had any regrets. He could still have done so much more, but the time he was here counted for something. In my life, Jami's, yours, and so many others'."*

*Damn it, most people tried not to talk about Tim too much, like they were afraid bringing him up would hurt, but Silver—and Landon—didn't make discussing Tim seem unnatural. He almost smiled as he glanced over at Silver. "I see him. Usually as a boy, but sometimes as a man. He's always grinning, or laughing. I'm sure a therapist would be able to explain it."*

*"Do you need an explanation? Your brother is still with you in some way. And I think that's good." She worried her bottom lip with her teeth. "I had a hard time when my mother died because I kept seeing all the bad things. But one night, I could swear I felt her with me. Tucking me in and singing to me. I don't remember her ever doing that, but the . . . vision, or whatever it was, helped me keep a part of her with me. A good part."*

*"That's all I remember with Tim. The good times."*

*"And you can hang on to them, Dean. Always."*

Every day seemed so long, as though he couldn't quite grasp that he was still here and Tim wasn't. Bringing his thoughts to the present, he went over all the things he'd read about grief in an attempt to help Jami. He'd seen his daughter sliding back and forth between several stages, but if he was to apply it to himself . . . he'd skipped several. He remembered the denial. The anger. The guilt. But acceptance had come too quickly.

Without even realizing it, he'd walked right through the house, not a word to anyone, to stand in the backyard once again. Tim's funeral was tomorrow, but part of Dean felt like he'd already laid his brother to rest. He'd found himself thinking about the game. About the rest of the season, the playoffs, the draft this summer. Part of him was ready to go on living, and he hated himself for it.

But at the same time, he couldn't hate himself for long. Because Tim would have wanted him to *live*. He would have wanted Dean to realize that in an instant, all he planned, all he loved, could be gone.

Footsteps crunched in the snow and without looking, Dean sensed it was Landon. They stood there for a while, neither speaking, just watching the darkening sky. Landon's presence, calming in the evening stillness, made everything so peaceful. For a few breaths, the pain inside lessened. When Landon brought his hand to the back of Dean's neck, light pressure in his fingertips soothing tense muscles, Dean let his eyes drift shut. Focused on the sensation like he told Silver to when they scened to relieve some stress.

"Jami's going back to the hotel with your mom," Landon said, stroking the side of Dean's neck with his thumb. "They won't leave until you come back in, but it looked like you needed a few minutes."

"I did. Thank you." He didn't want to move, because doing so would bring everything back. But what else could he do? He had to keep moving. Keep breathing and keep watching the days pass. These moments though, moments when time stood still, were a relief. They were rare, but they made it a little easier to face a world carrying on as though nothing had changed.

An hour after Jami and his mother had left, Dean lay in bed with Landon, Amia fast asleep between them. The pain had returned, like a huge shard of glass deep in his chest, cutting a little more of his insides out every time he breathed. But then he looked down at his daughter, a dreamy little smile on her lips, and warmth replaced the pain. Not completely, but enough to enjoy this time with her. He knew Jami had coped so far by doing the same, spending some time with him, his mother, Amia, her men, and her friends. As though being alone was unbearable.

He lifted his head, looking at Landon now, who stilled as Dean's gaze went over his face. He seemed to hold his breath as Dean brought a hand to his scruff-shadowed jaw. Smoothed a thumb over his lips.

The door opened, but Dean left his hand where it was as Silver came in. He met her eyes as she came around the bed, relieved to see there was no bitterness. Actually, she smiled as she leaned down to kiss him.

She carefully lifted Amia without waking her, then cradled their daughter in her arms and glanced over at Landon. Cooed softly as their baby stirred in her sleep. "I just want to hold her for a little while. I hope you're not upset that I'm taking her away from you?"

"Not at all. I've done the same." Landon wrapped his hand around Dean's wrist and pressed his lips to Dean's palm. "It helps to find all the little ways to feel alive. Every moment just seems that much more precious."

Silver nodded. There was a tenderness in her eyes as she looked at them. She opened her mouth as though she wanted to say more, but then simply blew Landon a kiss and slipped out of the room.

Dean wasn't sure what to make of that little exchange. Suddenly, all he wanted was to be closer to Landon. His pulse pounded under Landon's lips, beating hard through the tightness in his chest. He jerked Landon closer, slamming their lips together. The air that was sometimes so hard to draw in burst into his lungs as he rose up to tear off Landon's T-shirt.

Landon's muscles rippled as he leaned up to undo the buttons of Dean's shirt. A woman's softness had always been the most alluring thing to Dean, but something about Landon's strength, about the way his every rough touch matched Dean's bruising grip on him . . . gentleness would have Dean thinking. Carefully exerting his control over himself and his lover. But he didn't need that control now. Didn't want it.

He needed to lose himself for a little while. Breaking things and lashing out didn't feel natural, but this, this raw, brutal passion, gave him an outlet for the anger he'd fought not to express.

His fingers dug into Landon's jaw as they moved against one another. Their clothes, the comforter, and most of the sheets were on the floor. His dick was hard and the sensation of it grinding down on Landon's throbbing length was almost painful. Dean pressed his eyes shut when Landon shoved him up to wrap a hand around their erect cocks.

"Fuck." Dean let out a low growl as he slid his hand under Landon's head, bringing him close enough to claim his mouth. Part of him had known this might happen. Eventually. But not like this. He turned his head. "This is wrong. I can't be careful enough to—I might hurt you."

Landon let out a low laugh, the sound a little strained, as though he hadn't laughed in a very long time and had forgotten how. "That's why I'm here instead of Silver. I can take it, Dean. I want to. Do whatever feels right."

Control returned, but just enough for Dean to get the supplies he needed. He still fucking loved this man. He didn't want their first time to be something either of them would regret. But he couldn't consider anything beyond that. He wasn't a sadist, but there was a grim satisfaction within as he stared down at Landon, watching his jaw clench as Landon took that first, slow penetration.

"Don't stop." Landon groaned as Dean eased out almost all the way. "Damn you, don't stop."

"I'm not sure I can." Dean bit Landon's bottom lip, one hand still on the back of Landon's head, the other on Landon's shoulder as he slammed in. "Not sure I want to. But you need to know I'm using you. To breathe, to feel something other than pain."

"Good." Landon swallowed hard. Blinked fast. "Because I'm using you too. I need to know we can still do that."

Dean pressed his hand to Landon's face, forcing Landon to look at him. "Do what?"

"Feel more than how much it hurts inside." Landon's hips bucked, and he shuddered as Dean made his thrusts fast and shallow. "I'm not a masochist, but I need the pain to be physical—which probably sounds stupid because it's so much worse for you."

"Not stupid." Sweat beaded over Dean's upper lip. He licked it away before leaning down for another kiss. "I can do that for you.

Just don't hate me after."

"I can't. I love you too fucking much."

"Say that again." Dean brought his hands down to Landon's hips, keeping up a vicious rhythm he wouldn't have dared with someone softer, someone delicate. With Landon, he couldn't hold back. Didn't even bother to try. "When I'm done."

# Chapter Twenty Seven

Cort ignored the amused look from his cellmate as he washed the blood from the cuts in his knuckles. His jaw ached from the broom that had been broken across the side of his face, tearing open skin that had been taped together by the resident medic. In the polished metal mirror above the sink, he checked out the crusted crimson mess of his cheek.

This was a message from Roy, warning him not to talk.

Like he was that fucking stupid. Thankfully, some new guy had been brought in for a "random" holdup on a liquor store and had grabbed the guy before he could jab the broken end of the broom into Cort's stomach. The new guy, Adam, had a message for him too.

*"Sutter knows what went down. He's got your back."*

That was good, but Cort knew his stepfather could only do so much. Dad still had to make nice with Roy—he was too tangled in the man's business to make an obvious move against him. And that bit of support would disappear if Cort went against the twisted biker codes. Sutter might still have his back if Cort decided to go after Roy himself. He'd find somewhere to bury the body. But not if Cort tried to handle this with legal shit.

Which made Cort more than a little worried about Ford. Sutter wasn't one of Ford's biggest fans. Not that Ford had many. Sutter wouldn't go after Ford if he found out what Ford was doing, out of respect for Cort, but he might turn a blind eye if one of his men decided they wanted a bit of extra cash to do the job.

Cort had used his one phone call to get in touch with Ramos for the lawyer, but he wished he'd thought of all this sooner and had just called Ford. Told the kid he should make a deal without having to testify. Give information or something. If Ford took a public stand against his father, Cort wasn't sure he could protect him. Unless . . . well, there was still the option of disappearing if he got approved for bail. And could stomach screwing Ramos over.

But he didn't want that life for Akira. And the more he thought about it, the harder it was picturing life without her.

How fucked up was that? Wanting to leave her behind to move on without him had been one of the noblest things he'd ever considered. He'd had it all figured out. But then he'd poked holes in his own plan. Akira might try to find them. Either he or Ford might break down and contact her to make sure she was okay. Which would be more dangerous than sticking around and keeping things on the down low.

Not what he wanted for her either. If Ford pulled this off, at least he could be there for Akira. She wouldn't be alone. Like she was now.

Cort didn't try to fool himself. Dominik was a temporary fix. He couldn't see Akira letting him hold her at night. See her trying to make a life with Dominik as her man.

Or maybe he just didn't want to see it. Which made him a selfish bastard. Dominik could give her normal. Stable.

But he didn't love Akira, not like Cort. Or Ford.

What must she be thinking now? Was she angry? Was she wondering if their time together had meant anything? He ambled over to his bottom bunk in the cell and dropped hard onto the thin mattress. Rubbed his face with his hands, wincing as his fingers brushed over damaged flesh. If he recalled the team schedule right, there should be a game coming up soon. Maybe that would distract her for a bit.

Keep her from hating him too much for leaving her behind with no warning. So long as nothing else went wrong.

* * * *

Ford's hands shook as he pressed ignore on his phone. He'd

been avoiding his father's calls since getting his bond release. Which his father had paid after the lawyer pulled some strings with a judge on Kingsley's payroll. A "thank you" wouldn't do any good, so he hadn't bothered. He had the perfect excuse—Kingsley wanted results, didn't he?

Only, Ford knew he was treading on dangerous ground. His father expected a devil-may-care attitude from him, but with how unstable Kingsley was, he might not take this well.

*I don't got no choice.* Ford flipped open the Ice Girls' files he'd abandoned when he'd gotten arrested. Flipped them closed again. Nothing in them couldn't wait. In a few hours the Cobras would hit the ice for the first time since Tim's death. There had been a debate on whether or not the Ice Girls should perform.

He and Silver had decided to let them put on a show. Two songs would be played in Tim's memory, both from his favorite band. One in memory. One while the Ice Girls danced to give the fans a sense of hope that the team wouldn't give up.

Right now, there was only one person he needed to know hadn't given up. He'd promised Akira he'd see her as soon as it was safe.

He had to make it safe. So he paged his secretary and asked her to send the Ice Girls' captain and assistant captain to his office.

Akira and Sahara stepped into his office ten minutes later. Akira had made the same decision as Sloan—who'd taken his place as the Cobra's assistant coach—and asked her girls to come in early. The girls, and the players, needed to be in the Forum. To see it had changed, but . . . hadn't. Tim was still here in some way. In spirit or whatever people wanted to believe. And so was Madeline. But not in a way that should make anyone sad. They were still cheering every one of them on.

His shorty was pale, but there was a determination in her eyes, telling him she'd resolved to be strong for her girls. In her cute little black and gold skirt and cut-off Cobra jersey, she stood at the other side of his desk, not even blinking as he went over details she didn't need to hear. She knew what she had to do.

And she knew that wasn't why she was here.

"Thank you, Sahara." Ford stood and straightened his black suit jacket, a weak smile on his face. He couldn't manage anything better. "I'd like a moment with Akira, if that's okay."

Sahara nodded, but didn't smile back. "I wouldn't consider it if Cam wasn't standing in the hall." She paused. "But . . . are you sure—?"

"I am. This is work. My 'father' understands my position with the team. There's no reason for him to suspect—"

"Are you *sure*?" Sahara's glare proved she hadn't forgotten all Jami had gone through because of him. She'd never held it against him before, but she had every reason to worry now. Things were all kinds of fucked-up.

But Ford knew Kingsley. He was an arrogant bastard. And he wouldn't think Ford would hide anything with all that was at stake. Ford wouldn't take any stupid chances, but being insanely careful at this point would do nothing other than make Akira miserable. She didn't comment as he and Sahara spoke, but he saw a glimmer of hope in her eyes and had to keep that alive.

"I won't take any chances with her, Sahara." Ford met Sahara's eyes. "She's safe here with me."

Sahara gave him a curt nod, squeezed Akira's hand, then walked out. He went behind her to close and lock the door. The second the lock clicked, Akira closed the distance between them. Tears wet her lips as she kissed him, her fingers threaded through his hair, her whole body shaking as he pulled her into his arms, gentling the kiss as he stroked her back. He brought his other hand to the back of her neck, and his firm grip seemed to calm her. She stopped shaking and peered up at him, as though her own reaction surprised her. Her gaze shifted from his abruptly.

He caught her chin, forcing her to look at him again, reading her easily. "It's okay, Akira."

"It's not. There's too much going on for me to just let go and—"

His lips quirked at the edges. "Let go and what?"

She wrinkled her nose at him. "You know 'what.' I need to focus on tonight. On my girls. On how we're going to get Cort out of jail."

"I see." Ford held his smile, but understanding didn't come without a bit of regret. He'd almost forgotten that what they shared was tentative without Cort. He didn't need her worrying about . . . what exactly? That her time with him would be some kind of betrayal to Cort?

*Cort would want me to give her whatever she needs.*

But she might not be sure what that was.

*And I know what it's not. She shouldn't dwell on things she can't control.*

Akira cleared her throat, blushing and tracing her tongue over her bottom lip. "I should probably go." She glanced toward the desk. "You probably have work to do."

"Nothing that can't wait." His eyes narrowed as she placed her hands on his chest and tried to push away from him. He framed her jaw with his hand and tightened his grip on the back of her neck. "Going somewhere?"

Her eyes widened and her pupils dilated. Her pulse quickened under his fingers. She wet her bottom lip again. "I should."

"I disagree." With his hold still firm on the back of her neck, he brought his other hand down to the soft curve of her hip, resting it there as he stroked the delicate flesh of her stomach with his thumb. "It would please me if you'd stay."

She shivered, inching a little closer to him, her expression making it clear she didn't realize she was doing so. "What else would please you?"

He chuckled, sliding his lips along her cheek, speaking low in her ear. "If you'd call me 'Sir.' And mean it."

A breathy little laugh escaped her. "You have to earn that."

"Haven't I?"

There was a mischievous little sparkle to her eyes as she eased back, challenge in her gaze. "Not yet."

He inclined his head, the smile leaving his lips, his level stare one she wouldn't mistake. She'd told him as clearly as she could what she needed from him. Not to be in control. To let go, which she couldn't do on her own.

Without a breath of warning, he brought his hands down to the bottom of her little jersey and pulled it up over her head. Tossed it aside, then brought his hand to her throat. "You know your safeword. I expect you to use it if you're afraid or in pain." His lips slanted in a cruel smile. "Otherwise, I suggest you be very, *very* quiet."

Akira swallowed, her lips in a sweet little O, her cheeks nice and red. She bit back a yelp as he lifted her up by the hips, stepping past his desk to drop her in his big, black leather office chair.

He clucked his tongue as he leaned over her, dragging her bra strap off her shoulder with his fingertips. "You can be quieter than that, pet."

"Ford—"

"Shh." He pressed a finger to her lips and lowered his lips to her throat. "Where's my good girl?"

She squirmed, then let out a choked gasp as he set his teeth into her skin, not hard enough to bruise, but enough to hurt a little. He ran his tongue over the small dents in her flesh, enjoying the fresh, clean taste of her. Breathing in the subtle scent of flowers and honey that made his mouth water and his dick strain against his zipper. He bit her again, harder, and her back arched. She whimpered as he scraped his teeth along her collarbone.

He whispered with his lips hovering over the swell of her breasts, displayed nicely with her push-up bra. "Clasp your fingers behind your neck and lean your head back."

The way she complied, without even a token protest, levelled him out in a way he only ever did when a sub truly gave him control over her. Only, this was more. That kind of power was heady, but with Akira, it took him even deeper. There was nothing but the two of them. Nothing more important than the trust she showed him.

He used his chin to nudge the cup of her bra off one breast, then caught her rosy little nipple with his teeth and flicked his tongue over the tip. Reaching down, he tapped her inner thighs for her to open for him. When she hesitated, he put some pressure on her nipple.

Her thighs spread even as she bowed her body even more for him. He slipped his fingers into her panties, groaning at the slick silkiness of her pussy, wet folds surrounded by smooth lips he wanted to kiss just as hard and deep as he would take her mouth.

But not just yet.

Akira wasn't a masochist, but he knew she enjoyed the right edge of pain with her pleasure. He dipped one finger inside her as he bared her other breast to give it the same attention as he had the first. He tugged her nipple with his teeth as he slowly fucked her with his finger. Added a second finger and licked the areola around her nipple in a slow circle. Sucked the whole nipple into his mouth. Released it and brought his mouth to her abandoned breast to nip the side as he drove his fingers deep inside her.

A desperate little cry escaped her. Her butt was on the very edge of the seat, lifting a little as she clung to him, urging him to go deeper.

Instead, he drew his fingers out almost all the way. Moved just the tips in and out beyond the tightening ring of muscle. Laid soft kisses on her breasts, along her collarbone, up the length of her throat. He bit her neck again and slammed his fingers in hard.

She started shaking. Clawing at the back of his neck. Her pussy was so fucking wet he wasn't sure how long he could keep this going before his throbbing dick had him mindless of anything but being inside her. But he had no right to exert control over her if he couldn't keep a firm leash on himself.

Breathing hard, he barred one arm across her back, moving his lips, his teeth, between her breasts, putting pressure on her hot little pussy with four fingers. He positioned his fingers so they'd fit inside her, but only dipped them into her a little, the stretching more about the sensation than about getting his whole hand inside her.

Which, strangely enough, had him thinking about Cort. He was pretty damn sure he'd never thought of another man when he was with a woman, but this delicate body he was playing with didn't belong to him alone. And that didn't feel as weird as it would have once.

It was another opportunity to have some fun with her.

Fisting his hand in Akira's hair, he languorously continued pushing his fingers inside her, a half smile on his lips as he made her look at him. "Too much?"

"No." She bit her bottom lip, shaking her head quickly as he began pulling his fingers back. "No, Sir. It—it feels good."

"Hmm." He let out a rough laugh and kissed her cheek. "Brave little girl—taking a man as big as Cort." He pressed until his second knuckles strained against her. "But you can't take him all, can you?"

"No." She bucked, as though wanting to take more, her little wince showing him she couldn't. "I wish I could . . . But he said—"

Another laugh and he withdrew his fingers, flattening his hand over her hot mound and gently rubbing the heel of his palm over her swollen little clit. "What if I told you there was a way?"

"How? My body won't change, and he's—"

Ford straightened quickly and jerked her to her feet by her wrist. He kissed the tip of her nose, keeping her off balance with a touch of gentleness, while his tone was gruff. "Put your hands against the wall."

She ducked her head, giggling a little as she spun around and took the perfect position to be frisked. "Do I need to ask where you got this idea?"

He winked at her as he took out his wallet, dropping it on his desk after taking out a condom. "This is nothing compared to the games I want to play with you. Good cop, bad cop, and a very bad little perp that will do anything for a 'get out of jail free' card."

"Mmm, sounds almost as fun as being the naughty schoolgirl."

"At the club?"

She wiggled her butt a little as she spread her legs a bit farther apart. "Uh-huh."

Weird, but the idea of her playing with Cort didn't bug him at all anymore. Cort *and* Dominik? Yeah, that irked him. If Akira was gonna have two men, Ford needed to be one of them.

But what if she still wanted Dominik? He hadn't considered that until Cam had brought it up, weeks ago. Maybe he should have.

Holding back a sigh, he moved to stand beside her, draping her long, slick, black ponytail over one shoulder to press his lips to the other. "You enjoyed playing with both of them?"

"I did." She glanced back at him, a tender smile on her lips. "Dominik and I needed that one last time."

*Good. Very good.* And not only because he wanted Akira for himself and Cort. He liked Dominik. Loved Akira. Closure was best for them both.

"You are the most beautiful, giving person." He pressed his eyes shut as it hit him how fucking lucky he was to be here with her. To call her his, even if only in part. "You do know I won't be able to let you go?"

"Why would you have to?" Her brow creased, and he cursed himself for ruining the moment. Knowing her, she'd probably wonder what else could go wrong.

And before long, thinking about what already had.

He didn't give her a chance. He tore the condom wrapper with his teeth and squeezed her butt under her skirt, brushing his fingers over the damp cotton between her thighs. "I never will. And that is *all* that matters."

Stripping her completely to relish in the sight of her gorgeous body would have been perfect, but just having her shirt off was risky. Cam would let him know if anyone questionable came toward Ford's office, but Akira might need to get dressed and get out in a hurry.

No time to waste. The needy little sounds she was making drove him to distraction. He rolled the condom over his painfully hard dick, then shifted the little bit of cloth covering her. Positioned himself against her with one hand on her throat. Then slid in deep.

The way her snug pussy undulated around him told him how close she was. But she'd been trained well. He could fuck her for hours and she would take it, not coming until he allowed it, enjoying every second. Only, that was the control she'd given to another man.

He wanted her pleasure, wanted it to sweep her under and set her loose. He refused to give her the option of holding back. So he wrapped her ponytail around his fist. And used the one thing that he knew would toss her over the edge.

"Shall I show you?" He kissed her neck, tasting her wild pulse. She seemed to struggle not to move.

Her words were barely a whisper. "Show me?"

"Yes." He thrust in and out, angling his dick until she shuddered and stopped trying to hold still. Then he bit her shoulder and placed his hand on her ass, sliding his fingers under her panties, along the crease between her cheeks until he reached the small, tight hole. He pressed down and let out a low growl as her pussy squeezed around him. "Show you how you will take all of him. How you will take us both."

\* \* \* \*

Akira couldn't hold back much longer. She wanted to show Ford she could be a sub with him, and yet, he was making it hard to do what she was supposed to. To submit as well as she had for Dominik. And as a Dom, Ford had to want that.

At first, she hadn't really believed that he'd trained as a Dom for any reason but to appeal to her, but there was no mistaking that look. That *tone*. He might have started out for all the wrong reasons, but this was natural to him.

Cort had a naturally dominant personality, only it wasn't quite the same. Not in a bad way, just . . . different. His lines weren't as clear. Or weren't now, anyway. That could change.

*As long as it's what he wants.*

She hadn't thought much about Cort before, which almost made her feel guilty, but not enough to stop. She wasn't sure she *could* stop.

Knew she didn't want to.

The slow drag of Ford's dick, the way he pushed into her, brought her focus to the way every inch of him played at her body. It was like he had some secret manual telling him what buttons to push to drive her insane. A manual she hadn't read, so she had no way to prepare for the way her nerves flared, the way her muscles jumped, her whole body quivered. His finger slipping deeper into her back hole added a grittiness to the pleasure. Some part of her said it was dirty, naughty, but that turned her on even more.

More so when his chest rumbled with laughter as she lifted her hips to allow him to penetrate her deeper in every way. Another bite on her neck had her making a pleading, high-pitched sound she couldn't stop. He covered her mouth, speaking low into her ear. "Your pussy is so fucking tight, but here? We'll have to work on opening you up for him."

*Oh my God!* She was torn. She should want Cort here with them, but Ford had made it okay to be alone with him. Had included Cort in a way that made now perfect, and later an erotic fantasy that would come true. She became a candle so hot it couldn't retain its form. Spilling free and held together only by his hands, his kiss, his body. Her thoughts scattered as another thrust rocked her core, causing all that liquid heat to ripple out and flow all over her, through her veins, over her sweat-slicked skin.

She shuddered as she felt Ford find his own release, then whimpered as he drove in hard, dragging out another aftershock of pleasure. When he drew out, she groaned, her body so sensitive the motion had her twitching and clenching down on the emptiness.

Incredibly, it didn't take her too long to find her bearings again. She ducked her head, smiling a little as he helped her fix her clothes. After getting her jersey back on, he even had her sit on his desk, facing away from him so he could comb through her hair with his fingers and do it up in a neat braid.

"I used to do my mother's hair when I was a kid." A wistfulness curved his lips as she turned to him. "Guess I haven't forgotten how."

Pressing one hand to his cheek, she studied his face. "You must miss her so much."

"I do. Sometimes I wish . . ." He sighed and shook his head. "I'm grateful that she didn't suffer. That she didn't have to see how things are between me and Kingsley. She wanted me to be a better person than I was. Maybe I can be that for her now."

"You can. You're already *much* better." She leaned forward to kiss him. "You're someone I'm not afraid to love."

"Yeah, well, you probably should be."

"I'm not."

His brow furrowed. He stared at the floor. "I'll do my best to make sure that's not a mistake. But you have to go back to Dominik—at least for a little while. Once this thing with my father is over, once Cort is cleared—"

"But he will be? I mean, does he have a good lawyer?"

"The best. Sebastian made sure of it." Ford pressed his tongue into the center of his top lip thoughtfully. "I don't think Cort knows about Tim, though. Since he was working with my father, he might blame himself. Might think he deserves to be punished."

That brought Akira's thoughts back to the questions she couldn't ask on the phone. She had to ask them while she had a chance. "What was Cort doing for your father? I don't understand."

Ford made a face, as though he'd tasted something disgusting. "Damn it, if I'd known sooner . . . Kingsley still wants to use the team to make the dirty fucking money he makes look clean. He couldn't get me to do it, but he found ways to use Cort. Don't hold this against him, but the whole thing with Dave Hunt—"

*Poor kid.* Akira frowned. She hadn't liked Hunt, but most of that was from her own issues. "Cort got Angel to—"

"Yeah."

"But that has nothing to do with what happened to Tim." She

chewed at her bottom lip when Ford refused to meet her eyes. "What aren't you telling me?"

Pressing his eyes shut, Ford tipped his head up to the ceiling. "I don't think my father would have gone after Tim unless his name was mentioned."

"Cort—" She was going to be sick. Madeline and Tim were dead because of *Cort?* She bent over, arms crossed over her bare stomach. "I can't—if he—"

Shoulders squared, Ford looked down at her, his jaw hard. "Don't do that. There was no way Cort could have known what my father would do. Cort was trying to keep me alive, and my father would have killed me to make a point. And then he would have found someone else to pressure. Tim was the head coach. My father might not have considered him on his own, but anyone involved with the team would have put Tim in the line of fire. And Tim would never have gone against the team."

"It wasn't 'anyone,' though." Akira swallowed back the bile in her throat. "It *was* Cort."

"No. It was my father." Ford grabbed her arms and pulled her against his chest. "You hated me for so long because of what happened to Jami. And I get that. But don't do that to Cort. He's gonna need us. Remember how much you love him. Remember why. He didn't think twice before stopping Lee, even though he knew he could end up back in jail. That's who he is."

"There had to be another way. Not with Lee, but with Kingsley—"

"He didn't see it. But I'm doing what I can to get enough on Kingsley to put him away for a very long time. Just please—" Ford kissed her hair, her cheeks, massaging her arms as though his touch could somehow make her understand "—please don't mistake who the monster is here. It's not Cort."

Right. Ford was right. She still felt nauseous, but pinning Tim's death on Cort didn't sit right. It was horrible enough that Cort would take the blame on himself. Despite her immediate reaction, she knew there was only one person responsible for taking Tim and Madeline away from those who loved them.

*Kingsley*.

A deep, sizzling rage had her wondering if she could go after Kingsley herself. Get a gun and just . . . but no, that would be stupid. Ford—of *all* people—was trying to deal with the man legally. Which was good. But it scared her. She fisted her hands in Ford's shirt. "I get it. This isn't Cort's fault, and I'll help him see that. But what about you? When Kingsley finds out you're—"

"He won't. The detective I talked to wants me to be a 'confidential informant.'"

"Should you be saying that in here?" She held her breath. Damn it, they'd already said too much. "What if—"

"Laura met up with Cam earlier today. Gave him some easy, hi-tech way to check the room." Ford's lips curved slightly. "Security is pretty tight here. Kingsley would have had a hard time bugging the place. My bar, my house, my *phone* . . . different story."

"But your office is safe." Something occurred to her. "I didn't even—I mean, what we did . . . I didn't even think about being in an office. And that's where . . ."

Ford cupped her cheeks in his hands, a broad smile on his lips. "*That* is amazing. I can't do much for you, but at least I did something right."

She closed her eyes as he kissed her, feeling a moment of peace. A bit of the submissive mentality, maybe, but knowing what she'd said, what she'd done, made him happy, was wonderful. "You've done a lot of things right, Ford."

"Thank you, shorty." He groaned at a soft tap at the door. "All right, the rest of the world wants us back. I don't know how long it'll be before I can steal you away again, but this will be over soon, and then me, you, and Cort—"

"We'll have the rest of our lives." Or was that expecting too much? It was what she wanted, but . . . She wrinkled her nose. "I mean, we'll have time to—"

"You were right the first time." Ford led her to the door, one hand on the small of her back, and pressed his lips to the side of her neck. "Anything worth having is worth fighting for, right? We've all fought hard. So we've earned forever."

"Forever." She took a deep breath and nodded. "That sounds right. That will get me through the next few days."

*Or longer.* Her chest was tight as she left Ford's office and let Cam walk her to the elevator. *It might take longer. But it will be worth it in the end.*

# Chapter Twenty Eight

Deafening, eerie silence fell over the Delgado Forum. Filled to capacity, but the emptiness Max had sensed around him when he'd stepped on to the ice earlier, before all the lights were on, before any of the staff, or players, or fans had arrived, seemed to linger. Listening closely enough, whispers could be heard in the crowd, but the sound couldn't penetrate the loss of a voice gone forever.

The tribute for Coach was about to begin. A thickness in Max's throat made him swallow hard as he glanced over at the men along the bench. Dominik met his gaze and gave him a subtle nod. Sloan, taking his place behind the Cobra bench for the first time in a suit instead of a jersey, cleared his throat quietly behind Max, putting a hand on Max's shoulder as Max stood to join the rest of the first line on the ice.

Keane's voice came through the speakers, deep and steady as he spoke about Tim's tragic death. He brought everyone's attention to the Jumbotron to "Celebrate the life of the Dartmouth Cobras' beloved coach, Tim Rowe."

"Hear You Me" by Jimmy Eat World played as the screen showed a picture of Tim as a young boy, in his Halifax Hawks jersey, a big smile to proudly show off lost baby teeth. More pictures of him through his years in the minors. Then video clips of him as the Cobras' assistant coach.

Max's eyes moistened at a clip of Tim standing before him and Sloan, tearing them out for a sloppy play, then laughing abruptly at some stupid comment Max had made. Max couldn't remember what he'd said, but he remembered how Tim could get him feeling like nothing he'd done couldn't be fixed. He always believed each and every one of his men could do better. *Would* do better.

And they had. For Tim, every single player had worked their butts off to reach their potential because Tim accepted no less. He fought with them to keep the fire burning, the love of the game, the passion. He fought for them on the ice, picking his battles, but downright feral when he thought someone had done them wrong. Even now a scene played out where it looked like Tim wanted to strangle a ref.

That had Max grinning. Hell, the refs respected Tim because he was usually so level-headed. But when he got that look in his eyes, half of them would prefer dealing with Sloan while he'd been captain. Or Dominik once he'd gotten the position. The ref on screen looked embarrassed as Tim stood on the bench, shouting and making a slashing motion, pointing to Carter's bloody lip.

Off to Max's side, Carter made a rough sound, bowing his head and rubbing his gloved hand across his face. A few of the other men had tears streaming down their cheeks. The cameras showed the players standing at the bench, all staring up at the Jumbotron, all looking a little lost. A little broken.

As a clip played of Tim hugging Tyler after a game winning goal, Max glanced over and saw Tyler bend over, his shoulders hunched, head down. Zovko placed a hand on Tyler's back and said something to him that had Tyler nodding and lifting his head. He stopped trying to hide his tears. And smiled a little at the scene playing where Tim came into the hotel room and dumped ice water over a young, very hungover Sloan.

Arms crossed over his chest, Sloan seemed to inhale slowly, but he had a broad smile on his face. The tightness eased from Max's chest. It was gonna hurt them all for a long time, carrying on without Tim, but they still had what he'd given them. They'd always have that.

The tribute finished with a picture of Tim in his coach's uniform at a practice, pride in his smile as he looked over them all taking a knee in a circle around him. His minor league #38 with the Hawks' logo on one side, and the Cobras' on the other, showed at the base of the image and was worn as a patch on each player's jersey. The jerseys would be auctioned off, proceeds going to Tim's charities.

Cheers and applause from the crowd. Players from both teams rapped their sticks on the boards. Max and those on the ice lifted their sticks one-handed, pointing straight up, in a gesture of thanks to their coach. Keane went over the charities the team would donate to in Tim's name. The charity Tim's family had started for him and Madeline.

After Max and the first line returned to the bench, a large carpet was set up in the center of the ice for the Ice Girls' dance. Some of the fans grumbled, probably having expected Tim's family to come out to accept condolences, but it was just too damn soon for that. Tim and Madeline's funeral had been that very morning, small and private, with only family and the team.

This, the tribute, the dance, was for the fans. As a remix of Jimmy Eat World's "The Middle" played, the energy in the Forum changed. Akira led her girls in a powerful, blood-pumping performance that seemed to remind everyone why they were here. The heavy weight of sadness lifted. The air seemed a little easier to breathe.

By the time the puck dropped, the atmosphere around the ice was no different than at any other game. The Islander players had taken a moment to show their respects, but now they were simply opponents.

There was a game to win. Instructions Sloan had given in the locker room that every man carried in the forefront of his mind. No one asked "how" or "why." They needed direction. "Start easy and stay out of the box" was simple enough. Max knew the reasons, but few did. The odds leaned toward the Cobras losing this game. The team was an emotional wreck. Some might figure they could "do it for Tim" . . .

Easier said than done. In the end though, they had to come out ahead. With Hunt between the pipes. With half the team still uncertain whether the game really mattered anymore because, despite the rousing tribute, they hadn't had a chance to get past the sight of Tim's name carved in stone and the scent of damp earth on his grave.

Losing wasn't an option. Not with Kingsley still out there, held at bay only because Ford had convinced him that he didn't need to make another move to get what he wanted from the team.

If that changed, the next face up on that screen could be any one of them. Tyler, whose red-rimmed eyes were hard with determination. Carter, whose pale face made his game-earned scars stand out against the stone set of his jaw. Demyan, Pearce, Dominik, or any player who made an impact could find themselves in Kingsley's line of fire.

Max would be damned if he'd let that happen. But that proved a distraction in itself, because he couldn't stop watching the other men. Trying to see them as Kingsley would, wondering who stood out. Who might be vulnerable.

"I hear you've got my leftovers now, Mason," Grant Higgins said under his breath as he shoved against Dominik, off to Max's left at the face-off. "Knew she'd be the Cobras' little fucktoy soon as she came down here."

*Shit!* Max skidded up to Dominik as the puck hit the ice, blocking him before he could go after Higgins. Higgins laughed, spinning around to follow the play.

And flew backward when Demyan cracked him in the jaw with his fist.

The Islanders crowded around their fallen teammate. The Cobras converged behind Demyan, Ramos quickly hauling him back before Demyan could answer Higgins's teammates' invitations to drop the gloves. Behind the bench, Sloan called for a time-out. One hard look from him was all it took to get Demyan to head to the locker room when the ref threw him out for game misconduct.

But Max hardly noticed that. He hardly heard a word Sloan said to them. He couldn't stop himself from trying to get in Kingsley's twisted mind and see who the next target would be.

There was only one logical choice. Max stared at his best

friend, his pulse thrumming in his head as Sloan got the men to calm down. As Sloan made it way too obvious that the new "head coach" wasn't really in charge.

Sloan caught Max's arm seconds before time-out ended, leaning over the boards, his tone low. "Talk to me, Max. Why are you looking at me like that? What's wrong?"

How the fuck was he supposed to answer that? *"I'm afraid that you're next. I wish you'd sit back and not make it so goddamn clear that you're running the show."* When the hell was this going to end?

He couldn't lie to Sloan. So he gritted his teeth and faced him. "I wish you'd stayed in Calgary."

"You're full of shit." Sloan gave Max a hard shake. "You know what we've gotta do. Go do it. Don't worry about me."

"Tell me how I'm supposed to do that?"

"Stick on the ice. Head up. You know how to play the fucking game."

Guts churning, Max put his hand over the #38 patch on his chest. "I'm not gonna let your number be the next one we're wearing."

"Right back at you, Mr.-Fucking-Catalyst. And by the way, you might wanna keep your mouth shut. Knowing too much might be an issue." Sloan's grip tightened on Max's arm. "You hearing me?"

"Yeah." A sharp inhale and a nod and Max was able to get his head back where it belonged. To put his stick on the ice. Keep his head up.

And play the fucking game.

\* \* \* \*

Tied at one. Third period. Tyler wasn't sure why Callahan looked so agitated, or why Perron couldn't seem to stop pacing every time they went in the locker room. He was pretty sure he was missing something, but all he could think about was the promise he'd made to Chicklet.

The same one he'd made to Raif.

Play for Tim. Tyler was doing his best, but sometimes it felt like he was alone out there. Fuck, some of the guys were playing like they'd forgotten how. If Hunt hadn't turned into a freakin' wall during the second, they'd be trailing by at least six. Raif had their only goal on a sweet breakaway. The Islanders were playing real good, so they weren't giving away many chances like that.

He wouldn't worry, though. Dragging in a lungful of crisp air, Tyler took the face-off at center ice. Ignored the chirping from the man in front of him. Scooped up the puck and tucked it back to Pearce. The sharp slice of his blades carried him across the rink. He knew without having to look that the puck was coming back to him. Perron made a solid pass. Tyler dodged a hefty center. Deftly circled two defensemen. Feigned a high shot.

And cut the puck cleanly between the goalie's pads.

Ramos hugged him. Perron and Pearce slammed into his sides. He was surrounded by a team that seemed to suddenly come alive. But it wasn't until he was on the bench that it hit him that what he'd done mattered. And not by just putting them ahead by one.

Raif put an arm over his shoulders and kissed the top of his helmet. "*Dobar posao,* Ty. Well done."

"For Tim." Smiling kinda hurt, like his face wasn't used to it anymore. But as he glanced across the bench to where Callahan stood, he could picture Tim, standing there like Raif said he would be. Watching Tyler with that look in his eyes saying he'd expected no less. Tyler's smile grew even bigger. He whispered, "Thanks, Coach."

And Tim smiled back.

# Chapter Twenty Nine

Worn jeans held up by a thick belt, a beaten-up leather jacket, and a white wifebeater. Ford knew he was pushing it with the outfit, but Kingsley would expect as much. The man didn't know the "new and improved" Ford. He'd never believe in the man who wore a suit to the office. Who took paperwork seriously. Who had responsibilities. Who'd come to love the goddamn fucking team.

Kingsley would want the Ford he could look down on. The punk who came home reeking of weed, a cigarette hanging from his slanted lips. A wad of crumpled bills in his pocket from strippers desperate for whatever he had to sell. Cheap perfume and lipstick on his clothes. Beer, smoke, and attitude.

He'd grown up a little, so he didn't have to go to the extreme of stumbling into Kingsley's house drunk, but dressing respectably wouldn't seem normal. Better he looked like he'd come straight from the bar. And only because Kingsley's last text involved the possibility of losing limbs if he was ignored again.

Ford didn't really believe Kingsley would do anything drastic. This wasn't the fucking movies. No hands held on thea table to be broken with hammers . . . well, okay, it had been done. But Kingsley didn't get that messy himself.

*I'm still his son.*

Not for real, but he'd been portrayed that way too long for Kingsley's partners to care about the technicalities. If Kingsley couldn't control the man he'd raised, he had no power at all. So his form of discipline would be swift. No visible marks that he could avoid. He'd given Ford black eyes only twice in his life. A bloody lip once.

Sending thugs to get Ford in line was a great big neon sign that Kingsley wasn't quite stable. Because he'd dealt with everything from Ford getting in trouble at school to teenage defiance in one of two ways. Threats based on violent acts he'd let Ford witness from the age of seven, or lashing out quickly with a slap or a punch to the gut, followed by a carefully-worded warning. One that wouldn't be given again.

And Ford had seen enough to know what *those* meant. Men who were there every day, Kingsley's favorites, would suddenly disappear. A misstep and they were just gone. This life was a balancing act, and Ford knew what happened when you fell.

You never got back up.

Laura was staring at him as he tried to explain why he'd ignored Kingsley's phone calls. Tried to make her understand how doing something that might seem stupid to most made sense. If he didn't want Kingsley getting suspicious, he had to be the man Kingsley knew. Push as far as he could without passing the hard limits.

Wording it that way finally got through to her. She took a deep breath and nodded. "All right. But how likely is it that he'll say something we can use tonight?"

"I don't know. He might." Ford rolled his eyes when Detective Hamilton shot him a hard look. "I wouldn't have called you if I didn't think there was a chance."

The detective placed the tiny, felt bug against the inside of Ford's belt, his fingers hooked to the leather as he met Ford's eyes. "Don't lead the conversation. Let him talk."

Ford smirked. He couldn't help it. Kinda had to get "in character," right? "You're getting kinda friendly, *Detective*." He smirked as the man's eyes hardened. "If I'm gonna be your bitch, maybe a few beers first? I'm a cheap date."

"I bet." Hamilton scowled as he released Ford's belt. "Don't be an idiot about this. You're no use to anyone dead. And I'm your only hope of getting out of there alive if things go south."

"If I do everything you say?"

"Exactly."

"Pal, I play things your way—be a good boy—Kingsley will know something's up." Ford tipped his head back to stare at the ceiling of the van. His heart raced to the point that he could feel the web of veins pulsing hard in every limb. He was being a complete asshole, but what else could he do? The only other option was showing how fucking scared he was. And if he couldn't hide that here, he couldn't hide it once he got past those gates. So he didn't worry too much about pissing off the cop. "So, yeah. I'm gonna be an idiot. Don't come in and rescue me or anything. I'll be fine."

Laura grabbed his arm, her tone harsh. "We're here if you're not. I get why you're doing this. I respect it because Akira's a good girl and Cort . . . he did what he had to for Jami. I want him out, too." Her brow furrowed. "But I'll be the uniform at their doors if anything goes wrong. I'll insist. Don't make me do that."

"I'll. Be. Fine." Hell, maybe if he repeated it often enough, he'd believe it himself. "Record everything. Hopefully we'll be halfway done when I walk out those doors."

"You need something to say if you're in trouble, Ford."

Now that was just funny. Again, he was the "safeword Dom." His brows shot up. "How's that gonna work? A safeword is something you wouldn't normally say."

"Not with us. Pick something normal for you." Laura raked her fingertips through the slick hair above her tight ponytail. "Like . . . 'this is fucked-up.'"

All right, he could do that. Kingsley wouldn't even blink at those words. And Ford kinda liked knowing saying that could save him. But . . . "Fine. What do I say for I'm okay?"

Laura glanced over at Hamilton. "'I get it'? We're listening to everything, so we won't react if things sound in control. But if we're not sure, that would be a good sign that you've got things handled."

"Right. I can slip either in easy. Just don't do anything unless I say either one."

"Ford—"

"Swear it." He refused to do this halfway. Going in there had some risks. But they'd just get worse if he had to worry about cops storming in. "I'm a big boy. This is what I know. I'm trusting you to be there if I need you. All I ask is that you don't fuck this up if I don't."

It was Hamilton who gave Ford the assurance he needed. He smacked Ford's shoulder hard, then gestured him toward the back door of the van. "You've got it, kid. We're here if you need us. And we won't make a move if you don't."

"Thanks." Ford cracked his neck and cast one last sideways glance at the detective. "You still think I'm one of the bad guys, don't you?"

Brow arched, lips quirking, Hamilton inclined his head. "Damn right, I do. But that could change."

"Watch me." The edges of Ford's lips curved slightly as he stepped on to the street. "And it will."

Ford felt pretty damn good as he sauntered up to Kingsley's front door, but his bravado faltered as the lock clicked open. The butler let him in, and suddenly Ford's common sense had something to say.

*You might not be a bad guy, but since when are you some kind of hero?*

No, he didn't think he was a hero. Cort had been Jami's hero when he'd saved her from Lee. Tim had been a hero to the Cobras. Ford was just finally doing something good. Something that should have been done a long time ago.

The reasons for Akira's lasting hatred came back to him as he followed the butler down the long hall, familiar priceless trinkets on ornate tables at either side of him, an elegant, thick runner dulling the heavy thunk of his boots. He hadn't spoken up before, hadn't tried to stop his father, and too many people had been hurt. It was too late to fix that.

But he could make sure it never happened again.

Kingsley was in the kitchen, his suit jacket abandoned on the back of one of the wooden chairs around the small, glass breakfast table. He stood at the sink, back to Ford, staring at the water filling the sink. Something about his stance made Ford's pulse pick up speed. Common sense was shouting for him to turn around and get the fuck out of there.

Common sense had never held much sway with Ford. No point in letting it call the shots now.

"You were arrested." Kingsley's tone was cold, every word spoken with exaggerated clarity. "Because of Cort, yes?"

"Yes." Ford held his breath, unable to find strength in the cockiness he'd planned to lean on. There was something in the air, a sense of being on the edge of a cliff without the power to step back to safety. He'd played this all wrong—he could tell just by the way Kingsley stared at him over his shoulder. The man was questioning Ford's worth. And Ford had to remind Kingsley he was still good for something. "They've got nothing on me. Your lawyer had me out of there really fast, and I was able to—"

"To what? Please tell me you're not going to take credit for the Cobras winning that game. I watched it. The assistant coach managed to reach some of the players. One of the young ones . . . Vanek, I believe?" Kingsley shrugged when Ford didn't reply. "He moved beyond the 'tragedy' and seemed to recall what he's being paid to do."

Ford didn't like that Kingsley was singling out Callahan and Vanek. That wouldn't lead to anything good. And the passing mention being recorded would only be useful if Kingsley made a move. He watched as Kingsley picked up a bottle of bourbon off the counter and filled two tumblers. "Working around the coach's death won't be easy."

"I expected as much. But the team must make the playoffs."

"I agree."

"Good. Then, so far, we're on the same page." Kingsley handed Ford one of the glasses, then took a sip from his own. His calm was unsettling. "The backup goalie played better than expected."

"He's talented." Ford gulped down his bourbon, mouth as dry

as sun-scorched sand. The liquor only made it worse. But he held Kingsley's level gaze, trying to read the man. "That's why we drafted him."

"'We.' It's amusing that you word it that way. As though you were somehow involved." Kingsley shook his head, laughing quietly. "Only, you weren't. For all your 'involvement' with the team, you don't seem to have much influence."

"I'm where I need to be. The GM won't be around much— he's grieving. My little sister is trying to be there for him. Keane is new, so he'll need someone who *knows* the team. That's my angle." Sounded good, but it didn't look like Kingsley was buying what Ford was trying to sell. His expression never changed. So Ford tried a different approach. "The players come to my bar. I'm in a good position to get inside information and—"

"Nothing more than anyone who reads the team blogs can learn. You cannot change the outcome of the games."

"I can. I've just gotten started. Give me a chance to see who I can use."

"Why would anyone trust you? They all know you're a criminal. Your face was in the papers. The news coverage was quite embarrassing." Kingsley clucked his tongue as he held his hand out for Ford's glass and refilled it. He circled Ford slowly as he spoke. "Tell me how you plan to play this. I'd hoped to hear all about it when my lawyer freed you, but you decided I didn't need to be kept informed."

"There was nothing to say. I didn't want to waste your time."

"You *are* wasting my time. I've yet to be convinced that you'll be of any use to me." Kingsley stopped behind Ford, and it took all of Ford's willpower not to bolt. He swallowed hard as Kingsley whispered close to his ear, "I won't spare you for your mother. That time has passed."

Ford's heart stuttered at the mention of his mother. His throat locked. He pressed his eyes shut. "I know that. But she loved you. She'd want me to do what I can for you."

"Perhaps." Kingsley's hand fell hard on Ford's shoulder. "But

I'm not sure there's much you *can* do. And your defiance is trying. All I ask is a little gratitude, and you couldn't even give me that."

*I fucked up.* Damn it, he wasn't dealing with the man who'd raised him. He was dealing with someone much more dangerous. Unpredictable. He cleared his throat. "I'm grateful. And I will repay you."

"How?"

"The team will make the playoffs."

"I don't need you for that."

"Don't you? Losing a man like Tim, a coach that handled his team like they were all blood, could easily put the Cobras in last place. I've gotten to know the players well enough to work around what you—" Ford cut himself off. Too late. He wasn't supposed to lead the conversation, but his last statement came too close to an accusation.

"Ford, I don't like what you are implying. Do you think I had something to do with the coach's death?" Stepping away from Ford, Kingsley moved to stand at the counter, casually resting his hip against it. "It was an accident. Very sad. Tim was such a strong man. So dedicated to the team. I admired his conviction."

"I'm not implying anything."

"Good. So back to your situation. Cort's little crisis of conscience is quite unfortunate. You could have been considered an accessory to his crime."

"Your lawyer fixed that."

"He did."

"So what do you want from me?"

"A 'thank you.'" Kingsley's tone changed. Became sharp, betraying his tenacious grip on control. He reached out and latched on to the back of Ford's neck. "Know this. You are *nothing* to me. Nothing but a reminder of so many mistakes. A reminder I don't need."

The old man was strong, but it was the shock of being forced face-first into the sink that kept Ford from fighting back. Eyes wide open, he struggled against the grip on his neck, thrashing as water filled his mouth. He clamped his lips shut, struggling to hold his breath. His mind raced as he tried to find a way to survive and came up with nothing. How many times had he lay at Kingsley's feet as a boy, staring up at the man, hearing his mother pleading for her husband to stop? All Kingsley had done then was shove Ford and reach for the gun at his belt. He'd done that many times, but Ford had known his mother's screams would save him.

Ford had learned when to shut his mouth, but at some point, he'd stopped being afraid. Because Kingsley's love for his mother had spared him more often than not. But now that she was gone, nothing could stop Kingsley from ending Ford. From getting rid of his one last shame.

Lungs burning, Ford pushed at the edge of the sink, his life flashing like a stream of stills behind his closed lids. Akira finally turning to him with love in her eyes. Cort smiling over a bowl of cereal as he made it okay for them to share a woman who they'd both live and die for. He wrenched his head back and gasped in air, shouting before Kingsley could shove his head back into the water.

"I get it!"

Wrong words. If he was smart, he'd call in the fucking cavalry. Only, if he was rescued, he'd really be useless. Kingsley had set Lee on Jami. He'd had Tim killed. Yes, maybe he would kill Ford as well. He clearly wanted to.

But Ford had one last card to play. And if he was gonna die, at least he'd know he'd laid it on the table first. "I get it!" The words to keep the cops from coming in. Now for something to make Kingsley want to keep him alive. "I'm the last Delgado! The only one they know can get past this!"

"I'm not sure you want to remind me you're a Delgado, boy," Kingsley said, even as he released Ford. "The Delgados have no power. Because of you."

"They have some. And it's all mine now that my sisters are dealing with Tim's death. They trust me. They want to believe I'm a good person."

"Silly girls. One would think they'd know better, considering how quickly their father turned on them."

"The man's senile. When they look at me, they see their dead brother. They'll expect me to step up for the family." Ford braced his forehead on the edge of the sink. His body shuddered as his muscles tensed for fight or flight. "Keane hasn't shut the Delgados out. He'll listen to me."

"And what do you think you can do? Give me a name. Cort did that, at very least."

Ford kept his head down as he winced. Damn it, he didn't need a reminder of the guilt Cort would carry once he found out about Tim. And he couldn't fucking take that on himself. He knew what giving a name would mean. He coughed weakly, hunching his shoulders. "I need time."

"I've given you time. And support." Kingsley snarled. "To which I received nothing but disrespect."

"It won't happen again. I was . . ." Ford coughed hard, still feeling like he was drowning. Even though he knew very well, once his brain started working right again, that Kingsley had never intended to kill him. If it ever came to that, Kingsley would leave the job to someone else. This was just another form of discipline. Another warning. One Ford would take seriously. "I was stupid. I assumed I had plenty of time to figure this out."

"Because you're 'my son'?" Kingsley snorted as he pushed away from Ford. "You really are stupid. I'd cherish my own blood. You were never more than the bastard of the woman who meant everything to me. Now that she's gone . . . if you weren't her child, you'd be dead already."

"You were a father to me. I tried to be a son you'd be proud of." Just saying that hurt. Ford knew he'd never succeeded. Even before he'd found out that Kingsley wasn't his real father. And Kingsley's sharp laughter cut deep. He ground his teeth. "But you're right. It was always for her. I think I knew all along how little I meant to you."

"Then give me something, Ford. You don't want to waste my time? So far you've done nothing but. And wasted my resources as well. If Cort implicates you –"

"He won't."

"How do you know that?"

"You chose him, Dad." Calling Kingsley "Dad" made Ford feel sick. But he could tell the word put a little chink in the man's ice-cold armor by the telling twitch of his lips. So Ford pressed on. "I was your son for years, and you chose him to protect me. He's still doing it."

"Is he really? He might get a lesser sentence if he gives up information. And he knows too much."

*Shit.* If Kingsley believed that, Cort wouldn't make it out of jail alive. Ford scrambled for a way to shift the man's attention away from Cort. "He's got his own family to deal with. I don't know why he turned himself in, but I don't think he's stupid enough to make a deal. Either way, I've got nothing to worry about. He's got nothing on me."

"Fine. So you believe you have enough power to help me with the team?"

"I'd be dead if you didn't know I do."

"True. And what will you do with that power?"

"Whatever you want me to." Ford cleared his throat roughly, fighting the urge to cough against the wet feeling in his chest. All he had left was to give complete control to his "father." And hopefully that would be enough. "I don't have a name for you now, but I'll get you one."

"You have two days." Kingsley used the dishcloth hanging on the stove handle to dry his hands. "And you will give me someone easier to manage than the coach. I'd hoped eliminating him would put us in a position to bring in our own man, but that's proved impossible since Callahan accepted the job as assistant coach so quickly. However, if he is useful, perhaps it will work out after all."

Ford's jaw ached as he fought not to smile. *I've got you, you bastard.* He inclined his head, tone level. "You're right. I'll see what I can do."

Outside, away from the security cameras at the gate of

Kingsley's property, Ford walked past the cable van parked in front of a neighbor's house, then got into his own car. He drove for a few blocks and stopped at a gas station. Got out to wait for the cable van to pull up.

And couldn't contain his grin as Laura joined him. "He admitted to having Tim killed. You heard him, right? You waiting for a warrant so you can arrest him?"

Laura frowned. Not the reaction he'd expected. She looked him over and shook her head. "You're soaked. Whatever he 'admitted,' we didn't get it. I wanted to go in when we lost the transmission, but we heard you shouting that you were okay. What happened?"

He'd been all excited, warmed by adrenaline despite his wet clothes and the sub-zero temperature, but that faded as he absorbed her words. He'd thought he'd had it all.

*I have nothing.*

"Doesn't matter." Ford couldn't meet Hamilton's steady gaze when the man came out of the van. He knew what he'd see in the detective's eyes. He wouldn't be surprised that Ford had failed. Raking his fingers through his hair, Ford stared at the packed snow on the pavement beneath his feet. "Just give me another chance."

"Ford, we can't let you put yourself in danger." Laura touched Ford's arm, letting out a heavy sigh when he jerked away. "We'll find another way to bring him down."

"Please." He bit hard into his bottom lip, feeling like he was gonna lose it. Prove exactly what a worthless punk he really was. Hamilton would love that. Slow, even breaths brought him to the calm headspace he only ever reached at the club. He was finally able to lift his head and face them. "All I'm asking for is one more chance."

Hamilton grabbed his shoulder, his lips thin as he met Ford's eyes. "No one expected you to get everything we need first time out."

"So this isn't over?"

"Not by a long shot." Hamilton gave Ford a look that Ford

never would have expected from the man. One that held respect. And he told Ford exactly what he needed to hear. "You'll get your chance."

# Chapter Thirty

Cort shook himself hard at the chill as he left his car and stepped into the blowing snow, enjoying a breath of cold air even as it sliced at him, eager to freeze him to the bone. He didn't mind, though. Only three days behind bars and he'd pretty much accepted that he'd never walk free again. But Sebastian's lawyer, Jason Purcell, had worked a fucking miracle.

Hell, Sebastian had said he'd pay bail, but with Cort's habit of running, he hadn't thought he'd stood a chance. He snorted as he glanced down at the lump of the ankle monitor, covered by the hem of his threadbare, dark blue jeans. The judge obviously hadn't been completely convinced, but he agreed Cort had enough ties to the team to stick around. And the sweet lady at the bail office where he had to check in had even agreed to let him come down here to see his stepdad for a few hours. Some kinda exception to Cort having to be either at work or at home.

Walking across the parking lot to the large cabin that served as the small-town bar, a place where the local MC held most of its meetings, Cort spotted the old black Chevy that Ford liked using during the winter. At the other side of the lot was Akira's little white Firefly. They were both here. Ford had probably trailed Akira to make sure neither of them was being followed. Kept her safe.

Cort's jaw ticked as he got closer to the bar and heard the rough, drunken laughter inside. He hadn't been thrilled when Laura had relayed Ford's message that he and Akira would meet Cort here. His dad, Sutter, would look out for Akira if he knew what she meant to Cort, but if Dad thought she was Ford's piece . . .

He quickened his pace, shoving the door to the bar open and looking around quickly, ready to break some fucking necks if Akira even looked scared. He barked out a laugh when he saw her at a corner booth leaning against Ford and giggling at something Cort's dad said before kissing the back of her hand.

"Dad, I don't want to have to mess up all your perfect teeth. Hands off my ol' lady." Cort smiled wide as Sutter rose and came toward him, then grunted as Sutter squeezed the air out of his lungs in a rough bear hug.

"Fuck that!" Sutter let out an amused snort, his gaze flicking to Cort's cheek. His eyes hardened for a split second, but he didn't comment on the wound. "If you make that cute little girl your 'ol' lady,' I'm gonna fuck you up."

Cort slapped his father's back. "You know what I mean. Just wanted to make things clear."

"Ford already did." Sutter smirked and jerked his chin at a beefy biker—probably a local—nursing a bloody nose. "Your boy's lucky I knew it would piss you off if you showed up and found him out in the snow with a few holes in his gut. I settled all the bullshit." The grip on Cort's arm tightened as Cort shifted in the direction of the biker, red flashing across his eyes. Sutter knew him too fucking well. "He apologized. All he did was pull her over to the jukebox and talk dirty. Let it go." Most other men wouldn't dare try to hold Cort back. But Cort had never lifted a hand to his father. Not even when he was a cocky little shit of sixteen and Sutter had knocked him on his ass for taking a cop's daughter out for a good time. If Cort listened to anyone, it was this man.

And maybe his lawyer. Jason was pretty cool.

Glancing over at Akira, Cort saw the dirty look she was giving Ford for making her stay put. He gave his father one last squeeze and nodded at Ford to let him know it was okay to let her go.

The second Ford slid out of the booth, Akira bolted. Ran across the bar and threw herself into Cort's arms. He picked her up, kissing her, laughing as her hair clung to his lips even as she tipped her head back, her mouth on his, her fingers digging into his shoulders. He tasted the salt of her tears, heard her sob, and his heart broke a little. He'd put her through so much. Too much.

But things were gonna get better. He couldn't help believe his lawyer's assurance that he might not serve any time at all. That he had a solid case. It wouldn't be too long before he, Akira, and Ford got the life they wanted. He couldn't buy a big, fancy house, but he could get some place decent. If he didn't let pride get in the way, maybe he'd let Ford pitch in. Between the two of them, Akira would have everything she needed. Everything she deserved.

"It's okay, Tiny." Cort kissed Akira's wet cheeks. "I messed up. I'm trying to fix it, but things must have been hard for you. I'm sorry."

"It's not your fault, Cort." She was trembling. Still crying. Fuck, he had a lot to make up for.

Hopefully, she'd give him a chance to prove she'd stood by the right man. That his being arrested was the end of his being a fucking criminal. Maybe being here didn't help much, but he'd make sure she was never in a place like this again.

Ford's scenario of Cort coming home covered in grease while Ford came home in a suit, both working hard to be good men for her, sounded perfect right now. She needed something to look forward to.

"Tiny, it's my fault I waited so long. I'm not sure how much Ford told you . . . he got me to come clean. Which was the right thing to do. I did some bad things because I thought I had to. I considered letting you go so you could have better than me." He dried her tears with his fingers, shaking his head. "But I'm thinking I can be better. If you can forgive me."

"You don't need my forgiveness. I love you. Ford told me everything, and for a minute . . . No, not even. I want you in my life." She blinked fast and glanced back at Ford. "He doesn't know, does he?"

Ford let out a heavy sigh and latched his fingers behind his neck, staring at the floor. He cleared his throat. "He doesn't know."

*Know what?* His temper flared. He kept his arms around Akira, looking around at the men in the bar. None of them met his eyes, but whatever. Sutter would tell him who needed to die. Maybe he hadn't mentioned it yet because he wanted to keep Cort out of trouble, but fuck that. If someone had hurt Akira, they were gonna pay.

"Who?" Cort framed Akira's little face in his big hands. Kept his tone soft for her. Prayed she could tell him what had happened and know he'd never let it happen again. "Akira, talk to me."

"Tim's dead, Cort," Akira whispered as she brought her hands up to his face. "Kingsley did it. *He* did it." She moved with him when he stumbled away from her. "Tell me you understand that. It's not your fault."

Cort's knees gave out. He dropped to them hard.

*No . . . No!*

He wrapped his arms around Akira's legs, needing her close. Knowing he should send her away. This couldn't be happening!

But it was. It had. She wouldn't have said Tim was dead if it wasn't true.

*Fuck . . . oh, God, what have I done?* He pressed his forehead against her thighs, his soft, delicate woman. *I should let her go. I've destroyed something—someone so much better than me.*

"Look at me, son." Sutter's voice. His bruising grip on Cort's shoulder reached through the darkness where Cort was falling. "Tell me what you want me to do. I'll bury the fucker. Just say the fucking word." He made a gruff sound as he shook Cort. "This isn't on you. I'm not letting you fucking do this to yourself."

"I told Roy . . . I told him I had Tim." Cort brought a hand to his face. Pressed his fingers into his closed eyelids. "I did this."

*Dead. He's dead.* If only Cort had—fuck, Akira couldn't forgive him for this. She shouldn't. He couldn't forgive himself.

"Cort, you didn't know." Ford's soft tone made Cort want to get up and punch him. How could he say that when so many had hated Ford—including Akira—for so long for his mistakes? Jami had almost been raped. But she hadn't been. And she was still alive. So it was nothing compared to what Cort had done.

*You know what you've gotta do, Nash.*

438

"Take her, Ford. Get her away from me." Cort released Akira. As he should have done in the first place. He'd never be the man for her. At least she had Ford and Ford loved her. And Ford wasn't too far gone to be there for her. He felt a gentle hand on the side of his throat and jerked away. "Get her out of here!"

"No." It sounded like Ford and Sutter had spoken at the same time. Cort could almost feel them staring each other down. It was Ford who continued. "I think she might object. And I refuse to take her away from you, so that's not gonna work. She had to watch us both be hauled in for bullshit. We're both here now. I won't have her feeling alone again."

"She's not alone. She has you." That's what Ford had wanted. Why couldn't he just go with it? It would kill Cort to lose her, but better that than her being with someone whose hands would always be soaked in innocent blood. "You owe me, Ford. You better fucking remember that and give her . . . give her everything. Every fucking day you better look at her and know you've gotta work hard to deserve her."

"You're right. I owe you that and a lot more. So here's what I'm going to do." Ford held his hand out, not moving until Cort took it. Then he jerked Cort to his feet. "I'm gonna make this real clear. Neither of us is going anywhere."

"You're gonna make her stay with a killer?"

Akira latched on to Cort's wrist and glared at him. "He's not making me do anything. And you're not a killer." She held up her hand before he could object, her eyes narrowing into angry slits as she finally let herself really see the damage done to his face. "Who did that?"

"I was in prison, sweetie. Shit happens."

"Not anymore."

"You can't know that. I—"

"Don't argue with me, Cort. I won't let Roy Kingsley hurt any more of the people I love."

*She doesn't understand.* "He's not the only one to blame—"

"Yes. He is." She poked him in the center of the chest. "Now, stop it. I missed you, and I just want you to hold me and promise you're never going to leave me again."

He shouldn't make that promise, but she trapped him with her beautiful eyes, eyes that had shed too many tears already, and made him see she wouldn't accept anything else.

At first, he couldn't speak. His mouth was dry and even the thought of letting go of his guilt . . . only, he wasn't really letting it go. Whatever he said, his part in Tim's death would always haunt him. "Akira, I love you. It wouldn't be right for me to—"

"Cort, you didn't know Tim very well, so let me say what he would if he were here." Ford took off his thick leather jacket and dropped it on the table. He put an arm around Akira's waist and a hand on Cort's arm. "The game's not over. You played a small part, and if you think you fucked up, get back out there and try harder. Learn from your mistakes and all that shit."

Cort let out a rough laugh. "He wouldn't have said it like that."

"Probably not." Ford gave Cort a crooked smile. "He would have said it better. But you get the point."

"I get it." Cort looked from Ford to Akira. Nodded slowly. "I can't promise they won't put me away for a long time, but if they don't . . . I'll stay."

"Good." Akira bit her trembling bottom lip, squaring her shoulders as she turned to Ford. Her eyes widened as she stared at Ford's neck. "Damn it, Ford! What happened to you?"

Ford blinked, brought his hand to his throat, then winced. "It's nothing."

The collar of Ford's jacket had covered the marks, but they stood out now, blue and purple bruises like someone had held his throat. Cort ground his teeth. "Our lady asked you a question."

"Not one I can answer now." Ford glanced at Sutter pointedly. The waitress came over, winking at Ford like she knew her timing was perfect when he quickly nodded and ordered them all some beers. Ford returned to his seat, leaning back, an easy smile on his lips. "Sutter told me we can hang out here after the place closes. He cleared it with the owner."

Akira folded her arms over her breasts. "That's great. But first you're going to tell me if Kingsley is the one who left those bruises on you."

Ford gave her a level look.

"You're not going back, Ford."

"I have to. I handled it, shorty. That's all you need to know."

Answer enough. Cort knew Ford wanted him to stay out of it, but too fucking bad. *I'm going to kill Roy.*

Apparently, Akira had the same plan. She faced Sutter and held out her hand. "Give me your gun. I'm going to kill that bastard."

Sutter grinned and reached back to pull out his gun.

Tossing his own homicidal to-do list aside, Cort grabbed the gun before Akira could wrap her small hand around it. He put his hand on Akira's shoulder to make her sit, then scowled at his father. "Seriously, Dad?"

"What? I want a front-row seat for this!" Sutter chuckled, bending over to kiss Akira's forehead. "Cort's right, though. Let someone else take out the asshole. You're a good girl—keep my boy out of trouble, 'kay, sweetheart?"

"I'll do my best." Akira shot Sutter a crooked, yet grim smile. "But only if you promise to help me bury the body when I get that gun back."

Helpful as he was, Ford was laughing as he brought his fresh beer to his lips, looking at Akira like he thought her being bloodthirsty was sexy as hell. Not that it wasn't, but Cort wasn't about to let Akira slip into the life he and Ford were struggling to get out of.

So he exchanged a look with Sutter he knew his father would understand. Sutter called out that the bar was "closed" and walked out as the place emptied. Leaving the three of them alone.

Akira paled a little as Cort flattened his hands on the table. He leaned close, tone level as he met her wide eyes. "Tiny, I don't even like you swearing. This is much worse."

She swallowed hard. "I'm sorry."

He bent down a little more to whisper against her lips. "Not sorry enough. But you will be."

\* \* \* \*

A shudder ran over Akira as Cort pulled her to her feet, the gleam in his eyes a little scary, but wickedly promising. She glanced over at Ford, who gave her a slanted smile, and knew she wouldn't be getting any help from him. He looked eager to see how Cort would punish her.

Despite being a bit nervous, little tingles went over every part of her body that Cort's gaze touched. She pressed her thighs together as she grew hot and moist, licking her lips because deep down, she really hoped he'd follow through. Even if the discipline wasn't pleasant, she wanted it to feel real. Wanted to be taken in hand and out of her own head.

Cort shrugged off his jacket and laid it on the floor at her feet. "Kneel, Tiny."

"Yes, Sir." She knelt on the jacket, tipping her head back to look up at him.

"Eyes down." He tapped her cheek lightly at her hesitation and her lips parted. "Safeword applies, but don't use it unless you have to. I won't slap you, but if even little taps are a hard limit, say so now." Cort studied her face when she just stared at him. "Nod if you understand."

She nodded quickly and lowered her gaze. Her pulse began a rapid tattoo as Cort's presence thickened around her, his authority a big, heavy blanket, weighing her down and comforting her all at once. All his past uncertainty was gone. Or very well hidden.

"I've been thinking about punishments—I had a lot of time to think in jail." He arched a brow at her quick glance up, not continuing again until she looked down at his scuffed-up, salt-stained black boots. "My issue with punishing you is if I have to overpower you to do it, if I have to spank you while you're struggling, I end up feeling like an abusive dick and—" He held a hand up when Ford cleared his throat and moved to stand. "I'm not saying it's abusive. You doing it to her won't bug me. But it doesn't feel right for *me* to do it."

"Got it," Ford said, tone relaxed as he settled back down. "Do what you're comfortable with."

Cort circled her slowly, and since she couldn't see his face, she found herself focusing even more on his voice. On the low, steady resonance, the controlled way he said each and every word. "This is going to hurt. It won't last long, and when I'm done, Ford and I will make up for all the time you were alone. But it's very important to me that you learn your lesson and never even *consider* picking up a gun and taking matters in your own hands. We clear?"

She nodded.

He tugged her hair. "Say the words, Akira."

"Yes, Sir. Very clear." Her vision swam. She'd wanted real, and now she had it. This punishment wouldn't be for fun. He might sound all calm, but there was no mistaking that what she'd done really bothered him. "I'm sorry, Cort." Her voice hitched. "I need you to know how sorry I really am."

"And what will happen if I accept your apology? If I just let it go?"

The suggestion made her blood run cold. Was he taking away the offer of a clean slate? She meant every word, but saying them wasn't enough. She needed him to make her *feel* them!

Tears trickled down her cheeks. "Please, Cort—*Sir*, there has to be more!"

"There will be." His knuckles grazed her cheek, brushing her tears away. "But I need to know this isn't for me. It feels . . . important that punishments do something for you too."

"They do." She swallowed, wishing she could meet his eyes. Let him see how much his doing this meant to her. "They mean I'm worth forgiving."

Off to the side, she heard Ford shift in his chair. Sensed some kind of silent exchange between the men.

Ford stood and came to her side. He put his hand under her chin, urging her to lift her gaze. "You're worth so much to us both.

Don't forget that." He smiled and tapped her nose. "I have a feeling I know what Cort's going to do. Breathe through it and you'll be fine. This will be his thing. I'm a little more random with my punishments."

This she knew. She'd heard rumors about Ford being pretty damn creative. The girls he topped would bitch about how mean he was, but they'd always have a dreamy look in their eyes. Like being with him was worth going through the worst.

Now *she* was with him. And she would go through the worst if she earned it.

Hopefully, that wouldn't happen too often.

"You got some rope, Ford?" Cort asked from behind her.

"Yeah." Ford let out a positively evil laugh. "Give me a minute. Got that and a few other things in my car."

Cort didn't say a word after Ford walked out. He stayed behind her, only his even breaths letting her know he hadn't left too. She tried not to shift on her knees as they started getting sore, but it felt like she'd been kneeling forever. The creases in Cort's jacket dented her skin through her jeans. She tried to move her weight from one knee to the other, get on a smoother spot.

Clearing his throat, Cort tugged her hair again. "Be still."

*Oh God!* Her cheeks heated as liquid warmth pooled down low. Cort wasn't playing at being a Dom. Not anymore. She could hear it in his voice and it was damn sexy. He knew she was his to command and control. Which had her feeling beautifully and wonderfully owned.

This wasn't about going through the motions, wasn't a game. She belonged to him and to Ford.

Her lips quirked as something occurred to her. *I'm in really big trouble.*

When Ford came back, Akira planted her most serene expression on her face, sure by how closely he watched her, how easily he read her, that her punishment would be much more intense if he figured out how much she was anticipating it.

His smirk told her she hadn't hid it too well, but he didn't comment. He pulled a length of rope out of his toy bag and turned to Cort. "You gonna do something simple or do you want me to fix up something fancy?"

"Something fancy." Cort put his hand on the side of her neck, stroking her throat with his fingertips. "I want to take this slow."

"Mmm, I like that idea." Ford took a knee behind her and drew her wrists to the small of her back, speaking softly. "How flexible are you, shorty?"

The question made her blush. She ducked her head. "Pretty flexible."

"Excuse me?"

"*Sir.*" She looked at him over her shoulder and wrinkled her nose. "Formal much?"

"You prefer it that way, pet." He fisted his hand in her hair and slid his hot lips across her cheek. "You've been naughty enough for one night, don't you think?"

Her eyes widened and she nodded quickly. The tingles were back, and her panties were getting uncomfortably damp. The only way to make this better would be to let go. To submit and be in the moment. Even if some of the moments wouldn't be pleasant.

"Flexible, Sir. Please let me show you."

"Good girl. And I will." Ford met Cort's eyes as Cort crouched in front of her. "Shirt on or off?"

"Can we get it off after?"

"Hmm . . . might be tricky, but I could cut it off."

*Cut it off? What am I gonna wear home?* She pressed her lips together and gave Cort her sweetest, pleading look. "Please, Sir. I like this shirt, and it's so cold out that I—"

Cort held his hand up and inclined his head. "Reasonable request, little one." His fingers went to the buttons of her shirt. Once they were all undone, he let Ford pull it off. Her bra followed and her nipples grew tight and hard. He covered her breasts with his hands as Ford began to wrap the rope above and below them. "Akira, you are so beautiful like this. Exposed, fragile, and all fucking mine."

"Yours?" Ford asked as he positioned her hands together between her shoulder blades. "Don't you mean 'ours'?"

"You know she's ours. But she's always mine. Always yours. Not sure if that makes any sense." Cort shook his head as though frustrated with his inability to express himself clearly. "It's not all about sharing. We both love this woman and she loves us. The only other option was killing you, and I happen to like you most of the time, boy."

Ford's brow creased slightly in response to the "boy," but then he laughed. "Glad me living was an option." He deftly bound Akira's hands together and stood after testing the ropes. "Comfortable, shorty?"

"Yes, Sir." Akira had the silly urge to give both men a great big grin. The way they interacted definitely kept things interesting. How many subs could say their Doms were like brothers, but threatened each other's lives so casually it had become an inside joke?

This was theirs, this understanding, this life, and even though the future was uncertain, she'd never been happier. She almost forgot about the punishment as Cort and Ford stood in front of her, admiring Ford's ropework.

Cort smoothed her hair over one shoulder and Ford met her eyes. "Don't forget what I said, Akira. Just breathe through it. He knows how to avoid permanent damage, but you might forget when it gets bad."

"Eyes down," Cort said with his hand on her shoulder. "Tell me what you did wrong."

"I asked your father for his gun." Akira took a deep breath, waiting . . .

"That's right." Cort pressed his fingers and his thumb into a spot at the base of Akira's neck. Hard.

The pain stabbed into her, tensing her muscles and wrenching a shocked cry from her throat. Her eyes teared and she instinctively tried to pull away.

"Be still." Cort smoothed his hand over her hair. Put his

fingers against one of her palms. Then drove them into the flesh between her thumb and her finger. "Scream if you have to. It won't bother anyone."

Shock delayed the pain. She gulped back a sob, pressing her eyes shut as he found the pressure point in her other hand. It hurt so bad, but once she absorbed the pain, she felt herself leaning closer to him every time he touched her. Knowing the sharp agony would come, but not trying to escape it.

"You are a wonderful person. You help, not hurt." Cort framed her face with one hand, working a pressure point in her thigh with the other. "No matter how angry you are, this will not change. I won't allow it."

She shook her head as she lost her tenacious grip on control and simply spoke her mind. "I hate him for what he did to both of you. I want him to pay!"

"He will, baby girl." Ford's gentle caress on her cheek contrasted so much with Cort's painful touch above her knee that she could only gasp and stare at him through her tears. "He'll pay without ruining you, or Cort. When he goes to hell, it will be alone. I won't let him drag either of you down with him."

Her nose was all runny. She probably looked gross, but she didn't care. All she saw were the bruises on Ford's neck. How close she'd come to losing him. "What if he kills you, Ford? It's not worth your life for either me *or* Cort to try to be good people. There has to be a way we can help you!"

Cort's fingers hovered over the throbbing spot he'd first pressed into on her neck. He swallowed audibly and nodded. "She's right, Ford. There has to be something we can—"

"There isn't. But you bring up a good point." Ford raked his fingers through his hair. "You have to choose, Cort. Either you try to keep me safe, or you look out for her. You can't have it both ways."

"Don't ask me to do that."

"I'm asking. And I need an answer right fucking now. This punishment works because she's not getting blood on her hands.

I'll do anything to get that through her head." Ford went still. "Will you?"

"Yes."

"No!" Akira's whole body tensed as Cort pinched the nerve in her neck just hard enough to make her scream. "Please! I'll be good. I won't go after Kingsley, but I need to know Ford will be okay!"

"So do I, Tiny." Cort rubbed her arms. Helped her stand and held her against his wide chest. "But if we're going to be together, I have to trust him. With you . . . and with this. If you don't trust him as well, what we're doing is for nothing."

Akira's whole body shook hard. All her nerves were taut, tender, as though waiting for the next burst of pain. But something in her brain had clicked. Maybe because of what Cort had said. He trusted Ford, and he didn't give trust easily. He'd protected Ford for so long. If he was willing to stand back and let Ford do what he had to . . .

So would she.

"I trust him." Her lips curled slightly at the edges. "He's a survivor. And he's a lot smarter than Kingsley."

"True." Cort framed her face in his hands. "So will you be looking for a gun to kill him with anytime soon?"

*How can I not?* Akira jutted her chin up. Cort slid his finger along the sore spot at the base of her neck. And everything inside her screamed *"Hell no!"* She quickly shook her head. "No. I don't want a gun. I don't want to kill anyone. *Ever.*"

"I like hearing that."

"All settled then?" Ford wrapped his arms around her waist and kissed her shoulder. "Time to play with our good little girl?"

A soft touch on her palm as Cort drew a slow circle above the ropes had Akira tensing, not entirely convinced the punishment was over. Cort had gotten to know her pretty well. Might not be sure she'd gotten the message.

Might even know her well enough to figure that she'd keep her hands off guns, but may consider a nice, sharp carving knife if

Kingsley threatened either of her men again.

*Damn, I hope not.* She gave him a wide-eyed, innocent look over her shoulder, and he let out a throaty chuckle. "Not so good, but we'll keep her in line."

He pressed against her, simply holding her close like he couldn't help it, but she could feel him, fully erect beneath his jeans. Ford's teeth grazing her throat had her squirming with need as he stripped off the rest of her clothes. Her pulse was thrumming pure, boiling lust between her thighs, and her brain was fuzzy and light. Like being tipsy without the sour aftertaste of hard liquor. She pressed her eyes shut as Ford kissed her, as she felt him shift to pull something out of his pocket and unzip his jeans.

"Get up here." Ford tapped her chin, sitting back on the table and lifting her up to straddle him. She panted against his lips as he fitted himself against her, sliding in slowly, his gaze locked on her face when she opened her eyes. She was so ready his hard length glided in with no resistance, stretching her just enough to send a spark flittering along her nerves. But it was his words that had her tightening around him, swallowing and trying to breathe. "Remember what I told you about taking us both? Are you ready?"

"Yes!" She didn't even have to think about it. She'd lost them both for a little while, and now that she had them, there was nothing she wouldn't do. She tugged at her arm restraints, her breasts swollen and heavy in their bindings, and tried to take Ford in deeper. "I want it all. Please—oh, God! Please!"

Cort made a sound between a groan and something that sounded like words. She only caught the last bit. "—don't understand."

"There's lube in my bag, Cort. She wants to feel all of you." Ford stroked her back as she tried to rise up. Kissed her cheek. "Don't move. Get used to the feeling of me inside you before he joins us."

Akira nodded, resting her head on Ford's shoulder as Cort went to Ford's toy bag. She clenched as she heard Cort move behind her, trembling with need as his body heat blanketed her, erasing the bit of cold that touched her flame-licked flesh. But he didn't touch her. Didn't say a word.

"Cort?" Ford's grip tightened as he spoke, his scruff scratching the bare flesh of her throat. "It's okay. She wants this."

"Here?" Cort's hand curved around her hip. He pressed his lips to the other side of her throat. "Like *that*? She's not—"

"She knows she's not a fucking sweet butt, man. This isn't a night of drunk fun after doing illegal shit and being all rowdy." Ford raked his fingers through her hair, biting her bottom lip as he circled his hips beneath her, stirring the fire within. "Tell him, shorty. Tell him you want all of him, no matter how dirty and fucking nasty some people might think it is. This is something you're giving him—something you've given no one else."

She couldn't say all that. But . . . but she could say enough to make it okay for Cort. She giggled as she breathed out the words. "Only your sweet butt, Cort."

"Damn it, this is all kinds of fucked-up." Cort groaned and grasped her ass in his big hands. "All fucking kinds."

"Yo, stop saying that." Ford grinned against her lips. "Them's my safewords with the pigs."

"Jesus, you're not wearing a wire now, are you?"

"Fuck no!"

"You're both fucking hypocrites!" Akira scowled at Ford when he laughed. God, he was lucky she loved him. "I get punished for swearing."

"Not by me, I love hearing you talk dirty." Ford nipped her chin. "Tell the man to fuck your ass, shorty. I think he's shy."

Cheeks blazing hot, Akira glanced back at Cort. He gave her a lopsided smile and shook his head. "Ignore the dickwad. Just tell me if it hurts too much, Tiny."

The lube was cool as Cort slicked it between her ass cheeks, his fingers covered in it as one, then two, penetrated her tight hole, but his chest against her back was blazing hot. Her mouth formed a wide O as she tried to breathe, as he pressed the thick head of his dick into her. A burning pain, almost unbearable. Pressed in deeper, easing back. She adjusted a little and then there was more. And more.

Her eyes stung and she swallowed back a sob. She wanted this, but she wasn't sure she could do it. He was just too big.

"Say it." Cort spoke near her ear. So soft. "The word is red."

"No, I—" Her voice hitched. She shook her head. "There must be a way—"

"There is." More cool moisture as he slid out. His fingers inside her, two again, then a third straining to fill her. She wasn't used to being so wet back there and found herself tensing even though she was telling herself she needed to relax. He kissed her bare shoulder. "Press back against me."

"It's too much." The tension had her feeling tight. Small. There was no way to give him what she wanted to. And she knew him. He wouldn't just take it. She pressed her eyes shut. "I'm sorry."

"Don't be." He nuzzled her throat, his fingers driving in a little harder, making her gasp. "I'm not done with you. You can't tempt a Dom like that and change your mind, Tiny. Unless you safeword, I *will* have you."

"Fuck." Ford put his hands on her hips, breathing hard, echoing her own reaction with his words and the way his dick thickened inside her. He hissed as she grew even more hot and slick around him. As she clenched down in response to Cort working those three fingers in despite her body's slight resistance. "You're turning *me* on, Cort."

Cort chuckled. "Bitch."

"Fuck you." Ford closed his eyes and ground his teeth as Cort twisted his fingers inside her. "Jesus!"

The man was speaking her mind. Sweat dewed her flesh as she leaned on Ford, lifting a little to take what Cort gave her, pleasure rippling within as Ford moved with her, pushing in and panting against the other side of her throat.

"Brace yourself." Cort kissed her cheek, and through the corner of her eye, she saw him smile at Ford as he penetrated her with the head of his cock. There was something possessive in his stare. As though he was letting Ford know taking her like this was something more. Like he wanted Ford to acknowledge he was in charge.

And Ford . . . Ford seemed too lost in the sensations to care. She'd have expected Ford to challenge Cort. To feel the need to prove himself as a Dom and leave her in a place of being torn between two alpha males. Which might have been hot, but this was better. Ford was already inside her. And Cort was moving in, an inch at a time, stopping and whispering for her to keep pressing back, to open for him. He drew out almost all the way at one point to add more lube. Slid in and out, spreading it.

His solid pelvis finally connected with her ass. She was stretched open and unbelievably full. There were tears in her eyes, but not from pain. He'd managed to slip past that so carefully. Getting used to having both men inside her took a few moments, but the second she relaxed, Cort began to move.

Ford cursed, grinding in as though wanting more of the friction he was feeling inside her. Pleasure ripped her in two, fierce and scalding hot. She thrashed and twisted around, grateful for the tight grip on her arms from Cort. The solid hold Ford had on her hips. She came apart but was grounded, almost as though a surge of electricity had passed through her, causing her to jerk uncontrollably, but there was no danger because they had her. She leaned into Ford's chest, whimpering as Cort slid out, her nerves so tender, the stretching of the head of his cock leaving her, then driving back in was overwhelming.

"Again." Cort latched on to the back of her neck. His entire length slammed into her over and over, but his tone was almost indifferent. "Scream for me."

She threw her head back, lips parted, and screamed. Cort pounding into her, Ford rising up and down with the motion, had her coming, then climaxing over the peak she'd reached as though pleasure leaped from the edge and soared.

Ford slowed his pace, smiling against her lips as he kissed her.

He breathed out so many beautiful words, but the only ones she could remember were, "Damn it, I love you."

"I love you, Ford." She clung to him, trembling as he licked the tears from her cheeks. His smile scared her a little. "What—?"

Cort growled in her ear. "More."

He lifted her right off Ford with his thrust. Ford brought her down hard. She saw white spots in her vision as yet another orgasm was forced out of her, but it was Ford's expression of ecstasy and Cort's low grunt as he shoved in one last time that gave her what she really needed. All they'd given her was amazing.

That she could give it back meant so much more.

\* \* \* \*

Ford lifted his head at the rustling across the bed in one of the small rooms above the bar. He heard the persistent buzzing and watched Cort sit up, reaching over to grab his phone. A mumbled acknowledgement, then the crack as Cort slammed his phone down on the nightstand.

Akira, thankfully, didn't even budge. They'd worn her out. And strangely enough he felt more relief that she was able to sleep than pride at what he'd accomplished. Hell, he was getting soft.

He sat up and jerked his chin at Cort as the other man pulled on his jeans. "The cops?"

"My babysitter. She was real nice, but she could get in shit if I'm not where I'm supposed to be. I should have been home hours ago." Cort's expression filled with pain as he looked down at Akira. "I don't want to wake her up."

*I don't blame you.* His poor shorty had gotten a raw deal in picking two men on the edge like him and Cort, but she'd made her choices. And she was strong enough to take whatever came with them. So he met Cort's eyes. "How would you feel if she didn't wake you up because she had to take care of shit?"

"You're right." Cort chuckled at Ford's smirk. "Asshole."

"Love you too, you bastard." Ford looked Cort over, for a split second wondering . . . yeah, no. He shuddered as the thought skimmed through his hazy brain. Too much like incest. He laughed when Cort's brow arched. "Sorry, just thinking."

"I don't even want to know."

"Sure you do. Unfortunately, I can't ever be your bitch."

"That's a relief." Cort gave Ford a lopsided smile as he sat on the edge of the bed. "You're too pretty to be my type even if I was into dudes."

"You're a dick, you know that?"

"My dick scare you, pussy?"

"Sure. Let's leave it at that."

"Agreed." Cort gently nudged Akira. "Hey, Tiny. I gotta go."

Akira smiled with her eyes closed. "No, you don't. Pretend I'm sleeping so I can enjoy you two working out the details of your affair."

*This girl is gonna kill me!* Ford snorted as Cort stared at Akira like he'd never seen her before. The man wasn't good with subtle stuff. Or teasing.

And his shocked response was totally expected. "You want me to fuck Ford?"

"Mmm, that would be hot." Akira rolled on to her back and peeked at them. "How about only if I can watch?"

Cort glanced over at Ford like he needed an out and couldn't think of one. Ford took pity on him. "Shorty, that would be like Dominik doing his brother. Not gonna happen."

"Eww! Okay, you just ruined the mental image for me. Thanks *a lot*." Akira sighed when Cort frowned and shook his head. "I'm joking. Seriously, I wish you didn't have to go."

Nodding slowly, Cort pressed his lips together. "Right. So we're clear on me not fucking Ford?"

Akira giggled. "Are we?"

*What a brat.* Ford grinned. "That's Cort saying 'red,' Akira. Be nice. His brain doesn't work this early in the morning." His lips twitched as Cort rubbed his face with both hands. Akira's comments seemed to have aged the man a few years, and he already looked damn tired. "She's clear. Besides, you used up all the lube I brought, and I ain't taking your fucking sausage dry."

"Coffee. Need coffee." Cort tipped his head back, muttering a prayer to the ceiling. "You're both crazy."

"Absolutely!" Ford's smile faded as Cort's phone went off again. He really had to get out of here before he got in shit. "You better—"

"I know." Cort pulled Akira to her feet and buried his face in her hair. He went utterly still, speaking softly. "I hate this."

Akira's fingers dug into Cort's shoulders. She drew back a little and gave a sharp nod. "So do I, but it'll be over soon. You'll be clear. You did nothing wrong."

Cort wet his lips with his tongue and shook his head. "Akira—"

"I'm right. Just say I'm right."

Damn it, Ford couldn't look at Cort after that. The man couldn't even meet Akira's eyes. He didn't believe justice would work in his favor. His unshaven face, the shadows under his eyes, his whole demeanor shouted defeat. He loved Akira, so he wouldn't dash her hopes, but he had none for himself.

And Ford knew nothing he did could help Cort. Not really. He swallowed hard as he watched Cort and Akira just staring at each other, watched the light fade from Akira's eyes. Fuck, Cort had to get through this! Akira wouldn't do well with conjugal visits. Prison would destroy Cort. Other than great sex and all the mushy love stuff, what did any of them have to look forward to?

*There's one thing.* Ford slid over to the other side of the bed to grab his jacket off the floor. Took out his cigarettes and tapped one out of the pack. He placed the filter between his lips, speaking around it. "You two should get married."

Cort blinked at him, shaking his head when Ford held out a smoke. "What?"

"Married. You know, that thing people in love do? I'm sure we can plan all that frilly shit around your court stuff. I'll be your best man." He lit his cigarette, then blew out a puff of smoke, laughing

455

when both Akira and Cort stared at him like he was crazy. "What? It's a good idea." He shrugged. "You don't marry her, then I will."

"You're a fucking idiot." Cort growled, gently setting Akira aside. "You think I want her spending the rest of her life shackled to a fucking thug?"

Akira smacked Cort's chest. "Does that mean you *don't* want to spend your life with me?"

Poor Cort looked lost again. He quickly shook his head. "No! Just . . . I might be in jail for a long time."

"They won't let me . . ." Akira's cheeks turned a pretty shade of red. "If we're not married, I can't—"

"No fucking way. I'm not letting you visit me in prison."

"You don't get to decide that!"

"I'm your Dom!"

Ford smirked with his cigarette against his lips. "Actually, I plan to collar her. And she's right. If she's not Mrs. Nash, you two won't have any fun. I'll have to take care of her needs all on my own." He cocked his head. "Not that I mind."

"Fuck that." Cort growled again, like a bear woken up from hibernation half starved. He wrapped an arm around Akira's waist and kissed the length of her throat. "She's still mine. She'll always be mine."

"Good, then how about you tell our woman she's right— because she is—and get your ass back home. You've got a great lawyer. A solid case. Right?"

"Yeah . . ."

"Then don't fucking give up. I'm looking into that white picket fence we all want, and I need to know you're fighting for your freedom." The cigarette was doing nothing to calm Ford's nerves. His throat was tight and the smoke just made it worse. He dropped it in one of the many beer bottles littering the floor. Then cleared his throat. "Hugs all around and get going."

Nodding slowly, Cort drew Akira against him fully. Whispered something in her ear. Then grinned when she squealed and nodded. He took her hands between his and looked over at Ford.

"Sucks doing it without a ring, but she doesn't care. She's gonna be my ol'—"

"Your wife, Cort. Damn!" Ford laughed, but his guts gave an unpleasant little twist. And he wasn't sure why until Cort left and Akira came to sit beside him. Her words confirmed what the real issue was.

"Are you okay with me wearing your collar and being his wife? Really?"

His smile had her relaxing the press of her teeth into her bottom lip. "Of course I am. I wouldn't have suggested it otherwise."

She relaxed, crawling in bed with him for a few more hours' sleep. But he couldn't even keep his eyes closed. He had one more day to either give Kingsley what he wanted or . . . well, since that wasn't gonna happen, he had to get what the cops needed to put the man away. For all his talk of not giving up, he couldn't take his own advice.

*I'm more than okay with you being ours. It would be fucking perfect. But . . .*

But reality was a cruel fucking bitch. At least he knew Akira would have Cort. And if shit went bad for Cort . . . well, what's five to ten? They'd have the rest of their lives.

Short of a miracle, Ford was almost out of time.

"I know you're not sleeping." Akira wiggled closer to him and put her delicate little hand over his face. "Close your eyes and listen to me."

He closed his eyes. Held his breath as she spoke.

"I don't want you anywhere near Kingsley, but you have to do this. I get that. But you know why I'll let you?"

*Let me?* He grinned, ready to laugh off her words, but her hand covered his mouth.

"He needs to be stopped. And you can do it. For Tim. For Cort. For all the people Kingsley's hurt." She kissed his chest, then used it as a pillow as her tone grew soft. "For me. So we can be together out in the open without ever being afraid again."

*Shit.* She made him . . . she made him believe that he could do this. That he'd somehow find a way. He'd never had anyone believe in him so completely, and yet, she did. His brain started working on overdrive, coming up with all kinds of plans that he trashed once he really thought them over.

But in the end, when he finally drifted away, he was the one who couldn't help believing.

There had to be a way.

# Chapter Thirty One

Cort's jaw ticked as he glanced at the reflection in the dressing room mirror of the snooty fucking store. Scott Demyan stood behind him, trying to keep a straight face. And he'd better, because if the man laughed again, Cort was going to flatten his pretty face. The thought was asphyxiated as he fought to get some air past the noose—er, *tie*—the fucker's image consultant, Stephan Vaughn, tightened around his neck.

The little guy was kinda weird, but Scott had gone on and on about how great he was, and since Sebastian had come along to foot the bill, Cort didn't say much about being handed over to the man's dubious care. Stephan had even let Cort pick out a few suits of his own. Real nice of him.

'Cept he turned every one of Cort's choices down with the same kinda comment. "You look like a made man! We're going for a 'not guilty' verdict, aren't we?"

Well, yeah, they were, but did the guy have to make him look like fucking Clark Kent?

Stephan had a comment about that too. "Clark Kent *is* a good guy."

*Fucking hell.* Cort scowled when Scott snorted, then his face heated as Sebastian circled him, giving him a *very* slow once-over from every angle. He didn't give a shit that both men were bisexual, it was just . . . damn, he'd never had a man look at him like he was edible.

"Relax, *hombre*." Sebastian chuckled as he stopped in front of Cort to straighten his lapels with a sharp tug. "You are very appealing, but it is clear that your tastes veer closer to the other side of the spectrum."

Cort's brow furrowed. *What spectrum?*

Sebastian's lips quirked slightly. "I would have considered you a challenge once. I believe it is rare any man or woman is completely straight."

"I'm rare. Very rare." And that sounded damn stupid. Especially since the man had just stopped looking at him like a piece of meat. For all Cort knew, the man loved his men "rare." He cleared his throat and looked over at Stephan. "We done?"

"'Are we done?' you mean. You don't want to come across as uneducated." Stephan fussed with the tie again, probably thinking Cort would seem smarter if he couldn't breathe enough to talk. "Yes, we are done here. I will have two more suits made for you, one in charcoal and the other in navy."

"Navy?" The only "navy" Cort knew of was the color on those cute dresses little girls wore. Fine, he didn't look horrible in this suit—a pair of glasses and he could play out a little fantasy with Akira . . . rip off the shirt to reveal that cool "Man of Steel" getup and have her be Lois Lane . . .

"Are you listening to me, Mr. Nash?"

Cort rolled his eyes. "It's Cort. And no."

Scott covered a laugh with a cough loud enough to get everyone in the store staring at him. Cort grinned when Stephan sniffed and Sebastian gave Scott a warning look. The attention being off him for a split second was all it took to get his head back where it belonged. He wasn't gonna come off as innocent on his own. These people were all trying to help.

Might be a good time to stop acting like a dick.

Chewing on the inside of his cheek like the flesh was a hunk of tobacco, Cort squared his shoulders and turned to Stephan. "Sorry, man. Just not used to all this dressing-up shit. I'm a mechanic." *That's all I am now. All I want to be. Normal like.*

Cocking his head, Stephan studied him. "Yes, I think you could easily pass for that. But you must tone back on the swearing." His brow shot up when Cort snorted, thinking about how Akira had called him and Ford hypocrites. He managed to focus on Stephan's words when the man continued. "I've gone with the ideal of wearing to court what you would to church—"

"I ain't never gone to church."

"Oh dear, please don't say that in front of the grand jury." Stephan sighed. "It really would be best if you let your lawyer speak for you as much as possible. You look presentable, not overly wealthy, not a slob . . ." Stephan's lips slanted. "And not a thug. If we had the time, I'd have you grow your hair out a bit more, but you're attractive enough that I don't believe it will matter."

*Jesus, not him too!* Cort slid a finger under his tie. "I really am straight."

"Irrelevant, but so am I." Stephan shook his head and smacked Cort's hand. "Leave it alone!" His eyes widened in horror as he stared at Cort's hands, like they were covered in blood rather than just a little black in the creases and dark in the thicker calluses. "How did I miss that? Your hands are filthy!"

"They ain't—they're *not* dirty. Just stained." Probably permanently. He shrugged when Stephan grumbled something under his breath. "Want me to wear some leather gloves or something?"

"Might be a good idea." Scott folded his arms over his chest, looking serious for the first time. "You wouldn't want to leave fingerprints on anything."

"Mr. Demyan, you are trying my patience," Stephan said, tapping his chin thoughtfully, ignoring Scott's snort. "I don't suppose you would consider a quick manicure, Cort?"

Cort didn't even bother dignifying that with an answer. He just stared at Stephan.

"Very well." Stephan stepped to Sebastian's side, looking at Cort like he was some kind of fancy piece of furniture in a store window they were planning to buy. "Passible, Mr. Ramos?"

Eyes hard, Sebastian stepped closer to Cort. His lips thinned as Cort fisted his hands by his sides. "The suit is appropriate, but, Cort, you will gain no sympathy if you come off so aggressive."

"Not meaning to." Cort winced when Stephan rubbed his face

with both hands, muttering a prayer. This wasn't going real good. "Sorry, *I'm* not meaning to be aggressive."

"Did you even graduate high school?" Stephan frowned. "This really won't do."

Cort ran his tongue over his teeth. "No. I'm a dropout."

Scott stepped forward. "But he's a smart guy. And Ramos got him a good lawyer. He ain't gonna have no trouble." He smirked at Stephan's irritated look. "Hey, I don't see no press. I do fine with them now. Cort will do all right with his lawyer there to help him out. He's gotta talk to the detective and the Crown Prosecutor in less than an hour. Don't stress him out."

Just the mention of the people he'd have to face, people who wanted to keep him behind bars, stressed Cort out. But he was grateful that Scott had his back. The man had gotten past his own bad rep, so maybe he understood some of what Cort was going through.

Kid wouldn't do good in jail, though. He was too pretty. Too much of a smart-ass. Least Cort was going into this knowing he could handle himself inside. He might not come out whole, but he'd probably come out alive.

"I better go." Cort gave the three men a genuine smile, letting his shoulders relax as he held out his hand to shake each man's before he continued. "I really appreciate all you've done. If you ever need *anything,*—" he met their eyes, shifting his gaze from one man to the next to make sure they knew he meant it "—you give me a call."

Sebastian gripped his hand the tightest, for the longest, and smiled back. "This man, the one speaking to us now, will go free."

Cort laughed. "Shit, you've almost got me convinced that's true!"

"It is. But first you must believe." Sebastian jerked him in for a rough, backslapping hug that erased all Cort's worries about the man wanting in his pants. This was Jami's man. A man who was grateful that Cort had saved his girl. Maybe even a friend. And he had one last thing to say before he released Cort. "Believe it. Then you will convince them as well."

\* \* \* \*

The coffee tasted nice and rich, but most of the heat that seeped into Akira's body was from the whiskey she'd added to it. A bit of a change from the Irish Cream she'd had the first few mornings since she'd come back to Dominik's place. The man had a wonderful variety in his liquor cabinet, and she'd been sampling from each and every bottle. Not a productive pastime, but . . . she couldn't find it in her to care.

She didn't look up as Dominik came into the room. Didn't comment as he took her mug and poured the contents down the drain in the kitchen sink. She'd already had three cups and was feeling pretty good. Nice and mellow.

Dominik stood in front of her, then sighed and crouched down. He'd never brought himself to her level as her temporary Master, but they were just friends now, so she guessed it was okay. A little unbalancing—still okay.

She hadn't heard a single thing he'd just said. Wrinkling her nose, she looked at him. "Excuse me?"

"I said, 'Your Masters wouldn't be pleased if they saw you like this.' Your habit of drinking whenever you're sad is getting out of hand."

"Today should be an exception. Cort's getting his trial date, and Ford's dealing with his father and—"

"Things have been hard lately. I get that. But all these exceptions are leading to you drinking every day." He put his hand on her shoulder, massaging the tight muscles with his fingertips. "You're better than this, Akira. Stronger. Your men need you to be."

"There's nothing I can do for them! I'm not ready to go to another funeral. I don't want a quick wedding before Cort gets locked away for ten years and—"

"A wedding?" Dominik drew in a sharp inhale and

straightened. At first she wondered if he was upset, but then a wide grin spread over his entire face. "Congratulations, little one! We need to celebrate! I'll get the champagne!"

*He's lost his mind.* Akira frowned at him, then glanced over at the whiskey on the counter. She wanted more of *that*, not champagne! "I thought you wanted me to stop drinking?"

"I do, but this is a very *good* exception." He tossed her his keys. "Bring my car out front. And call your girls."

"You're not making any sense." Akira pushed out of her chair, watching Dominik over her shoulder as he went through his liquor cabinet. "I can't drive. I've been drinking. And do you seriously want me to get my girls together to get drunk over me getting engaged?"

Dominik went still. His muscles tensed. "No, that's not what I want. Cort and Ford trusted me to take care of you. And right now I feel like I'm doing a shitty job of it. I managed to get you past your fears, managed to help you find yourself in the scared little girl you'd been for so long. But I'm failing miserably at showing you how to deal with all the crap life might throw at you."

"It's not your fault, I just . . ." *I'm just doing what I asked Cort and Ford not to. I'm giving up.* The thought had her more than a little disgusted with herself. Dominik felt responsible for her, but she was the only one who could make sure her men didn't come home to a woman wallowing in alcohol and ice cream. She'd had girls come to her with all kinds of problems, everything from breakups to illness and deaths in their families. And she told each and every one the same thing.

*"Keep living."* Take the time you need to be sad, to mourn, then find a reason to carry on. Those you love want that for you. And Akira knew Cort and Ford would be upset to see her let herself go.

Not that they'd care that she'd gained a few pounds, but they'd hate knowing how often Dominik had carried her to bed after she'd passed out on the sofa after a few too many. That she'd cancelled practice for the Ice Girls a few times. That she went days eating too little, or too much.

Enough was enough. Yeah, things had been rough, but Dominik was right. She was better than this. Her girls were counting on her. Her men would need her to toughen up if things *did* go bad. And would want the woman they loved to be waiting for them whenever they finally came home.

She bit her bottom lip and met Dominik's eyes. "Can we make it non-alcoholic champagne, Dominik? I'm hoping I can fit in practice with the girls before the game tomorrow."

His smile alone was enough to make the step toward dealing with things worth it. He inclined his head and put the bottle he'd taken out away. "That I can do. I'm very proud of you, Akira."

The statement warmed her, but she quickly shook her head. "I haven't given you a reason to be proud of me yet." She did up her jacket, then pulled on her boots. "But I will."

* * * *

A meeting at the courthouse, a building no different than the many others he'd been in. A touch of classic appeal with paintings and statues of judges and Justice herself. Everything was big, every sound echoed with an ominous finality, but it was the cold Cort felt every time he entered a building like this that brought back the same grim reality.

He was guilty. Even if he was innocent, he was somehow guilty. Didn't make sense, but there was no debating the accusation in the still eyes on the walls. Painted immortality, all knowing.

Some fucking sci-fi images in the back of his head had him snorting and his lawyer cast him a questioning glance over his shoulder. From Clark Kent to Han Solo. He was losing his shit.

"Are you quite all right?" His lawyer, Jason Purcell, slowed his pace. "You remember what I said, don't you? The prosecution will offer a deal to get this done with quick. I'll refuse."

Cort scratched his jaw, giving the lawyer that was about a foot shorter than him and looked like he should be on a skateboard instead of in a suit, a questioning look. "You sure that's a good idea?"

"I know it is. I represent a lot of high-profile criminals, Cort. I'd get them a deal." The tiny man's brown eyes narrowed. "You don't need one."

*If you say so.* Cort rolled his shoulders and went with his new habit of putting one foot in front of the other. And just moving forward. Nothing would happen *today* to keep him from walking out those doors again. He was still free.

For now.

He blinked when Jason grabbed his wrist, only then realizing he'd been rubbing both wrists like cuffs had just been taken off. Jason inclined his head when Cort gave him a sheepish smile, then spoke low. "Don't show them you're nervous. Believe it or not, they all know you did the right thing."

*Bullshit.* Cort snorted. "I murde—"

"What did we say about using that word?"

"Don't."

"Excellent." The midget made Cort feel like a kid when he talked like that, but something in his smile reminded Cort of the one Sutter gave him sometimes. Like, "You're a dumbass, but it's all good."

That got him down the long hall. He spotted Laura and Detective Hamilton standing outside huge, dark wood double doors. Laura smiled. Hamilton kinda grunted a greeting—it was something at least.

Beyond the doors was a . . . library? Cort blinked at the walls lined with leather-bound books, the long, polished wood table, and a man with the friendly smile who rose as Cort and Jason walked in.

The man came around the table and held out his hand. "Mr. Nash, I am—"

"It's Cort." *Shit, I shouldn't have said that.*

Big, friendly smile fading, the man's eyes became sharp and assessing. He wasn't old, despite the flecks of gray in his dark hair. His suit, unlike Cort's, looked right on him. Like he was comfortable in it. He gave Cort a sharp nod, then gestured to a chair.

"Perhaps it would be best if you let your lawyer speak." His lips thinned, and his tone was a lot like an adult would use with a child with learning disabilities. "Unless someone says 'So, Mr. Nash . . .' or maybe 'Answer the question, Mr. Nash.' We'll get you used to answering to being called that so you don't get confused."

Jason scowled, stepping between Cort and the prosecutor "Tony—"

"Mr. Skeans. Let's form good habits with your client, Mr. Purcell."

All right, Jason looked like he was going to lose it. He gave Mr. Skeans a stiff smile, then gestured for Cort to take a seat. Cort's jaw clenched as something passed between the lawyers that he couldn't quite read.

He liked Jason. Which meant Skeans being a jerk to him was an issue.

Not one Cort could do anything about. Which pissed him off. He dragged his chair out and plunked down on it.

Skeans's brows shot up. He turned to Jason. "Have you worked with this man at all? He *does* realize he's not in . . . what do bikers call it? Church?"

"Cort's never been to 'church,'" Jason said curtly before taking a chair beside Cort. The man had clearly misinterpreted what Cort had meant by that when they'd talked about Stephan's wardrobe rule, but that didn't matter. Cort was making his lawyer look bad. And he didn't want that.

He sat up and pulled his chair closer to the table as Skeans went around to sit across from them. Put his hands on the table and tried to appear nice and calm.

Skeans ignored Cort, but some of his words seemed directed Cort's way. "I am Assistant Crown Prosecutor Skeans. Tony Skeans, but your client will call me 'Mr. Skeans.'"

Jason nodded. Glanced over at Cort as though to make sure he understood.

Cort wanted to say he got it, but followed Jason's lead and nodded too.

"Perfect. Now." Skeans turned to Cort. "You are currently charged with murder. We have reviewed your file."

Putting a hand on Cort's forearm before he could comment—the man was getting to know him pretty well—Jason faced Skeans. "We are open to hearing the Crown's thoughts on a plea deal."

"You're not getting one."

*What the fuck?* All the assurances Jason had given about this meeting, about having the upper hand, were gone. Cort moved to stand. Jason grabbed his arm and jerked him down.

Then practically snarled at Skeans. "Then what's the point of this meeting?"

"If he gets arrested for coming after me, you'll lose whatever advantage you have in this case. Besides the fact that without a choker chain, I'm not sure you can control your boy." Skeans smiled at Cort. "Heel."

*Okay, fuck this shit.* Cort carefully set Jason aside and placed his hands on the table. "I'm no fucking dog. But I'll listen to this man because I respect him. Don't waste his fucking time or—"

Jason stood beside him. "Cort!"

"Threats don't go over well with a judge, Mr. Nash." Skeans leaned back in his chair and grinned as the door opened. "This should be interesting."

Detective Hamilton practically barked at Cort as he held the door open for a small, curvy woman with curly blond hair. "Sit the fuck down, Cort!" He glared at Skeans when the prosecutor laughed. "He slugs you and I ain't arresting him. Seriously, Tony?"

"It's 'Mr. Skeans.' Mr. Nash needs consistency." Skeans steepled his hands on the table. "Please excuse us. Mrs. Norris, can I help you?"

"The *judge* needs your signature on something. If you have a moment?" Mrs. Norris was giving Skeans the same look people often gave Cort. The "Are you mentally challenged?" look.

Skeans got up and headed out without a word.

Rather than back out and close the door, Hamilton stepped in, leaving Laura to watch the hall as he approached Cort. He held up his hand to Jason, his expression grim. "I won't ask your client a single question, Purcell, I just wanted to explain something to him." Hamilton turned to Cort at Jason's nod. "Not sure if Skeans is just being his usual, *wonderful* self, but to his credit, you'd suck in front of a jury right now. I'd probably lose it dealing with Skeans's shit too, but in the end, he's on the same page I am."

"What page is that?" Cort probably shouldn't talk to the guy without checking with Jason, but . . . the man seemed on the level.

Hamilton rolled his shoulders, glancing back toward the door. "The evidence doesn't look bad for you. Some even say the fucker got what he deserved."

"And what do you say?"

"Said all I'm going to. Just don't let me see you back in here after we set you loose."

*Set me* . . . Cort held his breath as Skeans returned. His pulse was thumping hard between his ears as Skeans started talking, using legal terms that Cort didn't understand. He got the gist of some of it, but—he rubbed his hand over his face, not sure he'd heard Skeans right.

He was gonna sound stupid again, but he didn't really give a shit. "What?"

"I cannot say for certain, but the evidence in this case is not in favor of the Crown." Skeans tapped his steepled fingers together as he watched Cort's face like he'd just told Cort he'd won the fucking lottery.

But this was better. So much better.

Cort blinked. Swallowed. Tried to find words.

Jason squeezed his forearm as he addressed Skeans. "So there is a chance there won't be an indictment against Mr. Nash?"

Skeans inclined his head. "It is a strong possibility that Mr. Nash will never be prosecuted. But it is what it is and will be in the hands of the Crown's jury."

It took leaving that room, crossing the long hall, and stepping outside for a breath of snow-sweetened air before Cort could really absorb all that had come out of the meeting. His court date wasn't for another month. Nothing was definite, but . . . but things were looking fucking good. For the first time, he had hope. Hope he wasn't trying to grasp for Akira's sake, or Ford's.

He still had his freedom. And the way things sounded, he just might get to keep it.

# Chapter Thirty Two

A kira whooped as she hung up the phone with Chicklet and scrambled to get her jacket on. She drove her car to the small motel on the edge of town where Cort's message said to meet him. After parking, she darted across the lot, slipping on the icy pavement several times in her rush, but she made it to the room in one piece.

The door flew open and she almost fell through it. Cort chuckled and grabbed her, lifting her up into his arms and planting kisses all over her face as he kicked the door shut.

"Are you sure, Cort?" She wrapped her arms around his neck, not letting go even as he sat her on the bed with the ugly green ivy-print comforter. "There's not enough evidence to convict you?"

"That's what the lawyer said." Cort stripped off her jacket, kissing along her throat as soon as he had it bared. "The detective said the same. This isn't done with. I'll still have a trial, but . . . it looks good, Tiny. Real good."

Akira framed his face in her hands and kissed him, shifting as needed so he could take her shirt off. She'd been so afraid for him, she could tell going back to jail would have broken him. Now, all she wanted was to have him as close as possible. And by the bare lust in his touch, rough despite the tenderness in his eyes, she could tell he felt the same.

This, this moment of hope that wasn't so desperate anymore— she wanted to share this with Ford too. He'd be so relieved. He was still dealing with a lot.

"Did you get the message to Ford?" She gasped as Cort finished stripping her and flipped her over, dragging her over the edge of the bed so she had her feet on the floor and her body bent over the mattress.

Cort pressed his hand to the center of her back, keeping her in place. "Chicklet tried to get in touch with him, but he didn't answer. He could be in a meeting."

This celebration *should* include Ford, and yet, she was burning up, and Cort wasn't giving her time to think of anything other than *his* hands. *His* body. She needed Cort. Needed to feel her . . . her fiancé taking her with all the energy of a man who'd escaped being caged. Needed to feel him so filled with life, looking at his future like it would be a good thing.

Looking at *their* future like she was, like they were finally getting all they'd ever wanted.

She expected him to take her hard and fast, to feel the full force of all those chains being gone. She braced for it. He moved against her. Stepped back.

His hand came down hard on her exposed butt and she yelped.

"Cort!" The fiery pain spread and her core throbbed in time with the heat, causing her hips to thrust back even though she should probably get her ass out of the danger zone. She glared at him over her shoulder. "I thought you'd never punish me like—"

"I'm not punishing you. I'm doing this for fun." He winked at her. Hauled back. Then chuckled when she pressed her eyes shut. "And because I can."

He smacked her butt again. Rubbed it and bent down to kiss away the blossoming pain. It hurt so bad, but she remained still, trying not to grunt each time his hand came down. This wasn't a sensual spanking, and yet . . . it was still erotic. Cort was testing his limits with her, using his freedom as a Dom to play with her body in whatever way he chose. And *that* was what had her trembling with lust as each solid smack came down.

So often, he worried too much about pleasing her. Which had her worrying that she wasn't pleasing him. That he'd go deeper into the lifestyle simply taking her lead. That he might still be doing it to satisfy *her* needs.

Which didn't *satisfy* her at all. *This* side of him, this man who took all she would give him and more, he fulfilled her in every way.

A vicious slap resounded and the stinging spread across her throbbing flesh. Tears filled her eyes as she rested her forehead on the bed, sucking in air between wet lips, trembling as she wondered what he'd do next. She winced as he pressed his fingertips into the burning flesh at the swell above her thighs.

"I went too far." He traced what felt like finger-shaped welts a little higher up. "Why didn't you tell me I went too far?"

She hissed as he drew his fingers over a spot that would likely bruise later. Then she forced the words out because she had to say them. And he had to *really* hear them. "You didn't go too far. You finally took what you wanted. Which is everything I have to offer."

"Fuck, Akira, I want *you*." He let out a throaty moan as he slid his finger between her abused butt cheeks, making her twitch as his fingertip hit the little bundle of nerves still tender from the last time he'd taken her there. He pressed a little, one hand on her back to keep her still as he penetrated her. The sensation of taking his thick finger dry was gritty, with a dark pleasure-pain that she wasn't sure she liked. Her protests died on her lips as he whispered, "Shh, you know I won't do anything that will hurt you." He pumped his finger slowly, letting out a low laugh at her breathy little cry. "In a lasting way."

"I know." She panted as his finger dragged in and out, her pussy tightening and releasing as the emptiness of her hot, moist folds became more pronounced. She almost begged him to touch her, to fill her up in every way, but the desire was shallow. The deeper need was for him to continue just as he was. Acting as though he knew she belonged to him.

He bent down and lightly nipped along the base of her spine. "I stopped by a store to pick up a few things on the way." His pelvis bumped against her, driving his finger in a little deeper. "I'm going to play with you, Akira. There are so many things I've wanted to do to you—"

"Please, Master!" She swallowed, a little uncertain what exactly he had planned, but loving that her choices were gone. That he wasn't asking anymore. She tried to lift her hips, to show him how much she wanted it all.

His finger went still. He slapped her thigh with a sharp *Crack!* "Don't move unless you're told to, pet. You've been trained to know better."

She whimpered, keeping her head down, trembling as something in his presence shifted. Her brain clicked into that sweet mode of obedience. "Yes, Master."

"Good girl." He stroked her back. Withdrew his finger completely. "Legs open wide, head down, and arms straight. I want those pretty breasts nice and available."

Her nipples drew up into achy little points at the words alone. She spread her thighs and positioned her arms. Her whole body quivered with anticipation as she heard him walk away. She bit her lip when she heard him washing his hands in the bathroom. Seconds later, he crossed the room and there was the rustling sound of a plastic bag.

A *snap* made her jump. She froze when he placed his hand on her butt and it felt different. Like it was covered in a thin glove.

"I told you I wouldn't hurt you too much, but when I saw this, I knew I had to see it inside you." The second she tried to peek, his hand shifted to the side of her neck. She yelped as his fingers dug into the pressure point and pain streaked across her nerves. "Trust, Akira. Close your eyes and just do as I say."

She nodded, shaking and chewing at her bottom lip as she pressed her eyes shut. She heard a soft, liquid sound, then felt his finger against her again, much smoother with the glove and slick with lube. He pushed it in and out, then added a second. Pulled out, drizzled more lube between her cheeks, then eased them in again. A third finger had her breathing with her mouth wide open. The stretching was almost . . . almost more than she could take.

"Open for me, sweetheart. Give me a number for how bad it hurts."

*Eleven! Twelve!* A fragile part of her practically screamed as his knuckles breached her, but she forced herself to relax and let him in. It was uncomfortable, but there was enough lube to ease the way. And once she calmed down a bit, she realized it didn't hurt that much at all.

Just a little bit. "Three."

"Good. Now press back against me so I can loosen you up." He waited until she'd followed his instructions, then made a soft, humming sound of approval. "Perfect. How does that feel?"

The motion of his fingers going in and out had her struggling not to move with him. Her arousal had her so wet she was surprised her juices weren't spilling down her thighs. But with her legs spread so wide . . . her cheeks heated.

His fingers went still. "You tensed. What is it?"

She held her breath. Then spoke in a rush. "I just hope I'm not . . . dripping, Sir."

He laughed. "Damn it, Tiny, you're too cute." His free hand covered her pussy, and she gasped at the surge of pleasure. "Mmm, you're so fucking wet. But you're right. Mustn't make a mess. Stay just like that."

Suddenly empty. Completely lacking any contact with him, she let out a low whine. And clamped her lips together, embarrassed that the pathetic sound had come from *her*. She'd heard others whine at the club, but she'd always been a good sub for Dominik. And a *good* sub didn't *whine*!

Rustling again, coming closer, then below her. She didn't dare look, but Cort was quick to explain what he'd done. "I put the bag down, baby. No need to worry about dripping on the nasty carpet."

Her already fiery cheeks flared with hot blood rushing to her face. She'd never found humiliation arousing, but Cort seemed to be inadvertently exposing her to a side of herself she'd never known existed.

Or maybe it was intentional. He drew an ungloved finger along her slit, then brought it to her lips. "Open."

She opened her mouth, trembling as he slicked her own juices over her lips and then pressed his fingers deep into her mouth. She'd tasted herself on Ford's lips, on Cort's, but this was different.

475

Sucking on his fingers, she got a real sense of how slippery she was. Slightly sweet, a little salty, headier than the aroma of her arousal.

His fingers dipped into her ass once again, his other hand still half in her mouth. And this time, there was no pain. Only her body reacting to everything he did, stretched and taut as piano wire, contained but tuned to play the perfect note on the softest touch of a key.

He played her gently at first, but again, abruptly, stopped. The music was gone and the chord—the one that lingered just before the intense chorus—hung in the air. Only this time, she didn't shift to ask for more. Didn't let out so much as a sigh of complaint.

She simply waited for him to continue the song.

"Show me, Tiny. Show me how much you can take." Cort positioned something hard against her back hole. "But don't forget that I'm trusting you to tell me if you need to stop."

He didn't wait for her to reply. The tip of the smooth, unyielding object went into her slowly, becoming wider and wider. A quiet voice in her head reasoned that it was probably a butt plug. She would get past the widest part and would find some relief as it fit snugly inside her.

Only, it just kept getting wider. Burning more and more. She whimpered as it stretched her beyond what Cort had when his dick had filled her.

"So beautiful. I knew you would look beautiful taking this in." Cort's words were barely a murmur, but what they did to her made the pain negligible. He stopped for a few seconds, kissing her side. "Yellow or red?"

"Neither." It was close, but she shifted her hips back, adjusting and pushing against the full sensation until it slipped in a bit easier. And there was only one thing she needed from him now. "Please, Master, tell me what seeing this does for you?"

Cort groaned. "Fuck, it's just a bit wider than my dick, but it's clear glass with a big round silver ring at the end for me to pull on. The way you're stretched around it has me so fucking hard . . ."

Finally, the plug was all the way it. She hissed through her teeth as the ring of muscle clung to the slimmest part. The invasion of the wide, solid glass within was uncomfortable, but not unbearably so. She felt like she was glowing all over from Cort's reaction alone.

The sound of Cort taking the gloves off had her clenching every muscle from her belly down. Would he take her now? Would he do all she'd only dreamed he'd one day be capable of doing?

He covered her with his body and cupped her breasts. "Ready for more?"

"I'm ready for anything, Sir." Her arms shook as his brief, supportive hold left her. She sensed him at her side. He pinched one nipple between his fingers.

Tiny teeth bit into her and she choked back a scream.

"Breathe through it. I tried these on myself while doing 'research.' Looked kinda funny on me, but after a second or two, it wasn't too bad." He petted her hair. "Here comes the other."

Her whole body jerked, and she made quiet little noises that she hoped he wouldn't take as "stop"—or worse—"red." The weight of the nipple clamps made her breasts feel heavy and sensitive. She heard the jingle of a chain and felt it swinging against her belly as Cort positioned himself behind her.

The rip of a condom wrapper was familiar. His dick slipping between her folds, then driving in, had her arms folding. The huge butt plug made the thickness of his heavy cock such a ruthless invasion she had no problem remaining perfectly still. He'd claimed her in every single way, and all there was left for her to do was absorb the pleasure he gave.

"So *fucking* tight." Cort stopped and she could feel his fist at the base of his dick, preventing him from going in too deep. "I was hoping to do this with Ford fucking your mouth, but . . ." He eased out, then surged back roughly. "Next time. And next time, the plug will be bigger." He began a steady rhythm that had her brain shutting down completely and her body more than willing to take more and more and more. His next words tore her into tiny threads set ablaze. "I wouldn't try my fist in your pussy or your ass, but . . . damn, to see Ford do it—"

"Ah!" Akira screamed and bucked as her orgasm threw her like the world had exploded beneath her. She felt Cort everywhere. Could see how it would be when Ford was with them, how both men would overwhelm her by doing things to her that she'd never even considered. Her mind went blank. Stars danced behind her closed lids.

Her hips rose, then fell as Cort pulled at the plug, and she choked on a sob. So much to take, her body couldn't focus on one thing. She almost didn't hear him telling her to let go of the plug.

But a very primitive part of her was ready to do anything he asked. She pressed against the plug. It popped out.

"A fresh one for your pussy, pet." Cort told her before pulling out and thrusting a wide, smooth shaft into her pussy to replace him. He slammed his dick into her ass and kept moving. He was always moving, and it was as though she'd never stop climaxing. She reached the peak again and again, diving over then finding herself tossed up as though some invisible force hit her on the way down. She soared with the last and opened her eyes.

There were beautiful colors splashed across her vision. She giggled even as the last wave crashed into her. So pretty. Little fireflies danced in the air. Tiny specks of pain shimmered red below them, but they couldn't touch her. They were such a long, long way down.

"Don't move." Cort held her side with one hand and touched her cheek with the other. "Stay where you are, baby. You look so happy."

*Happy.* The word shimmered like white sand under the sun. Happy didn't sound right, but it was close. Free and contained didn't make sense. Alive and worn to that last breath came close. Everything was shifting around her, and then there was warmth. Strength wrapped around her. A solid place to land if she ever did.

"I'll stay." She smiled as her eyes drifted shut once again. "You want me to stay."

"I do." Cort framed her face with his hands, and she could see his face in high-definition. Clear and rough and perfect. "I'm not sure if this will hurt. I hope it doesn't yank you back down."

He shifted and her breasts flared, shooting her up higher. She hovered there, so high above, but still looking up at him.

And whispered with a smile still on her lips, "I'm not sure I'll ever come down."

\* \* \* \*

The knife carved across Ford's ribs, and he clenched his teeth to keep from crying out as he swung blindly. His blood ran down his side and soaked into his jeans. He fought to get free as he saw Cam take a knife to the shoulder.

Not the first Cam had taken. Ford knew he had to stop this. But the pain had him seeing nothing but red. And no matter how hard he fought, he knew he couldn't stop them.

He would die. But nothing hurt worse than knowing Cam, who'd been so loyal, who'd become a friend, would lie next to him under a pile of dirt. Cam's family would never know what had happened to him. He'd just be gone forever.

Inside the bar, the loud music from the band he'd hired was still playing. The Cobras who'd come in after losing tonight's game were shouting over the violent base of "Burn it Down," a song by Linkin Park, which the band was doing a decent cover of. They were bitching out the refs. Each other.

They had no clue Ford and Cam were out here. Both had been in Ford's office at the back of the bar when Kingsley's thugs showed up. Cam had "convinced" them to leave by pulling out his gun. The men had said they would go if Ford came and let them deliver his father's message.

*Stupid!* Ford grunted as a fist rammed into his stomach. He bent forward, cursing as he watched Cam hit the ground hard. He lurched forward to try to protect Cam, reacting on instinct alone because there was really nothing he could do.

One of the thugs raked his fingers into Ford's hair, then slammed him into the wall. A shredded sensation across his face and arm, then no pain at all. But there was the cold kiss of the gun the man pressed against Ford's cheek.

The back door to the bar clicked and Ford heard light, familiar laughter. "Sloan, it's disgusting out here—no, Sir, I wouldn't *dare* turn down an offer like that!"

"Oriana!" Ford threw himself at the thug, and the gun went off. All sound vanished for what seemed like a very long time. Ford collapsed against the wall as his sister came into view. There were specs of blood on her face. Crimson blotches on her white T-shirt.

Her lips formed his name. Sloan shoved her back and lurched forward, Max a step behind him. Suddenly there were so many people, big men, a good half of the team and some regulars. Ford blinked at Silver who seemed to appear in front of him out of nowhere. He reached out and grabbed her wrist. Looked for somewhere safe to hide her.

"Call Laura! We've got them!" That was Luke. Sound returned and Ford's heart pounded against his ribs. He held on to his little sister while seeking out Oriana, whispering an incoherent prayer that Luke had made Jami stay inside.

Dominik growled, on his knees beside his brother. He held his hands over Cam's stomach. "Look. At. Me. Cam, don't you fucking close your eyes. Damn you, I told you not to take this fucking job!"

"I'm sorry, Dominik," Ford whispered, not sure the man could hear him. But that couldn't matter now. He tugged at Silver's wrist. "Oriana—you have to help her!"

"What?" Silver's eyes went wide. Her small hand covered the cut on his side as she shouted. "Oriana! Oria—"

"I'm right here, sweetie." Oriana came over, touching Silver's cheek before crouching down in front of Ford. "The ambulance is on the way. The cops should be here any second." A cold smile slid across her lips. "The men who attacked you *might* still be alive when they get here."

"He's bleeding." Silver's voice was thick with fear. She was so pale; Ford wanted to tell her he was okay, but there was something more important.

"Oriana's bleeding too. I'll be fine, just make sure she—"

Oriana frowned. "I'm not . . ." She glanced down at her shirt. Her hand went to her throat. "It's not my blood."

A few feet away, Sloan had one thug on the ground, and White was fighting to get Sloan's hands off the man's neck. Sloan shoved White away, strangling the thug with one hand. Chicklet joined them, slipping between White and Sloan, her eyes hard as she got right in Sloan's face while prying his fingers away from the thug's throat.

Sloan was in a blind rage, but he didn't seem to be hurt.

There was a crowd around the two other thugs. Luke was struggling to hold one down. Lost his grip on the man's wrists and grunted as an elbow stuck his jaw. Sebastian jerked the thug to his feet and cracked him in the temple with a solid fist, knocking him out cold.

The last thug wasn't fighting. Zach stood over him, a foot resting on the shiny, bald head. Speaking to Scott who was sitting on the ground, holding on to Max. Blood seeped between Scott's fingers as he pressed his hand to Max's shoulder.

Ford swallowed and tears blinded him as Scott shouted something at Max, then at Zach as Max lost consciousness and slumped against Scott's side. *He'd* done this. First Cam, and now Max.

Oriana's screams tore through his chest and shredded his heart. She ran to Max, tripping just as she reached him, dropping to her knees by his side.

Ford twisted away from Silver and pushed to his feet. He ignored her attempts to stop him and jerked his chin at Landon and Dean who'd moved to stand behind her. "Get her out of here." His soul felt dead. As much as he loved Akira, as much as he'd wanted a future with her and Cort, there was no way he could have that anymore. There was only one thing left for him to do. "Go home and give my niece a kiss for me. And tell everyone . . . tell everyone I'm sorry I didn't do this sooner."

"Where do you think you're going?" Silver's nails dug into his arm. She sidestepped to block him, then hissed in his face. "You're hurt. You're staying right here and waiting to go to the hospital."

"No." Ford met her eyes, his tone completely lifeless. "I'm going to end this."

Rather than arguing, she gave him a curt nod. "Good. Then take out your fucking phone and call your detective friend."

"Why? There's nothing he can do. I have nothing."

"Your father's assistant is in the bar, enjoying your father's favorite whiskey. I was gonna tell you the next time I saw you because you said the bar wasn't safe." Her lips thinned as though she'd just realized how right he'd been. "But maybe it will be useful now."

"What the fuck are you talking about, Silver?" Ford couldn't waste any more time. He thought about the gun he had under the bar. Since he didn't give a shit about being caught, it didn't matter that the gun was registered to him. If it was the last thing he ever did, he'd have the barrel stuffed in his father's mouth by the end of the night.

"The guy's on oxy. I saw him buy it from a dealer I recognize." She bit her lip at the sharp look Dean shot her way. "I can't change what I know, but maybe, for once, it will be good for something."

"If the cops pull him over and find that on him . . ." Landon gave Ford a grim smile. "This might be exactly what you need. How much would your father's assistant know?"

Ford felt numb. He opened and closed his mouth a few times. There was no way it could be this easy. But the word finally came out. "Everything."

He pulled out his phone, walking away from the chaos, down the alley to where he could hear the phone ringing. The detective said "Hello," but Ford didn't reply for a long time. His brain didn't seem willing to function.

"I know it's you, Ford. What the fuck do you want? Do you know what time it is?"

Approaching a brick wall and resting his forehead against it, Ford drew in a shallow breath. "Kingsley's assistant. My sister just saw him buying oxy. Is there any way you could—"

"Where are you?"

"My bar. I think I just killed two people."

"Jesus Christ! Stay there!" Hamilton shouted. He went quiet for about a minute, then sounded a bit calmer. "What's the man's name? If he's on the road—"

"Cops are coming. He probably took off."

"His. Name. Ford."

"Patrick Tinibu." Ford took a deep breath. "But it doesn't matter. I'm going to kill my father now."

"I didn't hear that. And you are staying right there." Hamilton sounded like he was moving. There was the growl of a motor. Then another sharp command. "You hear me? Stay where you are. I'll come find you."

"Okay." Ford had no intention of following Hamilton's orders. He stared blindly down the alley after Hamilton hung up, closed his eyes, then turned. There were so many lights flashing. Sirens wailing. But none of it pierced the icy shell surrounding the frozen remains of the good man he'd wanted to be. He walked to the back door of the bar, grateful that Silver was too distracted by Oriana struggling with Sloan to get to Max to notice him. Inside his bar, he went straight to the lockbox under the counter. Put in the combination. Took out his gun. Loaded it.

A click behind him had him standing and turning with his gun between his fists.

Laura glared at him, her own gun out and pointed steadily at his head. "Put it down, Ford."

"I can't." And he really couldn't. But he had to make her understand so she didn't try to stop him. "Three people are dead because of me."

"Three people? Ford, you're in shock. You're hurt. Hamilton called me since I was already on my way here to see Chicklet. He told you to stay put. You really don't want to piss him off."

"It doesn't matter. Kingsley isn't here. I can't kill him here."

"No, you can't. And you're not going to." Laura's finger

hovered over the trigger. "Don't make me shoot you, Ford. I like Akira. I think Cort is a good guy, in a weird way. They'll be upset if I hurt you."

"You'll have to kill me to stop me." Ford took a step forward, ready to walk past her. She blocked him with an easy side step, her gun still pointed at him. "Laura, I don't want to—"

"No. You won't shoot me. I'd have pulled the trigger already if I didn't believe that." She took a slow inhale, her gaze level. "Listen to me. This is over for you. One way or another, it's over. Lay the gun on the counter and we'll forget this ever happened."

"I can't."

"You will." She sucked her teeth as her phone buzzed, but didn't so much as twitch. "That's probably Hamilton. If you put the gun down, I'll answer and let you know what's going on."

"There's only one way to stop Kingsley. I have to do it." Ford ground his teeth as Laura took a step forward. His hands were shaking. So fucking cold. He put the safety on his gun and put it on the counter. Fuck, he wouldn't risk anyone else's life because he'd fucked up. But he would pick up that gun again once he got her out of here. "Either arrest me, or let me go. You know what Kingsley did. He killed Tim, Laura. Don't you want him dead?"

Laura's lips parted. For the first time, her solid stand wavered. But then she shook her head and kept the gun on him one-handed as she answered her phone. "Yeah?" Her throat worked as she swallowed. "You have him? And he's ready to talk? *Already*?" She let out a tight laugh. "That's fucking dirty. I love it!" She chatted for a bit, all smiles, then hung up and inclined her head. "They've got Tinibu and he's squealing. He ignored being read his rights when one of the cops mentioned a murder charge. He's begging to testify against Kingsley. Hamilton thinks they'll have a warrant within the next few hours."

Ford fisted his hands at his sides. Again. Too easy. This couldn't be real.

"Let me go." Ford brought his hand to his face, and his stomach heaved as he saw the dried blood covering it. Whose blood? Who else had he hurt? His head spun and his knees almost gave out, but he leaned heavily on the bar to stay on his feet. "It needs to be over. I can do that. I *have* to!"

"Who else did you kill, Ford? Hamilton told me you think you killed someone, but the men who attacked you are alive."

"Cam. Max. I might as well have slit their throats. It would have been less painful." His voice hitched. He'd ruined his sister's life. Taken her husband from her. And Cam . . .

"They're both stable. On the way to the hospital," she said, all matter-of-fact. "And it's not your fault that they got hurt."

"It's all on me. You're a fool if you believe otherwise."

"Ford, you need a doctor. Come with me and—"

"No."

"Fine." Laura gestured with her gun for him to sit. "Then I'm calling someone you'll listen to."

He sat, and it didn't take long for him to figure out who she'd called. But the second he moved to stand, Laura glanced pointedly down at her gun.

"He's in bad shape, but I'm not sure I can get him to go to the hospital. You wanna come get him?" Laura smiled. "Oh, he's not going anywhere. Got a bullet with his name on it—yes, I love you too, Akira."

"You can't let her come here! It's not safe!" Ford shot off the chair and snarled as a hand settled on his shoulder. He cast a killing glare over his shoulder, stiffening as Sebastian arched a brow at him while holding him in place. "Where's Jami?"

"With Luke and her father. She insisted I come see to it that you were not 'doing anything stupid.' I tend to indulge her, but she had good reason to worry." Sebastian tightened his grip when Ford tried to stand again, then reached out to slide Ford's gun across the counter to Laura. "I could hate you for what you put Jami through. But I do not blame *you*. The man who tried to hurt her is dead. The one who sent him will pay."

"Only if you let me go!" What didn't they understand? The law couldn't bring Kingsley down. He would find a way out. Ford refused to let that happen.

"I disagree. I have to believe he will spend his life in jail. Lose all he has. Suffer for a very long time." Sebastian's jaw hardened. "If you convince me otherwise, you can count on my being by your side, hunting him down like the rabid dog he is. A bullet for Tim. A bullet for Jami. That's all I ask."

Good. Very good. Maybe Sebastian *did* understand. Ford put his hand over the one Sebastian had on his shoulder. "It's a deal."

"Fuck, you two do know I can't be hearing this shit?" She scowled at Sebastian. "You're not helping."

Sebastian's tone took on an edge Ford had heard him use with Luke and Jami at the club. His eyes were dark. Deadly. "Arrest us both then, pet. Because if justice is not served . . ." His accent thickened as he spoke, and he seemed to struggle to find the right words. "I will seek it out. For the woman I love, there is nothing I would not do."

"Jami is *fine!*"

"No, she isn't. Kingsley's actions nearly broke her. I work to put the pieces together."

"You're doing a damn good job." Laura bit her bottom lip, almost as though arguing with Sebastian was more than she could take. "Please. I need both of you to sit down and relax. This is my job. You can't . . . please don't talk to me like that, Sebastian."

Ford hadn't realized how long the conversation had been going on. Before he knew it, Hamilton was in the empty bar, speaking softly to Laura and asking her to wait outside. The shock came when he looked at Ford and laughed.

"It's over. What don't you get?"

Ford frowned. "Kingsley needs to die."

"No. He needs to pay. And he will." Hamilton glanced over at Sebastian, then moved closer to Ford. "The info you gave me about the assistant was gold. I won't be sleeping tonight. I need to be there when Kingsley is hauled in. Which he will be unless he runs."

*No, Cort's the one who runs. And hopefully he won't have to. Because*

*Akira will need him.* He met Hamilton's eyes. "Kingsley won't run. He knows his lawyers can get him out of anything."

"Not this. Hell, Ford, you do get that the law sometimes works in favor of what's right? I can't give you details, but Kingsley is done."

"Won't happen."

"Oh, it's happening." Hamilton grinned. "Laura told me she called your woman. If you won't go to the hospital—and honestly, don't blame you, looks like a few bruises and a little cut—then at least let her take care of you. You lucky bastard."

*Lucky?* No, but Ford *was* a bastard for wanting to see Akira. For wanting Cort to give him a rough hug and tell him things would be okay. For being that fucking weak.

"But Cam . . . Max—"

"They're both alive. And I doubt either of them regret stepping up to help you." Hamilton laughed and slapped Ford's shoulder. "I know I wouldn't."

The man was in a pretty good goddamn mood. It was touching that the man was saying all this shit, but Ford couldn't absorb any of it. A part of him wanted to trust that there was some kind of justice out there, but he couldn't. All this shit was what Hamilton told himself so he could pick up his badge every day and think he could make a difference.

Ford knew better.

# Chapter Thirty Three

Blue lights, but no sirens. Sirens would be better. With sirens, the silence wouldn't add to the eerie quality of the night, all that flashing blue making the pulsing shadows jerk around. The glow around the alley made the darkness beyond seem deeper, or maybe just more permanent. Like it might still be there when the sun came up.

Or maybe Cort was just too used to what was usually left behind at a scene like this. Ford being here wasn't okay. What had almost happened to his boy made his blood boil. He cracked his jaw as he passed the small group of people talking to the cop watching the perimeter. Halfway across the alleyway, he could see Sebastian standing by Luke with his hand on the younger man's shoulder. Both looked washed out by the blue lights, but only Luke looked shaken. Sebastian's expression was unreadable as he nodded to the cop questioning them. Several other Cobras and a few random guys Cort didn't recognize were being questioned as well, but out of them all, Cort knew Sebastian was the one he'd need to talk to if he wanted the facts and nothing but.

Movement to Cort's side stopped him short before he reached Sebastian. He clenched his fist, but made sure to look before swinging.

Good thing too. Punching a fucking cop would probably get his bail revoked.

"Sir, this is a crime scene," the cop said, glaring at Cort, his hand hovering near his holstered gun. "You can't be here."

*Like fuck, I can't!* Cort took a deep breath, forcing himself to calm down. The cop must be a stupid, cocky rookie. Odds were, he didn't know Cort *was* supposed to be here.

"Laura called me. I was asked to pick up my friend." Cort gave the cop a stiff smile and turned away from him.

The cop's hard grip on Cort's arm halted him abruptly. He jerked away. Heard the familiar slide of gunmetal against leather and moved without pausing to think. His fist met flesh. The wrong face was in front of him. He didn't resist when Hamilton shoved him back. His brain couldn't manage more than one word.

*Fuck.*

Hamilton's grin as the man swiped away a trickle of blood brought Cort's brain to two words. This time out loud.

"Oh fuck."

"Yeah, I'd say." Hamilton rolled his eyes and spat as he brought his attention to the other cop, who stood a few feet away with his gun aimed in their general direction. "Goddammit, put that away, Baker!"

The other cop, Baker, fumbled with his gun as though not sure whether he should stash it or just drop it. Cort was able to breathe a little easier when the gun was safely back in Baker's holster. Rookie didn't look like he should be wielding anything bigger than a fucking pen for parking tickets.

Of course, Baker hadn't just punched a goddamn detective in the face.

*Fuckfuckfuck.*

"How many times do I got to tell you to keep it in your fucking pants, Baker? We both know what happens when you get too excited. Gotta work on that."

Cort stared at Hamilton.

Baker sputtered, scowling at Cort when Cort glanced his way. A few of the other cops within hearing snorted. Baker's lips thinned under his sorry attempt at a mustache. "He said someone named 'Laura' called him."

"That would be Tallent." Hamilton's lips twitched, like he was amused by how much redder Baker's face was getting. "Any other reason for the pre-ejac?"

He might be wrong, but Cort was pretty sure the cop standing a few feet away was pissing himself laughing and not having a seizure. But this shit was all kinds of fucked-up. Why hadn't Hamilton dropped him in the back of a squad car yet?

*I hit him. I fucking . . . fuck!* So close to being free. Cort had tasted it. Then he'd tossed it away.

Hamilton's hard smack on his arm made him jump. Baker was gone. And Hamilton was smirking at him. "Your one and only freebie, big guy. Go get your boy. It's been a long day, and I don't feel like babysitting the two of you all night. Put in a lot of hours keeping you out of jail and him alive. Don't make me regret it."

"No, sir." Cort wanted to go straight to Ford, but he couldn't move. The cuffs were gonna come out any minute.

Hamilton arched a brow. Then grinned. "My truck's been giving me grief. If I bring it by your shop tomorrow . . . ?"

Cort opened his mouth. Closed it. Nodded. "I'll take care of it. No charge."

"Good man." Hamilton jutted his chin toward the back door of the bar. "Now get the fuck out of here."

That got Cort moving. He forgot about talking to Sebastian and just headed into the bar, wanting to be out of sight before the detective changed his mind. Cort was pretty sure he had a damn stupid smile on his face. Not being hauled off to jail put him in a pretty good mood.

But what he saw inside had him ready to hit someone. Again.

Just *not* Hamilton.

"What the fuck, Ford!" Cort sucked air through his teeth and lowered his voice when Ford's waitress—another one with a stripper name that he couldn't recall—skittered backward like a startled mouse. Ford had his shirt off and the girl was taping some gauze to his side.

The blood was already seeping through the lopsided bandage. Ford needed stitches, at very least. There were bruises forming all over his sides and his chest, not to mention the ones on the side of his face. Hell, the scrapes on his arm and cheek made it look like Ford had fallen off a motorcycle—actually, Cort was pretty sure the damage hadn't been this bad when Ford *had* totalled his first bike.

Ford didn't even lift his head. Cort wasn't sure the boy had heard him.

"Ford—"

"I want him dead. I was going to go kill him." Ford rubbed his face with the hand he'd had his head propped up on. "They wouldn't let me. Laura stopped me."

"Remind me to thank her." Cort put his hand on Ford's shoulder. Motioned for the waitress to go away. Maybe it was a good thing Ford hadn't gone to the hospital. Cort couldn't keep both Ford and Akira safe, and he recognized the tone Ford was using. Cort's usual method of handling Ford contemplating murder was to knock the stupid kid the fuck out and let him "sleep" it off.

But Ford wasn't a kid anymore. And he didn't look like he could take another hit.

Besides, he wasn't wrong for wanting Kingsley dead. Cort wanted the son of a bitch dead too. A few months ago, he would have done it without thinking twice.

Now? Kingsley wasn't worth risking a future he was actually looking forward to. One with Akira. One with Ford.

If Cort could patch Ford together and get the man thinking straight, maybe he could make that future a reality. He sighed after a few minutes of watching Ford, knowing that he had to say just the right thing to get Ford off that fucking stool. Out of the bar and in the car.

Nothing short of offering Ford a loaded gun and a lift to Kingsley's front door occurred to Cort. He scratched his jaw and sighed again. "Don't forget, Akira's marrying me. So she can't visit you in jail."

"She won't want to. Not after I've killed people she loves."

"Fuck, Ford! Can I crash your pity party with some facts?" Cort rubbed his forehead, wishing someone had done the counseling bullshit before he'd gotten there. "Laura told me everything. No one's dead. Not even the fucktards that came after you."

Ford lifted his head, his eyes narrowed. "Tim's dead."

Cort went still. Ran his tongue over his teeth. Resisted the urge to punch Ford a second time. "You tell me that's not on me, then take it on yourself? Enough of this crap! Get off your goddamn ass. Bad shit went down, but you're still alive. Our woman is at a sleazy motel being watched over by a bunch of bikers while you're sitting here sulking about not being able to put a bullet in your old man. Get the fuck over it!"

"*Cort!*" A chair hit the floor as Laura hurried across the room, casting a glare over her shoulder at Hamilton who was watching them from the other side of the room, doing a bad job at holding back a snort. Reaching them, Laura gave Ford a sympathetic look. "I know you're angry. I was hoping Akira would come, but—"

"I'm not sure it's safe for Akira yet," Cort said, keeping his eyes on Ford and hoping the man agreed. Fine, Cort might not be all the kisses and cuddles Laura clearly thought Ford needed, but Ford couldn't be so far gone that he'd want Akira here.

Ford shook his head. "Cort's right. Akira can't be seen with me. Not yet."

"So she's safer with the bikers?" Laura folded her arms over her chest. Shook her head. "Ford, I think you should go to the hospital. Have Akira meet you there. You know she'll worry if she sees you not being taken care of."

Pressing his fingertips into his eyelids, Ford shook his head. "She'll see me taken care of." He seemed to pull himself together as he straightened and looked to Cort. "I mean, if you don't mind?"

"I don't mind." Cort smiled a little as Ford tried to be all tough and stand on his own. The boy he'd looked out for might be all grown-up, but the stubborn little shit was still in there. So Cort did no more than he would have ten years ago. "You good?"

"Yeah." Ford sounded like speaking was a challenge, never mind standing. His jaw tensed as he leaned heavily on the bar. "Just give me a sec."

"Men!" Laura gave Cort a dirty look then reached for Ford.

Hamilton held her back. "Cort's got this. If Ford wants to be an idiot, let him."

"*You* should have tried harder to get him to the hospital."

"Probably. But not sure they can fix stupid."

"Damn it, Hamilton!"

Cort snorted when Ford glanced at the cops, then back to him as though he was fucking confused. Which Cort completely understood. Pigs never came off as human, but Hamilton and Laura? Hell, if Ford or Cort had come across cops like them years ago, maybe they would have stayed on the straight and narrow.

*Yeah, probably not.*

"Cort . . ." Ford's lips curled a little as he tried to push away from the bar. Disgusted with his own weakness, if Cort was reading him right. He finally sighed and held his arm out. "Not sure I can do this on my own."

Easing Ford's arm over his shoulder, Cort carefully gave Ford enough support to stand. He ignored Laura's "Are-you-*both*-brain-dead?" stare and headed for the door, speaking quietly to Ford. "You probably *should* see a real doctor, kid."

With a sidelong glance, Ford nodded. "Yep. But you'll patch me up?"

"Only if you promise not to whine like a little bitch."

"Do I ever?"

Cort snorted, instantly recalling a handful of times. Ford had puked the first time Cort had given him stitches. Of course, he'd had half a bottle of Jack first, so that may have had something to do with it. He decided not to rib Ford about it. "Naw, you always were a tough little shit."

"Thanks." Ford's steps faltered as they walked across the mouth of the alley. Crimson droplets created a clear path through the snow. He shuddered, his grip on Cort's shoulder tightening slightly. "They're really okay?"

No need to ask who Ford meant. Cort nodded. Smiled broadly. "They really are. And I'm telling you now, Cam's getting a fucking raise." After helping Ford into the car, Cort stood there, just watching Ford settle in, feeling the cold air fully filling his lungs for the first time since he'd gotten here. The iron fist that had seized his insides loosened its grip. He slapped the roof of the car and let out a rough laugh. "Dominik might hate you for what happened to his brother. But I owe Cam for saving mine."

\* \* \* \*

Akira threw open the door to the motel as Cort pulled up. Her big smile faded as he went around to the passenger's side to help Ford out. Without a word, she ducked back inside and grabbed a blanket. Ford didn't have his coat. And the way he was moving . . .

*He's hurt. Oh God, please let him be okay!* But she wasn't going to panic. This was something she'd have to get used to. She loved her men too much to walk away from them, no matter how much trouble they got in. So long as they came back to her in one piece, she should probably be grateful.

Snow melted through her socks as she ran out to put the blanket over Ford's shoulders. She covered her mouth with her hand when he stumbled. Sutter's presence at her side gave her something to lean on as Cort brought Ford inside. Sutter rubbed her arms as they followed, then left her in the doorway to go get something from the car he'd parked at the other end of the lot.

When Cort had left over an hour before—the bastard basically *commanding* her to stay here with his father and a few bikers keeping an eye on her—she'd paced the room for about ten minutes talking to Jami on the phone so she could at least find out what had happened. Jami had gone back to Silver's place to stay with the baby so the nanny could go home to her own kids. Silver was with Oriana who refused to leave Max. Half the team was at the hospital.

And Akira had been stuck here. The one time she'd peeked out the window had gotten Sutter banging at her door and wordlessly pointing to the other side of the room when she opened it. Then calmly telling her to put the bolt lock on. Damn it, she *had* liked the man until he'd gone into watchdog mode. She'd have liked him more if he'd given her the gun he'd offered her the other day and maybe sat and talked to her for a bit.

Instead, he followed Cort's instructions to the letter. The bikers weren't allowed near her. She wasn't to touch any weapons. Cort's rapid-fire orders came back to her as she watched him settle Ford on the bed on top of the towels Sutter spread out. As he carefully peeled off Ford's shirt and took the medical kit Sutter handed him.

*"We need you safe, Tiny. I can't help Ford if I don't know you're safe."* Cort ran his knuckles down her cheek. *"And you know Ford. He'll go nuts if he thinks I'm putting you in danger."*

*"But I'm fine being guarded by criminals?"*

*"Don't you trust my father?"*

*She could've slapped him for asking her that. "Of course I do, but I should be going with you!"*

*Cort's eyes had darkened and his whole demeanor became so unyielding he was more than a little scary. She moved to take a step back, but he put his hand on the nape of her neck and spoke very, very softly. "Do you have any idea how close we came to losing Ford? I'm not giving Kingsley a chance to get to you. Ever. You are going to stay here and do exactly what my father tells you to."*

And she'd done exactly that. Hated every second, but had gotten around to admitting that this was her life now.

There was part of her that couldn't come to terms with it. That wasn't sure she could keep her relationship with Ford and Cort hidden. That didn't want to worry if one or both of the men would leave one day "for her own good." Only, this wasn't the time to bring that up. She ground her teeth as Sutter roughly repositioned Ford on the bed and Ford's face lost all color. Sutter held Ford down as Cort opened what looked like a small bottle of clear spirits.

*Enough is enough.* She squared her shoulders and stepped up to Sutter. "Get out."

"What?" Sutter blinked at her, then looked over at Cort. "Son, she really shouldn't be watchin'—"

Akira held up her hand before Cort could say a word. "I'm helping you take care of him. Deal with it." She frowned at Sutter. "Mr. Nash, I almost like you, but you've made it clear how you feel about Ford. Go make sure no one comes in here to finish—" She cut herself off as Cort peeled off the bloody bandage. There was fresh blood oozing out of the sliced flesh on Ford's side. Her stomach rolled and her eyes teared, but she dug her nails into her palms to keep her tone steady. "Make sure they don't come to finish the job."

Sutter nodded and gave her a bracing smile. "Will do, cutie. And if it helps, Ford's had worse."

That didn't help. Not at all. But she just nodded at Sutter and waited for him to leave before turning to Cort. "Tell me what I need to do."

For a second, it looked like Cort was going to argue with her, but instead, he held out the bottle. "You're not strong enough to hold him down—"

Shifting to a half-sitting position that made the wound ooze even more blood, Ford winced and put his hand on Cort's wrist. "I don't need to be held down. Don't let her do this."

"No one's 'letting' me do anything. It's not an option. Now lie down." She pried Ford's hand off Cort's wrist, easing him down as she turned to Cort. "Was the hospital not safe?"

Cort shrugged. "Hard to tell. Either way, he refused to go."

"Like Sutter said, I've had worse." Ford brought a hand to her cheek, his crooked smile tight with pain. "Cort's good at this, shorty. Why don't you go take a nice hot bath, put some music on your phone, and—"

"Shut up." Akira glared at Ford, itching to shake him for being such an idiot. Such a damn lovable idiot that she'd almost lost tonight. "Either we bring you to the hospital, or I'm going to be right here putting you back together with Cort."

"But you'll want to come to the hospital?"

"I *will* come to the hospital."

"Kingsley wants me dead—in a way that sends a message to the people who work for him, not quick and easy. He'd have offered good money. There's no way to tell who else might come after me." Ford took a deep breath and dropped his head back on the pillow. "This is a mistake."

"Well, you've both made plenty. Maybe it's my turn." Akira tried not to look at the wound as Cort sat on the bed, holding Ford's wrists with one hand and placing the other on Ford's shoulder to keep him in place. The scent of blood had her breathing fast through her mouth. The pain Ford tried to hide made her want to cry. She glanced up at Cort. "This will hurt him, won't it?"

"Yes. Let him take a swig of the vodka first. It'll help."

Her palm was slick with sweat. She almost dropped the bottle as she moved to offer it to Ford. She laughed nervously and twisted the top off, taking a few burning gulps before bringing the bottle to Ford's lips.

Ford was shaking hard against her side. He pressed his eyes shut as he swallowed. Opened them when she took the bottle from his lips. His eyes were tender as they met hers. "Akira, I'm so sorry. I never wanted this for you."

Tears spilled down her cheeks. She leaned down to kiss him, answering her own question. She *hadn't* been sure if she could keep going like this. Pretending to be with Dominik so no one would know who she really belonged to. But in the end, did it matter what everyone else believed? She knew the truth. It was her truth, and Ford's, and Cort's.

The rest of the world didn't matter. The three of them had stolen this moment together. They'd steal many more. And maybe, one day, things would change.

She'd still be here, with them, one way or another.

"Are you ready, Ford?" Cort's brow furrowed when Ford closed his eyes again, almost as though he wasn't so sure about what they were doing. But he finally inclined his head to Akira.

"Pour it over the cut."

Tipping the bottle, Akira made sure to pour the vodka over the length of the narrow wound. Her stomach heaved as diluted blood spilled down Ford's side. Ford tried to wrench away, but Cort leaned almost full on him, seeming to read Ford's desperate look, quickly covering Ford's mouth with his hand to smother his agony-filled scream. The sound that escaped tore right into Akira's heart.

She sobbed and pressed wet kisses on Ford's cheeks. "I didn't want to hurt you! Shit! Tell me how to make it stop!" Without realizing it, she'd grabbed Cort's wrist and had her nails digging into his flesh. "Make it stop!"

"It'll pass in a bit, Tiny. Let him have a bit more to drink." He winked at her, even though by the gray cast to his skin, he wasn't enjoying this any more than she was. "Why do you think we use vodka instead of medical stuff?"

"Because you're insane?" But Akira quickly gave Ford a few sips when Cort moved his hand. The last swallow had Ford relaxing a bit, though he was covered in sweat and trembling. Akira let out a shallow laugh. "Is this how you guys deal with getting cut up and shot all the time?"

Cort didn't look like he wanted to answer. Ford, however, groaned and chuckled. "Pretty much. Sutter dug a bullet out of Cort's arm once, and you should have heard the way Cort yelled when his brother poured whiskey over the hole."

"Shut up, Ford." Cort growled, moving away from Ford and wrapping one arm around Akira's shoulders as she swayed. "Tiny, this is the last time, I promise—"

"You can't promise me that, Cort." She blinked fast as the room tilted and spun around her. She tipped the bottle to her lips, her whole body suddenly numb.

"I want to."

"But you can't." She peeked at Ford's wound. Planted her hands on the mattress to keep from falling off the bed. "Do you have to sew him up now?"

Eyes narrowed, Cort studied the cut, then shook his head.

499

"No, it's not that deep. The butterfly bandages will work just fine. Do you trust me, Tiny?"

She did, but the way Cort asked meant more than she could say. He already knew Ford trusted him—they'd been through this before. Cort was making sure she had faith in him to take care of the man they both loved—well, in different ways, but still. This had all started without her having a say, but she had a feeling that if she insisted on Ford going to the hospital, neither man would question her. She knew the risks.

And the risks, and her very real trust in Cort, were what had her nodding and holding Ford's hand as Cort laid out a sterile blue cloth and took out the butterfly bandages. Despite the primitive usage of vodka, Cort put on sterile gloves to deal with the bandages. The practiced ease with which Cort placed the tiny bow-shaped strips made her feel a lot better. Actually, it didn't look that bad once it was all held together and neatly bandaged. Cort dealt with all the scrapes on Ford's arms and face pretty quick and even put some yellow stuff on the bruises.

Ford seemed to be okay. He fell asleep after Cort let him finish off the vodka, still holding Akira's hand. But she was afraid to move. Didn't want to wake him up.

"Lie down next to him. He'll sleep better knowing you're there." Cort smoothed her hair away from her face after removing the gloves. His expression held confidence, but slipped a little when she held his gaze. "I wouldn't have given him a choice about going to the hospital if—"

"I know." Akira pressed a finger to Cort's lips, chewing on her own as she thought about how much she hated that this was the norm for her men. She would deal, but she wanted better for them. Only, there was no way she could make that happen. Kingsley was too powerful. With a word, he could take everything from them. Cort's DIY medical treatment of Ford wasn't all that bad when she considered the alternative. Then again, if he'd pulled out duct tape at any point, she'd have put her foot down. "I'm not sure I'll sleep much tonight. I'm gonna be paranoid about him getting an infection or . . . I don't know, just something going wrong. I'd feel better if Oriana could come check on him, but she's with Max, right?"

"She'd come if we asked her to. She loves Ford."

"But Max got shot." The impact of saying that out loud had her shaking hard. She'd been a fan of Max's for a long time and now considered him a friend. Actually, more of a big brother. If anything happened to him—

Cort put his hand over the one she had clasped with Ford's. "Laura told me about that. The bullet went straight through— didn't do any major damage. Missed his heart completely."

Ford grunted. He clearly wasn't really sleeping. His brow furrowed. "Cort, you're gonna scare her."

"Why? From what I heard, Max didn't even know he'd been hit right away. He helped take down one of the guys."

*But he could have been killed instantly.* Akira scrubbed away fresh tears with the heel of her palm. She had to toughen up. Being with Ford and Cort meant this kinda thing would happen a lot. If Sutter needed Cort, how could Cort say no? And as long as Kingsley was alive, Ford would always be in danger.

Moving to Africa would be a good alternative. Or maybe Alaska. Bulky parkas would definitely slow bullets. She planted a brave smile on her lips at Cort's questioning look. "What would you think of getting a place together soon?"

"After we get married? Do you still want to get married?"

Ford snorted without opening his eyes. "Why don't you ask her where she wants to move?"

Damn the man. He knew her too well. She wrinkled her nose. "Alaska?"

Cort frowned. "Really? But what about the Ice Girls? The team? All your friends?"

There was no good answer to that. She had to make a choice. One that would break her heart one way or another.

Apparently, Ford disagreed. He sounded drunk, but Akira really wanted to believe what he said next. "We're not going anywhere. I'm not supposed to kill Kingsley, but maybe someone will in jail. If he goes to jail."

"What are you talking about?" Cort voiced Akira's thoughts. What Ford was saying meant hope, but why wouldn't he have said something sooner? Why was he still talking like Kingsley was a threat?

Ford shrugged, winced, and groaned. "Don't buy it. Kingsley will find a way out of this. His assistant will spill, but then someone will kill him, and there will be no one to testify but me."

"Does Hamilton know about this?" Cort asked, sitting up. He hissed out a curse when Ford didn't reply. "Damn it, Ford! Answer me!"

"Hamilton is happy. He thinks it's over." Ford dropped an arm over his face. His breathing slowed. "It's not over. It will never be over."

Akira swallowed hard. The pain and the alcohol had left Ford an incoherent mess. But as she met Cort's eyes, she saw her own hope reflected in the ruddy green depths. It wasn't over yet. They still had to be careful.

One day though, one day soon this might all be nothing but a nightmare they could all wake up from. And forget.

# Chapter Thirty Four

"**D**ad! Come here! Oh, God, this is amazing!"

Dean cradled Amia against his shoulder, careful not to jostle her even as he hurried from her nursery down to the living room. Jami sounded like she was practically in tears. Only her words kept him from panicking. "Amazing" couldn't mean more bad news.

Perched at the edge of the sofa, one hand covering her mouth, the other held tight by Luke who sat beside her, Jami stared at the TV. Sebastian nodded a greeting to Dean before returning his attention to the news.

Soft fussing from Amia shifted Dean's focus, and he bent down to grab her little stuffed gray bunny from the coffee table, his gaze only half on the scene playing out on the large screen. Police officers and men in suits. Questions being shouted from the crowd as the officers cleared a path. Flanked on both sides, hands in cuffs, an irritated expression on his face, was a man Dean instantly recognized. The man who'd had his brother killed.

The reporter listed off the charges, never forgetting to state that the crimes were "alleged." There were so many Dean would never have suspected, even though he'd heard a bit about Kingsley's reputation over the past couple of weeks. But it was the last that made it hard to breathe.

"Come, *hermanita*." Sebastian came to Dean's side, patting Dean's shoulder before holding his arms out for Amia. Amia gurgled and went readily to the other man, who'd been treating her like his precious *hermanita*, "little sister," since she'd been born. The only reason Dean didn't hesitate to let him take her. Because he couldn't acknowledge Sebastian. Couldn't shift his gaze from the screen.

And then he couldn't hear anything but what the hard-eyed, crimson-lipped reporter was saying, "In addition to current charges, there is a pending investigation into the recent deaths of Tim and Madeline Rowe in which there are suspicions that Roy Kingsley hired the driver involved in the collision—who is still at large—to arrange the accident, though it is still unclear why the beloved coach of the Dartmouth Cobras would have been a target. The gambling charges laid on the previous coach and several players lead to the speculation that Mr. Rowe was offered a similar deal. And turned it down."

Dean laughed and the sound was disturbing to his own ears. He felt Jami's eyes on him and blinked back the threatening tears. "Of course he turned it down. My brother was a good man."

"The best." Luke cupped Jami's cheeks, drying her tears with his thumbs. "Justice, boo. I know it doesn't bring him back, but it's something."

Jami simply curled up in Luke's arms, not saying a word. And Dean couldn't blame her. It was hard to see how Kingsley being arrested made a difference now. Who gave a damn about justice?

*Tim would have.* Dean went to sit beside his eldest daughter, stroking her back and whispering to her all the things he knew Tim would have if he was still here. "Uncle Tim would have hated knowing Kingsley was still out there, that the man could hurt others. He'll be at peace now, baby."

"But Kingsley's still alive." Jami finally lifted her head, glaring at the TV as Kingsley was placed in the backseat of an unmarked car. "Why should he get to keep living, while someone like Uncle Tim—"

"That's the thing, Jami. He doesn't get to keep living." Dean followed his daughter's gaze, a tight smile on his lips. "Look at the bastard. He doesn't know it yet." A grim satisfaction filled Dean, numbing the pain just enough to make it bearable. "But his life's already over."

* * * *

Max tried not to wince as pain shot up his arm. Sloan didn't seem to realize his hand was on top of the bandages on Max's shoulder.

Until Oriana elbowed him in the gut. "Will you be careful?"

Sloan grinned at her, not fazed by the jab. "There's my brat. I was wondering when you'd get enough spunk back to earn a punishment."

Standing by the foot of Max's bed, leaning against Bower's side, Silver shot a narrow-eyed glare at Sloan. Her lips curled away from her teeth, and Max had a feeling she was going to say something unfortunate.

Until Bower's hand shifted from her shoulder to the back of her neck. Bower arched a brow at her as though to say "Speak, and you'll regret it."

Silver huffed and snapped her gaze back to the TV. She cleared her throat. "Do you think the charges will stick?"

Oriana frowned, reaching blindly for Sloan's hand as she stared at her sister's back. "Why wouldn't they?"

Good question. Max watched Silver shift away from Landon as though she wasn't sure he'd want to touch her as she spoke. "With a good lawyer, you can get out of almost anything. Why would they listen to the testimony of a drug addict? What if telling Ford about the assistant was just enough to give everyone false hope? Kingsley didn't look all that worried."

"Silver, his assistant was competent enough to handle all his business. I don't think they'd have gotten a warrant on his testimony alone. He'd have to have some evidence or . . . ?" Landon looked over at Sloan and Max, like he was sure one of them would know. His lips thinned when they both shrugged. "It doesn't matter. You were able to use your past to do something good, pet. If not for you, your brother would have spent the rest of his very short life looking over his shoulder."

Oriana held her hand out over the bed, taking Silver's even as

Landon took his place by his fiancée's side. She caught Silver's eye. "Face it, sis. You're a good person. What you did for Ford—"

"What *I* did? What about your husband?" Silver grinned at Max. "You just had to be a hero, eh, cowboy?"

Max's cheeks heated. He shrugged, which sent the sensation of being branded like one of his dad's calves right through his chest. And Sloan, the fucker, grinned. The twisted bastard really needed some quality time with Oriana and his favorite whip.

There was no way Oriana would leave the hospital while Max was stuck here though, so he decided to torture his best friend a little. He gave Bower a warm smile. "Apparently you missed Bower tackling the guy with the machete. Sweet moves, goalie. I was worried about you. Couldn't handle losing you, and not just 'cause of what you do for the team." He swallowed real hard. Real loud. "You know what I'm sayin'?"

"I do. But I did what I had to. Seeing you go down wasn't easy for me . . ." Landon winked at Max, then rested his chin on Silver's shoulder. "Damn. It's times like this that make me realize how important you guys are to me. We're all family and—"

"Fuck, do you two need a minute alone?" Sloan made a sound of disgust, inching away from the bed like all the sappiness was contagious. "Hug it out or something. You sound like a couple of chicks."

The "chicks" burst out laughing, Silver turning in Bower's arms to kiss him while Oriana patted Sloan's cheek, her tone indulgent. "Are they making my big, bad sadist uncomfortable? Do you want me to tell them to go?"

"I'm sorry, but you'll all have to leave," the nurse said briskly from the doorway. She held up her hand before Oriana could object. "You may stay with your husband, Mrs. Perron, but he needs his rest."

Silver and Bower left the room with a quick goodbye, but Sloan didn't budge. His fist pressed into the pillow behind Max, the muscle in his jaw ticking with irritation. One look at him had the nurse paling a little. Oriana licked her lips and glanced nervously at

Max.

"May we have a moment, ma'am?" Max asked, digging his fingers into Sloan's forearm before his best friend could snarl at the nurse like he looked ready to. He spoke low when the nurse nodded, backing out without closing the door. "We don't want no trouble, Sloan. She's just doing her job."

Sloan hunched his shoulders. Bowed his head. Nodded. "Fine. Just get better so I can get you the fuck out of here. I fucking hate hospitals. Never thought I'd be in one because some son of a bitch goes and shoots you."

That was as close as Sloan would come to saying he'd been afraid for Max. All the emotional stuff lately was getting to be too much for him, and he was shutting it out completely. Max was tempted to send Oriana home with Sloan just to keep an eye on him, but Sloan would never allow it.

"Call me in the morning. I'll bring you some biscuits and gravy. I know how much you like it." Sloan moved to straighten, scowling when Max refused to release him. "What do you want, Max?"

Like hell he was letting Sloan go anywhere like this. He met Sloan's dark eyes. "We're a family—"

"Don't start that shit, pal. I'm not—"

"Stop it. I want you to stay." And Max really did. He didn't want to make things difficult for the nurse, but he needed both Oriana and Sloan with him. He kept his tone polite as he called out to the nurse. "Ma'am, if they can't both stay, I'd like to be released."

Oriana opened her mouth. Closed it. She wasn't gonna question his decision. *Good girl.*

The nurse, however, had no problem doing so. "Sir, I really can't advise that. You were very lucky, but there's still the risk of infection and—"

"Then you agree he can stay?"

She pursed her lips. "Need I ask why you need both of them?"

Max smiled at her. "Reckon you don't unless you really want to know."

Blushing, the nurse shook her head and retreated from the room.

At his side, Sloan groaned. "Great, now she's gonna think I'm fucking you."

"And since when do you care what anyone thinks?" Max watched Sloan drop into the big gray armchair that would convert into an uncomfortable bed for him to sleep in tonight. He noticed that the tension had left Sloan's shoulders. Now he just looked tired. "Admit it, you're just glad you get to stay. Tell me you love me and quit your damn moping."

Wrapping his arms around Oriana's waist, Sloan dragged her onto his lap. Kissed her cheek as she leaned back. Then grinned at Max. "Yeah. I'm glad."

With one long finger, Oriana traced the collar of Sloan's black T-shirt, speaking in a mock whisper. "And you love him."

"He knows I do." Sloan reached over, putting his hand on Max's forearm. And said one of nicest things anyone had ever said to him. "I lost my fucking mind when I saw you were hurt. Almost killed that guy. Still want to. If that don't prove I love you, too fucking bad."

\* \* \* \*

They slept pretty well in the motel room, so well that Cort woke up first and only because his phone was buzzing. He picked it up and he saw he'd missed a few calls. He dialed for his messages, slipping from the bed to listen to them. One from Sebastian. Two from Sutter—he went over to the window to look out into the parking lot—his dad had gone back to crash at the club. Which he wouldn't have done if they weren't safe.

And they *were* safe. All the messages gave Cort the same information, enough to make it true.

But he couldn't quite absorb the facts. Not about Roy being arrested. Not that Roy's brothers had cut all ties with him. That every associate the man had ever worked with had already done all they could to erase any trace of him from their businesses, legal or not. Sutter made sure to point out no one would take up a hit on Ford now, not with all of Roy's assets frozen and his entire corporation under investigation.

"Cort?" Akira sat up, holding the sheets to her chest, her wide eyes full of fear. He hated what all this shit had done to her. The fear was bad enough, but the way her eyes hardened when he didn't answer was worse. "How fast do we need to get out of here? Is Ford stable enough to—"

"We don't have to go anywhere." Cort strode up to the TV and turned it on. Surfed through the channels until he found what he was looking for. "It's over."

"Over?" Akira stared at him like she didn't know what the word meant. When he jerked his chin at the TV, she locked her eyes on it. Didn't move. Held her breath.

Folding his arms over his chest, Cort leaned against the wall, splitting his focus between the TV and the bed. Ford was awake now, had himself propped up on the pillows Akira had piled up for him. He fisted his hands in the ugly leaf-print comforter, his throat working as he swallowed again and again. He hardly blinked until Akira rested her head on his shoulder, shaking and crying as though she was completely overwhelmed with relief.

"It's really over?" Ford put his arm around Akira and stared at the TV. "But . . . he has connections."

Cort shook his head. "Not anymore."

"Money?"

"Nope."

"This can't be . . . fuck, look at him, Cort!" Ford glared at the TV like it took all his strength not to get off the bed and shatter the screen. "Maybe you're right, but he's not feeling it. He's not afraid, and he would be if I had him choking on the barrel of my gun!"

This was true. If Ford had ever gotten close enough to put a gun in Kingsley's face, the man would probably have been afraid. Cort went over to the bed and sat on the edge, meeting Ford's eyes as Akira whispered soothingly to him. "He's not scared because he still thinks he'll get out of this. Wait until he goes to trial after a few days behind bars. He'll be cocky as hell until they sentence him to life."

"If he gets out on bail—"

"Then we'll deal with it. I don't want to be stupid about this. The three of us still have to be careful, but I'm not too worried. My dad is keeping an ear out, and he decided we don't need to be watched anymore." Cort smiled when Akira let out the breath she'd been holding. She was trying so hard to be strong for them, but this couldn't be easy on her. "We can all relax today."

"I'm happy with today." Akira sat up, holding her tongue between her teeth as she trailed her fingers over Cort's scruffy cheek. "You both need to shave. Will you let me do that for you, Master?"

Damn, he wasn't sure he'd ever get used to her calling him that. During a scene, the title felt natural, but beyond that . . . unless she didn't want to be outside of those dynamics right now. Offering to shave him might be her way of saying she needed the security of giving up control for a little while. She was paler than he liked. There was a tension around her eyes and she was being pretty quiet.

He rubbed his chin and his lips tilted up at the edges. "You can shave me after, pet. But I need your help with something first."

She gave him a hesitant smile, her gaze following him as he went to fetch the medical kit. He sat behind Ford, shoved the blankets aside, and held his hand up when Ford opened his mouth.

"The wound needs to be cleaned, Ford. Give me your hands." He snorted at the wide-eyed stare Ford shot over his shoulder. "Where's that trust, buddy?"

"My hands are fine. I don't know what you're doing behind me, but . . ." Ford's forehead creased as he continued to look back at Cort. "If you're planning to play, Akira needs to be in the middle."

"Not this time. Just give me your fucking hands."

Ford put his hands behind him, grumbling. "Pushy bastard."

Cort smirked, then used some medical tape to bind Ford's wrists. Surprisingly, Ford didn't bitch. He just cocked an eyebrow as if to say "What the hell are you doing?" Instead of explaining, Cort glanced over at Akira. "Unzip his jeans, Tiny. I'll help you get them off him."

Muscles tensing, eyes narrowed, Ford tried to twist away from Akira. She gave him an impish grin as she quickly opened his jeans, exposing his fully erect dick so she could lay a gentle kiss on the tip.

Groaning, Ford strained against his restraints, his hips rising of their own accord to keep his cock close to her mouth. Cort took advantage of the movement to lift Ford by his arms. Supported by only Cort's hold, knees bent and feet flat on the bed, Ford couldn't stop Akira from pulling his jeans down.

"Shit, Cort. What are you doing?" Ford shuddered as Akira lowered her head between his thighs, taking him slowly between her lips. "I'm not a sub. This doesn't feel—"

"Doesn't feel what, Ford? I'm not asking you to submit to me." Cort shifted over, carefully removing the bandage to inspect the wound on Ford's side. Didn't look too bad. No infection, but it still needed to be cleaned. He folded one leg on the bed by Ford's hip, bracing the other behind Ford's back in case he needed the support. "I've gotta take care of this. Just seeing what I can do to make it fun."

"Fun?" Ford's lips parted as Akira began sliding her lips faster up and down his cock. He didn't seem to notice Cort opening the bottle of vodka, but when the liquid spilled over his broken flesh, his back bowed. "Fuck!"

"Don't let him come, pet." A dark rush of power spread through Cort's veins, as though a tap had been turned on full blast, letting loose a stream of pure heat. He wasn't trying to Dom Ford, but there was something about taking control of him that was heady. There was nothing sexual about the sensation. Just a primal need to dominate fully.

Ford went still as Akira slowed her pace and wrapped her hand tightly around the base of his dick. His tone was firm, but lacking the anger Cort had prepared for. "My turn next time. This time . . ." He let out a sharp laugh. "That fucking hurt, but . . ."

Cort bared his teeth in a feral smile. He'd been hoping a bit of pleasure would help Ford get through the pain, but this was so much better. "It felt good, didn't it?"

"Damn you! Yeah, it did." Ford hissed as Cort poured a little more vodka over the wound. He spoke through his teeth as Akira swirled her tongue around the head of his dick. "That doesn't mean I'm gonna start kneeling for you."

The idea of having Ford kneeling to him wasn't really appealing, but at the same time—would depend for what. Even thinking about Ford sucking his dick or anything like that felt wrong, but . . .

"What if you're on your knees while I'm practicing with the flogger? I need more experience—wouldn't be more than you helping out a friend."

"I could do that." Ford jerked as Cort pressed his fingers into his side, just below the wound. He seemed to be having trouble getting enough air to breathe. "And just so you know, a Dom can like all kinds of things. Can get off on pain."

"You getting off on this, Ford?"

"Fuck yeah."

"Good. Very good." Cort pressed a little harder as he checked the small bandages, replacing the ones that weren't holding securely. He caught Akira's eye and his dick went from half-hard to fully erect, throbbing and straining in the confines of his jeans. There was a lust-filled glaze to her eyes and her cheeks were flushed. Ford's reactions might trigger one part of him, but Akira's set him off completely. Toying with Ford wasn't enough anymore.

He kept himself in check long enough to finish patching up the wound. Then he pulled Ford away from Akira, trying not to be too rough as he positioned Ford against the headboard. The movement had Ford growling and struggling—apparently the man's trust only went so far when he was naked and Cort was manhandling him.

Giving Ford a crooked smile, Cort stood and jerked Akira to her feet. A wild, reckless part of him wanted to rip her clothes right off her, but he forced himself to take his time. Handle her gently as he removed her shirt, her bra, and kissing along her throat as he cupped her breasts in his hands. She moaned, writhing against him as he rolled her nipples between his fingers and thumbs.

He opened her jeans and slid one hand down, dipping his fingers into her hot, soft flesh, so wet and swollen and ready for him. He nipped her shoulder, watching Ford trapped on the bed, with no choice but to wait until Cort wanted to include him.

"She needs us, Ford." He pushed her jeans down to her knees so Ford could see his fingertips delving into her. See them coming out shiny and slick with her juices. "She smells fucking delicious. Do you want to taste her?"

"I fucking hate you right now, *pal.*" Ford struggled to get off the bed. His head thunked against the wall as he winced in pain. "Do you want me to beg?"

Wrapping Akira's hair around his fist, Cort brought her to the bed, making her kneel in front of Ford.

But not *too* close.

"That's exactly what I want. She's worth begging for." Two fingers, three, pushing up into her until she gasped and started pleading for him to take her. For him to give her to Ford. For *something.* "Don't you agree?"

"I think we're gonna need Sloan's help in your training, you sadistic asshole." Ford pressed his eyes shut. And gave in. "Yes, she's worth it. Please, let me have her."

"Taste her?"

"Yes!"

Cort positioned Akira over Ford's thighs, legs parted. He grabbed a condom from his pocket and handed it to her. "Put this on him, Tiny. I think he's earned this."

He brought his fingers to Ford's lips. Smirked when Ford's nostrils flared and his eyes opened. Ford glared at him. Licked his lips. "Next time, I'm gonna make you pay."

The rough feel of Ford sucking on his fingers made Cort's dick twitch. He was kinda looking forward to seeing how Ford would take his revenge. But until then . . .

He withdrew his hand, slid it between Akira's thighs, and got his fingers nice and wet again. This time, Ford didn't hesitate before opening his mouth. He licked Cort's fingers and moaned.

"Next time." Cort latched on to Akira's hip with one hand, encouraging her to take Ford's dick into her body. "This time, you take whatever I'm willing to offer."

* * * *

Akira's brain had ceased functioning. She'd witnessed so many different things at the club—or even just at home when Sebastian and Luke were around. The dynamics between Luke, Sebastian, and Jami were so comfortable, so easy, she never questioned it. Ford and Cort were so different from Jami's men. Her whole body was set ablaze when she watched Ford sucking Cort's fingers, but it wasn't the sensual exchange she'd observed between others.

It brought to mind the nature shows she'd watched. A wolf baring his fangs to his brother, looking ready to tear his throat out, but simply playing. She wasn't sure if that would make sense to anyone else, but she was comfortable here, submitting fully while they clashed.

And the way they clashed made her a very, very lucky girl. Ford tipped his head back to claim her lips, tugging at her bottom lip with his teeth before smiling at her. "How about we switch your position around, shorty? If Cort's done fucking with me, maybe he'll enjoy having *your* pretty mouth on him."

Cort made a low, hungry sound as she rose off Ford, temporarily distracting her from the dull ache between her thighs while Ford wasn't inside her. Cort's finger smoothed over her lips. "Mmm, nice and soft. And less likely to use teeth, ain't you, pet?"

Akira giggled, shifting her position so her back was to Ford, her thighs parted over his, facing Cort who'd moved to the middle of the bed. Her men were too much. She was pretty sure Cort would be a lot *safer* with his pride and joy in *her* mouth. She wouldn't put it past Ford to let Cort go that far with him just to make a very painful point. After undoing Cort's black jeans, she nuzzled her cheek against his thigh. Laid soft kisses along the length of him, thick and dark, veins pulsing rapidly against her lips as she moved up to the broad head of his cock.

"No teeth if you don't want me to use them, Master." Akira glanced up at Cort, smiling as his eyes drifted shut. "But I can be gentle."

He gathered her hair in his hand, not pulling, just holding it out of the way. His voice was gruff as he fisted his other hand at the base of his dick, his grip rougher than hers would ever be. "Show me."

Wetting her lips, she opened her mouth, flattening her tongue as she took as much of him in as she could without choking. She loved the feel of his smooth flesh, loved the way his thigh tensed under her hand as she slicked her lips over him, losing herself to the rhythm. Neither man was giving her any direction anymore. She grazed her teeth lightly over the sensitive spot beneath the head of Cort's cock. Shifted her hips as the emptiness between her thighs cooled.

Tried to keep her focus on what she was doing. Bobbed her head a little faster when Cort groaned. Giving him pleasure made her happy, but there was something missing. The emptiness seemed to spread. She closed her eyes, slowing and breathing through her nose. Her brain wouldn't shut up. Sucking a man's dick, even her Dom's dick, could be hot if she was lost in the moment, but she wasn't. She started lifting her head.

There was a strange glint in Cort's eye. His smile wasn't the nice, sweet one she was used to. It was the other one, the one that made her pulse race, the one that scared her just a little.

"I do prefer your mouth on me. You're getting good at that." Cort looked past her, almost dismissing her. His hold on her hair tightened until she could feel the pull at her scalp. "Do you want me to untie you?"

Ford's tone was just as frightening as Cort's smile. "You gonna make me beg?"

With a cruel laugh, Cort replied, "Damn right, I will."

"Go fuck yourself." Ford kissed up Akira's spine, making her shiver as he whispered, "Put me back inside you, my beautiful girl. I want you to ride me."

Without hesitation, Akira reached between her thighs, took hold of Ford's dick, and lowered herself on to him. The slow, wet stretch as she filled herself with him was sweet torture. She slid up and down, tensing just enough to keep him in place. Then she braced her hands on the bed to maintain her balance as she rode him.

"Fuck, that's good, baby."

Akira arched her back, swirling her hips, the approval in his tone making her almost as hot as the languorous drag of his cock deep within. But then Cort grabbed her wrists, bringing them to his hips and throwing her rhythm off completely. She slammed herself back so Ford's dick wouldn't slip out of her.

"Open." Cort waited for her to get a good grip on his hips, then delved his hand into her hair again, the other positioning his dick. He made a sharp, negative sound when she moved her hand. "Just your mouth."

Her eyes teared at his first, deep thrust, but as she glided down onto Ford, the helpless position Cort had put her in forced her to go with the motion. To relax and let him lead the way. He fucked her mouth, driving her back onto Ford until she was mindlessly riding and sucking and feeling. Her saliva spilled over her lips, so the wet sound of Cort filling her mouth was no different than the sound of her coming down on Ford. She wasn't prepared for the rapid buildup of pressure within, coiling heat that released in a violent burst of ecstasy.

She gasped when Cort left her lips, pushing her up straight so she was taking Ford in at a different angle. Cort placed her hands behind her neck. Pressed her breasts together over his cock, slick with her saliva. "Work those strong legs, Tiny. He's close."

The muscles in her thighs burned as she kept riding Ford. Beneath her, he struggled to thrust up, and each of his soft curses made her clench down on him a little more. She watched Cort sliding his dick between her breasts, her lips parting at the sharp pleasure of him pinching her nipple. His gaze never left her face. Something in his expression told her he was on the edge of release, but holding back for some reason.

He wasn't done with her yet.

Her eyes widened as he put a hand on her shoulder. He gave her a lazy grin. "No rush."

Ford didn't seem to agree. He shuddered, pressing his forehead between Akira's shoulder blades. "I'm going to kill you, Cort."

"Revenge will be a lot more fun. Quit bitching and ask me to let you go."

"Like fuck."

Cort shrugged, lifting Akira completely off Ford, nipping her chin when she frowned at him. "Don't give me that look. I'd swallow my pride and beg for you."

Ducking her head, Akira pressed her face against his chest, breathing in the scent of fabric softener that clung to his cotton T-shirt, light enough that it didn't mask the headier scent of *him*. Grease, soap, and the faint smell of sweat. His words eased the unpleasant sensation of denial. Her body wanted to keep going, but she'd show him she could be patient.

Much as Cort and Ford seemed to struggle for dominance, Cort was the one who really seemed to *need* to be in control this time. She didn't understand, but she wouldn't question it.

She'd wait for Ford to. Which didn't take long. "What's your deal, man? There some reason you need to be in charge of both of us?"

"Yes." Cort's tone was firm, but something about the way he stroked her back made it clear he was happy with her. So she stayed where she was, sitting on the side of the bed, just enjoying the vibration of his deep voice against her cheek. "I'll have to let you take over at the club when you're teaching me stuff. I need this now."

She could sense the tension leaving Ford. Hear the understanding in his tone as he spoke. "All right." He went still. Cleared his throat. "Untie me. I need her—however you're willing to give her to me."

Letting out a low growl of satisfaction, Cort moved away from her. He stood, pulling off his shirt and tossing it aside. He removed his jeans, then took a condom and a folded blade out of his pocket.

Ford's jaw ticked as Cort opened the knife. He slid over, giving Cort his back. Hissed in a breath when Cort reached around to put the flat of the blade against his throat.

"I think you're right, Ford." Cort grabbed on to Ford's shoulder, holding him still before he could react on instinct and try to get away. "I'm going to see if Sloan will help train me."

"You're one scary fucker, Cort." Ford stared at Akira, drew in a shuddery breath. "I wouldn't put up with you if not for her."

"Which works out perfectly for all three of us." Cort winked at her, withdrawing the knife from Ford's throat, bringing it down to cut Ford's restraints. "We'll try this again when I know how to do it safely."

*Good idea.* Akira relaxed as Ford put his arms around her, smiling as he kissed her. The whole situation was thrilling, even though it was a bit messed up. At one point, she might have worried how this would work out. She knew both men loved her. Knew they cared about each other. But knowing there was something they could give one another, even if it wasn't sexual, made her feel like they all fit together. Like this would last.

"Lie down, Ford." Cort stepped off the bed, ignoring Ford's dirty look. He didn't say another word until Ford lay down on the bed. "Chill out, I want to try something."

"Put the knife away and we can try anything you want." Ford put his hand on Akira's hip, stroking her belly with his thumb. The touch made her twitch, and she fisted her hands by her sides as he slid his hand so his thumb could reach her clit. The tiny nub was so swollen it pushed past the lips of her pussy. Ford seemed to forget all about the knife as he toyed with her. "You have all you need to tempt me."

Cort chuckled. "Are you waiting for my permission to take her?"

Ford's thumb went still, pressing against her clit in a way that had her fighting not to spread open and beg for his hand on her. He cursed under his breath. "Asshole."

Akira yelped as Ford lifted her up to lie over him, holding her against his chest with one arm across her back while he drove into her. He framed her jaw with one hand, licking along the seam of her lips before dipping in with his tongue. She moved with him, groaning when he lowered his hands to latch on to her hips and keep her still. He slammed up into her until she threw her head back, lost in the reckless, overwhelming sensation.

A hard smack on her ass jolted her. Ford's dick slipped out.

Cort's fitted against her slit, finding purchase and driving in. She cried out as he spread her open. He pressed the tip of one finger into her back hole.

Pulled his dick out. Ford slid into her.

One man, then the other, Ford thrusting in deep, Cort keeping to shallow dips that drove her insane. Two fingers worked their way into her from behind. She rested her head on Ford's shoulder as his cock slipped against her belly and Cort pounded into her. As he left her empty and used her own moisture to penetrate her ass with his dick. Only an inch, then another, entering her painfully slow.

She winced, tried to breathe through it. Pushed back against him to ease the way.

Ford's fingers scissored over her clit. His dick glided into her pussy, no deeper than Cort's. Another *smack!* and her back arched.

Both men filled her. She screamed as her nerves flared with sensations and the orgasm rolled inside her, over her, like she'd swum out into rapids and couldn't reach the surface. Every time she came close, a touch, a movement, would drag her back under.

The second the waters seemed calm, the second she managed a gasp of air, Ford snarled out a curse and the pulsing of his dick threw her into the violent depths.

Cort's fingers bruised her hips as he rammed into her from behind, once, twice, then dropped down on her, his hand slapping on the bed, shaky arm holding most of his weight as he came. He tensed when she tightened around him. Kissed her shoulder and tried to slide out.

"Wait!" She trembled, partially because it hurt, partially because the pain almost set her off. And she wasn't sure she'd survive going under again. "Just . . . please just give me a second."

Ford chuckled, still half-hard inside her. "No."

He ground into her, which made Cort swear and buck. The rapids still had a hold on her. Wanted to keep her. She screamed herself raw, sobbing as she thrashed, every last bit of strength she had left gone to stop from drowning in rapture. And smiling as she took her last breath.

# Chapter Thirty Five

Snow whipped through the air violently, lashing at Ford as he strode up to the prison's main entrance. He hadn't been to a prison since Cort had served time. Hadn't expected to end up coming for his father.

*Not my father. He's not my father.*

He shouldn't be here. He should be at the Forum. He had work to do. Things were a mess with the GM gone and the team just a few games away from being out of the playoffs. For the last two weeks, he'd spent every spare moment he had with Akira and Cort, the rest with his sisters, because family had never meant so much to him as it did now.

*But why now? He wasn't family!*

He gasped in the frigid air before walking into the prison. Swiped at the melting snow on his face as he approached the communications desk to speak to the uniform behind the glass. To tell the woman why he was here.

*Why the fuck am I here?*

His tone was level as he spoke, giving her nothing but the facts. He was here to see his father. The officer who'd called him said he'd be expected. The woman asked him to have a seat. So he did. He sat in the waiting room. On the stiff plastic chair.

Feeling nothing. Which was good. He shouldn't feel anything.

Earlier this afternoon, he'd met Akira and Cort for lunch at a small place close to Cort's shop, but he refused to discuss the news. Wasn't sure how to deal with the sweet sympathy in Akira's eyes, or the concern in Cort's.

He'd gotten exactly what he'd wanted. Not by his own hands, but did it really matter?

Kingsley couldn't hurt anyone he loved. Ever again.

"Mr. . . . Delgado?" A guard approached Ford, holding out his hand as Ford stood. "Please follow me."

Ford followed the guard, going along with all the man's instructions as he was searched, not having to take much out of his pockets because Laura had told him what not to bring. She'd even told him how to behave, but that wasn't gonna be an issue. He was feeling too numb to mouth off. He did exactly what he was told. Signed whatever was put in front of him.

"This is highly irregular, but your detective buddy called in a favor." The guard rolled his eyes. "Not sure why he thinks you'd want to see your father—"

"He's *not* my father."

"Then why do you want to see him at all?"

Ford just stared at the guard. After a few minutes, the man shrugged and told Ford to wait. His footsteps echoed down the hall as he walked out. Then there was some religious guy there, the prison chaplain, old and gray and frail, holding Ford's hands in his and telling Ford how sorry he was for Ford's loss.

*I didn't lose anything. This is what I wanted.*

"Would you like to see him now, my son?"

Blinking at the old man, mouth dry, Ford simply nodded. He stayed close to the chaplain as he led the way down several halls with cement walls and barred windows. The idea of Cort being stuck in a place like this, for years, stole chunks of time. Whenever he'd visited Cort, all he'd seen was a big room with a bunch of tables. It hadn't been the fucking Ritz, but it didn't look like his vision of hell either. But the shouts that seemed so far away, yet so close, like the voices came from deep, dark pits within those walls, all belonged to the damned. The tang of mold and stale air, the cold that seeped into his bones . . .

Yeah, this was a different kind of hell. A hell Kingsley would never leave.

A clock ticked on the wall in the prison infirmary, in a small room away from the prisoners who were sick or had been beaten or some other shit. He could still hear them, but he felt removed from it all as the chaplain lowered the sheet and took a step back.

And there he was. Roy Kingsley. Ford blinked, laughing bitterly into the hand he used to cover his mouth, hating that there were tears streaking down his unshaven cheeks. He should be celebrating. Breaking out a bottle of champagne. The old bastard had gotten exactly what he'd deserved.

He was dead.

Kingsley's flesh was gray, his eyes closed, no color to be seen except for the thick line of black and purple bruises on his neck. No one believed Kingsley had hung himself in his cell. Not once had he betrayed any fear that the charges wouldn't be dropped. One of his brothers had visited him in prison. Was being investigated now because he'd said goodbye and told Roy he'd gone too far and there was no turning back.

*No turning back.*

Ford had expected his uncle to call him, and maybe he would, but right now he had a feeling the Kingsley family knew he wanted to cut all ties and pretend he'd never had any part of them. But what if coming here changed that? What if they thought he'd want revenge?

He didn't. Yeah, it was hard not to look down at Roy's still face and remember the few occasions the man *had* been his father. When his mom had brought Ford home after a T-ball game when he was five and Roy had left his office to ruffle Ford's hair with a smile and a "Good job, buddy!" The day Ford graduated from elementary school with honors and Roy had brought him out for dinner at a local buffet. The first time Ford shot a gun and took out the center of the target with ten rounds, which earned him Roy's prized 1896 Colt. When Ford came to him and promised to take the Delgados down and the old man said he was proud of Ford for the very first time.

Then again, maybe he was grasping for the good things he'd wanted to believe in. Something had always been off. The same man who'd hug him in front of his mother would speak casually of killing him for fucking up when she wasn't around. Had gotten so angry he'd held a gun on Ford in front of her because he was done pretending to care about her bastard child.

*That* was what Ford wanted to remember. *That* would make it easy to stand over the body of Roy Kingsley and be happy he was dead. This man had hurt his mother, never letting her forget that he barely tolerated *her* son. Jami, Cort, and so many others had suffered because of this man. Tim and Madeline were dead because of him.

He didn't deserve a single tear. Ford rubbed the moisture on his cheeks away with his fists. He nodded when the chaplain spoke, but didn't look at him until the chaplain held out a clear plastic bag.

"I'm sure your father would want you to have this."

"This" was Roy's effects. The suit he'd worn coming here since his brother was providing another. His wedding ring, his wallet. Not much else. Ford retreated from the bed and dumped the contents on an empty metal table. He grabbed the wallet and found pictures of his mom, so many pictures, from her as the eighteen-year-old girl Roy had married to the broken woman of almost forty before she died. Ford held on to them and backed up to the door.

"Burn the rest. I don't want it."

The chaplain looked sad. "You may change your mind, son. I will keep it in case—"

"Keep whatever you want. I won't change my mind. He's dead." Ford shook his head hard. Spun around and burst through the door. Only the guard kept him from running right out of there. From getting far, far away. He kept a quick pace as the guard brought him back to the main exit. Gave him back his own things. Had him sign out.

The fresh blowing snow outside, the biting cold, was a relief. He'd left Roy Kingsley behind. Forever.

*For-fucking-ever.*

Didn't feel as good as it should. He skidded on the slick pavement and fell into the snow. And stayed there, letting his hands and knees go numb.

"Ford?"

*No!* He shook his head, refusing to look up. He knew Akira's voice. Felt her presence. Felt Cort's nearby.

Neither of them should be here. He hadn't told them he was coming. Why would he? They didn't belong here. This was hell and he'd left his last link to it behind. And it would stay there. Because *that man* didn't breathe anymore. His heart didn't beat. He could never hurt someone Ford loved again.

"C'mon on, buddy. You gotta stand up." Cort didn't wait for Ford to move. He latched on to Ford's forearms, dragging him to his feet and holding on tight when Ford tried to jerk away. "It's okay."

Ford laughed in a way that sounded a little crazy to his own ears. He tried to sound sane when he spoke. "He's dead. Of course it's okay!"

Akira's soft voice reached him as she cuddled up to his side while Cort hugged him. "No. It's okay for you to mourn him. He doesn't deserve it, but you do."

"I don't need to mourn him. There's no grieving process for a fucking murderer!" Ford saw Tim. Saw Madeline. And then he saw countless others who'd died because of Roy. Shedding a single tear was like pissing on their graves. But he couldn't stop. He shoved at Cort and tipped his head back, shouting at the swirling snow and the clouds above. "I wanted to do it! I wanted him dead! Thank you, God! Thank you for—for making sure he couldn't—" His voice broke in a sob. And he didn't know if the tears were for Roy, or if they were for all the lives he'd broken before finally meeting his end. A sick part of Ford hoped it had been painful. A softer side didn't want to know. He shouted so loud his throat felt like he'd swallowed acid. "Let it be over!"

Cort's hold on him tightened. "It's over, Ford."

Akira kissed his wet cheeks, whispering, "It's over."

They were right. It was over.

*It's finally fucking over.*

\* \* \* \*

The future was damn uncertain, but after a month of spending most nights at Ford's apartment above the bar, Akira was fed up. Their life was in a holding pattern, and every effort she made to take things to the next level was met with hesitant enthusiasm. Cort would come home from the shop and sit with her at the small kitchen table while she showed him all the houses she'd found, liking them all, but telling her they should wait a little before picking one. Maybe until after the trial?

Ford showed a bit more interest, even helping her narrow down the choices, but he wouldn't let her touch her savings and didn't have "enough for the kinda place she deserved."

Basically, he wanted her to wait, too. And she would if . . . they didn't feel what she felt when they walked through the doors of the house she'd fallen in love with.

The men were indulging her, she had no doubt about that, but as Cort pulled up in front of the stone and iron-gated property, she watched his expression shift from casual interest to actual consideration.

He leaned his forearms on the steering wheel. "Nice and secure. I like that."

"I thought you would." Akira threw her door open, the fat droplets of cold rain not bothering her at all as she waited for her men on the sidewalk. Another car pulled up and the Realtor came out, a sweet older woman Sebastian had put her in touch with. Her name was Nancy, and she'd already let Akira visit the house twice. She came right over and hugged Akira like they were old friends. Akira gestured to Cort and Ford. "These are the men I told you about, Ford and Cort. The men I will spend the rest of my life with. Guys, this is Nancy Foley."

Cort grinned and held out his hand. "A pleasure, Mrs. Foley."

One brow arched, Ford glanced from Nancy to Akira. "You sure you want to be sharing that with just anyone, shorty?" He gave Nancy an apologetic smile. "Sorry, I'm sure you're very nice, but people can be really judgemental."

Nancy inclined her head. "You're absolutely right, Mr. Delgado, but one of the perks of this area is there are a number of people who value their privacy. Mr. Ramos, who lives only two blocks away, bought his house for that very reason. Both he and Akira also mentioned that security would be very important."

"It is." Cort walked past them, studying the intercom and the large iron gate. "People gotta get buzzed in?"

"Yes. There is a camera integrated into the intercom so you will have a visual of all your visitors. The security company the previous owners worked with is very good, but I have other recommendations if you'd like."

Cort nodded slowly, stepping aside so Nancy could tap in the code on the keypad. He spoke quietly to the Realtor, then strode across the grass, disappearing around the side of the house.

Akira bit hard on her bottom lip, not sure if she should follow him, or stay with Ford who was staring at the length of fence like it disturbed him somehow. Nancy, thankfully, just went straight to the front door to unlock it, leaving it open when she went inside.

"Doesn't it bother you?" Ford came to Akira's side, taking her mitten-covered hand in his bare one. He held his hand out toward the fence. "Knowing we probably need this?"

She squeezed his hand, tugging a little to get him to the wide porch. "I don't think we need it, but I think it will take a long time for either you or Cort to believe that. I want a place where you'll both feel safe."

The edge of his lip crept up a bit. "It's more about *you* being safe, but Cort's gonna be the one to decide that."

"And you'll trust whatever he decides. In the meantime, you get to be the first to see exactly why I think this place is absolutely perfect." She drew him into the house, holding her breath as he stood in the entryway. There was a mirrored coat closet, and white French doors open wide to reveal the spacious living room. From here they could see the kitchen, the areas separated by a white marble island that had three white leather stools lined up on one side.

Any woman who enjoyed cooking would die for a kitchen like this, with all the counter space, the steel appliances, the neat gadgets and light pouring in from the picture windows. But Akira could see them all in there, making meals together. Or maybe Ford sitting at the island doing paperwork while she and Cort cooked. The trees in the backyard were just tall enough to give them plenty of privacy, so she had a few fantasies of surprising the men with an elaborate breakfast in the morning, wearing nothing but a cute little frilly apron.

Actually, she'd already bought the apron.

"Your cheeks are all pink." Ford came up behind her and wrapped his arms around her, his lips close to her ear. "What are you thinking about, pet?"

Turning in his arms, she gave him a sultry smile. "Oh, I can't tell you. I can only show you—*if* we get the place, that is."

"Brat." He tipped her chin up with a finger and kissed her softly before whispering. "Show me the rest."

She brought him around the house, getting more and more excited as he asked her about her plans for each and every room. His eyes were hooded as he checked out the huge Jacuzzi bathtub in the bathroom. He went quiet when they left the master bedroom, a thoughtful smile on his lips as he walked around the third bedroom.

"The smaller room will be the guest bedroom?" he asked as he stood at the window, looking down into the yard where Cort was speaking to Nancy. "And there's office space in the basement?"

"You can use this as an office if you want." She bit the tip of her tongue, curious to know what was on his mind as he shook his head.

"No, I'd have other plans for this one. I mean, hypothetically. And if Cort liked it too."

"You like it?" Akira bounced up on her tiptoes and threw her arms around his neck. "Because I love it, and I hoped you would too, but I wasn't sure—"

He placed a finger over her lips. "It's perfect, shorty, and I would love for the three of us to have a place like this. But I'm not rich anymore, and a place like this won't be cheap. I'll see what I can do, okay?"

Before she could tell him she had it all figured out, the sound of the doors opening downstairs drew his attention. He took her hand and led her down to the kitchen to join Cort.

"There's place for all our cars. I'm not crazy about the lighting outside, but we can fix that," Cort said, sounding distracted as he checked the locks on the windows over the sink. "It's secure."

For some reason, Cort checking out the house like he was there as a bodyguard, instead of considering it as the place they'd all live together, irritated her. She listened to him grilling Nancy about the alarm system and rolled her eyes.

"There's a pool table downstairs—custom-made, the old owners are willing to leave it here for a really good price." She'd had Nancy ask them about it, sure that a game room would be a good selling point for her men. When Cort nodded while fiddling with the locks on the back door, she held her fists tight to her side, turning to Ford rather than giving into the temptation to throw the fake fruit on the counter at him. "And there's a bar and enough room for a den if you want to have the guys over—"

"The guys? We start letting players hang out here and we might never get rid of them." Ford's tone was light, but something about how he talked about living here reminded her of when her dad used to talk about winning the lottery. Like it was nice to dream, but that's all it was. "Unless you're thinking of letting Sutter and his pals hang out here?"

Cort didn't look up from the locks as he practically growled. "No fucking way."

Ford chuckled, resting his arm on her shoulders casually, jerking his chin toward the door in the hall. "I want to see this pool table. If they're willing to sell it, I might buy it for my bar. I've been thinking about making the place a bit classier."

As they headed downstairs, Akira swallowed against the lump

in her throat. All the times she'd come before, the possibilities had seemed endless. But now she had to accept the facts that she'd been dreaming way too big. She'd gotten carried away, and it was time to face reality.

They might have all this together someday.

But not today.

\* \* \* \*

Cort refused to even consider the house if it wasn't as close to a fucking fortress as possible, no matter how perfect it was in every other way. No matter how much he loved the way Akira's eyes lit up the second the place had come into view. Damn, he hated that his being so paranoid had dimmed the hope in her eyes, but he was taking this seriously.

Which was what she wanted, wasn't it?

He walked around upstairs alone, leaning in the doorway of the master bedroom, a smile tugging at his lips as he envisioned how the room would look with the huge bed he'd found in an antique shop a few blocks away from the Forum. The snooty salesperson had turned up his nose the second Cort walked through the door, but he'd changed his attitude when Cort paid the huge deposit. He made decent money at the shop, and didn't have to spend much of it since he was staying with Ford. Which meant he had the money for a few nice things.

Less saved up now though, since the bed alone cost three weeks' paychecks—from the garage and the bar—but the solid oak pillars, the overhead, iron canopy frame, gave him some damn kinky ideas he knew Akira would be into. The bed had a leather headboard, which he knew Ford had a thing for—Cort figured it was a comfort thing, more than style, but either way, the bed would suit them all.

So would the house, but . . . he sighed as he roamed around the second floor, mentally picking the smallest for Ford's office and the other for future noisy, messy, and adorable possibilities, even though he really couldn't figure out how they would make this work. The down payment alone was more than the three of them could manage together. Selling his car might help, but then there was the mortgage. He calculated the numbers Nancy had given him and rubbed his temples with his fingers as he made his way to the first floor, then to the basement where Akira was still showing Ford around. He could pay his third, Ford would have no problem paying his, but what about Akira? His Tiny was proud; she'd want to pay her share. Wouldn't give her much to spare, but he and Ford would make sure she had everything she needed. Anything she could ever want.

*Her Doms are gonna spoil her, whether she likes it or not.* His lips slanted as she finally looked back at him, and what she saw in his eyes had her paling, her lips parting as though she'd been about to say something, but changed her mind.

Ford leaned against bar, built into the wide space under the stairs, and folded his arms over his chest. "Nice place, eh, Cort?"

Cort inclined his head. The den and the game room looked like the ideal place to hang out and unwind after a long day at work, and that pool table was fucking nice—sturdy like the bed he was buying, probably wouldn't budge if he bent Akira over it and—

"Just say it, Cort!" Akira stomped her foot, then blushed, like she felt silly, and mirrored Ford's crossed-arm pose. "The way you looked at me before I was wondering if maybe you were . . ." She sighed, blinking in that way she did when she was trying not to cry. "Never mind. Coming here was stupid. Let's go back to Ford's place so you can fuck me. I can tell that's all you want to—"

Covering Akira's mouth with his hand, Ford looked over at Cort. "Duct tape or a ball gag?" His jaw hardened. "Bite me again, shorty, and I ain't waiting until we get to my place to punish you."

Akira went still. Cort smirked, which had her narrowing her eyes, likely considering all the things in the room she could throw at him. She reached out for a decorative wine bottle on the bar.

"I'd stop and think about what you're doing, Tiny." He watched her jerk her hand back, then latched his hand to his wrist behind his back and strolled across the den, pleased to find another door which lead to a room about the same size as the master bedroom. "I think a spider gag would be appropriate. But only if the attitude doesn't change after we've cleared a few things up."

He continued into the room, taking measured steps to see how much space he had to work with. Ford had mentioned Scott Demyan made things with wood in his spare time; he could probably give them a good price on a few custom pieces. Like a spanking bench—or maybe that cool throne they had at Blades & Ice. A bondage frame right in the middle so he could . . . he retreated eight steps from the center of the room. All right, not enough clearance for a full length whip, but maybe—

"What do we need to clear up, Cort?" Akira approached him, blushing at his expectant look. "Sir?"

Tapping his chin with a finger, he surveyed the room, nodding slowly. "Our neighbors are far enough, but I think I still want to soundproof this room."

"I . . ." Akira licked her lips, her eyes sparkled, and she took a deep breath, speaking in a rush. "I figured Ford could have his office here."

"Naw, he can take the room upstairs."

"But he had other plans for the room beside the guest room."

Cort met Ford's eyes, pretty sure they had the *same* plans for that room. Then he cocked his head. "Hey, why the hell do we need a guest room?"

Akira blinked. "Umm . . . for guests?"

"Perfectly good motel down the street." That settled, he held out his hand, pulling Akira into his arms, absorbing all the excited energy that practically vibrated off her. He wondered if there was any way to just buy the place today and get rid of the Realtor so they could start christening each and every room. He lowered his lips to Akira's. "This is gonna be our dungeon, sweetheart. One level up is where I'm gonna have you for breakfast, and above that is where Ford and I will hold you in our arms every fucking night for the rest of our lives."

She was holding her breath, staring at him and blinking fast again. But he wouldn't mind her tears now. He tasted the first one that spilled free as she whispered, "Do you mean it?"

"Yeah. Already got the bed." He took his phone out of his pocket to show her the picture. "We've all gotta sit down and figure out how we'll manage the deposit, but—"

"I've got that covered. I hope you don't mind, but when I talked to Sebastian about maybe taking this place he told me he'd help us out. We'll pay him back, of course, but he has the money and he really doesn't mind and—"

He held up a finger, close to her lips, and nodded. "Okay."

Ford, who'd been standing off to the side, silent for their whole exchange, took a step back, shaking his head like they were both crazy. "Okay? This is insane! Cort, don't get her hopes up. You know very well we can't have all this—"

"All what, Ford?" Cort kept one arm around Akira. Held his hand out to Ford. "Come here."

Ford shook his head. "I still don't get it. I'm waiting for . . ."

"For more bad shit to happen?" Cort put his hand on Ford's shoulder when his best friend finally came to them. "I get that, but are we gonna stop living, waiting for it?"

The way Ford closed his eyes and dropped his head back made it clear that he didn't know how to do anything besides wait for the next blow. He was trying, but his expectations didn't go much beyond hoping they'd all survive.

"Why don't you tell Akira what you want that other room for, Ford? You let yourself see it, even if only for a minute." Cort tightened his grip on Ford's shoulder when Ford shook his head. "Tell her."

Swallowing audibly, Ford met Akira's eyes. "Was just a thought—not any time soon." He gave her a sheepish smile. "I could see us raising kids here. Cort would make an amazing father."

"So would you." Akira hooked her finger to the collar of Ford's shirt, her gaze hot as she looked up at him. "I've seen you with your niece. There's nothing sexier than a man who's good with kids."

"When we're *all* ready." Cort cleared his throat, his attention suddenly split between how happy both the people he loved looked, and how much more security this place would need if he had a little baby to watch out for. If Akira gave them a little girl, he'd need to start collecting guns—and make sure he had solid lockboxes for all of them. And when his little girl grew up, he'd have to keep her far, far away from the Dartmouth Cobras. And bikers. And men in general.

*Fuck, why did I bring this up again?*

"Yes. When we're all ready." Ford snorted, his expression knowing. "Neither of us knocked her up, Cort. Take a deep breath, man."

"Yeah, well, you feeling fucking better, asshole?"

"So long as you're not gonna have a heart attack, old man. Shit, can your face get any redder?"

"Okay, no way are we even discussing kids again until you both clean up your language." Akira folded her arms over her chest. "And, for your information, I am making being punished for swearing a hard limit. This is bullshit!"

Cort hooked his arm around her, pulling her back to his side where she belonged. "I will consider your request, pet." He looked from her to Ford. "So we doing this?"

Ford held out his hand for Akira's, lacing their fingers together as they moved into the game room. He rested his hip against the pool table, inhaling slowly. "This . . . damn it, can we? I mean, what is 'this'?"

"Freedom. Our future. A place we can all feel safe." Cort ran his hand up and down Akira's side as she wrapped her arm around his waist. He cupped the back of Ford's head so their foreheads touched. "It's home."

# THE END

**Visit the Dartmouth Cobras**
**www.TheDartmouthCobras.com**

# Game Misconduct

## THE DARTMOUTH COBRAS #1

The game has always cast a shadow over Oriana Delgado's life. She should hate the game. But she doesn't. The passion and the energy of the sport are part of her. But so is the urge to drop the role of the Dartmouth Cobra owner's 'good daughter' and find a less . . .conventional one.

Playmaker Max Perron never expected a woman to accept him and his twisted desires. Oriana came close, but he wasn't surprised when she walked away. A girl like her needs normal. Which he can't give her. He's too much of a team player, and not just on the ice.

But then Oriana's father goes too far in trying to control her and she decides to use exposure as blackmail. Just the implication of her spending the night with the Cobras' finest should get her father to back off.

Turns out a team player is exactly what she needs.

*"Ms Sommerland takes us on an extremely incredible journey as we watch Oriana's master her own sexuality. She comes to realize that there is more out there that she craves and desires, than she has ever realized." Rhayne —Guilty Pleasures*

*"With a delicious storyline and kinky characters outside of the norm, Game Misconduct pushes you outside of your comfort zone and rewards your submission with phenomenally erotic sex. If you're a fan of hardcore BDSM, then this book is going to top your list of must reads!" Silla Beaumont —Just Erotic Romance*

# Defensive Zone

## THE DARTMOUTH COBRAS #2

Silver Delgado has gained control of the Dartmouth Cobras—and lost control of her life.

Hockey might be the family business, but it's never interested Silver. Until her father's health decline thrusts responsibility for the team he owns straight into her hands. Now she has to find a way to get the team more fans and establish herself as the new owner. Which means standing up to Dean Richter, the general manager and the advisor her father has forced on her. The fact that their "business relationship" started with her over his lap at his BDSM club shouldn't be too much of a problem. Their hot one-night stand meant nothing! But how can she earn his respect when he sees her as submissive? Can they separate work and the lifestyle she's curious to explore?

Balancing her new life away from Hollywood, living among people who see her as the selfish Delgado princess, has her feeling lost and alone until Landon Bower, the Cobras new goalie slips into her life and becomes her best—and only—friend. The time they spend together makes everything else bearable, but before long his eyes meet hers with more than friendship, reflecting what she feels. Which could ruin everything.

Two Dominant men who see past her pretty mask and the shallow image she portrayed to the flashing cameras. A gentle attack from both sides that she can't hope to block unless she learns how to play.

But she's getting the hang of the game.

# Breakaway
## THE DARTMOUTH COBRAS #3

Against some attacks, the only hope is to come out and meet the play.

Last year, Jami Richter had no plans, no goals, no future. But that's all changed. First step, make up for putting her father through hell by supporting the hockey team he manages and becoming an Ice Girl. But a photo shoot puts her right in the arms of Sebastian Ramos, a Dartmouth Cobra defenseman with a reputation for getting any woman—or, as the rumors imply, man—he desires. And the powerful dominant wants her...and Luke. Getting involved in Seb's lifestyle gives her a new understanding of the game and the bonds between players. But can she handle being caught between two men who want her, while struggling with their attraction to one another?

Luke Carter's life is about as messed up as his scarred face. His mother is sick. His girlfriend dumps him. When he goes to his favorite BDSM club to blow off some steam, his Dom status is turned upside down when a therapeutic beating puts him in a good place. He flatly denies being submissive—or, even worse, being attracted to another man. He wants Jami but can't have her without getting involved with Sebastian. Can he overcome his own prejudices long enough to admit he wants them both?

Caught between Luke and Jami, Sebastian Ramos does everything in his power to fulfill their needs. His two new submissives willingly share their bodies, but not their secrets. When his own past comes back to haunt him, the fragile foundation of their relationship is ripped apart. As he works to salvage the damage done by doubt and insecurity, he discovers that Jami is hiding something dangerous. But it may already be too late.

# Offside

## THE DARTMOUTH COBRAS #4

A pace ahead of the play can send you back to the start. And put everything you've worked for at risk.

Single mother and submissive Rebecca Bower abandoned her career as a sports reporter to become a media consultant with her brother's hockey team. A failed marriage to a selfish man makes her wary of getting involved with another. Unfortunately, chemistry is hard to deny, and all her hormones are dancing when she gets close to the Cobra's sniper, Scott Demyan.

Zachary Pearce 'came out' to the world last season to shift attention away from a teammate. And his one night with Scott Demyan had been unsettling. There could be more there, if only Scott was a different person. Instead, a night of sensual BDSM play with Becky leaves him wanting more, but she thinks he's gay and questions his interest. It's been a long time since a woman has attracted him both as a man and a Dom, and he'll do everything in his power to prove she's the only one he needs. Or wants. His one time with Scott was a mistake.

Scott might have forgotten what happened in his childhood, but the effects linger, and he specializes in drunken one-night stands...until he meets Zach and Becky and sees what he's missing. But neither one believes Scott can be faithful. Although he's trying hard to clean up his act to avoid getting kicked off the team, they want more from him. He's willing to make changes, but the most important one—putting their happiness before his own—means he'll probably end up alone.

# ABOUT THE AUTHOR

Tell you about me? Hmm, well, there's not much to say. I love hockey and cars and my kids...not in that order of course! Lol! When I'm not writing—which isn't often—I'm usually watching a game or a car show while networking. Going out with my kids is my only downtime. I get to clear my head and forget everything.

As for when and why I first started writing, I guess I thought I'd get extra cookies if I was quiet for a while—that's how young I was. I used to bring my grandmother barely legible pages filled with tales of evil unicorns. She told me then that I would be a famous author.

I hope one day to prove her right.

For more of my work, please visit: www.Im-No-Angel.com

You can also find me on Facebook and Twitter.

# PRAISE FOR BIANCA SOMMERLAND'S BOOKS

"The Trip is a book that comes real close to my limits in some ways. Almost non-consensual and yet not quite. Very hard and gritty in places and yet it's written in the style I've come to expect from Bianca Sommerland's books -- with flair and great skill and the ability to take the reader right down into the heads of the people in the story and live what is happening. One of those books that leaves you thinking afterwards too. Highly recommended."

*-Cari Silverwood*
*Author of the Pierced Hearts series*

"I just have to start by saying that this book is not for the faint of heart or the easily offended. Secondly, I have to say to the author, Bianca Sommerland, I give you a standing ovation. Deadly Captive was dark, sinister, erotic, intense, sexy and dangerous. Wow!"

*—Karyl*
*Dark Diva Review of Deadly Captive*

"My heart broke a little for Shawna. The entire set up made sense and from a personal note, I've been in the same situation. That's when I completely connected to the story and I was moved to tears."

*—BookAddict*
*The Romance Reviews review of The Trip*

"Collateral Damage blew me away! Once I started this book, I did not put it down and read it in one go. Nicole's story is harrowing and raw, and Bianca Sommerland does an amazing job evoking so many emotions as you read how Nicole struggles to survive."

*-Julie*
*Read Our Lips Book Review Blog on Collateral Damage*

"As in the first book in the series, the plot is fast-paced and gripping, and evil and violence await the reader at every flip of the page. This book has a few more moments that allow for respite, an opportunity for the reader to catch their breath, but the moments of light, though bright, are short lived. I couldn't put the book down and was completely engrossed, horrified, desperate for revenge, and aching for the connection between Vince and Nicole. This chapter in the story, punctuated by an intense climax, is finished but it is clear there is more terror to come."

*-Gillian*
*Tattooed Book Reviews on Collateral Damage*

39531143R00330

Made in the USA
Charleston, SC
10 March 2015